A Star Above It
and other stories

volume 1 of selected stories

Chad Oliver

Edited by Priscilla Olson

The NESFA Press
Post Office Box 809
Framingham, MA 01701
2003

FIRST EDITION
August, 2003

International Standard Book Number:
1-886778-45-0

To Chad—
For leaving us so much of himself
in these stories

First Appearances

"Blood's a Rover", first printed in *Astounding Science Fiction* 49:3, May 1952

"The Land of Lost Content", first printed in *Super Science Stories* 7:3, November 1950

"The Ant and the Eye", first printed in *Astounding Science Fiction* 51:2, April 1953

"Artifact", first printed in *The Magazine of Fantasy & Science Fiction* 8:6, June 1955

"Any More at Home Like You?", first printed in *Star Science Fiction Stories* #3, edited by Frederik Pohl, New York: Ballantine Books 96, 1954

"Rewrite Man", first printed in *The Magazine of Fantasy & Science Fiction* 13:3, September 1957

"The Edge of Forever", first printed in *Astounding Science Fiction* 48:4, December 1951

"The Boy Next Door", first printed in *The Magazine of Fantasy & Science Fiction* 2:3, June 1951

"A Star Above It", first printed in *Another Kind* by Chad Oliver, New York: Ballantine Books 113, 1955

"The Mother of Necessity", first printed in *Another Kind* by Chad Oliver, New York: Ballantine Books 113, 1955

"Night", first printed in *Worlds of If* 5:1, March 1955

"Technical Advisor", first printed in *The Magazine of Fantasy & Science Fiction* 4:2, February 1953

"Between the Thunder and the Sun", first printed in *The Magazine of Fantasy & Science Fiction* 12:5, May 1957

"The One That Got Away", first printed in *The Magazine of Fantasy & Science Fiction* 16:5, May 1959

"Transfusion", first printed in *Astounding Science Fiction* 63:4, June 1959

"Guardian Spirit", first printed in *The Magazine of Fantasy & Science Fiction* 14:4, April 1958 [reprinted as "The Marginal Man"]

"The Gift", first printed in *Future Kin: Eight Science Fiction Stories,* edited by Roger Elwood, Garden City, NY: Doubleday & Co., 1974

"To Whom It May Concern", first printed in *A Spadeful of Spacetime,* edited by Fred Saberhagen, New York: Ace Books 0-441-77766-X, February 1981

"A Stick for Harry Eddington", first printed in *The Magazine of Fantasy & Science Fiction* 29:2, August 1965

"Old Four-Eyes", first printed in *Synergy 4,* edited by George Zebrowski, San Diego: A Harvest/HBJ Original, Harcourt Brace Jovanovich 0-15-687703-1, May 1989

Contents

Introduction: Chad Oliver (Howard Waldrop) 13

Blood's a Rover 19   *10*

The Land of Lost Content ... *Walmartians* 59   *10*

The Ant and the Eye .... *Culture & war* 75   *10*

Artifact ... *on Mars?* 109   *10*

Any More At Home Like You? ... *Keith & Professor* ... 131   *9*

Rewrite Man ... *Harry of future & Newspaper* ... 145   *8*

The Edge of Forever 165

The Boy Next Door 187

A Star Above It 195

The Mother of Necessity 229

Night 243

Technical Advisor 259

Between the Thunder and the Sun 271

The One That Got Away 315

Transfusion 327

Guardian Spirit 363

The Gift 399

To Whom It May Concern 419

A Stick for Harry Eddington 437

Old Four-Eyes 453

A Star Above It

Introduction: Chad Oliver

The guy's been gone ten years now, and it's still hard to write about him.

Symmes Chadwick Oliver was born on March 28, 1928, in Cincinnati, the son and grandson of doctors; his mother had been a nurse when she met his father.

He grew up in Cincinnati (Ledgewood, to be precise; more later). He did all the usual kid stuff, baseball, bicycling, reading. He was a flyfisherperson from the time he could hold a rod. He saw the first reissue of *King Kong;* after that he watched the tree outside his window every night for the sign of the big ape's approach.

Then when he was twelve he was hit with rheumatic fever. Gone were bicycles, flyrods, baseball bats. There was Chad in his bed for a year, watching other kids fish, wreck their bikes and miss skinners. What was left to him was reading and listening to jazz records.

What he read, besides books, was mostly the air-war pulps: *Dusty Ayres and His Battle Birds; G-8 and His Battle Aces.* He wrote letters to the editors; he got back letters from Robert O. Erisman that ended "Clear Skies and Tailwinds".

One day by mistake, he was brought, along with the usual air-combat stuff, one of the old encyclopedia-sized *Amazing Stories.* Chad leafed through it, came across Edmond Hamilton's "Treasure on Thunder Moon", read it and pronounced it "the greatest piece of literature ever written!"

Out of bed jumps Chad (rheumatic fever be damned!), gets on his bike, hotfoots it to the nearest newsstand and buys up *everything* that looks like *Amazing.*

Soon the letter columns of the SF magazines were full of things signed "Chad Oliver, the Loony Lad of Ledgewood."

By and by Chad was out of bed for good; by and by the US was sucked into the vortex of the last World Unpleasantness by Pearl Harbor.

Chad's father got a commission in the Army. They pulled up their Ohio roots and found themselves in Crystal City, Texas.

Chad lived in the Crystal City complex, which was one-half German-Italian POW camp, and one-half Japanese-American relocation camp, where his father was the doctor. "At the German-Italian POW camp the machine guns pointed *in,*" said Chad once. "At the Japanese portion, the guns pointed *out,* in case some farmer decided to get a little rough justice for what was happening on Guadalcanal or in the Solomons."

He went to Crystal City High School, and as he said, "Football saved my scrawny ass." He went in as S.C. Oliver, 96 lb. weakling; out comes Chad, the Boy Who Walks Like A Mountain. He liked it so much that when the camp was closed and his father restationed in Corpus Christi, he rented a room in town and finished out his senior year of gridiron glory.

Unlike everyone else in town, who went to Texas A&M, Chad entered UT, where he majored in English.

The war was over; he and his father, in search of bigger and better trout, crossed over Slumgullion Pass in the summer of 1946, and in Lake City, Colorado, stopped at the little falls in front of the grocery store on the Lake Fork of the Gunnison. There was a guy fishing there with a cane pole and some worms. They asked him if he knew where a good place to fish would be. The guy reached down and pulled up a stringer with two seven-pound cutthroats on it. "This is as good as any," the guy said.

Chad and his father looked at each other, and said, like Dean Jagger in the movie, "This is the Place."

Meanwhile Chad lucked out and got a succession of brilliant profs, including some in his anthropology electives. That didn't stop him and Garvin Berry from publishing the first SF fanzine in Texas, *The Moon Puddle,* in 1948, where they used such pseudonyms as L. Sprague de Willy.

Along about 1950 Chad took off for UCLA to get his graduate degrees in English and anthropology. His life was changing in big ways. He sold his first story (more later); he met other writers in LA, and he met BeJe.

They were married, in Forrest J Ackerman's living room, on November 1, 1952 (they wanted to get married on Halloween, but Chad had classes that day . . .). Ray Bradbury was best man. You can't get any more fannish than *that.*

Life for Chad became a blur of writing, teaching, fishing, and eventually, field work among the Kamba of East Africa, in the late 1950s and early sixties. He also returned to UT to teach.

As if that weren't enough, he did a jazz radio show four hours a week as the Masked DJ, or whatever he was called.

Eventually there were two *kinder,* Kim (a she) and Glenn (a he). In the fullness of time he became a grandad.

Inevitably, Chad became chairman of the anthropology department at UT. He immediately made two rules: that the chairmanship would become a rotating one, so *he* wouldn't be stuck in the job forever; and, that the chairman had to teach the 300-student Intro to Anthro course. ("You meet every student who's going to be in the department for the next four years; you don't get rusty just teaching graduate seminars.") Non-majors always packed the place the day Chad ran through *all* the primate distress calls, from gibbon to human. ("Man, the ape that walks like a chicken," as he used to say.)

He also worked to set up and refine Plan II Studies, whereby all the bright kids (as Chad had been) could skip most of the crap. He won, eventually, every teaching award UT had to give. He probably influenced the lives of 20-30,000 students; people would come back to college 15 years later, wander into his office like it was a public convenience, and tell him *he'd* changed their lives.

When he wasn't in Africa, or teaching and writing (his other specialty was the Plains Indians—more later), or dealing with the Headaches of Academe, he was trying to make a viable trout fishery of the Guadalupe River in Texas, the southernmost place they can live in the U.S., and fighting with the Guadalupe-Blanco River Authority over minimum flows. He served as President of the Texas Chapter of Trout Unlimited a few times; for his pretty much damn thankless efforts they gave him their Conservation Award in the early '90s.

Also by and by Chad had *three bouts each* with *two* entirely separate kinds of cancer. He was a tough guy—he probably had eighteen good months in the last eight years of his life. He kept on doing everything—teaching (except for the last six months), writing and fishing—right up until the end.

He passed away, ironically enough, on Isaak Walton's birthday, August 9th, 1993. He had turned 65 in March; it should have been his year of retirement from UT.

You have here, in these two volumes, Chad the Writer. He had been sending off stories since he was 14. One day (more later) one didn't come back. Then another didn't, and another and another, and so it went.

He wrote his first novel (at 24), *Mists of Dawn,* for the Winston SF juvenile series, a time-travel story of Neanderthals and those pesky Cro-Magnons (us). Then came *Shadows in the Sun* in 1954, in which a transposed Crystal City is found to be full of aliens. *The Winds of Time* came out in 1957. ("What ever happened to that handsome devil in the author photo on the back of that book?" I once asked him. "They killed him and replaced him with me," Chad said.) Then came *Unearthly Neighbors* (1960), *The Shores of Another Sea* (1971) and *Giants in the Dust* (1976). Those were the SF novels.

Chad plugged away for years in SF, getting all the prestige he could eat, but damned little else. Eventually he sat down and wrote about his second love, Westerns, and he got awards out the old wazoo. *The Wolf Is My Brother* (1967) won the Western Writers of America SPUR award (it *really is* a pair of spurs). *Broken Eagle* (1989), the Little Bighorn novel he'd researched for 25 years, won the Western Heritage Society Award as Best Novel (and at the awards ceremony both BeJe *and* Chad danced with James Garner, another honoree). He didn't live to see his third Western, *The Cannibal Owl* (1993,) in print. (He had 18 pages left to do when he was told he had to go in for *yet another operation.* "Ten, and I would have done it that night," he said. "Eighteen was too much." A week after he got out of the hospital, he sat down and finished the book in two days and mailed it off.)

Those are his novels.

Chad had only two collections published in his lifetime: *Another Kind* (1955) and *The Edge of Forever* (1971).

Chad sold his first story, "The Boy Next Door," to *F&SF* in 1950 (although his second sale, "The Land of Lost Content", was published first, in *Super Science Stories*). He hit the ground running and never looked back, publishing stories nearly every year of his 43-year career. There was just plain *a burst* of sales twice in his career: early in the Fifties, another in the late 80s and early '90s. Some of those last ones got him Nebula nominations.

Running through his bibliography are many titles from A. E. Housman's poems, an early literary love of Chad's: "The Land of Lost Content", "Between the Thunder and the Sun". When Harlan Ellison wanted to title his sequel to "A Boy and His Dog," "Blood's a Rover", he wrote to Chad as a matter of courtesy to ask if it were okay, as Chad had used *that* title on a story in 1952. "Why are you asking me?" Chad wrote back. "Why aren't you asking the *Housman* estate? That's who *I stole it from . . .*"

From the subject matter of his novels—either dealing directly with anthropology, or with contacts between cultures and aliens—Chad was thought by some to deal almost exclusively with these themes. You'll find in these two volumes the depth and breadth of the things he was interested in, from the jazz-world of "Didn't He Ramble?" to the *Twilight Zone*-type story (seven years before the TV show premiered) of "Transformer", a story that should stay in print, all the time, somewhere, forever.

What you have here is forty-something years of the man and the writer, alpha to omega, absolute first to last. Besides everything *else* he did, it's a body of work anyone would be proud of.

If you haven't made these word-journeys before, I, as the usual phrase goes, envy you. But I *really do.* Those of us reading him all along were always surprised by the guy. No matter what had happened before; the next one wasn't going to be like that. There *is* the pastoral tone, as they say, all the way through. There's an elegiac tone too, in some of them—not just in the later ones, though. Check out "King of the Hill"—that was in the middle, and pretty much says it *all* about us, i.e., *homo sapiens*—manlike but not so wise.

Here's Symmes Chadwick Oliver at his best.

Or to those of us who miss him so much, plain ol' wonderful Chad.

Howard Waldrop
Austin, Texas
May 2003

BLOOD'S A ROVER

Clay lies still, but blood's a rover;
　Breath's a ware that will not keep.
Up, lad: when the journey's over
　There'll be time enough to sleep.
　　　　　　　　—A. E. Housman

I

Night sifted through the city like flakes of soft black snow drifting down from the stars. It whispered along the tree-lined canyons between the clean shafts of white buildings and pressed darkly against windows filled with warm light. Conan Lang watched the illumination in his office increase subtly in adjusting to the growing darkness outside and then looked again at the directive he held in his hand.

It still read the same way.

"Another day, another world," he said aloud. And then, paraphrasing: "The worlds are too much with us—"

Conan Lang fired up his pipe and puffed carefully on it to get it going properly. Then he concentrated on blowing neat cloudy smoke rings that wobbled across the room and impaled themselves on the nose of the three-dimensional portrait of the President. It wasn't that he had anything against President Austin, he assured himself. It was simply that Austin represented that nebulous being, Authority, and at the moment it happened that Authority was singularly unwelcome in the office of Conan Lang.

He looked back at the directive. The wording was friendly and informal enough, but the meaning was clear:

> Headquarters, Gal. Administration.
> Office of Admiral Nelson White,
> Commander, Process Planning Division.
> 15 April, 2701. Confidential.

One Agent Conan Lang
Applied Process Corps
G.A. Department Seven
Conan:

    We got another directive from the Buzzard yesterday. Seems that the powers that be have decided that a change in Sirius Ten is in order—a shift from Four to Five. You're it. Make a prelim check and report to me at your convenience. Cheer up—maybe you'll get another bag of medals out of it.

Nelson.

    Conan Lang left the directive on his desk and got to his feet. He walked over to the window and looked out at the lights sprinkled over the city. There weren't many. Most people were long ago home in the country, sitting around the living room, playing with the kids. He puffed slowly on his pipe.

    Another bag of medals. Nelson wasn't kidding anybody—wasn't even trying to, really. He knew how Conan felt because he felt the same way. They all did, sooner or later. It was fascinating at first, even fun, this tampering with the lives of other people. But the novelty wore off in a hurry—shriveled like flesh in acid under a million eyes of hate, a million talks with your soul at three in the morning, a million shattered lives. Sure, it was necessary. You could always tell yourself that; that was the charm, the magic word that was supposed to make everything fine and dandy. Necessary—but for *you*, not for them. Or perhaps for them too, in the long run.

    Conan Lang returned to his desk and flipped on the intercom. "I want out," he said. "The Administration Library, Division of Extraterrestrial Anthropology. I'd like to speak to Bailey if he's there."

    He had to wait thirty seconds.

    "Bailey here," the intercom said.

    "This is Lang. What've you got on Sirius Ten?"

    "Just like that, huh? Hang on a second."

    There was a short silence. Conan Lang smoked his pipe slowly and smiled as he visualized Bailey punching enough buttons to control a space fleet.

    "Let's see," Bailey's voice came through the speaker. "We've got a good bit. There's McAllister's 'Kinship Systems of Sirius Ten'; Jenkins'—that's B. J. Jenkins, the one who worked with Holden—'Sirius Ten Social Organization'; Bartheim's 'Economic Life of Sirius Ten'; Robert Patterson's 'Basic Personality Types of the Sirius Group'; 'Preliminary and Supplementary Ethnological Surveys of the Galactic Advance Fleet'—the works."

    Conan Lang sighed. "O.K.," he said. "Shoot them out to my place, will you?"

    "Check—be there before you are. One thing more, Cone."

    "Yes?"

"Been reading a splendid eight-volume historical novel of the Twentieth Century. Hot stuff, I'll tell you. You want me to send it along in case
you run out of reading material?"

"Very funny. See you around."

"So long."

Conan Lang switched off the intercom and destroyed the directive.
He tapped out his pipe in the waster and left the office, locking the door
behind him. The empty hallway was sterile and impersonal. It seemed
dead at night, somehow, and it was difficult to believe that living, breathing human beings walked through it all day long. It was like a tunnel to
nowhere. He had the odd feeling that there was nothing around it at all,
just space and less than space—no building, no air, no city. Just a white
antiseptic tunnel to nowhere.

He shook off the feeling and caught the lift to the roof. The cool night
air was crisp and clean and there was a whisper of a breeze out of the
north. A half moon hung in the night, framed by stars. He looked up at
it and wondered how Johnny was getting along up there, and whether
perhaps Johnny was even then looking down on Earth.

Conan Lang climbed into his bullet and set the controls. The little
ship rose vertically on her copter blades for two thousand feet, hovered a
moment over the silent city, and then flashed off on her jets into the west.

Conan Lang sat back in his cushioned seat, looking at the stars, trying
not to think, letting the ship carry him home.

Conan Lang relaxed in his armchair, his eyes closed, an icy bourbon
and soda in his hand. The books he had requested—neat, white, uniform
microfilm blowups from the Administration Library—were stacked neatly
on the floor by his side, waiting. Waiting, he thought, sipping his drink.
They were always waiting. No matter how much a man knew, there was
always more—waiting.

The room closed in around him. He could feel it—warm, friendly,
personal. It was a good room. It was a room filled with life, his life and
Kit's. It was almost as if he could see the room better with his eyes closed,
for then he saw the past as well as the present. There was the silver and
black tapestry on the wall, given to him by old Maharani so long ago, on
a world so far away that the very light given off by its sun when he was
there had yet to reach the Earth as the twinkle of a star in the night sky.
There were his books, there were Kit's paintings, there was the smudge—
the current one—on the carpet where Rob had tracked dirt into the house
before supper.

He opened his eyes and looked at his wife.

"I must be getting old, Kit," he said. "Right at the moment, it all looks
pretty pointless."

Kit raised her eyebrows and said nothing.

"We tear around all over the galaxy like a bunch of kids playing Spacemen and Pirates," he said, downing his drink. "Push here, pull there, shove here, reverse there. It's like some kind of half-wit game where one side doesn't even know it's playing, or on which side of the field. Sometimes—"

"Want another drink?" Kit asked softly.

"Yes. Kit—"

"I know," she said, touching his shoulder with her hand. "Go ahead and talk; you'll feel better. We go through this every time there's a new one, remember? I know you don't really mean things the way you say them, and I know why you say them that way anyhow." She kissed him lightly on the forehead, and her lips were cool and patient. "I understand."

Conan Lang watched her leave the room with his empty glass. "Yes," he whispered to himself. "Yes, I guess you do."

It *was* necessary, of course. Terribly, urgently necessary. But it got to you, sometimes. All those people out there, living their lives, laughing and crying, raising children. It hurt you to think about them. And it wasn't necessary for them, not for him, not for Kit. Or was it? You couldn't tell; there was always a chance. But if only they could just forget it all, just live, there was so much to enjoy—

Kit handed him a fresh bourbon and soda, icy and with just a trace of lemon in it the way he liked it, and then curled up again on the couch, smiling at him.

"I'm sorry, angel," he said. "You must get pretty sick of hearing the same sad song over and over again."

"Not when you sing it, Cone."

"It's just that sometimes I chuck my mind out the nearest window and wonder why—"

There was a thump and a bang from the rear of the house. Conan Lang tasted his drink. That meant Rob was home. He listened, waiting. There was the hollow crack—that was the bat going into the corner. There was the heavy thud—that was the fielder's glove.

"That's why," Kit said.

Conan Lang nodded and picked up the first book off the floor.

Three days later, Conan Lang went up the white steps, presented his credentials, and walked into the Buzzard's Cage. The place made him nervous. Irritated with himself, he paused deliberately and lit his pipe before going on. The Cage seemed cold, inhuman. And the Buzzard—

He shouldn't feel that way, he told himself, again offering his identification before entering the lift to the Nest. Intellectually, he understood cybernetics; there was nothing supernatural about it. The Cage was just a

machine, for all its powers, even if the Buzzard did sometimes seem more—
or perhaps less—than a man. Still, the place gave him the creeps. A vast
thinking machine, filling a huge building, a brain beside which his own
was as nothing. Of course, men had built it. Men made guns, too, but
the knowledge was scant comfort when you looked into a metallic muzzle
and someone pulled the trigger.

"Lang," he said to himself, "you're headed for the giggle ward."

He smiled then, knowing it wasn't so. Imagination was a prime requi-
site for his job, and he just had more than his share. It got in the way
sometimes, but it was a part of him and that was that.

Conan Lang waded through a battery of attendants and security personnel and finally reached the Nest. He opened the door and stepped
into the small, dark room. There, behind the desk where he always was,
perched the Buzzard.

"Hello, Dr. Gottleib," said Conan Lang.

The man behind the desk eyed him silently. His name was Fritz
Gottleib, but he had been tagged the Buzzard long ago. No one used the
name to his face, and it was impossible to tell whether or not the name
amused him. He spoke but seldom, and his appearance, even after you got
used to it, was startling. Fritz Gottleib was squat and completely bald. He
always dressed in black and his heavy eyebrows were like horizontal splashes
of ink against the whiteness of his face. The Buzzard analogy, thought
Conan Lang, was more than understandable; it was inevitable. The man
sat high in his tower, in his Nest of controls, brooding over a machine that
perhaps he alone fully understood. Alone. He always seemed alone, no
matter how many people surrounded him. His was a life apart, a life whose
vital force pulsed in the shifting lights of the tubes of a great machine.

"Dr. Lang," he acknowledged, unmoving, his voice sibilant, almost a
hiss.

Conan Lang puffed on his pipe and dropped into the chair across from
Gottleib. He had dealt with the Buzzard before and most of the shock
had worn off. You could get used to anything, he supposed. Man was a
very adaptable animal.

"The smoke doesn't bother you, I hope?"

Gottleib did not comment. He simply stared at him, his dark eyes
unblinking. Like looking at a piece of meat, thought Conan Lang.

"Well," he said, trying again. "I guess you know what I'm here for."

"You waste words," Fritz Gottleib hissed.

"I hadn't realized they were in short supply," Lang replied, smiling. The
Buzzard was irritating, but he could see the justice in the man's remark. It
was curious the number of useless things that were said all the time—useless, at any rate, from a purely communicative point of view. It would have

been sheerly incredible for Gottleib—who after all had been checking his results in the computer—*not* to have known the nature of his mission.

"O.K.," said Lang, "what's the verdict?"

Fritz Gottleib fingered a square card in his surprisingly long-fingered hands, seeming to hover over it like a bird of prey.

"It checks out," he said sibilantly, his voice low and hard to hear. "Your plan will achieve the desired transfer in Sirius Ten, and the transfer integrates positively with the Plan."

"Anything else? Anything I should know?"

"We should all know many more things than we do, Dr. Lang."

"Um-m-m. But that was all the machine said with respect to my proposed plan of operations?"

"That was all."

Conan Lang sat back, watching Gottleib. A strange man. But he commanded respect.

"I'd like to get hold of that baby sometime," he said easily. "I've got a question or two of my own."

"Sometimes it is best not to know the answers to one's questions, Dr. Lang."

"No. But I'd like to have a shot at it all the same. Don't tell the security boys I said that; they'd string me up by the toes."

"Perhaps one day, Dr. Lang. When you are old like me."

Conan Lang stood up, cupping his pipe in his hand. "I guess that's all," he said.

"Yes," said Fritz Gottleib.

"See you around."

No answer. Cold shadows seemed to fill the room.

Conan Lang turned and left the way he had come. Behind him, drilling into his back, he could feel the eyes of Fritz Gottleib following him, cold and deep like the frozen waters of an arctic sea.

The ship stood on Earth but she was not of Earth. She was poised, a mighty lance of silver, a creature of the deeps. She waited, impatient, while Conan Lang slowly walked across the vast duralloy tarmac of Space One, Admiral White at his side. The sun was bright in a clean blue sky. It touched the ship with lambent flame and warmed Conan Lang's shoulders under his uniform. A slight puff of breeze rustled across the spaceport, pushing along a stray scrap of white paper ahead of it.

"Here we go again," said Conan Lang.

"That's what you get for being good," the admiral said with a smile. "You get good enough and you'll get my job—which ought to be a grim enough prospect even for you. If you're smart, you'll botch this job six ways from Sunday and then we'll have to give you a rest."

"Yeah—play a little joke, strictly for laughs, and give 'em an atom bomb or two to stick on the ends of their hatchets. Or take 'em back to the caves. There are plenty of delicious possibilities."

The two men walked on, toward the silver ship.

"Everything's set, I suppose?" asked Conan Lang.

"Yep. Your staff is already on board and the stuff is loaded."

"Any further instructions?"

"No—you know your business or you wouldn't be going. Just try to make it as quick as you can, Cone. They're getting warm over on Research on that integration-acceleration principle for correlating data— it's going to be big and I'll want you around when it breaks."

Conan Lang grinned. "What happens if I just up and disappear one day, Nels? Does the galaxy moan and lie down and quit?"

"Search me," said Admiral Nelson White. "But don't take any more risks than you absolutely have to. Don't get the idea that you're indispensable, either. It's just that it's tiresome to break in new men."

"I'll try to stay alive if you're positive that's what you want."

They approached the ship. Kit and Rob were waiting. The admiral touched his cap and moved on, leaving Conan Lang alone with his family. Kit was lovely—she always was, Conan Lang thought. He couldn't imagine a life without her.

"Bye, darlin'," he whispered, taking her in his arms. "One of these days I'm coming back and I'm never going to leave you again."

"This is till then," Kit said softly and kissed him for keeps.

Much later, Conan Lang released her and shook hands with his son.

"So long, old-timer," he said.

"Hurry back, Dad," Rob said, trying not to cry.

Conan Lang turned and joined Admiral White at the star cruiser. He did not look back.

"Good luck, Cone," the admiral said, patting him on the back. "I'll keep the medals warm and a light in the cabin window."

"O.K. , Nels," said Conan Lang.

He swung aboard the great ship and stepped into the lift. There was a muted hum of machinery as the car whispered up through the pneumatic tube, up into the hollowness of the ship. Already it seemed to Conan Lang that he had left Earth far behind him. The endless loneliness of the star trails rode up with him in the humming lift.

The ship rested, quiescent, on Earth. Ahead of her, calling to her, the stars flamed coldly in an infinite sea of night.

II

Conan Lang walked down the long white corridor to the afterhold, his footsteps muffled and almost inaudible in the murmur of the atomics. It *would* be a long white corridor, he thought to himself. Wherever man went, there went the long white corridors—offices, hospitals, command posts. It was almost as if he had spent half a lifetime walking through long white corridors, and now here was yet another one—cold and antiseptic, hanging in space eight light-years from Earth.

"Halt."

"Lang here," he told the Fleetman. "Kindly point that thing the other way."

"Identification, please."

Lang sighed and handed it over. The man should know him by now; after all, the ship was on his mission, and he was hardly a subversive character. Still, orders were orders—a principle that covered a multitude of sins. And they couldn't afford to take chances, not *any* chances.

"All right, sir," the Fleetman said, returning the identification. "Sorry to bother you."

"Forget it," said Conan Lang. "Keep your eye peeled for space pirates."

The guard smiled. "Who'd want to steal space, sir?" he asked. "It's free and I reckon there's enough to go around."

"Your inning," acknowledged Conan Lang, moving into the afterhold. The kid was already there.

"Hello, sir," said Andrew Irvin.

"Hi, Andy—and cut the 'sir,' what do you say? You make me feel like I should be extinct or embalmed or something."

The kid smiled almost shyly. Conan Lang had half expected to find him there in the hold; Andy was always poking around, asking questions, trying to learn. His quick brown eyes and alert carriage reminded Conan of a young hunting dog, frisking through the brush, perpetually on the verge of flushing the grandfather of all jack rabbits.

"It doesn't seem possible, does it?" asked the kid.

Conan Lang raised his eyebrows.

"All this, I mean," Andy Irvin said, gesturing at the neat brown sacks stacked row upon row in the brightly lighted hold. "To think that a couple of sacks of that stuff can remold a planet, change the lives of millions of people—"

"It's not just the sacks, Andy. It took man a good many hundreds of thousands of years to learn what to *do* with those sacks."

"Yes, sir," the kid said, hanging on every word.

"No 'sir,' remember? I'm not giving you a lecture, and you don't have to look attentive. I'm sure that elementary anthropology isn't *too* dumfounding to a guy who took honors at the Academy."

"Well—"

"Never mind." Conan Lang eyed him speculatively. The kid reminded him, almost too much, of someone else—a kid named Conan Lang who had started out on a great adventure himself too many years ago. "I . . . um-m-m . . . guess you know you're going to work with me on Ten."

Andy looked like Conan had just handed him a harem on a silver platter. "No, sir," he said. "I didn't know. Thank you, sir."

"The name is Conan."

"Yes, sir."

"Hellfire," said Conan Lang. How did you go about telling a kid that you were happy to have someone around with stars in his eyes again? Without sounding like a fool? The answer was simple—you didn't.

"I can't wait," Andy said. "To really *do* something at last—it's a great feeling. I hope I'll do O.K."

"It won't be long now, Andy. Twenty-four hours from now you and I go to work. The buggy ride is about over."

The two men fell silent then, looking at the neat brown rows of sacks, feeling the star ship tremble slightly under them with the thunder of her great atomics.

It was night on Sirius Ten—a hot, humid night with a single moon hanging like frozen fire in the darkness. A small patrol craft from the cruiser floated motionless in the night sky, her batteries pouring down a protective screen around the newly-cleared field. Conan Lang wiped the sweat from his forehead and washed his hands off in the clean river water that gurgled through the trench at his feet.

"That about does it, Andy," he said wearily. "Toss 'em a Four signal."

Andy Irvin turned the rheostat on his small control board to Four and flipped the switch. They waited, listening to the faint murmur of the night breeze off the river. There was no change, nothing that they could see, but they could almost feel the intense radiation pounding into the field from the patrol ship, seeping into the ground, accelerating by thousands of times the growth factor in the seeds.

"That's got it," said Conan Lang. "Give 'em release."

Andy shot the patrol craft the release signal and shut off his control board. The little ship seemed to hover uncertainly. There was a humming sound and a spot of intense white light in the sky. That was all. The ship was gone and they were alone.

"It's been a long night, kid," yawned Conan Lang. "We'd better get some sack time—we're liable to need it before morning."

"You go ahead," Andy Irvin said. "I'm not sleepy; the sunrise here ought to be something."

"Yeah," said Conan Lang. "The sunrise ought to be something."

He walked across the field and entered a structure that closely resembled a native hut in appearance but was actually quite, quite different. Too tired even to undress, he piled into bed with his clothes on and rested quietly in the darkness.

The strange, haunting, familiar-with-a-difference sounds of an alien world whispered around the hut on the soft, moist breeze from the sluggish river. Far away, an animal screamed hoarsely in the clogging brush. Conan Lang kept his eyes closed and tried not to think, but his mind ignored him. It went right on working, asking questions, demanding answers, bringing up into the light many memories that were good and some that were better forgotten.

"Kit," he said, very softly.

Tired as he was, he knew there would be no sleep for him that night.

The sunrise was a glory. The blue-white inferno of Sirius hung in the treetops across the field and then climbed into the morning sky, her white dwarf companion a smaller sun by her side. The low cumulus clouds were edged with flame—fiery red, pale blue, cool green. The fresh morning winds washed the field with air and already the young plants were out of the ground, thirsty for the sun. The chuckling water in the trenches sparkled in the light.

With the morning, the natives came.

"They're all around us," Conan Lang said quietly.

"I can't see them," whispered Andy Irvin, looking at the brush.

"They're there."

"Do you . . . expect trouble, sir?"

"Not yet, assuming we've got this deal figured right. They're more afraid of us than we are of them."

"What if we *don't* have it figured right?"

Conan Lang smiled. "Three guesses," he said.

The kid managed a wry grin. He was taking it well, Lang thought. He remembered how he'd felt the first time. It didn't really hit you until that first day, and then it upped and kicked you in the teeth. Quite suddenly, it was all a very different proposition from the manuals and the viewers and the classrooms of the Academy. *Just you, all alone,* the alien breeze sighed in your ear. *You're all alone in the middle of nowhere,* the wind whispered through the trees. *Our eyes are watching you, our world is pressing you back, waiting. What do you know of us really? What good is your knowledge now?*

"What next?" Andy asked.

"Just tend the field, kid. And try to act like a ghost. You're an ancestor of those people watching us from the brush, remember. If we've got this figured wrong—if those survey reports were haywire somewhere, or if someone's been through here who didn't belong—you should have a little warning at least. They don't use blowguns or anything—just spears, and they'd prefer a hatchet. If there's trouble, you hightail it back to the hut *at once* and man the projector. That's all."

"I'm not so sure I care to be an ancestor," Andy Irvin muttered, picking up his hoe. "Not yet, anyhow." He moved off along a water trench, checking on the plants.

Conan Lang picked up his own hoe and set to work. He could feel the natives watching him, wondering, whispering to themselves. But he was careful not to look around him. He kept his head down and dug at the plants with his hoe, clearing the water channels. The plants were growing with astonishing rapidity, thanks to the dose of radiation. They should be mature in a week. And then—

The sun blazed down on his treated skin and the sweat rolled off his body in tiny rivulets. The field was strangely silent around him; there was only the gurgle of the water and the soft sigh of the humid breeze. His hoe chopped and slushed at the mud and his back was tired from bending over so long. It was too still, unnaturally still.

Behind that brush, back in the trees—a thousand eyes.

He did not look around. Step by step, he moved down the trench, under the hellish sun, working with his hoe.

The fire-burned days and the still, hushed nights alternated rapidly. On the morning of the third day, Andy Irvin found what they had been waiting for.

In the far corner of the field, placed on a rude wood platform about four feet high, there were three objects. There was a five-foot-square bark mat, neatly woven. There was a small animal that closely resembled a terrestrial pig, face down, its throat neatly slashed. And there was a child. It was a female baby, evidently not over a week old. It had been strangled to death.

"It's . . . different . . . when you see it for yourself," Andy said quietly, visibly shaken.

"You'll get used to it," said Conan Lang, his voice purposely flat and matter-of-fact. "Get the pig and the mat—and stop looking like a prohibitionist who just found a jug of joy water in the freezer. This is old stuff to ancestors."

"Old stuff," repeated Andy without conviction.

They carried the contents of the platform back to their hut and Conan Lang wrapped the body of the child in a cloth.

"We'll bury her tonight after dark," he said. "The pig we eat. It won't do any harm to sit on the mat where they can see us while we're eating it, either."

"Well," Andy muttered. "Glad to see you're not going to eat the baby, too."

"You never can tell," smiled Conan. "We anthropologists are all crazy, or hadn't you heard?"

"I've heard," agreed Andy Irvin, getting his nerves under control again. "Where's the hot sauce?"

Conan Lang stepped back outside and picked up his hoe. The blazing double sun had already produced shimmering heat waves that danced like live things in the still air over the green field. The kid was going to be all right. He'd known it all along, of course—but you could never be *sure* of a man until you worked with him under field conditions. And a misfit, an unstable personality, was anything but a joke on an alien planet where unknowable forces hung in the balance.

"Let's see if I've got this thing figured straight," Andy said, puffing away on one of Conan's pipes. "The natives are afraid of us, and still they feel that they must make us an offering because we, as their supposed ancestors, control their lives. So they pick a system of dumb barter rather than sending out the usual contact man to ferret out kinship connections."

"You're O.K. so far," Conan Lang said. "I guess you've studied about the dumb barter system used on Earth in the old days; it was used whenever trade took place between groups of markedly unequal strength, such as the African pygmies and trading vessels from the west. There's a fear factor involved."

"Yes, sir."

"Forget the 'sir.' I didn't mean to lecture. I think I'll start calling you Junior."

"Sorry. The bark mat is a unit in a reciprocal trade system and the pig is a sacred animal—I get that part of it. But the baby—that's terrible, Conan. After all, we caused that death in a way—"

"Afraid not," Conan Lang corrected him. "These people practice infanticide; it's part of their religion. If the preliminary reports were correct—and they've checked out so far—they kill all the female children born on the last three days of alternate months. There's an economic reason, too—not enough food to go around, and that's a pretty effective method of birth control. The baby would have been killed regardless—we had nothing to do with it."

"Still—"

"I know. But maybe she was the lucky one after all."

"I don't quite follow you there."

"Skip it—you'll find out soon enough."

"What are you going to leave them tonight?"

"Not sure yet," Conan Lang said. "We'll have to integrate with their value system, of course. We brought some mats, and I guess a good steel knife won't hurt things any. We'll worry about that later. Come on, farmer—back to work."

Andy Irvin picked up his hoe and followed Conan Lang into the field. The clear water bubbled softly as it flowed through the trenches. The growing plants sent their roots thirstily into the ground and the fresh green shoots stretched up like tentacles into the humid air of Sirius Ten.

That night, under the great yellow moon that swam far away and lonesome among the stars, they placed exchange gifts of their own on the platform. Next morning, the invisible traders had replaced them with four mats and another dead pig.

"No babies, anyhow," Andy Irvin said, puffing industriously on one of Conan's pipes. They had decided that cigarettes, as an unfamiliar cultural trait to the natives, were out. Now, with Andy taking with unholy enthusiasm to pipe smoking, Conan Lang was threatened with a shortage of tobacco. He watched the smoke from the kid's pipe with something less than ecstasy.

"We can have smoked ham," he observed.

"It was your idea," Andy grinned.

"Call me 'sir'."

Andy laughed, relaxed now, and picked up the pig. Conan gathered up the somewhat cumbersome mats and followed him back into the hut. The hot, close sun was already burning his shoulders. The plants were green and healthy looking, and the air was a trifle fresher in the growing field.

"Now what?" Andy asked, standing outside the hut and letting the faint breeze cool him off as best it could.

"I figure we're about ready for an overt contact," Conan Lang said. "Everything has checked out beautifully so far, and the natives don't seem to be suspicious or hostile. We might as well get the ball rolling."

"The green branch, isn't it?"

"That's right."

They still did not get a glimpse of the natives throughout the steaming day, and that night they placed a single mat on the platform. On top of the mat they put a slim branch of green leaves, twisted around back on itself and tied loosely to form a circle. The green branch was by no means a universal symbol of peace, but, in this particular form, it chanced to be so on Sirius Ten. Conan Lang smiled a little. Man had found many curious things among the stars, and most of them were of just this unsensational but very useful sort.

By dawn, the mat and the circle branch were gone and the natives had left them nothing in return.

"Today's the day," Conan Lang said, rubbing the sleep out of his eyes. "They'll either give us the works or accept our offer. Nothing to do now but wait."

They picked up their hoes and went back into the field. Waiting can be the most difficult of all things, and the long, hot morning passed without incident. The two men ate their lunch in silence, thankful for the odorless injection that kept the swarming insects away from them. Late in the afternoon, when the long blue shadows of evening were already touching the green plants and the clean, flowing water, the natives came.

There were five of them and they appeared to be unarmed. One man walked slightly in advance of the others, a circular branch of green leaves in his hand. Conan Lang waited for them, with Andy standing by at his side. It was moments like this, he thought, that made you suddenly realize that you were all alone and a long, long way from friends. The natives came on steadily. Conan felt a surge of admiration for the young man who led them. From his point of view, he was walking into a situation filled with the terror of the supernatural, which was a very real part of his life. His steps did not falter. He would, Conan supposed, be the eldest son of the most powerful chief.

The natives stopped when they were three paces away. Their leader extended the circular green branch. "We would serve you, fathers from the mountains," the native said in his own tongue.

Conan Lang stepped forward and received the branch. "We are brothers," he replied in the same language, "and we would be your friends."

The native smiled, his teeth very white. "I am Ren," he said. "I am your brother."

Conan Lang kept his face expressionless, but deep within him a dark regret and sadness coursed like ice through his veins.

It had begun again.

III

For many days, Conan Lang listened to the Oripesh natives preparing for the feast. Their small village, only a quarter of a mile from the field, was alive with excitement. The women prepared great piles of the staple ricefruit and broiled river fish in great green leaves on hot coals. The men chanted and danced interminably, cleansing the village by ritual for the coming visitation, while the children, forgotten for once, played on the banks of the river. On the appointed day, Conan Lang walked into the village with Andy Irvin at his side.

It was a crude village, necessarily so because of its transient nature. But it was not dirty. The natives watched the two men with awe, but they did not seem unfriendly. The supernatural was for them always just on the other side of the hill, hidden in the night, and now it was among them, in the open. That was all. And what, after all, thought Conan Lang, could have seemed more supernatural to them than a silver ship that dropped out of the stars? What was supernatural depended on one's point of view—and on how much one happened to know about what was *natural.*

The box he carried was heavy, and it took both arms to handle it. He watched Andy puffing at his side and smiled.

"Stick with it, kid," he said, walking steadily through the watching natives. "You may earn your pay yet."

Andy muttered something under his breath and blinked to get the sweat out of his eyes.

When they reached the clearing in the center of the village, they stopped and put their boxes down. Ren, the eldest son of the chief Ra Renne, approached them at once and offered them a drink from a large wooden bowl. Conan drank and passed the container on to Andy, who grinned broadly and took a long swallow of the warm fluid. It was sweet, although not too sweet, and it burned pleasantly on the way down. It was, Conan decided instantly, a great improvement over some native fermented horrors he had been subjected to in times past.

The natives gathered around them in a great circle. There must have been nearly five hundred of them—far more than the small village could accommodate for any length of time.

"We're celebrities," Conan Lang whispered out of the side of his month as he waited to be presented ceremonially to the chiefs.

"You want my autograph?" hissed Andy, his face just a trifle flushed from the drink he had taken. "I make a real fine *X.*"

The feast followed a pattern familiar to Conan Lang. They were presented ceremonially to the tribe, having identified themselves as ancestors of four generations ago, thus making themselves kin to virtually all the tribe with their complicated lineage system, and also making refutation impossible since no one remembered that far back. They were seated with the chiefs, and ate the ritual feast rapidly. The food was good, and Conan Lang was interested in getting a good taste of the ricefruit plant, which was the basic food staple of the Oripesh.

After the eating came the drinking, and after the drinking the dancing. The Oripesh were not a musical people, and they had no drums. The men and the women danced apart from each other, each one doing an individual dance—which he owned, just as the men from Earth owned material property—to his own rhythm pattern. Conan Lang and Andy Irvin contented themselves with watching, not trusting themselves to improvise an authentic dance. They were aware that their conduct was at variance with the somewhat impulsive conduct usually attributed to ancestors in native folklore, but that was a chance they had to take. Conan was very conscious of one old chief who watched him closely with narrowed eyes.

Conan ignored him, enjoying the dancers. The Oripesh seemed to be a happy people, although short on material wealth. Conan Lang almost envied them as they danced—envied them for their simple lives and envied them their ability to enjoy it, an ability that civilized man had left by the wayside in his climb up the ladder. Climb—or descent? Conan Lang sometimes wondered.

Ren came over, his color high with the excitement of the dance. Great fires were burning now, and Conan noticed with surprise that it was night.

"That is Loe," he said, pointing. "My *am-ren,* my bride-to-be." His voice was filled with pride.

Conan Lang followed his gesture and saw the girl. Her name was a native word roughly translatable as *fawn,* and she was well named. Loe was a slim, very shy girl of really striking beauty. She danced with diffidence, looking into Ren's eyes. The two were obviously, almost painfully, in love—love being a part of the culture of the Oripesh. It was difficult to realize, sometimes, even after years of personal experience, that there were whole worlds of basically humanoid peoples where the very concept of romantic love did not exist. Conan Lang smiled. Loe was, if anything, a trifle *too* beautiful for his taste. Dancing there, with the yellow moon in her hair, moving gracefully with the leaping shadows from the crackling fires, she was ethereal, a fantasy, like a painting of a woman from another, unattainable century.

"We would give gifts to the chiefs," Conan Lang said finally. "Your Loe—she is very beautiful."

Ren smiled, quickly grateful, and summoned the chiefs. Conan Lang rose to greet them, signaling to Andy to break open the boxes. The chiefs watched intently. Conan Lang did not speak. He waited until Andy had opened both boxes and then pointed to them.

"They are yours, my brothers," he said.

The natives pressed forward. A chief picked the first object out of the box and stared at it in disbelief. The shadows flickered eerily and the night wind sighed through the village. He held the object up to the light and there was a gasp of astonishment.

The object was a ricefruit—a ricefruit the likes of which had never before been seen on Sirius Ten. It was round, fully a foot in diameter, and of a lush, ripe consistency. It made the potato-sized ricefruits of the Oripesh seem puny by comparison.

It was then that Conan Lang exploded his bombshell.

"We have come back to show you, our brothers, how to grow the great ricefruit," he said. "You can grow them over and over again, *in the same field.* You will never have to move your village again."

The natives stared at him in wonder, moving back a little in fear.

"It cannot be done," a chief whispered. "The ricefruit devours the land—every year we must move or perish."

"That is over now," Conan Lang said. "We have come to show you the way."

The dancing had stopped. The natives waited, nervous, suddenly uncertain. The yellow moon watched through the trees. As though someone had flipped a switch, sound disappeared. There was silence. The great ricefruit was magic. They looked at the two men as though seeing them for the first time. This was not the way of the past, not the way of the ancestors. This was something completely *new* and they found themselves lost, without precedent for action. Ren alone smiled at them, and even he had fear in his eyes.

Conan Lang waited tensely. He must make no move; this was the crisis point. Andy stood at his side, very still, hardly breathing.

A native walked solemnly into the silence, carrying a young pig under his arm. Conan Lang watched him narrowly. The man was obviously a shaman, a witch doctor, and his trembling body and too-bright eyes were all too clear an indication of why he had been chosen for his role in the society.

With a swiftness of motion that was numbing, the shaman slit the pig's throat with a stone knife. At once he cut the body open. The blood stained his body with crimson. His long, thin hands poked into the entrails. He looked up, his eyes wild.

"They are not ancestors," he screamed, his voice high like an hysterical woman's. "They have come to do us evil!"

The very air was taut with tension.

"No," Conan Lang said loudly, keeping his voice clear and confident. "The *barath-tui,* the shaman, has been bewitched by sorcerers! Take care that you do not offend your ancestors!"

Conan Lang stood very still, fighting to keep the alarm off his face. He and Andy were helpless here, and he knew it. They were without weapons of any sort—the native loin cloth being a poor place to conceal firearms. There was nothing they could do—they had miscalculated, moved too swiftly, and now they were paying the price.

"We are your brothers," he said into the ominous silence. "We are your fathers and your father's fathers. There are others who watch."

The flames leaped and danced in the stillness. An old man stepped forward. It was the chief that Conan had noticed watching him before.

"You say you are our brothers who have taken the long journey," the old chief said. "That is good. We would see you walk through the fire."

The wind sighed in the trees. Without a moment's hesitation, Conan Lang turned and walked swiftly toward the flames that crackled and hissed in the great stone fire pits.

There was nothing else in all the world except the flickering tongues of orange flame that licked nearer and nearer to his face. He saw the red, pulsing coals waiting beneath the twisted black branches in the fire and he closed his eyes. The heat singed his eyebrows and he could feel his hair shrivel and start to burn.

Conan Lang kept moving, and moved fast. He twisted a rigid clamp on his mind and refused to feel pain. He wrenched his mind out of his body, thinking as he had been trained to think, until it was as if his mind floated a thing apart, free in the air, looking down upon the body of Conan Lang walking through hell.

He knew that one of the attributes of the Oripesh ancestor gods was that they could walk through flame without injury—a fairly common myth pattern. He had known it before he left Earth. He should have been prepared, he knew that. But man was not perfect, which would have been a dangerous flaw had it not been his most valuable characteristic.

He saw that his legs were black and blistered and he smelled the suffocating smell of burning flesh. The smoke was in his head, in his lungs, everywhere, choking him. Some of the pain was coming through—

He was out. He felt Andy's hands beating out the rivulets of flame that clung to his body and he forced the clean, pure air of night into his sick lungs. The pain, the pain—

"Stick with it, Cone," Andy whispered in his ear. "Stick with it."

Conan Lang managed to open his eyes and stared blankly into a hot-red haze. The haze cleared and he was faintly surprised to find that he could still see. The natives were awestruck with fear—they had angered their gods and death was in the air. Conan Lang knew that the shaman who had denounced him would quite probably be dead of fear before the night was over—if he did not die before then of some less subtle malady. He had endangered the tribe without reason, and he would pay with his life.

Conan Lang kept his face expressionless. Inside, he was on fire. Water, he had to have water, cold water—

Ren came to him, his eyes filled with pain. "I am sorry, my brother," he whispered. "For my people, I am sorry."

"It is all right, Ren," Conan Lang heard his voice say steadily. "I am, of course, unharmed."

Conan Lang touched Andy's arm and moved across to the chiefs. He felt Andy standing behind him, ready to catch him, just in case. He could feel nothing in his feet—quite suddenly, he was convinced that he was standing on the charred stumps of his legs and he fought to keep from looking down to make sure he still had feet.

"You have doubted your brothers who have come far to help their people," he said quietly, looking directly into the eyes of the old chief who had sent him into the flames. "We are disappointed in our people—there are sorcerers at work among you, and they must be destroyed. We leave you now. If you anger your brothers again, the Oripesh shall cease to be."

He did not wait for an answer but turned and started away from the clearing, back through the village. Andy was at his side. Conan Lang set his teeth and moved at a steady pace. He must have no help until they were beyond the village; the natives must not suspect—

He walked on. The great yellow moon was high in the night sky, and there was the face of Loe with stars in her hair. The moon shuddered and burst into flame and he heard himself laughing. He bit his lips until the blood came and kept going, into the darkness, into nothing. The pain clawed at his body.

They were through the village. Something snapped in Conan Lang— the steel clamp that had carried him through a nightmare parted with a clean *ping*. There was emptiness, space. Conan Lang collapsed. He felt Andy's arm around him, holding him up.

"You'll have to carry me, kid," he whispered. "I can't walk at all."

Andy Irvin picked him up in his arms and set out through the night.

"It should have been me," he said in bitter self-reproach. "It should have been me."

Conan Lang closed his eyes and, at last, nothing mattered any more, and there was only darkness.

A week later, Conan Lang stood in the dawn of Sirius Ten, watching the great double sun lift above the horizon and chase the shadows from the green field that they had carved out of the wilderness. He was still a very sick man, but Andy had pulled him through as best he could and now the star cruiser was coming in to pick him up and leave a replacement with the kid.

The fresh leaves of the ricefruit plants were shoulder high and the water in the irrigation trenches chuckled cleanly, waiting for the full fury of the sun. The tenuous, almost hesitant breeze crawled through the still air.

Conan Lang watched the green plants silently. The words of the dead *barath-tui,* the shaman, echoed in his brain. *They are not ancestors,* the man had screamed. *They have come to do us evil!*

They have come to do us evil . . .

How could he have known—with only a pig and a stone knife? A crazy shaman working the discredited magic of divination—and he had been *right.* Coincidence? Yes, of course. There was no other way to look at it, no other *sane* way. Conan Lang smiled weakly. He remembered reading about the Snake Dance of the Hopi, long ago back on Earth. The Snake Dance had been a rain-making ceremonial, and invariably when the very early anthropologists had attended the dance they had got drenched on the way home. It was only coincidence and good timing, of course, but it was difficult to tell yourself that when the rain began to pour.

"Here she comes," said Andy Irvin.

There was a splitting whistle and then a soft hum as a small patrol ship settled down toward the field on her anti-gravs. She hung there in the dawn like a little silver fish seen through the glassite walls of a great aquarium, and Conan Lang could sense what he could not see—the massive bulk of the sleek star cruiser waiting out in space.

The patrol ship came down out of the sky and hovered a few feet off the ground. A man swung down out of the outlift and waved. Conan Lang recognized him as Julio Medina, who had been lifted out of another sector of Sirius Ten to come in and replace him with Andy. The ricefruit was green and fresh in the field and it hurt Conan to leave his job unfinished. There wasn't a great deal to do now until the check, of course, and Julio was a very competent and experienced man, but there was still so much that could go wrong, so much that you could never anticipate—

And he didn't want anything to happen to the kid.

"So long, Cone," Andy said, his voice very quiet. "And—thanks. I won't forget what you did."

Conan Lang leaned on Andy's arm and moved toward the ship. "I'll be back, Andy," he said, trying to keep the weight off his feet. "Hold the fort—I know it'll be in good hands."

Conan Lang shook hands with Julio and then Julio and Andy helped him into the outlift. He had time for a brief wave and a final glimpse of the green field under the fiery sun, and then he was inside the patrol ship. They had somehow rigged up a bunk for him in the cramped quarters, and he collapsed into it gratefully.

"Home, James," he whispered, trying not to think about what would happen if they could not save his legs.

Conan Lang closed his eyes and lay very still, feeling the ship pulse and surge as it carried him out into the dark sea from which he had come.

IV

The doctors saved his legs, but years were to pass before Conan Lang again set foot upon Earth. Space was vast and star cruisers comparatively few. In addition, star ships were fabulously expensive to operate—it was out of the question for a ship on a mission to make the long run from Sirius to Sol for the sake of one man. Conan Lang became the prize patient of the ship medics and he stayed with the star cruiser as it operated in the Sirius area.

A star cruiser on operations was never dull and there were books to read and reports to write. Conan Lang curbed his impatience and made the best of the situation. The local treatments applied by Andy had been effective enough so that the ship medics were able to regenerate his burned tissue, and it was only a question of time before he would be strong again.

The star cruiser worked efficiently and effectively in support of Administration units in the Sirius area, sliding through the blackness of space like some leviathan of the deep, and Conan Lang rested and made himself as useful as he could. He often went up into the control room and stood watching the visiplate that looked out upon the great emptiness of space. Somewhere, on a far shore of that mighty sea, was a tiny planet called Earth. There, the air was cool and fresh under the pines and the beauty of the world, once you got away from it and could see it in perspective, was fantastic. There were Rob and Kit, friendship and tears and laughter.

There was home.

While his body healed, Conan Lang lived on the star cruiser. There was plenty of time to think. Even for a race with a life span of almost two hundred years, the days and the weeks and the months can seem interminable. He asked himself all the old questions, examined all the old answers. Here he was, on a star ship light-years from home, his body burned, waiting to go back to Sirius Ten to change the life of a planet. What thin shreds of chance, what strange webs of history, had put him there? When you added up the life of Conan Lang, of all the Conan Langs, what did you get? Where was Earth going, that pebble that hurled its puny challenge at the infinite?

Sometimes, it was all hard to believe.

It had all started, he supposed, with cybernetics. Of course, cybernetics itself was but the logical outgrowth of a long cultural and technological trend. For centuries, man's ally, the machine, had helped him physically in his adjustment to his environment. What more natural than that it should one day help him mentally as well? There was really nothing sinister about thinking machines, except to a certain breed of perpetually gloomy poets who were unable to realize that values were never destroyed but were simply molded into new patterns in the evolution of culture. No, thinking machines were fine and comforting—for a while.

But with the dawn of space travel, man's comfortable, complacent progress toward a vague somewhere was suddenly knocked into a cocked hat. Man's horizons exploded to the rims of the universe with the perfection of the star drive—he was no longer living *on* a world but *in* an inhabited universe. His bickerings and absurdities and wars were seen as the petty things they were—and man in a few tremendous years emerged at last from adolescence.

Science gave to men a life span of nearly two hundred active years and gave him the key to forever. But there was a catch, a fearful catch. Man, who had had all he could do to survive the conflicts of local groups of his own species, was suddenly faced with the staggering prospect of living in an inhabited *universe.* He had known, of course, about the millions and millions of stars, about the infinity of planets, about the distant galaxies that swam like island universes through the dark seas of space. But he had known about them as figures on a page, as photographs, as dots of unwinking light in a telescope. They had been curiosities, a stimulus to the imagination. Now they were vital parts of his life, factors to be reckoned with in the struggle for existence. In the universe were incredible numbers of integers to be equated in the problem of survival—*and the mind of man could not even learn them all, much less form intelligent conclusions about future actions.*

And so, inevitably, man turned again to the machine. But this time there was a difference. The machine was the only instrument capable of handling the data—and man in a million years could not even check its most elementary conclusions. Man fed in the facts, the machine reached the conclusions, and man acted upon them—not through choice, but simply because he had no other guide he could trust.

Men operated the machines—but the machines operated men.

The science of cybernetics expanded by leaps and bounds. Men made machines to develop new machines. The great mechanical brains grew so complex that only a few men could even pretend to understand them. Looking at them, it was virtually impossible to believe that they had been born in the minds of men.

The machines did not interfere in the everyday routine of living— man would never submit to that, and in problems which he could understand he was still the best judge of his own happiness. It was in the larger problems, the problems of man's destiny in the universe in which he found himself, that the great brains were beyond value. For the machines could integrate trends, patterns, and complexes of the known worlds and go on from there to extrapolate into the unknown. The machines could, in very general terms, predict the outcome of any given set of circumstances. They could, in a very real sense, see into the future. They could see where Earth was headed.

And Earth was headed for disaster.

The machines were infallible. They dealt not with short-term probabilities, but with long-range certainties. And they stated flatly that, given the equation of the known universe, Earth would be destroyed in a matter of centuries. There was only one thing to do—man must change the equation.

It was difficult for man, so recently Earthbound, to really *think* and *act* in terms of an inhabited universe. But the machines showed conclusively that in as yet inaccessible galaxies life had evolved that was physically and mentally hostile to that of Earth. A collision of the two lifeforms would come about within a thousand years, and a life-and-death struggle was inevitable. The facts were all too plain—Earth would lose and the human race would be exterminated.

Unless the equation could be changed.

It was a question of preparing the galaxy for combat. The struggle would be a long one, and factors of reserves, replacements, different cultural approaches to common problems, planets in varying stages of development, would be important. It was like a cosmic chess game, with worlds aligning themselves on a monstrous board. In battles of galactic dimensions, the outcome would be determined by centuries of preparation before contact was even made; it was not a romantic question of heroic spaceships and iron-jawed men of action, but rather one of the cultural, psychological, technological, and individual patterns which each side could bring to bear—patterns which were the outgrowths of millennia of slow evolution and development.

Earth was ready, or would be by the time contact came. But the rest of the galaxy—or at any rate as much of it as they had managed to explore—was not, and would not be. The human race was found somewhere on most of the star systems within the galaxy, but not one of them was as far advanced as were the men from Earth. That was why Earth had never been contacted from space—indeed, it was the only possible explanation, at least in retrospect. And the other galaxies, with their totally alien and forever nonunderstandable principles, were not interested in undeveloped cultures.

The problem thus became one of accelerating the cultural evolution of Earth's sister planets by means of diffusion, in order to build them up into an effective totality to combat the coming challenge. And it had to be done in such a manner that the natives of the planets were completely unaware that they were not the masters of their own destiny, since such a concept produced cultural stagnation and introduced corrupting elements into the planetary configurations. It had often been argued that Earth herself was in such a position, being controlled by the machines, but such was not the case—their choice had been a rational one, and they could abandon the machines at any time at their own risk.

Or so, at any rate, argued the thinkers of Earth.

The long months lengthened into years and, inactive though he was, Conan Lang spent his time well. It was good to have a chance to relax and think things through; it was good for the soul to stop midway in life and take stock. Almost, it was possible to make sense out of things, and the frantic rush to nowhere lost some of its shrieking senselessness.

Conan Lang smiled without humor. That was all very well for him, but what about the natives whose lives they were uprooting? Of course, they were human beings, too, and stood to lose as much as anyone in the long run—but they did not understand the problem, *could* not understand it. The plain truth was that they were being used—used for their own benefit as well as that of others, but used none the less.

It was true that primitive life was no bed of roses—it was not as if, Conan Lang assured himself, the men from Earth were slithering, serpent-like, into an idyllic Garden of Eden. All they were doing was to accelerate the normal rate of change for a given planet. But this caused far-reaching changes in the culture as it existed—it threw some people to the dogs and elevated others to commanding positions. This was perhaps no more than was done by life itself, and possibly with better reason, but you couldn't tell yourself that when you had to face the eyes of a man who had gone from ruler to slave because of what you had done.

The real difficulty was that you couldn't *see* the threat. It was there all right—a menace beside which all the conflicts of the human race were as nothing. But it had always been difficult for men to work before the last possible moment, to prepare rather than just sit back and hope for the best. That man was working now as he had never worked before, in the face of an unseen threat from out of the stars, even to save his own existence, was a monument to his hard-won maturity. It would have been so easy, so pleasant, just to take it easy and enjoy a safe and comfortable life—and beyond question it would have meant the end of the human race.

Of one thing, Conan Lang was sure—whenever man stopped trying, stopped working and dreaming and reaching for impossible heights, whenever he settled back in complacency, on that day he shrunk to atrophied insignificance.

Sirius Ten had been a relatively easy project because of the planet-wide nature of its culture. Sirius Ten had only one huge land mass, and one great sea. The natives all shared basically the same life pattern, built around the cultivation of dry ricefruit, and the teams of the Applied Process Corps were faced with only one major problem rather than hundreds of them as was more often the case. It was true that certain peoples who lived on the shores of the sea, together with one island group, had a variant culture based on fishing, but these were insignificant numerically and could for practical purposes be ignored.

agilit ananin

The dry ricefruit was grown by a cutting and burning method, under which a field gave a good yield only once before the land was exhausted and the people had to move on. Under these conditions, individual ownership of land never developed, and there were no inequalities of wealth to speak of. The joint families worked different fields every year, and since there was no market for a surplus there was no effort made to cultivate more land than was really needed.

The Oripesh natives of Sirius Ten had a well-developed cult of ancestor worship, thinking of their dead as always watching over them and guiding their steps. Since whatever the ancestors did automatically had the sanction of tradition behind it, it was through them that the Corps had decided to work—it being simply a question of palming off Corps Agents as ancestors come back from their dwelling place in the mountains to help their people. With careful preparations and experienced men, this had not proved overly difficult—but there were always miscalculations, accidents. Men were not like chemicals, and they did not always react as they were supposed to react. There was always an individual variable to be considered. That was why if a Corps Agent lived long enough to retire you knew both that he knew his stuff and that he had had more than his share of plain old-fashioned luck.

Sirius Ten had to be shifted from Stage Four to Stage Five. This was a staggering change in economics, social structure, and technology—one that had taken men on Earth many centuries to accomplish. The men of the Applied Process Corps had to do it in a matter of a few years. And so they set out, armed with a variety of ricefruit that grew well in marshy land and a sound knowledge of irrigation.

With such a lever they could move a world.

It was three years to the day when Conan Lang returned to Sirius Ten. The patrol ship came in on her anti-gravs and he waited eagerly for the outlift shaft to open. His heart was pounding in his chest and his lips were dry—it was almost like coming home again.

He swung his newly-strong body into the outlift and came out of it in the green field he had planted so long ago. He look a deep breath of the familiar humid air and grinned broadly at the hot, burning sun over his head. It *was* good to be back—back at a place like so many other places he had known, places that were as close to a home as any he could ever have without Kit. The breeze whispered softly through the green ricefruit and he waved at Julio, who came running across the field to meet him. These were, he knew, his kind of people—and he had missed Andy all these years.

"Hey there, Julio!" he laughed, shaking Medina's hand. "How goes it?"

"Pretty good, Conan," Julio said quietly. "Pretty good."

"The kid—how's the kid?"

"Andy is dead," said Julio Medina.

Conan Lang stood stock-still while an iron fist smacked into his stomach with cold, monotonous precision. Andy dead. It could not be, *could not be.* There had been no word, nothing. He clenched his fists. It couldn't be true.

But it was. He knew that with ice cold certainty.

"It just happened the other day, Conan," Julio said. "He was a fine boy."

Conan Lang couldn't speak. *The whole planet,* his mind tortured him. *The whole stinking planet isn't worth Andy's life.*

"It was an accident," Julio said, his voice carefully matter-of-fact. "Warfare has sprung up between the rival villages like we figured. Andy was out after information and he got between them—he was hit by mistake with a spear. He never had a chance, but he managed to walk away and get back here before he died. The Oripesh don't suspect that he wasn't a god and could die just like anyone else. He saved the rest of us by coming back here—that's something."

"Yeah," Conan Lang said bitterly, "that's something."

"I buried him here in the field," Julio Medina went on. "I thought he'd like that. He . . . said good-by to you, Conan."

It had been a long time since Conan Lang had had tears in his eyes. He turned without a word and walked away, across the green field and into the hut where he could be alone.

V

From that time on, by unspoken mutual consent, the two men never again mentioned the kid's name. They gave him the best possible write-up in their reports, and that was all that they could ever do for Andy Irvin.

"I think we've about done it here, Conan," Julio told him. "I'd like to have you make your own check and see if you come up with the same stuff I did. There's a lull in the raiding right now—the natives are worried because that spear hit an ancestor by mistake and they're pretty well occupied with rituals designed to make us feel better about the whole thing. You shouldn't have any trouble, and that ought to about wind things up."

Conan Lang nodded. "It'll be good to get home again, eh, Julio?"

"Yes, you know that—and for you it should be for keeps."

Conan Lang raised his eyebrows.

"It's no secret that you're due to be kicked upstairs," Julio said. "I rather think this is your last field job."

"Well, it's a nice theory anyhow."

"You remember all us old men out here in the stars, the slave labor of the Process Corps. Bring us all home, Conan, and we'll sit around in the shade and drink wine and fish and tell lies to each other."

"Consider it done," said Conan Lang. "And I'll give you all some more medals."

"I've got medals."

"Can't have too many medals, Julio. They're good for what ails you."

"They're not good for what ails *me*," said Julio Medina.

Conan Lang smiled and fired up his pipe. *The kid,* his mind whispered. *The kid liked that pipe.* He thrust the thought from his mind. A man had to take death in his stride out here, he told himself. Even when it was a kid who reminded you of yourself a million years ago—

A million years ago.

"I'll start in tomorrow," Conan Lang said, puffing on his pipe. "Do you know Ren, Julio?"

"The chief's son? Yes."

"How did he come out?"

"Not well, Conan. He lost his woman, Loe, to one of the men we made wealthy; he has not been the same since."

"We're great people, Julio."

"Yes."

Conan Lang was silent then and the two men stood together in the warm evening air, watching the great double sun float slowly down below the horizon as the long black shadows came marching up from the far edge of the world.

Next morning, Conan Lang was off with the dawn on his final check. He pretty well knew what he would find. Julio Medina was an experienced hand and his information was reliable. But it was always a shock when you saw it for yourself. You never got used to it. To think that such a tiny, seemingly insignificant thing could change a planet beyond recognition. A ricefruit—

It was already hot when he passed the native fields. Their ricefruit plants were tall and healthy, and their irrigation channels well constructed. He shook his head and walked on to the native village.

Where the open, crude, friendly village had stood there was a great log wall. In front of the wall was a series of deep and ugly-looking moats. Behind the wall, he could see the tops of sturdy wooden buildings, a far cry from the huts of only a few short years ago. Conan Lang made no attempt at concealment but walked openly up to the moats and crossed them on a log bridge. He stopped outside the closed gate.

"You will remember me who walked through the flames," he said loudly in the Oripesh tongue. "You will open the gate for your brother as he would visit you."

For a moment nothing happened, and then the gate swung open. Conan Lang entered the village.

The native guard eyed him with suspicion, but he kept his distance. Conan Lang noticed that he had a bow by the log wall. There was nothing like constant warfare for the production of new weapons, he reflected. Civilization was bringing its blessings to the Oripesh with leaps and bounds.

Conan Lang walked through the village unmolested, taking rapid mental notes. He saw storehouses for ricefruit and observed slaves being marched off to work in the fields. The houses in the village were strong and comfortable, but there was a tense air in the village, a feeling of strain. Conan Lang approached a native and stopped him.

"Brother," he said, "I would see your chiefs. Where are they?"

The native looked at him warily. "The Oripesh have no chiefs," he said. "Our king is in council."

Conan Lang nodded, a sick feeling inside him. "It is well," he said. "Ren—I would see him."

The native jerked his thumb contemptuously toward the back of the village. "He is there," he said. "Outside."

Conan Lang moved through the village, watching, missing nothing. He went all the way through and came out through the back wall. There, the old-style native huts baked in squalor under the blazing sun. There was no log wall around them, although they were inside the moat system. A pig rooted around for garbage between the huts.

"Slums," Conan Lang said to himself.

He walked among the huts, ignoring the fearful, suspicious eyes of the natives. He found Ren preparing to go out into the fields. The chief's son was thin. He looked tired and his eyes were dull. He saw Conan and said nothing.

"Hello, Ren," said Conan Lang.

The native just looked at him.

Conan Lang tried to think of something to say. He knew what had happened—the chiefs and their sons had been so busy with ritual work for the tribe that they had lagged behind in the cultivation of the new ricefruit. They had stuck to the old ways too long and their people had passed them by.

"I can help you, my brother," Conan Lang said softly. "It is not too late."

Ren said nothing.

"I will help you with a field of your own," said Conan Lang. "Will you let me help you?"

The native looked at him and there was naked hate in his eyes. "You said you were my friend," he said. Without another word, he turned and left. He did not look back.

Conan Lang wiped the sweat from his forehead and went on with his work. The sensitive part of his mind retreated back in to a dark, insulated corner and he let his training take over. He moved along, asking questions, watching, taking mental notes.

A little thing, he thought.

A new kind of plant.

A week later, Conan Lang had completed his check. He sat by the evening cook fire with Julio, smoking his pipe, watching the shadows in the field.

"Well, we did a good job," he said. "It's awful."

"It would have come without us," Julio reminded him. "It does no good to brood about it. It is tough, sometimes, but it is a small price to pay for survival."

"Yes," said Conan Lang. "Sure."

"Your results check out with mine?"

"Mostly. It's the same old story, Julio."

Conan Lang puffed slowly on his pipe, reconstructing what had happened. The new ricefruit had made it valuable for a family to hang on to one piece of land that could be used over and over again. But only a limited amount of the land could be used, because of natural factors like the presence or absence of available water. The families that had not taken the plunge right away were virtually excluded, and the society was divided into the landed and the landless. The landless gradually had to move further and further from the main village to find land upon which to grow the older type of ricefruit—sometimes their fields were so far away that they could not make the round trip in a single day. And they could not get too far away and start over, because of the tribal warfare that had broken out between villages now that valuable stores of ricefruit were there for the taking. The old joint family co-operation broke down, and slaves became economically feasible.

Now that the village need not be periodically moved, it too became valuable and so was strongly fortified for defense. One old chief, grown powerful with fields of the staple ricefruit, set himself up as a king and the other chiefs went to work in his fields.

Of course, Sirius Ten was still in transition. While the old patterns were being destroyed, new ones, less obvious to the untrained eye, were taking their place. Disintegration and reintegration marched hand in hand, but it would be tough on the natives for a while. Process Corps techniques had speeded up the action almost beyond belief, but from here on in the Oripesh were on their own. They would go on and on in their individual development—although no two peoples ever went through exactly the same stages at the same time, it was possible to predict a general planet-wide trend. The Oripesh would one day learn to write, since they already had a crude pictographic system for ritual use. When the contact finally came from the hostile stars in the future, what histories would they have written? Who would they remember, what would they forget? Would there be any twisted legend or myth left that recalled the long-ago time when the gods had come out of the mountains to change the lives of their people?

That was the way to look at it. Conan Lang tapped out his pipe on a rock. Just look at it like a problem, a textbook example. Forget about the people, the individuals you could not help, the lives you had made and the lives you had destroyed. Turn off that part of your mind and think in terms of the long-range good.

Or try to.

"We're all through here, Julio," Conan Lang said. "We can head for home now."

"Yes," said Julio Medina. "It has been a long time."

The two men sat silently in the darkness, each thinking his own thoughts, watching the yellow moon sail through silver stars.

After the patrol ship had been signaled, there was nothing to do but wait until their pickup could be co-ordinated with the time schedules of the other Corps men and the operational schedule of the star cruiser. Conan Lang busied himself with his reports while Julio sprawled in the shade and devised intricate and impossible card games with a battered deck that was old enough to be in itself of anthropological interest.

Conan Lang was playing a game, too. He played it with his mind and he was a somewhat unwilling participant. His mind had played the game before and he was tired of it, but there was nothing he could do about it. There wasn't any button that would turn his mind off, and while it was on it played games.

It was engaged in putting two and two together.

This was not in itself uncommon, although it was not as widespread as some people fondly imagined it to be. But Conan Lang played the game where others did not see even one, much less a set of twos with a relation-ship between them. There is nothing so hard to see as what is termed obvious after the fact. Conan Lang's mind had played with the obvious all his life; it would not let well enough alone. He didn't like it, there were times when he would have preferred to junk it all and go fishing without a thought in his head, but he was stuck with it. When his mind wanted to play the game, it played and that was that.

While he waited for the patrol ship, his mind was playing with a set of factors. There was the history of Earth, taken as a vast overall sequence. There were thinking machines, atomic power, and the field techniques of the Process Corps. There was the fact that Earth had no record of ever having been contacted by another world—they had always done the contacting themselves. There was the new principle that Admiral White had spoken to him about, the integration-acceleration factor for correlating data. There was the incredible, explosive energy of man that had hurled him light-years into space. There was his defiant heart that could tackle the prodigious job of reshaping a galaxy when the chips were down.

Conan Lang put two and two together, and he did not get four. He got five.

He didn't know the answers yet, but he knew enough to formulate the right questions. From past experience he knew that that was the toughest part of the game. Incorrect answers were usually the products of off-center questions. Once you had the right question, the rest was a matter of time.

The patrol ship came for them finally, and Conan Lang and Julio Medina walked across the soil of Sirius Ten for the last time. They crossed the field where the green plants grew, and neither tried to say what was in his heart. Three had come and only two could leave. Andy Irvin had lived and worked and dreamed only to fall on an alien planet light-years away from Earth that could have been his. He was part of the price that was exacted for survival—and he was also a kid with stars in his eyes who had gotten a rotten, senseless break.

After the patrol ship had gone, the green leaves of the ricefruit plants stretched hungrily up toward the flaming sun. The clean water chuckled along the irrigation trenches, feeding the roots in the field. Softly, as though sad with all the memories it carried, the lonesome breeze whispered through the empty hut that had housed the men from Earth.

VI

Through the trackless depths of interstellar space the star cruiser rode on the power from her atomics. The hum that filled the ship was a good sound, and she seemed to quiver with pride and impatience. It did make a difference which way you were going in space, and the ship was going home.

Conan Lang paced through the long white corridors and walked around the afterhold where the brown sacks of ricefruit had been. He read in the library and joked with the medics who had salvaged his burned body. And always ahead of him, swimming in the great emptiness of space, were the faces of Kit and of his son, waiting for him, calling him home again.

Rob must have grown a lot, he thought. Soon, he wouldn't be a boy any longer—he would be a man, taking his place in the world. Conan remembered his son's voice from a thousand quiet talks in the cool air of evening, his quick, eager eyes—

Like Andy's.

"Dad, when I grow up can I be like you? Can I be an Agent and ride on the ships to other worlds and have a uniform and everything?"

What could you tell your son now that you had lived so long and were supposed to know so much? That life in the Process Corps filled a man with things that were perhaps better unknown? That the star trails were cold and lonely? That there were easier, more comfortable lives? All that was true, all the men who rode the ships knew it. But they knew, too, that for them this was the only life worth living.

The time passed slowly. Conan Lang was impatient to see his family again, anxious to get home. But his mind gave him no rest. There were things he had to know, things he *would* know before he went home to stay.

Conan Lang had the right questions now. He had the right questions, and he knew where the answers were hidden.

Fritz Gottleib.

The star cruiser had hardly touched Earth again at Space One before Conan Lang was outside on the duralloy tarmac. Since the movements of the star ships were at all times top secret matters, there was no one at the port to greet him and for once Conan was glad to have a few extra hours to himself. Admiral White wouldn't expect him to check in until tomorrow anyway, and before he saw Kit he wanted to get things straight once and for all.

The friendly sun of Earth warmed him gently as he hurried across the tarmac and the air felt cool and fresh. He helped himself to an official bullet, rose into the blue sky, and jetted eastward over the city. His brain was seething and he felt cold sweat in the palms of his hands. What was it that Gottleib had said to him on that long-ago day?

"Sometimes it is best not to know the answers to one's questions, Dr. Lang."

Well, he was going to know the answers anyhow. All of them. He landed the bullet in the space adjoining the cybernetics building and hurried inside, flashing his identification as he went. He stopped at a switchboard and showed his priority credentials.

"Call the Nest, please," he told the operator. "Tell Dr. Gottleib that Conan Lang is down here and would like to see him."

The operator nodded and spoke into the intercom. There was a moment's delay, and then he took his earphones off and smiled at Conan Lang.

"Go right on up, Dr. Lang," the operator said. "Dr. Gottleib is expecting you."

Conan Lang controlled his astonishment and went up the lift and down the long white corridors. *Expecting* him? But that was impossible. No one even knew the star cruiser was coming back, much less that he was coming here to the Nest. Impossible—

All around him in the great building he felt the gigantic mechanical brain with its millions of circuits and flashing tubes. The brain crowded him, pressed him down until he felt tiny and insignificant. It hummed and buzzed through the great shielded walls.

Laughing at him.

Conan Lang pushed past the attendants and security men and opened the door of the Nest. He moved into the small, dark room and paused to allow his eyes to become accustomed to the dim light. The room was silent. Gradually, the shadow behind the desk took form and he found himself looking into the arctic eyes of Fritz Gottleib.

"Dr. Lang," he hissed softly. "Welcome to the Buzzard's Nest."

The man had not changed; he was timeless, eternal. He was still dressed in black and it might have been minutes ago instead of years when Conan Lang had last seen him. His black eyebrows slashed across his white face and his long-fingered hands were bent slightly like claws upon his desk.

"How did you know I was coming here?" Now that he was face to face with Gottleib, Conan Lang felt suddenly uncertain, unsure of himself.

"I know many things, Dr. Lang," Fritz Gottleib said sibilantly. "Had I cared to, I could have told you ten years ago the exact date, within a day or so, upon which we would have this meeting. I could even have told you what you would say when you came through the door, and what you are going to say five minutes from now."

Conan Lang just stared at him, feeling like an absurd little child who had presumed to wrestle a gorilla, His mind recoiled from the strange man before him and he knew at last that he knew nothing.

"I do not waste words, Dr. Lang," Gottleib said, his eyes cold and unmoving in his head. "You will remember that when we last met you said you wanted to ask some questions of the machine. Do you remember what I said, Dr. Lang?"

Conan Lang thought back across the years. *"Perhaps one day, Dr. Lang,"* Gottleib had said. *"When you are old like me."*

" Yes," said Conan Lang. "Yes, I remember."

"You were not ready then," Dr. Gottleib said, his white face ghostly in the dim light. "You could not even have framed the right questions, at least not all of them."

Conan Lang was silent. How much *did* Gottleib know? Was there anything he *didn't* know?

"You are old enough now," said Fritz Gottleib.

He turned a switch and the surface of his desk glowed with dull red light. His face, reflected in the flamelike glow, was unearthly. His cold eyes looked out of hell. He rose to his feet, seeming to loom larger than life, filling the room. Moving without a sound, he left the room and the door clicked shut behind him.

Conan Lang was alone in the red room. His heart hammered in his throat and his lips were dry. He clenched his fists and swallowed hard. Alone—

Alone with the great machine.

Conan Lang steadied himself. Purposefully, he made himself go through the prosaic, regular motions of lighting up his pipe. The tobacco was healthily full-bodied and fragrant and it helped to relax him. He smoked slowly, taking his time.

The red glow from the desk filled the room with the color of unreality. Crimson shadows seemed to crouch in the corners with an impossible life of their own. But was anything impossible, here? Conan Lang felt the pulse of the great machine around him and wondered.

Trying to shake off a persistent feeling of dreamlike unreality, Conan Lang moved around and sat down behind Gottleib's desk. The red panel was a maze of switches which were used to integrate it with technical panels in other sections of the building. In the center of the panel was a keyboard on an open circuit to the machine and set into the desk was a clear square like a very fine telescreen. Conan Lang noticed that there was nothing on Gottleib's desk that was not directly connected with the machine— no curios, no pictures, no paperweights, not a single one of the many odds and ends most men picked up for their desks during a long lifetime. The whole room was frightening in its very impersonality, as though every human emotion had been beaten out of it long ago and the room had been insulated against its return.

The machines never slept and the circuits were open. Conan Lang had only to ask and any question that could be answered would be answered. The red glow in the room reminded him of the fire and he shuddered a little in spite of himself. Had that really been over three years ago? How much had he learned in those three years when he had seen the Oripesh change before his eyes and had had time for once to really think his life through? How much did he still have to learn?

Conan Lang took a long pull on his pipe and set the desk panel for manual type questioning and visual screen reception. He hesitated a moment, almost afraid of the machine at his disposal. He didn't *want* to know, he suddenly realized. It wasn't like that. It was rather that he *had* to know.

Framing his words carefully, Conan Lang typed out the question that had been haunting him for years:

IS THE EARTH ITSELF THE SUBJECT OF PROCESS MANIPULATION?

He waited nervously, sure of the answer, but fearful of it nevertheless. There was a faint, all but inaudible hum from the machine and Conan Lang could almost feel the circuits closing in the great walls around him. The air was filled with tension. There was a brief click and one word etched itself blackly on the clear screen:

YES.

Conan Lang leaned forward, sure of himself now, and typed out another question.

HOW LONG HAS THE EARTH BEEN MANIPULATED AND HAS THIS CONTROL BEEN FOR GOOD OR EVIL?

The machine hummed and answered at once.

THE EARTH HAS BEEN GUIDED SINCE EARTH YEAR NINETEEN HUNDRED A.D. THE SECOND PART OF YOUR QUESTION IS MEANINGLESS.

Conan Lang hesitated, staggered in spite of himself by the information he was getting, Then he typed rapidly:

WITH REFERENCE TO GOOD, EQUATE SURVIVAL OF THE HUMAN RACE.

The screen clouded, cleared, and the words formed.

THE CONTROL HAS BEEN FOR GOOD.

Conan Lang's breathing was shallow now. He typed tensely:

HAS THIS CONTROL COME FROM WITHIN THIS GALAXY? IF SO, WHERE? IS THERE USUALLY AN AGENT OTHER THAN EARTH'S IN CHARGE OF THIS MACHINE?

The hum of the machine filled the blood-red room and the screen framed the answers.

THE CONTROL HAS COME FROM WITHIN THE GALAXY. THE SOURCE IS A WORLD KNOWN AS RERMA, CIRCLING A STAR ON THE EDGE OF THE GALAXY WHICH IS UNKNOWN TO EARTH. THE MAN KNOWN AS GOTTLEIB IS A RERMAN AGENT.

Conan Lang's pipe had been forgotten and gone out. He put it down and licked his dry lips. So far so good, But the one prime, all-important question had not yet been asked. He asked it.

IF THE PLAN IS FOLLOWED, WHAT WILL BE THE FINAL OUTCOME WITH RESPECT TO RERMA AND THE EARTH?

The machine hummed again in the red glow and the answer came swiftly, with a glorious, mute tragedy untold between its naked lines:

RERMA WILL BE DESTROYED. THE EARTH WILL SURVIVE IF THE PLAN IS CAREFULLY FOLLOWED.

Conan Lang felt tears in his eyes and he was unashamed. With time forgotten now, he leaned forward, asking questions, reading replies, as the terrible, wonderful story unfolded.

Far out on the edge of the galaxy, the ancient planet of Rerma circled her yellow sun. Life had evolved early on Rerma—had evolved early and developed fast. While the other humanoid peoples of the galaxy were living in caves, the Rerma were building a great civilization. When Earth forged its first metal sword, the Rerma split the atom.

Rerma was a world of science—true science. Science had eliminated war and turned the planet into a paradise. Literature and the arts flourished hand in hand with scientific progress, and scientists worked surrounded by cool gardens in which graceful fountains splashed and chuckled in the sun. Every man was free to develop himself as an individual and no man bent his head to any other man.

The Rerma were the human race in full flower.

But the Rerma were few, and they were not a warlike people. It was not that they would not fight in an emergency, but simply that they could not possibly win an extended encounter. Their minds didn't work that way. The Rerma had evolved to a point where they were too specialized, too well adjusted to their environment.

And their environment changed.

It was only a question of time until the Rerma asked the right questions of their thinking machines and came up with the knowledge that their world, situated on the edge of the galaxy, was directly in the path of a coming cultural collision between two star systems. The Rerma fed in the data over and over again, and each time the great machines came up with the same answer.

Rerma would be destroyed.

It was too late for the equation to be changed with respect to Rerma—she had gone too far and was unfortunately located. But for the rest of the human race, scattered on the far-flung worlds that marched along the star trails, there was a chance. There was time for the equation to be changed for them—if only someone could be found to change it! For the Rerma had the knowledge, but they had neither the manpower nor the driving, defiant spirit to do the job themselves. They were capable of making heroic decisions and sticking by them, but the task of remolding a star system was not for them. That was a job for a young race, a proud and unconquerable race. That was a job for the men of Earth.

The ships of the Rerma found Earth in the earth year 1900. They knew that in order for their plan to succeed the Rerma must stand and fight on that distant day when galaxies collided, for their power was not negligible despite their lack of know-how for a long-range combat. They must stand and fight and be destroyed—the plan, the equation, was that finely balanced. Earth was the only other planet they found that was sufficiently advanced to work with, and it was imperative that Earth should not know that she was being manipulated. She must not suspect that her plans were not her own, for a young race with its pride wounded is a dubious ally and an ineffective fighting mechanism.

The Rerma set to work—willing even to die for a future they had already lived. The scientists of Rerma came secretly to Earth, and behind them, light-years away, their crystal fountains still sparkled sadly in the sun.

Rerma would be destroyed—but humanity would not die.

Conan Lang sat alone in the red room, talking to a machine. It was all clear enough, even obvious, once you knew the facts. Either there were no advanced races in the galaxy, which would account for Earth having no record of any contact—or else the Earth *had* been contacted secretly, been manipulated by the very techniques that she herself was later to use on undeveloped worlds.

He looked back on history. Such profound and important changes as the Neolithic food revolution and the steam engine had been produced by Earth alone, making her the most advanced planet in the galaxy except for the Rerma. Earth had a tradition of technological skill behind her, and she was young and pliable. The Rerma came—and the so-called world wars had followed. Why? Not to avenge the honor of insulted royalty, not because of fanatics, not because of conflicting creeds—but in a very real sense to save the world. The world wars had been fought to produce atomic power.

After 1900, the development of Earth had snowballed in a fantastic manner. The atom was liberated and man flashed upward to other planets of the solar system. Just as Conan Lang himself had worked through the ancestor gods of the Oripesh to bring about sweeping changes on Sirius Ten, the Rerma had worked through one of the gods of the Earthmen—the machine.

Cybernetics.

Man swept out to the stars, and the great thinking machines inevitably confronted them with the menace from beyond that drew nearer with each passing year. Young and proud, the men of Earth accepted the most astounding challenge ever hurled—they set out to reshape a galaxy to give their children and their children's children a chance for life.

And always, behind the scenes, beneath the headlines, were the ancient Rerma. They subtly directed and hinted and helped. With a selflessness unmatched in the universe, those representatives of a human race that had matured too far prepared Earth for galactic leadership—and themselves for death on the edge of the galaxy. They had unified Earth and pushed and prodded her along the road to survival.

When the Rerma could have fled and purchased extra time for themselves, they chose instead—these peace-loving people—to fight for another chance for man.

Conan Lang looked up, startled, to find the black figure of Fritz Gottleib standing by his side. He looked old, very old, in the blood-red light and Conan Lang looked at him with new understanding. Gottleib's impatience with others and the vast, empty loneliness in those strange eyes—all that was meaningful now. What a life that man had led on Earth, Conan Lang thought with wonder. Alone, wanting friendship and understanding—and having always to discourage close personal contacts, having always to fight his lonely battle alone in a sterile little room, knowing that the very men he had dedicated his life to help laughed behind his back and compared him to a bird of prey.

"I've been a fool, sir," Conan Lang said, getting to his feet. "We've all been fools."

Fritz Gottleib sat down again behind his desk and turned the machine off. The red glow vanished and they were left in the semidarkness.

"Not fools, Dr. Lang," he said. "It was necessary for you to feel as you did. The feelings of one old man—what are they worth in this game we are playing? We must set our sights high, Dr. Lang."

Conan Lang waited in the shadows, thinking, watching the man who sat across from him as though seeing him for the first time. His mind was still groping, trying to assimilate all he had learned. It was a lot to swallow in a few short hours, even when you were prepared for it beforehand by guesswork and conjecture. There were still questions, of course, many questions. He knew that he still had much to learn.

"Why me?" Conan Lang asked finally. "Why have I been told all this? Am I the only one who knows?"

Fritz Gottleib shook his head, his face ghost-white in the darkened room. "There are others who know," he said sibilantly, "Your superior officer, Nelson White, has known for years, of course. You were told because you have been selected to take over his command when he retires. If you are willing, you will work very closely with him here on Earth for the next five years, and then you will be in charge."

"Will I . . . leave Earth again?"

"Not for a long time, Dr. Lang. The integration-acceleration principle will keep you busy—we are in effect lifting Earth another stage and the results will be far-reaching. But you will be home, Dr. Lang—home with your family and your people.

"That is all, Dr. Lang," Gottleib hissed.

Conan Lang hesitated. "I'll do my level best," he said finally. "Good-by, sir . . . I'll see you again."

Conan Lang put out his hand to the man he had called the Buzzard and Gottleib shook it with a firm, powerful grip.

"Good-by, Conan," Fritz Gottleib said softly.

Conan Lang turned and walked from the dark room, leaving the man from Rerma sitting alone in the shadows of the Nest.

The little bullet rose vertically on her copter blades through the evening sky, hovered a moment in the cool air under the frosty stars, and then flashed off on her jets into the west. Conan Lang set the controls and leaned back in the seat, at peace with himself at last. There *was* meaning to it all, there was a purpose—and Andy and all the others like him on the far trails had not sacrificed their lives for nothing.

Conan Lang breathed the clean air of Earth and smiled happily. Ahead of him, waiting for him, were Kit and Rob and he would never have to leave them again. He opened the lateral ports and let the wind hurl itself at his face.

THE LAND OF LOST CONTENT

That is the land of lost content,
 I see it shining plain,
The happy highways where I went
 And cannot come again.
                              —*A. E. Housman*

The trial by Council was unreal to Brighton; a confused fantasy of smoke, shadows, and droning voices. All of the people—tragic reminders of a dying race—were there in the old Council chamber, but they filled hardly a third of the seats. Lawrence, the aged Head of Council, and his ten Council Members faced Brighton and Lynna and the people. His voice, still strong with the strength of a once-powerful man, echoed hollowly through the vault.

"You know the laws of our people?"

"Yes."

"Yet you have gone to the forbidden land?"

"Yes."

"You are aware that you may be punished by death if this Council so decrees?"

"Yes."

"Speak, then, in your own defense."

Brighton faced the Council, feet wide apart, eyes blazing. This was insane. His crime was that he was alive in a world of corpses. What could he say to these people? How do you talk to the dead, the dying, the uncaring?

He tried.

"Look around you," he commanded. "Look at the empty seats. With every meeting of the Council there are fewer of us. Soon there will be none left, and then whom will the Council have to rule?"

A rustling in the shadows.

"Lynna and I are known to you, all of you. We have all lived together in peace; we have done you no harm, we have committed no crime against you. We have tried to find life in this sick world, life for ourselves and for our people, and we have not let children's superstitions stand in our way. We have found a way to life—to the roof of the world!"

Electricity in the air.

"This is your chance, our chance. What are you afraid of? What have you to lose—you *cannot* lose anything on a journey from death to death. Are you going to allow meaningless laws to cut you off from a chance for life? If you kill us, you kill yourselves. Think—for once in your lives, *think!*"

Angry murmurs.

"He mocks the law!" cried Wentworth.

"Let him speak," Lawrence said wearily.

"Crazy, crazy," voices whispered.

Brighton said, "Listen to me!"

His mind filled with his dreams of the roof of the world, he talked—talked for hours and told his people what he knew, what he thought, what he believed. They laughed at him.

"Are you through?"

"Yes—yes, I'm through."

The Council debated out loud, in open session.

"Broke the law, that's what counts!"

"Impossible . . ."

"Never been done before . . ."

"Always been that way. . . ."

"Defy the gods . . ."

"Wrong to change . . ."

"Insult . . ."

"Our wise ancestors . . ."

"Crazy . . ."

"Kill him!" yelled Wentworth. "Kill him!"

Mutterings among the people.

Lawrence raised his hand. There was silence.

"I am an old man," he said quietly. "I see death all around me. We are too few to kill each other needlessly. This man, and the woman with him, have not harmed our people. But they have broken the law."

He paused. Then: "They have broken the law," he repeated gravely. "That fact cannot be altered. No man can be permitted to break the law with impunity. Our ancestors, in their wisdom, gave us the laws by which we live. It is our duty to see that they are enforced."

He looked at Brighton and Lynna, regret in his eyes.

"It is the judgment of Council," he said, "that the prisoners shall be executed when seven sleep periods have expired. That is all. The Trial by Council is over."

Brighton took Lynna by the hand and the Council Guards led them out of the chamber. The people watched them blankly. They didn't care; it made no difference to them. They were apathetic, slow, already dead. Brighton and Lynna emerged into the cold world of rocks and caves and shadows.

"The fools," he whispered slowly. "The blind, dead, stupid fools!"

Brighton had begun to think when he was twenty years old. The others, almost all of them, were dying—slow and pale and weak. But Brighton still had the spark. He began to ask questions.

He did not question the people, for he knew that he would find no answers among them. He turned to the world around him. He flung his questions at the clammy rock that made a vault of gloom above his head. He asked the cold water, the air, the fires in the pits. He asked the black shadows that crawled on the walls of the world.

His mind was a whirlpool of confusion, and his strange eyes made him a stranger to his people. His eyes blazed through them, beyond them, seeking, demanding. He was dissatisfied, but he did not know what was wrong, or why. He neither knew what he was looking for, nor where to seek it. But he tried. He had to try.

Was the world all there was? What would happen if you dug further into the rock—what if you dug and dug until—until what? Would you come to an end to the rock, an end to the world? How *could* it end? What could possibly lie beyond matter? Air? Nothing? If there were nothing there, what held the world together?

What about the old songs that no one understood? The legends, the superstitions, the gods who had lived on the roof of the world? Why were his people dying?

Brighton had to know. He had Lynna, and a few friends. But the others were suspicious of him, He was haunted by an age-old, timeless spectre—the ghost of loneliness that stalked through the world with him, the terrible loneliness of the man nobody understands.

He decided to go to the Old Man.

The Old Man had had a name once, but it had been forgotten. He was just the Old Man. His face was lined, and he had a dirty white beard. He lived in an isolated niche in the wall of the world and everybody thought he was crazy.

He had used to talk a great deal in his youth, but few people had ever listened seriously to him. Minds were sluggish and the fires of life were burning low. He had gradually been driven within himself, and now he sat nodding before the fire pit, silent and alone.

The Old Man looked at Brighton and saw himself—as he had once been. Skin that was pale but not dead, black hair, sensitive features, restless eyes. And something else. Something forever beyond analysis that set Brighton apart.

"Sit down, lad," the Old Man said. "I have been waiting for you."

Brighton sat at his feet. He instantly recognized that he had at last found someone to talk to, and so he said nothing. He listened. The Old Man talked and spun a web of dreams in his mind.

He told the stories he had heard from his father, who had heard them from his father before him. Wonderful, incredible stories about the gods who had lived on the roof of the world, in an enchanted land of warmth and light.

There had been many gods, the Old Man said. Many more than the number of people who now lived in the world. Perhaps there had been as many as a million of them, although that was, of course, hard to believe. They had grown and prospered. They built fantastic cities and had green, succulent things to eat instead of eyeless fish and synthetics.

But even the gods had not been perfect. They had fought one another and conceived better and better means of destroying themselves—nothing like the crude clubs and knives the world used now. They made killing their business. Being gods, they were terribly efficient—they finally set off an inferno of flames and plague germs and death. They annihilated themselves.

Almost. A few escaped, hiding in a hole in the roof of the world. But they were trapped. They were afraid to go back into the flames and the germs. Upheavals of rock had sealed them in. Their fear of the horror from which they had escaped translated itself, in time, into laws and taboos and superstitions. Generations crept by, and the gods began to die. They became stagnant and dull. They forgot that they had ever been gods. The world around them was the only world they knew and they lived in the darkness like animals.

Brighton stood up, tense, his fists clenched.

"We are the gods," he said slowly. "We are the gods!"

"We were the gods," the Old Man whispered. "Once."

He turned back to the fire pit and closed his eyes. Brighton looked at him but couldn't speak. His mind in a turmoil, he ran back through the rocks to Lynna.

The next sleep period, in the silence and the flickering of the smoldering fires, Brighton set out to find the roof of the world. With Lynna, he picked his way through the rock passages, their flaring torches casting grotesque shadows on the world around them.

"What will we find?" asked Lynna. Her hushed voice was hollow in the darkness.

"I don't know," Brighton said. "Nothing, probably. But we may find everything."

"Everything?"

"Everything that counts."

They were silent then. For a long time they passed through old and little-used passages, where twisted columns hung from above and pushed up from below. The cold water oozed through the wet walls.

"You're very sure, aren't you?"

"Yes."

They stopped on a high shelf. The world lay before them, dark and still. Brighton shivered and put his free arm around Lynna. He lifted his torch high and listened to the slow drip of water somewhere in the vast sable distance.

"Look," he said softly. "Look at the rocks and the emptiness and the cold. We don't belong here. We aren't made for this. This is for the snakes and the fish, the white fish without eyes. You know what I'm trying to say—you know, don't you, Lynna?"

"I know. We have to try to find something else—have to try even if we never find it."

"Lynna, you know why."

"Yes. For us," Lynna said, and smiled at him.

Brighton nodded and held her closer. For them. For them and for others like them. In her own way, Lynna understood. He was grateful for her. If she hadn't understood, if there hadn't been someone to turn to in this bleak world—Brighton didn't like to think about it.

They went on through the empty passages, pausing occasionally to replenish their torches with chunks of the rock that burned. They were alone and tired and uncertain. But they went on. Something made them go on.

"This part of the world is forbidden," Lynna said. "What if the Council finds out?"

"They are fools."

"But they are the law."

"The law will have to be changed."

"Do you think that there really are . . . things out here? Like the stories say? What if there are?"

"I don't know."

They went on. They crawled and stumbled and climbed until their legs turned to lead and their minds went blank with fatigue. Then they made a fire pit and slept on the damp rocks. Somewhere, water dripped coldly.

When they awoke, they both thought they heard sliding, reptilian sounds in the dark recesses of the world. They looked at each other, but said nothing. They swallowed some food concentrate, drank chill water from their containers, and set out again through the rocks.

They were utterly alone in the world—more isolated than ever because of the faint slithering and the lonely drip of the water in the silence. Brighton was worried. What if he were wrong? What if the world went on like this forever, all rocks and desolation and cold? What if he found a passage to the surface and it proved to be a hideous tunnel that crawled with death and disease from the roof of the world? Most legends, most superstitions, had a grain of truth in them somewhere.

"How much longer?" Lynna asked. Her voice was tired.

Brighton shook his head. "If we go back," he said, "we go back for keeps."

They went on.

"The world is getting smaller," Lynna said suddenly. "It doesn't feel as big."

She was right. They quickened their steps, pushing through the rocks with new spirit and energy. The walls of the world closed in on them almost perceptibly, until they found themselves in a narrow cave. The end of the world danced before their eyes in the flaring light of their torches—a pile of broken, jumbled rock that clogged the passage.

Brighton thrilled, his heart hammering in his throat. He scrambled forward and pulled at the rocks. They were too large to move. But they were loose. He sat down on a boulder and looked at Lynna.

"We've found it," he said quietly. "The way to the roof of the world. The way back."

"We may have found it," Lynna said. "But we can't use it. We could never get all those rocks out. They may go on for miles."

"We can't use it *now*," Brighton corrected her with new confidence. "We'll go back and get help."

"What if they won't help? What if it doesn't go anywhere? What if death still lies at the other end?"

Brighton kissed her.

"They've got to help," he whispered. "And there is death all around us where we are; the people are dying. They don't have much to lose. We've got to try."

They started back. The rocks cut at their feet and their torches threw twisted shadows on the walls of the world. When they stumbled back into the inhabited part of the labyrinth of caves, Wentworth was waiting for them with the Council Guards.

Condemned to death, Brighton slept the sleep of exhaustion in the prisoner's cave—a dank hole in the eternal rock, a cell within the greater rock prison that was the world. He dreamed the same dream over and over again. He was running across a flat, endless surface, gasping for breath, his feet torn and bleeding. He could see an enchanted land of warmth ahead of him—see it clearly with its brilliant greens and blues. He had to get to it, *had to!* He fought his way nearer and nearer, his heart pounding in his throat. He forced his tired body across the featureless plain. He fought for air, bit his lips until the blood came and trickled down his chin. He was closer—he could almost touch it! He reached out for it, sobbing—and watched it writhe away into a hideous horror of rocks and death and cold black water full of blind, laughing fish.

He woke up in a cold sweat. Someone was calling him.

"Brighton? Brighton, can you hear me?"

He scrambled to his feet, shuddering. He leaned against the wall of the cave and made himself relax.

"Yes," he said. "I can hear you. Who is it? What do you want?"

"It's Wilson," the muffled voice answered. "Hang on—we're going to get you out of there. You're taking us up."

Lynna pressed close to him, rubbing the sleep out of her eyes.

"What about the guards?" Brighton asked. "Can you move that rock away from the entrance? Who's with you?"

"Don't worry," Wilson's voice assured him. "We'll get you out."

Brighton felt hope surge up within him again. There were others, then! The people were not all dead, not all fools. The Old Man had been at the trial, silent, thinking his own thoughts. And there must have been others—others in whom the spark of life still smoldered under the ashes of the centuries, others who still thought for themselves. They had been lost in the crowd where they had always been, not saying anything, waiting.

He heard the chink of metal and the murmurs of the men as a metal bar was rammed in behind the rock. The rock groaned and swung back. He felt light-headed and dizzy. They were free.

He walked out with Lynna into the sleeping world, taking deep draughts of the cool air. He shook Wilson's hand wordlessly and looked around him. There were four others with Wilson—Hatcher, MacDonald, James, and Hayes. Two guards lay sprawled on the rocks with their skulls crushed.

"We had to do it," Wilson said, nodding at the dead bodies. "There was no other way."

Brighton looked a question at him.

"We believed you," Wilson said simply. "We're ready to take a chance with you, no matter what the others think."

Brighton did not waste words in thanks. "Are there any others?" he asked.

"Over at my place," Wilson replied.

"Let's go then," Brighton said. "We've only got a few hours to work in, and we've got plenty to figure out."

The seven shadowy figures moved quietly among the flickering fire pits, their shuffling feet sending hushed echoes through the darkness of the sleeping world.

There were nineteen of them in all, besides Brighton and Lynna—nine men, nine women, and the Old Man, who was alone. Against them stood the world with its three hundred people.

Brighton listened to them talk and forced himself to think clearly. He had to think straight now and he knew it. This was their chance. If they missed it, there would never be another. He watched the others, eyes narrowed, as they crouched around the blazing fire in an inner cavern of Wilson's home.

There was Wilson, who wanted an armed rebellion—twenty-one of the living against a world of the dead. There was Hatcher, who wanted to keep the whole affair secret and furtive. There was James, who wanted to force the Council to back them up. And there was Hayes, who was in favor of doing something in a general way, but who was too cautious ever to decide upon a single course of action.

He listened to them all, weighing and balancing carefully what each man said. He had to be right. He had to be sure. Time was running out; the world would be awake soon, and he and Lynna must not be found in Wilson's home. He turned to the Old Man, who had been sitting motionless before the fire, eyes glittering, saying nothing.

"What do you think?" he asked him. "What should we do?"

The Old Man looked up, his dirty white beard etched in the glow from the fire. His weary face was stamped with the strange contradictions of time—resignation and rebellion, bitterness and love, despair and hope.

"Brighton," he said quietly, as if the two of them were alone, "you are a leader. The others feel your strength and they trust you. The decision is yours to make. I am very old; perhaps I have lived too long already. But the others—the people here in this room, the death-touched automatons left in the world, the countless generations that may never be born—are depending on you. A burden of inconceivable significance, a destiny that no one here may possibly grasp, rests on you. It is too much to ask of any man; no man can be infallible, no man can be right every time. And yet, for reasons that you know, you must try. You must do the best you can."

Brighton looked at him, and at the others huddled around the great fire. He was staggered by the realization, full and complete, of what the Old Man had said. The dark, tangled webs of fate and the unguessed and unknowable paths of history had somehow, incomprehensibly, led to this—to this fugitive cavern, to these few souls, to him. And he was no superman, no being touched with supernatural powers. He was only a man. Was that enough?

He faced them all, with icy doubt gnawing inside him and a resolved determination in his lonely eyes—eyes that were lonely for the life he had never lived, the world he had never known.

"We must make a break, clean and simple," he told them flatly. "It is too late—it may have always been too late—for stealth and politics and halfway measures. We have got to choose one way of the other and stick to it. There will be no going back."

Silence. The fire threw great shadows on the walls.

"We must leave here—now, within the hour—and hack and tear our way through to the roof of the world—to life or to death. If there are any among you who are afraid, now is the time to get out. You will not be harmed, and no one need ever know that you were with us in this room."

For a moment, nothing. Then, slowly, wordlessly, two men got to their feet—Hatcher and Lewis. Taking their women with them, they walked out of the cavern. They were ashamed and did not look back.

"All right," Brighton said to the rest, his heart warming to them. "Thank you for your confidence. We haven't much time—get all the tools and the food and the weapons you can carry and bring them back here. We start in an hour. Be careful; don't let anyone see you. If you are seen, it is your responsibility to make sure that it is not reported to the council before we have a chance to get away. Good luck."

There was a murmur of voices. Men and women filed out of the room, smiles on their faces. Brighton was proud of them. He put his arm around Lynna and read approval in the Old Man's eyes. He stood silently, gazing into the fire, thinking.

While the world was still hushed with sleep, Brighton led them out. Seventeen shadows filed through a ghost world they were leaving forever, loaded down with all they could carry. They were careful to make no sound. Furtively, almost holding their breaths, they slipped through the world like sleepwalkers in a sleeping land.

Brighton set a fast pace through the twisted tunnels. No one complained. The dark figures picked their way steadily through the rocks, their flaming torches throwing crawling shadows on the wet walls of the world. Voices murmured, and echoes crept back and forth, chasing themselves through the dead tunnels.

Brighton led them on, his eyes restless in the uncertain light. The sounds of clambering feet almost concealed the cold, distant drip of water—but he could still hear it. It trickled relentlessly in his brain. He was tired, and he knew that the others would have to stop and rest. He stopped them in a small alcove and watched with burning eyes as they collapsed in exhaustion on the hard rocks. He forced himself to stay awake, his hand on Lynna's shoulder as she slept.

Unasked, Wilson sat with him, shivering. Brighton looked at the prone figure of the Old Man. He was pathetic in his weakness, and yet, even in sleep, his strength was evident. He had said nothing since their flight, but had kept up wordlessly. Brighton wondered about him—the one man who had understood him best. How long could he last? What kept him going? Would he ever see the world of his dreams?

"How much further?" Wilson asked.

"We should make it in a few hours now," Brighton said.

"Do you think we can really get through?"

"I don't know. We have a chance."

"What if we break through and find that the world is still deadly, the way it was when the gods fled from it?"

"Well, if it is, we won't have much time to worry about it," Brighton smiled. "We'll have to wait and see; that's all."

Wilson yawned and gazed blankly at the darkness around them. Brighton watched him with tired eyes. He was a good man, Wilson. He deserved something better than death. Brighton felt sick inside. Could he bring them through, all of them? Or was he leading them only to suicide? The blind leading the blind! He shook his head and pressed his fingers to his throbbing temples. It was hard to keep awake—he noticed that Wilson was dozing now. He was alone.

Brighton stuck it out for five hours and then he got the others up. They yawned and trembled in the chill of the caves. They looked at the darkness around them and listened to the cold drip of the water. They didn't know that Brighton had not had any rest. They swallowed some food concentrates and drank some water.

They went on.

When they stumbled into the blocked tunnel that marked the end of the world that they had known, Brighton wasted no time. He was numb with exhaustion and his eyes were streaked with red, but he drove his unwilling brain to think clearly. He divided the men and women into shifts and instructed them in clearing away the choking rocks. He got the work started and left word that he was to be called at the first sign of anything unusual. Then he found a welcome hollow in the wall of the world and surrendered himself to instantaneous sleep.

Brighton's sleep was a strange fantasy of white emptiness across which black splotches of sound marched from the world around him. He was aware of, but did not hear, the disembodied mutter of voices, the clatter of rocks, the clank of tools.

The hours whispered by, until the white blankness became alive with black spots that whirled and expanded and grew into oceans of black through which poured currents of phantom sound. Something . . .

"Brighton!"

"Wake up, Brighton. Wake up, wake up, wake—"

He moaned and rolled over on the damp rocks.

"Brighton—the people, the Council! They're coming!"

Sleep vanished as if it had never been; consciousness hit Brighton like a splash of cold water. He leaped to his feet, senses acutely alert.

It was true. Someone was coming. He could hear the sounds of voices and scuffling feet. He turned to James, who had awakened him.

"Quickly now! How many of them are there?"

"About a hundred, I think." James' voice was frightened, nervous. "That's what Hayes said; he saw them first."

Brighton nodded, surprised at his own calm.

"Come on," he said, working his way back to the others. They stood among heaps of excavated rock, waiting for him. There was no panic, but they looked uncertain. He took over, reassuring them with his confidence.

"Take it easy," he told them. "We can handle anything they can throw at us."

Can we? A voice within him whispered.

"Two of you hide in the rocks on each side. The rest of you line up. Grab anything that you can use as a weapon. Don't do anything until I give the word."

It's five to one against us if they fight.

"Now just hang on—don't worry."

What if we lose? What if we lose?

They waited.

The light of their torches preceded the men from the Council. The sound of their voices became an ominous, muted rumble. Wentworth came into view, with the others behind him. Brighton couldn't count them all.

"We've got the Decree of Council," Wentworth said smugly. "We're not going to let you defy the gods and destroy the world!"

The others roared their approval.

"You've got five minutes to get out of here," Brighton told him flatly. There was no hint of his inner anxiety in his voice.

Wentworth laughed—fat, pompous, dead-white. "You're not bluffing us, Brighton! We're five to one against you. Maybe you don't like this world, but we do—and intend to go on living in it. You're not going to kill us with your wild ideas!"

The others pressed forward behind him, shouting.

"We're not bluffing," Brighton said coldly. Something within him laughed at this patent lie. "If you come any closer, not one of you will live ten seconds."

Wentworth hesitated and Brighton knew that he had to follow through with something—anything. It was now or never. He tried to relax his tense muscles and motioned the others to stay where they were. He advanced toward Wentworth alone, his closed hand, palm upward, outstretched.

"We're not bluffing," Brighton repeated, walking slowly forward. "Before you murder yourself and everyone with you I think you'd better have a look at what I have in my hand. Not all the old weapons were lost. We've found some of them, and we're ready to use them."

Wentworth watched him uncertainly. Would it work? Brighton knew that the centuries of dull lethargy had not been without effect; these people had no stomach for a real fight. Wentworth couldn't be *sure* that there was nothing in his hand—and Wentworth was anything but eager to risk Wentworth's life.

Brighton stopped when he was still several paces from Wentworth. His hand remained outstretched but at too high an angle to enable Wentworth to see anything clearly. He was cool now; he had himself under control. He isolated the corner of his mind that was a black pit of fear. He refused to think about what would happen if he failed.

"Have a look, Wentworth," he said softly. "Have a look and then see how much fighting you want to do."

In spite of himself, Wentworth edged closer. "You haven't got anything in your hand," he said without conviction.

"You'd better have a look, Wentworth. In two minutes my men will use their weapons. Have you ever seen a man burned to a black cinder?"

There was silence except for the nervous breathing of the men. Wentworth was afraid to move closer and Brighton stood where he was, waiting.

"One minute, Wentworth," Brighton said.

The men behind Wentworth murmured uncertainly. Wentworth moved closer, hesitantly, straining to see what was in Brighton's hand. Brighton waited until exactly the right moment. Then, with desperate speed, he took one quick step forward, caught Wentworth's fat shoulder with his outstretched hand, and spun him around. Wentworth shrieked and Brighton whipped his right arm into an iron lock around his neck. His left hand unsheathed his knife and pressed the sharp blade into Wentworth's flabby neck until the blood came. The thing was all over in seconds.

"All right," Brighton whispered coldly. "Tell them to get out of here— fast, or you're a dead man."

Wentworth's pale body trembled with fear. "Go back," he screamed. "Go back, go back!"

His men whispered among themselves and began to press forward, fingering their weapons. Brighton cut into Wentworth with the knife.

"No," Wentworth yelled. "Don't come any closer. He'll kill me—and you'll be responsible, all of you. You know the penalty for killing a Council Guard! The gods will avenge me! Go back—go tell the Council what happened. Go back, go back—"

The men stopped in confusion. They looked at Wentworth, the sweat pouring from his white face. They looked at Brighton, his eyes meeting theirs with steady strength. They looked at the men lined up against the end of the blocked passage, ready and waiting. Slowly, muttering, they turned and began to retrace their steps through the dark tunnel of twisted rock. The light from their torches vanished and the sound of their voices was lost in the distance.

Brighton put his knife away and turned the shaking, terrified Wentworth around.

"The hero," he whispered. "The hero!"

He hit him once and left his fat body lying in a heap on the rocks. He didn't know whether he was alive or dead, and he didn't much care.

"Come on," he said to the others. "Let's get back to work."

Time dragged on and the hours blended together into one blurred vision of sweat and metal and rock. They hacked and tore the rocks out of the tunnel and piled them in the wide passage through which they had come, accomplishing the double purpose of clearing the tunnel and establishing a protective wall behind them. They dug and chipped and hauled until it seemed that they had never done anything else.

They had no way of knowing what sort of progress they were making— the rocks ahead might extend for miles or inches. They didn't know. It might never end. No one, not even Brighton, knew for certain where they were going. The world around them might well be all there was.

The end was a shock. One minute there was the interminable rock ahead of them and the next—light. A tiny square of light, no larger than a man's fist and more brilliant than fire. It hurt their eyes. They fell back, staring at it.

Brighton couldn't think. In a daze, he crawled into the tunnel and tore at the choking mass of rocks with a strength he never knew he possessed. The intense, incredible beam of light stabbed through his white skin. It widened perceptibly as he strained at the rocks. Others joined him and they fought the rocks in a frenzy of unreasoning joy.

They were suddenly—out. They were out, and Brighton staggered down a rocky hill, trying to adjust his stunned eyes. He couldn't see, but an unaccustomed warmth swept over him and he was conscious of a ball of fire floating over his head. The soft air was sweet and moving gently. He fell face downward in some spongy stuff that was like moss but wasn't. The heat beat on his back. He stared at the strange floor of this new world and touched it with his hands. It was green.

His vision cleared a little and he made out a cool shadow beneath a dark shaft with green branches. He crawled into it and called to the others. He didn't know what he said, but they came. He was beyond thought. His eyes were adjusting. He could see.

It was impossible—wonderfully, deliriously impossible. After a lifetime of darkness and encircling rock, he saw color and broad, rolling fields. A vivid blue with drifting patches of white arched over his head. Green plains surrounded him and he could see towering mountains in the distance. The sweet air caressed his face.

He found Lynna's hand and pressed it wordlessly. They had found it. They had found what had been the home of the gods. It lay all around them, and the gods had come home again.

"Look," Wilson said finally. "The ball of fire—it's falling."

It was true. The sun was settling gently in the west, throwing long, cool shadows across the green world. Outlined on the horizon they could see the jumbled ruins of what might once have been a city.

The Old Man was silent, tears in his eyes, content just to look at last on the world he had dreamed of for so long. Brighton watched the hot sun settle across the green fields and knew what it meant to be happy.

"It will be back," he said, nodding at the distant ball of flame. "It must go around the world."

They were silent as the soft shadows crept across the land and they lighted their torches. It was not yet dark, but they could sense the coming of the night.

"I say let's go back and close that tunnel," Hayes said finally. "We gave them their chance and they didn't take it. This is our world now—we fought for it and we found it. They haven't earned a share in it."

"They wouldn't fit in," James agreed. "We should start over now. We've got a chance really to do something—and they're not going to ruin it!"

There was a general murmur of agreement.

The Old Man shook his head. "There is room enough for all," he said quietly.

Brighton sat in the cool breeze and wondered. It was true that the others had had a chance and not taken it. Indeed, they had actively opposed them and would have killed them all if they had been able. They had condemned him to death, and Lynna with him. They were riddled with superstition, dull, weak. They could contribute little and might do great harm.

Still—he didn't know. They were his people, he had lived his life among them. They could not all be bad. And there were the children—pitifully few with their lost, hopeless eyes.

"No," he said finally. "We won't block the tunnel again. If we're going to start over again, that would be a bad beginning. We won't seek them out—they would kill us if we did. But if they come to us in peace we won't harm them. It is not for us to say who is to die and who is to live."

He whispered to Lynna and left her where she was. Alone, he walked through the green grass and the soft breezes of a summer evening, torch in hand. He could not know the strange cycles and destinies that were lost in the waiting vastnesses of time. He was ignorant of the full significance of this tiny moment, lost and forgotten in the shadows of history. But he did sense, as for the first time he saw the splendor of the stars, that he and what he had done had an importance far beyond his wildest imaginings.

He walked through the starlit field of what a few hundred years before had been Atlantis, breathing the sweet night air. He wondered about the future, and about himself and his people. Could they succeed where gods had faltered? He shook his head. Probably, almost undoubtedly, they would fail.

But they would try, for that was what it meant to be a man.

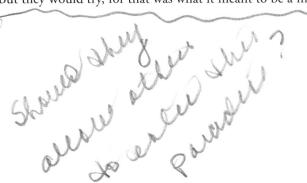

THE ANT AND THE EYE

NICO: Saidyah, do you know what space is?
SAIDYAH: It is the little road the ant travels between two
blades of grass: it is the great empty road my eye travels on its way
to the stars.

From "Time is a Dream,"
by Henri-René Lenormand

Robert Quinton could feel it coming.

He opened his eyes, yawned, and tried not to look at the multiple color tones that rioted over the walls of the sleep sphere. He let the fresher work him over briefly and tried to pretend that this was just a day like any other day. He selected a predominantly blue-toned tunic, which was downright hypocrisy, and checked to make sure all the viewers were off. Then he secretly lit a cigarette.

"Getting to be a regular sot," he observed.

It was curious how the local customs got under your hide. The Merans on Procyon III took their stimulants via the smoking route, with a fair-sized cigarette being about the equivalent of a straight shot of high-powered Scotch. He had to be cautious about his smoking. By now, he actually *did* feel like he was sneaking a quick one whenever he fired up for a smoke.

Quinton finished the cigarette, carefully destroyed the butt in a disposer, and walked out of the sleep sphere into the open air. It was morning on Meran, and the primary sun was radiating a cheerful greenish-yellow. Cool, fresh breezes whispered up from the valley floor, and the world smelled like flowers. Quinton took a tube to a Five Transfer, where Ncarl was waiting for him.

"Blue harmony," greeted Ncarl, smiling. He was dressed in a gray tunic, indicating that he was in rather mediocre spirits.

"Blue harmony," Robert Quinton returned the greeting, quite as naturally as he would have said "good morning" on Earth.

"An odd time for a message, I believe," Ncarl said courteously. "I hope nothing is clashing."

"That makes two of us," Quinton agreed, settling himself in the tube for Communications.

Ncarl shook his head, somewhat self-consciously. It was a trick he had picked up from Quinton. "Black is in the air, " he said.

"It may just be a routine message," Quinton suggested, knowing full well that it wasn't.

"You're a liar," Ncarl said.

"Isn't everybody?" asked Quinton.

The tube hummed to a halt. Quinton tried to ignore the cold knot of worry that chewed his stomach, and followed his friend into the hum of Communications.

Quinton kept his mouth thoroughly shut. Even now, he did not trust himself to attempt casual contacts with Merans he did not know. The system was too intricate; he let Ncarl guide him through the color maze to the Contact Booth. Speaking a bit too rapidly to enable Quinton to follow his words, he checked with the booth operator, a dour-looking individual dressed almost entirely in black. Not for the first time, Quinton was grateful that he had Ncarl around. In making relatively early connections with diverse cultures, you saved a lot of time by having a more-or-less objective informer on hand—in the case a man who corresponded to the Meranian version of a fellow anthropologist.

"All harmony," Ncarl said finally, as the black-clad operator left. "He's got it all set up for you."

"Thanks, Ncarl, I'll check with you as soon as I find out what the deal is."

Robert Quinton stepped into the booth and closed the door behind him. He sat down in the operator's chair and closed the contact switch. For a long moment, there was nothing. Quinton sat there, a tall, rather thin man, beginning to gray at the temples, with his usual quiet smile absent from his face. He was outwardly calm, but he wasn't kidding himself. The boys wouldn't call him off schedule just to pass the time of day. Of course, they might just be after information . . .

A bell *dinged* with its customary abruptness and the communicator rattled briefly. Quinton read the message: THIS IS BAC XII. IDENTIFY.

He jabbed the keys in return. QUINTON BAC UN. PROCYLON III. XX5L. WHAT'S COOKING, DAN?

Again a moment of silence. Then: UN BAC IMPERATIVE OFFICIAL. RETURN AT ONCE VIA BAC XII PICKUP POINT SIX UNIT 12.7. REPLACEMENT CUMMINGS. REPEAT IMPERATIVE. END OFFICIAL. THE JIG IS UP DARLING. MY HUSBAND KNOWS ALL.

Quinton grinned and tapped out his acknowledgment of the orders. Dan had a way of taking the bite out of unpleasant situations—but the situation remained. He opened the contact switch again and took a deep breath. Back to Earth again, after less than a year. *What could have gone wrong?* He didn't fool himself—no man was utterly indispensable in the UNBAC setup. If they had to yank him home in a hurry, that meant that things were in the stage where shades of ability and slight favorable factors were considered vital. And that meant—

He got slowly to his feet. The old uncertainty flooded him with doubt, but it didn't show on his face. He kept his thoughts to himself and left the booth. Ncarl was waiting for him and guided him out of Communications back to the tube.

"I've got to go home, Ncarl," he answered his friend's unspoken question. "They're sending a replacement—name is Lloyd Cummings, a good man—and I don't know when I'll get back."

The hum of the tube filled the silence.

"When?" Ncarl asked finally.

"Tonight. I'd appreciate it if you'd come along to the pickup and let me introduce you to Cummings. This doesn't mean the end of our work, of course—but I regret the delay."

"No. But I will miss you, Bob."

"Yeah. I know."

The two men parted at the Five Transfer. Ncarl walked off through the green forest, and Robert Quinton went back to his Meranian home to pack his gear. It would be good to be with Lynn and Baby again—a man needed his family. And Earth, old Earth, for all his acid comments, was still his planet—and the strangest of them all.

But—*What had gone wrong?*

It was a soft night on Meran, and sad as only the hush of night can be. The warm wind played in the summer grasses and the crystal stars looked down. There was something infinitely poignant about the night. It reminded a man of all the things that he had not done, all the loves he had never known. Sometimes, Quinton felt pretty sharp during the day—but the night whittled him down to size again.

"I hear her," said Ncarl.

Quinton looked up, although he knew that he could not possibly see the great cruiser against the stars. He could hear her, though; or, more properly, he could *feel* her. From far out in space, she was only a rumbling vibration, a muted murmur. Invisible, she yet dominated the land—massive, poised.

The two men watched, and shortly a tiny streak of flame arched through the night sky and hissed out of the heavens above them. The jet flames winked out and a small spaceboat hummed in on her copter blades, landing with scarcely a jar in the open field in front of them. The entry port hissed open and warm golden light spilled out of the ship. Two men stepped down, and Quinton and Ncarl went to meet them.

"Good to see you, Bob," greeted Lloyd Cummings, the UNBAC man. And then, switching easily to Meranian: "You must be Ncarl; I have looked forward with great harmony to meeting you."

Quinton smiled, seeing that Cummings knew his stuff as usual. Cummings introduced him to Engerrand from the spaceboat, and that was that. Quinton had left complete notes and advice in his sphere, and Cummings was fully competent to go on from there. Quinton didn't waste his time asking questions—Cummings wouldn't know the answers, of course. He shook hands all around and followed Engerrand into the spaceboat.

Looking back, he could see Ncarl and Cummings walking off together under the stars. The soft Meranian night touched his face. It seemed to know that he was leaving, that he would not be back. It was trying to say good-by.

If it were important enough to call him home, it would definitely not be a case of elementary-my-dear-Watson and back to Meran again.

This was for keeps.

The entry port hissed shut behind him. Robert Quinton sank into a seat and lit a cigarette. The spaceboat lifted on her copter blades for what seemed to be a long time, and then the jets erupted with a slamming roar that dwindled slowly down into a muted rumble.

"It won't be long now," Engerrand said. "I'll bet you hate to leave."

Quinton smiled. "No," he said. "It won't be long now."

Twenty-three days later, Robert Quinton by-passed the sprawling, wheeling Space City by switching over at Lunaport, and an UNBAC shuttle landed him at the divisional headquarters of the United Nations in New York.

He had a quick look at New York before entering the Shaft, and the New York of 2034 was the same town it had always been. It was reassuring, somehow, to know that Little Old New York was still there. The shining copters lazed along in six-level traffic under the bright afternoon sun and a transcontinental rocket flashed by high overhead. The women's skirts were a trifle longer this year, with a faint filmy area at the knees—quite daring, really. The air was fairly clean with the piped-in solar energy, but he could see traces of New York "fog" hanging over the city. Several large freight copters were sluggishly lumbering along the lower levels, headed

toward the coastal sub bases. The colorful old art vendors, with their natu-
ral-abstraction projectors, were everywhere.

New York hadn't changed a bit.

At the Shaft, Quinton energized his credentials and went straight up
to the Fifteenth Level, detouring around the showy administrative and
public areas. His code signals admitted him directly into Lorraine's private office, which was situated in an inconspicuous part of the Shaft that
nobody paid much attention to. The office itself was on the prosaic side,
except for the man sitting in it.

"Hi, Boss," Quinton said, extending his hand—three weeks and two
days after receiving the UNBAC imperative on Procyon III, eleven light-
years from the Earth.

"What kept you?" grinned the Boss, shaking hands.

"Lovely intergalactic spy, as per usual," Quinton said. "Good to see
you, Mart." He surveyed the Boss. A bit more gray at the temples, perhaps, but otherwise Martin Lorraine looked about the. same—which was
to say that he looked like the tri-di conception of a handsome scientist,
which in turn was one good reason why he fronted UNBAC. Another
good one was that he knew his stuff six ways from Sunday.

"Sit down," said Mart, "and I'll try to fill you in. I guess you're wondering what the score is."

Quinton smiled. "You might say that, yes," he said. "What's up—is
the world coming to an end?"

Martin Lorraine looked him right in the eye. "Something like that,"
he said, and didn't smile.

Quinton sat down. He took his time, lit a cigarette, and blew a neat
smoke ring at nothing in particular. He didn't say anything.

"I'll give you a quick outline," the Boss said, leaning forward, his hair
studiously awry as though to cover up his indecent good looks. "We'll
smuggle you out to New Mexico to take over pronto, if the brass doesn't
spot you first. There won't be time to make a report on the Meranian
stuff, but I'll get Rog to fake something for the front office to keep the
Wizards of Finance happy."

Robert Quinton waited silently. He was an outwardly slow man, and
had often been called a lazy man due to his habit of doing nothing when
there was nothing to do. He had heard the end of the world announced
before—but not by Mart. He thought of his child.

"No Judgment Day junk, of course," the Boss said, reading his thoughts.
"No end in *any* sense if we can catch it in time. But we're stumped, Bob—
it's getting away from us."

"Facts," suggested Robert Quinton.

"You live with 'em a while, then. One year ago, the computer survival probability curve took a nose dive. It's still going down."

A little man with an ice hammer began to beat on Quinton's stomach with monotonous precision. "Figures?" he asked—outwardly calm.

"Point ten," Lorraine said.

Robert Quinton didn't move. He was stunned, literally. Point ten. *That meant the odds were nine to one against the survival of civilization as he knew it.* And computers didn't make mistakes.

"Time?"

"Hard to say. Thirty, forty years, maybe."

On the face of it, to the untrained eye, that didn't look so bad; forty years was a long time. It was like worrying about another Ice Age. But the catch was that with every second the odds got worse. When things got that critical, it was act fast—or not at all.

"Any leads?"

"Precious few. We can't find—"

The viewer buzzed and lit up, and broad brass-encrusted shoulders with a head on them came into view. Martin Lorraine smiled politely as though he hadn't a care in the world, promised that he'd check on the ore constants the very second that he saw Robert Quinton, and switched off after a few concluding pleasantries.

Neither man paid the slightest attention to the interruption.

"Nobody knows?" Quinton asked.

"Outside of Little UNBAC, no. The stock market is rising, the papers are full of rhapsodic editorials, the Space City weightless games came out as expected. The economy's sound, most everybody is happy within human limits, and there are no ominous clouds on the horizon. There isn't even a horizon. In short, this isn't a crisis period. No one is viewing with alarm. Everything is just ginger-peachy."

"Like the guy shooting marbles in that nice sunny place below the reservoir," Quinton offered after a brief pause. "Having a fine time, but he unfortunately isn't on to the fact that someone has opened the dam a short distance up the valley."

"Exactly. Someone—or something."

There was a long silence in the little office room. It was much too still. Quinton could hear his watch ticking, and he didn't like the sound.

"I'll be going, Mart."

"Catch a copter on the roof. The transcon for New Mexico will be waiting at the port, and I've already notified Lynn and your daughter that you're coming. I'll be down as soon as I get through another round of

bigwig conferences to get money for you guys." He paused. "I don't have
to tell you to watch your step."

"No., You don't have to tell me."

"Take care of yourself, Bob—and give Lynn a kiss for the Boss."

"See you shortly, Mart. Maybe we'll both get back to Meran one of
these years."

He left Lorraine's office. No one paid any attention to him, save for a
casual nod here and there; everyone was busy with Big Problems. He caught
the lift for the roof. *Maybe we'll both get back,* his voice echoed in his mind
as he smiled vacantly at the lift's other passenger. And another echo laughed
at him:

And maybe we won't.

When Robert Quinton stepped off the transcon at New Mexico Station, Lynn and Baby were waiting for him in the desert sunshine. He
walked toward them, heart pounding, the old thrill racing like electricity
through his veins.

He never remembered afterward what they did or what they said in
those first magic moments together after their periodic separations. There
were only impressions, confused and fleeting, and the smell of the sun
and the sky. Lynn was incomparably beautiful because he loved her, and
Baby was ten years old and beginning to look like her mother.

"We've been lonely, Bob—"

"Daddy, Daddy, did you bring me a surprise—"

"Getting old, gray hairs, supper's waiting—"

Being apart was no fun, but maybe it had its compensations. Any two
people got pretty used to each other when they were together every day, but
when they were forced apart and then came back to each other it was like
falling in love all over again. These meetings, these first breathless moments,
were beyond value—and what else, in all the worlds, really mattered?

Nothing, nothing, nothing, his mind whispered exultantly.

But already, as they walked slowly across the tarmac to where their
copter waited, the long shadows of the afternoon sun crept blackly at their
side, and a cool north wind rustled across the land.

Early the next morning, Robert Quinton walked into the UNBAC
computer station and went directly to Carr Siringo. Siringo hardly looked
up when he entered, and Quinton didn't try to hurry him—having found
from long experience that Siringo had a distinctly negative reaction to
being pushed. Quinton deposited himself on a metal stool, lit a cigarette,
and waited.

If Martin Lorraine looked like a tri-di conception of a clear-eyed, noble scientist, it was equally true that Carr Siringo reminded one instantly of the prototype of all mad fiends out to blow up the planet with an invisible ray. He had been compared variously with the Devil and a cockeyed angel, usually the former, and it didn't take much imagination to see why. Siringo was short, fat, and bald, and he was never still. He ate prodigiously, worked hugely, and lived in Gargantuan style. He worked on problems because he loved problems for their own sake, and once he had the solution he lost interest completely and launched himself into something else. He didn't care a hoot for the world, humanity, or anything else apart from the incredible world of his own mind. There was a firm conviction among his co-workers that he would never die as other men died, but would simply vanish in a puff of blue flame on some distant day when he really got wound up on a problem he couldn't solve. He was indispensable, or course, and Quinton respected him for what he was, although he never felt entirely comfortable in his presence. On his part, Siringo called Quinton a "humanitarian," and when he said it, it was an insult.

"Back to save the world, hey?" Siringo said finally, without looking up from the computer, in precisely the tone of voice he would have used to remark, "I hear your wife has leprosy."

"Probably not," Quinton said slowly, declining to lose his temper. "There's always a chance—a good chance—that the factors will change favorably without any help from us. There's always a chance that a broken copter will fix itself if you just let it sit and swear at it every day as you walk to work. I just like to play Hero, that's all."

Siringo laughed shortly and changed the subject. "What'd you get on Meran?" he asked with a flash of interest. "How about that consanguineous family system? What about the mental tri-di? What is the significance of banded clothing? What are—"

Quinton blew a smoke ring at his face. "You tell me, I'll tell you," he said. "What've you got?"

Siringo raised his absurdly thin eyebrows. "Talk to Wonder Boy," he advised. "And after you tell us dummies what to do to save Beloved Terra, come on back and we'll have a beer."

"Try not to smash anything," Quinton told the man who was probably the finest technician in the world. He left then, and didn't hear, or want to hear, the pungent remark that filled the room behind him.

"Wonder Boy" was John Bordie, whose official title was Chief Correlator, and whose actual job it was to sort through the mass of data sparked off by

Siringo and try to make some sort of sense out of it. Prolonged contact in the tiny UNBAC station had made him regard Siringo as something either more or less than human, and he welcomed Quinton with all the enthusiasm of a fellow tourist on a desert island.

"Meran must have been nice," he said after they had exchanged greetings. "We'll have to talk about it sometime, Bob."

Quinton smiled. *Nice? How did you translate stars into words?* "Yes," he said. "We'll have to talk about it."

Bordie got down to business. "Here's what we've done, Bob," he said. "We've put every available man on it, sparing just enough to fake the usual station activities and make the joint look respectable. We've arbitrarily divided the possible causes for the down-curve into five classifications, and worked them through the mad Genius and his computers."

"Um-m-m. The usual five?"

"Generally speaking, yes. Extraterrestrial, embracing such star systems as we know, the planets on which we have colonies, Luna, and the space station; Cultural; Technological; Personal; and Unknown—the latter being anything not caught by the first four. We've been going full blast, cutting security precautions to a minimum. But the Snake dropped another point the last time we checked it; Lorraine doesn't know that, and he won't be happy."

Quinton didn't say anything.

"We've abstracted the essentials for you, and you can pick them up in Classified. Tentatively, I'd say we'd ruled out any non-earthly cause, but you'll have to interpret for yourself. I don't put any stock in that Unknown stuff—that's Siringo's baby. Aside from that, we know precious little. If we could only work out in the open—"

"But we can't," Quinton finished for him. "If anyone finds out what we're up to, we won't have to wait for any world to end. Our name won't even be mud."

John Bordie shrugged. It was too late to start worrying about that; that was something they all had to live with—or try to.

"Any concentration at all?" asked Quinton.

"Not much. There's the usual stuff—the press yapping about the morals of the teen-agers, a couple of new religious cults, lots of good protest literature about inhuman scientists, some national incidents of a minor sort, some joker down in Mexico who says he's the Aztec Cuauhtemoc and wants to change the name of Mexico City back to Tenochtitlan and start a holy war against Spain, a spurt in membership in the Anarchist Party, and Aunt Tillie back under a doctor's care with a backache. You name it, we got it. What a planet."

"There must be some concentration," Quinton suggested, smiling.

"Well—maybe. I'd say the United States, but maybe that's just national pride."

"What does Siringo think?"

"God only knows, and I wouldn't put any money on *that.*"

"Well, let's start breaking the United States down into areas, John. It might turn up something, and at any rate it'll give Siringo a chance to work off some of that nervous energy. You got an analyzer I can use, for what I don't get done at home?"

"Sure—use Four. I'll slap a restricted on it until you give me the clear wave."

"Fine. I'll go digest this stuff, and then we'll start asking questions." Quinton drummed his fingers absently on his knee. "Can you spare Conway? I'm going to need a bright boy."

"Check. My best to Lynn, and tell Baby I'm waiting for her to get a little older."

"You won't have to wait long—and you'd better start loading the parcheesi dice; I hear the kid is getting pretty sharp."

"Beginner's luck," Bordie said sourly.

Robert Quinton picked up the data abstracts at Classified, and left the Station for home. Even on viewer tape, the abstracts were bulky. He knew that he was in for a protracted siege of learning. A man couldn't even keep up with his own planet any more, much less the universe. He had a momentary vision of an extensive interstellar civilization, and felt decidedly sorry for anyone mixed up in it.

It was early afternoon in New Mexico, and on the hot side. The land as seen from his copter looked sleepy and pleasant, with the green farmlands rolling along under him like eternal verities. They seemed to say that they had always been there, would always be there, and that he was a fool for not tossing the abstracts overboard and taking off for the nearest trout stream.

But Robert Quinton felt oddly cold in the hot sun. A century ago, that green farmland had been desert. It only seemed eternal, obvious. Once it had been obvious that the blazing sun above his head had gone around the Earth below him—you could *see* that that was true, and had always been true.

A century ago, desert. And a century hence—?

The long days passed, and they were good days. Robert Quinton worked, and worked hard. There were red streaks in his eyes and he was hard to live with. There was a terrible, driving urgency behind his every move, with rest when he could fit it in. But it wasn't exciting work, and there was nothing dramatic about it. It was grinding, digging work—and it had to be done.

Just the same, it was good to be home.

Every man has a place he calls home, no matter how many places he may live in. In Quinton's case, it was an old-fashioned Frank Lloyd Wright type of house that blended in with the soft browns and greens of the New Mexico hillside. It had a small, clean stream that bubbled through the living room and out into the patio, and the glass-and-rock walls were open and spacious. Quinton had often wondered why he was so conservative in his housing, but somehow he just didn't care for the turret-and-gingerbread style of the modernists. And this was a good house, *his* house, made into a home by the years that he and Lynn had lived in it. It had his kind of soap, his kind of casualness, his kind of books, and it was his kind of house.

Then, too, there was the statue. It stood arrogantly on top of the piano, and it had originally been a whisky ad. It was the bust of an elderly, aristocratic gentleman with a monocle and a somewhat bemused expression. Into the base of it Quinton had carved a name: *Cuthbert Pomeroy Gundelfinger.* This was sort of a private deity, and a very useful one. Whenever someone came to visit him that he did not know, Quinton simply waited until he saw the statue. If he laughed, he offered him a drink. If he asked who Cuthbert Pomeroy Gundelfinger was, he made polite conversation and waited for the caller to leave.

At the moment, Lynn was picking fresh fruit out in the garden, and Baby was avidly watching the tri-di. It was a science-fiction story she was watching, and Quinton smiled to himself as he glanced at it. It was routine stuff about the Twenty-fifth Century, involving the usual space pirates, matter transmitters, a mad scientist who looked enough like Siringo to be his twin brother, and a clear-eyed hero in a blue and silver uniform who was dashingly engaged in saving the world. Why was it, he wondered, that all these stories envisaged technological marvels by the bushel, but seemed to assume that social structure and culture wouldn't change in over four centuries? Why were they fighting all of today's local issues in the Twenty-fifth Century? Why, it was less than a century ago that nations had still had colonies, and nobody had even heard of Charles Sirtillo or Intelism!

And why did they persist in imagining that saving the world was a popular pastime? It wasn't, and never had been. Quinton lit a cigarette, no longer smiling. Saving the world was for crackpots, idealists, and impractical dreamers; everyone knew that. It was a standard joke, and world-savers were about as popular as plague carriers. The popular man, the practical man, was the guy who did the expected thing, the socially approved thing, and never questioned whether it was right or wrong. If everyone else was doing it, why then, naturally it *was* right.

They had a name for world-savers.

Suckers.

Quinton put it out of his mind. This was a battle that he had fought with himself long ago, and he had won. He worked on, sifting through the abstracts, getting the feel of the situation. The sun was warm outside, and there was a lazy insect hum in the air, but he stuck with it.

There was nothing else to do—for him.

The days raced by and became weeks.

Computers chattered and banged and clicked. Analyzers sorted, chewed, classified. Data flowed into New Mexico Station in daubs and tricklets and underground rivers. The UNBAC men sweated and argued and threw rocks at the trees.

It was all very dull, to an untrained eye. They discussed culture correlations and integrative principles, diffusion receptivity and Uncle Charlie's beef against the tax collector. They sat up all night with a computer. They lost sleep and insulted each other with vast regularity and fineness of distinction. And they worked together on the toughest problem of all— putting two and two together to get four.

When it came, the setting was anything but impressive.

John Bordie leaned forward over the smoke-burned table and frowned at his parcheesi dice. Martin Lorraine, AWOL from his New York office, did his level best to look sloppy in a Y-shirt, but only succeeded in looking like the typical tri-di hero exhibiting Pose 7-X-4b, Casual Masculinity Without Pipe Or Dog. Bob Quinton slouched his long frame in a chair, his hands in his pockets, a cigarette glowing unhealthily from the corner of his mouth. Carr Siringo charged up and down the room like an impatient dragon; you could almost see the fire squirting out of his nostrils.

A young man hurried into the conference room with a microplate. He was terribly earnest and excited when he handed it to Lorraine, and probably didn't even hear Siringo's contemptuous snort.

"We've got it," Lorraine announced briefly. "The curve took an upswing on M-97. It's a man."

Robert Quinton smiled broadly.

"Clean living," suggested Siringo.

John Bordie fingered his dice. "We've got to be *sure*," he said.

"This is as sure as we can get it until we try it for keeps," Martin Lorraine told him slowly. "The hypothesis has been tested from every angle we can work, and the survival curve has indicated we're on the right track."

"And where do we go from here?" Bordie asked.

"Well, let's see what we've got," Quinton said. "We've established two facts: the factor that's causing the Snake to drop is a personal one—that is, it's a man we're after—and the threat is located in the United States—according to Siringo, somewhere in Texas, Arizona, Louisiana, New Mexico, or California. The obvious procedure from here is to narrow that area down and then find him, whoever or whatever he is. And then—"

There was a short silence.

"We'll cross that bridge when we come to it," Lorraine said decisively.

"As the man said when he stepped off into the chasm," muttered Carr Siringo with an unpleasant grin.

Quinton turned, started to speak, and then held his tongue. Carr *was* irritating—but he had a habit of being right. As usual, Siringo had placed his stubby finger unerringly on a very knotty aspect of the problem.

Quinton replaced his infinitesimal fraction of a cigarette with a fresh one, feeling for all the world like an alcoholic on a prize binge. They were looking for a human being, that was definite. In a way, that made it easier. In another way, it spelled out trouble.

The catch was, of course, that the man—if it was a man, and not a woman—hadn't *done* anything much yet. In all probability, he was not even a well-known personality. He might even be a child. He was certainly no wild-eyed schemer in a black coat making atom bombs in a secret lab high in the mysterious Ughflutz Mountains—or at least that wasn't likely.

He might be anyone, anything.

It was not so much as *who* he was that made him important. It was *when* he was and *where* he was.

They were looking for Hitler—a man made dangerous by the conditions around him. They were looking for Hitler—*while he was still a house painter or a corporal in the German army.*

It was tough, of course. It was always tough. But it was far simpler, and a lot less bloody, than going after him when it was too late, when he was already a powerful dictator, when you had half a world to fight instead of just one man. *Just* one man? Quinton smiled. They were dealing with a human being, and that could be messy—and dangerous.

"O.K., Siringo," Quinton said. "Let's go into a huddle. We'll see if we can't narrow that area down to something we can work with; we can't do anything until we do that. When we get the picture in focus, we'll see about stepping off that chasm."

Carr Siringo's face was expressionless. "It's your funeral," he said.

The men got up from the table. John Bordie smiled a cold smile and tossed his dice on the table with a practiced hand. In spite of himself, Quinton watched the bouncing cubes of ivory with fascinated attention.

Snake eyes.

The mother spider spun her web across the land.

The slender invisible threads from UNBAC crept out across fields and towns, villages and county fairs, probing. At first they were widely spaced, resting on Louisiana, New Mexico, Arizona, Texas, and a part of California. The days slipped by.

The web grew tighter, stronger.

California dropped out, and then Arizona. Only fragile wisps clung to New Mexico and Louisiana, and then even these disappeared. The web contracted over Texas, seeking, hesitating. It grew smaller, smaller—

It tightened over Texas. It inched down from Fort Worth and Dallas, across from Laredo and San Antonio. The computers hummed and buzzed though a haze of cigarette smoke, testing, eliminating. *What would happen if—? Supposing that he were here, what would—? If the X concentration is here, and the Y factor there, then—?*

The web tightened. It gripped a tiny area bounded by Bay City, Houston, Beaumont, and the Gulf of Mexico. It shrunk still more, contracting like a shallow puddle in the sun. It flowed together, stopped. The web made a black dot on the map of the Texas coast.

"That does it," said Martin Lorraine, his usually too-handsome face lean and ugly with strain.

"Galveston," said Robert Quinton, sinking down into a chair. "Our man is in Galveston."

"Chalk up another one for you, Carr," John Bordie said. "Nice work."

Carr Siringo stopped his pacing, shook his head impatiently, and walked swiftly out of the room. It was almost as if he had been caught off base by Bordie's words; Siringo had lived so long in his private world apart from freely-expressed emotions that he foundered when he unexpectedly found himself being complimented. He was like a fish in air. Not for the first time, Quinton wondered what had happened, long ago, to make Siringo the kind of man he was—and also not for the first time, he decided that he did not want to know.

So their man was in Galveston, he thought. Now they would have to start a precise screening process of the city's fifty thousand inhabitants. It would be a difficult job, and time-consuming, but it would not be essentially different from the techniques used to narrow the critical area down to one city. Without the computers, of course, the job would have been impossible. Even with the computers, there was going to be plenty of leg work involved.

But it *could* be done.

Who was he, this man set by chance into the fuse area of an explosive situation yet unborn? What was he doing now? Was he a genius of a sort, or just an ordinary guy who happened to be in the wrong place at the right time? He could be *anything,* Quinton realized. An idiot can change history as profoundly as a brilliant schemer—or even a germ.

"Me for coffee," said Martin Lorraine.

Quinton and Bordie nodded and followed him out of the Station into the New Mexico night. A half-moon slept in shadows. The stars twinkled as they had for the millions and billions of years of Earth's existence, and seen so, on a summer night from Earth, they were only stars again. Robert Quinton smiled a curiously sad smile.

It was good to see them just as stars once more.

The three men walked through the cool night air to Harry's, where a red neon sign still shone cheerily in the night. Harry's stayed open late, catching straggling Station workers and occasional night-fliers on the road to Folsom. They walked in and perched on counter chairs, while Harry, unbidden, got the sausage and eggs and coffee working. The music box was still for once, and the men did not talk.

They were all thinking about one man. A man they had never met. A man whose very name they did not know. Quite possibly, he, too, was sitting in a late hash house, smoking and sipping coffee, thinking—

Robert Quinton sat very still, feeling the silver moon rays paint the hills outside. His thoughts turned, as they often did, to the little town of Folsom a few miles down the road, where long ago flint artifacts had been found with fossil bison, establishing positively the antiquity of man. Ancient man in a New World that Columbus had "discovered"—some twenty thousand years too late. Quinton looked down at the plastic floor. Under that floor was the land, and across that land men like himself had once hunted the mammoth with spears and sung strange songs beneath the same cold moon that still drifted through the night seas.

No man knew what had happened to the Folsom people—or to the later Pueblo groups who had walked off and left their homes to the desert winds long before the white man came. Quinton closed his eyes. Here in the southwest, men had built a civilization before—and had vanished into nowhere, leaving only ghost structures and a few mute pieces of chipped flint to mark their passing.

A cool night wind swished across the grasslands and rattled the windows.

"Let's go home," said Robert Quinton.

"There's our man," said Pat Conway, three weeks later.

Robert Quinton followed the psychologist's pointing finger and saw him. The man came walking out of the courthouse, his hands in his pockets, absently whistling convenient extracts from "But Oh! Those Bars on Mars," the old drinking song. He looked like the guy next door, the guy who sat next to you at lodge meetings.

He was the most dangerous man in the world.

Quinton eyed him closely. The man was of medium stature, a bit on the thin side. He looked hard and muscular, but that could have been imagination. He had very light, straw-colored hair, brushed straight back. He was dressed conservatively in a green business cape with a brown-and-yellow neckline. He was tanned and he had a ring on his left hand. As they watched, he stepped into a shuttle and hummed off westward, toward the old causeway.

"No need to follow him," Conway explained, steering Quinton to their parked copter. "We can pick him up again on the way to his house."

They got into the copter and lifted up into a cloudy gray sky. Quinton let Conway handle the controls, and when they had gained some altitude he looked down and watched the Gulf toss and roll restlessly off the island, sloughing off white breakers that bubbled in and broke on the colorless sands. It felt like rain, and there were very few bathers on the beach.

"Doesn't look like much, does he?" asked Conway.

"No," agreed Quinton. "Neither did Napoleon for that matter."

Conway grinned. "But take Josephine, now—"

Quinton relaxed a little, listening to the hum of the copter. Conway was a good man to have around, a good man to work with on a job like this. He knew how to laugh. Pat's appearance was deceptive, to say the least. He was thin and animated, with a lively and expressive face. He cut his hair short to the vanishing point and affected violent clothes and suspenders. He looked like he was perpetually on the verge of going into it a soft-shoe routine on a burlesque stage—which he had been known to do upon occasion—and he had fooled a good many people who couldn't look beneath the surface.

The copter intersected the shuttle route and lazed along above it, following it across the island toward where the almost abandoned causeway stretched away to the mainland. It looked like a toy dropped by a child, but Quinton could see a few old men fishing on the gray spans. His eyes returned to the shuttle beneath him, the shuttle that carried the man who had unwittingly called him home from the stars.

The man's name was Donald Weston. It was an average sort of name, the kind that you wouldn't look at twice. The viz books were full of names like Donald Weston. It was a non-dangerous, pleasant sort of a name. Donald Weston was twenty-seven years old, and had been educated at a small Texas secondary college. Since his graduation four years ago, he had been doing moderately well on the surface, though not sensationally so. He was an officer in the Galvez Syntho Supply Company, which was engaged in selling special supplies to the Mars and Venus colonies. It was a very ordinary sort of a job.

Recently, Weston had shown mild symptoms of political ambitions. He had announced as a candidate for City Councilman, a position of minor importance, but one that could serve as a stepping-stone toward bigger things. The UNBAC scanner had gone over Weston with a finetoothed comb—his old school records, his associates, his background—and had found very little of interest. There were a few intriguing hints of outside activity, but for the most part Weston seemed almost painfully average.

Camouflage, Quinton wondered, *or accident?*

The gray clouds turned a shade darker. Big, fat drops of rain began to patter down on the copter cowl, and Quinton saw the fishermen far below start to scurry for shelter. Hissing rain sheets swept in across the Gulf and thunder rolled faintly in the west.

As the copter hovered discreetly in the distance, they saw Weston hurry out of the shuttle and run through the rain to his small suburban home. There was a warm glow of light as the door opened, a glimpse of a woman with golden hair, and Weston was gone.

"Well, back to the salt mines," Conway said, and turned the copter in a slow arc.

Quinton looked at the slanting rain and listened to the fast drops patter on the cowl. He felt a cold chill inside him that was not due to the rain, and Conway's light talk didn't ease it much. They had seen their man, and both of them knew what that meant. They had to get him, and it wasn't going to be easy. They were outside the law, men without legal status, and if they got into hot water they would have to get themselves out—or not get out at all. They could expect no help from UNBAC if they failed. They could not even *ask* for help.

It was cat and mouse—and no ordinary mouse, either. Sometimes the cat didn't get back.

Below them, almost invisible, the gray buildings of the city huddled together to keep warm. A city full of people, Quinton thought, and one small copter lost in the sky. It was a deadly game they were playing, and the city didn't even know. Had it known—if it found out—it would turn on them with the mindless ferocity of a beast gone mad.

Quinton looked down, thinking. The sea leaped and roared in a rising wind, and now the beach was deserted. An old beach umbrella rolled along the sand, waiting for the sun.

"Take a look at this," said Pat Conway.

Robert Quinton looked up from the paper, where he had been reading one of Weston's campaign speeches, and took a sheaf of film blowups from Conway's outstretched hand. He glanced at the psychologist questioningly.

"We got a chance to get inside last night while the Westons were out lapping it up at a business party," Conway explained. "A couple of the boys and myself picked the house over, and we got a sheaf of manuscript in Weston's handwriting under a false bottom in an upstairs desk. We photographed the lot—seems that our boy fancies himself to be another Machiavelli."

"Um-m-m," said Quinton.

"Just a clean, red-blooded American boy," Conway observed. "A credit to the force."

Robert Quinton started to read the blowups and felt the cold knot tie itself like ice in his stomach. He lit a cigarette, but the smoke seemed cold, black, gritty—

Weston's manuscript was charming stuff.

Night.

Black, black night and the red blood flowing. It swirls and eddies around my legs. It soaks me and mixes with my blood.

In the black night.

I walk through the black world, and it is red. I see it but I cannot speak. It is too red. I walk through the world, and I think.

In the black, black night.

They do not see me. I am alone. I will be one of them, a part of them. And they will be a part of me, slowly. Redly. I only want to help them, but they cannot see me. It is too black. It is very hard, but I will do it. For them.

I love them.

I walk on.

In the black, black night—

There was more, much more, and Robert Quinton read it all. When he had finished, he did not speak. He put the blowups down, got to his feet, and walked out of the building. Out into the open air, the blue sky, the people and the sunshine.

So that was Donald Weston. Not much, now. A clever man, a warped man. Perhaps even an evil man, although Quinton was wary of the word. He wasn't particularly dangerous—yet. Not until his moment came, a moment yet lost in the twisted paths of future time. But the moment would come, inevitably. It was in the cards.

The cards had to be reshuffled.

What was it that the man had written? *"I only want to help them, but they cannot see."* Was that so very different from what UNBAC was trying to do? *Was it?*

Robert Quinton watched the people passing him. All kinds of people. Men, women, children. Drunks, lovers, dreamers. Kids on their way to the beach and businessmen on their way back to work. Happy people, sad people. Contented people and people who would one day throw themselves from copters just to get away from it all. They weren't worried about survival, these people. That wasn't fashionable, and never had been. They just wanted to be let alone, and Quinton didn't blame them.

Was there a difference, a difference between a Weston and an UNBAC? There was one difference: *reason.* Reason, logic, science, humanity. Words, of course. Just words—but a man had to have something, had to believe in something down deep, even when believing wasn't popular. Man had been given a mind, and with that mind he had evolved science. Science was a tool. Were they wrong to use it?

Were they just kidding themselves?

The people who walked by him wouldn't like him, if they knew. They would turn on him, hate him, fear him. Weston, on the other hand, was a man they could put their trust in, believe in. He was a regular guy.

Robert Quinton walked on down the beach, alone in the crowd. The sea breeze whispered in his ears and the hot sun burned his shoulders under his shirt. Tomorrow, they would go after him.

If they failed—

"Sit down, sit down," said Donald Weston pleasantly. "Drink?"

"Thank you," said Robert Quinton, smiling. "Scotch and soda, if you don't mind."

"Fine, don't mind at all," Weston assured him, his voice warm and exceptionally friendly. "Honey—"

Jo, his wife, vanished into the kitchen to fix the drinks. She was a magnetic, blue-eyed blonde, the kind that dominated a room just by being in it. Quinton sat back in his chair, relaxed, and surveyed the room. It was just as Conway had described it to him; comfortable, but not pretentious, in good taste. A few books were in a case against one wall. They were of the type usually displayed in homes not much addicted to reading—several book-club best-sellers, a treatise on how to keep your figure slim by living on orange juice, a family Bible, a volume of condensations from the *Reader's Digest,* and a set of Greek and Roman classics, from Homer to Marcus Aurelius. The latter were spotlessly clean and unread. Jo emerged from the kitchen, smiled engagingly, and handed him his drink. She had fixed one for herself, but her husband did without.

"I'll try to come right to the point," Quinton said, after sipping his drink. "I know you're a busy man."

Weston waved the remark aside, his straw-colored hair neatly combed as always. "Lots of time," he assured him. "I've been looking forward to meeting you; I'm very flattered, really, that you think I have any possibilities along those lines."

Jo smiled.

"Our business is finding men with potentialities," Quinton said truthfully. "Finding them and lining them up before they get too expensive. It's just good business."

Jo produced an ashdisposer when Quinton fumbled for a cigarette, and he paused to light up. Weston didn't smoke, his green eyes sharply alert in contrast to his easy-going manner.

"I know you've read our letters with care, Mr. Weston, and looked over the literature we sent you. I think you will agree that we have made a generous offer?"

"Certainly, certainly," Weston said. "I appreciate it."

"Your name was suggested to us by various sources here in Galveston, Mr. Weston, and—"

Weston waved his hand. "Please," he said. "The name is Don."

Jo smoothed her long skirt over her silken legs.

Robert Quinton found it difficult not to let down his hidden guard. These people *were* charming, and no doubt about it. Sitting here with them, in their homey living room, it was virtually impossible to fear them. They were typical to an extreme, even idealized. And yet—

"Black, black night, and the red blood flowing—

"Don, then—and my name is Bob. Your record in college, and your enviable reputation here in town, together with your often-expressed interest in the Mars Colony, has convinced us that you are one of the men we are looking for. Now, I'm not going to make you any sales-talk; you know as well as I do the prospects and opportunities you would have with our company on Mars. There's no question of success or failure involved; it's purely a matter of how far you can go. We think you could go a long way with us."

Or without us, Quinton thought. He remembered: it was not so much *who* he was that made him deadly. It was *when* he was and *where* he was. The *who* and the *when* couldn't be changed. That left the *where. They had to get Donald Weston out of Galveston, and do it legally.*

"It's a break, all right," Weston said. "We know that."

Quinton nodded, feeling the sweat in his hands, and took a deep drag on his cigarette. "You bet it is. I know that you two have talked it all over, and have looked up our company's standings and ratings to check on what we've told you. I've taken the liberty of bringing some papers with me this evening, and the rest is up to you." Quinton crossed his mental fingers—tight. He smiled. "What do you say, Don?"

"I'm afraid our answer is no," Donald Weston said, smiling back at him. "I've decided not to accept the position."

Robert Quinton's heart took a long nose dive to nowhere. He kept his face expressionless, except for a polite look of disappointment. Their strategy had failed completely. Donald Weston was going to stay right where he was. *How much did the man know?*

Quinton looked into the other's eyes. They stared back at him, guilelessly. They were open, frank, friendly—on the surface. And their green depths were frigid with the cold hardness of ice.

"I'm mighty sorry to hear that, Don," Quinton said. "I find it hard to understand—"

Jo Weston brushed a soft blond hair out of her blue eyes. "It's just a marvelous chance for Don," she said. "But with the election coming up and all, we really feel that our place is here, at least for the present."

Jo Weston. What part was she playing in the invisible game?

Quinton stood up, nodding. "I see your point, of course," he said. "I won't overstay my welcome—but if you should happen to change your mind in the near future, just get in touch with us. We'll be glad to see you at any time."

"Thank you very much," said Donald Weston, his rather boyish face very earnest. "We'll certainly think it over."

I'll bet you will, thought Quinton. He said: "Well, thanks very much for the drink. Perhaps I'll see you around sometime."

"Perhaps," agreed Donald Weston, smiling,

Little man, what now?

Robert Quinton said good-by and walked out through the night to his copter, and death walked at his side.

"We've underestimated our man," Robert Quinton said slowly. "Weston didn't tumble for it, period."

"How much does he know, do you think?" asked Pat Conway, perched on the edge of the bed in Quinton's Galveston apartment.

"No telling; I can't read him. But Weston is a smart one, Pat, and so is that bombshell wife of his. We're not dealing with any pawn, and that's for sure. He must suspect something, or else why would he turn the offer down? We've got to watch our step, boy."

"I don't entirely get it, Bob," objected Conway, his thumbs hooked in his suspender straps. "It looks like this All-American Boy pose of his is strictly for the birds, but *why?* He can't possibly know he's the key pivot in a developing cultural situation, he hasn't done much of anything—or has he? What's he got to be afraid of?"

Quinton shrugged. "My guess would be that he's just plain old-fashioned smart. He's got big ideas, and he's playing the political game. This just-call-me-Don stuff is just about what you'd expect, after all. He's setting himself up as a regular Joe for the voters, that's all."

"It's more complex than that, I think," Conway said. "He's probably got his finger in some pies we haven't even smelled yet. He's no dope, and he'd have covered his tracks. Did you notice his eyes?"

"I noticed them," Quinton nodded.

There was a long silence.

"Nuts," Conway laughed shortly. "We're still gulping over the Evil Eye."

"Maybe," said Quinton. "Maybe we'd better be."

They had both seen "simple" situations blow up in their faces before. In this game, the rules changed while you played, and you changed with them—or else.

"Well, the next step is clear, anyhow," Conway said, breaking the uncomfortable silence.

"Unfortunately," Quinton agreed.

He was just getting to his feet to fix himself a drink when it happened. His scalp prickled and there was an explosive *poof.* Quinton dropped like a stone, twisted, and fired a chair at the wall switch. The lights went out.

He lay very still, hardly breathing, listening to his heart pound in his ears. There was silence, utter and complete. Quinton strained every muscle in his body, trying to hear. But there was nothing. Not a whisper. He waited a long time, wondering why he was still alive.

"Pat." His voice was very low. "Pat."

Silence. Quinton felt a sick dread wash through him. The killers were gone now, but he didn't want to turn on the lights. He didn't want to see. He tried again, without hope.

"Pat."

Nothing. Or—was that shallow breathing he heard in the room with him? Silently, Quinton wormed his way across the floor to the bed. He held his breath and felt ahead of him on the floor. Pat was there, and the floor was wet and sticky. Quinton let out his breath through set teeth. He felt sick and tired.

Quinton explored the body with a practiced hand, not daring to take a chance on the lights. There *was* a heartbeat, a faint one. The wound was in the chest, low on the right. That wasn't good, but it could have been worse. Pat was still breathing, but he wouldn't be for long. Not without help.

The hospital was out of the question. Quinton couldn't afford to get mixed up with a shooting at this stage of the game. There was just one thing to do.

He crawled over to the closet and fished the special wave radio out of its hiding place in the wall. Regulations or no regulations, he wasn't going to let Pat die if he could help it. He beamed New Mexico Station, setting the dials by means of a tiny red light on the set, and sent a code message: UNBAC IMPERATIVE OFFICIAL. CONTACT: BORDIE, NEW MEXICO STATION. CONWAY SHOT GET THE DOC AND COME A'RUNNIN'. REPEAT IMPERATIVE. QUINTON.

He lifted Conway's wet body carefully to the bed and dressed the wound as well as he could with his first-aid box. Conway moaned once and his heartbeat remained faint. Quinton clenched his fists, the old hate trembling through his body.

If Pat died—

He sat down by the still figure on the bed, his gun in his hand, and listened to the shallow, fast breathing.

It was going to be a long night.

It was four o'clock in the morning when the doctor came, and he didn't come with Bordie. He came with Carr Siringo.

"Bordie was delayed," Siringo told Quinton, looking him in the eye as though daring him to challenge his word. "I had to come down this way anyhow, so I brought the doc."

Quinton ignored the words and accepted the facts. "Thanks, Carr," he said. "I won't forget it."

Siringo plopped himself down in the kitchen and insisted on talking about the significance of banded clothing on Meran. At first, it irritated Quinton, but then he calmed down and even became interested in the ideas Siringo was sparking off with such brilliant nonchalance. Quinton's mind was sharp with early-morning clarity and he thrust and parried the rapier-like cuts from the short, bald man, trying grimly to hold his own.

It was after five when the doctor walked through the door and sat down on the kitchen table, and Quinton suddenly realized that Siringo had neatly and effectively been taking his mind off the still form in the next room. Quinton eyed him accusingly in the gray light of dawn, and Siringo returned his gaze imperturbably.

"Well, Doc?" Quinton asked.

The UNBAC doctor shrugged. "Maybe," he said.

"You'd better get some sleep, son," said Carr Siringo.

Robert Quinton hesitated, and abruptly discovered that he was exhausted. Something snapped way down deep, and told him he wasn't as young as he once was. His throat was dry and his eyes burned. He nodded slowly, left the room, and turned in.

He didn't look at the figure on the other bed.

Robert Quinton looked at the man sitting across from him and wanted to smash his face in. Instead, he smiled pleasantly.

"That's it, Pond," he said. "We've picked you for the job, and you can write your own ticket."

Wiley Carruthers Pond made pyramids with his smooth hands and listened intently. He had iron-gray hair and an aristocratic, noble face. He was forty years old, was liked by small children and babies, spoke loud and often of his service to the people, and was a first-class heel.

"I'm not sure I understand you, Mr. Quinton," he said.

"You don't have to understand, Pond. All you have to do is sit in for four years and collect twenty thousand a year from us, plus your regular salary as Councilman. We'll get you elected, and no strings attached."

"It's most irregular, Mr. Quinton," Pond said, his eyes gleaming.

Quinton clenched his fists, thinking of Conway. He hated the guts of Wiley Carruthers Pond, a fact of no importance whatsoever. Pond had political connections in Galveston, and aside from that he didn't matter. Donald Weston did.

"Well?" Quinton said.

"After all, Mr. Quinton, a *Councilman.* Then, you're paying me—"

"Yes or no," Quinton said, his eyes hard. "I haven't got all day."

Pond eyed him narrowly. "Of course," he said, "my only interest is to help the people. If for some reason you feel that I could be of more service to them as a Councilman, then I must say that no position is too humble for service. No man can be too proud to serve, Mr. Quinton."

"Yes or no," Quinton repeated.

Pond leaned forward. "All I do is serve. and keep quiet, and collect twenty thousand a year, right? You'll sign a contract assuring me that I won't be asked to act in any way contrary to my principles?"

"Of course," Quinton assured him. "You're in no danger. Our interest begins and ends with getting you elected."

Wiley Carruthers Pond stuck out his well-manicured hand. "It's a deal," he said. "May I say that I am grateful to you for your interest in the people of Galveston? It's men like you, Mr. Quinton, who—"

Quinton cut it as short as he could. He had played this scene before, too many times with too many people, to take any pleasure in it. He came to terms in a hurry, and walked away by himself. He felt like he needed a good bath.

Pat Conway was still alive, but he couldn't be moved. The doctor stayed on, and Quinton and Siringo played poker on the kitchen table.

That wasn't the only game they played.

Money was no object, and the men from UNBAC knew their stuff. What little they didn't know, Wiley Carruthers Pond and the local machine filled in with a vengeance.

Both Galveston papers announced Pond's candidacy on their front pages, and printed flattering, smiling pictures. Both Galveston papers began to run his life story of unselfish service to the people of Galveston, climaxed now by his decision to serve in a minor capacity where he could directly and intimately help the little people. At the same time, editorials were printed about Donald Weston that painted him as an unscrupulous political schemer, unfit to represent the people of the City of Oleanders.

Whenever one turned on the tri-di, there was the beaming, hearty, trustworthy Wiley Carruthers Pond, indulging in heart-to-heart talks with the people. Viz phones rang all over the island, and the canned face and voice of Wiley Carruthers Pond assured the listeners that he was on *their* side, first, last, and always.

There was more, much more. There were whispering campaigns, clever and vicious political jokes, and slanted "news" stories. Weston's tri-di talks were edited, and commentators "interpreted" them with cutting sarcasm.

It was dirty, slimy, and ugly. It was the Big Leagues, and it made Quinton sick of himself and of the work he had to do.

It was rotten, clean through.

Robert Quinton paid out the easy money and talked with oily voices on the blacked-out viz phone. He got down in the dirt all day long, and at night he sat up and listened to Conway's shallow, gasping breathing in the next bed.

He talked to his soul.

Somehow, he had never imagined that it would be like this.

Robert Quinton had been born in 1994.

That meant that the first space station had been built and the Moon had been reached twenty years before his birth. It meant that the inner planets had been touched and a tentative colony set up on Venus ten years before his birth.

That meant that the United Nations, after half a century of bitter ups and downs, had gradually absorbed enough power to make itself an authority to be reckoned with in world affairs. The United Nations, of course, was an inevitable product of space expansion.

That meant that before he ever drew a breath the great solar energy stations had largely supplanted atomic energy as a cheap power source, and had brought tropical areas into positions of new importance as vast natural hothouses for the cultivation of the necessary plants.

In 1990, a practical interstellar drive had been found—and promptly hushed up as being too dangerous a toy for a still-unstable planet to play with thoughtlessly. That was four years before Robert Quinton was born.

That same year, Robert Quinton, Sr., a cattle rancher in New Mexico, had met Anne Torneson, his future bride, at a stock show. The senior Quinton had been born in 1954, and his wife in 1958.

When Quinton was a child, he hadn't been markedly different from other children of his age and time and place. He banged around the barn and got treed by a bull and watched the rockets flash by in the blue sky over his head. While the first genuine social science was coming to life after the ferreting out of the true interrelationships between psychology, anthropology, sociology, and economics, young Bob Quinton was discovering how to pick up sleepy rattlesnakes by their tails and snap their heads off with a flick of his wrist—a practice not encouraged by his mother.

While Bob Quinton was losing sleep over traditional school baseball games, a vitally important principle began to dominate scientific thought. It was quite simple. It had been around for a long time in medicine and elsewhere. It had been succinctly stated by an old general of the '50s named Omar Bradley: *"The way to win an atomic war is to make certain it never starts."*

The principle? It's tough, if not impossible, to cure a cultural disease such as war—but you can *prevent* them before they ever happen.

Preventative medicine—applied to cultures.

It wasn't that simple in practice; neat plans never are. Culture patterns had lagged desperately behind technological advances. In a world of atomic fission, politics were hardly out of the Feudal Ages. The course of civilization was still charted by "common sense" and "everybody knows" and "the natural way to do things." There were no legal channels through which wars could be prevented in the only way they *could* be prevented—and legal changes were incredibly slow with nuclear clouds on the horizons, based as they were upon prior decisions going all the way back to the Roman Empire.

The scientists had the solution. Could they *use* it?

Their answer was, inevitably, a patchwork, makeshift system that operated undercover, in the shadows. They went to work, a selected few of them, to try to hold the world together until some sort of a balance was attained.

They were outlaws, of course. So was George Washington.

The survival probability curve, commonly known as the Snake, was developed by integrating the cybernetic computers with selected social data from all over the world. The curve was *not* designed to maintain the *status quo,* or to block progress in any form. It was not designed to "control" cultures or individuals in any particular direction. It was non-political, without preference for any one faction or system, whether conservative, liberal, or in-between.

The Snake was concerned with exactly one item: the survival of free civilization. It was designed solely to enable the world to last long enough to work out its own problems in its own way. When the curve nosed down, it did not mean simply that a change was coming; that didn't matter. It meant that unless conditions were changed it was *finis* for Earth., Kaput.

The End.

The survival probability curve was built around one guiding principle: "Control" must be kept to an absolute minimum, and not utilized at all unless it were imperative for survival. All cultures must be allowed to develop in their own way, so long as they did not positively threaten the free existence of mankind. It was about as radical as the concept of liberty.

It was spraying the stagnant waters before the mosquitoes hatched.

Bob Quinton grew up exploring the forest preserves and the hills of New Mexico, wandering in the purple canyons and picking up beautifully chipped arrow points from the rocks. Had you asked him his problems, he would have wondered what was the matter with you. He wasn't interested, and he had more important things on his mind.

But he was hooked, nevertheless. He was hooked from the day he found his first arrow point, read his first book, looked at the stars. He went fishing along the clean mountain streams, and he soaked up the sun. But new ideas were in the air—and Bob Quinton inevitably soaked up more than just Vitamin D.

By 2010, UN exploration ships had contacted Procyon and Centaurus. They had contacted four other systems as well—and the ships had never returned. The contacts were hushed up until a major war threatened between India and China, and then life on other worlds was announced.

Bob Quinton was fourteen years old.

The patchwork pattern of the self-styled "culture tinkers" took form. It took shape as UNBAC—the Business Advisory Council of the United

Nations. BAC gave tips and planned developmental patterns for the commercial interests of Earth, and it got tax-free support funds. Most of UNBAC, the part that people saw, made itself extremely useful and had the reputation for being the only practical part of the UN.

The rest, the secret part, wasted its time on survival.

Bob Quinton went to college and majored in anthropology. He had fun and drank a lot of beer and married a classmate. The world was calm and pleasant for ten years, on the surface, and the belief was loudly proclaimed that a New Golden Age had arrived—the date of the first one being tactfully not mentioned.

He saw a lot of the world, and a lot of other worlds. He went up fast and he grew up fast. In some dimly-perceived but acute way, Bob Quinton felt that a lot of things depended on him, and upon men like him. He seldom talked about them, and when others did he usually felt uncomfortable and bored. The obvious didn't need elaboration. But he felt them.

In the silence of space.

In the stars in the eyes of a child.

It should have been dashing, romantic. There should have been bands playing and medals and people cheering. It should have been a richly rewarding and pleasant life.

But it wasn't.

It was tough and dirty and bitter.

So Robert Quinton worked on, in the late summer of 2034, in the island city of Galveston. Few people even knew he was there, and fewer still cared. He did things he hated and saw a friend cut down before his eyes.

He worked, fists clenched, a smile on his face. He worked, and when he was through the average citizen could not have told Wiley Carruthers Pond from Thomas Jefferson.

Or Donald Weston from the Devil.

They flew Conway, still alive, back to New Mexico Station and left Robert Quinton alone in his apartment. That same night, Jo Weston came to see him.

She walked in quietly, out of the darkness. She slipped off her light summer jacket and sat down in Quinton's best chair. She crossed her astonishing legs and eyed him questioningly.

"Drink?" she asked, in a voice that was cold honey.

Quinton nodded, unsurprised. "Guess I owe you one or two," he said. It wasn't a particularly original remark, but he didn't care. This, too, was a scene he had played too many times before. It was getting more than a little stale. He mixed her a stiff Scotch and soda, took one himself, and waited.

"I don't understand you, Mr. Quinton," Jo said finally.

"Call me Bob," Quinton said.

Jo smiled, her teeth white and sharp. Her golden blond hair caught the soft highlights of the room and her blue eyes invited.

"You're out to get my husband," Jo said steadily. "Why?"

"I don't know what you're talking about," Quinton said. He looked into her frosted blue eyes. *She knows,* his mind whispered. *She has to know.*

"Don't lie to me, Bob," Jo said softly. "Another drink?"

Quinton fixed it for her, and watched the slight flush creep up her smooth neck while she drank. *A flush,* he thought irrelevantly, *is caused by blood. There was more blood right across from where she sat, just a dark spot on the rug now. Pat's blood.* Quinton lit a cigarette.

"Bob," Jo whispered. "I want you to stop it."

Quinton looked at her. "I love my wife," he said evenly.

Jo stiffened, her smile vanishing. "Don't play games, hero," she said quietly. "I'm not kidding."

"Neither am I," Quinton said.

They stared at each other. Quinton would have bet a small fortune, had he had one, that Jo could have counted the times men had said no to her without using any fingers at all.

"I . . . I don't understand," she whispered. She began to cry, softly.

"That isn't worthy of you, beautiful," Quinton said. "It won't work."

The crying stopped.

"Fix me another drink, lover," Jo said.

Quinton walked into the kitchen and mixed the drink. When he came back into the room he looked down the muzzle of a small pistol held in Jo's white hand.

"You drink it, lover," Jo said. "You're going to need it."

Quinton sat down and sipped at the Scotch. He didn't say anything. He was calm, relaxed. He had played this scene before, too.

"You're going to take the heat off," Jo Weston said, the gun steady in her hand. "You can play this little game any way you want to play it, but the pressure's going to stop. You're leaving town, hero—one way of the other."

Quinton raised his eyebrows.

"You don't think I'd kill you," Jo said coldly.

She fired with startling quickness and a slug slammed past Quinton's ear and buried itself in the chair. He jumped, spilling some of his drink He hadn't expected that.

"I think you would," he said, "if you could."

The tiny Skippy from Quinton's sleeve spring leaped into his right hand and he fired instantly, without seeming to aim. There was a light *poof* and Jo dropped her gun. Her hand had a sliver of silver needle though it. Her fingers were dead. She didn't make a sound.

"Sorry, baby," Quinton said, and meant it.

He went to her, scooped up the gun, and led her to the kitchen. He pulled out the needle with a practiced hand, washed the wound, and dressed it with the same kit he had used on Pat. Then he led her back into the living room.

Jo just looked at him, her blue eyes tight with pain.

"Here," Quinton said, handing her the rest of the drink. "You'll be able to use this."

Jo tensed her slim figure, breathing hard. She smiled icily and threw the drink in his face. Then she turned on her heel and walked out the door.

Quinton wiped his dripping face with his handkerchief and watched her go. She hurried down the dark street alone, her heels clicking on the pavement. Her head was up, proudly.

A factor, Quinton thought, *a number in an equation?*

Or only a woman in love with her man?

Quinton watched her until she passed out of sight. She was both, of course—but that was words. What good were words?

He walked back into his apartment and closed the door.

When it was all over, Quinton didn't wait for the final returns. The election itself hadn't been too much of a problem—such things had been arranged on Earth long before UNBAC had come into being. Quinton didn't bother with Pond; they were through with him, except for the money.

He went out to the Weston home, out by the causeway where the old men still sat fishing in the afternoon sun.

Jo opened the door. "What are you doing here?" she asked coldly. "Get out."

"Let him in," Donald Weston said over her shoulder. "Let him in, you fool."

Jo stepped aside and Quinton walked in. The living room was just as he had left it. The volume from the *Reader's Digest* was still ajar in the bookcase. But Donald Weston had changed. Quinton sat down and lit a cigarette. He didn't look at Jo's eyes.

"A tough break about the election," he said. "I was sorry to hear it, Don."

Donald Weston smiled, but only with his mouth. His deep green eyes bored through Quinton like an ice drill. Quinton felt centipedes crawling up his spine.

"Our offer is still open, Don," he said pleasantly. "How about it?"

Donald Weston sat down, his face blank, his straw-colored hair neatly combed as always. He was breathing too fast. "Suppose I say no," he said, his voice a little too high. "Suppose I decide to stay here."

Quinton took a drag on his cigarette, feeling death all around him in the little room. "I wouldn't know about that," he said. "The decision, of course, is up to you."

"Is it?" Weston asked, his voice tightly under control. *"Is it?"*

Quinton shrugged.

"Still playing games, Mr. Quinton?" Jo asked. Her hand curled tensely on her chair arm, making her white scar stand out against her white skin.

Quinton smoked his cigarette. *She might have been queen of the world,* he thought.

"Cards on the table, Quinton," Donald Weston said. His green eyes were narrowed to slits. "Quickly."

"I don't know what you're talking about," Quinton said.

Donald Weston stood up, fast.

"Let's put it this way," Quinton went on, every nerve alert and screaming. "I don't think you'd do very well on Earth, Don. You never would be able to do yourself justice. On the other hand, we can always use you on Mars. Our company can always use men like you. You'd be comfortable there, and you'd get considerably more than your share of things. We'd want you to be happy, you understand. On Mars, you'd be set for life— though, of course, it wouldn't be feasible for you to come back to Earth. If you should stay here . . . well, it's a gamble, isn't it?"

Weston clenched his fists, breathing hard. "I don't have any choice," he said flatly, keeping a steel vice in his voice. "Is that it?"

"I'm afraid I don't quite understand you," Quinton said, listening to the blood race in his ears. "I'm just offering you a job, that's all."

Weston stared.

Jo laughed, unpleasantly.

Quinton waited, his cigarette burning down short against his fingers.

There was a long silence, filled with the hoarse breathing of the man who had called Robert Quinton light-years across the galaxy.

"I'll take your job," Weston said finally. "I'll take it."

Robert Quinton smiled broadly and inserted his cigarette butt into the ashdisposer. "Mighty glad to hear that, Don," he said, getting to his feet and extending his hand

Weston ignored the hand. "When do I leave?" he asked shortly.

"I think tomorrow would be excellent," Quinton told him.

"One time's as good as another," Weston said. A small muscle twitched in the side of his jaw.

"Fine. If you'll drop by my office in the morning, we'll fix things up. A ship will shuttle you to New York tomorrow afternoon, and by ten tomorrow night you'll be Marsbound."

Jo sat very still, her eyes closed.

"I'd like to say, Don," Quinton said, "that I think you've made a very wise decision, We'll do the best we can for you, and that's straight."

"Get out of here," Donald Weston whispered, his voice shaking. *"Get out of here."*

"See you in the morning, then," Quinton said. "Good afternoon, Mrs. Weston."

He walked out the door and headed for his copter. He was wet with sweat and he needed a drink. This was all wrong, he knew that. He had seen worlds saved before, on the tri-di. He had read books. He had had his own dreams. Worlds were saved by heroes, in a blaze of glory, saved cleanly out among the stars, man to man.

Not like this.

Not by an old man, down in the dirt, cold with sweat.

He walked to his copter and he didn't look back. He didn't have to. He felt them behind him, boring into him. *Eyes.* Icy green eyes, and blue ones lined with red. Eyes that had looked upon a world—full, deep eyes.

Empty, now.

It was the next night, and the lights were low.

The election had caused some local flurry, but not much. No one even knew that Donald Weston was gone. The post-election remarks of Wiley Carruthers Pond were back on the second page of the Galveston *Daily News,* the big headlines having gone to the space games. It all was moderately interesting to native Galvestonians, but not exactly hot copy now that it was over. The wire services, of course, didn't even bother to pick it up.

The music throbbed across the dance floor, and Lynn was in the silver gown he liked so well. In Quinton's pocket was a gram from Siringo that told him that Conway was improving, and had a chance to live.

"This is nice," Quinton said, holding his wife's hand across the little table.

Lynn smiled at him—the private smile. "We'll never grow up," she said. "We should be past this stage by now."

"We're too smart," Quinton said. "We know better."

A ship flashed by overhead—only a rumble and a murmur in the night outside. You could hardly hear it over the music. Quinton closed his eyes, watching the ship in his mind. He saw it climb past the planets, out to the crystal stars. To far Centaurus and to Procyon beyond.

The stars called to him, and one day he knew he would have to answer them again.

But this was for now.

He looked around him, at the soft lights, the dancers. He heard the tinkling of glasses and the relaxed laugher of men at play. They didn't know. They had never felt the stars burning inside them. For them, there was only the night and the whispers and the music.

For Robert Quinton, too—for now.

He stood up, smiling. "Let's dance," he said, and held out his arms to his wife.

ARTIFACT

Late August, 1971.

Far above a field in New Mexico, above the blue sky itself, a ship decelerated and floated down toward the Earth. The close star that had seared through blackness lost its nakedness and became the golden sun. White clouds touched the ship that had come from emptiness.

Hundreds of miles away, across half the state of Texas, Dr. Dixon Sanders sat in his university office and looked out the window. The cool breeze felt good after a hot summer, and the August rains had stroked green across the land.

He did not know that man had landed on Mars for the first time.

He did not know what men had found there.

Three days later, Sanders got the call from Washington.

One hour after he had received the call, he climbed into a jet and was flown to a field in New Mexico. There was no spaceship in sight. He saw only a thick concrete blockhouse, two spidery structures that looked like radio towers, anti-aircraft missiles and sheds. There were jets patrolling the skies.

A copter lifted him four miles to a neat new settlement in the desert. The houses were white and compact, and concealed irrigation channels had turned the area into an oasis with green trees, grasses, vines and flowers. A big lettered roof sign read:WELCOME TO GILA MONSTER SINKHOLE. a smaller sign was more official: GREENACRE, NEW MEXICO. U.S. GOVERNMENT PROPERTY. LANDING PROHIBITED.

They landed.

A shaded roof path carried them across six houses, and at the seventh there were three military policemen guarding the roof door. They walked inside and a cool stairway led down into a rustic reception room. Two more MPs opened a side door for them.

Sanders stepped inside. He still knew a general when he saw one, and the impulse to salute was almost uncontrollable.

"You're Sanders?"

"That's right."

"A pleasure to meet you, sir. Have a chair, won't you?"

Sanders sat down, slightly stunned at being addressed as *sir* by a general.

"I'm General Ransom, Sanders. Intelligence. I want you to know how much we appreciate your coming up here like this."

"No trouble at all." Sanders wanted a cigarette. The general was a big, pleasantly ugly man with gray hair and sharp blue eyes. Sanders rather liked him.

"You realize, naturally, that what you see and hear in this place must be treated as top secret information. We're counting on your discretion."

"I understand that, General Ransom."

"Okay." The general paced across the room and then sat down behind his desk. He unlocked a drawer and took out a small box. The box was three inches on a side. It was ordinary enough in appearance, although it was metallic. The general drummed his fingers on his desk. Then, abruptly, he slid the top off the box and handed the box to Sanders. "In your opinion, Dr. Sanders, what *is* that?"

Sanders took the box and looked inside. "Can I take it out?"

"Certainly."

He took the object out and held it in his hand. It was a piece of brown rock two and a half inches long by two inches wide. He examined it carefully. The top of the rock was smooth and worn. The bottom had been neatly chipped by pressure flaking to make a V-shaped edge. The flake scars were clearly visible. Looked at from the side, the object was slightly concave on its worked edge. He gripped it, holding it with the smooth top surface in the palm of his hand.

"Well, Doctor?"

"I assume this is important, for some reason?"

"Very important."

He picked his words with care. "It's made out of flint or chert, or something closely resembling it. The bottom edge has definitely been worked— I'd say by means of indirect pressure flaking. In my opinion, it's an artifact—a tool made by man. It may be a scraper; that's a common tool used to flesh hides and that sort of thing. Hard to tell what it was used for, though. It's a fairly crude implement, but it's well made of its type. Nothing too unusual, I'm afraid."

The general leaned forward. "How old is it?"

Sanders shrugged. "Sorry, but I can't tell that from the scraper alone. Most of them are pretty much alike, and you'll find them all over the world and from the early Pleistocene right on down to the present. If it was found in association with bones or charcoal or pottery or projectile points—damn near anything—or if it was found eroding out of a datable geological stratum, I might be able to take a stab at it."

"It was found all by itself, on the surface of a desert," General Ransom said, smiling.

"Then dating would be just guesswork, really."

"But it *is* an artifact?"

"I'd say so, yes. I didn't know you boys were so interested in primitive cultures."

"That," said the general, "would depend on where the primitives *are*."

"Apaches on the warpath again?"

"No—though we do have one over at the field who's a first class rocket engineer. I wish the Apaches were all we had to worry about. Tell me, Doctor: if you, as an archeologist, had to find out more about this little gadget—who made it, how old it is, that sort of thing—how would you go about it?"

Sanders frowned. "I'd go back to where it was found and try to find another one in place. If we could get one in a dig—excavate it, that is, in association with some other stuff—we should be able to give you more information on it."

"Would you be willing to undertake such a search, Doctor, if the government asked you to do so?"

"Certainly, if it's important. I have classes to think of, of course. Where did it come from, anyway—somewhere around here?"

"That's one way of looking at it, Dr. Sanders. It came from Mars."

He was a little slow on the uptake. Then it hit him. "But that means—"

"Exactly," said General Ransom.

He was a little surprised at his own calm acceptance of the fact that men had landed on Mars, but then he had been expecting it, really, along with everybody else.

But an artifact was something else again.

An artifact was a tool made by man.

Or by something like a man?

"Why me?" he asked. "I'm no spaceman. I like it here."

"I'll be perfectly frank with you. Our expedition was made on a strictly hush-hush basis; that isn't necessarily the way I would have preferred it, but with the world situation the way it is, that's the way it had to be. Sooner or later, the news has got to be released. We've got a knotty little job ahead of us at the United Nations. We have no right to keep that artifact quiet, and when we talk about it there are some questions that have to be answered. Do you understand me?"

"Well, I see why you need an archeologist. Why me?"

"We can't force you to go."

"I realize that. I just want the reasons."

Ransom ticked them off. "One, you can be trusted. Two, we feel you're the man for the job—well trained, but with a shot or two of imagination. Three, you're in good shape physically—though an examination will have to clear you officially, of course. Finally . . . may I be blunt?"

"Sure."

"Your wife divorced you, I understand."

The old pain stabbed at him, but he kept his face expressionless. "That's right."

"Your parents are dead. You have one son in the oil business. You don't get on with him too well."

"Yes."

"You've chosen to work at a small private college. Your absence can be covered."

"In other words, I won't be missed if I don't come back."

"I wouldn't put it quite that way."

Sanders looked at the artifact in his hand. He put it back in the box and handed it to Ransom. "I'll do what I can."

"We're grateful, Sanders. You can pick your medal if you want one. And don't worry: we'll get you there and we'll get you back. That ship can carry three men. Your pilot will be Colonel Ben Cooper—he made the first flight, so he's the best we've got. You pick the other man. You know what we want, and you know who you can work with best."

Sanders didn't hesitate. "That'll be Ralph Charteris over at Santa Fe. He's thirty-eight, he knows his stuff, and he's technically unmarried. He's a research man, so nobody'll think it's funny if he disappears for a spell."

"Got you. Takeoff will be in ten days. You'll want to get things in shape."

"Okay."

The two men shook hands.

The ten days went by in a hurry.

He made out a will, a job he had been postponing for years, and managed to spend a day fishing with two friends in Matagorda Bay.

He phoned his son Mark in Houston. Their talk was unsatisfactory as usual, full of forced heartiness. He couldn't tell him where he was going, and he was glad when the call was over.

He didn't call Ellen.

The ship lifted on schedule.

Within an hour, there was no blue sky.

He thought briefly of himself: forty-two years old, on the thin side, horn-rimmed glasses. He probably looked a lot like a professor. He felt singularly out of place in a spaceship.

He looked at the screen. He saw cold stars and a frozen sun. He saw black distances and long, long silences. He saw his own life far away and lost: a life that had been too lonely, and too fast.

He stopped looking.

The atomic drive was soundless except for a high, irritating vibration that seemed part of the ship. Magnets kept him anchored and after an initial vertigo the weightlessness meant an annoying indigestion and little else.

They had some good bourbon, and it helped.

They were neither hot nor cold.

Ralph Charteris was a big blond giant of a man, and little Ben Cooper always referred to him as the biggest mass on the ship. "Let's talk about rocks, Sanders," he said. "Tell me what the devil that scraper was doing on Mars—figure it out in true Boy Scientist fashion so we can turn around and go home."

Sanders smiled, sipping his bourbon. He liked to talk, although he knew it was just a device for getting outside himself. "I'll give you six fast answers, Ralph."

"Fire," Ralph said, chewing on an empty pipe.

"Here's the deal. A ship—the first one, mind you—lands on a supposedly uninhabited planet. It's mostly all desert and a yard wide, as I understand it, and the air is shy on oxygen. We've all been solemnly assured by our astronomical colleagues that people like ourselves couldn't exist on Mars. Oh, maybe some outlandish freak without any carbon molecules in his carcass, but not *people*. So what do they run right smack into? An artifact. Nothing queer or strange or alien. Nothing to make them swat their helmets and holler, 'There's Martians, by gum!' Just a perfectly ordinary scraper—it's a miracle that botanist spotted it at all. So what's the most logical explanation, the one that strains the credulity the least?"

"It's a hoax," Ralph said quietly.

"You thought of it too, hmmmm? The simplest way for that scraper to get there would be for one of the men to have picked it up on Earth, carried it to Mars, tossed it on the sand, and then 'discovered' it. The botanist could have done it."

"I don't much think Schlicter was a dishonest man, Sanders," Ben Cooper said.

"Remember Piltdown," Ralph said.

"Exactly. I don't say that Schlicter planted that scraper—I just say that's the simplest explanation."

"Let's have some more ideas."

"Here's another: the artifact is not native to Mars, but was left there by a party of interstellar travellers. In that case, the catch is why they would leave a flint scraper behind. I can't figure a culture with spaceships and scrapers."

"Maybe they were shipwrecked," Ralph suggested. "Maybe one man was left behind, thrown on his own resources."

"Can't see it," Ben Cooper objected. "What's he supposed to scrape with that thing—sand pies? We didn't spot any animal life to speak of, except for those little things that looked like moles."

"Still, we can't rule it out," Sanders said. "Try this: there has been some contact between Earth and Mars we don't know anything about. A ship came here maybe half a million years ago, dropped the scraper for some reason, and hightailed it back home."

"This space travel does great things for the imagination," Ralph said sourly.

"I'm trying to name possibilities, no matter how far-fetched. I'm aware, I think, of the mythological nature of Atlantis, Mu, Lemuria, and the Lost Continent of Lake Erie. Remember the old dictum of Mr. Holmes: eliminate the impossible, then hang onto what's left."

"What *is* left?"

"Number four: just like the last one, but the ship came from Mars, picked up the scraper on Earth, came back home and dropped it. Maybe it happened a million years ago. Since that time, Mars has lost her civilization and her cities are covered with sand. And *don't* tell me civilizations can't disappear."

"Sounds pretty gassy to me."

"They had to dig to find Troy. They had to dig to find some Biblical towns. You already have to dig to find some of the army forts on the American frontier—and they're only a few hundred years old."

"It's your theory, friend."

"Number five," Sanders continued, running a hand through his sandy hair. "Man evolved on Mars and then migrated to Earth, maybe half a million years ago when water got scarce. In other words, the primate evolution evidence on Earth is misleading."

Ralph Charteris bit down hard on his pipe stem, and then remembered to relax. "You're kidding. How about the South African stuff—Australopithecus and all that? How about Pithecanthropus? Sinanthropus? Neanderthal? Swanscombe? How come when they got to Earth they went back to living in caves and rock shelters? Dammit, Sanders, you're trying to make me sore."

"Not at all. Here's my parting shot: that artifact was left on Mars by some representatives of a galactic civilization. It was left there on purpose, for us to find, as a kind of I.Q. test. They want to see how we handle the situation. How's that?"

"You're a wild man with a theory, Sanders."

"Listen, Doc," Ben Cooper said slowly. "What do you *really* think?"

Sanders looked at him and shook his head. "I don't know, Ben," he said. "I just don't know."

They didn't have much to say after that.

They started up a poker game with magnetized cards.

They waited.

Seventeen days later, the ship landed.

They put on their airsuits and stepped outside.

There was no wind and they stood in utter silence. The ship had come down on the flat top of a mesa. Small, thorny plants with tiny green flowers were scattered loosely between worn outcroppings of reddish brown rock. The mesa was not high, and at its base was the desert, a motionless sea of gently rolling sand, so light brown that it almost appeared white.

The sky was a deep blue, very close to a cold black directly overhead but somewhat lighter near the close horizon. There was one large dirty yellow cloud hanging just over the desert floor to the south.

Sanders shivered, although it was not yet cold. He blinked his eyes, grateful for the filter lenses in his airsuit. The sun was brighter than he had ever seen it on Earth, and it was a fierce, naked brightness that pelted the low hills and deserts with shattering attacks of light.

Here, in the lost immensities of a strange and silent world, his glib theories of a few days ago could find no expression. Here were fundamentals, and the raw truths of simplicity.

Quite casually, as though unimpressed by the enormity of the moment, a creature that looked too much like a gopher for comfort stuck his head out from behind a rock and surveyed them with decided suspicion.

Sanders eyed the gopher the same way.

"Well," Ralph said into his suit mike, staring out at the glaring wastelands, "I'd settle for a needle in a haystack any day."

A planet is huge, Sanders thought. *You cannot imagine how great it is. Suppose some creature came to Earth searching for artifacts, and all the people were gone. Where would he look? How long would it take? How many undiscovered sites are there on Earth, even today?*

"Ben," he said, "can you see where the scraper was found from here?"

Ben Cooper shook his head. "I set her down as close as I could figure to where we landed before, but it's hard to get your bearings here. We're close, I'd say—maybe fifty miles. We could get the copter out and spot it—we left a big circle of rocks on the sand."

Sanders looked out. It was like standing on the beach of an ocean. There were winds on Mars, and dust storms. When the winds blew, the sands shifted. It was a lousy spot to do archeology.

"What do you think, Ralph?"

Ralph put his hands on his hips. Even he was dwarfed by the vastness around him. "No point in digging up the Sahara, I guess. The scraper was a surface find, and Schlicter said he couldn't find a site under it. If there's one artifact, and this deal is on the level, there must be more."

"I'll buy that. How about this mesa?"

Ralph shrugged. "We don't know what we're doing. How do we know where they lived? One place is as good as another."

Sanders examined the ground. "Lots of erosion. But those rocks and plants have held the soil down pretty well. Probably phenomenal root systems on those plants—no water that I can see. It beats the desert. It *feels* like the kind of a place . . ."

The excitement grew in him.

"Let's have a look," Ralph said.

The three men split up and started to search the mesa, moving in the peculiar bent shuffle of a man trying to spot flaked stones on the ground.

The ship stood quietly behind them; it rested on the thorny plants and was nothing against a backdrop of emptiness.

The sun was white and cast sharp black shadows. The temperature was a comfortable fifty degrees Fahrenheit. There was no breeze, and not a sound.

Sanders wanted a cigarette, but couldn't figure out how to light one in his airsuit. He moved rapidly, his eyes on the ground, looking for rock concentrations, or fired rocks, or bones, or flake chips. He found that the slight gravity affected him hardly at all, except that he felt stronger than usual.

He was content.

This was the part of archeology he liked best: you were alone, far from the cities, and the next hill was never too far away.

It took him three hours to find what he was looking for. By then the sun was lower, and it was growing cold.

"Over here," he said into his suit mike.

He didn't touch anything. Ralph and Ben came over in great leaping bounds, and the three of them got down on their knees and stared.

It wasn't anything much. The soil looked a little darker than the surrounding area, and there was some cracked rock. The darker soil made an irregular circle about four feet in diameter. There was a green flower growing in the middle of it.

There were flint chips.

There was one core, with long flake scars on it.

"Get the camera," Sanders said.

The night was very cold and filled with stars. Phobos was visible, but unimpressive. The men slept restlessly.

Next day, they went to work.

They mapped the site and plotted a north-south line and used string to lay out the area in two-foot squares. They got their notebooks and centimeter sticks ready.

Sanders and Ralph got out their small triangular trowels and began to scrape the surface of the site, very gently. Ben Cooper watched. At first, he almost held his breath.

After six hours without results, it was less exciting.

They took it down in two-inch levels and filtered all the dirt through a fine mesh screen. They worked all day and found one flint chip.

The next day they found nothing at all.

Late in the afternoon of the third day, when they were ten inches down, Ralph's trowel scraped something hard. He stuck his trowel in the hip pocket of his airsuit and took out a small whisk broom. Very carefully, he brushed the dirt away.

Sanders came over and watched.

The uncanny thing was the complete familiarity of the scene. They had both dug sites like this a hundred times, and with the same results.

Ralph uncovered a broken projectile point.

They measured its exact position in the site and photographed it in place. Then Ralph lifted it out and handed it to Sanders. The base of the point was intact, with two neatly chipped shoulders. Both sides of the thin point were nicely flaked. The tip was broken. The whole thing, without the tip, was a little over three inches long and an inch wide.

"Arrowhead?" asked Ben.

"Probably not," Ralph said. "Too big for that."

"Unless," Sanders smiled, "whoever made it was a giant."

"Cut that out, Sanders."

"Okay. Provisionally, it's a spear point or a knife. That's what it looks like to me."

"Bag it."

Sanders placed the point in a cloth bag and labeled it. Then he took up his trowel and went back to work in his own square.

When night fell, they had found nothing else.

They stuck with the site for ten days. Before they were through, the gophers had gotten used to them and came over to watch them dig. The site played out at the four foot level. They had found two scrapers, one more broken point, and a piece of charred bone. The bone was not human; it was quite small and seemed to be a femur of some sort. There was no pottery.

"Well," Sanders said, "we may be able to get a radiocarbon date on that bone when we get back, but I don't know how good it'll be. Otherwise, we don't know beans about the geology—if that's the word I want—and there's no telling how old the stuff is. It wasn't left here yesterday, though."

"We *do* know something now."

"Yes. These artifacts are indigenous; nobody brought 'em here. It looks like we've got the remains of an old hunting and gathering culture, but we can't very well generalize from one site."

"In other words," Ben Cooper said, "there were Martians."

Sanders walked over to the edge of the low mesa and looked out across the desert sands, his mind filled with questions.

The silence came in from a long way off.

The desolation was old and patient and overwhelming.

"Come on," he said. "We've got a lot of work ahead of us."

Sites were not difficult to find.

The land had evidently been abandoned for a long time, and had been undisturbed. They spent a month sinking test pits and making surface collections, and then took the big-bladed copter from the ship and made two long flights in opposite directions.

Wherever they went, the story was the same.

Widely scattered artifacts, all of which could have been fitted into the Paleolithic of Earth without too much difficulty. Nothing that could be classed as Neolithic. No pottery, no traces of agriculture.

No skeletons.

No cities, no towns, no villages.

The land, Sanders thought, must always have been desperately poor. The food supply was uncertain, the water scarce. People must have lived in small, widely separated bands, spending every minute trying to stay alive. It would have been tough.

The lack of skeletons was not particularly surprising; old skeletal remains were always rare, and a man dropped more artifacts than bones in a lifetime.

They saw one large snake that vanished into the rocks before they could catch him.

"There's just one question left," Sanders said slowly, "and that's the big one. Are we dealing with an extinct form of life, or aren't we?"

"I was wondering myself," Ben said. "You take back in New Mexico and Arizona, now. You find lots of old places like the ones we've been digging up—some of 'em go back maybe ten thousand years, they tell me. Just the same, the Indians are still there."

The silence of centuries covered the land.

"The country seems abandoned," Ralph said, sitting on a rock. "These people weren't far enough along for space travel. So where could they have gone?"

"Let me ask you a question, Ralph," Sanders said. "If you're in a strange country and you're looking for a place where people have lived, what would be the quickest way to find it on Earth?"

"Go where the water is," Ralph answered without hesitating.

"Next question: where *is* the water?"

"Around the poles is the only place," Ben said. "We flew over all that country last time and mapped the ice fields. There's no water at all anywhere else."

Sanders looked away, across the deserts, beyond the horizons. He felt small and lost and old.

"Let's go," he said.

They left Ben Cooper with the spaceship, not entirely against his will. There was a strong two-way radio in the copter, and they all felt that it would only be sensible to hold one man in reserve.

The copter took off, a glittering bird under the morning sun.

The flight lasted three days. It was monotonous for the most part, an endless waste of silent sand, broken occasionally by low and rocky hills. They saw no animals from the air, and only a few cactus-like plants rooted in the shifting sands. There was one bad dust storm that boiled across the desert floor, but they got above it without difficulty.

There were no canals. There were not even streaks that might have resembled canals. The canals, Sanders thought, were like the Western Sea, the Northwest Passage, the Seven Cities of Cibola. Like all dreams, they were seen best from far away.

As they drew near the polar ice, even the days were bitterly cold. The sky was almost black and there were thin blue mists of ice crystals in the air. The desert sand below them became splotched with a dark, cold, swampy green. The hard snowdrifts were violet in the light of the frozen sun.

The copter landed near the edge of the polar ice on a narrow ridge of slick, mossy rock. The land closely resembled some parts of Earth, where you get up above the timberline in cold mountain air and water from glacial lakes trickles down across the gray wet rocks.

They got out.

They heard the frozen silence, and that was all.

Sanders looked around slowly, feeling the cold eat through his clothing and chill his feet. There was a lake of white-violet ice to his left, like glass in the snow and the rocks. He stared at it for a long time.

"Ralph, have we got any line in the copter?" he said into his suit mike. It seemed odd not to see his frozen breath before him. "Anything we could use for a hook?"

"We might be able to rig up something."

They found some wire and torched a hook out of a spare copter ring. Sanders walked over to the lake, his feet coming down uncertainly on the light, crisp surfaces. He took the torch and carved out a small, neat circle in the ice.

There was deep black water beneath the ice.

He put a chunk of canned meat on the hook and lowered it into the hole.

"Here goes nothing," he said.

They waited, stirring the water occasionally to keep the ice from forming. They got good and cold. The silence was absolute.

An hour passed.

Another hour.

Something bit the hook. The wire jerked in Sanders' gloved hand and he would have lost it if it had not been wound around his wrist.

The wire cut through the black water with a *sssss.*

"Can you hold him?" Ralph whispered.

"I think so."

It was strong and heavy and full of fight. Sanders played it tautly, feeling it jerk against his wrist. He was sure he had it hooked. He began pulling the wire in, a loop at a time. His heart hammered in his chest and he was short of breath. If he could keep it from darting under the ice, snagging the line—

He saw it: a flash of gold in the cold black water.

He pulled, not too fast.

It flopped out on the ice and both men dived for it.

They held him as he squirmed under their gloves. They laughed and hollered unreasonably. They had him!

They ran a wire through his gills and held him up, still wiggling heavily.

He was a beauty: a slim firm five-pounder, sleek and solid gold with jet black fins. He looked more like a golden mountain trout than anything else, and he was the most beautiful fish Sanders had ever seen.

"Get him in the water. We don't want to kill him."

They lowered him into the icy water on the stringer and then anchored the line to a stub of mossy rock. They looked at each other, grinning happily.

"There's a food supply here," Sanders said.

"Look!"

He followed Ralph's pointing finger and saw a small black shape on the ice. It slithered away as he watched, moving toward the swampy country beyond. It looked like a cross between an otter and a seal.

"This is where the life is, Ralph. This is where he's got to be."

The emptiness and the silence closed in around them, but the wire into the water was taut and moved as they watched, back and forth across the hole in the ice.

Three days later, they found him.

He was not three hundred yards from the copter.

He stood quietly on the violet ice, watching them.

He could not have been mistaken for a human being of the type that they had known. But he was a man, and could have been nothing less.

"Don't scare him."

The man was not frightened. He was small, only slightly over four feet tall, and warmly dressed in black skins. He held a spear balanced in his right hand, and Sanders could see that he had an atlatl to throw it with. His face was very white with a high flush of red around the nose and on both cheeks. His eyes were narrow and there was no hair on his face. He wore a skin hood that covered his head, neck, and ears.

He neither advanced nor gave ground.

He never saw an Earthman before, Sanders thought. *He hasn't learned to be afraid.*

"Get the fish," Sanders said.

Ralph hauled up the golden fish and handed it to Sanders. "Let me go first," Sanders said. "He won't worry so much about just one of us."

He took the fish and held it in his hand where the man could see it. He walked toward him, slowly.

The man stood his ground.

Sanders got close enough to touch him. He noticed that his eyes were brown. He held out the fish with his right hand. With his left hand he pointed first to the fish and then to the man. He smiled.

The man took the fish, sniffed it, and broke its neck with one quick jerk. He put the fish in a pouch he carried around his waist. He smiled back, showing white even teeth, He put his spear down on the ice and pushed back his hood. He took a bone comb out of his straight black hair and handed it to Sanders.

Sanders took it. He pointed to himself. "Sanders," he said slowly. "Sanders."

The man caught on instantly. "Narn," he said, pointing to himself. His voice, picked up by Sanders' suit phones, was high and musical. He said nothing else,

Sanders led him over to Ralph. He introduced them and the man repeated Ralph's name. Then he repeated Sanders' name and pointed to Sanders. He smiled, happily.

The three men stood on the ice, completely stumped by the frustrating wall of language.

He has a language, Sanders thought. *Certainly he doesn't live alone, because he is a man. His people must hunt and fish and gather what plants there are here. No agriculture, no cities, no nothing. This land won't support but a handful. How many? Fifty? Sixty? A hundred? They never had much of a chance on this world. What happens to them now? What happens to them now—after they've met the men from Earth?*

There was no wind, there was only cold.

Desolation was all around them.

The man in the black skins looked at the shining copter curiously.

"Narn," he said again, and pointed.

Sanders turned to Ralph. "Guess he wonders what it is," he said.

Ralph pointed to himself, and then to the copter. He pointed into the dark sky and moved his finger in an arc to the ground.

Instantly, Narn grew agitated. He tried to talk, rapidly, and then abandoned the attempt. He pointed at the copter, and then into the air. His eyes were bright and excited.

"He thinks we came from the sky in the copter," Ralph said.

"Didn't we?"

Narn pointed again at the copter and tugged Sanders' arm.

"He wants to see it up close, Ralph."

"Okay by me."

Narn hurried across the ice, easily, without effort. Sanders and Ralph couldn't keep up with him. When they reached the copter, Narn was already patting its sides and trying to lift it off the ground.

"Boy," Sanders said, shivering in the cold, "we don't awe this guy any."

"Does he really want to go up?"

Narn settled that question. He pointed insistently up into the clear air. He grinned from ear to ear.

"Roll all the windows down," Sanders said. "We'll keep our suits on."

He helped the man into the copter and strapped him in a seat. Narn was not happy about the strap, but seemed to trust them. He looked around eagerly.

Ralph took the copter up five hundred feet and then loafed along over the rocks and the ice and the wet green mosses. Narn stared from the copter to the ground and back again. He did not try to speak. He watched Ralph intently. The look in his eyes was almost religious in its intensity.

Sanders stayed at his side.

They had been in the air ten minutes when Narn spoke.

"San-ders."

Sanders turned and smiled.

Narn pointed at himself, and then at the copter controls.

"This," Ralph said slowly, "is about where I get out."

"San-ders."

"My God," Ralph said. "He can't fly this thing."

Sanders leaned forward. "How do you *know* he can't!"

"He's never even *seen* a copter before."

"San-ders. San-ders."

Sanders looked at Narn and wondered. "He's about the last of his kind, Ralph," he said finally. "He's lived on a world that's tough beyond belief, lived there maybe for millions of years. He's used what there was, gone as far as he could in a hopeless ecological situation. He's survived."

"Sure, sure. I'm all for him. Adaptability. High intelligence. But no man can go from a spear-thrower to a copter in ten minutes."

"He's a different kind of man, Ralph."

Ralph shrugged. "It's your life. You get up here with him."

Sanders unbuckled the strap that held Narn to his seat. He led him to the controls of the hovering copter, squeezing past the white-faced Ralph Charteris. Narn sat down, cautiously. Sanders stood just behind him.

The man seemed absurdly small in the pilot's seat. He looked at Sanders. Sanders nodded, smiled, and crossed his fingers.

Very slowly, duplicating the motions he had seen Ralph make, the man moved the wheel and strained to reach the floor pedal. The copter lurched and lost altitude. Sanders started to reach for the controls, but Narn did not panic. Carefully, exactly, he compensated for the fall.

The copter straightened.

Sanders stumbled back and sat down.

"Well, I'll be damned," Ralph said.

The man piloted the ship for fifteen minutes, across violet fields of ice, flying steadily through the air. An icy wind blew through the ship, but Sanders hardly noticed it. He was completely stunned.

Narn, too, had found an artifact.

He took the ship back to almost exactly the position it had held when he had taken over the controls. He was tense and there was sweat on his face. It was terribly hot for him in the copter, even with all the windows open.

He let Sanders land the copter.

Narn hurried to get outside and sat down on the ice, resting.

After a few minutes, he got up and embraced each of the men in turn. "Narn," he said proudly. "Narn."

The man in the black skins pointed across the ice and beckoned.

"He wants us to go with him," Sanders said.

Ralph was still trying to get his thoughts straightened out. "I don't know," he said. "One of us will have to stay with the ship."

Sanders nodded. "I want to go, Ralph. I'll take the pocket radio and throw out a beam so you can track me. Will you give me twenty-four hours, and then come and get me?"

Ralph hesitated. "Okay, Sandy," he said finally. "You watch yourself. These boys are nothing to fool around with."

Sanders smiled at Narn. "We'll get along," he said.

They shook hands, and Sanders set off with Narn across the violet ice.

The bitter cold ate into him, turning his bones to ice.

They went a long, long way, across the cold and the rocks and the silences. Sanders felt his age, and it was hard for him to keep up. He damned his own inability to talk.

He had never seen such loneliness.

Here, Sanders thought, *here before me is the ultimate in isolated cultures. Here is a culture that has had to figure it all out for itself, with no help from anywhere. Here is a man who flew a copter the first time he saw one. Here is a simple man that some would call a savage. What might he become— now? How far might we go, together?*

It took them three hours. Sanders was sore and his feet were numb with cold before they carne to a valley of ice and rocks. The excitement of what he saw revived him a little.

The valley was pocked with caves: black holes against the faded light of the faraway sun.

They picked their way up a smoothly inclined path and paused before a cave entrance. Sanders couldn't see a thing, but Narn took him by the arm and led him inside.

Some twenty paces beyond the outside hole they came to what could only be called a door. Narn pressed three places on it very carefully and it swung open. A soft green glow spilled through the opening and in its gentle light, Sanders could see that the door was beautifully made of hides stretched over a bone frame.

They walked through semi-darkness now, their footsteps hollow in the vault of the rocks. Gradually, the greenish light shifted to a warm yellow. Sanders noticed that the source of the illumination was hidden in the cave roof over their heads: glowing rocks that seemed to be built into the cave itself. He guessed that the rocks were of natural origin, but their cunning arrangement betrayed the revising hand of man. He knew little enough about indirect lighting, but this was as efficient a system as he had ever seen.

They stepped down into a large, well-lighted room. A tiny fire—hardly large enough to toast a marshmallow comfortably—flickered in the center, and around it sat a woman and a child. Smaller caves branched from the cavern and lost themselves in the rocks.

Sanders saw something that took his breath away.

The child was holding a toy cart in his arms.

The cart had wheels on it.

God, he thought. *A Stone Age culture lost in the ice, and a toy cart with wheels. It had to be a toy, of course—they have no domesticated animals to pull a real cart. Narn's people are so few, so isolated. All his inventions had to come from a handful of people, without help from outside. There was a brain in that skull. . . .*

He noticed a light sled, with bone runners, standing against a wall. After the wheeled cart, it came as something of an anticlimax—though it was certainly more useful in the polar ice and snow.

"San-ders," Narn said.

The woman took her child's hand and moved back, shyly. She stood by a basin of crystal-clear water, her eyes on the stranger. She said nothing.

Sanders stood still, uncertain what to do. He felt as though he had stepped backward in time a million years, back through an enchanted cave, that wound through ageless rock, back through history to an age when man was only a whisper in the wind. . . .

He felt his palms sweating inside his airsuit.

Narn shook his head.

"Don't afraid," the man in the black, sewn skins said carefully. "Don't afraid, San-ders."

He's learning our language already! What have we found?

A hand touched his arm.

He started, surprised back to reality. Narn's boy was smiling gravely, pulling at his sleeve.

Sanders walked slowly to the center of the room, and sat down before the tiny fire. He saw that the fire was really a kind of lamp—a stone dish of fat with a wick in it. Narn's woman took her place opposite him. There was only friendliness in her eyes.

Somehow, something passed between them. A little of the loneliness that Sanders had always had with him melted and was gone.

The lamp-fire threw steady shadows on the cave walls.

Narn sat down by his side.

Sanders was suddenly very aware of his exhaustion, but he couldn't relax. His body ached with cold and fatigue, and his mind was so saturated with emotion that he felt a certain blankness. He was vaguely hungry, but he could not eat in his suit. He was tired, with dark circles under his eyes, but he was not sleepy.

He felt curiously at home.

He sat there, smiling, and he was glad that words were not necessary.

Finally, he stretched out by the tiny fire, looked at Narn, and closed his eyes.

Sleep was a long time in coming, and when it came it was nothing to write home about. Solid rock is not the ultimate in mattresses, and he was keyed up to a point where he could not relax. He dozed fitfully, and his own spasmodic snores woke him up twice. His stiff, aching body did the trick the third time, and after that he knew that he had all the sleep he was going to get.

He lay still, trying to keep his thoughts from bouncing back and forth between scrambled eggs and Gargantuan steaks. He listened to the silence.

"San-ders?"

He looked up. Narn was squatting by his side.

"I'm awake," Sanders said, not knowing whether or not he would be understood. "You have insomnia too?"

Narn frowned at the last question, evidently storing it away for future reference. He pointed to one of the caves that branched out from the central cavern. "Come?"

Sanders got up. His body was one large ache.

Narn led him across the floor of the room, and into a dark hole. The passage was narrow and poorly lighted at first, but it gradually broadened as they walked. Sanders felt a little better. He guessed that Narn was going to show him something—another family, perhaps, or even an underground river.

The cave opened up, abruptly, into a high cavern perhaps fifty yards in diameter. The light was astonishing—soft greens and yellows and pinks, washing down from glowing rocks set into the very roof of the chamber.

Narn stopped, and pointed.

Sanders suddenly forgot his pains and his weariness. He held his breath so long that the blood pounded in his forehead before he remembered to breathe again.

He said nothing, for what he saw was beyond words.

The walls were alive. A man smiled down on him, and he could see his white even teeth and the glint of humor in his brown eyes. A landscape of violet ice lost itself in frozen immensities. A golden fish twisted in dark water, rising to a lure. A yellow storm boiled across a bleak desert, and cold stars were serene and splendid in the heavy velvet of an arctic night.

It was beyond reality, beyond his wildest dreams.

Paintings, yes—but you had to remind yourself of that. Their colors were vividly real, and enhanced by a masterly use of the light from the glowing rocks.

The perspective was perfect, the style naturalistic.

That wasn't all.

There were neat, geometrical marks in bands under the paintings. Writing, beyond a doubt, covering panel after panel—and there were more caverns beyond.

Written history, on the walls of a cave—going back how many hundreds of thousands of years?

There were other marks that looked suspiciously like mathematics, a series of triangles that almost had to be geometry.

Sanders sat down, right in the middle of the cavern. He was stunned, and more than that.

The toy cart had been enough of a jolt, even after Narn had flown the copter.

After all, toy carts had been found in Mexico archeologically, and the main differences were in the relative sizes of the two populations, and in their respective degrees of isolation.

This was a different kettle of fish.

This was almost a miracle.

There was an excellent naturalistic cave art in the Upper Paleolithic of Europe, but it was a far cry from the paintings in *this* cave. And the Cro-Magnons were millennia away from writing, to say nothing of mathematics.

Sanders sat there, lost in the rush of his own thoughts.

Even on Earth, you had to be careful when you reconstructed a culture solely from what survived of their technology. The maze of the Australian kinship systems could never be forgotten; the Maya invented the concept of zero with a Neolithic economy. And here were a people blocked technologically by a hopeless environment, forced to channel their culture along other lines. . . .

A new kind of people.

"You like?" asked Narn.

He watched Sanders with pleasure sparkling in his eyes.

"I like," Sanders said fervently. "More?"

Narn smiled, and led the way into another cavern lost in the rock beneath the ice.

Sanders almost forgot about Ralph Charteris and the copter. When he and Narn walked back through the central cavern and out into the valley, they had only a few minutes to spare.

They stood in the long valley with the sky almost black above them.Sanders almost forgot about Ralph Charteris and the copter. When he and Narn walked back through the central cavern and out into the valley, they had only a few minutes to spare.

They stood in the long valley with the sky almost black above them.

The cold was bitter and very still. A thin blue mist of ice crystals was motionless against the snow.

A cold, hard world.

Sanders looked into Narn's eyes, and saw there a wordless hope.

Sanders knew that hope.

When the copter came, a dot against the black sky, they both knew that one chapter had ended and that a new one had begun.

It was *their* copter now.

Side by side, they waited for it to land.

Far above them, shining through the pale disc of the sun, the stars burned in an ocean of loneliness.

ANY MORE AT HOME LIKE YOU?

The ship came down through the great night, across a waterless sea where the only islands were stars and the warm winds never blew.

It glowed into a high, cold yellow when it brushed into the atmosphere above the Earth. It lost speed, floating down toward the distant shore that marked the end of its voyage. It whistled in close, feeling the tug of the world below.

At first, only darkness.

Then lights.

A new kind of darkness.

The ship angled up again, trying to rise, but it was too late. It crashed gently and undramatically into a hillside and was still.

Journey's end.

The ship's only occupant, cushioned by automatic safety devices, was shaken but unhurt. He spoke rapidly in a strange language into a microphone. He wiped his forehead with a handkerchief and climbed out of his broken ship, his hands trembling. A damp and chilly night closed in around him.

If he could get away before he was seen it would simplify matters greatly. He looked around. He seemed to be about a quarter of the way down a brush-covered hill. There were lights on the black ridge above him, and a string of lights marking a canyon road below him. There was a house on the hill, not fifty yards away. He would have to hurry. . . .

No. Too late for that now.

A flashlight moved toward him along the path, picking him out. He had been seen. His hand moved toward his pocket, nervously.

A voice, "What happened? Are you all right?"

He tried to remember his instructions. He must be very careful. Everything depended on these first few moments.

"I'm all right," he said, blinking at the light. "There's been an accident."

The light shifted to the ship that had smashed into the brush. "What's that? I never saw a plane like that before."

Be careful. "It's an experimental model."

"You a test pilot?"

"No."

"You an Air Force man?"

"No."

"I think you'd better come inside. It's cold out here."

He hesitated.

"I'll have to report this, you know. You got any identification?"

He tried to change the subject. "Where am I? I lost my bearings."

The man with the flashlight waved down below. "That there is Beverly Glen. Up on top is Bel-Air Road, right at the end of it."

"What city is this?"

"Man, you *are* confused. This is Los Angeles. Come on inside."

Los Angeles.

He followed the man along a path flanked by orange trees to a small bungalow. He walked into the house, into the light. A refrigerator hummed in the little room back of the kitchen.

"Let's have a look at you," the man with the flashlight said.

The man from the ship stood still, his face expressionless. He was quite young, tall, with straw-colored hair. He was dressed in sport clothes.

"You *look* okay," the man said, still holding his flashlight. "My name's Frank Evans."

"I am called Keith."

"Keith what?"

"Just—Keith."

"Ummmm."

A young woman came in from the living room. She was dressed in matador pants and a red shirt, but was passably attractive.

"My wife, Babs," Frank Evans introduced them. "This guy is Keith Somebody. He was in that ship that tore up the hill."

"I thought this was the Arizona desert," Keith said, trying to smile.

"I'd hate to see you make a *real* mistake, mister," Babs said throatily.

"So would I," Keith said seriously.

"You got no identification, you say?" Frank repeated.

"No. It's not necessary."

"Well, I have to report this. You understand. Unidentified aircraft and stuff. You got nothing to worry about if you're on the level. Phone the cops, Babs."

The woman went into the living room. They were alone.

"Care for a beer?" Frank asked.

It's too late. I'll have to play along. "Thank you."

"Come on in and be comfortable while we're waiting," Frank said. "You were lucky to get out of that one alive."

He followed Frank into the living room, which was painted a singular shade of green, and sat down on a couch. He lit a cigarette and noticed that his hands were still shaking.

"You like bop?" Frank said suddenly.

"Bop?"

"You'll like *this*," Babs said, coming in from the telephone. "Frank knows his music."

"It'll help you relax," Frank said. "Hi-fi and everything. I work in a record shop over in Westwood." He adjusted a mammoth speaker. "You go for Dizzy? Thelonius Monk on piano. Great bongo solo, too."

Noise filled the room.

The man called Keith sipped his beer nervously and was almost glad when the police arrived ten minutes later. The two policemen looked at the wrecked ship, whistled, and promised to send a crew out in the morning.

"You'd better ride in with us," one of them said finally. "You must be pretty well shaken up."

"I'm all right," Keith said.

"I think you'd better ride in with us. Just a formality, really."

Don't get into any trouble. Don't antagonize anyone. "I suppose you're right. Thanks for the beer, Frank."

"Don't mention it. Hope everything turns out okay."

The policemen led him up a narrow, winding asphalt trail to Bel-Air Road. A black police car, with a red light on top that flashed monotonously on and off, was parked on a bluff. There were people gathered around the car.

Keith paused a moment, ignoring the crowd. They were high above the city, and he could see Bel-Air Road winding down the hill like a string of white Christmas tree bulbs. Far below was the city of Los Angeles, a design mosaic with a billion twinkling lights.

"I guess I'll have to go all the way to the President," he said wearily.

"Yeah," said one cop, not unkindly. "Come on, we'll see if the door's unlocked at the White House."

They got into the black car and went down through the night, past all the palaces of the Bel-Air elite. It was cold and damp, and a long way down.

The next day the papers had the story, and they kicked it around joyfully.

Four of them played it strictly for laughs:

COFFEE SPILLED IN BEL-AIR AS SAUCER FALLS. PROMINENT
MARTIAN ARRIVES HERE FOR VISIT. SPACE INVADER FOILED
BY SMOG. INTERPLANETARY PATROL GETS SIGNALS MIXED
One tabloid, with tongue firmly in check, ran it straight.
FANTASTIC SHIP FALLS IN BEL-AIR; SCIENTISTS TO
INVESTIGATE
All of the papers carried pictures of the crashed ship, which looked
nothing whatever like a saucer, flying or otherwise. All of the papers car-
ried pictures of the man called Keith, and the overwhelming impression
given by the photographs was that of his extreme youth. He could not
have been over twenty-five, by Earthly standards, and it was difficult to
take him seriously as a menace.

The second day after the crash the papers had two further bits of concrete information to pass along to their readers. The first was that engineers were subjecting the ship to a surprisingly intensive analysis. The
second was that Keith had taken to writing down in a strange script all
the conversations that occurred within his hearing. By this time, of course,
the stories were buried in the back pages of the papers.

In a way, the most interesting thing was what the newspapers *didn't*
print. The usual follow-up story was conspicuous by its absence. No one
tried to explain the so-called flying saucer away as a promotion stunt for
a new George Pal movie. No enterprising reporter dug up the leads that
would connect Keith to the Pacific Rocket Society, the Los Angeles Science Fantasy Society, the White Sands proving grounds, the Rosicrucians,
the November elections or the end of the world.

And Keith wasn't volunteering any information. He went out of his
way to be agreeable, and he kept on taking careful, detailed notes on what
people said to him. After the third day, there were no more stories. As far
as the readers were concerned, Keith had been a three-day wonder who
had run his course, and there were two diverting new Hollywood divorces
to fill up the headlines.

What the papers knew, but couldn't print, was that Keith had been
quietly hustled off to Washington.

Eventually, after being shuttled through the Federal Bureau of Investigation, the Central Intelligence Agency, and the UnAmerican Activities
Committee, Keith reached the State Department.

He was still taking elaborate notes, often asking a person to repeat a
word or phrase that he had not heard clearly. His writing might have been
anything from Aztec to the International Phonetic Alphabet, so far as
anyone could tell.

John William Walls of the State Department looked so much like a diplomat that he could hardly have found employment as anything else short of a whiskey ad in *The New Yorker*. He was slim to the point of emaciation, immaculately dressed, and his perfectly brushed hair was graying at the temples. He drummed his well-manicured nails on his highly polished desk and pursed his thin lips.

"Your case poses many extremely serious problems for us, Keith," he said, smiling disarmingly.

Keith scribbled in his notebook. "I didn't mean to cause any trouble," he said. His hair was freshly cut, but he had deep circles under his eyes. He lit another cigarette and tried not to fidget on his leather chair.

"Of course you didn't, Keith. But the unpleasant fact remains that we must deal with actions, not intentions. You have placed this government in a quite intolerable position."

"I'm sorry, I have tried to explain my willingness to co-operate fully with the authorities here."

John William Walls leaned back in his chair and built pyramids with his long, clean fingers. "Your reticence really gives us very little choice in the matter, Keith," he said, warming to his topic. "I wish to be entirely frank with you. Your ship is unquestionably of extra-terrestrial origin. You have come through space, from some unknown world, and landed on our territory without official permission. Do you realize what this means?"

"I'm beginning to," Keith said.

"Of course." Walls inserted a cigarette in a long ivory holder and lit it with a gleaming lighter. "Let us proceed, then. You have crossed the void between the worlds in a ship of very advanced design. There is no getting around the fact that you represent a civilization far more powerful than our own. Candidly—for I wish to be entirely honest with you, Keith— you are stronger than we are. You would agree to that?"

"I suppose so."

"Yes. Exactly. Now, we would like to believe that you have come to us with peaceful intentions. We would like to believe that you have come here to facilitate peaceful commerce between our two civilizations. We are, I may say, willing to make some concessions. However, we would *not* like to think that your intentions toward us are hostile. We should really be forced to take stern measures if we had reason to doubt your good will. I hope I make myself entirely clear, Keith. We want to be your friends."

The implied threat was not lost on Keith. He looked up wearily, the stub of a cigarette burning in the corner of his mouth. "I have no hostile intentions. I've told you that, just as I've told about one million senators and policemen. You'll just have to take my word for it."

The refined mouth of Mr. Walls curved gently into a smile. "We are
grown men, Keith. We have larger considerations to think about. It is
imperative that we nail this thing down, so to speak. You have been briefed
on the political situation that exists on this planet. It is necessary that we
establish the relationship between our two civilizations on a firm founda-
tion. Do you understand me?"

"Well—"

"Clearly, there is no alternative." John William Walls crossed his long
legs, being careful not to disturb the razor crease in his trousers. "I think
you will agree that we have extended to you every courtesy. The time has
now come for you to demonstrate your good will in return. We have indicated to you the proper way to proceed, and our staff is willing and able
to give you every assistance. I trust you will not disappoint us."

Keith wrote earnestly in his notebook. He remembered his instructions. "I've told you that I don't want to cause any trouble," he said. "We'll
play it your way."

Mr. Walls beamed, his well-tended face radiating pleasure like shav-
ing lotion. "I knew we would be friends, Keith. I'm proud to have had a
small part in the birth of a new era."

Keith started to say something, but changed his mind. Nervously, he
lit a fresh cigarette.

Within a week, photographs of Keith shaking hands with the President appeared in every newspaper in the world. The President looked
exceptionally serious, and Keith looked very young, and vaguely troubled.
The government played its hand with considerable skill. Keith was kept
under wraps while the tension built up, and around the world people
wondered and worried and hoped.

This concise editorial appeared in *The New York Times:*

"A young man has come from nowhere to our planet. He has come in
a ship so advanced that it makes our finest aircraft look like the amusing
toy of a child. It may be assumed that the civilization which designed and
built that ship has also designed and built other ships.

"The emissary they have sent to us appears to be a rather shy, person-
able young man. He seems well-intentioned, although the evidence on
this point leaves much to be desired. We can meet this man on his own
terms if we wish, if not as equals, then at least as friends.

"But as we look at this man, so much like ourselves, we cannot but
wonder why *he* was chosen for this task. We know nothing of his world.
We know nothing of the people he represents. They may, as he says, wish
to be our friends. They may be offering us the greatest opportunity we
have ever had.

"We remember the Indians who first lived in our land. The first white men they saw did not frighten them. They thought these men were god-like, and they admired their strange ways and vastly superior technologies. The Indians knew nothing of the white men who were still to come.

"We look today at this young man who has come among us. We look at him and like him and admire the ship in which he came. We would ask of him only one question:

"Are there any more at home like you?"

The editorial was widely quoted, and seemed certain to bring another Pulitzer Prize to *The New York Times.*

Late in January, Keith lived up to his obligations by addressing the United Nations. There was, of course, tremendous popular interest in his speech, and the television and radio crews turned out in force.

Keith took careful notes all during the elaborate introductory speeches, and seemed genuinely interested in listening to what the assorted delegates had to say. His appearance was still on the haggard side, and he looked anything but eager.

He took his place under the bright lights before the cameras and microphones with reluctance. His hands were trembling. He had to clear his throat several times.

Once he got going, however, his speech was impressive.

"I have come to a New World," he began in English, pausing to permit accurate translation of his words. "I have come across the greatest sea of them all. I have come not at the head of an armed flotilla, but alone and defenseless. I have come in peace and in friendship, to extend the hand of welcome from one civilization to another."

There was spontaneous applause from the assembled diplomats.

"It is time," he went on with greater confidence, "that you put your differences aside and take your rightful place in the family of the worlds. War must be a thing of the past, so that we may all march forward side by side down the long corridors of Destiny. On all the planets of a million suns, there is no stronger might than friendship, no finer aspiration than the harmony of strong men."

More applause.

He talked for over an hour in the same vein, and finally concluded: "Be proud of your great world, and yet know humility too. I have come to say something good about the human race, and to hold out to you the torch of confidence and faith. Remember my visit well in the years that are to come, and I pray that you are today all my friends, even as I am yours."

He brought the house down.

Everyone seemed satisfied.

Several days passed before a few people began to wonder about the speech they had heard. What, they asked themselves, had Keith really said, beyond glittering generalities and vague sentiments about friendship?

Most people, having never heard any other kind of speech, continued to accept it as a masterpiece.

Keith was troubled and nervous, and locked himself up in his suite. He worked with almost desperate haste on his notebooks, going over even the most trivial phrase again and again. He refused to see anyone, pleading that he had an urgent report to prepare for his government.

When he did leave, much to the consternation of the Secret Service, he simply disappeared. The last person to see him was a paper boy at a busy intersection. He swore to investigators that Keith had paused at his stand and bought a paper, muttering to himself what sounded like, "God, I just can't go through with this any longer."

There the matter rested.

Keith reappeared somewhat furtively several days later on the third floor of the Social Sciences Building of Western University in Los Angeles. He had dyed his hair black, and he walked quickly down the hall past the Anthropology Museum and stopped at a closed office door. A white card on the door had a name and title typed on it: *Dr. George Alan Coles, Professor of Linguistics.* He took a deep breath and knocked.

"Come in!"

Keith walked inside and shut the door behind him

"Are you Dr. Coles?"

"I have that dubious distinction, yes." The man behind the desk was slightly built and his rimless glasses were almost hidden behind the fumes from a virulent black cigar. "What can I do for you?"

Keith took the plunge. He had tried to follow his instructions to the letter, but the strain had told on him. There came a time when a man had to act for himself. "Dr. Coles, I'm in terrible trouble."

Coles lowered the cigar and looked more closely at the young man before him. He arched his rather bushy eyebrows. "Dyed your hair, didn't you?"

"I didn't know it was that obvious."

Coles shrugged. "Keith, I've seen your picture in my morning paper every day for what seems to be a lifetime. I can't claim to be any Sherlock Holmes, but I've patterned my existence on the assumption that I'm not feeble-minded."

Keith sank into a chair. "I was going to tell you anyway, sir."

"Look here, young man." Coles waved his cigar. "You really can't stay here. About half a billion people are looking for you, at last count, and if the Board of Regents stumbles over you in my office—"

Keith lit a cigarette and wiped his hands on his trousers. The circles under his eyes were more pronounced than usual, and he was in need of a shave. "Sir, I'm desperate. I've come to you as one man to another. You're my last hope. Won't *you* listen to me?"

Coles chewed on his cigar. He took off his rimless glasses and polished them on a Kleenex. "Lock the door," he said finally. "I'll hear you out, but I'll hate myself in the morning."

A ray of what might have been hope touched Keith's face. He hurriedly locked the office door.

"Cards on the table now, young man. What the hell is going on here?"

"Believe me, sir, this is all damnably embarrassing."

"As the actress said to the bishop," Coles said, knocking off the ash from his cigar.

Keith took a deep drag on his cigarette. "My people will be coming for me very soon," he said. "I got a message off to them when I crashed. If they could have only got here sooner, this whole mess would never have happened."

"That's Greek to me, son. I had hoped you might be able to make more sense in person than you did at the United Nations."

Keith flushed. "Look," he said. "There's nothing complicated about it, really. You just don't have the picture yet. You'll have to toss out all your preconceived notions to begin with."

"Haven't got any," Coles assured him.

"Here's the first thing, then. There *is* no galactic civilization. I'm not the representative of anything."

Coles blew a small cloud of smoke at the ceiling and said nothing.

Keith talked fast, anxious to get it all out. "I landed in Los Angeles by accident; you know that. I'd hoped to come down in the Arizona desert, where no one would see me and I could go about my business in peace. But, dammit, I was spotted right away, and from then on I never had a chance. I had strict instructions about what to do if I was discovered by the natives—that is, by the citizens of Earth—"

"Just a second." Coles crushed out his cigar. "I thought you said there *wasn't* any galactic civilization."

"There is a civilization out there, sure, if you want to call it that," Keith said impatiently. "But not that *kind* of a civilization. There are hundreds of thousands of inhabited worlds in this galaxy alone. Don't you see what that means, just in terms of your own science?"

"Well, the notion did pop into my cerebrum that the communications problem would be a tough nut to crack. I admit I did wonder a little about this mammoth civilization of yours. I couldn't quite figure how it could *work.*"

"It *doesn't* work. There's some contact between us, but not a lot. Why, one whole planet couldn't hold the government officials for a set-up like that! There isn't any uniform government. War isn't very popular except for would-be suicides, so each of us goes pretty much our own way. The plain fact is—excuse me, Dr. Coles—that we don't really give a hoot in hell about the planet Earth. The last time one of us visited you, so far as I know, was in 974 A.D,. and I expect it'll be a few more centuries before anyone comes again."

"Ummm." Dr. Coles prepared another cigar and stuck it in his mouth. "I believe your speech mentioned the hand of friendship clasping ours across the great sea of space—"

"I'm sorry." Keith flushed again. "I did have to say all that hokum, but it wasn't *my* idea."

"I'm glad to hear it, frankly. I'd hate to think that our friends out in the stars would be as tedious as all that."

"All I did was to be agreeable!" Keith shifted on his chair and rubbed his eyes. "Our instructions are very explicit on that point: if you get found out in a primitive culture, play along with them and stay out of trouble. If they think you're a god, be a god. If they think you're a fraud, be a fraud. You know—when in Rome, and all that. I tried to be what I was expected to be, that's all."

Coles smiled a little. "Once we found out you were a spaceman you were cooked, hey?"

"Exactly! I not only was a spaceman but I had to be *their* kind of a spaceman. They couldn't even consider any other kind. I never had a chance—it got to the point where I was either the emissary from a benevolent super-civilization peopled by fatherly geniuses or I was some kind of monster come to destroy the Earth! What could I do? I didn't want to cause any trouble, and I didn't want to go to jail. What would you have done?"

Coles shrugged and lit his cigar.

"I haven't handled things very well," Keith said nervously. "I've botched it all. It was rough learning English from radio broadcasts—you can imagine—and now everything is ruined."

"Let's start at the beginning, young man. What the devil *are* you any-how? An anthropologist from the stars doing an ethnological study of poor, primitive Earth?"

"No." Keith got to his feet and paced the floor. "I mentioned a previous visit by a student in 974? Well, I wanted to follow it up. I'm studying the vowel-shift from Old English to the present. We'd predicted a shift of the long vowels upward and into diphthongal types. I'm happy to say I've been able to confirm this, at least roughly."

Coles put down his cigar. "You're a linguist, then?"

Keith looked at the floor. "I had hoped to be. I'll be honest with you, sir. I'm still a graduate student. I'm working on what you'd call a Ph.D. I came here to do a field study, but my notes are hopelessly incomplete. I'll never be able to get another research grant—"

Dr. George Alan Coles put his head in his hands and began to laugh. He had a big laugh for such a small man. He laughed so hard the tears streaked his glasses and he had to take them off. He had the best laugh he had had in years.

"I guess this is all very amusing to you, sir," Keith said. "But I've come to you for help. If you just want to laugh at me—"

"Sorry, Keith." Coles blew his nose, loudly. "I was laughing at us, not at you. We've built ourselves up for a huge anticlimax, and I must say it's typical."

Keith sat down, somewhat mollified. "Can you help me? *Will* you help me? I'm ashamed to ask, but my whole lifework may depend on this thing. You just don't know."

Coles smiled. "I do know, I'm afraid. I was a graduate student once myself. How much time do we have?"

"Three days. If you can help me, just give me a hand this once—"

"Easy does it." Coles got to his feet and went over to a section of the metal bookcases that lined his walls. "Let's see, Keith. I've got Bloomfield's *Language* here; that's got a lot of the data you'll need in it. We'll start with that. And I've got some more stuff at home that should come in handy."

Keith wiped his forehead, his eyes shining.

He had learned many words in English, but somehow none of them seemed adequate to express his thanks.

Three nights later it was clear and unseasonably warm. The two men drove up Bel-Air Road in Coles's Chevrolet, turned out the lights, and parked on the bluff.

Silently, they unloaded a crate of books and journals and started down the winding asphalt trail to the house where Frank Evans lived.

"We'll have to sneak along the back of their house," Keith whispered. "If we can just get out past that patio we'll be okay."

"Shouldn't be difficult," Coles panted, shifting the crate. "I don't think they could hear a cobalt bomb with all that racket."

The hi-fi set was going full blast, as usual. Keith winced.

They made it undetected, and proceeded along the dark path under the orange trees. They went fifty yards, until they could see the brush scar where Keith's ship had crashed.

Coles looked at his watch. "Five minutes, I figure," he said.

They sat on the crate, breathing hard.

"Dr. Coles, I don't know how to thank you," Keith said quietly.

"I've enjoyed knowing you, Keith. It isn't every professor who can draw students from so far away."

Keith laughed. "Well, if they ever figure out how that ship of mine works, maybe you can send a student to me sometime."

"We'll both be long dead by then, but it's an intriguing idea anyhow."

Exactly on schedule, a large sphere, almost invisible in the night, settled into the hillside next to them, A panel hissed open and yellow light spilled out.

"Good-by, sir."

"So long, Keith. Good luck to you."

The two men shook hands.

Keith lifted the crate into the sphere and climbed in after it. He waved and the panel closed behind him. Soundlessly, the sphere lifted from the Earth, toward the ship that waited far above.

Coles worked his way silently back along the path to the house, and up the asphalt trail to his car. He paused a moment, catching his breath. As Keith had done before him, he looked down on the great city glittering in the distance. Then he looked up. A blaze of stars burned in the sky, and they seemed closer now, and warmer.

He smiled a little and drove back down the hill, into his city.

REWRITE MAN

"Your throat is full of frog," Barbara Dodson informed her husband. "I can't hear you."

John Dodson toyed briefly with the idea of correcting his wife's phrase, but being an old married man—seven years now—he decided to ignore it. He waggled the newspaper on his lap and said: "There's something funny about this paper."

"Pogo?" Barbara suggested, sipping her coffee.

"You don't follow me. I mean something is *wrong* with this paper."

"It's not the best in the world," Barbara agreed. "Those typos . . ."

John frowned. "Look," he said. "Haven't you noticed that there's never anything *interesting* on the front page like there used to be? Just the UN and Russia and politics and weather. It's the same every night—they don't change anything but the dateline."

"Your coffee's getting cold," Barbara said, sensing that John was off on another inscrutable tangent.

John gave her scant attention. He gripped the paper more firmly, as though determined to choke the truth out of it. "What's become of all the flagpole-sitters and goldfish swallowers? Isn't Marilyn doing anything these days? Aren't there any more flying saucers? And what's happened to all the sex criminals?"

"I'm sure I don't know, dear," Barbara said, somewhat demurely.

Something scratched insistently at the door.

"Here comes one now," she said. "Let him in, will you?"

John reached over, and by stretching heroically managed to open the door without quite getting up. Their dog, a house-filling German shepherd, padded in solemnly. He tracked garden-dirt with great precision across the living room rug, curled his bulk up at Barbara's feet, and went to sleep with an air of relief.

John started to swing the door shut.

"Wait a minute," Barbara said. "Someone's coming."

John brightened. A car crunched up their driveway, stopped, and doors slammed. There were footsteps.

A head with a large smile on it poked itself through the doorway.

"Busy?" a familiar voice boomed.

"Are you kidding?" John asked. "Come on in, Bill, and bring that woman of yours with you."

Bill Wineburg charged into the room, rubbing his hamlike hands together in anticipation. His wife, Sue, a tiny creature of fluff and honey, drifted along in his wake.

Perhaps fifteen minutes were devoted to platitudes of assorted varieties, after which John and Bill settled down to continue their interminable bout of two-handed stud poker. The girls drank coffee, leafed through utopian home-decorating magazines, and chattered he-said-and-then-she-said girl talk.

The dog, Brutus, twitched his ears contentedly.

Along about eleven, just as the game was breaking up for the night, Sue said to Barbara: "Wasn't that *crazy* about Claudette?"

"Claudette?"

"Claudette Cruchette—*you* know, the actress? The one with those perfectly enormous—"

"I remember now. What about her?"

"Didn't you see it? She's entered a *convent.* Isn't that—"

John spun around in his chair, knocking a pile of red chips to the floor. "Where did you hear about that, Sue?" he asked, pointing his index finger like a six-gun.

Somewhat taken aback, Sue waved her tiny hands aimlessly. "In the *paper,* silly. Don't you even *read* it any more?"

John snatched up the crumpled paper, held it out to her. "This paper?"

Sue glanced at the headline—IKE SAYS YES TO UN—and nodded. "What other one is there? It's right there on the front page."

"Show me."

She took the paper curiously, and examined the front page. "That's funny," she said after a moment. "It doesn't seem to be here."

"Maybe it was somewhere else in the paper," Barbara suggested.

Bill shook his head. "Nope. Right there on the front page. Saw it myself."

"There was a picture and everything," Sue said. She thumbed rapidly through the rest of the paper. "I can't understand it. You must have a later edition or something."

"There's only one evening edition," John said.

"Someone's censoring your paper, boy," Bill laughed. "Cutting out all the sexy parts."

John was not amused.

After Bill and Sue had left, he sat in his chair staring morosely at the paper. Barbara had to remind him twice what time he had to get up the next morning before he would listen to her.

Before he went to bed, he took the paper, folded it carefully, and put it on the shelf in the closet.

"There's something fishy going on around here," John said, switching off the table lamp by the bed.

"Now, now," said Barbara, kissing him goodnight. "I'm sure there's some perfectly simple explanation."

"For instance?"

Silence.

John had a tough time getting to sleep, and his dreams were lulus.

The next day was Dreary Thursday, only a slight improvement over Awful Monday, and John's mind was not on his work. It was a slack period anyhow, with very little for the computer to chew on, and he was able to do his job without too much concentration.

He was by nature an imaginative man, much intrigued by some of the philosophical writings of India, and he was also a mathematician, forever concocting charming games with rules so intricate that no one else could ever fathom enough about them to give him a decent contest. Whenever his work was routine—he ran a small IBM machine for an insurance firm—he often let his mind roam on more interesting topics.

Now that he actually seemed to be involved in something odd, he found it decidedly stimulating.

He watched his associates closely, but saw nothing unusual. They were the same old gang they had always been. When he went out for lunch, he paused several times to lounge in doorways, eying the passing crowd to make certain he wasn't being followed.

Nobody followed him.

His lunch was decidedly ordinary, if somewhat greasier than usual.

Nothing happened in the afternoon.

Another man might have shoved the whole business from his mind, but not John. A fact was a fact. Something was screwy about his paper, and he was fully prepared to wrestle with it the rest of his life if necessary.

These things didn't just happen.

There was a *reason* for everything.

Wasn't there?

He waited impatiently until five o'clock, and then hurried out of the building. It was a lovely September evening, crisp and cool, with the sun putting on a spectacular display of rose and purple as it drifted down below the tops of the big hotels. John walked up to the paper boy on the corner, stared at him suspiciously, and passed him by. He got his car out of the lot and deliberately drove in the opposite direction from his home. He tooled the car through heavy traffic out across the bridge into the south end of town. He picked the number five at random, and then proceeded until he came to the fifth drugstore, which was a good way out. He parked his car, went inside, and pulled the fifth newspaper out from under a pile by the cigarette counter. (There was only one evening newspaper in the town.) He tossed the man a nickel and went back to his car.

He didn't read the front page. He just took out his pen and wrote *Drugstore* on the upper right hand corner. The paper absorbed the ink, but it was legible.

Then he went home.

Brutus jumped up on him and tried to lick his face. He started to tell the dog to go fetch the paper, which he saw stuck in the hedge where the route man had thrown it, but changed his mind and retrieved it himself.

Bru hung his head in dismay.

John thumped his way into the house, slamming the door behind him.

Barbara stuck her head out of the kitchen. "Hi," she said.

John muttered something unintelligible. He ripped open his evening paper and spread the front page out on the floor. Then he opened up the copy he had picked up at the drugstore and spread *that* on the floor.

"What in the world are you doing?"

"Ummmmm."

John's eyes flicked rapidly from one front page to the other. He saw it almost at once. He got up and pulled all the blinds and locked the door. He walked decisively into the spare bedroom and found a soft red pencil in his desk. He went back to the papers and outlined two stories, one in each edition. It wasn't easy to draw on the rug, but the lines were clear enough.

"Johnny, what's the *matter?*"

"Look at this, honey."

Barbara dried her hands on her apron and got down beside him.

"Why, that's just crazy," she said after a moment.

"Exactly."

"I'm going to call the paper right this minute. I'm—"

"No. Don't do that. Lets see if we can't figure this thing out."

Barbara stared at the papers. "What is there to figure?"

"As the man said, that is indeed the question."

There was nothing threatening about the two front pages, nothing sinister. It was just that there were two entirely different stories, one in the copy he had picked up at the drugstore, and another one in the copy be had gotten by subscription. Except for the one story, in the lower left hand corner of each paper, the front pages were identical.

The paper that had *Drugstore* written on it featured a little yarn with a headline that read: MIAMI BATHING BEAUTY NIPPED BY SHARK. There was a cut of a well-stacked young brunette in a minimal bathing suit, smiling bravely at the carcass of a shark on a sandy beach. The story itself was nothing very sensational, and was probably brewed in the overactive mind of a press agent. The girl had been swimming, the story said, when she had been attacked by a shark. Handsome life guard Bruce Bartholomew, a veteran of the Pacific theater, had just happened to have his rifle handy, and had plugged the shark. (There was no photograph of Mr. Bartholomew.) The girl had stated that she would go on with her swimming, "because swimming means more to me than anything else in the world, and I know Mom and Dad are counting on me."

That was all there was to the story.

In the paper that John had rescued from his hedge, there was no trace of the bathing beauty story. Instead, there was a perfectly innocuous item about fishing on Lake Travis, which was a few miles outside the city limits. The story had no business on the front page, and had been padded with several fillers because it wasn't long enough. The headline was: TRAVIS BASS STILL TAKING LURES.

The story read:

Austin, Sept. 5 (Spl.). Local anglers will be glad to learn that the bass in Lake Travis are still hitting fairly well on lures, Mr. Harold X. Rogers announced today. Mr. Rogers stated that several parties had taken boats out from his dock in the morning and afternoon hours, and each boat had returned with three or four bass and several perch.

"The recent spraying to eliminate parasite fish has not harmed the game fishing," Mr. Rogers said. "I can see the bass jumping out there all day long, and this is really one of the prettiest seasons of the year for lake fishing."

One of the bass weighed in at three pounds, and several others were also nice ones. The perch were small.

* * * *

The duckbilled platypus is a mammal but it lays eggs like a chicken. It lives in Australia.

* * * *

The biggest man ever to play football in the United States was Jasper "Moose" McGill, who weighed 450 pounds.

* * * *

"Well?" asked John.

"I don't get it," said Barbara.

"Neither do I. But I'm *going* to, understand?"

Barbara sighed. "We're going to have fish tonight. I hope you don't mind."

John didn't answer her. He got up and rummaged through his desk in the bedroom until he found a partly empty scrapbook. (The first twelve pages were taken up with stamps, a hobby he had abandoned.) He got some scissors and glue and went back to the papers on the living room floor.

"There's something funny going on around here," he announced, and began to snip away with a vengeance.

Outside, the wind shifted around to the north, and it began to grow cold.

"Now look," he said, after the fish had been transformed into bones and they were drinking their first cup of after-dinner coffee. "We're intelligent people, and we should be able to figure this thing out."

Barbara, who was not terribly interested, smiled brightly. She was a tall, leggy blonde with friendly blue eyes and a sweet smile that had been known to melt ice cubes at twenty paces. The smile, however, had no perceptible effect on John.

"Someone or something is messing with our newspaper," he said, lighting a cigarette and puffing on it with his I-smoke-but-it's-just-a-habit-I-don't-really-enjoy manner. "You agree with that?"

"Some*thing?* What do you mean by that?"

John waved his cigarette. "How do I know? I'm just trying to include all the possibilities."

"Well." Barbara looked over her shoulder nervously. The wind had died away to a whisper, and it was quiet outside. You could close your eyes and imagine you were all alone in the world. . . .

"OK," John went on, frowning. "We agree. Next question: *Why?* If you yank a story about a bathing beauty out of someone's paper and substitute a story about bass fishing, what are you up to?"

Barbara moaned inwardly. *Why not just call the paper?* she thought. But no, that would be the last thing Johnny would ever do. She felt a warm glow. She loved her man, and wouldn't change him for the world. Still—

"Maybe it's some fishing fanatic," she suggested lamely. "He's starting a private campaign to keep girls out of the water because they spoil the fishing."

John gave her a look of polite contempt. "Let's make the question more general. If you take *any* story out of a man's paper and put in another one, what are you up to?"

Barbara drained her coffee and waited.

John ground out his cigarette. "That's right," he said, as though she had said something. "There are only two basic possibilities. Either you are hiding something from him, cutting out a story you don't want him to read, or else you are trying to tell him something—inserting a story you do want him to read. Now, which is it?"

"Well," Barbara said, determined to play along, "maybe he's trying to keep all the sexy stories away from you. Doesn't want to arouse your libido or something."

John considered this quite seriously. "Maybe," he said. He smiled a secret smile. "But let's take it from still another angle."

He'll forget all about it in a week, she thought. *But what a week!*

"Why me?" John demanded. "Why single me out? What's so unusual about me?"

"You're different, dear."

"Everyone's different, one way or another. I'm nobody important. I run a little computer, but there's nothing secret about it. I'm twenty-six years old, I've never been in any trouble, I don't have access to any classified information. I fiddled around with psychology in college before I got tired of running rats through mazes. Why me?"

"The Naval Reserve? Radar?"

"Hmmmm. Could be. But I'm not really any expert. It just doesn't figure."

Barbara poured some more coffee and stacked the dishes in the sink. *Suppose there's really something to it. Suppose something's AFTER my Johnny.* She shivered.

"Have you ever heard of Charles Fort?" John asked suddenly.

"No. Where is it?"

John muttered something under his breath. "This isn't solving the problem. There's just one thing to do."

"Which is?"

"I'll keep on getting two copies of the evening paper every night. I'll save them and analyze the differences between them. If this means anything, some pattern is bound to emerge sooner or later. And don't say anything about this to anyone, honey."

"I won't," she assured him sincerely. "Where are you going?"

"I'm going to listen to the radio tonight. See if they're censoring that, too." He paused. "Lucky we don't have a TV set. That would really complicate matters."

Barbara turned to the dishes.

John got a notebook and pencil and switched the radio on. The radio was on the kitchen table, where they could listen to it at breakfast time, and it was somewhat temperamental. However, it came on in fine style tonight.

"*. . . and scientists continue to urge attention to this problem in the aftermath of the political campaign,*" the radio blared. "*The radioactive fallout from the hydrogen bomb tests constitutes a grave genetic hazard to future generations, and scientists stress the fact that . . .*"

John scribbled away diligently.

Barbara washed off the dishes with a ragged sponge, being as quiet as she could. And, somehow, she was unable to shake off a queer feeling of unease, almost of fear.

There *was* something funny going on.

If someone's after my Johnny . . .

She broke a plate when she was drying it, which was something she hadn't done in years.

Two weeks passed. The crisp green of September gave way before the slippery yellow of October.

John had established these facts to his own satisfaction:

One, someone (or something) was definitely and systematically altering the front page of his newspaper.

Two, discreet questions revealed that none of his friends were having similar problems.

Three, the interference did not extend to other media of communications. His radio was okay.

Four, there was no discernible pattern to the thing. The stories cut out of his paper were minor items, usually of the human interest type, but that was their only common thread. The new stories, *his* stories, were trivial to the point of incredibility.

Then, on the fourth of October, as he was pasting the usual two clippings in his scrapbook, he hit the jackpot.

"Look at this!" he hollered triumphantly.

"I don't see anything," Barbara said, puzzled.

"Look again. Don't you *see?*"

Dutifully, Barbara read the two stories again.

The first story, the one in the paper that John had surreptitiously bought in a crosstown supermarket, carried the headline: WOLF IN MAN'S CLOTHING JAILED. The story related the curious predatory adventures of one David Elmer Toney, who had been hunting for deer in the Texas hill-country in the vicinity of Kerrville. Mr. Toney had not had much luck when he happened upon a neatly fenced-in field that was snow-white with grazing sheep. Mr. Toney felt an itch in his trigger finger, and he let fly with his rifle. The dauntless marksman downed sixteen sheep before he was disarmed by an apoplectic rancher. "I don't know what came over me," Mr. Toney was quoted as saying. "I guess I just don't like sheep."

There was a photograph of Mr. Toney; he looked reasonably normal.

The second story, from the paper that John was now thinking of as his own special edition, was headlined: AUSTIN MAN LIKES JELLYBEANS.

The story read:

Austin, Oct. 4 (Spl.). Texans may eat beef every day, and some of them may even enjoy a friendly beer or two, but Mr. Harold X. Rogers of Austin practically lives on jellybeans. "I don't know just what it is about them," Mr. Rogers stated, "but I really go for jellybeans. Most days I just skip other foods so I can eat more jellybeans."

According to Rogers, this habit dates back to his childhood, when he used to carry a sack of jellybeans in his saddlebags while working cattle on his father's West Texas ranch. "Jellybeans don't make you short-winded like cigarettes do," he observed, "and it was hard to roll those old cigarettes in the dust and wind."

Mr. Rogers is convinced that jellybeans are an excellent source of high-energy food, but he confesses that he really eats them "just for the fun of it." He estimates that he consumes five pounds daily.

* * * *

The wombat never eats its young alive, scientists say.

* * * *

Friedrich Gottlieb Klopstock was a German poet.

* * * *

John eyed his wife's face expectantly. Then, noting its vacant expression, he threw up his hands in despair. "The name, honey! The name!"

"Klopstock?"

"Not Klopstock! *Rogers.* Harold X. Rogers!"

"So who is Harold X. Rogers?"

"I don't know. But look here." John flipped back through the pages of the scrapbook until he found the first clipping, the one about bass fishing on Lake Travis. "See? Same name: Harold X. Rogers. That time he was operating a boat dock on the lake, and now he's eating jellybeans."

"Maybe that means something significant to *you,* dear, but—"

"It's the first sign of a pattern, that's why it's important. No other name has repeated itself in any of these stories. This is the first instance of a commonality. Suppose this Rogers, whoever he is, is trying to communicate with me . . ."

"Then why not put his name in *all* the stories?"

John frowned. "Good point," he muttered, glancing at his wife in mild surprise. "Well, look at it this way. He doesn't want to make it too easy."

"Why?"

"How do I know? Maybe it's a contest of some kind, or a game, or a test. The real question now is: who is Harold X. Rogers?"

Barbara sighed. "Before you think of something devious, why not try the phone book?"

John snapped his fingers and charged out into the hall. He snatched up the telephone book, flipped it open, and ran his finger down a column. "Rogers, Rogers," he said. "Lots of them. Ah!"

"Find it?"

"Yeah. Harold X. Rogers. Address on Sixth Street—some kind of business address, probably. GReenwood 2-5059."

"Maybe you shouldn't call him, Johnny. I mean, wait until we can find out something . . ."

"Nonsense!" said John, hot on the trail. "This is D-Day, H-Hour."

He dialed the number, listened a moment, and hung up the receiver. "What's wrong?"

"Busy."

He waited five minutes, pacing the floor with Brutus padding along behind him, and tried again. "Still busy."

He kept on trying until after midnight, but the number was always busy.

"Just one thing to do," he announced.

"Now, Johnny, you're *not* going down there in the middle of the night, Harold X. Rogers or no Harold X. Rogers!"

John hesitated, then nodded. "Of course not, honey. I'll drop in on him tomorrow during my lunch hour—it's only a few blocks from where I work."

Barbara knew that wild horses couldn't keep her husband away from there the next day, so she just crossed her fingers. "You will be careful, won't you?"

"Sure, baby. I can take care of myself."

Brutus eyed his master dubiously.

Nobody slept much that night, and it seemed that dawn would never come.

For John Dodson, the next morning passed with all the rapidity of a turtle plodding across a field of glue. He worked impatiently, glancing at his watch every few minutes. And he thought: *It's amazing how deep a rut we all get into. Even when something like this turns up, we still check in at work and save adventure for our lunch hour!*

He felt no fear, not even a vague uneasiness. After all, what was there to be afraid of? His sole emotion was eagerness, like a kid on Christmas morning.

John was always attracted to the unusual and the romantic. As a boy, the finding of an arrow point or an old rusty spur had been enough to set him off on day-long fantasies. Growing up, he had discovered, involved a certain hardening of the mental arteries, and it was a genuine thrill, it was *exhilarating,* to be actually mixed up in something different.

Bring on your flying saucer pilots and your men from Mars! Bring on your sinister gang of murderers! Anything to put a bit of spice into living!

Of course, he wasn't really expecting anything of the sort. When he had been younger, he had sought out all the haunted houses for miles around and explored them thoroughly, but the last thing he had figured on running into was a genuine certified ghost.

Well, who was Harold X. Rogers then, and what did he want?

John inclined toward the notion that the whole deal was a test of some sort, perhaps part of a contest. Probably tied in somehow with TV; maybe they would give him fifty thousand dollars in nickels and then he could quit his job and go uranium hunting in Utah. . . .

A buzzer sounded.

Noon.

Time for lunch.

Food was a million miles away from John's mind, for once. He grabbed his topcoat and hurried outside. It was a chilly gray day, with a faint drizzle of rain in the air.

Four blocks down Congress, then five blocks to the left along Sixth Street—

There.

An old, dirty stone building, three stories high, sandwiched in between a noisy beer hall and a cut-rate men's clothing store. He paused a moment, sizing the place up. Jukebox music spilled out of the beer parlor into the wet street:

"Oh I had a gal in San Antone
"She was rustled by ano-ther;
"Now all I do is set and moan
"She's run off with my bro-ther, . . .

Shivering a little, John stepped inside the doorway and pushed open the reluctant door. He found himself in a dingy hall, with a flight of wooden stairs leading up to the second floor. He mounted the stairs, half expecting them to collapse under his weight, and at the second floor landing he came to another door.

It was an ordinary wooden door, and it had a button in the panel to the right. Underneath the button a small white card was stuck to the wood with a thumbtack. The card read: HAROLD X. ROGERS.

John felt an unreasonable surge of triumph.

He held his breath and listened, but the place was silent as a tomb. The only sound came from the bar next door, where the cowpoke was still lamenting his sibling's perfidy.

He pressed the button.

There was no ring or buzz that he could hear, but a yellow bar of light suddenly appeared under the door. He thought he heard a swelling hum, like an activated dynamo, but it passed quickly.

"Come in!" an excited voice called.

John opened the door and stepped inside. He was in a large, rather barren room. The only substantial piece of furniture in the place was an ancient roll-top desk. Behind the desk stood a short, balding, red-faced man. The man was built on the rotund principle, and had obviously been eating something besides jellybeans.

"Are you Rogers? Harold X. Rogers?"

The man stared at him, the enthusiastic welcome light dying out in his eyes and being replaced by a look of disappointment that he tried heroically to hide.

"I am Rogers," he said in a careful, precise voice. "Who are *you?*"

"My name is Dodson."

There was no response from Rogers.

"*John* Dodson."

The fat man sat down in a swivel chair behind the desk. He made no attempt to shake hands.

"I figured out your little deal in the paper," John continued doggedly.

"Oh," the man said, *"that!"* He waved a plump, well-manicured hand airily, as though the matter was of no consequence whatsoever.

"Yes, *that.*" John was beginning to get annoyed. "'Don't you think I'm entitled to some sort of an explanation?"

"Not necessarily." Mr. Rogers folded his hands and leaned back in his chair. He was trying hard to give an impression of boredom, and he might have succeeded except that his hands were trembling violently. . . .

John frowned. There was no way he could force the man to talk. He toyed with the idea of threatening some sort of legal action, but Rogers had promised nothing, there was no obvious intent to defraud—

"Ummmm," said Mr. Rogers, trying to sound casual. "You—er— worked it all out for yourself, is that right?"

John nodded.

"No—ummmm—help from anyone, is that correct?" The man's diction was still oddly precise, as though he were speaking a foreign language.

John shrugged. "I talked it over with my wife."

"She made suggestions, perhaps?"

"One or two, yes," John said, remembering the telephone book. "But I came here to ask *you* the questions."

"Impossible," stated Mr. Rogers flatly. "Quite, quite impossible." He darted a look into the corner of the room, almost as if he expected to see something there. His pink forehead was gleaming with sweat.

John glanced into the corner.

There was nothing there.

"Well!" said Mr. Rogers, suddenly getting to his feet. "Must be going!"

"Wait a minute, dammit! You can't—"

Mr. Harold X. Rogers paid no attention. He walked hurriedly to a side door in the room, opened it, stepped inside. Just before the door closed behind him, John caught a glimpse of a large dull gray metal sphere in the room, flickering with tiny flames that reminded him of little lightning flashes.

"Hey!"

Too late. The door was shut. There was a high whine, like the dynamo-sound he had heard before, and then silence.

The lights went out.

In the darkness, John reached out and tried the door. It wouldn't budge. He fumbled in his pocket and pulled out his cigarette lighter. He spun the wheel, and on the fifth try he got a light.

Bewildered, he crossed over to the desk, looked at it. There was nothing on the desk. He pulled open the drawers, one by one. In the bottom right drawer, there was a piece of scratch paper. He flattened it out on top of the desk, and held the light down where he could see it.

It was covered with marks. Not writing, he saw instantly. Some kind of formula—

He stared at it more closely. There were lots of brackets and equal signs, and a number of curious squiggles that looked vaguely familiar. One a tiny circle with an arrow on it, another a circle with a plus sign attached. . . .

Of course! They were the astronomical symbols for Mars and Venus. He felt a curious wild excitement. His mind raced ahead, throwing off conjectures and postulates like sparks. Mars and Venus. The closest planets to Earth. Earth was in the middle—

"What the devil," he muttered.

He decided to make a copy of the chart, but before he could get his pencil ready for action his lighter went out. He spun the wheel without results, hammered the treacherous gadget into the palm of his hand without results, and cursed it roundly, also without results.

He groped over to the door by which he had entered and ran his hand over the wall. He found a light switch and flicked it, but the lights refused to come on.

And it was getting late.

He could, of course, take the scrap of paper along with him. John, however, had a healthy respect for the law, and he certainly had no right to rifle Mr. Rogers's desk. He stumbled across the room, replaced the paper in the drawer, and left the place.

The juke box was still blasting out its philosophy of agony from the beer parlor. John glanced at his watch, saw that he only had two minutes left on his lunch hour, and practically sprinted back to work.

He was damp from the rain.

He was hungry.

He was completely baffled.

Who *was* Harold X. Rogers? Why had he gone to all the trouble of doctoring up a man's newspaper, and then been disappointed when the man came to see him? What had Mr. Rogers been afraid of during the interview? What had that strange metal sphere been in the next room? It wasn't any printing press, that was certain.

For that matter, where had Mr. Rogers gone?

And *how?*

And those squiggles, those signs for Mars and Venus . . .

John tried to ignore the rumblings in his empty stomach and the churnings in his equally empty brain. He did his work methodically until almost four o'clock.

Then, quite suddenly, he dropped what he was doing.

"Tell the Old Man I was taken sick," he hollered to Ben.

He grabbed his coat, ran out of the building, got his car out of the lot, and headed for home.

And, law-abiding citizen or not, he broke some speed regulations getting there.

When he got home, there was already a car parked in his driveway. It was a perfectly ordinary blue sedan, and he had never seen it before. It did not belong to any of his friends, and it had no business being in his driveway.

He knew who had driven it there, however.

John glided to a stop at the curb and got out of the car. He left the door partially open, careful to make no sound. He stepped across the soggy lawn and paused at the front door.

The door was slightly ajar.

He could hear voices in the living room.

One of the voices belonged to his wife, Barbara.

The other one belonged to Harold X. Rogers.

Of course, he thought. *Mr. Rogers was never after me at all. He wanted Barbara. That was why he was so disappointed when I walked into that office of his. He was testing Barbara all the time. He asked me if she had helped me out with the solution, and I didn't deny it. He wants my wife. What for?*

He listened.

"You do not seem to understand, Mrs. Dodson," the man named Rogers was saying in an exasperated tone of voice. The words were not so precise as they had been before; he was slurring them a bit as he got excited. "I am a man from the *future,* I have traveled through *time* to make this contact with you."

Future? Time? What about—

"That's really swell," Barbara said. There was the clink of a coffee cup against a saucer. "I appreciate it, but you should really talk to Johnny about things like that. He's always been interested in crazy theories, and I—"

"No, no, *no*. You are *impossible!* No, I don't mean that. Please, you must forgive me."

"That's quite all right. Johnny says things like that all the time."

"Imbecile! I mean, look. Listen. Attend! I will attempt to explain one more time."

"About this Edgar Vincent Winans of New York? Really, Mr. Rogers, I'm quite happy as I am—"

"Bah. *That is not the point.* Do you care nothing at all for the human race?"

There was silence, as Barbara earnestly tried to decide what to do.

"Look. Listen. Attend. You have heard of the hydrogen bomb, I trust?"

"Oh, yes."

"Well! The radiation from the fallouts of these bombs has certain very harmful effects on the germ plasm, on the *genes*. It leads to an increased frequency of mutations—"

Genes. Mutations. Those symbols: one a tiny circle with an arrow on it, another a circle with a plus sign attached. Astronomical signs for Mars and Venus, yes. But also the symbols for male and female in a genetics computation. Those brackets and equal signs. Barbara and Edgar Vincent Winans . . .

"Mr. Rogers, I never discuss politics."

Mr. Rogers said something in a foreign language, paused, and tried again. "My dear Mrs. Dodson. In a few hundred years, in *my* time, these mutations have had serious consequences for the human race as you know it today. In fact, we are faced with *extinction!* A new race of men has come into being—"

"Oh, yes, those supermen you were telling me about."

"They are *not* supermen!" screamed Mr. Harold X. Rogers. He spluttered for a moment, then continued in a relatively normal tone of voice: "They are not supermen. Only different men. They are strong, they are powerful. And they wish to isolate normal men, people like us, for the good of the race! The *arrogance,* the nerve—"

"Now, Mr. Rogers, don't let yourself get all excited."

"Well! We must fight back, we normal men. How, you ask? I will tell you. We must go back in time, we must prevent certain matings before children are born, we must assure other matings which will produce superior *human* beings to aid us in our struggle! If we fail, our race is doomed. *You,* Mrs. Dodson, have a crucial genetic contribution to make to the future! It is *imperative* that you have no children by your present husband.

Instead, our computations show that you and Edgar Vincent Winans of New York City—"

"Please, Mr. Rogers! I try to be broad-minded and all that, but you are making it very difficult for me."

"Bah! This ridiculous sex taboo. Look! Listen! Attend! It is a question of *science,* a matter of random assortment and recombination; it has nothing to do with your infantile ideas about sex!"

"I just don't see it that way, I'm afraid."

"Then you refuse?"

"Well, I hate to say no—I always have trouble saying no to people about charity drives and things—"

"Mrs. Dodson, consider! Your decision may mean the obliteration of the human race!"

"Well, I'm really awfully sorry, Mr. Rogers, but I really couldn't. I'd like to help you out, really I would, but I love my Johnny and I simply have no interest at all in this Edgar Winans of yours."

"Love! You speak of love at a time like this! Mrs. Dodson, you are a fool, a colossal, stupendous, incredible *fool!*"

"Now look here, Mr. Rogers. Mr. Rogers! Keep away from me, Mr. Rogers! I'll call Bru—"

John decided that it was time he made his entrance. He took a deep breath and stepped through the doorway.

"Hold it, Rogers!" he said

The short fat man with the red face whirled. His face grew even redder. He pointed a trembling finger. "You! Murderer! Race-slayer! Mutant-breeder!"

John spread his hands. "I mean you no harm, Rogers. What you were saying may have been the truth, for all I know. But you can't talk to my wife that way, sir. Get out of my house before I throw you out."

Harold X. Rogers hesitated.

John doubled up his fist, which was of impressive dimensions.

Mr. Rogers spat out something in that foreign language. John could not understand it, but he knew it was no compliment. Then the man from the future stormed out the door, fuming with rage.

"Johnny!" breathed Barbara.

John received his hero's reward, then disentangled himself.

"Baby, I've got to go out again," he said. "You lock all the doors and don't let anyone in until I get back."

"But, Johnny—"

"I won't be long, honey. But there's something I just *have* to find out. You see, if that man was telling the truth . . ."

He left her there in the living room, ran outside, and climbed back into his car.

He pulled out into the heavy five o'clock traffic and headed for town as fast as he could go.

Sixth Street was a wet ribbon, reflecting the white headlights of the homeward-bound automobiles in cold, silvered puddles. John rounded the block three times before he found a parking place.

The dirty stone building was still there, even more gloomy in the damp dusk. The cut-rate men's clothing store was cheerful with warm yellow light, and doing a brisk after-work business. The beer joint was filled with the low murmur of drinking men, and the juke box was moaning:

> *"Gimme your love, you great big doll,*
> *"I'm hungry for your smile and that ain't all. . . ."*

John pushed open the hesitant door and stepped into the unswept hallway. He took the wooden steps two at a time and paused at the second floor landing.

The thumbtacked white card was still in place: HAROLD X. ROGERS.

Was he too late?

No—he heard sounds from inside, and light showed beneath the wooden door. John pressed the button.

There was no reply, but the noises from the other side of the door increased in volume. Two voices, speaking a strange tongue, and a sound of scuffling—

John opened the door and stepped inside the barren room.

He stopped, staring.

Harold X. Rogers was there all right, but he was in the process of leaving. The red-faced fat man, in fact, was suspended in mid-air, held in the arms of a man who looked like a perfectly proportioned giant.

"You!" screamed Mr. Rogers, kicking his legs futilely.

The other man raised one eyebrow in salute, and smiled in greeting. He was a good seven feet tall, and he was golden. He *glowed*—that was the only word for it.

The giant said nothing to John. He just carted Harold X. Rogers through the side door as though Mr. Rogers were a sack of sawdust.

"They've won!" cried Mr. Rogers as he vanished into the other room. "Murderer! Idiot!"

John watched, but kept his distance. The huge man lifted Mr. Rogers into the dull gray metal sphere and then climbed in after him, waving courteously to John as he disappeared. There was a clank as the portal into the sphere closed. Tiny flames flickered over the surface of the metal.

There was a humming whine, like a dynamo.

The sphere—*wasn't*.

The room was empty.

John shivered in the sudden silence. He felt as if he were in a cave far underground, with tons of rock sealing him off from the sounds of life. Then the hush lifted. He heard the juke box, the squish of tires on the street outside, the call of a newsboy.

He turned and left the room.

He had found out what he needed to know. The man had told the literal truth. He had come out of the future on a mission to save the human race as he knew it. He had set up the test with the newspaper as a check on Barbara's intelligence—even genetics could be misleading at times, and he had to be *sure*. No doubt he had taken the paper back with him into the future to have it altered, or even taken them all at once. Time travel made many things possible. . . .

And he had failed.

Barbara had turned him down.

The delicate balance had tilted the other way.

John got back into his car, and set out for home. He was not depressed at all. In fact, he was elated. He *did* amount to something! He was, in truth, a very important man.

What had Rogers called him?

"Mutant-breeder."

Why, he and Barbara were going to become two of the most significant parents in history!

Of course, old Homo sapiens was going down the tube in the process.

Well, he thought, *who am I to stand in the way of evolution?*

He drove on home and pulled the car into the driveway. He let himself into his home with his key. He felt mighty good.

When they had finished eating, Barbara yawned at him contentedly.

"I'm certainly glad no one will be fooling with our paper again," she said, folding it back to the comic section. "That funny man gave me the creeps."

John nodded and turned to the dog curled up by the stove.

"Well, Brutus," he said, "how would you like to have an exceptionally interesting little playmate in a year or so?"

Barbara looked up from the comics, eyes wide with delight.

Brutus thumped his tail.

THE EDGE OF FOREVER

Dale Jonston gripped the palisade logs until his knuckles went white with strain and tiny droplets of blood began to form under his fingernails. The humid air choked his throat and a cold sweat beaded his forehead and trickled down the inside of his ETS shirt.

Start, his tense mind whispered. *Why don't you start?*

The massed black clouds rolled over his head like a dark sea suspended in the air. Drums of thunder throbbed in the west and an electric hush charged the atmosphere. Lightning flickered in ghost-flames around the distant peaks of the Hills of the Dead.

It was the Time of the Terror—and the Terror was coming.

"It will be soon now," a low voice echoed his thoughts.

Dale Jonston jumped inwardly at the sound and then forced himself to relax. He turned around. A tall native stood there watching him, a faint smile playing across his proud face. In the murky haze the light blueness of his skin was all but invisible.

"Good to see you, Lkani," Dale Jonston said. "This weird weather of yours has just about got me down—you almost scared me to death creeping up on me like that! Don't you ever make any noise?"

"Perhaps you should tie a bell around my neck," the native suggested. "Is not that what you do to keep track of the animals on your planet?"

"Your sense of humor can be a trifle . . . startling, Lkani."

Dale Jonston eyed the native thoughtfully. These people never ceased to surprise him, and he had been stationed on Rohan for two years now. The planet was referred to officially as Procyon Twelve, of course, but no one who had ever been there called it by that colorless name. When in Rome—

"It is coming," Lkani said quietly, pointing out into the gathering darkness. "My people have all gone from the Changing Lands—they are waiting in the hills. They will not have to wait long."

Dale Jonston felt his jumpy nerves begin to settle down. He shouldn't let it get him this way, he realized. But this brooding weather did something to

165

a man. It was like waiting for a bad hurricane back on Earth, when you sat around interminably in the still air and watched the barometer fall. It had been like this for weeks now.

And there were the Others—the people of mystery that no man had ever seen, custodians of a civilization that spanned the far-flung stars. Somehow, in the mutter of the thunder and the clouds of darkness, he knew that they were near. Watching. Waiting—

"You know we'd be glad to have you on the Post," he said. "We've got room for fifteen or twenty, and our buildings may be able to take what's coming better than your settlement in the hills."

"I will stay with my people," Lkani said. "We have been through the Terror before—you have not."

"You've got a point there at that."

The motionless, dead-smelling air pressed down on them heavily. The yellow squares of light in the windows of the Post buildings looked safe and comfortable. Dale Jonston was glad that they were there.

"You had better get inside before it comes," Lkani said.

"I guess I'll have time for *that,* anyway," Jonston replied.

"It comes fast." Lkani smiled.

"Well, if we can be of any help to you just whistle or beat on a drum or something."

"If *we* can help *you* just flash us a radio signal or send up a magnite flare," Lkani countered.

"You win," Dale Jonston laughed. "Sometimes I wonder just who is kidding who around here."

"Here it comes," said Lkani.

The charged air trembled and thunder blasted savagely across the plains. Great livid bolts of lightning slashed jaggedly down and tore at the crouching vegetation. The sound swelled to a shuddering roar that pounded the ears with physical force.

"Merry Christmas to all," Dale Jonston whispered dazedly. "And to all a—"

He never finished. He had a split-second's warning as a fresh wet smell hurtled in from the plains and then it hit. Rain! Rain such as no man on Earth had ever imagined—rain that slammed down in a blinding torrent, rain that thundered and pounded and choked.

Ten years it had been pent up in a monstrous reservoir—and now the Gates of Hell were opened wide!

He felt his feet slipping out from under him and he coughed desperately as water clogged his lungs. The rain beat at him with a million wet hammers and he knew he was going down. The ground under him was already a sea of mud.

A strong arm came out of nowhere and supported him as he stumbled back toward shelter. He gasped and coughed and tried to wipe the blinding sky river out of his streaming eyes. He staggered into the main Post building and the door shut behind him.

"Lkani!" he choked.

He was alone—Lkani was gone.

He leaned against the log wall, fighting to get his breath. The rain pounded down on the Post as if determined to rip it to shreds. Thunder roared as the gods went mad.

Quite suddenly, Dale Jonston was chillingly aware that he was a long, long way from home.

Dale Jonston paced up and down the floor of his office, puffing on his pipe and listening to the hammer of the rain on the roof. It never stopped, that rain—it ebbed and flowed with savage fury, but it never stopped. It made Earth's mightiest cloudbursts seem like gentle drizzles and it went on forever.

"Sit down, Dale," said Tom Troxel. "You're making *me* nervous."

"Sorry," muttered Dale Jonston, seating himself behind his desk.

"It's only rain," Troxel offered.

"Sure—and the H-Bomb is only atoms."

"Take it easy—you can't stop the rain and there hasn't been any trouble yet."

"*Yet*—that's the word I don't like."

"What can happen? So it rains for six months or a year—it won't kill anybody."

"Won't it?"

There was a splitting hiss followed by a jarring blast of thunder. The rain droned on and it was cold in the room.

"I don't follow you," Troxel said.

Dale Jonston got to his feet again and walked over to the duraglass window. He stood there and watched the rain wash across the glass like tiny breakers. That was all there was to see—the rain and the darkness.

"Do you know what it's like out there now?" he said quietly. "It's been raining like this for three weeks now and no one knows for sure how long it will go on. Those lowlands have been saturated, drenched. They're wild swamps now, filled with great white worms crawling up through the soft ground. The natives are all crowded together on the hilltops and the caves are roaring underground rivers. The natives call this the Time of the Terror and they're not just coining phrases for the fun of it. There's a reason— things *happen.*"

"You think the natives will act up?"

"No, they're intelligent people and they're better adapted to these conditions than we are. I'm not much worried about the natives."

"Then—"

"You know man's greatest enemy is not alien natives, not monsters, not the Others—but himself. Man is his own destroyer. He always has been, down through history back on Earth, out in space when he got to the planets of his own solar system, and now here. He won't change just because he's on a planet that belongs to another sun."

The rain thundered down and a cold wind whined around the little buildings of the Post. The light on Jonston's desk threw blurred shadows on the log walls. Troxel shivered and lit a cigarette.

"Yes," Jonston went on, puffing slowly on his pipe. "I'm worried about us—us, the mighty Earthmen. I tell you, you take any group of selected spacemen, men who have been carefully conditioned and psychologically screened—you take 'em and coop them up somewhere for a year. Put pressure on them; don't let them see a living person except themselves. They *may* come through O.K.—and they may not. And we're not dealing with trained spacemen here, Tom. Intelligent workers, sure, but not trained spacemen."

"I'm receiving you."

"Take any two ordinary people—good friends, maybe—and lock them in a room for a year. Watch what happens; the growing tensions, the little arguments, the brooding hostility that develops. Multiply that by a hundred or so, toss in this infernal rain and a planet light-years away from home, complicate the situation with great worms and God only knows what else, add a few natives—"

"And don't forget the Others," Troxel added with a grin.

"I'm not forgetting them—not for a minute. They're an unknown factor, and hence doubly dangerous. Tom, I wish *you* were in charge of this Post. I'd sit around with a fiendish leer on my face and concoct enough gruesome situations to make your hair stand up on end and sing the 'Deep Space Blues'."

"I hear the swamp is full of dinosaurs, too."

Dale Jonston looked at his prematurely bald junior officer and gave up. He was glad he had a man like Troxel around. It took a lot to panic a man with a sense of humor, and Troxel was no fool. Jonston realized that Troxel was deliberately forcing him to relax, and he appreciated it. He needed to calm down, and no mistake. It wouldn't do for the commander of the Post to blow his top at a time like this.

He opened the bottom left-hand drawer of his plastic desk and took out a bottle and two glasses.

"We'll see if we can conjure up a couple of pink elephants to add to your menagerie," he said. "Have a drink."

Troxel's eyes brightened as he hitched his chair up to the desk.

"Hm-m-m—Old Rocket Fuel," he enthused. "That's what Admiral Groten was drinking just before he passed away, poor man. You know what his last words were?"

"Afraid not."

"He said, 'I don't see how they can make a profit on this stuff at twenty cents a fifth'."

"I told you that man was his own worst enemy," Jonston said with a smile. "Jokes like that might well destroy civilization."

"Right you are," Troxel agreed cheerfully. "Let's drink our first drink to the Others."

Jonston raised his glass.

"To the Others," he said quietly.

Outside, the great storm lashed out at the planet, churning the lowlands into swampy ooze and pelting the mountains with a driving deluge of rain. It was a chaos of thunder and lightning and wind. And, if you were of an imaginative turn of mind, you could hear, between the Post and the Hills of the Dead, the slithering of the great white worms . . .

It was night on Rohan and the Post was still. Dale Jonston sat alone at his desk, listening to the monotonous hammer of the rain on the roof. There was no visible difference between night and day, but you always knew, somehow, when night had come. You felt a strange chill in your blood and your mind did odd things with the shadows on the walls.

He permitted his tired body to relax. It had been a hard day; they were all hard. Conferences with psychologists and anthropologists—anthropologists were indispensable in space-travel, he reflected, since they were the only scientists on Earth who were trained to understand alien cultures—supervision of projected entertainments, paper work, and the thousand and one urgent little problems that were forever coming up in the management of any community. He fired up his pipe. Funny how much civilized man depended on tobacco . . .

He had held up pretty well, he figured. He had been keyed up to start with and had stayed more or less at the same pitch, while the rest of the Post had grown progressively more tense as the weeks and the months dragged by. Even Troxel was showing it now—there was a report on his desk from Dr. Moreland that noted the chief psychologist's concern over Troxel's condition.

All he could hear in the night silence of the Post was the sound of the thunder, the rain, and the wind—all scrambled together into a roaring awareness of the storm that never stopped. The lightning teamed up with his desk lamp to throw grotesque shadows on the log walls.

Sometimes, the distance got you. You wouldn't think about it for days; you might even kid yourself into thinking that you had it licked, that you were conditioned to the deeps of space. Then it would hit you—if the great double star of Procyon should happen to explode, *it would take over eleven years for the light of the explosion to reach the Earth.* That's a long way to be from home—a long way from the green fields and the trout streams and the girl you hoped would be waiting . . .

He sat back in his chair, puffing slowly on his pipe, eyes closed. You could never explain a planet like Rohan to the people back on Earth; it was one of those places that only the spacemen would ever know. You might show them pictures, talk to them. You could tell them that Rohan was a world where everything was adapted to a peculiar, seasonal rain cycle. Due to the pull of the double star, an odd inclination of the planet's axis, and great quantities of the spongelike substance frondal in the upper atmosphere, it only rained once every ten years—and then it really *rained.*

You could tell them of the wonderful storage roots of the plant life, and of how they cast off millions of globular seeds just before the storm. The plants were largely destroyed by the pelting rain, but the seeds floated in the black muck and germinated after the storm.

You might describe the intelligent, blue-skinned natives of Rohan, and tell how deceptive their simple culture was from an anthropological point of view. Their economy was a standard hunting-and-gathering one, and they lived in small groups on the great plains. When the rains came, they retreated to the hilltops, where the unusual crowding and emotional tensions brought about the periodic Time of the Terror. They lived then from storage bins and small mammals which took refuge with them on the high ground and fish in the few caves which were not transformed into torrential underground rivers.

You could tell them about how the great plains turned into abysmal swamps filled with the crawling white worms that had been dormant underground during the dry season. You could tell them all about everything—except what counted. You couldn't tell them how it *felt.*

Dale Jonston nodded sleepily, too tired to go to his room.

Men flamed up from the Earth and fought their way to the stars for many reasons—ambition, greed, glory. But there was only one thing that kept them on a planet once they had reached it—and that was a composite reason of economics. It might not always be so but now, in the infancy of interstellar travel, that was how it was working out.

The planet had to *produce*. So it was with Rohan, a planet rich in mineral substances and medicinal plants nowhere else available. The Proclamation of Equal Rights for All Intelligent Life had nipped exploitation in the bud, to man's everlasting credit. Trade was carried on pretty much on a mutual-benefit basis, within the limits of human failings and the alien psychologies and cultures found on the far-flung worlds. The natives of Rohan were indifferent; they had their culture and were perfectly content to let the men from Earth have theirs. Earth had nothing to offer them except terrestrial civilization, and Dale Jonston often considered that to be at best a dubious blessing. He thought of Lkani, with his shrewd intelligence and quick humor. Lkani was by no stretch of the imagination an "inferior being"—indeed, Dale Jonston sometimes wondered just which race was tolerating which on Rohan. . . .

The storm roared on, tearing at the building. The rain poured down until you couldn't remember a time when the sun had shone and the sky had been any other color than black. The men were getting sick of the sight of each other. They laughed too much and too loud. You'd be sitting around and all of a sudden get an almost uncontrollable urge to sock somebody—anybody.

And then you would remember that you were a man, and that the Others were watching.

The Others. Who were they, what did they want? No man had ever seen them, but they were there—there in the vastnesses of space, waiting, watching. They were there in strange contacts on radar screens, there in alien artifacts found on distant worlds, there in the whispered legends that a thousand thousand primitive tribes whispered around their campfires in the sky.

It was rather painfully obvious that man, despite his once self-centered assumptions, was not the only intelligent race in the galaxy. He was out to carry his civilization to the stars—and someone was already there! Somewhere, sometime, they must meet. And then—what?

The best minds on Earth had wrestled with the problem and had come up with a few simple propositions which were unusual only in that they began to show the common sense of man's maturity. One, there was already in existence a galactic civilization of a high order. Two, Earth could not hope to fight it—it must *join* it. Three, the men from Earth must first prove that they had finally grown up before they could expect any overtures from the Others.

Always, down the black rocket trails between the stars, men could feel their presence. Somewhere, lost in infinity, the Others watched and judged.

Dale Jonston got wearily to his feet and switched out the light. He walked slowly through the long halls to his room, nodding at the sentries as he passed them. The rain beat down with a terrible relentlessness and lightning hissed down on the swamps.

Here he was, he thought—one tiny man in this outpost on the edge of forever. And something big was going to happen; he knew it positively with that subconscious sixth sense that made him a leader. Something big—something that might well change the whole future history of that strange species that the universe called man.

It seemed as though he had hardly dropped off to sleep when Dale Jonston came to his senses with a start. He sat up in bed, rubbing the sleep out of his eyes. The storm sounded wet and unpleasant outside and he was glad that he had the warmth of the Post to protect him. He glanced at the glowing dial of his watch. Four in the morning. What in the world—

Then it came again, whining dismally through the night. The alarm siren!

He leaped out of bed and pulled on his uniform, his mind spinning with half-formed conjectures. He ran out of his room into the hall. Lights were coming on all over the Post.

"What's up?" panted Lin Carlson, catching up to him in the corridor.

"Don't know—come on."

Carlson—chief anthropologist at the Post—nodded and they pounded down the hall to Jonston's office. The siren was wailing like a lost soul. Jonston flipped on the telecom.

"Hello, Control," he said tensely. "Get me the Watchtower and stand by."

The steady, relaxed face of the defense co-ordinator flashed on the screen.

"O.K., Williams—Jonston here. Let's have it."

"Over at the main gate, sir. Two sentries knifed—don't know what the deal is yet but I figured I'd better turn in the alarm. I've already told Control to call a red alert."

"Check. Anything else?"

"That's about it—too early to tell what happened. Can't get a thing on the radar. Should I turn the floodlights on?"

"I'll handle it, Williams. Stand by. Over."

Jonston jiggled the telecom switch.

"Hello, Control. See that the floodlights are turned on and get hold of Lieutenant Burks—I want an immediate personnel check. Tell the radio room to try to get through to Earth. Tell Burks I'll expect a report here in half an hour—Carlson is here with me. That's all."

He switched off and turned to Carlson.

"Any ideas, Lin? Natives?"

Carlson shook his head and finished buttoning up his ETS shirt. "Don't think so. Of course, I can't tell for sure—but I'd bet a considerable fortune if I had one that those natives are safe. I've studied them for years—it's unthinkable."

"That's my opinion too, frankly. But we can't take chances with that atomic pile in here."

"The Others, maybe?"

"They're still an X factor, Lin—there's no way to tell. Where the devil is Troxel?"

"Still pounding his ear probably. He could sleep right straight through Armageddon."

Jonston drummed his fingers on his desk and thought of Dr. Moreland's psychological report on Troxel. It couldn't be, of course. Still—

"Let's get down there to the main gate and see what goes," he said.

Carlson nodded and they hurried through the Post together. Jonston noted that all the men were properly deployed and that there was no panic—yet.

The sentry house at the main gate was connected to the rest of the Post by a log tunnel. The gate was simply a door in the palisade wall, and the sentry house was a lonely place indeed during the Time of the Terror; visitors from across the swamps were few and far between.

They went down the tunnel and the storm was very close. The logs were moist and cold. Five armed men greeted them in the sentry house. Their faces were pale. The two bodies on the floor were covered with uniform coats. Jonston looked them over.

"Knife wounds all right," he said slowly. "In the back."

"It's Marks and Richards, sir," one of the men said needlessly. His voice was taut. "They . . . they—"

"They came a long way to die," Jonston finished softly. "All quiet out here now?"

"Yes sir."

"Take it easy, then—but keep your eyes open."

He turned away, beckoning to Carlson, and they made their way back to his office. Lieutenant Burks was waiting for them.

"What did you find, Burks?"

"'All present and accounted for, sir, as far as I can tell. Except—"

"Yes?"

"I can't locate either Lieutenant Troxel or Dr. Moreland, sir. I thought perhaps that you'd seen them somewhere."

"No," Jonston said slowly. "No, I haven't seen them."

He sat down behind his desk and began to fill his pipe. The thunder and the rain seemed to isolate the little room, as though it were all by itself, drifting in infinity. He felt an awful chill race through his veins. Two men knifed in the back and—

"They'll show up, Dale," Carlson said.

Dale Jonston hoped so with every atom of his being. If only Troxel would come barging in, with his smile and one of his countless jokes about the weather. He could see him, in his mind's eye, sprawled in his chair, saying seriously, "It's like I always say, Dale. Everybody talks about Mark Twain but nobody *does* anything about him—"

His thoughts came to an abrupt end as the door banged open. A wet, bedraggled caricature of a man stumbled into the room, his clothes soaked with mud. It was Dr. Moreland.

"I tried to stop him," Moreland choked. "I tried to stop him."

Carlson and Burks helped the psychologist to a chair. His eyes were bright and he was breathing with difficulty. Jonston went around and stood by his side, one hand on his rain-drenched shoulder.

"Try to tell us what happened, Doc," he said.

"It was Troxel," Dr. Moreland whispered, taking a deep breath. "I was worried about his psych report and went around to check on him. And . . . and—"

Carlson handed him a drink. Moreland gulped it gratefully.

"Go on," Jonston said.

"He wasn't in his room. I found him right after he knifed the sentries—he went out the main gate into the storm. I . . . I tried to follow him, catch him, but . . . the storm—"

"I understand," Jonston said, a sick feeling in his heart. "Did he have anything with him—any weapons?"

"I . . . I think he was carrying something. I tried to get him but the swamp—Dale, it's . . . it's horrible out there—"

Jonston listened to the hammer of the rain on the roof. The lightning hissed down on the swamps and the thunder rolled heavily through the black skies. He could feel the cold sweat on his forehead.

"There's just one thing to do," he said. "We've got to go out there and get him."

Dale Jonston tried not to think of Troxel as his friend. He was just a factor in a problem that had to be solved. That wasn't an easy way to look at it, but it was the only way. He knew that Troxel, as junior officer at the Post, had access to the arsenal. There were atomic bombs in the arsenal—and when there's a madman at your door with an atom bomb it's already later than you think.

Copters were useless in the storm that raged across the face of the planet, and the ship from Earth wasn't due for another two months. Dale Jonston smiled without humor. It was strictly a family affair.

"We'll never find him out there," Lin Carlson said. "Never in a million years."

"We've *got* to find him."

"A man might live for a while in that storm," Carlson pointed out. "But he could never locate anyone else—he couldn't see two feet in front of him. And if the person being hunted doesn't *want* to be found—"

"I'll find him," Jonston said.

"*You?* You can't go out there—you're in charge here."

"That's why I'm going."

"Don't throw your life away, Dale," Carlson said. "It's all very well to be a hero, but what good will it do? You'll go out there into that swamp full of worms and we'll all be worse off than we are now."

Jonston smiled. "Don't worry, Lin. I'm not going to throw a fit of heroics for dear old Terra—I think as much of my hide as the next man. I think I can find Troxel or I wouldn't go. You see, I'm not going alone."

"I don't get it."

"Very simple, really—Lkani. He can cross those swamps and he must have some way to see where he's going. If he'll help us—"

"I think you're making a grave mistake," Dr. Moreland said, shaking his head. "To put the safety of this Post into the hands of a savage—after all—"

"Lkani is not a savage," Carlson interrupted angrily. "A man of your education, Dr. Moreland, should certainly have better sense than to—"

"Knock it off," Jonston said wearily. "This is hardly the time for an argument."

He looked at the lines of tension in Carlson's face and at Dr. Moreland's too-bright eyes. He felt the strain himself—it was like sitting on a powder keg while a paranoiac looked at the fuse and played with a cigarette lighter. There was no longer any time for discussion. He had to *act*.

"O.K., Burks," he said. "Start firing magnite flares across the Hills of the Dead where Lkani and his people are. Get with it."

Burks left and Jonston settled back and tried to relax.

"What do we do now?" Carlson asked.

"Cross your fingers, friend. That's all—just cross your fingers."

The storm lashed at the Post with new fury as if challenging any man to go against it in mortal combat. Jonston thought of Tom Troxel out there, sick and dangerous. *This is the price you pay,* his mind whispered. *This is the price you pay for your ticket to the edge of forever.*

The hours passed. The faces of the men were white with strain. Any minute, any second, the blast could come. And they could only sit and wait. And wait. And *wait.*

The telecom buzzed.

"Jonston here."

"It's the native chief, sir—Lkani. He's at the main gate. He says—"

"Never mind what he says. See that he's comfortable—I'll be right down."

He flipped off the telecom and got to his feet.

"Can't I go along?" Carlson asked. "Maybe I—"

"Thanks, Lin—but if one man can't do this job then two men or a dozen can't do it either. You hold the fort."

"Well—good luck."

"I still think—" Dr. Moreland began, then thought better of it.

Dale Jonston, already dressed in boots and plastic slicker, hurried out of his office and down the tunnel to the main gate. The rain pounded gleefully on the roof, sensing a victim. Lightning burned furiously through the storm. Jonston shivered. If they couldn't find Troxel—

Lkani was there waiting for him. His blue face was glistening wet in the cold light of the sentry house.

"I saw your flares," he said.

"You don't know how glad I am to see you, friend," Jonston said. "We're in a mess."

He explained the situation to the native, wasting no time. Lkani listened carefully, nodding his head from time to time. The storm howled mournfully around the log house and the rain came down in torrents.

"I understand," he said finally. "I will try to help you, of course—but it will not be easy."

"If you ever want a medal, Lkani, I'll get you a dozen or so."

"I'm afraid they would be of little use to me," Lkani smiled. "Are you ready?"

"As ready as I'll ever be."

"Then let's go."

Two of the sentries opened the gate and a wet hell blasted in. Dale Jonston's heart hammered in his throat. He looked at Lkani and tried to smile. This, emphatically, was *it.*

Shoulder to shoulder, the two men walked out into chaos.

The thick mud sucked at his feet and the rain pounded his body. Dale Jonston's skin crawled under the cold lashing of the wind and he noticed wildly that the rain smelled like metal. *Like standing under Niagara in a raincoat,* he thought numbly.

He couldn't see; he plodded on in a nightmare fantasy of unreality. He was afraid and his stomach felt hollow and cold. He held closely to Lkani's arm and forced himself to keep going. Where? Somewhere—anywhere that Lkani went. Through the storm, through the sea of rain, through the darkness.

The rain choked in his lungs. He couldn't think but his mind was spinning with livid images. And questions—questions that screamed in his head, questions that had no answers. How could any man, sane or not, stay alive in this shrieking attack of the elements? How long could *he* take it? How could Lkani find his way through the swamp—how could he know where he was going, much less how to get there?

A man might live for a while in that storm, Carlson had said. *But he could never locate anyone else.*

Jonston gasped for breath and pulled his feet through the muck. Lightning sizzled through the wet air and hissed into the swamp behind them. The thunder crashed with an ear-splitting roar. It was too much for any man to take—but Jonston kept his head down and went on. There was no other way to go.

His mind began to think about the thousands of slithering white worms that undulated through the swamp and terror crept like ice through his veins. His feet were tense and uncertain in the mud, as though he were walking through the ocean surf back on Earth with jellyfish between his toes.

Lkani stopped.

"What's the matter?" Jonston yelled above the pounding of the storm.

Lkani pointed and Jonston followed his arm. There was something in the muck, something dark. Jonston knelt against the force of the rain and rolled it over.

Troxel. Troxel—with his neck cut almost in half by a knife.

Dale Jonston got numbly to his feet and stood there swaying in the blast of the storm.

"Tom," he whispered.

That was all. There was no time for anything else. He had to whip his mind into action, had to *think*. Lkani was silent in the wind-driven downpour, waiting. Jonston clenched his fists. *THINK.* The rain hammered at his face.

Troxel was dead in the swamp, knifed. He hadn't killed himself, that was obvious. In all probability, he hadn't killed the sentries, either. *Troxel wasn't the man they were after.* O.K. Someone had cracked, and it hadn't been Troxel. Who, then?

Jonston thought back. He shook his head, half in anger and half in fear. He had been tricked, neatly and completely. Feinted out of position like the greenest cadet.

"Dr. Moreland," he breathed.

Of course. It was Dr. Moreland who had made out the psych report on Troxel, Dr. Moreland who had "seen" Troxel knife the sentries, Dr. Moreland who had come in wet from the swamp, Dr. Moreland who had been afraid to call in Lkani.

And he was inside the Post and he outranked every other officer.

Dale Jonston looked down at the thing that had been his friend and made himself think the problem through. He ignored the thunder that blasted through the darkness, ignored the choking rain, ignored the cold wind that whistled through his slicker. *Think—*

Dr. Moreland had cracked under the strain of the storm and too many tense mental problems of others. He wasn't a villain; he was sick. But he had to be stopped. He had tricked Jonston out of the Post and he had killed three men with a knife. He couldn't go on like that, Jonston realized. He would either have to stop killing altogether, which wouldn't be likely, or—

Or he would have to destroy the entire Post, himself included. How could he do that? There were atomic bombs in the arsenal—but Jonston doubted that Dr. Moreland could get into the arsenal alone. Even though he outranked the other officers, he was a psychologist and would have no business in the arsenal. The other men were not fools; they would become suspicious and that wouldn't do. What else then? Jonston shivered. The atomic pile, used to power the mining tools. There would be guards in the arsenal, or supply men at least, because they were on the alert for an attack from *without.* But the atomic pile—Moreland could get to it— could tamper with it.

No man in his right mind would alter the pile, of course. But that was just the point. Moreland was no longer sane.

Dale Jonston could visualize the scene—Moreland in the room with the pile, warning the others that they must not approach him. Yes, Moreland would have to let them know what he had done—have to taunt them with his cleverness and feel like God with the power in his hands. A working knowledge of psychology was not by any means restricted to the psychologists in the Extra Terrestrial Service—it was standard equipment.

Lightning hissed into the swamp again and the rain slammed down harder with the push of the thunder. Jonston smiled coldly. *All right, genius,* he thought. *You've figured out what you should have known all along—now what are you going to do about it?*

He put his mouth next to Lkani's ear and hollered above the storm. If this didn't work—

"Lkani, Moreland's going to detonate the pile. It will destroy your people as well as mine. What can we do?"

Lkani was tall and dark in the driving rain. His steady eyes measured Jonston carefully.

"Just think the facts of the situation," a voice spoke clearly in Jonston's stunned brain. "Then follow me."

Dale Jonston stood there staring.

So, his mind whispered, *he can read minds, too.*

The storm lashed out at them with sentient fury and the darkness covered the two men like a shroud.

No matter what men say, and no matter how good an act they may put on for the world, there is within all men a pragmatic core that always knows what the true score is. And within that core, despite their outward egotism, men usually underestimate themselves. Dale Jonston would never have believed for a minute that he could take what he was taking and go on asking for more. But he could—and he did.

He didn't think about it. He just kept plodding forward, holding on to Lkani's arm and pulling first one foot and then the other out of the eternal mud. The rain beat at him and the wind tore at his clothes. He felt as though his lungs were on fire and his eyes burned in his skull. Every second he expected the blinding flash from the Post—the flash and the end.

But they were moving away from the Post, he sensed. Toward the Hills of the Dead. He shuddered, feeling the unthinkable coils of the great white worms slither past them in the darkness. Why didn't they attack? There was just one answer—Lkani. Lkani was the answer to a lot of questions.

The footing became a little surer under them as the clinging muck turned into firmer stuff. Jonston realized that they would never have got through at all if Lkani had not known how to avoid the bottomless pits and suckholes that must have made up the greater part of the swamp. That Moreland had gone as far as he had was a miracle of a singularly unwelcome variety.

They were climbing now, he knew. Climbing into the Hills of the Dead where the natives buried their lifeless friends and the wind whistled through the mountains. Torrents of rain water gushed in mighty rivers down the hillsides and lightning hissed in the sky. Jonston held on.

Suddenly, it was over. They were out of it and Dale Jonston could only stand numbly and wait for feeling to return to his battered body. He stood there, soaked to the skin, and looked out at the raging storm. Gradually, he became aware of the fact that he was in a cave. Someone put a bowl of hot liquid in his cold hands and he drank it mechanically.

Lkani thought ahead and they were waiting.

The fluid was strong and warm and good, like a cross between a heavy soup and a sweet liquor. It picked him up amazingly and he began to feel almost human again.

"We haven't much time," Lkani said.

"I'm O.K.—let's go."

They started into the cave and Dale Jonston noted with surprise that the air was dry and warm. There must be some sort of a force field across the cave entrance, he reasoned. Simple natives indeed! And yet the smooth floor of the cave seemed to be completely free from mechanical contrivances of any sort; the blue-skinned people cooked over roaring wood fires and evidently made their homes in smaller, branching caves. Force fields and caves, mind reading and a primitive social structure—Dale Jonston shook his head at the mounting paradoxes.

"Where are we going?" he asked.

"Can't explain," Lkani answered shortly. "Trying to keep the man from pulling the rods on that pile."

Coercive thought projection, Jonston's mind observed.

He followed Lkani without comment through the cave. The sounds of the storm were muted by distance now, but far ahead of him he could hear the muffled roar of a swollen underground river. He tried not to think of Moreland at the Post—face too pale, eyes too bright, with his finger on the trigger of eternity. If that pile cut loose—

It was all up to Lkani now. Dale Jonston accepted the situation as it was, without trying to assert a meaningless authority of his own. He knew superior intelligence when he saw it and he was ready to co-operate. He followed the native tensely and kept his eyes open. Lkani, he noticed, had picked up a tubular device of some sort that looked like an uncommonly thick flashlight with a pistol grip attached.

Primitive man, Jonston thought, laughing at himself.

The sound of the river was closer now, and they quickened their steps. Why are we going alone? Jonston wondered. Why don't the rest of them come with us? A part of his mind sensed the truth: *I've* got to be the one who does the job. Lkani will make it possible, but I've got to do it. Why?

They passed a branching cave that was larger than the others and Jonston looked inside. It was brightly lighted from within and he caught a fleeting glimpse of a slim tower of silver that strained toward the dark heavens above.

A spaceship—in a cave!

Lkani went on and Jonston stayed right behind him. Abruptly, the air turned cold and moist; there was no gradation from warm to cold—it was just suddenly and precisely *cold*. There was still light in the cave, coming from a faint mineral glow in the rocks.

Jonston shivered and kept on going, his mind beginning to stagger under the strange import of the things that he had seen. The churning roar of the river washed chillingly through the damp cave and phantom echoes shuddered among the rocks.

Time, he knew, was running out.

The river hissed by like a great serpent below them, fat and swollen with tons of rain and hurling itself angrily at the walls of its rock prison. Dale Jonston stood with Lkani and looked uneasily at the narrow ledge of sharp rock that wound along above the boiling torrent.

"That the way?" he asked, knowing the answer in advance.

Lkani nodded and swung down to the ledge, holding carefully to the metal tube. Jonston trembled in his wet clothes and followed him.

"You've got me all wrong, friend," he panted. "I'm an ETS man—not the Human Fly."

Lkani smiled and kept on going. Jonston took a deep breath and tried to cling to the slippery rocks. The churning river tumbled wickedly below them, filling the cavern with booming spray. He was cold and afraid and he felt very small. He tried to joke to himself, as men always do when they feel death at their throat. But nothing is very funny when you're walking the Last Mile.

Time ceased to be as they clawed and fought their way along the treacherous ledge. Their fingers were cut and bleeding and their exhausted muscles were numb with fatigue. The world was the next rock, the next curve, the next inch. Below them, the black river chanted its song of hate—and waited.

Jonston gasped with relief as Lkani turned off into a cave that branched away from the river. He stood gratefully still for a long minute, getting his wind and listening to the roar of the cheated torrent. His chest ached with strain and his torn clothes were streaked with blood where he had touched them with his hands.

"Come on," Lkani said.

They ran through the comparatively dry cave, forcing their bodies as if they were something apart from them, like automatons in which their minds temporarily resided. Lkani still carried the tube in his hand and he set a murderous pace. Jonston kept up with difficulty, breathing in short, painful jerks of air. His mind was a spotty screen of black and white upon which Moreland's face was stamped in livid flame. Time—there *couldn't* be any more time.

Lkani stopped, his chest heaving. He stood rigidly with his eyes closed. Beads of sweat stood out on his forehead. Jonston watched silently, fighting to get his breath. The great river was a dark murmur behind them.

"All right," Lkani whispered. "We're directly under the pile room, and he's up there. I'll open a hole and you get him—and *don't miss.*"

Jonston set himself, his heart beating wildly. Lkani aimed the metal tube at an angle toward the upper part of the cave wall. He set two dials very carefully and pressed the switch.

There wasn't a sound—but a spherical section of rock ceased to be. It simply wasn't there any more. Dale Jonston hurled himself into the hole and hoisted himself through.

The scene that confronted him was like a picture that he had seen many times before. He had imagined it so intensely that every detail was familiar to him. The indicators set in the lead shield were gyrating feverishly and the very air in the glaringly white room was tensely charged. Moreland crouched at the door, his too bright eyes staring out of his too white face.

He screamed when he saw Jonston and threw himself crazily at the lead shield, clawing for the damping rods. Jonston caught him with a flying tackle—and Moreland exploded like a wild thing in his arms. He shrieked and tore and lashed out with superhuman strength. Something hit Jonston on the side of the head and white lights danced in his brain.

Jonston wrenched loose somehow and fell to the floor. He rolled and got up again, sick and dizzy. Moreland was rushing in, screaming his hate, his fingers tensed like white claws. Jonston backed away, calling on reserves of power he wasn't sure he possessed.

One punch, he thought desperately. *One punch is all I've got.*

Moreland loomed up in front of him and Jonston threw his punch from the heels up. It smacked into Moreland's face with a sickening crunch. The shock of the blow traveled back through Jonston's arms and went off with a white puff in his brain.

That was the last thing he remembered.

"You've been out for thirty-six hours," Lin Carlson said.

Dale Jonston looked around shakily. He was in his own bed in the Post and his body ached dully. The light from the floor lamp splashed whitely across Lin Carlson's face.

"Lkani," he said, not recognizing his own voice. "Where's Lkani?"

"He went back across the swamp after he unlocked the door of the pile room—that tunnel the natives dug caved in."

"I see," Jonston said, not seeing at all. Tunnel caved in? That was nonsense—

"Sure glad to see you awake again," Carlson smiled. "You really saved our necks, Dale. If you hadn't fixed those damping rods, we'd all be in the unhappy hunting ground for sure."

I never touched those rods, Jonston thought.

"The credit belongs to Lkani," he said.

"He's some native, I'll say."

"Yeah—some native."

"He left a note for you," Carlson said, handing him a sealed envelope. "And we've got Moreland doped to the gills—we'll send him back on the first ship to Earth. Maybe they can do something for him."

"Everything else O.K.?"

"Guess so—except that none of us quite understands what happened. Lkani didn't do much explaining and—"

"Tell you all about it some day, Lin. Right now, I wonder if you'd go tell the cook to scare up some breakfast for me? I'm half starved."

"Will do," Carlson said, getting to his feet. "See you later."

He left the room and Dale Jonston was alone. He twisted his bruised body over in the bed and tore open the letter. His hands, he noticed, were shaking. There were two sentences on the paper:

"There was no atomic explosion—that is what counts. Stop and think and you will understand."

Dale Jonston fumbled for his pipe, filled it with fragrant tobacco, and lit it. He closed his eyes and relaxed, inhaling the smoke slowly. Lkani, he sensed instantly, had somehow planted a message in his brain. Or perhaps he was in contact now from across the swamp—

No matter. It came softly into his mind—softly but with bell-like clearness.

You are an intelligent man, the voice spoke in his mind. *You cannot see two and two and fail to put them together to make four. We have gambled on your intelligence and your discretion—and we know that you will act accordingly, both for our people and for your own.*

You saw force fields and spaceships, telepathy and a tool that realigns the dimensional plane of atoms. You must have guessed that we are a part of that civilization which you know only as the Others. Much that may seem mysterious to you is not strange at all; like so many things, it is relatively simple once you know the facts.

You have had difficulty in associating what appears to be a primitive culture with an advanced civilization, but that is only because you have confused complexity with progress. Your own anthropologists have known for many years that simple cultures are often better integrated than your own, and better serve the needs of the individual. It has been a truism of your people that you have knowledge and refuse to apply it.

If you will stop and think about it, the "Time of the Terror" is quite as graphic a term as "A Psychological State of Tension Induced by Periodic Storms"—but I will not trouble you with an analysis of why we live as we do. We are happy and that, after all, is the only valid test.

We are but a tiny part of a tremendous civilization that spans the galaxy. Cultural maturity must be attained before a people can become a part of such an association—and there are many different types of civilizations involved. For example, we do not manufacture our own spaceships; our contributions are along other lines.

We have been watching Earth for centuries, waiting. Your presence here on Rohan is not entirely your own doing—it is one of a series of tests. You see the problem: a tense conflict situation with atomic energy readily available. There was no atomic catastrophe—and it was prevented by your own efforts. You asked for help and got it—and that, too, showed intelligence on your part.

You will understand, Dale Jonston, why this knowledge must stop with you. Your people are not yet ready to face the situation that exists, and unless they work their problems out for themselves they can never attain the stability that is essential for galactic co-operation. But the time is rapidly approaching—and you will live to see the day—when mankind sets forth on an adventure beyond its wildest dreams.

For we are not the only civilization in the universe.

That was all.

Dale Jonston opened his eyes. His pipe had gone out and he put it aside. It was too much to assimilate all at once. He looked around his room. The floor lamp threw dark shadows on the log walls. He thrilled with knowledge.

Not the only civilization in the universe—

Beyond the Others—what?

He shook his head, suddenly conscious of a strangeness in the air.

Something was wrong.

He got out of bed and stood still, listening. There wasn't a sound. That was it. *Silence.*

He walked shakily over to the window and pressed the button that changed the glass from opaque to clear. Mottled sunlight splashed into the room. He looked up into the sky where the massed black clouds were splitting and being forced apart by slanting rays of flame that transformed the sky into a brilliant mass of color—red and yellow and green, cold silver and warm gold, the clouds rolled by and the light came through. He opened the window and drank in the fresh, clean smell of the breeze that murmured in from the marshes.

It had been a tough climb up from Earth to the edge of forever, he thought—but it was a climb that had to be made.

He heard laughter drift up from around the Post and somewhere a guitar began to play. A rhythmic voice started an old, old song:

"Oh, I'm bound to go where there ain't no snow,
Where the sleet don't fall and the wind don't blow,
In the Big Rock Candy Mountains—"
Dale Jonston smiled happily.
"There's a lake of stew and of whisky, too,
You can paddle all around in a big canoe,
In the Big Rock Candy Mountains—"
The storm was over.

The Boy Next Door

It was five o'clock by the clock on the studio wall. Behind his glass partition, the balding engineer waved his right hand at Harry Royal.

"Hello again, kids!" Harry said in a hearty voice.

The youthful studio audience squealed with delight. A little girl in a pink dress smacked her hands together enthusiastically. Harry moaned to himself. What a way to make a living!

"Yes, sir," he said, careful to keep a big, cheery smile on his face. "Five o'clock again, boys and girls, and you all know what *that* means!" He winked at the adults in his audience—must be parents, he thought. Why else should they torture themselves? He said: "Ha, ha. Station ZNOX, right here in the good old Hotel Murphy, again brings you *The Boy Next Door,* the program where you get to hear your very own friends speak to you over the radio. This is your old Uncle Harry Royal, getting the old program under way again. How are you all this evening, hmmm?"

The kids in the audience assured him that they were fine. They always were, thought Harry grimly. They would be. He smiled wanly and tried to look like a good scout.

"Well, sir," he continued, "as you all know, old Uncle Harry picks one of your names out of the little old red box every day, Monday through Friday, and invites the lucky winner down here to the good old Hotel Murphy to talk over the radio." His smile felt a trifle limp and he engineered a fresh one. "This afternoon, our guest is young Jimmy Walls, from away out in Terrace Heights."

Applause. Harry wondered why. What had Jimmy Walls ever done? Set fire to the school?

Jimmy Walls eyed Harry gravely. He was an eager-looking boy in what was obviously a brand new suit. His straw-colored hair was slicked back precariously. He had bright blue eyes and his tie was crooked.

"Don't be afraid now, Jimmy," said Harry Royal.

"I'm not afraid," Jimmy Walls assured him.

"Well, well—that's fine, Jimmy, fine. There—stand a little closer to the microphone. Fine. Dandy. How old are you, Jimmy?"

"I'm eight years old, going on nine."

The same questions. The same answers. Harry Royal decided, not for the first time, that he hated kids. All of them.

"Mighty fine, Jimmy," he said. "Mighty fine. Yes, sir, that's fine. Where do you go to school, Jimmy?"

"I go to Terrace Heights School," answered Jimmy. He added: "When I go."

"When you go? Ha, ha. You don't mean to tell your old Uncle Harry that you skip school sometimes?"

"Sometimes," Jimmy admitted.

Harry worked on his smile again. Didn't they ever say anything new or interesting?

"You're not very bright, are you?" he wanted to say.

"What programs on good old ZNOX do you like best?" he said.

Jimmy Walls thought about it briefly. Then his blue eyes glistened. "Golly," he exclaimed, "I like *The Hag's Hut* best. I like *Terror in the Night,* too!"

Well, thought Harry. Just a nice, healthy, American boy. Nothing like horror programs for the little, growing minds.

"Ha, ha,'" Harry Royal chuckled dutifully."Don't those programs scare you, Jimmy?"

"They don't scare *me,"* Jimmy retorted indignantly.

"Ha ha. I see. Yes, I see." Harry Royal fumbled around for something to say, and came up with: "Why do you like those programs best, Jimmy?"

"I like the way they kill people," Jimmy replied instantly. "They sure are smart!" His blue eyes were bright with admiration.

That one stopped Harry Royal for a second, but he bounced back in a hurry. Nothing ever stopped Harry Royal for long, no, sir! "But they always get caught, don't they, Jimmy?" he suggested. "Crime doesn't pay, you know."

He winked broadly at the adults in the studio.

"Maybe,"hedged Jimmy Walls reluctantly.

"Hmmmm. Well, well. I see. Yes, sir." Better change the subject, Harry decided. Definitely. You never could tell about parents, studio brass, and the FCC. He chose a safe topic: "What have you been doing all week, old man?"

"Killing people," Jimmy Walls announced proudly.

Pause. Harry began to feel uncomfortable. "Ha, ha," he said, without humor. "Come now, Jimmy. Ha, ha. Come now—honesty is the best policy."

"I *am* honest," muttered Jimmy Walls insistently. He shuffled his feet, smearing the fresh polish on his shiny brown shoes. "Nobody ever believes me."

"Oh, I believe you, all right. If you say so, Jimmy. Ha, ha—just a regular cut-up, I guess! Do you use a knife, Jimmy? Ha, ha."

"No," Jimmy Walls stated flatly.

"Well, well. Yes, sir! This younger generation!" Harry winked hugely at the studio audience. Several of the adults smiled weakly, but the children sat very still, listening to Jimmy Walls raptly.

"You don't believe me, honest," accused Jimmy. "You're just saying that. You'll see."

Harry felt peculiar. Not worried, or afraid, or anything like that, he assured himself. Of course not. Just—well, *funny*.

"Well, Jimmy," he said, feeling quite clever, "if you kill people, why don't you get caught, eh? Crime doesn't pay, you know! Ha, ha. No, sir. Honesty is the best policy. I guess you listen to old ZNOX and try out everything you hear, hmmm?"

"*That's* not the way." Jimmy Walls looked disgusted.

"How do you do it then?" Harry was getting desperate. "You must be awfully smart."

"I'm not so smart."

Harry Royal worked up a new smile. He glanced at the clock on the wall. Seven minutes to go. He decided to try another angle.

"Then you were just kidding your old Uncle Harry, huh, Jimmy? Ha, ha. You have a lively sense of humor, all right."

"Golly, no." Jimmy Walls tugged nervously at his tight collar. "You don't understand. I've killed *lots* of people."

Harry Royal frowned. Then, remembering himself, he turned it into what would have to pass for a smile. Until the real thing came along, he thought to himself. He felt a little better. Time for the man-to-man angle, he decided.

"Well sir, Jimmy," he said heartily, "you want to be careful with that kind of talk. Yes, sir. Now, *I* understand, of course—old Uncle Harry understands kids pretty well, you bet. But other people might get the wrong idea. Then what will you do?"

"Uncle George will fix it," Jimmy said, after a short pause.

"Uncle George?"

"Uncle George."

Harry Royal felt an unaccustomed chill race down his spine. It felt like a cold centipede with little crystals of ice on its legs. Harry didn't like it. Something was wrong here. He knew it. Maybe Jimmy was just kidding him along—of course he was! Of course. But amateurs—kids at that—seldom carried out a gag over the air, even if they had one planned. There was something about a microphone—

"Uncle George must be quite a man," he heard himself saying.

"Oh gosh, no!" Jimmy protested.

"You mean he isn't remarkable, then?"

"I mean he isn't a *man,* Uncle George isn't."

Harry determined to keep talking. "I see, I see," he said, not seeing in the least. "A blue midget with twelve legs, maybe? Ha, ha." Harry managed a wink for the audience, but he had given up his smile. He noticed that several of the adults were looking startled, and one old lady was frowning her disapproval. That was bad. The children looked awed and envious—a composite picture of shining eyes and open mouths. Fiends, thought Harry.

"He is not a midget with twelve legs, Uncle George isn't," Jimmy Walls declared. "I'd be scared. Uncle George *looks* like a man."

"But he—isn't?" asked Harry, knowing the answer in advance.

"No."

"How do you know?"

"You can tell."

It was a mad conversation—mad for anywhere, but unthinkable for radio. Harry Royal was worried; he'd hear about this. He tried to smooth it over. "Well," he said jovially, "you out there in the radio audience must be having quite a time, ha, ha. Yes, sir. It isn't often that we get a real killer here on *The Boy Next Door,* ha, ha. But I'm sure that you all remember little Bobby Boyle, who slaughtered all those soldiers in Burma, and Stu Dailey from Westmont, who said he was a werewolf. There just isn't any limit to young imaginations, no, sir. Quite a healthy sign, too—-take it from old Harry Royal."

He turned back to Jimmy, who remained perfectly impassive during Harry's speech to the radio audience. "What do you want to be when you grow up, Jimmy?" he asked, searching for a safe subject. "A fireman? A G-Man?"

Jimmy Walls looked thoughtful. Then: "No," he said suddenly. His blue eyes glistened. "I want to be a—"

A horrible thought crossed Harry Royal's mind and he cut Jimmy short. "Let's talk about baseball," he boomed heartily. "Grand old game, baseball. I'll bet you like baseball, eh, Jimmy?" He wouldn't have bet much, he assured himself.

"It's all right, I guess." Jimmy wasn't very enthused.

"I'll bet you get real excited when you listen to a game, don't you?" continued Harry doggedly.

"No," said Jimmy, "It's not near as much fun as—"

"Football," supplied Harry Royal. "Football. Grand old game." He looked grimly at the studio clock. Two minutes to go.

"I didn't mean—" Jimmy began patiently.

"Ha, ha. Of course you didn't mean all that about killing people, Jimmy. Boys will be boys, yes, sir! Old Uncle Harry understands. You don't have to explain to him, no, sir."

For once in his life, Harry Royal didn't know what to say. He winked again at the studio audience and decided to end it before Jimmy started off on another grisly tangent. "Well, Jimmy!" he said cheerfully, "I've sure enjoyed having you up here on *The Boy Next Door,* and I'm sure that all your little friends have enjoyed listening to you, too. I'm sorry that the little old clock tells me that our time is up. Good-by, Jimmy Walls! We hope that you'll be back with us again real soon." Over my dead body, thought Harry.

"Good-by, Mr. Royal," said Jimmy politely.

"Yes, sir," Harry continued. "Ha, ha. We had quite a time this evening here on *The Boy Next Door,* and I hope that all of you enjoyed Jimmy Walls as much as your Uncle Harry did. Yes, sir. You all want to be on hand again tomorrow, same time, same station, when old ZNOX, here in the Hotel Murphy, will again present your favorite program and mine, *The Boy Next Door.* Until then, this is your old friend, Harry Royal, wishing each and every one of you a very pleasant good evening."

Harry signaled the engineer and cut off the microphone. He sighed shortly. What a mess! How could he ever explain it? Of course, it wasn't his fault; he had done all he could. But try to tell that to the brass in the office! He wasn't looking forward to the occasion.

The studio was almost empty now. The silence began to hang heavily over the sound-proofed room, with the only sounds drifting in from the hall outside. As he watched, the last of the audience filed through the door, and the door closed behind him. Even the engineer had left. The silence was complete.

"Mr. Royal?" questioned a small voice.

Harry turned around slowly, hoping against hope that he hadn't identified that voice correctly. But he had. It was Jimmy Walls, sitting in one of the metal chairs on the stage. "What are you doing here?" demanded Harry. He felt distinctly uncomfortable. "Haven't you got a ride home?"

"Yes, sir."

"But it hasn't come yet, is that it?"

"Yes, sir."

"Well, it'll be along shortly," Harry Royal assured him. "It was nice knowing you." He started to leave.

"Mr. Royal?"

Harry stopped. "Yes?" he questioned sharply.

"Mr. Royal, will you wait here with me until my ride comes? I'd be scared in here." Jimmy Walls looked small and afraid in the bright studio lights.

Harry Royal hesitated. He didn't like studios, especially empty ones. They gave him the creeps; they were too quiet. But he was in enough hot water now—if he left the kid in there alone, and the big wigs found out about it, it wouldn't help things any. After all, he told himself, it's just a little kid.

"*You* scared?" he laughed nervously. "That's a good one."

"I'd be scared all by myself, honest, Mr. Royal. Don't leave me here." Jimmy Walls looked up at him imploringly with big, blue eyes.

"Your parents coming here for you?" Harry asked, somewhat mollified.

"No, sir."

"I thought you said you had a ride home."

"I do, sir. Uncle George is coming."

That icy centipede tripped down Harry's spine again. He became acutely aware of the deserted studio, with its empty rows of staring seats. They were utterly alone. No one could hear through those sound-proofed walls. He looked narrowly at the small figure before him—young, blue-eyed.

He's just a kid. Relax!

"Uncle George," said Harry slowly. "That's the one who fixes things up for you?"

"Gosh, yes! He tells me just what to do. He sure is smart!"

"The one who looks like a man, but isn't?" Harry Royal wanted to hear his voice say that. It made him feel better; the whole thing was so ridiculous.

"Oh, you can *tell*."

"You certainly have some imagination, Jimmy." Harry hoped that it was imagination. It had better be imagination. He looked at Jimmy Walls speculatively. Jimmy Walls looked at him the same way.

"You'll be good," Jimmy said suddenly,

Harry felt the silence close in around him. He couldn't laugh, some-how. It wasn't funny any more. He decided that it was time for him to leave, ride or no ride.

Footsteps,

"Here comes Uncle George now," Jimmy said.

The steps paused outside the studio door. Uncle George walked in.

"See?" inquired Jimmy Walls proudly. "He *looks* human."

Harry Royal took a deep breath of relief. Uncle George *was* human. Of course he was! A nice little fat man with a red face who wheezed as he walked. Harry noted the conservative gray suit, the old hickory walking stick.

Jimmy Walls waved happily. "Hi, Uncle George!"

The cheery little fat man grinned at Harry Royal and patted Jimmy affectionately. "Hello, Jimmy my boy! Hello there!" He turned to Harry Royal and extended his hand.

"I'm George Johnson," he chuckled. He had a rich, mellow voice that bubbled with good nature. "I hope I haven't detained you? I heard the broadcast, but was unavoidably detained."

"Uncle George never goes out while the sun is up," Jimmy explained.

George Johnson laughed heartily, shaking Harry's hand. He had a firm, pleasant grip. "I hope Jimmy's talk hasn't upset you," he said solicitously.

"Not at all," lied Harry. "The boy has quite an imagination."

"Yes, yes! Jimmy's quite a talker, aren't you, Jimmy?"

Jimmy Walls squirmed nervously.

"Ha, ha," laughed Harry Royal. "Jimmy's been telling me that you help him kill people." He winked at George Johnson.

"He *does*," insisted Jimmy. "Don't you, Uncle George?"

George Johnson straightened Jimmy's tie for him and laughed jovially. "Now, Jimmy," he admonished. "You say good-by to Mr. Royal."

"Good-by, Mr. Royal," Jimmy said, a gleam of delight in his blue eyes.

"Good-by, Jimmy!" answered Harry Royal, unheeding. He felt fine now. "See you around, Mr. Johnson!"

"Quite possibly, quite possibly," bubbled Uncle George. He steered Jimmy Walls to the door and out of the studio. The happy little fat man turned back to Harry Royal, his red face beaming.

Harry Royal laughed and winked prodigiously.

Uncle George smiled and turned away again.

What is he doing? What is—

Harry Royal's heart pounded treacherously. His face paled suddenly and he clutched desperately at the dead microphone.

Uncle George was *backing* toward him from the studio door. That wasn't so bad. No. But in the exact center of the back of his balding head was a large, blue eye. And it *winked* at him with a hideous regularity, over and over again. Wink—step—wink—step—*wink*—

Harry Royal caught a fleeting glimpse of little Jimmy Walls. His small, eager face peered intently from the studio doorway, shining blue eyes wide in anticipation.

A STAR ABOVE IT

There's no road has not a star above it.
—*Emerson*

I

The room around them was big and solid and familiar. It had a hard-wood maple floor, brightened considerably by several genuine antique Navajo rugs in patterns of warm reds, blacks, and grays. It had soft pine walls, with the knots showing. There were five good paintings, four of them modern and one a Gauguin almost two centuries old. The chairs were comfortable, the one desk substantial.

Wade Dryden leaned forward in his chair. His first reaction was only one of incredulity, but already the back of his mind was grateful for the no-nonsense style of the room. It gave him something to hang onto, and he had a feeling he was going to need it.

"They found *what?*" he asked, knowing well enough that he had heard it correctly the first time.

"Horses," Heinrich Chamisso repeated. His rather thin hand was flat on the desk, motionless except for his thumb. The thumb tapped rapidly, nervously. It was a mannerism that Wade was used to, but it wasn't unduly soothing to the nervous system. "H-o-r-s-e. *Equus caballus.* Old Paint."

Wade kept talking, determined not to allow the silence to fall in on him. "Maybe I got the date wrong, Hank. When did you say they spotted them?"

"The month was June, if you want it in terms of our own calendar." The circles around Chamisso's eyes were heavy, but the eyes themselves were clear and alert. The thumb kept rapping. "The year was 1445. There's no question about the date, Wade—the horses were reported by a regular Survey party, and we double-checked by sending a Security team back. Dave Toney turned in the final certification—you know him?"

"I know him." Wade felt a sinking sensation in the pit of his stomach.

195

"Permit me to anticipate your next request," Chamisso said with a faint smile. "The horses were found in Mexico. Central Mexico, to be precise. And *don't*, please, ask me if I'm trying to be funny. I've got half the World Council on my neck now, and I am not amused."

"What have you done about it?"

Chamisso shrugged. "What can I do? I've got Security teams checking the line from 1300 right on up to the present. All new requests for time permits are being stalled. There are over four hundred screened scholars already in the field, some of them way back in the Mesozoic, and three of 'em even in the Paleozoic; we can't just yank them back, but we're keeping an eye on them."

"All of which is fine and dandy," Wade said. "Of course, it won't solve the problem, will it?"

"Mostly window dressing," Chamisso admitted. "It sounds good to the Council; that's about all."

"Do they know how serious it is?"

"I don't know. I doubt it—but it's only a matter of time, naturally, and please excuse the pun."

"Let me guess the rest," Wade said sourly. "You've held an emergency meeting with the Time Security Commission, and you and Senator Winans have decided that I'll volunteer for the job."

"I'm afraid that's about the size of it, Wade. Maybe we'll squeeze through an appropriation to raise your pension if you get back."

"I'll go alone, I suppose?"

"Sorry—but that *is* the best way to handle it."

Wade Dryden reached down into his coat pocket and extracted a singularly unlovely pipe. He slid a cube of cheap tobacco into it, waited the necessary five seconds for it to ignite, and then blew a shaky smoke ring at nothing in particular. He stood up and began to pace the room, his feet slipping slightly when the Navajo rug skidded on the maple floor. His tall, lanky body seemed to be relaxed, but his narrow, pleasantly ugly face was tense.

"Horses," he said slowly. "Who would do a thing like that?"

Chamisso took a folder out of his desk. He pulled out a three-dimensional photograph and handed it to Wade. He didn't say anything.

Wade Dryden looked at the picture, and shivered.

It was a good photograph, taken for a time passport. The face was sharp and clear in the print; it was like holding a head in your hands.

The face that confronted Wade was smiling, just a little. It was a strong face—firm features, clear blue eyes, an air of comfortable amiability. The hair was white, and neatly combed.

If there was evil in that face, it was too subtle for any camera to catch. The face, trite as it seemed, was a nice face.

That was the chilling part.

"What's his name?"

The thumb tapped on. "Not a very sinister one, I'm afraid. His name is Daniel Hughes; everyone calls him Dan. He's sixty years old, and he's back there on a regular permit, issued by our Cincinnati office. He was screened, of course, and found eminently responsible—*too* responsible, maybe, but that's hindsight. Daniel Hughes is a historian by trade—got a Ph.D. from Harvard, the usual monographs, and the rest of the standard equipment. He's never been in any real trouble. He's well thought of in his profession. He's a specialist on the early high cultures of Middle and South America, particularly Central Mexico."

"Ummm." Wade looked at the picture again. "He's got all his marbles, I presume?"

"He's sane." Chamisso frowned. "He has a reputation for being on an even keel—very stable, easy-going, something of a plodder."

"He sure doesn't *look* like a guy who would try a stunt like that."

"How do you know?" Chamisso smiled coldly. "No one ever *tried* a stunt like this before, or even one remotely resembling it. Different kinds of crimes attract different sorts of personalities."

"You'd call *this* a crime?"

"Legally, yes. What else can I call it?"

Wade laughed. "I guess you'd call a guy who sets fire to the world a pyromaniac."

"I guess I would."

He looked at Chamisso, who met his gaze squarely. Wade shook his head. He'd known Charmisso for thirty years, and the man still surprised him.

Wade dropped the photograph back in the folder, returned to his chair, and sat down. He inspected his pipe to make certain that the fine ash in the bowl had disintegrated, then stuck the pipe in his pocket.

"Where did he get the horses?" he asked. "How many does he have?"

"He's got about fifty," Chamisso said. "Both mares and stallions. That number is not absolutely certain, but it's close. We don't know where he got them. We've been running down the line trying to find out, natu-rally—but no luck so far."

"He couldn't have had them with him when he left, could he? I don't think even the Cincinnati office could overlook fifty head of horses."

Chamisso changed hands, and his other thumb took up the incessant rapping. "No, he didn't have them at this end. There's been some fiddle-faddle somewhere along the line, of course, and somebody's head is going to roll for it, but that's not your problem. He must have stopped off some-where—it might have been 1900, 1800, anywhere—and picked 'em up on the way back. How that could have happened without any report being filed on it I don't know—but I will know."

"He could have gotten them in Europe in 1445," Wade suggested.

"Possible, yes. Probable, no. Columbus was still half a century away, and I'm sure he didn't swim those horses across the damn ocean."

Wade frowned. "There were even horses in America once, weren't there? Native ones. I mean?"

"That's a thought. There *were* horses in the New World, but they were extinct around the end of the Pleistocene. He *might* have picked up some horses back there, but it would have been almost impossible—he would have to had to domesticate wild stallions all by his lonesome, and then haul them maybe twenty thousand years from the end of the Pleistocene to 1445. I can't see that, frankly. Anyway, *how* he got them there isn't the question. The horses are there. That's all you need to know."

Wade leaned forward. "Hank, how serious do you think it is? On the level?"

The thumb stopped tapping. "We've been living with the cobalt bomb for over a century," Chamisso said. His rather frail body suddenly looked old behind his desk. "It hasn't gone off, thank God—but it *could* go off. Those horses are a time bomb, Wade, and I use the term intentionally. They *may* fizzle on their own—even with Daniel Hughes monkeying with the fuse. Their effect *may* be localized, and cancel itself out before it gets to us. But 1445 in Central Mexico is just about the right distance away from 1520, and that means Cortes. If we don't wipe this thing out now—wipe it out completely—there's a very good chance that our civilization will disappear, and us with it. That's how serious I think it is."

The words deepened the anxiety that Wade already felt. "You don't think a team would work better? Suppose I make a mistake?"

"Don't make a mistake," Chamisso said flatly. The thumb resumed its tapping. "In a situation like this, the less disturbance we make the greater our chances for success are. That means one man, at least at first. We've got human lives to think about, Wade; we can't fool around with per-sonal preferences. You know that."

Wade took a deep breath. He knew. "Okay, Hank. We'll play it your way. Where do I start?"

"Right here." Chamisso nodded at the folder. "First, you digest what we've got on Hughes. After that, I want you to go to some people who knew him—his wife is still here, by the way—and get your own impres-sions, Daniel Hughes is the key to this whole thing, and you'll have to know how to handle him. When you think you're ready—and take all the time you need, so long as it isn't over two weeks—we'll set you down smack on his roof in 1445, if he's got a roof. Then you're on your own. We'll have a Security squad standing by, but don't call on them unless it's absolutely necessary. If you slip up we'll have to send a really big team in to patch things up and remold the culture—and that just might not work at all."

Wade looked again at the smiling, white-haired man in the photograph.

Chamisso nodded. "Kill him if you have to," he said.

Wade scooped up the folder, left the room, and hurried outside to his copter.

The April sky was a wonderfully fragile blue, and there were no clouds to mask the warm Arizona sun. Wade lifted his copter to five thousand feet and let it drift on automatic. Green, irrigated farmland slipped by below him, and the desert was all dressed up in its Sunday best—caught in the first flush of spring, the cold winds of winter already forgotten, the searing heat of summer only a distant memory.

He spread the folder out on the counter before him, anchoring it under plastic against the breeze, and set the pages to turn slowly. He scanned the material, not trying to remember everything yet, but absorbing impressions.

The sun relaxed him; its heat tingled the back of his neck and warmed his shoulders. He could smell the land far below him—green and fresh from the spotty patches of irrigation, spiced with the strangely damp scent of sand from the desert. The air was quiet around him, his copter only a thin hum in the silence.

He thought about horses. Horses in Mexico, in 1445.

Every great technological advance made by mankind seemed to carry with it the seeds of man's destruction—or, as Wade had always felt, seemed to require a more mature responsibility on the part of its creators. Time travel had been possible for forty years, ever since they had "lost" that week at Cal Tech in 2040, and now it had turned on them for the third time.

Twice before, it had almost happened—by accident.

This time it was deliberate.

The folder contained a great deal of information about Daniel Hughes, and included abstracts of several of his monographs. One was titled *The Influence of Urbanism on the Folk Society in Central America after Teotihuacan.* Another was called *Cultural Unity and the Classical Toltecs.* Both were sound, scholarly works; hardly the products of a maniac.

Daniel Hughes was definitely not going to be any pushover.

Wade let the estimates of others filter through his mind. He saw the image of Daniel Hughes as seen by his wife, his professional associates, his neighbors. The impressions seemed consistent, and altogether unremarkable.

Therefore, they were wrong.

No one had really known Daniel Hughes—for the thing that he had done simply could not have been considered, much less carried out, by the rather colorless scholar portrayed in the folder.

Wade knew he would have to do better than that in his own interviewing.

The things he had to know were not in the folder.

The photograph came up again, and Wade held it stationary under the plastic.

The pleasant, smiling face looked at him, blandly.

Wade studied it again, then closed the folder. He set the copter controls for Ohio, and leaned back, grateful for the sun.

He looked down on the flowing horizon ahead of him, but he saw another kind of horizon.

The gray barrier of Time—deep beyond imagination, shadowed beyond comprehension.

Waiting.

II

The city of Columbus was like most of the cities he had known, although the total effect was not as depressing as in the neighboring cities of Cleveland or Cincinnati. It had the usual air of emptiness, of abandonment, and whole sections of old middle-class housing had been taken over by semi-nomadic squatters, who moved from city-shell to city-shell as the mood struck them.

All cities, of course, were anachronisms. The ancient threat of nuclear warfare had helped matters along, but the combination of automatic industries virtually run by computers and cheap, fast transport powered by solar energy had rendered the city obsolete.

Cities had been born from necessities: employment, protection, efficiency. When the necessities no longer existed, men returned to a more congenial way of life. Small, clean villages dotted the countryside, in which a man could get to know the people who went through life with him. Houses went up where there was land around them, and people could see the sky and the earth and hear the music of cool streams and restless winds.

The cities remained, but they were dying. Little by little, step by step, the trees and the grasses that had been briefly sheeted with sterile concrete and steel crept back—green shoots pushing up through unused streets, strong and patient roots digging beneath the gray foundations of the cities, finding earth.

A good many psychiatrists found themselves with nothing to do.

Columbus still retained a semblance of life, since it was held together by the machinery of the state government and by the old, tradition-coated campus of Ohio State.

Wade smiled at the quite handsome face of Dr. Frederick Clements, chairman of the history department, and wondered what it felt like to have an office in a city.

"What can you tell me about Daniel Hughes?" he asked.

Dr. Clements built delicate pyramids with his slender fingers and assumed an expression of considerable profundity. He managed to convey an air of tolerant distraction, as though he were making a small sacrifice of time from some Genuinely Important Research Project. Actually, he wasn't much of a research man; he was departmental chairman because he was a good politician and liked committee meetings, but he never thought of himself as anything but a dedicated scholar.

"I find it hard to believe that Dr. Hughes is involved in anything— ah—unsavory," Dr. Clements said.

"I didn't say he was."

"Come now, Mr. Dryden! You are the third Security man who has interviewed me about Hughes in a week. I am quite capable of putting two and two together in such a manner that the sum is four."

Bully for you, Wade thought. "Ever have any trouble with Hughes? Any—well, incidents?"

"No. Dr. Hughes did his work well and faithfully. He taught his classes in person, you know. He was not what you might call aggressive in his research—seemed quite content with his solid but unspectacular reputation. His students liked him."

"How about his private life?"

"I'm sorry, but the University makes it a point of policy not to pry into the personal lives of its faculty members. I can't give you any valid testimony on what Dr. Hughes may or may not have done apart from his academic career."

"You weren't personal friends, I take it?"

Dr. Clements hesitated. "I had the greatest admiration for Dr. Hughes," he said finally.

"I see. As a historian, what do you think of Hughes's work? Are you in agreement with it—the fundamental orientation of it, that is?"

Clements eyed him curiously. "I'm not sure I follow you."

Wade pressed his point. "You were associated with Hughes for a good many years, Dr. Clements. A man of your eminence might be supposed to have formed some, shall we say, points of difference? I understand that you are interested in the science of history?"

Clements took the bait. "That's rather shrewd of you, really. I had always rather felt—off the record, you understand—that Dr. Hughes didn't really believe in some of his own work. History, you see, is a product of cause and effect, like everything else. Therefore, it can be reduced to processual forms—you follow me? The alternative, we feel, is to regard man as somehow a supernatural being, not subject to the basic principles upon which our universe operates. Now, Dr. Hughes never argued with these postulates, at least overtly. His monographs, I must say, are quite scholarly—even a bit—ah—*dry*, if I may say so. In conversation, however, he was more interested in people—you know. He even tried once to write a novel, I believe."

Ah, thought Wade. *Paydirt*. "Was it published? Under some other name, maybe?"

Dr. Clements shook his head. "As far as I know, it was never finished."

"Did you read any of it?"

"No. I wasn't that—close—to Dr. Hughes. He never even discussed the book with me." There was a faint hurt in Clements' voice, and Wade liked the man a little better for it.

"Who would you say his best friend was, sir? Some historian?"

"I don't think so." Clements leaned back in his chair. "He didn't seem to associate much with his professional colleagues, although he was always pleasant enough with us." He smiled a little. "He used to get long letters from a chap in Canada. He'd read them in his office between classes, and laugh so hard it was really a bit—well, strange, you know."

"What was his name?"

"Karpenter. Herbert *Kay* Karpenter."

"The poet?"

"Yes, I believe it's the same one—Dr. Hughes used to get advance copies of his books from the publisher; I noticed them several times."

"I see. I want to thank you, Dr. Clements, and I hope we won't have to bother you again. You've been most helpful."

Clements smiled. "I enjoyed talking to you, Mr. Dryden. I hope everything turns out all right."

"So do I," Wade said.

The next day, he was in Canada.

The log house, which was a sophisticated version of a log cabin as it might have been envisioned by the legendary Frank Lloyd Wright, was on a tiny island set in a glassy cove of one of those emerald lakes which dot the great Canadian pine forests.

The island looked natural, but it was hard to tell.

Wade landed his copter in the rocky yard, took a good swallow of the fresh, pine-scented air, and knocked on the plank door.

After three minutes, he knocked again.

The door opened. A big man looked out at him with neither interest nor surprise. He was dressed in rough, unpressed clothes, and he could have used a shave and a haircut. The muscles in his arms did not come from pushing a pen, and his deep blue eyes were squinted slightly, as though in protection from cold winds and sunlight glinting off lake waters.

"Are you Mr. Herbert Kay Karpenter?"

"I'm Herb." His voice was loud and direct. "If you want my autograph, it'll cost you ten thousand dollars and a kick in the pants."

Wade grinned. "I'm Wade Dryden; I called you last night."

"Oh. About Dan. Come on in."

Herb Karpenter led Wade into his house, which was neat and clean and stuffed with books. They went through a surprisingly large living room, which had a wonderful rock fireplace and a superb buck head on the wall, and into Karpenter's study—a small, simple room filled with a desk and a litter of seemingly unrelated objects: books, tapes, stereos, a human skull, a cypress knee polished to a reddish sheen, a fly rod with the line thoroughly tangled on the reel.

"Sit down, Wade," the poet said, clearing one of the chairs with a sweep of his brown hand.

Wade sat down. The room virtually demanded a pipe, so he took his out and lit it.

"Dan's in trouble, is he?" Karpenter said, leaning against a window that looked out on a rather scrubby pine and the cold, clean water. "What's he done?"

Wade liked Karpenter already, and had made a mental note to read some of his work. He wanted very much to tell him the truth, but that was impossible. If the news ever got out, there would be a panic, and in a panic anything could happen.

"Sorry, Herb, but the law won't let me be very specific. Daniel Hughes *is* in trouble, yes. I'm trying to find out *why* he's in trouble. There's a chance I can get him out of it."

Karpenter chewed his lip. "Dan Hughes," he said slowly, "is a horse's fanny."

"More so than the rest of us?"

"I think so." Karpenter dropped into a chair, pretty well obliterating it. "Dan's got no more business being a historian than Thomas Wolfe would have had."

"Who's Thomas Wolfe?"

"Novelist—back around 1930. He wrote huge, sprawling, magnificent books. His stuff had life in it. You'll come around to his stuff sooner or later, if you live deep enough."

"Ummm. Dan was like this Wolfe?"

"No. But he might have been."

"I see."

"Like hell you do. Never mind, though. Dan was a guy like a lot of others I've known. He didn't have enough guts to do what he wanted to do, so he trapped himself in the old academic rat race. Result: competence. He never amounted to a hill of beans."

"I thought you were his best friend."

"I am." Karpenter picked up an eraser and flicked it at the wall. "You trying to say that you can't understand a man and like him too?"

"I guess not." Wade retreated briefly to his pipe. Karpenter's bluntness made him a little hard to get used to. "Did he want to write, is that it?"

"I don't know. He thought so, on and off."

"Did you read his novel?"

"I read what there was of it, yes. He called it *A Window on the Stars*. I told him to burn it."

"You didn't like it?"

"My friend, it stank."

"What was it about?"

"It was one of those impressionistic, stream-of-consciousness things. It was what I like to call a *whither* book. You know—Whither Man? Whither our tiny celestial sphere? Whither childhood and the little furry creatures of the forests? Whither whither? Claptrap."

"Could you be a little more specific?"

"No. Dan wasn't in that book. That's why it was what it was."

"Herb, what *was* Dan like? I've got to know."

Karpenter shrugged. "He doesn't fit into any slot," he said. "That was his problem, maybe. He had a mind—a good mind, an independent mind. He asked good questions. He liked to fish. He had a wife; he didn't love her. No kids. He was nervous most of the time, tense. He tolerated his work. He got drunk once in a while—usually here—and he was a good guy. Dan lacked roots, if you'll excuse the expression. He never quite found what he was looking for, because he never had a solid platform to look from. Hell, I don't know what Dan was like. He wasn't simple. One thing about people, you know—they can't be summed up too glibly. People surprise you sometimes, thank God."

"I hope I can get him back."

"Maybe he'd be happier where he is."

"I'll do my best, Herb."

Karpenter stood up. "You're not married, are you?"

"No," Wade said, surprised. "How'd you know?"

Karpenter smiled. "I'm a poet, man. Come on out in the kitchen and meet Faye. She'll have the coffee ready by now."

Karpenter's wife was a delightful person: not beautiful in any conventional sense, but she brightened the whole house. Her devotion to Karpenter was frank and open, and he returned it with interest.

The coffee was delicious.

Karpenter escorted him to the door. "When all this is over," he said, "you come on back and see us. We'll see if we're smarter than the trout."

"Thanks, Herb. I appreciate it."

The two men shook hands.

Wade looked at the warm house and the clean lake and the ferns growing between the rocks.He felt a regret deep down inside, a regret he had not felt so keenly for many years.

He climbed into his copter, took off into a twilight sky, and flew south into darkness.

The wife of Daniel Hughes, while her husband was in the field, had gone to live with a sister in California.

She greeted Wade with courtesy, and served him weak tea with evident pride, but it was obvious that she couldn't tell him much about Daniel Hughes. She was thin, wore clothes that had a retiring, apologetic air, and she was grimly interested in the Universal Minders, one of the several thousand lunatic-fringe metaphysical groups in Southern California.

"Did your husband seem at all—unusual—the last time you saw him, Mrs. Hughes?"

"Oh, no, no. Poor Daniel!" she said vaguely, "I was not feeling well, not at *all* well—my fever, you know—and dear Daniel was so thoughtful, getting his own breakfast and all. I really haven't been myself for some years, ever since—"

"I see," Wade broke in, smiling to show how sympathetic he was. "He was quite happy, was he?"

"Poor Daniel! Happy? Oh, yes, I suppose. So lost in his books, you know how scholars are! Sometimes he hardly knew I was in the house. And me with my fever, and it being so *difficult* for me to get around and all—"

"Yes indeed. Mrs. Hughes, do you perhaps remember a book your husband started to write, called *A Window on the Stars?*"

"Oh my, yes. That was dear Daniel's novel. He was quite excited about it once, I remember, though it hardly seemed *worthy* of him. I mean, not like his *serious* work, if you know what I mean. I really couldn't get through it—you mustn't tell him this—although I tried for just days and days—"

"Well, thank you very much, Mrs. Hughes. You've been very helpful to us."

She fingered her handkerchief. "Daniel—he's not in any—I mean, he hasn't *done* anything, has he?"

"Of course not. This is just a routine check. Don't you worry about him."

"He's so careless sometimes." She looked away, lost in herself. "If he should need me, Mr. Dryden—you will call me?"

Wade took her hand. Daniel Hughes had never needed his wife, or had never thought he did. "We'll call you," he said.

He finished his tea and left.

The copter lifted into a California fog, and Wade flew eastward toward Arizona.

He had done what he could here.

Now, he had to go back. Back to Daniel Hughes.

III

The Time Security Commission maintained what was technically known as an Orientation Center in Arizona, not far from the unique beauty of Oak Creek Canyon. Wade had never heard the Center referred to by its proper name; it was known as the Pumphouse to almost everyone except confirmed bureaucrats.

No one, of course, was permitted to travel in time unless he knew his stuff backwards and forwards. If a man wanted to go to Rome in the time of Cicero, he had to demonstrate a thorough knowledge of Latin and he had to understand the mores and folkways of Italy in the century before Christ.

One mistake was too many, if you were fooling with time. The unguessed consequences of a single action might well destroy a civilization—and it might be *your* civilization.

Given millennia, little things could snowball.

The Pumphouse existed to make mistakes almost impossible. It accepted no man at his own valuation; it took him in and pumped him full of what he had to know.

Wade spent ten days in the vaults of the Center, ten days in which he never regained consciousness. He lay on his back in a sealed room, and every six hours a food capsule was placed in his mouth and a glass of water trickled down his throat. He was drugged to the gills, completely receptive, and machines fed data into him through tiny electrodes fastened to his skull.

It was an eerie business, but theoretically you weren't supposed to remember any of it.

Just the same, Wade had had more than his share of nightmares after sessions in the Pumphouse.

For ten days, the machines were never silent.

He learned the language as it had been at that time and in that place: mostly Nahuatl, of course, but with a smattering of other Indian tongues. He learned the important cycles of the calendrical system, and he learned the sacred almanac, the tonalpohualli. He came to know the gods, and what they were like: Huitzilopochtli, the God of War, the Tlaloques, gods of the rain, and Tonatiuh, the Sun God, together with a thousand others. He learned the street plan of Tenochtitlan, and how to grow crops in the chinampas, the floating gardens.

The social system became a part of him, and he understood the priests and the farmers and what it meant to be an Eagle Knight. He learned how to chip obsidian, and what to do about a witch.

Most important of all, he learned how it *felt* to be alive in Central Mexico in the year 1445.

He felt the pride and the cruelty and the dignity and the laughter.

He came to understand why a man might go to his own sacrifice with joy in his heart, and how a priest felt looking down on his people from the summit of a stained pyramid. . . .

When Wade left the Pumphouse, he was in part a different man, and would be for the rest of his life.

Heinrich Chamisso shook hands with him at the Jump Box.

"That's quite a feather cloak you've got there; you be careful of it."

Wade smiled, his teeth white against the artificial copper of his skin. He looked decidedly strange. He was dressed in a long black robe, and his hair was matted with dried blood. His ears were shredded at the lobes. He had a feather cloak of black around his shoulders.

"Good luck, Wade."

"Be back in a century or three, Hank; don't wait up for me."

Wade stepped into the Jump Box and threw the relays that sealed the door.

He sat down in an armchair, carefully arranging his cloak so as not to crush the feathers, and waited.

The date was April 28, 2080.

The lights dimmed, briefly, and the year was no longer 2080.

He sat back and tried to relax.

From the inside, the Jump Box resembled nothing so much as a small apartment. The lead walls were painted a light, cheerful blue, and there was a bed, a bathroom, and a mirror. There were two pictures, chosen primarily for their utter lack of distinction. There was a shelf full of books, all of them relatively humorous in tone.

The Box always reminded Wade of a dentist's office.

He closed his eyes, wishing he could have taken his pipe along. It would take him four hours to go back in 1445, and there was nothing for him to do but wait. There was no window to look out of, and nothing to see if there had been one.

His thoughts raced ahead of him.

His mind threaded its way back through the tangled webs of history, back beyond Hiroshima and Lincoln and herds of bison on the Plains, back beyond the time of the white man in America, back to the mountains and the jungles of Mexico before there was a Mexico . . .

Back from 2080 to 1445—only a little more than six centuries, some 635 years, and the United States did not even exist in imagination.

Back along the time stream—

Back to Daniel Hughes.

Time travel, he thought, was a curious business—curious and yet shielded in an almost classic simplicity.

For many years, long before travel in time became a practical possibility, thinkers of various persuasions had gotten a kick out of fooling around with some of the supposed implications of time travel. Some had been serious, some only playful, but almost all of them had concerned themselves with riddles and paradoxes of one kind or another. They worried the idea, as a cat might worry a mouse.

Suppose, they said, that you went back in time and murdered your own grandfather? (A good many of the writers, Wade had always thought, exhibited homicidal tendencies at odd moments.)

Suppose that there were parallel time streams, alternate lines of possibility?

Suppose you met yourself somewhere in time?

The reality was at once simpler and more subtle.

There are no paradoxes in nature, unless man himself is a paradox. Paradoxes exist only in logical systems, in philosophical concepts—in short, only in the minds of men.

The tortoise, singularly unconcerned with the speculations of Zeno, keeps right on losing all races with the hare.

In a way, time travel was like that.

The oldest dream of all had failed to come true: the future remained a blank wall, utterly inaccessible. In a very real sense, the future did not yet exist at any given time; that was why it was the future. Since it did not exist, it could not be penetrated. There was always a chance that there *wasn't* any future.

There was only one way to move into the future. Every man, woman, and child on the Earth was a time traveller all his life—indeed, this was the very meaning of life. Together, and yet each alone, all human beings moved into the future, step by step, second by second, *at a constant rate that could not be altered.*

The past existed, because it had happened. It was there, written in the record.

The present existed: a tiny fluid bubble of activity, pushed along on the very tips of rigid, telescoping pencils of past development. The present, of course, was hardly more than an idea; it came and went with such speed that it was impossible to grip it, hold it, stop it, and say, "Now, right *now,* this instant, is the present." Even as you spoke, present became past.

Nevertheless, the microsecond of the present was crucial. Normally, in all of history there was only one point at which change could occur—in the flashing instant of the present.

What happened if the past was changed?

Suppose, for example, that Rome had been wiped out while still a village. Suppose the Etruscans had never lived. Suppose that there had been no Roman Empire. What then?

The answer was simple enough, on the surface. There *had* been a Roman Empire in the past that led to the present known by Wade Dryden, That *could not* be changed.

If it was changed, somehow, then this present was impossible.

What was impossible ceased to exist.

It *looked* like a paradox, yes. If the past existed, it could not be altered and still be the same past, leading to the same future. What happened?

Computers gave the answer.

Imagine a vast tree, with many branches. Imagine a root to this tree, a deep root that cannot be killed except by digging up the root itself. Imagine twigs and leaves, each unique.

Picture a woodman and an axe. Picture the axe chopping through the trunk of the tree, changing it.

Graphically enough, the phenomenon was known to the temporal scientists as Cutoff.

From the point at which the trunk was chopped, the tree falls. All the old branches and leaves still exist, but they are dead. The upper tree, once alive, is now just so much wood: it cannot live on the new base. It exists as a dead log. It is forgotten. It rots.

At the point of Cutoff, a new tree begins to grow from the living root. It may be a similar tree, but it will not be the *same* tree.

The moral of all this, if you happen to have your nest in the upper branches, is clear.

Woodman, spare that tree!

Wade glanced at his watch. Two hours had gone by, inside the Jump Box. Outside, to the extent that the term had any meaning while in the stress field, over three centuries had whispered by in the shadows. Where was he, or *when* washe? 1776? 1700?

No matter.

He shifted his position in the chair, and tried to fight off the nervousness that was growing within him.

Once Daniel Hughes had gone back to 1445, with the horses, he was there, part of the past. He could not, therefore, be stopped before he started.

There are no paradoxes in time travel.

What did those horses mean?

The first rule for a traveller in time was this: *don't be different.*

If you go back to Crete in the days when her people were the wonders of the world, you must think as they thought, look as they looked, and above all *do* as they do.

Don't change anything. Leave it *exactly* as you found it.

Altruism? Hardly.

The word was survival.

Consider those horses: horses in Mexico, in 1445.

There were no horses in the Americas in 1445, of course—not in the past that had led to the present in which Wade Dryden lived. The horse had been extinct there since the end of the Pleistocene, and would not reappear until the Spanish landed in 1519 at the site of Vera Cruz.

How important was the horse?

Well, there were at least three high civilizations in the New World before the Spanish came. The Maya had invented the concept of zero before the Hindus, and the Inca culture of Peru had actually entered the Bronze Age.

Culture evolves as energy is harnessed. Throughout the Americas, from the Eskimos of the North to the Ona of the South, the Indians were severely handicapped by their lack of efficient domesticated animals. They were growing corn by 4000 B.C., but domesticated animals were limited to the dog and the llama, together with such curiosities as the guinea pig and the turkey. Both the dog and the llama—and the related alpaca— were utilized for purposes of transportation, but they are ill-suited for the job, except under highly specialized conditions.

It is easy enough to attribute this lack of effective domesticated animals to some sort of ignorance or cultural mysticism; the facts, however, lie elsewhere. You can't domesticate a cow if there are no cattle. You can't tame a horse if there are no horses.

The New World abounded in game—deer, rabbits, bear, cats. But the *necessary* animals just didn't happen to be there. The bison, which looked like a possibility, could not be domesticated, even by much later scientific experimenters in the twentieth-century United States.

How important was the horse?

Look at the Plains Indians. Before they obtained horses from the Spanish, the fabled Indian of the American West hardly existed. No American

Indian rode a horse before 1600. The Cheyenne were growing crops in Minnesota. The Comanche were a poor Shoshonean tribe in the Great Basin. The Dakota Sioux, symbols of the Plains, were farmers from the Mississippi Valley.

The bison, or buffalo, was a source of food before the horse, but not a rich and dependable source. And the bison was the key to the Plains Indian known to American history. When the government killed the bison, they killed the Indian.

The horse came, from the Spanish in New Mexico. A cultural explosion took place. The Plains Indians became rich in food, and mobile enough to be dangerous. Many diverse peoples moved out onto the Plains. Still in the Stone Age, without knowledge of the motivations or techniques of organized European warfare, they fought the United States to a standstill until after the Civil War.

General Custer could well thank the horse for what happened to him that day on the Little Big Horn.

Now, suppose the horse had been introduced into a really *high* culture, before the Spanish arrived on the scene?

Cortes and his men had no easy time of it at first, despite their triggering of a native revolt against Montezuma II. Cortes, as shrewd and effective a general as ever lived, was defeated time and time again, his army cut to pieces, and he was only saved from disaster by the staunch support of his Tlaxcalan allies, who far outnumbered his own men. He finally subdued Tenochtitlan by shutting off the canals and starving the city out.

If there had been horses in Mexico in 1445, the story would have been different. There would have been cavalry, and, more importantly, a genuine empire held together, as was Rome's, by rapid transport.

The wheel would have been more than a toy.

The toughest culture in the New World would not have been decapitated in 1521. It might have held off the thinly extended Spanish ships for a century; it might have *never* been beaten.

With such a past, obviously, the world Wade knew in 2080 could not exist.

Therefore, those horses *must* be canceled out before they could take effect. Daniel Hughes had to be stopped, cold.

The Jump Box halted. A green light flashed.

Wade did not allow himself to hesitate. He unsealed the door and stepped outside. He knew exactly where he was, and he felt it all around him.

Surely, one of the strangest cultures the world had ever seen.

Central Mexico, in 1445. The Aztecs.

IV

He stood in a clump of trees just south of Coyoacan. Bright sunshine filtered down through the leaves, and the air was warm. There was dampness from the lake, however, and he knew that by evening it would be cold enough to be uncomfortable.

He stepped clear of the trees and followed a wide path to the little village of Coyoacan. He did not pause there, but started at once across the causeway that led north over the blue waters of Lake Texcoco.

Canoes dotted the lake and the causeway itself had a scattering of foot traffic. Most of the Indians he saw were men, who wore their hair long, and who were simply dressed in loin-cloths, together with mantles knotted on one shoulder and leather sandals. Those common tribesmen gave him a wide berth, and Wade kept his eyes straight ahead. One wealthy merchant, ornately dressed and sporting ornaments of jade and turquoise, ventured to address him. Wade returned the greeting briefly, but did not linger for conversation.

His priest's robes, of course, gave him a certain immunity to small-talk—and most citizens were content to remain as inconspicuous as possible in his presence.

The open water on both sides of him gradually gave way to patches of green, little mud islands planted with garden crops and tended by farmers from poled dugouts. The floating farms shortly became continuous and quite solid, as roots took hold in the lake floor, and the lake itself was reduced to twin canals that bordered the causeway.

Adobe huts were sprinkled over the farms, and ahead of him, framed by the volcanic craters of distant mountains, Wade could see more substantial houses.

He saw more people now: officials crowned with feathers, idlers, runners with tumplines. Boatloads of food floated in the canals, moving slowly into the city.

More than three hundred thousand people, Wade knew, lived in the city before him. This was no simple village. And yet, the quiet was astonishing. There was only the smooth ripple of water in the canals, the rustle of breeze from the mountains, the fragile hum of low voices. There were canals instead of roads, and in all the city there was not a single wheeled vehicle or pack animal.

He heard laughter from a red-washed patio, and caught the slaps of hands shaping tortillas.

There were more priests now, and the smell of incense in the balmy air. Some of them eyed Wade curiously, but he was not molested. One of the advantages of urban life, he reflected, was that it was impossible for everyone to know everyone else.

He walked on, and now he caught the odor of something besides incense. He knew what it was, but nonetheless he started when he saw the skull racks. There were four of them, poles set into a temple courtyard, and there were thousands of human skulls threaded like vertebrae on the stakes.

It was no wonder that the people gave a priest all the walking room he needed.

Passing through a great open plaza, where temple-dotted pyramids reached upward toward the sun and the palace of the war-chief, Montezuma I sprawled across one corner, Wade walked on beside the canal until he came to the Tlaltelolco market: a square of polished pavement, ringed with shadowed alcoves where merchants displayed their wares. Vegetables, mats, obsidian tools, feathers, jewels—each had its special place. Patient Indian women bargained and bartered, sometimes using cacao beans, and the scene had a curiously timeless, peaceful quality to it in the late afternoon sunlight.

Even here, however, the dominant motif of Aztec society could not be escaped. Past a double wall from the market were the temples of Tlaltelolco, and in the center of these buildings reared the huge pyramid of the War God, topped by a twin shrine to the squat Huitzilopochtli and the obsidian-eyed Tezcatlipoca.

The pyramids cast long, black shadows.

Wade felt oddly displaced in time. The city around him was vividly real—he could see it, hear it, smell it, feel it. The people he saw were alive and human—children, women, warriors, noblemen, slaves. There was laughter here, and horror too.

And yet he felt as though he were walking through history, as if all that he saw was somehow lost in the dust of centuries. He had walked along the route that Cortes would one day follow into the city of Tenochtitlan, the chief city of the Aztecs. And in the centuries that were still to come, Lake Texcoco would be dry and the island city of Tenochtitlan would become Mexico City, capital of Mexico, and in the fullness of time another Indian named Zapata would ride again against the Spanish. . . .

There was a sadness here, and the weight of years.

Wade shook off the mood that had gripped him. Unless he moved, and moved fast, the history he had known would die, and a fresh history would grow from the roots of the Aztec world around him.

He kept his face impassive and walked past a rack of grinning skulls into the gloom of a large temple.

There was a surprising lack of space inside the temple. While generous enough in its overall dimensions, the massive walls took up most of the room; since the Aztecs lacked the true arch, it took some doing to support the ornate roof structures. A little light filtered in between the pillars, but it was not a pleasant place.

Wade ignored a group of children being instructed in the mysteries of the priesthood and walked into a small chamber in the right side of the temple.

The priest was there: a short, somewhat plump man with sharp, dangerous black eyes.

Wade greeted him formally and did his level best to act as though he had every right to be where he was.

"Well?" the priest said in Nahuatl.

Wade hammed it up a little; it wouldn't hurt to be dramatic. "I am in the service of Tezcatlipoca at Texcoco," he replied in the same language. "I come to you as a brother, for you are known to be wise."

The priest snorted, unimpressed. "You have some purpose in coming to our temple, Texcocan?"

"I have brought you a message," Wade said sonorously. "I have seen omens, and other things."

The priest folded his arms. The black eyes looked anything but gullible. "Speak, then."

Wade did it up brown. "In this, the age Four Earthquake," he intoned, "I have had strange dreams and seen strange things in my city. I have seen in a dream a stranger coming among us, bringing horrible four-legged monsters such as I had never seen before. I have seen, only today, such a man in our city, and with him were fifty devil-beasts." He watched the priest narrowly, but it was impossible to tell whether the man knew what he was talking about or not. Surely, he must know about Hughes by now? "I tell you, brother priest of Tezcatlipoca, that these demons have been sent among us by Mictlantecuhtli, Lord of the Dead. This stranger says he is our friend, but he comes to lead us all to the land given over to the dead."

"What has that to do with us?" the priest asked, his voice emotionless. "You speak of Texcoco; this is Tlaltelolco."

He smiled coldly and played on an ancient antagonism. The advantages of hindsight were considerable, he reflected—for he knew what the priest could not knew, namely that Tenochtitlan would conquer and assimilate Tlaltelolco in a relatively few years. "This man of whom I speak," he said, "speaks in dreams to Montezuma of Tenochtitlan—and not only in dreams. He trains Montezuma's warriors in the use of the devil beasts, and he covets the temple of Tezcatlipoca in Tlaltelolco."

The priest stirred, and Wade knew he had struck home. The rivalry between Tlaltelolco and Tenochtitlan was becoming serious, and suspicions were easily aroused. "What do you want?" the priest asked bluntly.

Wade dodged that one and threw out a cloud of prophecy. "I say this to you, brother-priest: this man and the devil beasts must be destroyed. If they are not sent back to the Lord of the Dead, birds shall fly with mirrors in their heads. When the New Fire Ceremony comes ten years from now, your people will fast but the corn shall not grow. You will scarify your children, but the rain shall not come. When next the New Fire is kindled on the Hill of the Star, the fire will die and darkness everlasting shall forever reign over the land."

The priest seemed impressed; it was hard to say. Wade didn't tell him that there were going to be severe crop failures between 1451 and 1456, due to storms and frost, but when they came he knew his words would be remembered.

"I should like some evidence of what you say," the priest said. Whatever else he may have been, the man was no mystic.

Wade lowered his voice., "Within one day, the demon beasts will kill their victims in Texcoco. If they are not stopped, they will come here as well." He eyed the priest and added a practical note. "They threaten our positions," he said.

The black eyes of the priest were inscrutable.

Wade was getting uneasy; this boy wasn't swallowing everything by a long shot.

"Tell the others," Wade said. "Do not mistake my power."

He dropped two smoke pills to the stone floor behind him, and backed rapidly out through the puffs of black smoke that instantly filled the chamber.

He got outside before the priest could recover from the shock, and lost himself in the milling crowds in the plaza. So many priests were around that he was not conspicuous.

Step One had been completed, although he had no idea how successful he had been. Aztec society was a theocracy, run by the elaborate priesthood. If the priests were against you, your name was capital M-U-D.

He hurried to the shore of Lake Texcoco, appropriated a large canoe, and paddled eastward in the hush of twilight.

Ahead lay Texcoco, with its poet-king, Nezahualcoyotl.

And ahead lay the man he had come to find, Daniel Hughes.

The moon floated redly on the crests of the mountain ranges before Wade reached the town of Texcoco, eastward on the mainland. The night was still and damp, but his passage left a string of yapping dogs behind him.

He found the house of Daniel Hughes without difficulty. It was a simple wattle-and-daub home, hardly more than a hut, situated on the outskirts of Texcoco. Behind the house was a perfectly ordinary corral, built of logs.

He could see the horses, restless shadows caught in the silvering light of the rising moon.

There was nothing very sinister about them; they neither threatened nor promised. They were just there, in place, as though they belonged. They were just horses.

They didn't look deadly, like a cobalt bomb.

They weren't dressed for murder, like an army.

But they were, no matter what they looked like, the levers that could move a world. They were in the wrong place at the wrong time, and that was deadly.

Wade didn't hesitate. The horses were unguarded, and his own presence was unsuspected. There would never be a better chance than right now, and he took it.

A stallion nickered, suspiciously.

Wade moved cautiously to the log rail, spotted the water trough, and tossed half his supply of irritants into it. They made a light splash, and the horses began to mill nervously.

He backed away, careful to make no sudden motions. The irritants would not take effect for fifteen hours. They weren't designed to kill, but they were *guaranteed* to make the horses mean.

The right poison, of course, would have killed at least some of the horses outright. But he couldn't be certain that it would get all of them, and he had no way of knowing whether or not all of the horses were in the corral—Hughes might have some that Security hadn't spotted. In any event, he wanted to make the horses into something frightening, something supernatural, so that they could never be accepted into the Indian culture before Cortes landed.

Preventive medicine was still the best medicine.

This way, he didn't have to get all of the horses; he simply had to render them ineffective. A bunch of dead horses in the morning would just have proved that horses were vulnerable like other animals. Twenty or thirty maddened horses were something else again. Something unforgettable.

He went to the front of the house. There was no door, only a blanket hanging over a space in the wall.

He noticed a good rope with a loop in it hanging by the doorway. He smiled a little and knocked gently on the mud wall of the house next to the rope.

There was a moment of silence, then footsteps. The blanket was pushed aside.

Daniel Hughes looked out at him. He didn't look much like his picture. The white hair had been dyed black, the skin was a copper color, and he was dressed in a loin-cloth and an over-the-shoulder mantle.

The pleasant blue eyes, however, were unchanged. The air of affability, of sophistication, remained.

"Hello Dan," Wade said in English. "May I come in?"

The man didn't react at all—or, if he did, he recovered himself before Wade could catch it.

"It's rather late," said Daniel Hughes in a soft, polite voice. "But by all means step inside. I've been expecting you."

Wade was startled, to say the least, but he managed to keep it from showing. *By God,* he thought, *I'll be as suave as he is if it turns my upper lip into cement.*

He went in.

The inside of the house fully lived up to the promise of its rather drab exterior; it was furnished with mats and stools and something that would pass for a low table. The kitchen was in an adjoining shed, and what light there was came from the embers of a fire between the house and the kitchen.

It was warm and dry, though, and not uncomfortable.

A figure—little more than a shadow in the half-light—stepped gracefully out of one corner and moved without a word into the kitchen shed. Wade caught just a glimpse of a striking Indian girl, perhaps twenty years old, and then she was hidden from his view.

Daniel Hughes seated himself cross-legged on a mat.

"You have the advantage of me," he said quietly. "What is your name?"

"Dryden. Wade Dryden."

"Wade it is, then. From the Time Security Commission, of course. Isn't it curious to imagine that we are in something called *time?* I feel quite at home. Sit down, won't you?"

Wade sat down. The charm of Dan Hughes was very real, he decided—and there was a mind back of that somewhat bland smile.

Hughes folded his hands. "Beating around the bush doesn't amuse me, Wade," he said. "Suppose we get right down to cases. I flatter myself that I am not feeble-minded, and therefore I have, shall we say, anticipated a visit from the TSC. Would you be interested in my line of reasoning?"

"Shoot," Wade said, feeling that he was caught up in something he could hardly understand.

"Well," Hughes said, his blue eyes sure and steady, "I knew the horses would be spotted sooner or later by a Security team. That was obvious. Shortly thereafter, our friend Chamisso would send someone back here with the semantically curious mission of saving the world. Naturally, the TSC would wish to disturb matters as little as possible, so I assumed the man would come alone—as, I'm happy to see, you did. Now then, Wade— what do you suppose that agent would do when he got back here?"

Wade said nothing, but he felt the sweat in the palms of his hands.

Hughes laughed, gently. "Our friend would reason that Aztec society was a theocracy, and so he would start with the priesthood. I imagined he would pass himself off as a priest, go to one of the temples, and go through some mumbo-jumbo designed to make the priests worry about the horses. Then, I reasoned, he would probably do something to stir the horses up, and after that he would come here to preach some ethics. How close am I, Mr. Dryden?"

"Not very close, I'm afraid," Wade said.

Hughes raised one eyebrow. "Well, I went ahead on the assumption that I was correct," he said. "I went to the priests, one by one, and made a little prophecy to the effect that a stranger would be along shortly to tell them lies about my animals. I see by the look in your eyes, which you are trying most heroically to shield, that you have already fulfilled that prophecy, thus strengthening my position here no end."

Wade stood up, his heart hammering against his ribs.

"Do sit down, Mr. Dryden. We've hardly begun our little talk. I've made a bit of a study of the TSC, so I think I know your methods rather well. Naturally, you would underestimate me, since it is hardly admissible to your philosophy that a man like myself could be as smart as you are." He waved a hand. "I'm not a fool, Wade. You wouldn't dream of bringing a weapon back here, but my ethics are different. I assure you that my wife will not hesitate to use that rifle."

Wade looked into the kitchen shed. The Indian girl stood there in the shadows behind the fire, an old-fashioned repeating rifle in her arms.

"I really can't allow you to live through the night, Wade, but I would be singularly ungracious to cut you off without a word. What was it you came here to say?"

Wade felt little and helpless, filled with the acid of failure

Outside the hut, the moon stood high in the night, and a cold wind whispered down from the mountains.

V

Wade tried to get a grip on himself.

He had to think, he knew that. His brain was his only weapon. If he got rattled now, he was done for. There could be no question that he had been outsmarted; Hughes had checked every move he had made, before he had even made them.

Okay. Go on from there. What do you know about Dan Hughes?

For one thing, he had been a frustrated man, whether he showed it or not. He had wanted to write a novel but hadn't been able to bring it off. He hadn't fitted into the culture in which he had found himself, but he had brains to spare. He would be hungry for recognition, eager for anything that fed his starved ego.

And he could be hurt, when the time came.

Right now, he had to be kept talking.

Wade sat down, careful to keep his hands in front of him where they could be seen. He didn't know what signal would be needed to make the Indian girl pull the trigger, but he knew he could never get away with anything so crude as tossing a smoke pill on the floor.

"I came here to say that you are a murderer," he said. "You are the greatest mass murderer in history. I came here to tell you that you need medical care."

Quite suddenly, Hughes looked less cordial. He was of course, quite sane, and it was important to him that other people should understand that too. "You say I am a murderer, Mr. Dryden. Why?"

"That's obvious, isn't it? If those horses are integrated into this culture, our own civilization as we know it becomes impossible. In 2080, America will be an Indian nation—and everything that America ever did will be canceled out. The rest of the world will be equally different; different people will be born, and they'll live different lives. So you are murdering every human being that exists in our civilization."

Hughes pursed his lips in an oddly academic gesture. "Come now," he said. "You can't really be as sophomoric as all that. Hasn't it occurred to you that *you* are just as much a murderer as I am?"

The thought *had* occurred, unfortunately. Wade waited for the rest of it.

"You see," Hughes said patiently, "the horses are here now; that's a fact. If you destroy them, you're robbing the Aztecs of their chance for life. Cortes was no saint, Mr. Dryden, and you know it. He knew more about military tactics than the Aztecs could ever know, of course, and he came from a genuine empire, not an unstable tribal alliance like we have here in Mexico. If that future Montezuma and Cuauhtemoc have horses, however, that's enough to tip the scales against the outnumbered forces of Cortes."

"You're doing it deliberately, then?"

"You miss the point. As of *now,* it's the *Aztecs* who will win, In other words, the future belongs to their civilization unless *you* act. It will develop, of course—our own ancestors had lots worse than human sacrifice in *their* past. If you kill those horses, or prevent their use, *you are murdering every descendant of these people from now to the end of time.* Don't prattle about ethics to me, Wade. You're in exactly the same spot I am, and you know it."

"Look," Wade said, "our civilization is the one that did exist in 2080—you can't deny that. You're trying to play God; the decision you've made is beyond your powers."

"Nuts," Hughes said succinctly. "The minute history can be changed, choice enters the picture. Every culture you destroy at the whim of your own, you are making a value judgment. You are saying that you are superior to anything else that could have developed. That, I submit, is egotism of a high order indeed."

"You're making a value judgment."

"Certainly. I only wished to point out that you're in the same boat. The concept of *right* depends to a large extent on where you're sitting. What's right here is wrong in the year 2080. What's right in 2080 is just as wrong here."

Wade let that one pass. The man was a confirmed cultural relativist, and could not be argued out of his position by rational means. Therefore, argument was a waste of time.

The devil of it was that Hughes was not stupid. His position was sound enough to be dangerous.

"Why did you decide this culture was superior to your own, Dan? Let's just leave ethnocentrism out of it. I won't wave any flags at you. I just want to know."

Hughes smiled. "I don't think the Aztecs are better than we are," he said surprisingly. "I don't profess to know whether one way of life is better than any other way. I don't even know what 'better' means in that context."

"Why are you doing it then?"

Hughes met his eyes steadily. "I fell in love," he said. "I fell in love with an Indian girl. I don't think you can understand that, but that's all the explanation there is."

Wade turned slowly and looked behind him. The lovely Indian girl was still there in the shadows, the rifle cradled in her arms. *For her,* he thought. *For her, he would kill a world.*

And yet, from his point of view, why not? He had met the girl on an earlier research trip, and fallen in love with her. He could not take her back with him; she could not be smuggled into the Cincinnati station in 2080. And what was the dominant fact Wade had learned about Hughes? The man didn't fit. He was unhappy m his work, a failure at what he wanted to do. He did not care much for his wife. He had no children. His best friend was the poet, Karpenter, who was too honest to do much ego-feeding. Why should Hughes be passionately loyal to the civilization that had spawned him?

"But look," Wade said. "Why the horses? You can live your life here with the girl. There will be no Cortes in your lifetime. I think I could arrange for you to be let alone, if you would agree to be reasonable."

"Have you ever loved anyone, Wade?"

Wade didn't answer him.

"I want children," Hughes said. "I can't bring children into a world that's going to blow up in their faces—l *know* it's going to be wiped out;

it's not a conjecture. My wife here has given me the only happiness I've ever known. I'm going to do what I can for her people. If you think that's evil, I can't honestly say that I give a damn."

"No," Wade said slowly, "it's not evil. I don't know what it is."

Wade looked at the mat he was sitting on. He was deeply troubled; Hughes's arguments could not be shrugged off. He couldn't kid himself with any simple-minded truisms. As of right now, one civilization was as "real" as the other. You couldn't close your eyes and claim that one way was "right" because it had happened that way once. Who could say what kind of a world *might* have been?

There was no right or wrong in this situation.

Hughes was not evil, Wade was not a shining hero.

Very well. Reduce it to essentials. Their loyalties, their conceptions of honor, were different. Wade's life was in 2080. If he could not stop Hughes, he would be killed. He had no desire to be sacrificed to anything.

It was that simple.

He *had* to act. How?

Already, dawn was streaking the eastern sky, and the hut was cold with the chilled gray light of early morning.

Wade launched his attack.

He let fly at the other man's vanity, and he hoped his aim was accurate.

"I saw Dr. Clements before I left," he said. "Your boss told me your last paper—the one on urbanism—was so grossly wild he was going to have your degree revoked."

Hughes was visibly startled. "What? That's impossible. You can't revoke a degree. Clements is an ass. My paper was a damned good one, and he knows it. What the devil do you mean—"

"Your wife has killed herself," Wade said flatly, cutting him off.

"I don't believe you—"

"I saw Karpenter. Did you know that he kept a copy of your novel? I read *A Window on the Stars*. It was a failure, but you showed some promise in one section."

"Kept a copy? What section?"

Wade wasn't proud of what he was doing, but he hammered it home. "You're not in love, Dan. You've failed in your life and you're running away. You can't run away from yourself. You'll fail here. You'll always fail—"

Hughes leaped to his feet, his face white beneath its dye. He was breathing fast.

"You're a liar! A liar! I'll show you, all of you—"

Now.

Wade threw himself sideways on the mat, rolled, and hurled himself through the blanket that masked the door. Instantly, he cut to the side.

The rifle cracked and a slug *thunked* through the blanket.

He grabbed the rope from the peg by the door and sprinted for the corral. The horses snorted and neighed as he tore down the gate rails. He didn't hear the second shot, but he felt its wind on his cheek.

He yelled, climbed up on the top rail, threw his loop, and dived. He slipped completely over the stallion he had roped, but he scrambled up on its bare back again and held on for all he was worth.

He yelled again, and whipped the horses around him with the free end of his rope. They began to run.

The stallion under him quivered, but did not buck. He was a saddle horse; the marks were still on him. The bedlam in the corral swelled to a nightmare of plunging, rearing horses. He caught the thin crack of the rifle and a mare gave an oddly human whinny of pain as a slug slammed into the wrong target.

Wade dug his knees into the stallion's ribs and clutched the mane with his free hand. He gave some quite creditable cowboy yells and burst through the open gate at a full gallop. Almost all of the other horses followed the stallion, eyes rolling, breath coming in great snorts as they ran into the thin morning air.

Wade let the stallion have his head for a full ten minutes; it was almost impossible to guide him with the rope. He concentrated on staying aboard, cursing his flapping robe heartily as he jounced on the sweaty back.

He finally managed to slow him to a walk, and then to bring him to a nervous halt. The other horses milled uncertainly. Wade slid off, keeping the rope in his hand, and fashioned a fairly decent halter with the loop as a base. Then he scrambled back on the horse, giving thanks that the stallion seemed good and tame. The irritants he had put into the water hadn't had time to work, but the exercise might speed it up some,

He was exhausted, but the crisp air had revived him a little. He knew he was not out of the woods yet, and in fact his own plan had backfired against him.

Those irritants in the water meant trouble.

The Jump Box could only return to its original landing place near Coyoacan when he summoned it—and Coyoacan was a full fifteen miles away as the crow flew, and he was no crow. He couldn't swim the horse all the way across Lake Texcoco, and all the causeways were on the other side of the lake.

Therefore, he had to go around.

That meant he would have to circle to the north, where there was less population, and *that* meant a distance of perhaps fifty miles. There were some paths, but they were none too good.

There were two factors in his favor: if pursuit came, it would have to be on foot, unless Hughes himself got one of the horses, and communications were poor enough so that no one would be sure just where he was.

And Hughes didn't know about the irritants.

He headed north, holding the mustang to a steady running walk. Most of the other horses tagged along, following the stallion. The halter—it was a hackamore—worked pretty well, and Wade relaxed a little in the warming sun.

He passed a fair number of Indians, who either ran in terror into their huts or tried to keep up with him by running. His priest's robes prevented any overt hostility.

It was curious indeed, he thought, that this smooth running walk was faster than anything else in Central America. As long as he kept moving, he couldn't be caught.

Unfortunately, he couldn't keep moving,

By high noon the mustang was getting nervous, tossing his head and snorting. The irritants were taking effect.

Wade found a clump of trees, halted, and dismounted. He let the stallion get some water, and then tied him firmly to a tree.

After that, there was nothing to do but wait.

Wade climbed a tree, to be on the safe side, and made himself as comfortable as he could. The horses probably wouldn't stampede with the irritants if they weren't ridden, but Wade wasn't taking any chances.

He settled down for a miserable afternoon. The night was worse.

By morning, the irritants had worn off, and Wade mounted the mustang and set off once more in his great northward circle around the blue waters of Lake Texcoco.

It took him three days to come within sight of the causeway at Ticoman, north of Tenochtitlan.

He had managed to snag four fish in the lake, and had appropriated some tortillas at an unguarded farmhouse, but he was tired, hungry, and thoroughly disenchanted with the beauties of outdoor living.

The tiny transmitter that would summon the Jump Box was buried in his right femur, just above the knee. That transmitter was one thing that no time traveler could take a chance on losing, so it was surgically planted for keeps. Wade pressed the combination, and hoped that he would still be alive when he got to Coyoacan—if he got that far.

He took a deep breath and rode into the open. There were six other horses still with him.

He rode at a steady walk onto the causeway.

Indians ahead of him gave him one startled glance and began to run to keep out of his way. It wasn't any lack of courage on their part; they saw what they thought was one of their own priests riding an animal that must surely be supernatural, and their reaction was about what might have been expected in the Middle Ages if a priest flew into the church in a helicopter.

Wade kept going. The other six horses followed nervously behind him.

He waited as long as he could. They knew where he was now, and Hughes surely would have them stirred up if he was in Tenochtitlan. If he wasn't, the priests would mean trouble anyway—they were inclined to be skeptical about the supernatural.

He was right.

It was late afternoon before the lake narrowed to twin canals and the city rose out of the green floating gardens ahead of him. A squad of soldiers blocked the causeway, bows at the ready.

Wade maneuvered his stallion to one side, and whistled the other horses around him. He patted his mustang on the neck.

Then he yelled like a banshee, whipped the other horses with his rope, and slammed his heels into his stallion's ribs.

They hit the soldiers at full gallop.

A cavalry charge, even if you have been trained to combat it, isn't a pleasant thing to be in front of. If you've never seen a horse before—

The soldiers dived off the causeway into the canal. Their initial shower of arrows wounded one horse, but that was all.

It was now or never.

Wade hit the market at Tlaltelolco full tilt, screaming at the top of his lungs. He narrowed his eyes against the wind and scattered citizens right and left. He deliberately rode people down, and he galloped yelling through a temple, doing as much damage as he could.

He lost the other horses, but they kicked up a fuss on their own, since no one knew how to handle them.

He bent low over the mustang's neck, whispering in his ear, and charged into the plaza at Tenochtitlan, where he repeated his performance. He moved too fast for any defense to be organized against him, and he almost got away with it unscathed.

Almost.

Just as he hit the causeway to Coyoacan, a spear thrown from an atlatl caught him in the left shoulder, almost knocking him from his mount. It pulled loose and clattered on the causeway, but he could feel the blood trickling warmly down his back.

He slowed the mustang a little, saving him, and thudded toward Coyoacan as fast as he dared.

The sun sank behind the mountains beyond the lake and a cold mist drifted up from the water.

He rode on, half out of his head, muttering feverishly to his horse.

He was saved once again by poor communications. No one at Coyoacan knew he was coming, and he pounded through the dark village without incident.

At the clump of trees, he threw himself stiffly from the horse. The mustang stallion was foaming and covered with sweat, his flanks bloody from arrow creases. He sank to the ground, done for. Wade knelt beside him, too exhausted to cry.

He stroked the mustang's wet neck.

"Good-by, boy, good-by," he mumbled, his tongue thick, wanting desperately to say something that could not be said.

He dragged himself into the trees, stumbled into the Jump Box, and looked the door seal.

He collapsed on the floor, unable to make it to the armchair, and watched the cheerful room around him spin itself into blackness.

He felt a stickiness under him and thought vaguely that he was bleeding to death.

But it was all far away, and then it was nothing. . . .

VI

Wade was in the hospital for a long time, staring at the ceiling

One day, after May had already flowed into a warm, green June, Chamisso came to see him.

Wade tried to be interested in what Chamisso had to say.

"He got those horses back during the American Civil War." The words seemed to come from a great distance. "Bribed a Security man, of course. He must have saved up the money all his life."

All his life. All his life.

"You did a magnificent job, Wade. You can lie around in the sun and take it easy as long as you want to. Almost all the horses have been killed, you know, and the ones that are loose won't ever be used for anything. They think the horses were devils—that's what they thought when they saw the horses Cortes had in 1519, too. Time travel is a funny business, isn't it? I wonder . . ."

I wonder, wonder . . .

"And Dan?" Wade asked slowly.

A pause. "You know about Dan, don't you?"

He knew. He knew what happened to criminals in Aztec society. He saw it more clearly than the room around him. . . .

The dark block high atop the shadowed pyramid.

The priest in black.

A knife of razor-sharp obsidian.

A heart, held dripping toward the sun . . .

"It was necessary, Wade," Chamisso said. "Try not to think about it."

"Yeah. I'll try, Hank."

The days were long, long days.

It was August before Wade got out of the hospital.

He flew the same day to Canada, where the tall pines were still green against the soft pastels of autumn. He landed on the emerald lake this time and coasted to the plank dock. He went up to the log house and knocked on the door.

Herb Karpenter opened it, smiling a greeting.

"Dan's dead, Herb. Am I still welcome here?"

Karpenter didn't hesitate. "Of course. Come on in. We had a letter from Chamisso—Faye's got some coffee on, unless you'd like something stronger."

"Coffee's fine."

Wade felt the house as a living presence. Logs burned cheerily in the stone fireplace, and the neat, book-stuffed living room was sleepy with warmth.

Warmth.

They were warm people, Herb and Faye—warm because they had found a quiet life that still knew how to sing.

Wade reached out for it, grateful that they were willing to share with him. He had never known a happiness like this; most people never did.

Dan Hughes had known it—for a little while.

That night, he walked out of the house alone and went down to a rocky point under the stars. The waves slapped gently at the shore and his breath froze in the frosted starshine. He looked into the night, and the night seemed choked with phantom shapes.

Shadows.

Shadows of a million ways of life, a million cultures. Aztecs, Bantus, Polynesians, Australians, Apaches, Tasmanians. All trampled, crushed into the dust of centuries, so that *this* civilization might live . . .

Shadows. Only shadows.

Hs people had reached out for the worlds of the solar system and now those bleak planets belonged to man. And now, he knew, the starships were dreams on drawing boards, as all great adventures had once been dreams.

How far, how far must we go, to answer for where we've been?

A loon laughed eerily across the stillness of the lake.

Herb came out of the house and sat down next to him.

"Funny," he said, puffing on his pipe. "Funny to think that all this might have died because of one man—just one guy looking for something he never had when he lived in our world."

Wade skipped a flat pebble across the dark water.

"Old Dan liked it here, too," Herb said.

Wade nodded.

They were quiet then, lost in themselves.

Remembering, wondering—

And daring to hope—

Two men, sitting on the rocks beneath the blazing stars.

THE MOTHER OF NECESSITY

It isn't the easiest stunt in the world (the fairly young man said to the historian over a glass of beer) to be the son of a really famous man.

Now, Dad and I always got along okay; he was good to me and I like the old boy fine. But you can maybe imagine how it was after they kicked George Washington upstairs to Grandfather, and stuck my dad in his exalted shoes.

George Sage, Father of His Country!

People are always tracking me down and asking about George. You'd think he was some kind of a saint or something. Don't get me wrong—I think Dad is swell. But what can I say to all these weirdies who want to know about their hero? If I give them the real scoop, they think I'm insulting my own father just because I make him human, like you or me.

I've pretty well given up trying to tell the truth; nowadays I usually just mumble something about a dedicated life and let it go at that.

But you're interested in history. You want the facts.

Okay. I'm with you.

But remember: my dad was just a guy like a lot of other guys. He didn't go for all this saint stuff, and neither do I. I'll give him to you just the way he was; take him or leave him.

They call it Peace Monday now, that day when it all started. I was just a kid, but I remember like it was yesterday. It was a wet year, 2056 was, and that Monday was typical. It was gray and rainy outside, and you could hear the wind blowing, and you were glad you were in the apartment, where it was warm. . . .

George Sage was stumped.

His ample body—not fat, but with a detectable paunch—was absolutely motionless in the hammock. His graying hair hadn't been combed

229

all day. Distantly, he listened to the wind. His slightly glazed eyes examined nothing.

A slogan on the wall read: IT'S ALWAYS TIME FOR A CHANGE.

Lois, his wife, knew the signs. She was his only wife; she had to be sensitive to nuances. She tiptoed around the apartment as if the floor were liberally sprinkled with eggshells. She was glad that Bobby was staying in his room.

The silence thickened.

"Zero," George muttered cryptically, shifting in the hammock.

"What, dear?"

"There's nothing new under the sun," George amplified.

"Now, George," Lois said, trying to make a neutral noise.

"Don't nag, dammit! I'm plotting."

"I know you are, George."

"Sure," George said.

The silence flowed in again and congealed.

George breathed irritably.

Lois worked on her nails.

"Do you *have* to do that?" George asked finally.

Lois looked up innocently.

"Your nails," George explained. "You're scraping them."

"Oh." She put her equipment down, and tried to sit very still. Outside, the rain was getting heavier; she hoped that it would let up soon so Bobby could go out and play. She was a little worried about George; he wasn't a young man any more, and he hadn't been as successful as Lloyd or Brigham. He was losing his confidence in himself, and of course that made it hard for him to come up with anything really *sharp*.

They had always hoped that Bobby might grow up and live in one of George's systems; that would have been nice. But there was only Westville left now, and even George found Westville a bit on the stale side.

She crossed over to his hammock and gently ruffled his uncombed hair. It was curious, she thought, how his hair had turned; about one strand in three was white as snow, and all the rest as brown as it had been twenty years before when they had met in college.

"Troubles?" she asked gently.

"You might put it that way, as the man said when he walked the plank."

"Try not to worry about it, dear."

George muttered something impolite, and then looked at her frankly. "We've tried everything, Lo," he said, his eyes very tired. "You know that. The people out there have seen it all now, and you can't impress them these days just by tossing in a clan instead of a bilateral descent system. It all seemed kind of new and exciting once, but now—hell, I sometimes think there's nothing as dull as constant, everlasting change."

"Maybe that's the answer," she said, trying to help. "Maybe if you drew up one that was long on tradition—play on the let's-put-our-roots-in-the-soil routine—"

"Please. I may be an old man, but I've still got *some* pride. Anyhow, Lloyd tried a back-to-the-good-old-days gimmick in Miami just last year, and even he couldn't put it through. The devil of it is, there's just plain nothing new under the sun, to coin an inspired phrase."

"There never was, George."

"What?"

"You *always* used to say that, way back even before we were married. You said it was a little like writing—only ten and three-quarters basic plots, or whatever it was, but the trick was to string 'em together differently."

"Well," George admitted, "it's a long damned way from Homer to Joyce, but I guess the old boy's still Ulysses, no matter how you stick him together."

Lois waited patiently.

"Ummmmm," George said, and sat up in his hammock. "Maybe if we just filched an item here and there from different systems—even made a random assortment—and functioned them—"

Lois smiled, and resumed work on her nails.

George walked over to the library line, dialed a stack of books, and proceeded to his desk. He sat down and began making rapid notes on his scratch-pad.

Bobby stuck his blond head into the room, and yawned. "Mom," he asked, "can I play in here?"

"Not now, Bobby," Lois said. "Your father's working."

Bobby eyed the ample figure of George at the desk, shrugged, and went back to his room, monumentally unimpressed.

Three weeks later, it was another Monday and the rain had showed up on schedule. It was a weary drizzle this time, and it exactly suited George Sage's mood.

Will Nolan, his promotions officer, slouched back behind his big desk, extracted the lenses from his eyes, and studied the ceiling without interest.

"It's great, George," he said flatly. "A great, great pattern."

George began to sweat. That was the mildest comment he had ever got from Nolan in fifteen years—ever since his nomadic-reindeer-herder program. It wouldn't have been so bad, but George had his own misgivings, even more so than usual.

"Really swell," Nolan continued. "Of course, there may be some small difficulty with the Patent Office."

"In other words, you don't think it's original enough to get a patent on. And if we can't get a patent, we can't put it on the market. That right?"

"Well, George," Nolan said, shifting uncomfortably. There was a pause of singular length. "Well, George," he repeated.

"Will, you've got to push this through. I don't care how you do it, but it's got to be done."

"Nothing to worry about," Nolan said insincerely.

George eyed his promotions officer, more in sympathy than in anger. George had few illusions about himself; he knew that his career as an inventor had been on the mediocre side. Naturally since he wasn't one of the big boys, he couldn't expect the top agencies to handle his promotions. He and Will Nolan were in the same boat, and it was not the sturdiest craft ever built.

"Let's look on the bright side," George said, trying to sell himself as much as Nolan. "It's not subversive, is it? It doesn't violate any of the American Ways of Life, does it?"

"It's clean, George. Real clean."

"Okay. It's got good things in it, right? It's got a small town deal with country stores and neighborliness and a slow pace; that gives tradition. Security. You know. It's got a cosmopolitan nucleus, right in the center, that only operates on market days and holidays. When the people Go To the City, they know they're supposed to act like an urban population; that takes the tedium out of it, get me? It's a kind of alternating social organization, and it requires enough service personnel in the urban nucleus to handle anyone who doesn't go for rural life no matter how he's brought up. The big city gives 'em direction, expansion. Now look, Will, the sex angle is good, you've got to admit that. The teen clubs give the kids a healthy outlet, and the merit badges give them status while they're adolescents. Not only that, but the chaperons give the older adults something to do with their time—their valuable experience isn't wasted at all. When the kids get ready to settle down and get married, they'll go into it with their eyes open."

"Sex is always good," Nolan admitted.

"That isn't all," George went on, warming to his topic. "Look at the way I've got the small businesses distributed: kids start right in, manufacturing and selling equipment for the high school and the football team. Farm children supply the lunch wagons, city kids handle accounts at the banks."

"Free enterprise is always good," Nolan agreed.

"Sure, and I haven't neglected the spiritual side, either. Look at all the Sunday Schools, and how about that Pilgrim Society? I tell you, Will, this system has got *everything.*"

"Has it got a name?"

"Not yet, no."

"Got to have a name, George. You know that. Can't sell a system with-out a name. We'll need some slogans, too."

"Okay, okay. What are your writers for?"

Will Nolan inserted the lenses in his eyes and made a few notations. "It's great, George," he said. "If we can just get it by the boys in Patents."

"They *can't* turn it down. It'd be against the Constitution. What grounds would they have?"

"They wouldn't have a leg to stand on, of course, not with a great, great idea like this one. It's just that there isn't anything in it that's—well—*new*. You know."

George waved his hand with a confidence he was far from feeling. "Hell, there's nothing new about pyramids, the Roman circus, the Empire State Building, wigwams—not all by their lonesomes. But all in one society, that's different, different in *kind.*"

"I'll push it, George," Nolan said. "Try not to worry."

George Sage was getting decidedly tired of having people tell him not to worry, but he realized that this was no time to blow up about it. He took a cue from Lois and made a neutral noise.

"I'll call you," Nolan said.

George left the promotions building and wandered aimlessly down past the Washington Monument. It was still raining: a bored, gray drizzle with all the character of a clam.

He walked on, hands in his pockets, beginning the long wait that al-ways had emptiness at the end of it, emptiness that was neither success nor failure, but only existence.

"Damn the rain," he said. "Damn it anyway."

Election Day.

Perhaps it was of some significance—it had *better* be of some signifi-cance, George thought—that the weather could not have been more pleas-ant. A balmy sun coated the fields outside Natchezville with melted gold, and summer breezes whispered lazily through the sweet gum trees.

"Sit still, Bobby," Lois said. "Your father has to be careful not to fly our copter inside the city limits while voting is going on."

"Aaaaahh," Bobby commented, and continued to twitch around.

Not without some disgust at himself, George noticed that the fingers on his left hand were firmly crossed. Well, the election *was* important to him; if Natchezville didn't give him a tumble, he might as well turn him-self out to pasture. Nolan had just barely snaked it through the Patent Office, and Mr. George Sage was not precisely the fair-haired boy around Washington these days.

More like a bald-headed mummy, in fact.

The copter loafed along in the sunshine, and George swerved a few degrees to make certain he did not get too close to an ancient blimp that Nolan had dredged up somewhere. The blimp hovered over Natchezville, trailing a long airsign: LET'S GIVE OUR KIDS A BETTER SOCIAL ORGANIZATION THAN WE HAD—FULL CIRCLE MEANS A FULLER LIFE!

Not bad, George thought. Not bad at all.

Natchezville, spread out like a toy town below them and to their left, was a pretty little village, with its white houses gleaming in the sun. It was surrounded by large cotton plantations, for Natchezville was currently patterned after the Old South. If you looked closely, you could see belles in crinoline sipping tall drinks on pillared porches, and gray robots dancing in the slave quarters.

The Court House was a hive of activity as the voting picked up in tempo.

George switched on the TV. Yes, it was still there on Channel 7: a white circle flashing on and off, alternating with a bass voice that kept chanting: *"Full Circle—a design for living designed for living—Full Circle— a design for living—"*

George noticed that his hands were sweating, and wiped them on his handkerchief.

"We're lucky," he said for the tenth time, "that the competition isn't too hot this time around. Neither Lloyd nor Brigham has a system in the race—Natchezville would be pretty small potatoes for them. Really, we've got only three challengers going down there. Krause's Urbania routine is all right—but we've got that *plus* the rural appeal. Old Gingerton's Greenwich Village deal is strictly from senility, and the Mammoth Cave entry is just a dark horse."

Lois laughed dutifully.

George took the copter down almost to road level, where wagons and horses were plodding along toward Natchezville. He smiled and waved, but he was primarily intent on checking his roadsigns. Yes, there was one now, starting just ahead:

WHEN YOU MAKE YOUR TURN
ON YOUR ROAD AND MINE
DON'T BE SCARED
TO BE PREPARED
TO GO TO THE END OF THE LINE
FULL CIRCLE

"I like that, Dad," Bobby said. "That's good."

There was a conventional billboard not far ahead, but it was too close to the city limits for him to risk a close look at it. Basically, it seemed to show two stupendously healthy and starry-eyed children gazing worshipfully into a future filled with circles.

George waved again, and took the copter up.

"Damn this waiting," he said.

"Try not to worry, dear," Lois advised.

George thought of a cutting retort, but had been married long enough not to make it.

The copter hummed through the air like an insect, as the sunlight faded and night shadows darkened the land below. A cool breeze sprang up in the north, and Bobby was getting emphatic about his hunger.

It was close to midnight when the copter's private-line TV blinked into life.

It was Will Nolan, and George knew the result by the glow on his face.

"We're in!" Nolan said. "Not a landslide, George boy, but a great, great victory. Congratulations!"

George grinned his thanks, put his arm around Lois, and headed the copter for home. Bobby made gentle boy-snores behind them. Stars sprinkled the sky and the moon was close and warm.

"I'm so proud of you, dear," Lois said.

"It wasn't really anything," George said. "But wait until the Concordburg elections next year! I've got an idea cooking that'll set them on their ears."

The copter hummed on through the friendly night.

Of course, as you might suppose (the historian said to young Robert Sage over a second glass of beer), what happened to your father and to Fullcircle is hardly understandable except in terms of the social and historical context of the phenomena. If I may interrupt you for a moment, I think I can show you what I mean.

Looking at the whole thing now, it all takes on a sort of spurious inevitability, as though it couldn't have happened any other way. That's the crudest sort of teleological thinking, to be sure, and we must be careful of it.

Still, if we consider certain tendencies in American culture during the last seventy-five years of the century just past—say from 1925 until the year 2000—it helps us to explain your father and what happened to him.

Take two key ideas: individualism and progress. You are doubtless familiar enough with the notion of individuation, and the value American culture placed on the individual. You may not have realized that the idea of progress is a relatively recent one in history. A great many peoples failed to see that constant change necessarily meant improvement—how do you know that what you're getting is better than what you had, and what do you mean by *better?* But Americans believed in progress; it was part *of* their value system. If you weren't "making progress" you were as good as dead, in an individual as well as a national sense.

It was possible to demonstrate progress in some areas, such as technology. If by progress you mean efficiency, it could be shown that some tools were more efficient than other tools. Progress in terms of other spheres of culture was harder to define, but Americans believed in that kind of progress too. If you should ever go back and read some of the historical documents of that period, Robert, I'm sure you will be struck by the constant references to spiritual growth and social betterment.

Now, cultures are funny things. All of them change, but all of them are inherently conservative; they have to be. You can't have a culture—which is an integrated system—charging off in ten different directions at once. In America, the slogan might well have been this: the same, with a difference. In other words, you must preserve the traditions of your forefathers, but be more up-to-date than they were.

You probably know that our industry was not always robotized and controlled by cybernetic systems, but it is hard to imagine today that it was ever anything else. This was a fundamental change in our way of life. As long ago as the middle of the last century, a man named Riesman was already pointing out that our culture was becoming oriented toward the *consumers;* he called it "other-direction," I believe, and he noticed the increasing dominance of peer groups and the growing discriminations of taste. People were becoming sophisticated in what they consumed, you might say.

Atomic power, as you have read in your elementary history books, meant the end of old-style warfare. War was no longer an efficient instrument of national policy. It became necessary to win men's minds. At the same time, the physical sciences went into a bit of a decline. Most of the work went into the making of bigger and better super weapons, which were never employed in warfare but were simply set off first in isolated areas, and later on the Moon—in order to keep the other side too scared to fight. The social sciences, meanwhile, had got far enough along to know what made sociocultural systems tick.

It was rather neat, really. Americans had always loved gadgets, and as they became more sophisticated they turned to really fundamental gadgets: social systems. It was all phrased in terms of healthy variety and showing the world what we could do with free enterprise and respect for the individual; but what it was, in fact, was social gadgeteering.

Inventors had always been highly regarded in America, but now the focus of their inventions changed. It was all very well for Edison to have thought up an electric light, of course, but how much more rewarding it was to invent a way of life for a whole generation!

What came out of it all was a series of flexible, delimited social groups—about the size of the old counties—with variant social systems competing for prestige. Every village and town had always thought of itself as different from and better than its neighbor down the road—perhaps you have heard of Boston or of some cities in Texas—and now they could really put on the dog. Of course, they weren't *completely* different; that would have been chaos. They were all American, but with the parts put together differently. And there was a national service culture—a government—that was centered in Washington and had colonies in each area.

I hope you'll excuse me for talking so long, Robert, but I think all this has a bearing on what your father did. The defects—if that is the right word—of this way of running things were not apparent until after the Natchezville elections, where Fullcircle began. That's why I'm particularly anxious to hear about the next decade or so, when you were growing up. I recall that George lost the Concordburg elections the next year, but after that I'm a little hazy.

I have always wondered just how long it was before your; father knew what had happened to him . . .

"Look," George Sage said, with a moderately successful imitation of long-suffering patience, "do you have to shoot marbles right under my hammock?"

"It's raining outside, Pop," Bob answered, laconically chalking another circle on the living-room carpet.

"It's always raining," George muttered, half to himself. "It's been raining for a million years."

"Don't be depressed, dear," Lois said.

"Now *you're* turning on me! How the hell am I supposed to get any work done?"

"Don't swear in front of Bobby, George."

"Aaaahh." George stared grimly at his son. "You know plenty of worse words than that, don't you, Bobby?"

"Sure," the boy said solemnly. "And my name is *Bob,* not Bobby."

"Hell," George said again.

"Come on, Bob," Lois said. "You run get in the copter and go to the store with Mother."

"Can I pilot?"

"Of course," Lois said, hiding a shiver of anticipation.

They hurried up to the roof.

George was alone.

It was ten years since he had won the Natchezville elections with his Full Circle. Not one of his ideas had panned out since. To make matters worse, he was in competition with himself.

And losing.

He swung out of his hammock, made some half-hearted notes on the pad on his desk, and called Will Nolan. The promotions officer faded into the screen like a reluctant spirit.

"Great to see you, George boy," he said with an appalling lack of sincerity. "What's new?"

"That's what *I* want to know. Any new figures on that Frankenstein of ours?"

"It wasn't Frankenstein," Nolan corrected, removing the lenses from his eyes. "It was Frankenstein's monster."

"Monster, shmonster. What's the box-score?"

Nolan sighed, fixing his gaze on the ceiling. "Your little creation—it's written as one word now, 'Fullcircle,' you know—has spread to six more communities in the last two weeks. It's winning every blasted election. A great, great system!"

"Great," George agreed, in utter despair. "Still the same routine?"

"Yeah. Nobody puts it on the ballot, since nobody can get any royalties on it after the first time around; but the thing keeps winning as a *write-in* candidate. No advertising, no promotion, no nothing!"

"The best advertisement," George repeated wearily, "is a satisfied customer."

"Great." Nolan paused, at a loss for words. "Great."

"Will, what have I done? I'm just an average kind of guy, just trying to make a living; I'm no revolutionary, dammit!"

"Well, George—"

"That monstrosity—that Full Circle—I mean Fullcircle—is too good, that's what's wrong. It's got *everything!* All the joys of rural living, all the joys of the city—how can you beat it? *I* can't beat it, and I thought it up! Where will the damned thing end, Will? *Where will it end?*"

"I strongly suspect," Will Nolan said in complete seriousness, "that it's going to take over the world."

"Oh my God."

"Too late to invoke the Deity, my friend. We're headed for technological unemployment. A great, great situation."

"Maybe I'll get a pension," George said.

"I'll work on that angle. I should get one too; I sold it in the first place. Don't call me, I'll call you."

"So long, Will."

George cut the screen off and walked unsteadily back to his hammock. He closed his eyes but he could not relax.

"Survival of the fittest," he remarked to the wall.

He was no fool. He saw what was happening, saw it with hideous clarity. There was a fight for survival among social systems as well as in the animal kingdom; there were no primitive hunters left in London. The set-up in the United States, with its emphasis on local variations, would work fine, until a social organization came along that was markedly superior to all the rest. And then—

And then it spread.

Everybody wanted one.

It was the end of an era.

"I am Achilles' heel," George said.

The empty rooms began to get on his nerves. He slipped into his rainsuit and went down and out the little-used street entrance. The rain was a gray drizzle in the air, and Washington was hushed and colorless.

George walked, aimlessly.

His feet squished wetly on the old cement.

He didn't even feel like smoking.

It was two hours before he saw another human being. At first, the figure was just a dark shadow, coming toward him. Then, as it walked nearer, it took on substance and features.

It was Henry Lloyd. A few short years ago, he had been the most successful social inventor in the country.

Lloyd was looking very old.

"Hank!" George called out. "It's good to see you."

Lloyd stared at him icily.

"Monopolist," he said, and made a small detour to get around him. He said nothing more, and vanished up the wet street.

George Sage put his head down.

He walked slowly through the gray rain-haze, walked until night had come to the city. Then he headed back toward home, because he knew that Lois would be worried.

That wasn't the only reason, he supposed.

There just wasn't anywhere else for him to go.

So you see (Robert Sage said to the historian as they finished their third glass of beer) that it wasn't all milk and honey after Dad invented our way of life. There was a tough transition time, when Fullcircle was just catching on and a lot of people hated Dad's guts.

I'll tell you, getting that pension wasn't the easiest stunt in the world; there was a time when I thought we were all going to starve to death.

People get sore when I mention that; they figure I'm just some spoiled brat who likes to tell lies, but it's the truth.

All that Father of His Country stuff came later—much later.

Well, that's the way it was. I could tell you wanted the facts, so I've given 'em to you straight. It's been a pleasure talking to you.

What's that? Sure, if you insist. I'll get 'em next time—that a deal?

Tell you what. Old George doesn't live far from here. Mother's dead, you know, so Dad is all alone. He still won't admit to himself that it's all over; that's the way artists are, I guess. Like as not, he'll be sitting at that old desk of his, making notes and cussing the weather. He'll look busy, Dad will, but don't let that fool you.

He's lonesome, and likes to be able to talk to people.

I'm going over there now. Won't you come along?

NIGHT

Bob Wistert found the steel axes quite by accident.

He had been poking around in the station storehouse back of Thunderton's, looking for a replacement battery for his electric typer, when he had moved a crate and found the trapdoor. It pulled open easily, and there they were.

Steel axes.

Hundreds of them.

Their metallic heads gleamed in the white light.

"Good God," Bob Wistert breathed. Quickly, he slammed the trapdoor shut and shoved the crate back in position to hide it. He wiped his sweating hands on his trousers and stood very still. Listening.

A bird trilled cheerfully, digesting a worm. The twilight breeze rustled across the sand and lost itself in the tall trees beyond. The sea muttered and whispered insistently in its ancient conversation with the shore.

That was all.

He switched off the light in the storehouse and locked the door behind him. Soundlessly, he moved down the pathway. Both Sirius and her white dwarf companion were below the horizon now, but the sky was still a blaze of blue-white with sunset clouds laced with flame. Tony Thunderton's house was ahead of him, a bubble in the pinelike trees, and its plastic was clear. He searched the house with his eyes, but Tony wasn't there. He hurried on, anxious to get past the house.

"Hello, Bob," Tony said.

Bob Wistert stopped short. Tony was sitting in the yard, reading. He put aside his scanner and stood up. He was not a tall man and he was getting stout. His skin was bronze in the slowly fading light and his hair was black. He did not smile.

"Find what you were after?" Tony asked.

"Yes. Sure. Needed a battery."

"Good for you."

243

"Got to get back to Helen," Bob said. "Time to eat."

"Give her my regards."

He walked on, trying not to hurry. He could feel Tony's dark eyes following him down the path. When the trees screened him, he broke into a run. He entered his own house by the station wall and locked the door behind him.

"Helen! Where are you?"

She came out of the bedroom, straightening a clip in her brown hair. "What's wrong?" Her voice was taut, as though wound too tightly on a spring. "You look like Hamlet's old man filled you full of ectoplasm."

He took her hands, his tall, thin frame towering over his wife. "Honey, I've got some bad news."

"I can believe it. Are we in for a native uprising? Am I going to be burned at the stake like Jeanne d'Arc?"

"Dammit, I'm not kidding."

"Spill it, then. The suspense is killing me."

"Over in the storehouse," Bob said quickly, "I was looking for a battery. I pushed a crate out of the way and found a trapdoor. There's a cellar under there. It's full of steel axes."

Helen's face paled under her tan. She sat down.

"What are we going to do?" she whispered.

"You tell me," Bob said.

Together, moved by a common impulse, they turned and looked at the door.

Toward Anthony Thunderton's.

"He must be insane," Helen said.

Outside, the wind was gentle in the trees and an alien sun was lost beneath an old and lovely sea.

Almost imperceptibly, the twilight deepened. Night would not fall for ten Earth-days. When it did come, it would last for a long, long time.

There was no hurry.

"I knew there was something fishy about this place," Bob said. "I knew it the minute I got off that ship, the minute I spotted Thunderton."

"We've only been here a month. Maybe we ought to give Tony the benefit of the doubt."

"Look," he said. "When you see some joker coming at you with a lead pipe in his hand and blood in his eye, the only doubt you're entitled to is whether you can bash him before he bashes you." He hesitated and then spoke slowly. "It'll be over nineteen Earth-years before that ship comes back for us, Helen. We're the only people from Earth on this planet except for Tony—and Tony's been here for ten years. He's been alone here for five years, ever since his wife died. He's been a god—he's had absolute power if he wanted it. If he's flipped his wig out here, we've got to know about it—and fast."

Helen looked away. She looked at their home, at the soft blue chairs and the pictures on the walls and the lazy couch before the fireplace. Something died in her eyes. "We can't be *sure* he's using those axes," she said.

"He's using them all right, and he's not using them to shave himself with, either."

There was a long silence, broken only by the wind and the beat of the sea.

"I'll just have to go out and get some proof," Bob said finally. "We'll need photographs."

"He took you out to meet one group, didn't he? You didn't tell me about anything wrong there."

"I didn't see anything," Bob Wistert admitted. "That figures, though. He wouldn't show me the ones he'd been working on, not unless he's cracked more than I think he has. There's another band of them about twenty miles east of here according to the contact map. I can get to them before night. We've got to know."

"Take me with you, Bob. I don't want to stay here alone."

He kissed her lightly, ruffling her fragile brown hair with his hand. "No, lady. I can make better time alone, and you'll be all right here. Just keep the door locked and keep a gun handy. Don't let him in, Helen, no matter what happens."

She didn't argue. "You'll need some food," she said.

Packing was simple enough. He put his bed roll in his pocket and slipped the force field generator on his wrist. The food pills went into his belt slots. He pulled on his boots and was ready to go. Weapons were not permitted off the station, and it did not occur to him that he could smuggle one out in his pocket if he wanted to.

In any event, he wasn't worried about the natives.

"Don't worry, baby. Everything will be all right."

"Of course." she said.

He went out into the bright blue twilight, light-years from the planet Earth. When he had gone, Helen locked the door behind him and sat down in one of the blue chairs.

She began the wait that has never been measured.

She looked toward Anthony Thunderton's. "Damn you," she said in a flat, cold voice. "Damn you for killing the only thing we ever had. Damn your soul."

It took Bob Wistert five Earth-days to find the natives.

Through the tall green trees ahead of him, he saw a curl of blue woodsmoke in a grassy plain. He walked faster, his force field protecting him from the thorny brush that guarded the cool forest floor. Once, not long ago, the scene before him would have thrilled him with excitement.

Now, there was only a nameless dread.

The wind was in his face and he saw them before they saw him. They were few—perhaps thirty men, women, and children squatting around low orange fires. Their crude lean-tos with thatched grass tops were almost invisible against a soft backdrop of swaying grasses and incredible weeds and flowers.

The children were naked. The adults, however, were too sophisticated for nakedness. Their skin loin cloths were simple and unadorned, but both men and women were scarified and wore wooden ear plugs the size of half-dollars within their stretched ear lobes. Their teeth were filed and darkened. They were a small people, and their skins were faintly greenish.

All in all, they looked quite human.

Stones had been heated in the fire until they were good and hot, and had then been dumped into bark containers full of water. The water boiled and cooked a varied assortment of plants, insects, and meat. There was no pottery. The only visible weapons were stone-tipped spears and curved throwing sticks.

Bob Wistert made no attempt to hide himself. He walked straight toward the camp, his arms swinging easily at his sides. When the natives spotted him, they melted into the grass as though they had never been.

He stood by the bubbling bark basket and waited. These people knew Thunderton; they would soon recognize that he was of the same tribe.

Shortly, a young man stepped out of the grass, clapping his hard hands in greeting. A *young* man! Bob, even after only a month, knew how wrong that was.

He clapped his hands in return. "I come in peace," he said, speaking the language he had learned before coming to the seventh world of Sirius. "I am called Robert. I am the brother of Anthony, who is your brother."

"My brother, you are welcome here with the Nwarkton, the people. I am called Entun." His voice was clear and liquid. Bob had no difficulty understanding him, although the dialect was different from what he had heard before.

The others came out of the grass and shyly resumed their cooking. He noticed that the old men—there were four of them—seemed hesitant and confused. He kept his eye peeled, and he soon saw what he had come to see.

Steel axes.

Six of them.

Five of them were in the possession of young men. One was being used by a woman to knock clumsy branches from firewood. Bob kept talking politely, but he got all the pictures he needed with his ring camera.

"It is ready," Entun said. "Eat with us."

He could not refuse. He sat with the young man and ate some of the stew from a bark bowl. It was just as bad as it looked. When he had eaten, he stayed a decent interval with the Nwarkton, making the small talk that is the same everywhere. He told lewd stories, but only to the proper relatives. He could not tell which of the girls might be his "sisters," so he carefully avoided speaking to any of them.

He stayed for one sleep period, and then left, after a grim struggle with his breakfast.

No one had said anything about the steel axes.

He walked through the forest and the air was sweet and clean. It was darker now and the long shadows were less distinct. Sirius was only a glow of electric light in the west. It was strange, he thought. He, so close to that great star, could not see it. On Earth, light-years away across a sea of desolation, it was the Dog Star, the brightest in the heavens. And the light that could be seen on Earth, by some boy and girl in a hovering copter, had left the star almost nine years before Bob Wistert had set foot on the seventh world of Sirius . . .

He shivered in a growing twilight hush.

When he got home, Helen was waiting for him.

"I got the pictures," he said, sinking down on the couch. "There's no doubt of it now; I guess there never was."

"Tony came to see me," she said.

He sat up straight. "What did he want?"

She fixed him a drink and put it in his hand. "He wanted us to come over for dinner when you got back. I didn't let him in."

He knows. He must have seen me go.

Helen moved about the room, giving a poor imitation of calm unconcern. "How now, Horatio? Do we ride into the valley of death, all two of us?"

"Well, there's only one of him."

"We're going to go, then?"

He hesitated. "First, I'm going to log a little sack time. Second, I'm going to take a bath. Third, we'll go over and sample the cuisine at Tony's. Fair enough?"

"I'd just as soon got it over with."

He finished his drink and arranged himself on the couch, too tired to go to bed. He closed his eyes and waited for sleep.

Sleep was slow in coming. Thoughts came instead.

What is Thunderton up to? Is he going to ruin everything for all the people here? Is he going to ruin everything for us? Did Helen and I make a mistake in coming here? So many years to go—and what can we do? What can we do?

He tossed restlessly on the couch. Impatiently, he tried to sleep, tried to relax his mind.

The thoughts kept coming, nagging at him.

Questions, memories, promises, fears—

And dreams seemed very far away . . .

In 1975, the first man set foot on the moon of Earth.

Mars had been reached by 1981, and a landing had been made in 1983. By the year 2000, the solar system had been pretty well explored. It had proved to be fascinating, in much the same way as the Grand Canyon is fascinating. It was wild and good to look at, but it was desperately empty.

Some fifty years later, in 2051, the first expedition got back from Centaurus. After that, a more practical interstellar drive was only a matter of time. In 2062, the first of the true starships was launched. It moved with a new kind of motion through a new kind of space. It was more than just a faster spaceship, just as an airplane is more than just a faster automobile.

The starships were *different.*

From 2062 until 2090 was the period of the initial investigation of the nearer star systems. Life had sought out life.

One hundred and three Earth-like planets were found and there were humanoid people on every one of them. No planet was located that had a culture higher than Earth's, at least in a technological sense. As might have been suspected from Earth's history, Earth had specialized in technological development. Out of the one hundred and three planets which had intelligent life, only seventeen had attained an agricultural, Neolithic culture—and none had passed beyond that stage.

It became very clear why Earth had never been contacted from space.

Earth *needed* a frontier, and now she had one. One hundred and three planets meant many things to many people, but first and foremost they meant a fantastic new market potential. They were a shot in the arm for a planet geared to production. Potentially.

There were flies in the ointment.

Centuries are long, and they are full. No mere record of explorations and inventions can tell you much about a century. People live and work and die, and sometimes a single day is too much for the historians.

Earth had changed. It *had* to change, or there would have been no exploration of space. It *had* to change, or the first travelers to far Centaurus might have had no Earth to come back to.

Earth changed.

You can't sell a plow to a man who doesn't know what agriculture is. You can't sell a car to a man who has no roads. You can't take a man's money if he has never heard of money. You can't produce for a market unless the market's there.

The new planets could not be profitable markets until they were further developed. Outright exploitation, in the year 2100, was out of the question. Colonialism was a dead duck—and that was one duck nobody cared to dig up again.

Okay. Where do we go from here?

Socioculturology was a fairly well developed science; it was quite possible to predict mass developments under any given set of conditions. The scientists could deal with the situation—but the scientists didn't make the policy. A long wrangle broke out in the United World Council. What was ethical? What was practical? How could the job be financed?

Meantime, there the planets were. It was important to know more about the people who lived on them, and to maintain contact with them. Anthropologists went in for a year or so, and made their reports. But who was willing to go out in the middle of nowhere and stay there for twenty years, to establish squatter's rights for industry? It was economically unsound to rotate personnel; it took over a year to reach most of the planets, and it was expensive. Stations had to be maintained until teams could be lawfully sent into the area to develop markets.

Who would go? It took more than money to make a man leave his home for twenty years on an alien world. The man had to be qualified. It was no job for an adventurer

His job was to "really get to know" the natives. That meant, in practice, that he met as many of them as he could within a very restricted area; planets were big places. It was his job to maintain friendly relations. But *under no condition*s could he tamper with the native culture. He had to keep his hands off.

This was their world, and they must be permitted to live their lives undisturbed—for the present.

Bob Wistert turned on the couch. Why had he come, really? And Helen—what had she hoped to find here?

We were going to live a new life, close to the land. We were going to start over, just the two of us.

And now—

Exhausted, he slept. He dreamed that Anthony Thunderton was coming at him with a steel axe that glinted in iced moonlight.

When he awoke, it was dark enough to see faint stars in the sky, and there was no wind.

Anthony Thunderton met them at the door.

"Come in," he said.

They stepped inside. The living room was lean and spare with simple wooden furniture. It was not a cold room. There were bright rugs on the floor and the lights were soft gold. Over the fireplace was a painting of Thunderton's wife; her rather broad face, dark hair and black eyes closely resembled Thunderton himself.

"I'll put the dinner on," Thunderton said. "We'll eat in twenty minutes."

They sat silently, caught between anxiety and embarrassment. The house was neat and clean—surprisingly so, since Thunderton lived alone. He was back in three minutes, with Martinis on a polished wood tray. He handed them their drinks.

"Here's to continued good fellowship in our primitive wonderland," he said with a perfectly straight face.

He served them dinner on an open porch; the bugs were kept out by a miniature force screen. They had tender white meat from a rabbit-like animal, green salad, and ears of corn that Thunderton grew in a garden. When they had eaten, there was wine.

Bob Wistert was tense and nervous. There were a lot of years ahead of them. Sooner or later, they would have to get things straight. For his part, he wanted it to be sooner. Now. He watched Thunderton carefully, wondering. Despite his stoutness, Thunderton was not a big man—but he dominated the porch. He was not a man to fool with. Bob wasn't at all sure how to proceed.

Anthony Thunderton helped him.

"I guess you're wondering about the axes," he said quietly.

Bob hesitated, but Helen spoke up. "Yes," she said. "We were."

With great deliberation, Thunderton took out a cigar and lit it. His face was impassive. "There are many questions in the universe," he said. "For example, what brought you two all the way across space to this?"

He waved his hand and the night came closer. There was no moon yet and the station made a small circle of light in the darkness. The black trees were still. On the edge of the sand the cool sea drummed with long, even beats.

"Don't change the subject, Tony," Bob said.

"All questions are one in the end," Thunderton said. He smiled. "The hell with that, though. Suppose I tell you why you're here."

"Suppose you do," Bob said.

Thunderton folded his powerful hands and clamped the cigar more firmly in his mouth. "I don't know you very well, so you'll have to allow for errors. Still, I think I can hit it pretty close."

"We're waiting," Bob said, his irritation showing in his voice.

"I'll take you first, Mr. Wistert. I should hazard a guess that you are one of that strange breed known as the intense idealist. You probably write poetry or do something equally foolish in your spare time. Naturally, you will compensate for this by insisting that you're the most practical damned man that ever lived. You're interested in our charming native friends out there in the woods—you think they have a unique way of life which must be preserved. You think of yourself as their protector. You regard Earth as phony, so you've trotted out here to live in the Great Outdoors—with all modern conveniences, of course."

Bob leaned forward. "Listen, Mac, about one more crack out of you—"

Anthony Thunderton ignored him. "And you, fair lady," he said to Helen, "have always wondered why you weren't satisfied with your life. You've built an intellectual wall around yourself because you don't seem to *fit* anywhere. You've come out here with your man to find something you've never found. You won't find it here, either. It's in yourself if it's anywhere."

Helen said nothing.

Bob stood up. "If the 'Boy Psychologist' is through with his string of bromides, maybe we can get back to the axes."

"Maybe we can," agreed Thunderton, chewing his cigar.

"Do you deny that you've been giving steel axes to the natives?"

"Have you ever heard me deny it?"

"Forget the double-talk. Do you admit it?"

"Certainly. I'm proud of it, if it comes to that."

Bob stared at him. Thunderton sat there, calmly smoking his cigar. He might have said, "Why, yes, I often have prunes for breakfast."

"You must be stark staring nuts!" Bob said.

"Thank you, sir. You are a born diplomat."

Bob sat down again. He leaned forward, trying desperately to make contact with this man. "Look here, Tony. Don't you realize that those axes will utterly destroy those people out there? Don't you understand that they're human too? Can't you see that you're ripping their lives apart, leaving them with nothing? Do you think you're God?"

"To answer the first and least emotional of your questions, I do realize that the axes will destroy those people. That is my intention."

Bob slammed his fist down on the table. "You won't get away with it! You may be able to push those people around, but you can't push me around."

"Most heroic," Thunderton said. Carefully, he took a pistol out of his pocket and held it loosely in his hand. "I just don't want you to get carried away," he explained. "Rather good pun, if I do say so myself."

Bob looked at Helen, utterly at a loss for words. The man *was* insane, that was the only possible explanation—

"Now," Thunderton said, "if you will be good enough to pour yourself another glass of wine—don't try throwing it in my face, by the way, as it annoys me—I'd like to tell you exactly how I intend to destroy the natives. After that, I'll give you a short history lesson. After that, I'll put the gun away and we shall see what we shall see."

Bob thought of several rash plans, but settled for doing as he was told. The wine, at any rate, was good.

"Very well," Thunderton said. "Here are the details. I think you'll find them interesting."

Bob and Helen waited.

Around them, the long, long night was only beginning.

Thunderton replaced what was left of his cigar with a new one.

"Steel axes are curious things," he said with obvious relish. "You can chop down trees with them, bash in heads with them, or use them for money. On many worlds, a steel axe is a wonderfully effective new invention—a jump forward of maybe a hundred thousand years of time. On other worlds, a steel axe is a tiresome and outmoded antique. It sort of depends on where you are—or perhaps I should say, *when* you are."

"We know all that," Bob said. He was not pleased with himself for having said it, but he had been stung, and he wanted to sting back.

"Our somewhat ignorant friends out there in the forest," Thunderton said, jerking his thumb toward the dark wall of pinelike trees, "are still living in a stone-age culture. That means that their technology is pretty crude stuff, even if it did take the human animal the better part of a million years to get that far on Earth. A stone axe takes time to make, as you doubtless know, and flint has the unhappy property of shattering or losing its edge if you whack it into a tree too many times. A steel axe can save you a lot of time, it lasts longer, and it gets the job done more efficiently. Of course, that happens to be irrelevant."

"Why?" Helen asked.

Thunderton grinned around his cigar. "I don't give a hoot in hell how long it takes them to chop down a tree. I'm interested in knocking their culture apart in the quickest possible way."

Bob Wistert eyed the gun in Thunderton's hand and shifted his weight on the chair. *Why? Why is he trying to destroy them? What's in it for him? What kind of a man is he? What kind of a man—*

"Interesting business," Thunderton said. "I've made quite a study of it—can't afford to make mistakes, you know. There are two things about the native culture that are important. The first is that the society is set up in such a way that the old men, the tribal elders, run the show. They get the best food, the best women, and the best places around the fire. Those old buzzards are really powerful, too—their authority is real, and damned near absolute. Okay. I don't care. That's one way to do things. But look at this:

the symbol of their authority is the stone axe. An old man is the only person who can own a stone axe. If a woman or a boy wants to use one, they have to go to 'Old Man Mose' and get his permission. There's a complex taboo system thrown up around the stone axes, naturally. If you use one without permission, you've had it. It's a cute system; all the old men have to do is threaten to hold back the axes, and that's all the power they need."

I knew those axes were important. But Tony knows more than I do. Is it too late to stop him?

Thunderton puffed on his cigar. "The second important thing is that those axes have to be made out of a special kind of stone—and there are no such stones within two hundred miles of here. The old men have to trade for them. There's a network of trade that almost crosses this continent—and it's based on area specialization in the manufacture of stone axes. The tribal elders around here supply wood for the handles—that's all they do. Somebody else supplies the stone. Another tribe makes the axes. All the old men have trading partners in other villages, and regular trade routes they follow seasonally. Get the picture?"

"I'm beginning to," Bob said quietly.

"Let me fill in the details," Thunderton said. He smiled with genuine pleasure. "I go into this set-up with a crate or so of steel axes—I made 'em myself, by the way. I give the steel axes to the women and the young men. At first, they're afraid to take them. I take them aside and explain to them—look, these aren't stone axes! These aren't sacred! They can't hurt you—there are no taboos around them! Try 'em and see! Well, they *do* try them. No bolt of lightning strikes, they don't get sick and die. And damned if they don't work *better* than the old stone axes! Okay. The chain reaction starts. Nobody has to ask the permission of the old codgers anymore—they've got their own axes. The authority of the old men goes down the drain. The boys and young men stop giving the old men all the good deals. They figure they're already big shots—they've got something the old men haven't got. The stone axes are suddenly anachronisms. The old men get discouraged. Why make that long, hard trading expedition? Say! Maybe if they play their cards right *they* can get some of those new axes with the hard, sharp blades!"

Thunderton crushed out his cigar. "That does it. A few steel axes, and presto! The whole web of tribal interrelationships breaks down—why trade for something useless? The power of the gods is challenged. The social organization collapses; the younger generation starts feeling its oats. In a word, the old culture is *kaput*. Neat, eh?"

"Yeah," said Bob. "Neat."

Why has he done this thing? What kind of a man—

"You spoke of a history lesson," Helen said.

Anthony Thunderton stood up, the gun still held loosely in his hand. He looked out into the night, toward the sand and the sea and the quiet.

"Have you ever heard of the American Indian?" he asked.

Nuts. Stark staring nuts. Or—

He pointed the gun at Bob Wistert, casually.

"Well?"

"Come off of it, Tony. Of course I've heard of the American Indian. There's a statue in Washington. We learn about them in school. People write novels about them."

"Hooray. What do you think of the Indian, Mr. Wistert?"

Bob shrugged. "They were an interesting people. I guess they got a dirty deal. They were the first and all that."

Thunderton nodded. "I notice you use the past tense," he said. "I suppose that's the point, really. Did you find them quaint when you studied them, Mr. Wistert? Unique way of life? Sort of like the natives out there in the woods?"

"I don't know. That's not a fair question. Anyway, I didn't destroy them. That's more than you can say, whatever you're driving at."

"How do you know you didn't?"

"Look, I know you speak English. Try a little and forget the riddles."

Thunderton sighed. "Time for the history lesson. Topic for tonight: The American Indian. Listening time: two minutes. Hang on, boys and girls."

"I don't understand—"

"Be quiet, Bob," Helen said. "Let him finish."

He looked at his wife in astonishment.

"We'll skip all the romantic guff, with your permission," Thunderton said. "You know who the Indians were, and you've heard all about the broken treaties and the smallpox. Okay. How about after all that was over? How about when everything was friendly, when the Indians weren't a threat any longer? How about the reservations and all the people who admired the Indian ways of life?"

"I'll bite," Bob said. "How about them?"

"This about them: by the middle of the twentieth century, most people did not hate the Indians. They were colorful, interesting. Many people tried to preserve what was left of the Indian cultures. Sure, maybe the reservation schools were poor and under-staffed. Sure, maybe an Indian kid had nothing to look forward to because he couldn't get a good education and compete in the white world. Sure, maybe they were backward and caught in a trap. Didn't they make pretty pots? Didn't they weave colorful blankets? Weren't they *fascinating?*"

Thunderton sat down and spun the pistol on his finger. "Oh, people meant well, all right. Nobody bothered to tell the Indian about real estate deals and mineral rights and stocks and bonds and con men. Nobody bothered to make sure he could stand on his own hind legs and fight for his rights after he became a citizen. Nobody told him he might lose his land when he became 'free'. Hell, education was expensive. It was easier to just turn him loose and hope for the best. People meant well, most of them. It was all very high-minded. But this is 2104. Where are the Indians? Let's see—there's a statue in Washington, there's that *lovely* novel about the wicked cavalry troopers—"

"I see what you mean," Bob said. "But those natives aren't Indians, and this is 2104. We've learned a few things in the last century or so. They're working out a fair program back there in the Council, they'll figure out the right thing to do. I'm afraid I don't get the connection. Your speech was pretty—but *you're* the one who destroyed those natives."

Thunderton ignored him. "A few more points, Mr. Wistert. Maybe the policy will be a dandy one; scientific and all that. Back in Spain, along about 1520, they had an enlightened policy toward the Indians. But it was a long way from Spain to Mexico; some of the boys with Cortez didn't pay much attention to the nice policy. Okay. Suppose the policy they develop *is* a good one, and suppose, just for the hell of it, it's honored to the letter. So what? So they'll come out here and tell those natives what to do—for the good of the natives, of course. Why not ask the natives what *they* want? Excuse me; I detest idealists."

Thunderton poured himself a glass of wine with his free hand.

"Get this," he said. "Industry is coming out here, whether the natives like it or not. We're here, and they've got to change. I don't say it's right and I don't say it's wrong. That's just the way it works, Mr. Wistert. I've got maybe thirty years before the teams come in on Sirius Seven. I can't do much, and I can't reach many of the people on this planet. But, by God, when those teams come in here, there are going to be a few natives around who know what the score is. They're going to speak English, they're going to know how money works, and they're going to know about the law. They're going to have a chance. After that, if they throw it away, that's their business."

"But you're tearing them apart!" Bob said. "You're not teaching them anything."

"Mr. Wistert," Thunderton said quietly, "it is sometimes necessary to destroy before you can build. The old men were very conservative, and they ran the tribe. I had to give the young men a chance to change. There's one group you haven't seen yet. They may not be any wizards of finance, pal, but they know enough to get a lawyer."

"You'll go to jail. You can't set yourself above the law."

Thunderton laughed.

"How do you know you're right? Who are you to say you're smarter than the United World Council?"

"I never said I was right, Mr. Wistert. I do what I have to do. That's all."

Anthony Thunderton put the pistol down on the table in front of him. He stood up. He turned his back on them and walked into his house, leaving them where they were.

Bob Wistert picked up the pistol, looked at it, and put it back on the table.

"I don't know what to do," he said slowly.

Helen got up and took his arm. "Come on, honey."

"Where are we going?"

"Let's take a walk."

He stood up. Together, they walked off the porch, feeling a tingle as they passed through the bug screen. They walked along a pathway under the pinelike trees, until there were no trees and there was only sand.

They walked toward the sea.

Bob Wistert tried to think. He didn't understand. Why had Thunderton done it?

What kind of a man—

The sea was vast and lonely, silver-flecked beneath a million stars. It slid up the sand at their feet and made slow wet curves of phosphorescence and then whispered back to black depths and ageless currents.

He tried to speak honestly, forgetting the hurt inside him. "Helen, we have twenty years ahead of us here, on this world, with this man. I don't know whether he's right or wrong. I don't know what I should do, or shouldn't do. We've got to think of ourselves."

"Yes. We must think of ourselves."

"I didn't mean it that way." He managed a smile. "Our pay is already deposited on Earth; that makes it easier to be brave."

She kissed him. "You have me, Bob. You just have to do what you think is right."

"I don't *know* what's right."

"Maybe there is no right or wrong here. Maybe there are just two different ways of doing things. Maybe nothing we do will make any difference in the end."

The night filled the world around them. It would be night for two hundred Earth-days. Out there, in the forests and the fields, another kind of night had begun for the peoples whose world this was. An ancient, bitter night of misery and despair. A cold night, a night of shadows and destruction.

Still, the light would come again.

Beyond every night there was a morning.

"Who is he, Helen? Why has *he* come here?"

"Look at his face, Bob. Look at his eyes and his hair. Look at that painting of his wife. It's been almost six hundred years since the first Indian met Cortez. That's a long time—but not too long to remember the white man."

Broad face, bronze skin, black hair, dark eyes—

What kind of a man—

"What are we going to do?"

"I don't know," she said. "I haven't got any answers, not now."

He hesitated. "We have twenty years to go. We can help him or not help him, but I hope we can be his friends."

"I know this," she said quietly. "He is a lonely man."

They turned and put the dark sea behind them. Slowly, they walked through the sand toward the small light that burned in the trees.

When they got back, Tony had the coffee ready, waiting for them.

Technical Advisor

Gilbert Webster, slouched down in a soft chair at the conference table, radiated a distinctly fluid impression that he was on the verge of cascading away into a puddle on the rug. His long, thin face wore a funereal air, as though he were perpetually preoccupied with World Problems. As a matter of strictly objective fact, however, he happened to be thinking about his incipient ulcer.

"You are not a corpse, Webster," stated the patient voice of Daniel Purdy Bell. "Let's sit up and play Man."

Webster flowed into a more orthodox posture and cocked an eyebrow at the producer. "Whom are we impressing today, Purdy? If it's the League again, I left my Eagle Scout badge in the washroom—"

"Don't play dumb, Webster. Just be yourself. Dee Newton is due here any minute." Purdy Bell paused significantly. "*Dr.* Newton has a Ph.D."

"Oh, *Dr.* Newton!" exclaimed Webster in awed tones. "Is he bringing his gravity with him?"

Bell sighed. "Brief him," he told Cecil Kelley, the director.

"Technical advisor on the science fiction deal," Kelley explained shortly. "Physicist. Used to write the stuff. Won't interfere with your script except for the science angle—"

"Never mind, Cecil," Webster interrupted, lifting his hands in surrender. "I was only kidding—you know, a joke. Like in an egg."

Cecil Kelley shot him a look reserved for subspecies.

"It's no joking matter, Gil," said Purdy Bell, his face very tanned under his snow-white hair. "In this business you've got to keep up with the times. Science fiction is big right now, and it's going to get bigger. You can't pass off fool's gold for the genuine article, not today. People know too much. *Valley of the Moon* has got my name on it, and it's going to be Scientifically Accurate right down the line from Atom to Zygote. That's what Newton is for—nice Joe, too; speaks English, got his feet firmly on the ground. . . ."

The buzzer on the table burped apologetically and Bell flipped a switch.

"Dr. Dee Newton, sir," announced a voice like distilled honey.
"Send him in," said Purdy Bell.

Dee Newton didn't look like a scientist. Of course, Gilbert Webster
admitted to himself, such a thought raised the question of just what a scientist *did* look like. No doubt they came in all sizes, like Space Cadet hats.
Nevertheless, they shouldn't, somehow, look like Dee Newton. Newton
was a rotund, cherubic little man, nattily dressed, who seemed to be bubbling with silent laughter that percolated just below the surface. Webster
liked him on sight.

"I'm not the man to waste words, Dr. Newton," said Purdy Bell when
the introductions had been completed. "I'll run through the broad outline of *Valley* and you see what you think of it. Remember, what we're
after is Scientific Accuracy—you don't have to pull any punches for *us*."

"Fine," beamed Dr. Newton, obviously pleased. "Admirable."

"Here's the set-up: *Valley* is going to be class, in color, with a good,
sound story of a misunderstood guy who finds both himself and the girl
he loves in the dark reaches of Outer Space." Purdy Bell paused, in defer-
ence to Infinity. "Two ships have already reached the moon, you see, but
have not been heard of since they landed. Something happened to them
after they got there. This film deals with the Third Flight, sent by the
U.S. Army to find out what happened to them."

"Martians, of course," chuckled Dee Newton.

"Of course," agreed Purdy Bell. "What else? There's no air on the
moon—as I guess you know, Newton—so that rules out any moon people.
Accuracy! That's what this business needs more of."

"Agreed," said Dee Newton, lighting up a virulent black cigar.

" Yes," said Purdy Bell. "Now—it all starts off with a bang, to hook the
audience right from the beginning. This third job barely clears into Outer
Space when she runs smack into trouble with a capital T—a blazing meteor swarm, great in Technicolor. The ship twists and turns, piloted by
this guy nobody thinks is any good, and just barely manages to . . ."

"Whoa," objected Dee Newton, waving his cigar like a fiery sword.
"That won't do, I'm afraid."

"Something—ummm—wrong?"

"You might say that, yes. In the first place, Purdy, the chances of running into a meteor swarm between here and the moon are almost zero—
the ship has a better chance of getting smacked on the noggin than you
would have in your own back yard, but not much. And if the meteors *did*
happen to be around, they wouldn't be blazing in a vacuum. No friction.
In the second place, that's not a World War I Spad you're flying out there—
it's a spaceship, jet-controlled. You'd do well to curve it in an arc at all in
that short a time, much less do stunts in it."

"Hmmm," observed Purdy Bell. "Well, that's what we want—Accuracy! I tell you—suppose we cut it down to *one* meteor, just sort of glowing, and blast it out of the way. No fancy rays, of course; just some sort of radar-directed artillery—"

"No dice." Dee Newton smiled sadly. "At those speeds you couldn't hit the Empire State Building with a howitzer. Why not just forget the meteors?"

"No can do." Purdy Bell got to his feet and began pacing the room, the eyes of the three men following him like spectators at a tennis match. He jabbed his finger, six-gun fashion, at Newton. "That meteor may be just a chunk of rock to you, but to me it's Visual Appeal. Man versus the Unknown—in terms that the dumbest popcorn chewer in the third balcony can sink his teeth into, and no pun intended. The meteor stays in."

"You said you wanted accuracy," the physicist shrugged. "I've nothing against space opera, God knows—used to write it myself— but I don't see why it can't be *realistic*."

"Well," said Purdy Bell, "we'll see."

Gilbert Webster smiled sourly. Purdy had *meteor* written all over him in indelible letters a foot high. Webster went back to thinking about his ulcer while Newton and Bell haggled over the costs of technical accuracy on sets, and then jerked back to attentiveness when Newton shot off on a new tangent.

"Look here, Purdy," Dee Newton said, banging his pudgy fist on the polished table. "Don't you realize that space travel is almost in our grasp today? You can't just throw a fake set together on chicken feed and get by with it. These things cost money."

"I am aware of that," Purdy Bell assured him. "But I'm not in the gambling racket; an investment has to show returns. This business of building these fantastic sets over and over again . . ."

"Wait a minute," Dee Newton breathed, bouncing to his feet and standing there stock-still. "Wait—a—minute. Why do we *have* to go on faking these shots and rebuilding our sets? *Why?*"

"Ummm? I don't quite follow you."

Newton sat down again and leaned forward intently, eyes flashing with excitement. "Look here," he said. "How would you like to clear about 15,000,000 bucks on this picture?"

Purdy Bell smiled tolerantly.

"Look," Newton persisted. "Dammit, can't you see? I said that space travel is almost within our grasp, and it *is*. What it lacks is financing. Now, the government doesn't seem to be pushing it—and what's the other source of bigtime financing?" He paused, then answered his own question: "Hollywood."

Purdy Bell's smile vanished. "You mean—"

Newton was breathing very fast now, his hands shaking. "You give me $4,000,000 and *we can go to the moon and shoot the picture there.* We can keep it strictly hush-hush; the very first shots of the moon will be in *your* picture!"

"Four million dollars . . ."

"Million shmillion! Purdy, I thought you were a businessman. Why, man, you'll get the biggest audience in history—an exhibitor's paradise— it can't miss. Don't you understand? *It can't miss!*"

"You mean—film it on location," faltered Purdy Bell.

"On the *moon*," amplified Cecil Kelley.

"Well, I'll be damned," said Gilbert Webster.

One year later, a toy in fairyland, the ship rode a tongue of white flame into space. Ahead of her, waiting, hung the moon.

Gilbert Webster surveyed the interior of the club room with quiet satisfaction. Comfortable modern chairs and couches in a soft pattern of contrasting greens were arranged snugly in the chamber and a neat chromium bar functioned against the far wall. There were no windows. The air was fresh and clean, vaguely pine-scented, and a green light set into a black check panel signified that the automatic pilot had everything under control.

Dee Newton smiled, anticipating his thoughts. "It's real," he said.

Webster shook his head. "I *knew* that space travel was a possibility," he said, downing the last of his scotch and ice. "I believed in it, have for years. But it all went off with such precision, such clockwork! And artificial gravity and everything—more like a luxury liner than a pioneering vessel—"

Dee Newton puffed happily on his cigar. "That's one thing about a spaceship," he pointed out. "Either it works or it doesn't and there just isn't much in between. Why be uncomfortable when you don't have to be? I just used what knowledge I had, cut a corner or two with some notions of my own, and there you are—or more precisely, *here* we are. The ship is a bit unorthodox in some respects, but what's the difference?"

Gilbert Webster looked at the soft green wall that stood between him and nothing. "I've got to hand it to you, Dee." He paused. "*Dee*—I've been meaning to ask you about that name. Where'd it come from?"

The physicist hesitated, chewing on his cigar. "Long story, Gil," he said apologetically. "I'll try to cut it short. The D was originally short for Danton, and I always sort of felt like a fugitive from the French Revolution. Never could keep Danton and Robespierre straight anyhow, and the D just naturally evolved into *Dee,* which same I am stuck with." He smiled engagingly. "One of those things."

Cecil Kelley stuck his head into the club room then, and Webster was surprised to note the flush of enthusiasm on the director's face. Around the studios, it was legendary that Kelley hadn't really been impressed with a picture since *Gunga Din,* and before that there was a gap that ran all the way back to Charlie Chaplin's *City Lights.*

"Shooting in the control room," he advised them. "Come kibitz."

Dee Newton bounded to his feet, hot on the trail of technical flaws. Gilbert Webster uncoiled himself more slowly, not entirely elated at the prospect of hearing his own dialogue mouthed by Linda Lambeth and the current bobbysox dreamboats. In the best of times, trying to construct a workable script from one of Purdy Bell's "outlines" was not his idea of Paradise.

He followed the two men out of the club room and through a narrow metal corridor. It was hard to believe, in the cozy club room, that you were thousands upon thousands of miles in the middle of nowhere. Here, with the great emptiness whispering from the walls and the vertigo tugging at your stomach, it was different.

You didn't doubt it here.

The control room was buzzing with activity. A sound effects crew had switched on a transcription of a screaming jet, which was intended to represent the noise of an atomic drive, inasmuch as the actual drive devised by Newton was unimpressively subdued. Prop men had already fitted a dummy instrument panel over the real controls, in order to supply the thumping relays, knife switches, rheostats, knobs, buttons, televiewers, spark gaps, and multi-colored flashing lights that were conspicuously lacking in the genuine article.

Webster shook his head. Purdy Bell—who had judiciously elected to cheer them on from the safety of Mother Earth—even had to fake the real thing in the interests of Scientific Accuracy, which was an interesting exercise in semantics. But it was understandable enough, and Purdy *did* know his business, and had a private bank to prove it. It was just that he knew science in the same way that he knew Roman history—he had made a picture about it once. When Webster had ventured to suggest to him that perhaps Nero had not set fire to Rome at all, but had in fact been busily engaged in trying to put it *out,* Purdy had almost had him banished for heresy.

Dee Newton looked daggers at the phony control panel and waved his cigar at Webster. "Why can't they play it straight?" he demanded. "They've got such a wonderful opportunity; this idiocy isn't *needed.*"

"The popcorn all tastes the same, you know," said Gilbert Webster. "Sometimes I wonder why I don't just open the airlock door and step outside."

"There's no air out there, darling," protested Linda Lambeth, overhearing the last part of Webster's remark. "You couldn't breathe."

"That's the idea," Webster replied, watching her fluttering eyebrows without interest. Linda was a beautiful woman, by Hollywood standards, but a few years past her prime and beginning to acquire a certain desperate glamour. She had been written into the script on Purdy's orders; she was the lovely female reporter in love with The Guy That Nobody Understood. Webster had had nightmares visualizing a Purdy Bell Special in which Linda bathed in Martian goat's milk, but the great man had spared him that final *coup de grâce*.

Kelley clapped his hands together for order. "Okay," he said. "Let's take that discovery scene and let's get it right. This is a take."

The room cleared as if by magic, and Gilbert Webster found himself seated on the sidelines next to Dee Newton. He relaxed, taking a secret satisfaction in the fact that his body was able to assume positions never intended for the human organism, and settled back to watch. The alchemy of drama never failed to fascinate him, even though the raw product you saw with your eyes was by no means what would later appear on the screen replete with music and special effects. There was silence now, except for the toned-down whistle of the pseudo-atomics. Four men and Linda Lambeth took their places on the set. The men, for some obscure reason no doubt connected with Visual Appeal, had shapeless flour sack garments over the top halves of their uniforms—Purdy presumably remembered *Dawn Patrol* and wanted to protect his actors from flying oil. Linda was in a neat correspondent's uniform, as befitted a young girl reporter going to the moon.

"Okay, now," said Cecil Kelley. "You've just spotted it on the viewscreen. *React!* Don't just stand there. You're up against the Unknown, your lives depending on a guy you have no confidence in. Set? Action . . ."

Shadows blanketed the control room with crisscrosses of anxiety. Frosted stars swam in a deep black viewscreen. Somewhere, a high-toned radar *beep* whistled insistently at electronic intervals that were drawing inexorably closer together. A lieutenant, his face haggard, sank down next to the pilot.

"It's no use," he said flatly. "The computer doesn't *make* mistakes."

Linda registered Fear.

"That does it," said the gray-haired colonel, crumpling a chart into a wad in his fist. He shot a despairing look at the pilot. "To come all this way and then to . . ."

"If only we could *do* something," breathed Linda Lambeth. "I don't understand—why must we just sit here and take it? *Why do we have to die?*"

"Extended parabola of the space-time coordinates," the old colonel explained rapidly. "There's only one man who could get us out of this alive." He looked at the pilot. "And *he* doesn't happen to be with us."

For a long moment, the pilot did not speak. Then, slowly, he lit a cigarette. His voice was steady in the hum of the atomics. "Stand by for turnover," the pilot said.

The *beeps* from the radar came faster and faster.

"But the *orbits*," protested the lieutenant. "It's a *collision* orbit."

"Stand by," the pilot said.

"You—you haven't got a chance," whispered the old colonel.

"He'll do it," gritted Linda Lambeth. "He'll *do* it."

The radar *beeps* coalesced into a keening whine.

"Steady," said the pilot. "Look out, meteor—here we come!"

The atomics erupted into a rising roar.

"Cut!" yelled Cecil Kelley. "That's fine."

"Come on," said Gilbert Webster. "Let's have another drink." Why couldn't they be just a little more realistic? What harm could it do?

"The fate of the artist, my boy," Dee Newton said, reading his mind. "The fate of the artist."

The ship's forward braking jets flitted into atomic life. The cold face of the moon watched them come, impassively. Staring into the viewscreen, Gilbert Webster filled his eyes with what he saw.

"How long?" he asked quietly.

"Soon, my friend," said Dee Newton. "Very soon."

"Just think," gushed Linda Lambeth, "we're going to land on the *moon*."

"Someone should really say something appropriate," an actor said, in sepulchral tones that hinted he was just the right fellow for the job. "This is a momentous occasion in the long history of mankind, an occasion which I feel sure will . . ."

Gilbert Webster nudged Newton and together they slipped away from the voice, retiring to the bar where they could not hear. Newton excused himself and headed for the control room. Webster was alone, and it was just as well. There are some moments that cannot be shared.

Webster's heart pounded with a clean excitement he hadn't known since was a youngster in Vermont. They would have to land a camera crew first, of course, and then the ship would have to take off and land again, in order to get pictures of the landing. It would consume a lot of fuel, but Newton said that their supply would be sufficient.

There was no sensation of discomfort. The moon filled the screen. . . .

Webster tensed himself. Soon—very soon—man would be on the moon. And all because of a space opera!

Space operas or wars, he said to himself. *One or the other. You pays your money and you takes your choice.*

There was a low whine and a sudden thump.

Silence.

The ship had landed.

The door of the airlock clamped shut behind him. Gilbert Webster felt the cold silence of the moon press down on him, sealing him in. It made him feel oddly heavy, despite the slight gravity. The five men of the camera crew, standing uncertainly with their equipment, were grotesque caricatures of life—living jokes stuffed in spacesuits and turned loose on the moon.

"I don't know about the rest of you," he said aloud, "but I'm scared stiff."

"Man's first words on the moon!" one of the cameramen chuckled. "Take that down for posterity."

"Nothing to worry about," Dee Newton's voice rasped in his earphones. Newton was handling the initial landing party, while Kelley directed the actors for the ship landing, inasmuch as this end of things was purely a technical one. "Come on—we've got fifteen minutes to clear the blast area."

Webster followed the squat figure across the desolate lunar plain. He had a sudden impulse to reach up and touch the stars, so near did they seem. Stars, brushing his fingertips . . .

Walking was a pleasure in the light gravity and the men had no trouble carrying equipment that would have broken their backs on Earth. Looking back, Webster could see that the ship that had carried them between the worlds had already dwindled against the close lunar horizon.

"Okay," said the physicist finally. "Let's get set up—we don't want to miss this."

Webster checked his special suit watch. Five minutes to go. Newton had adjusted the automatic controls to lift the ship off the moon and bring her back again after an interval of half an hour. Nothing, he said, could possibly go wrong. Still, Webster worried. It would be disconcerting, to say the least, if the ship failed to return.

Thirty seconds.

"Okay," said Dee Newton. "Start the cameras."

The special cameras went into action as the crews activated the tracking mechanisms. A spot of white flame flickered around the ship's tail and a brief shudder shook the ground. The ship hesitated uncertainly for a moment, and then lifted on a column of fire. The complete absence of any sound at all gave Webster the creeps; it was like watching a silent film of Niagara, with tons upon tons of foaming water crashing down on the black rocks below, without a murmur, without a sound.

"What a picture," murmured Gilbert Webster.

"They're tracking her perfectly," said a cameraman's voice.

"Fine," said Dee Newton, and whistled three times into his suit mike. The whistles hurt Webster's ears, and he opened his mouth to protest. Or, rather, he *tried* to.

His mouth wouldn't open.

Out of the corner of his eye he saw that the cameramen, too, had frozen into immobility. Dee Newton, smiling cheerfully and evidently quite in command of the situation, balanced himself comfortably in his bulky spacesuit and began to hum "How High the Moon," with bop interpolations.

Somewhere in space, the ship from Earth began her slow turnover for the return to the moon.

Within minutes, circular vehicles running on tractor treads came crunching over the rocks and whisked silently up to their position. Gilbert Webster just stared, unable to move a muscle, feeling like the man who casually dug up a live dinosaur out of his backyard. The machines stopped and spacesuited figures clambered out briskly. Webster could see distinctly red features on the faces behind the plastiglass helmets. His stomach took a long dive into nowhere.

It just couldn't be, his mind illogically insisted. Not his own plot, the oldest chestnut in the business, really *happening*. It was like finding a banker actually trying to poison a waterhole in Texas. It couldn't be—

But it emphatically was.

What was it that Newton had said so long ago? *"Martians, of course."*

A confused jumble of thoughts chimed through his brain. So the Martians were telepathic—naturally. They *would* be. Webster wasn't surprised. Nothing surprised him any more.

Congratulations, Dee!

Stupid fools, most of them. Never suspected. . . .

Wonderful!

Newton waved at Webster and grinned. "Degrading business, this space opera," he said aloud. "But think of it—a really new twist at last! *A space opera with real live Earthmen in it!"*

Webster felt very ill.

"Don't worry, my friend," Newton said, reading his thoughts again. "I have plans for you, lad—big plans. I want accuracy in my pictures, and I like you. You've spent your whole life on Earth, while I only skimmed the surface. I want you for my technical advisor later—you won't be harmed, I assure you. We'll do 'em up brown together!"

Here she comes, the telepathy resumed. *Remember, no killing; we want no trouble with the SPCA. Stick to the paralysis, and we can use them all over again in other pictures.*

Linda Lambeth would be in heaven, Webster thought irrelevantly. One of the seven human women on Mars . . .

The ship from Earth eased down on her stern jets and settled on the lunar plain. The airlock door swung open. As indicated by Webster's own script, spacesuited figures clambered down a metal ladder, brandishing phony ray pistols in their gloved hands.

The Martian cameras worked feverishly. Webster wanted to groan, but couldn't.

"Rich, rich!" bubbled Dee Newton. "This is rich!"

Webster had to admit that it was. The Martian actors launched themselves from the rocks and advanced across the moon's surface, their paralysis beams mowing down the Earthmen like scythes going through wheat.

It was beautiful.

Webster took it all in, and was surprised to find that he felt quite good. Happy, even. It wouldn't be so bad, really. Technical advisor for a Martian film company, working under a stickler for accuracy like Newton! What if he was a Martian—Webster wasn't prejudiced, and it might even be a chance to do the job right at last. Webster didn't much care who the job was done *for*. Idly, he wondered how Ray Bradbury would go over with the Martians, and the more he thought about it, the better he liked the idea.

"They can't be any worse than people," he thought cheerfully, and when they released him to walk he followed the Martians willingly to their ship.

It was one year later and it felt like ten.

Gilbert Webster surveyed the set of *Down to Earth* with a feeling of horror. Dee waddled up, a rather globular mass of reddish protoplasm in his native state, and Webster grabbed him in dismay.

"But my God, Dee!" he exploded. "You say you want accuracy, and then you have your women going around New York with bare breasts. Civilized women haven't done that since Crete!"

The thing that had been Dee Newton smiled sadly. "I know, dear boy, he said with infinite patience. "It isn't quite, strictly accurate, but what can I do? The audience knows that these people are supposed to be mammals and how else call I show it in dramatic visual terms?"

Between the Thunder and the Sun

And least of all he holds the human swarm—
Unwitting now that envious men prepare
  To make their dream and its fulfillment one.
When, poised above the caldrons of the storm,
  Their hearts, contemptuous of death, shall dare
His roads between the thunder and the sun.
—George Sterling

I

It began as a perfectly ordinary day.

Evan Schaefer woke up a little after nine in the morning, which meant that he was a few minutes behind schedule and would have to hustle to make his first class on time. That was normal; it happened to him every Monday, Wednesday, and Friday. Tuesday and Thursday were better, because he had no classes before noon.

He piled out of bed, noted that his wife Lee was still asleep, and stumbled blearily into the kitchen where he punched the preset breakfast button. He yawned, decided that the house was a little on the cool side, and glanced into the scope. No one was below him. He flicked on the warning beam and lowered the house down to three thousand feet. Then he readjusted the window pattern for the prevailing wind system. A warm, balmy breeze drifted into the house. Golden sunlight touched the imitation redwood surfaces.

"Much better," Evan Schaefer muttered. He was proud of his house. They had had to cut corners on his professor's salary, but with the children gone—

He shut off the thought before the pain came.

He showered, dressed in his blue coverall, and did hurried justice to three poached eggs on toast, sausage links, and two cups of steaming fragrant coffee.

He glanced at his watch. It was going to be close. He knew he was forgetting something, but for a moment he couldn't place it. Something Bill had wanted . . .

Snapping his fingers, he ran up the curving ramp to his skylight study. His eyes ran over the shelves of books, tapes, and films.

"Boas, Boas," he said to himself. "Kwakiutl, Annual Report—"

The book should have been in the old Bureau of American Ethnology series, back around 1920. He found it finally, on the wrong shelf, in a microfilm edition.

He hurried back down the ramp and into the garage. The roof slid aside when he climbed into the copter cabin. He jetted up into the open sky and cut in the blades. The copter was too small for an antigravity unit, but he usually enjoyed the flight to the university.

Not when he was this late, however.

He took her up to the fast traffic lane and eased into the stream. He flew for five minutes over the rich green forest and then landed on the roof of his university office. He ducked down into it, snatched up his notes from his cluttered desk, and rode the elevator down into the underground lecture hall.

He was three minutes late when he mounted the platform and faced the five hundred students and the TV pickup.

"Good morning," he said. "Where were we, anyhow?"

The blonde in the front row made a big occasion out of checking her notes. "Something about the Oedipus transfer," she said.

She pronounced it *Eddie-puss,* of course.

Schaefer nodded.

"We were talking about the shift in the locus of authority to the mother's brother in some societies with matrilineal descent," he said. "Now, you'll remember that when Malinowski . . ."

The rest was routine.

There was nothing at all to indicate that this day was different from any other day.

When the class was over and he had disposed of last-minute questions from the eager-beavers, he took the elevator back up to his office. He felt drained, as he always did after a lecture. It was precisely the same feeling an actor had after giving a performance.

The word was *limp.*

He needed a few minutes with his pipe, and then some coffee with Bill. After that, he could face his advanced class on multilinear cultural evolution—tougher than his introductory sections, but more stimulating for him.

He stuck his key in the lock, opened the door to his office, and stepped inside.

He stopped.

There was a man in his office. Schaefer had never seen him before. He didn't took like a student. The man was tall, with a face that might have been handsome had it not been for the lines of strain around the full mouth, He was around 50 years old. There was an ashtray filled with cigarette butts by his right hand.

"Dr. Schaefer?" The voice was tense, as though the man was controlling it with difficulty.

"Well?" Schaefer was not alarmed, but he was annoyed.

"I would appreciate it if you locked the door," the man said.

"How did you get in here?"

"With a key."

Schaefer frowned, then checked the door. "It's locked."

The man relaxed, just a little. "My name is Benito Moravia," he said, and waited.

The name rang a vague bell, but Schaefer couldn't quite place it. He was reasonably sure that he had no Moravia in any of his classes, but then this man didn't have the took of a worried parent about him.

Moravia took a deep breath. "I'm head of the UN Extraterrestrial Division," he said. "I thought you might have heard of me; I hope you'll excuse the vanity."

Schaefer snapped his fingers. "Of course!" He shook hands with Moravia. "You took me by surprise, sir."

"I meant to."

Schaefer eyed the man. He *was* worried about something. "What can I do for you?"

Moravia laughed, shortly. "First of all, you can swear to me that what I tell you in this room will never be passed on to a living soul without my permission." He spread his hands helplessly. "This damned melodrama, this secrecy, it makes me sick. I have no choice, do you see?"

Schaefer felt a tiny electric thrill tingling through him. He was suddenly not tired at all. He sat down at his desk and leaned forward in his swivel chair.

"Shoot," he said.

"This is confidential." Moravia looked at him with nervous brown eyes. "You swear to it?"

"If that's the way you want it," Schaefer said, feeling a little silly. "What is it? Something about the Pollux stuff—they haven't gotten back yet, have they?"

"Not yet." Moravia shook his head. The light gleamed on his black hair. "The diplomatic mission won't return for another three years."

Schaefer fumbled for his pipe, stuck a cube of tobacco in it, and inhaled until he could taste the smoke. There was a taut emptiness in the pit of his stomach.

"You've got a new one."

Moravia didn't answer him directly. He reached behind him, to a table Schaefer kept in the office for students who had to take special exams, and picked up a heavy briefcase. He unlocked it, took some glossy three-dimensional photographs out of it. He handed them to Schaefer without a word.

Schaefer looked at the top one and swallowed hard.

Words weren't necessary.

There were no words.

A riot of color: green from chlorophyll, yellow and orange and violet from flowers, red-brown from the soil, blue from the sky.

Faces: a man's, a woman's, a boy's. Hesitant smiles, shyness, uncertainty. Darkish skins, wide eyes, tiny noses. Gray hair—no, it was fur, with white stripes in it. Canine teeth that gleamed in the light when mouths were opened.

Schaefer looked more closely. Diastema? He couldn't tell.

Bodies: very light, small-boned, with extremely long, graceful arms. The arms were longer than the legs.

"They're brachiators," Schaefer breathed.

Moravia nodded. "Yes, they often swing through the trees."

More pictures: caves, tents, thatched villages, adobe towns. Small fields planted with crops that looked like cereals. Some animals in corrals, ungainly mammals that were obviously milk-producers.

"Where is it?"

"Aldebaran. The fourth planet. One of the survey ships found it six years ago—the ship's been back five months now."

"Got a culture map?"

"Right here." Moravia slipped a sheet out of his case.

Schaefer studied it carefully. There were four large continental land masses and several big islands. The survey had been thorough on cultural distributions, although it was necessarily superficial in a trait-list sort of way. Most of the people clearly lived by hunting and gathering. There were three centers of agriculture; one continent seemed to lack it altogether.

There were no cities, although there were a number of large adobe towns in several areas. He checked the key with a sinking sensation. No writing. And no real working of metals, except for some raw copper.

He put down his pipe. "Damn," he said.

"Exactly," agreed Moravia. "We're stuck."

Schaefer got up and paced the floor. It was maddening. It was like glimpsing the promised land and then having the gate slammed in your face.

"No mistake, I suppose?"

"None."

Schaefer sat down again, clamped his pipe in his teeth. It had been rough enough when Pollux had been found, twelve years ago. That had been the first one, the first system with humanoid beings, the first positive evidence that man was not alone in the universe.

The end of a centuries-long search.

The fifth world of Pollux, 29 light-years from Earth, had a civilization, as defined by law: urban centers, writing, advanced technology. They even had spaceships, although they had not yet perfected an interstellar drive.

Schaefer still remembered the excitement, the promise, the thrill of that discovery. He had prayed that he might be selected to go along with the diplomatic mission as part of the scientific project. He had been passed over. He told himself that he couldn't have gone anyway, couldn't have left the kids to grow up by themselves while he spent the implacable years it took to reach another star system and return—

He shut off the thought.

The kids were gone now.

It didn't matter anyway. Pollux V had had a civilization roughly comparable to Earth's, which made it simple under the law. Earth could contact them again, talk to them, trade with them.

Aldebaran's fourth planet was a different kettle of fish.

Schaefer knew the law, and approved of it. There had been enough powers in the UN that remembered their own status as one-time colonies so that the law was a foregone conclusion.

Earthman's Burden?

Hunt the natives down if they look a little different?

Round them up and herd them into reservations?

No, thanks!

The law was explicit. If a planet was found with humanoid beings who were not prepared to defend themselves technologically or legally, there was just one policy: *Hands Off.*

No trade, no exploitation, no scientific missions.

No blather about progress and underdeveloped areas.

No well-intentioned slaughter.

It was the great triumph of mercy in law: *Let 'em alone!*

Schaefer understood that law, and believed in it. He knew the whole sordid story, concealed for so long: Tasmanians hunted like animals until they were extinct, Africans rammed into stinking ships and sold as slaves, Polynesians ravaged by disease. American Indians shot for game and tortured by Spanish explorers and then virtually exterminated simply because they were in the way.

It was a good law, the best law.

He handed the photographs back.

"Too bad," he said. "But there are more important things than science."

Moravia looked at the floor. "Yes. I knew you'd see that. That's why I came to you."

Schaefer waited, his palms beginning to sweat.

Moravia glanced around the office, his quick eyes taking in the good oil painting on the wall, the novels stuck in between the monographs and tapes and journals on the shelves.

"You see the problem," he said slowly. "At least, you see part of it. We cannot go back to the Aldebaran system. It would be ethically and legally wrong." He smiled faintly. "And we'd both lose our jobs if anyone ever found out."

Schaefer stared at the man. "You're not suggesting—"

Moravia ignored him. "We can't go back. We dare not risk making an exception that might be the beginning of the end for millions of free people out there. It's unthinkable."

Schaefer waited, feeling as though he had one foot waving over a chasm, with the other about to follow.

Moravia slammed his fist down on the table with a suddenness that made them both jump.

"We've got to go back! Heaven help me, we've *got* to."

The chasm yawned below Schaefer, black and waiting.

"Let's have it," he said.

Moravia took a deep breath. "Those people out there are in trouble."

"What kind of trouble?"

Moravia met his eyes squarely. They were haunted eyes, tired eyes. "They're dying," he said.

Schaefer digested that one, slowly.

"All of them?"

"No. Just one area. Only a few hundred thousand people." There was just a trace of irony in Moravia's voice.

Schaefer drew on his pipe. He knew the score now. He wished desperately that Moravia had never walked into his office or his life.

"We could help them, is that it?"

"Looking at it simply as a problem to be solved, yes. We could save many of them, to say nothing of generations to come. There are people out there dying. We know the answer. Legally, we can't deliver it."

"And morally?"

"You tell me, Dr. Schaefer."

The two men sat in the office, staring at each other.

II

It was early evening when Schaefer lifted his copter from the roof of his university office. There was a fat yellow moon in the sky, dimming the brilliance of the stars. He jockeyed into the fast traffic lane, a river of blinking lights that swirled in the soft night air.

Below him there was another river, a winding ribbon of silver in the moon's rays. The river glided through darkness now; he could not see the green beds of the treetops or the wind-waves of the grassland meadows. But he could smell the freshness of it, the life of clear water and the peace of trees, and he was glad it was there.

Houses floated above him, warm splashes of light like fireflies in the dusk, and he thought, *Antigravity did much more than just give us the key to space—it gave us back our Earth.*

He remembered when he was a boy, walking in the green wonderland of the forest, building rock dams across chuckling little streams, and he was grateful for those memories. He was glad that people no longer dirtied the land with their cities, and thankful that men had headed off the pollution of the Earth while there was yet time.

It had been close, too close.

It was so easy to turn grasslands to dust, forests to eroding mud-flats, flowers to steel, rivers to sewers.

He looked up at the faint stars, almost hidden by copter-bugs and houses. *God, I wouldn't know Aldebaran if I were looking right at it.*

Schaefer had never been in space, not even to the moon.

He knew, though, that Aldebaran was 53 light-years away. That was a far piece, in any league. Even with the interstellar drive, it would take a minimum of ten years, five years to get there, five to return. And it wouldn't be that simple.

He was no spaceman, his roots were in the Earth. His roots and his friends and his job. Ten or fifteen years was a big chunk out of a man's life. To be sure, *he* wouldn't age that much, not in the icebox, but everything on Earth would. Jim, Norm, Betty—they all would be past 60 before he returned. And in his own field he would be fifteen years behind. Fifteen years of journals . . .

And there was Lee.

He couldn't go without her.

What of her life? Would she be willing to go? Could she take it? He didn't attempt to kid himself about his wife. She was not so strong as she had been before they had lost their children. She had been an alcoholic for two years before they snapped her out of it.

He listened to the buzz of the copter in the night.

People are the problem. They always are.

He thought of Moravia's haunted eyes, and wondered.

His home loomed up below him, an island of green in a sea of twinkling lights.

Schaefer landed.

They sat on the couch together. The coffee was still hot in the heat-retaining cups on the imitation redwood table, but it was stale and bitter. Even the fresh night breeze could not completely clear away the film of smoke from the room, and the ashtrays were filled with his charred pipe-cubes and her lipstick-stained cigarette butts.

He was not tired. He was in that flat state of being wide awake, but knowing he had to get up in the morning for an early class. It was probably worse thinking about it now than it would be then.

It was three o'clock in the morning.

Lee had dark circles under her eyes, and there was a coffee stain on the blue silk of her robe. Her hair—a soft brown that she referred to as a nothing color—tumbled down around her almost-thin shoulders.

Moravia's photographs, maps, and charts were scattered on the floor.

"It's up to you, Ev. You know that."

He shook his head. "It's up to both of us. Always has been. I fouled us up once; that's enough."

"Maybe." *Two youngsters playing by the stream. Danny with his dark, serious eyes. Sue, all laughter and sunshine. They'd wandered off; he hadn't seen them. He'd been too busy with that fat old trout he'd snagged once, and missed. He had never even heard the screams when the kids had gone out too far in the swift water. He had never known, until the man had come to him with the two limp shapes in his arms. . . .*

"I don't know what to do," he said. "He says he can fix it up, get me a leave, cover my tracks. But fifteen years is a long time, Lee. There'll be questions. I won't ever be able to tell anyone where I was. I'll get no thanks for what I do. I could very easily lose my job. Maybe these are selfish considerations, but what the hell. I'm no knight in shining armor."

She laughed, a friendly laugh. "Nobody ever accused us of being heroes," she admitted.

"There's more than that. I don't know what the *right* thing to do is. It's easy for some people—they always seem to know what's right and what's wrong. It's never been easy for me. I believe in that law. I want no part of colonies that take a world away from its own people. I want no part of that ignorant arrogance that assumes that our ways are right and all other ways wrong. If we go out there, if we set the precedent for whatever reason, then what happens the next time, and the next?"

"Careful," she said, touching him. "The knight is showing through the armor."

He flushed. "Damn it all. How about our friends? What would they think of us?"

Lee didn't answer. There was a silence, and then she said, "Ev, are you still worried about me?"

The question took him by surprise. "I don't know," he said honestly. "Should I be?"

"I won't let you down again."

"You never let me down, Lee."

She leaned over and picked up a picture from the floor. They had both looked at it many times. It was a photograph of a child. Not a human child, perhaps, but they never thought of that.

A big-eyed, skinny kid—skinny except where his belly was bloated with hunger.

A shy smile, not asking for anything, not even hoping.

Just a hungry kid.

"Moravia knew what that picture would do to us," he said, not without bitterness.

"We have to go," Lee said. "There isn't really any choice, not for us."

He said nothing, his chin in his hands.

Lee got up with a whisper of warm silk. "Come on, honey. It'll be a long day tomorrow."

He got up, his mind blank, and followed his wife into their bedroom.

The lights went out, and their home was dark, with only the warning beacons burning beneath the stars.

The semester was almost over, and Schaefer was busy with his preparations for final exams. Writing them was no trouble by now, but all the secondary side-effects took time. There were students who had missed lectures, and wanted to be filled in on a week's work in fifteen minutes. There were students who were failing, and wanted to pass. (*"I'll do anything, Dr. Schaefer, anything! If I don't make a good grade, I'll be disinherited!"*) There were students who absolutely *had* to be on the moon the day of the final, and couldn't they *please* take their exam with some other section?

It was funny, in a way, but life went on. His head was spinning with unanswered questions and problems he could not discuss, but he still had a job to do.

He hadn't seen Moravia for almost a month.

And then, one afternoon, there he was, waiting in his office. He had another man with him—a smal,l wiry man, his dark hair shot with gray.

"Ah, Dr. Schaefer!" the little man said, cutting off Moravia's attempted introduction. "I am Tino Sandoval, your partner in crime." He smiled, showing very white, even teeth.

Schaefer shook his hand with genuine pleasure. "I've read your book, sir." He nodded toward a shelf and a title. *Spring Lake.*

"Excellent! Did you read it before or after you found out that you were going to have to work with me?"

"I read it years ago. It was wonderful."

Sandoval was flattered and embarrassed, and covered it with a flood of words. "It was a little thing. The critics in your country, they say I am a new Thoreau. He was from New England, I am a Mexican." He spread his hands in a thoroughly Latin gesture. "How can that be?"

Schaefer laughed, feeling more hopeful than he had felt in a long time. He knew that Sandoval was a top-notch ecologist, and he knew already that they would get along. That helped a lot.

"You two will have plenty of time to talk later," Moravia suggested, smiling. "Should we get down to business?"

"He has taken on your ways," Sandoval whispered loudly. "Always in a hurry! He wants to be an American."

Moravia lit a cigarette. If he resented Sandoval's remark, he gave no sign. "We're all set and the ship is ready," he said. "I can tell you that it wasn't easy."

He paused, searching for words.

"We talk a lot about spiritual values, about high purposes. Did you ever try to raise money, a lot of money, for a mercy mission—in secret, when the contributors can't even get a button for their money? When they know, absolutely, that it will never benefit them in the slightest? When they know they are even breaking the law?"

He looked haggard, Schaefer thought. And his eyes were more haunted, more troubled, than ever.

"A lot of people had to know. The Security Council had to know. The governments of many countries had to know—unofficially, of course, You can't build a spaceship and launch it in your backyard. Too many people know, and it can't be helped. If anything goes wrong, if the word ever leaks, governments will fall. It is terrible how a thing like this can snowball."

"In other words," Schaefer said, "we've got a bull by the horns."

"Exactly. If you get into trouble, we can't help you. If you are successful, we can't even thank you in public."

"It does not make for high morale," Sandoval said. His voice was suddenly shrewd, stabbing. "Who is going with us?"

"You will have twenty UN men under your direction. They're intelligent and well-trained."

"Good. And the ship? Who will command the ship?"

Moravia seemed to hesitate, then spoke swiftly. "Admiral Hurley will have thirty officers and men under him."

Tino Sandoval stuck a cigarette in a holder, lit it, inhaled deeply. "And this Hurley? You have every confidence in him?"

@his time Moravia did hesitate. "He's the best we could do," he said finally. "He knows his business."

"By business, you mean running a spaceship?"

"Yes."

Schaefer watched the two men fence with each other. He had been bothered by the same questions, but he was content to let Sandoval carry the ball.

"You have of course fed the situation and the personality components into a computer?'"

"Certainly."

"And the prognosis is that it will all work out OK, probably?"

Moravia hesitated again. "Probably," he said. "Look here, Sandy! I'm in this thing as deep as you are—deeper, in fact."

"You're not going," Sandoval pointed out bluntly. "We are. I mean no offense. If we can't trust you, who can we trust?"

The question hung in the air. There was no answer to it.

Schaefer felt uncomfortable and tried to change the subject. He looked at Sandoval. "Is your wife going too?"

The little man laughed and jabbed his cigarette holder at the air. "My wife? That is a good one, Evan!"

"I'm sorry. I assumed you were married—"

"Oh, do not be sorry, please! Is a man sorry because he has no chain around his neck?" His eyes twinkled. "There are many fish in the sea, Evan."

Moravia watched the two men with a curious expression in his eyes. Schaefer caught it, and wondered at it. Pride? Hope? Regret?

Evidently Sandoval also felt that it was time to let Moravia off the hook, for he steered the conversation into a new channel.

"My people, they were Indians not long ago," he said. "You are an anthropologist, Evan. Maybe you would like to study me?"

"I might learn something at that."

Sandoval laughed, and the room was free of tension.

"How long do we have, Ben?" Schaefer asked Moravia.

Moravia looked at him with dark, clouded eyes. "Three weeks," he said.

The three men fell silent.

Schaefer thought of a child's face, a child's hungry body.

That child would be dead by now, his solemn eyes forever closed.

But there were other children.

How many would die in three weeks?

How many would die in five years?

"Come on," he said. "There's lots to do."

III

The ship had a number, not a name.

It lifted away from the Earth on a column of silence, and yet the silence was filled with the tautness of power almost beyond comprehension. It lifted through rain and white clouds and blue skies, and then it was in the star-bright stillness where the winds never blew.

It passed the metallic doughnut of the old space station, useless now with antigrav takeoffs.

And then the heavily shielded atomics cut in with a hushed Niagara of sun-flame, and the journey had begun.

Schaefer and Lee and Sandoval sat in Sandy's room, which was hardly more than a big closet, and felt the immensity that surrounded them. It was the same feeling you had when you climbed to the top of a mountain and looked over the edge, down and down and down, but there was nothing to see.

There are no windows on spaceships.

They gradually relaxed, as the vibration of the atomics steadied and soothed. They looked at each other and spoke in low voices and thought about the icebox.

When they were four ship-days out, they knew it was time.

Admiral Hurley sent for them, as was the custom.

Until that moment, they had never met the man.

Hurley's cabin was not large, but it seemed spacious after their own. It was neat and clean and a trifle barren. There were pictures on the walls, all of ships: sailing craft leaning into the wind and spray, sharklike submarines surfacing into the sunlight, a shaft of steel against a lunar background, the squat mother-ship that had been the first to send her children for the touch-down on Mars.

The admiral was in full uniform. He was a tall, thin man, with a balding head that was pinkish in the light. His face was all sharp lines and crags; there was no softness in it. His eyes were an icy green, as though they concealed a bitterness he had long ago learned to live with.

He was neither friendly nor unfriendly. He was scrupulously polite, holding a chair for Lee, and he gave an impression of a man who would do his duty although the world collapsed around him.

Hurley waited until they were all seated and uncomfortable, and then he spoke. Even talking to them, he kept his distance. He addressed them as a group, not as individuals.

"We're about to switch over to the inertialess drive. It is our custom on shipboard to drink a toast before any passenger goes into the icebox for the first time. It helps to keep you warm, over the years."

He smiled a wintry smile, and they all laughed politely. Schaefer was certain that the man had made the same little joke every single time he had gone through this ceremony. Still, he could not dislike the admiral. They were different kinds of people, and that was all.

Hurley produced a bottle of sherry and four surprisingly fragile glasses. He poured the drinks, raised his in a toast: "To a successful mission."

They sipped. Sherry is not the most powerful drink in the world, but it warmed things up a trifle.

"You understand, of course, about the icebox. There is nothing to fear. We have never had an accident. You will all be injected with shots—a substance derived from the lymphoid tissue of hibernating animals, an absorbent of vitamin D, insulin, some simple drugs. Then your body temperature will be chilled. All your bodily processes will be suspended, and you will actually age only a week or so in the five years it will take us to reach our destination."

He poured more sherry. None of this was news to Schaefer, but since Hurley was enjoying his role of giving the scientists some elementary facts he did not interrupt.

"Naturally," Hurley went on, "there will be men on duty at all times. I myself can be at my post within an hour if need be; that is part of our training. We work in relays of several months each. Since you are civilians, you will not be called until we reach the Aldebaran system."

When he used the word *civilians* his voice was carefully neutral.

"We know we're in good hands, Admiral," Lee said, giving him her best smile. "We wish we could be of more help to you. We know this trip is not entirely to your liking."

Hurley thawed slightly, but did not reply.

Schaefer thought: *Ten years and more on a mission that must seem to him a mush-mouthed waste of time. Ten years to help some people he doesn't even think of as human. Ten years while others are out on the great adventure. Ten years with fuddy-duddy social scientists. No, Hurley doesn't relish this assignment—and who can blame him?*

"How many women are on this ship, Admiral?" Lee asked. "Some of the men seem a bit hungry, even when they look at an old crone like me."

Hurley took the bait, pouring some more sherry. "You're a most attractive woman, Mrs. Schaefer, if I may say so. I trust none of my men have—"

Lee blushed, synthetically. "Oh, no. They are perfect gentlemen. I'm just curious." She used her smile again.

"All the officers have their wives along," he said brusquely. "Privileges of rank, you know." He chuckled, and Schaefer decided that the admiral was probably a pretty good guy—in the Officers' Club, with other admirals.

"Isn't that—well, unstable?" asked Sandoval.

Hurley looked at him, and some of the ice came back. "There is only so much room on a spaceship, sir. And your party, with all the UN men, is taking up a good bit of it. The other men on this cruise were selected in part because they were unmarried. We had no choice."

Sandoval nodded, frowning.

"It isn't as bad as it seems, Mr. Sandoval. We're frozen most of the time, if I may remind you. On shipboard, the wives go along mainly so that there will be no age discrepancy when we return. There is no real problem—unless we have to stay in the Aldebaran system over a protracted period of time. On that matter, of course, I am under your orders."

Schaefer grinned. "You tossed that one right back in our laps, sir."

"That's the way it is."

Hurley stood up, indicating that the meeting was adjourned.

Schaefer was curious about why the time-deceleration effect did not apply on shipboard, since they were moving faster than the speed of light. He had read an explanation somewhere, and knew that it had something to do with the nature of the drive, but was ashamed to ask about it. The admiral had little enough respect for him now, and if he didn't even know about *that* . . .

Lee's skin glowed with the sherry. "Sweet dreams," she said to Hurley as they left.

His door closed behind them.

Schaefer and Sandoval kept Lee between them as they walked. It was almost as though they were huddled together for warmth, and despite the fact that there was no change in the temperature inside the spaceship a cold wind seemed to blow through the sterile white corridors. . . .

"There is nothing to fear."

Whenever a man told him that, Schaefer knew that it was time to get worried.

They took them separately, to avoid scenes.

When a man saw his wife seem to die before his eyes, when her breathing slowed until he couldn't see it, when the frost began to form on the tips of her hair—

It was better not to watch.

Sandoval went first, smoking a last cigarette in his jaunty holder.

Then Lee. She smiled at him, and he was acutely aware that he still loved his wife after twenty years of marriage. She still caught at his heart, still made him want to reach out and touch her just to be sure she was there. It wasn't just the hair or the eyes or the body. It was the warm certainty that she would understand, and her faith that he too could always accept her for what she was.

In a universe of miracles, that was the best one.

Then it was his turn.

They took him through an airlock into a small cold room. There was a white slab in it, more like an operating table than anything else. He took off his clothes and stretched out on it. His back tensed for the chill, but the table surface was warmed.

The doctor gave him his best bedside smile, checked his medical history a final time.

"See you in five years," the doctor said.

He used the needle, a big one. It stung, but not much.

Schaefer felt nothing at first, but when the medics lifted him onto a stretcher he found he had no sensation in his body. He tried to wiggle his fingers. Nothing happened.

The other lock opened.

The medics zipped up their suits and carried him through.

They were in the icebox. It must have been cold, for vapor clouds came out of the suits. His naked body did not feel it. He couldn't turn his head, but he saw enough. He saw more than he wanted to see.

Catacombs.

Glistening walls lined with cubicles. Forms in them, stiff and still. He could not see their faces, the faces were covered with masks and tubes.

They lifted him into his slot, and he felt nothing. He saw them insert two thin flexible tubes into his nostrils.

Then the mask.

He could not see. *This is the way death is. I cannot see or feel or smell. I cannot hear. There is no panic, no fear, no cold. There is nothing. I do not exist.*

His mind begin to blur. He could no longer think coherently, and then, from somewhere deep down inside of him, he found a new respect for the admiral, and for all men who sailed this strangest of all strange seas. . . .

That was all.

He ceased to be.

At first, it was no worse than waking up after a long nap on a hot, sticky afternoon. He hovered between sleep and awareness and dreamed rapid and pointless dreams. A part of him knew that he had been asleep and that he would be awake soon.

It was all rather pleasant and drowsy.

It stayed that way for what seemed to be a long time.

Funny. So hard to wake up. Tired? Hangover? Sick?

Sick! No, worse than sick. What . . .

Ice. White. Cold.

Vaults, slabs, bodies.

I'm dead, it's over, don't let me wake up underground, in a box, with wet earth all around me, with my body—

He was out of it.

He opened his eyes. There was the doctor's face, smiling. He moved his head. He was on the white table under the white light. The table was warm under him, but the room was cold, and he was cold.

"Easy now, Dr. Schaefer," the doctor said. "It's always hard the first time, but you're perfectly all right."

He tried to move, couldn't.

His lips shaped a word. "Lee?" His voice was the voice of a stranger.

"Your wife is fine, just fine. She's waiting for you in your cabin. You'll be carried there on a stretcher. We'll have some hot broth waiting. A special diet for a day or two and you'll be your old self again."

My old self, but I know what death is now. I'll remember. I'll always remember.

Then he was in his cabin, in the bed, with Lee next to him. They could hardly talk, but the hot broth helped.

It was two days before he felt human again.

Then there were notes to go over with Sandy, notes and plans and charts. When they were getting close, an officer appeared. "The admiral's compliments, sir. Aldebaran is visible in the control room viewer, if you would like to have a look at it."

They were escorted to the control room, a spotless oval chamber filled with computers. One entire wall was lined with dials, their surfaces red and green and yellow. A black bank of switches had four men on duty before it, seated in contour chairs, earphone bands across their heads.

Schaefer felt like an intruder, but he was fascinated.

Admiral Hurley stepped forward with a smile. "Have a good sleep?"

"I must have set the wrong dial," Sandoval said. "I think I overslept."

Hurley chuckled, very much at home here in his control room.

Schaefer thought, *On Earth, five years have passed. All my students will have gone, all my friends will be older.*

The admiral took Lee's arm and guided her to a panel as tall as she was. He nodded at a technician, and the slide rolled back.

They were looking out.

They saw beauty beyond belief, and loneliness that was almost painful to see.

A giant red sun blazed against a backdrop of night, with distant stars like diamonds around it. Streamers and fountains of brilliant gases erupted in flaring bursts. Scarlet prominences streaked the edges like the clouds of nightmare.

Distance was a word without a meaning. There was vastness everywhere, an endless depth that clutched at your stomach. Even that sun, 72 times the size of the sun Earth knew, was a brave candle burning in a cave of Stygian gloom.

"It's best not to look too long," Hurley said.

The panel closed.

They were back in the control room, back in familiar dimensions that a mind could grasp and understand.

"I thought you ought to see it," Hurley said.

"Thank you," Schaefer whispered. "It was worth the trip."

"We land in two days," the admiral said.

They were escorted back to their rooms.

There were few sensations in the hours that followed, but they could tell when the ship's power system switched over to antigravity. They waited the long wait.

In his mind's eye, Schaefer saw a planet, a blue world floating in space. He saw it grow larger, a balloon inflating. He saw continents and seas take form, and then trees and rivers and snow-kissed mountains.

He saw a strange, slim people, with long arms and eyes that watched and wondered—

A bell rang,

"We've landed," Sandoval said.

IV

A world is many worlds, and many peoples. A world is flame and ice, lush tropical jungles and brown desert sands, laughter and hate and boredom.

Their mission concerned just one part of one continent. They had no authority to visit the rest, no matter what fascinating things might be waiting there. But even one part of one continent was a large chunk of real estate; a man couldn't trot over it the way he could spring the length of a football field.

It was going to take time, and lots of it. Time to check on the inevitable changes that five years had brought. Time to find out the key facts the first expedition had not been authorized to investigate. Time to work out a solution to the problem faced by these people, and time to put that solution into effect.

Time, and more time.

The first contact ship had made some recordings of the local languages and dialects, and had mapped them. That was an enormous help, but it did not give conversational fluency, which was imperative.

There were no interpreters on Aldebaran IV.

And there could be no mistakes.

It would be pleasant, Schaefer thought, if it could have been done the flashy tri-di Space Patrol way. No pain, no trouble. You landed on Mudball VII, which looked just like Earth except that it had jagged mountains that it never could have had with an atmosphere. You stepped out in your razor-sharp uniform, mowed down a horde of slithering reptiles with your blaster, rescued a lovely but chaste female, and whipped up a jim-dandy whiz-bang invention on the spur of the moment. Then, as the enemy fled in consternation, you smiled your enigmatic smile and faded into stars and a word from your sponsor.

The actual plan was somewhat different.

The crew was to stay aboard the ship. Schaefer and Sandoval were to take copters and make extended studies of their special aspects of the problem. The UN men were to fan out with cameras and other recording devices and check for specific items of information.

It was going to take plenty of sweat, among other things.

Lee, of course, had to stay in the ship, at least at first. The whole business was tricky, and it was senseless to multiply the risks they would have to take.

When the time came, Schaefer adjusted his oxygen mask and went through the airlock to the waiting copter. The heat hit him like a fist when he stepped outside. A glare of sunlight almost blinded him until he got used to it, and swirls of gritty brown dust pulled at his clothes.

He stood blinking for a moment, watching Sandoval as the ecologist grinned at the dust with anticipation. He felt his boots sink into the shifting stuff, but not far; it was solid as a rock slab underneath.

He thought: *This is the step of no return. This is the step into a new world, the step that Cortés and Pizarro and all the others took. This is the step that breaks the law, breaks the precedent. Who will follow in these footsteps, if word ever leaks out? Who will swarm on these people, with honeyed words and grabbing hands?*

"Come on, Mac," a man yelled. "This crate's blowing away."

Schaefer waved, swung up into the cabin. He settled himself and nodded at the man. The man let go, and Schaefer lifted the copter into the sky, up past the shining obelisk of the great ship.

He headed west, keeping low enough to spot details beneath him. From here, the land was a vast baked mud-flat, checkered with dark crack-lines. Dirty blown dust-eddies played over the surface, and the mighty red sun beat down on it all like a malevolent furnace.

At first, there was no sign of life.

Within twenty minutes, however, he passed over what had once been a town. Broken adobe walls were drifted high with sand, and the square ruins of houses had black gaping holes for windows. The place was utterly lifeless now, just as the once-alive land around it was dead.

Once, he knew, all this had been green farmland, with trees and streams and fields of grain.

Now, it was nothing.

He flew on, an excitement growing within him.

Death was everywhere, but ahead of him, beyond the horizon, the living village waited.

He came to the fields first, and they were nothing to write home about. They were irregular plots of burned-over land that had never known a plow, but there were crops growing in them, including something that looked a good deal like maize. The plants did not seem to be doing well, and it wasn't hard to figure out why: water.

There was an irrigation system of sorts, small trenches fed by what should have been a good-sized river. The river terraces were clearly visible from the air, and it was obvious that the river was drying up. Schaefer doubted that it was a quarter of its former size, and the irrigation trenches weren't drawing that much water out of it by it long shot.

He saw people, too, poking pointed sticks. They looked up at him as he passed, and from his altitude they didn't look alien at all. He had the curious feeling that this was not another world, not a planet of another sun, but only the past of Earth; he felt that he had somehow gone back in time, to see his own ancestors fighting the hard fight with wind and sun and the long, long dry spells.

Then the village was below him.

It was a town, really, rather than a village. It was walled, just as the abandoned place had been, and it was basically a cluster of square adobe houses and dark crooked streets built around a central market plaza. Schaefer went down low, and he could see stout poles projecting from the sides of the houses over the streets. The slim, long-armed people were swinging through the hot air, hand over hand, from one pole to another. Apparently, they never walked if they could avoid it.

The town, even to his eyes, was not an attractive place.

It already had something of the decay of a ruin about it, but it was not clean as a ruin is clean, washed by patient rains and bleaching sunshine. There was garbage in the streets. *No wonder they travel on the walls above the streets. I'd do the same, if I could.* It was the sort of place that looked as if it was crawling with disease, and his skin prickled when he thought of it.

But then he saw the market below him as he hovered. It was a gay riot of color, and most of it was shaded by awnings. He looked down at what seemed to be a sea of faces, a million eyes all staring up at him.

He took a deep breath through his face mask.

"Ready or not, here I come," he muttered.

He hoped the information from the survey ship was correct,

If not—

Well, he probably wouldn't live long enough to realize that he'd made a mistake. There was no turning back now. He aimed his copter for a cleared space in the square, hovering until he was certain there was no one directly under him, and landed.

The copter blades shivered to a halt.

He climbed out, his empty hands in plain view.

In an instant, he was surrounded.

He stood there in the heat by his copter, and he was two people. One man faced the crowd with level eyes and a determined smile. The other stood back and watched, and felt a vague relief. Schaefer had never been a man of action, and he had often wondered how he would face up to a really dangerous situation.

He was unarmed, and he could have been quite literally torn apart if things went wrong. He was scared, deep down inside, but he could handle it.

It was a good thing to know about yourself.

He looked at them and they looked at him. They didn't press him too closely, and seemed more friendly than otherwise. He was the tallest man there, but hardly the most powerful. The people's arms were very long; their fingertips reached their ankles when they stood erect. The arms were slender and graceful, but they were strongly muscled.

He barely noticed the arms, however. It was the *feel* of the crowd that impressed him. They were a people of surprising dignity, even in a situation that was unfamiliar to them. Dignity—and courage too, he supposed, for they were probably as afraid of him as he was of them.

The people watched him with polite curiosity. They were very small-boned, and their tiny noses and wide dark eyes gave their faces an almost frail appearance. They were dressed in bright-colored tunics that left their arms completely free.

None of the men carried weapons. These were farmers and merchants, not soldiers. The rather elfin children were not at all shy, but they were well-behaved.

The girls, Schaefer had to admit, were a surprise. Despite their strangeness, they had an elusive grace and vitality, with warm and gentle eyes. Their long supple arms and white canine teeth were just different enough to be really interesting. In fact, he decided, the girls were as genuinely sexy as any he had ever seen.

That could mean trouble, here as well as anywhere.

It had its compensations, however.

The people were very patient, most of them standing in the shade of awnings that covered the market tables and booths. They waited for him to make the first move. Schaefer, standing in the hot sun by his copter, was only too glad to oblige.

He raised his left hand, the four fingers extended, the thumb folded into his palm.

There was a murmur from the people, and they moved back respectfully. Schaefer wanted to talk to them, but he knew it wasn't a good idea for several reasons. For one thing, his command of the language was too shaky. For another, he didn't know these people well enough to be sure he was saying the proper thing, even if he managed the grammar adequately.

So he waited, and they waited.

He could not *see* the suffering as he studied them. Most of the people did not look thin, and they did not appear to be starving. It was not a dramatic moment where hordes of famine-ridden men and women gazed up at their rescuer with adoration in their eyes. They didn't know why he had come, and they didn't even need his help visibly.

He knew they were dying, nonetheless. A whole town had once lived on that sun-baked plain he had seen, and now lived no more. The people before him were undoubtedly fewer than they had been the year before, and would be fewer still next year. It was a subtle question of the carrying capacity of ruined land, and when the population pressure got too great for the food supply people died. It was all simple and timeless and horrible. He knew the facts in a way they could never know them—facts gathered by experts on the survey team. Within fifty years, this entire portion of the continent would be dead—and there was no way out. These farmers were surrounded by tough hunting peoples that would never give up their territories.

So a few hundred thousand natives on a forbidden planet light-years from Earth were faced with extinction. No doubt it happened all the time, on worlds Earth did not know and never would know.

There were many men who could learn of such a tragedy and shrug. So what? Did they ever do anything for us? We've nothing against those savages, but it's their problem, not ours.

Schaefer looked at the people before him. He knew that he was not such a man, and he was glad of it.

There was a stir at the edges of the crowd, a buzz of voices.

Schaefer turned and made the sign again.

The priests were coming.

The religious officials wore long blue robes, although their arms were free. It was rather odd to see them come swinging along the wall-poles, hand over hand, their skirts swirling in the air. They did it with a solemn gravity that should have been ludicrous, but wasn't.

Once in the market square, they walked straight up to Schaefer and confronted him in a group. Schaefer made the sign, and it was returned.

The priest who seemed to be the leader said something that was too fast for Schaefer. Schaefer smiled carefully and said one of the sentences he had learned: "I come as your friend, and I wish to be taken to your temple."

The priest nodded impassively. He was a striking figure of a man, and the white-striped fur on his head gave him a certain man-of-distinction air. He was obviously no fool; when he saw that Schaefer did not handle the language well, he made no further attempt to speak. Again, Schaefer was amazed at the courtesy of these people. He was positive that the priest would do almost anything to avoid causing his guest embarrassment.

Beckoning to him, the priest turned and led the way out of the market. Schaefer fell in behind him without hesitation, knowing that his copter was safe where it was. The other priests kept him pretty well surrounded, but it was more of an escort than a guard.

He had a bad moment when the leader started to swing up to the wall projections above the street, but the priest looked at Schaefer's arms and changed his mind. He stuck to the ground, which was quite a concession considering the debris that littered the space between the adobe house walls.

Schaefer knew that they were wondering about him—a man who, by their standards, was an absolute freak. A man who had come out of the sky. A man who knew their sacred sign and a few words of their dialect. A man who resembled those beings seen several seasons ago, about whom so many stories had been whispered. . . .

Well, the important thing was to make contact with the men at the top. Schaefer was too well trained to start with the common people, whether he liked them or not. Once you got fouled up with factions, once you were an object of suspicion to the big boys, you never got anywhere in an alien culture. The fact was that humanoid beings, despite their individual differences, always followed certain laws. One such principle was that in an agricultural town of this type the secular and religious authorities were apt to be the same. In other words, it was likely to be a theocracy. This being the case, a man either got along with the priests, or he got out.

They led him into a house that was little different from the others they had passed, but inside there was a deep stairway lighted by smooth-burning torches. The temple, of course, was underground. Had this not been the case, he would certainly have spotted a pyramid-like structure from the air.

He followed the priests into a long, winding passage. The light was bad, and there was little to see. Eventually they came into a large chamber in which hundreds of oil-burning lamps were burning. The walls were hung with tapestries. In a depression at one end of the chamber there was a black altar. Spaced around the walls, rather like pictures placed over cloth, were little rings of black skins. Each skin was only a few inches across, but there were lots of them.

Schaefer was glad to see them. They meant that Sandy was right.

There was no ceremony. That was for show, for the people. It would come later, if it was needed. For the present, the priests wanted information, and they went about it in a no-nonsense manner.

Schaefer was escorted into the presence of a man who apparently was the priest-king, although there was no exact translation of his title in English. He sat on a couch in a small, austere room. He was a small man, even for his people, but he absolutely dominated the situation with the force of his personality. He fixed his dark alert eyes on Schaefer's face and Schaefer was startled by the familiarity of those eyes.

They were Moravia's eyes.

They were haunted eyes.

There was a whispered conversation between the priest-king and the man who had led Schaefer's escort. Then Schaefer was left alone with the ruler of the people.

There was a long silence.

Schaefer had an uneasy feeling that he was in the presence of a powerful man, who commanded strange gods. But when the man spoke his voice was calm and courteous.

"I am Marin," he said slowly. "I wait for your words."

Schaefer swallowed and made the speech he had learned. "I am called Schaefer. I have come to help you if you desire help. I come in friendship and without weapons. It is known that your lands shrink, your crops fail, your people die. Your tongue is new to me, and I must learn more of it. Then we will talk. It is my prayer that there will always be friendship between your people and my people."

Marin fixed his eyes again on Schaefer's face, and Schaefer was glad that he had been speaking the simple truth, neither more nor less. Marin was not a man to be trifled with.

Marin got to his feet, placed his left hand on Schaefer's right shoulder. His face was shadowed in the lamplight. His grip was strong. "Let it be so, Schaefer. Your prayer is good. Soon we will talk again. Until then, live in peace among us."

Marin himself led him out and introduced him to an old priest named Loquav, who was to be his teacher.

After that, Schaefer settled down for months of hard work.

He had a lot to learn before he spoke with Marin again.

A worry he could not identify nagged him as he worked. He sensed an urgency that drove him far into the night, studying by a flickering torch.

He saw eyes when he slept.

Moravia's.

Marin's.

Hurley's.

"It is my prayer that there will always be friendship between your people and my people."

What could go wrong?

He thought of Lee, missing her. And he wondered how Sandy was coming along. . . .

High in the mountains, where the eagle-winds cry out their icy power against the rocks, the snow was falling, in a blanket of white. It was too high for trees to grow, and there was little shelter on the wild outcropping where Tino Sandoval stood.

He was alone, his boots knee-deep in crusted snow, his eyes narrowed against the cutting wind. His breath, filtered through his mask that concentrated the natural oxygen in the air, was a cloud of freezing vapor that blew away even as it formed.

Far below him, miles away, he could see the flat plains baking in an autumn sun. The cold had not yet come to the lowlands, and still he stood with his legs half-buried in the middle of winter.

"Sunlight and plants and animals and water," he said to himself, speaking in a whisper that would have been audible had there been anyone to hear. Sandoval had often talked to himself at Spring Lake; indeed, he had written that no man was ever lonely when he could to talk to himself with understanding. "It is always the same, wherever man lives, in whatever time."

Sunlight. All life comes from the sun. Without the energy of a sun, there could be no life. Many peoples, including some of his own ancestors, had bowed down before the sun, and perhaps they had worshipped more wisely than they knew.

Plants. If the sunlight falls on bare soil, there is heat, which is lost when the cool night comes. But with grass or leaves it is a different story. The chlorophyll takes the sun's energy and builds with it, blending air and water and soil to make new leaves and new grasses. The energy is not given up with the night, but is stored. It waits patiently in green forests and waving fields of grass, and then the animals come. . . .

Animals. They eat the grass and plants and leaves, storing and concentrating the energy in their bodies. And then the grass-eaters are devoured in turn by the meat-eaters, and these may also be eaten, or may die and release their energy again to the living plants. Life is a vast pyramid. Each layer feeds on the layer beneath it, and all live on the sun that is the pyramid's base. Man stands alone atop the pyramid, and in his pride he imagines that he is independent. It is only when he is thirsty or when his land blows away that he remembers the rain, the magic of water. . . .

Water. Sandoval nudged the snow with his boot. Water had given birth to life, and life could not survive without it. On Earth, it had taken five thousand pounds of water to produce a single pound of wheat. The water began here, falling from the clouds as the snow that covered the ground and melted against his face. The snow would be on the ground all winter, waiting. Further down the mountain, where the trees grew, banks of snow should accumulate in the shade. It would melt only slowly, and the insulating blanket of conifer needles would prevent the freezing of the soil underneath. The water would sink gradually into the sponge-like humus, and filter down and down, until the mountain became a reservoir of stored water, until great underground rivers flowed and seeped into the soil, giving life. When it reached the plains, the dry vegetation would suck it up, and some of the water would bubble up to the surface in clear springs, and creeks and brooks would feed the rivers that ran forever to the sea.

That was under normal conditions, of course.

Conditions here were not normal.

That was the trouble.

The land had been touched by fire and flood and famine. The forests were gone, the grasslands dead. When the water came, it splattered out into the sun-baked plains that could not absorb it. The water gushed through straight gullies and into rivers, carrying what was left of the topsoil with it. The silt-filled rivers rushed the brown flood away to the sea, and it was useless.

Sandoval shook his head, turned, and began to trudge down toward his copter. The wind cut at his face and his feet were cold in his boots. It was so easy to bring death to the land. . . .

He passed through a fire-blackened forest, its branches naked against the winter wind. He knew the forest well, every tree of it. He and his men had worked hard these many months, and Sandoval had been happy. This was work he believed in, and work he loved.

He had killed a million beetles in that dead bark, planted a million trees in that barren soil, calculated innumerable bacteria counts for the forest that would come again.

And woodpeckers! They looked very much like the woodpeckers of Earth, although they were of different species. After all, he reflected, a woodpecker is such a specialized bird that it has to follow a certain design: a long sturdy bill to drill under the bark with, feet to grip the bark while it works, tail feathers with supporting tips to hold it steady. They had hatched enough woodpeckers to stuff a spaceship, and they had not forgotten the nuthatches who would finish the job by getting the insects in the bark crevices.

World-savers?

Yes, they existed.

Not men.

Woodpeckers.

He reached the sheltered valley where his copter waited. He climbed into it with reluctance, despite the cold outside. Sandoval was a man of the land, content to leave the sky for others. He took off and flew down the valley and out into the warm air over the plains.

He smiled a little, looking down at the rolling country. He knew the plains, too. They had broken its baked surface, ploughed it with heavy remote equipment from the ship, poked holes in it to hold the water when it came. They had dug huge contour furrows to hold back the flooding of the rivers. They had caught and were breeding grazing animals to eat the grass that was as yet invisible. And tiny gophers and ground squirrels and rats to paw and tug at the soil, keeping it loose for other rains. And predators to control the grass-eaters. . . .

It wasn't easy to give life back to a dead land.

But Sandoval knew satisfaction. This land would come back, even as it had on a ruined Earth. One day it would be green again, deep with cool grasses, and the towns would return. . . .

The ship glinted before him, silver in the afternoon sun. The sight brought mixed feelings to Tino Sandoval. For just a moment, his vision clouded, and the ship became another ship, a wooden ship on a sea of blue, its sails puffed with the wind. Sandoval was an Indian, and he remembered.

The face of Admiral Hurley was too much like the faces that stared proudly from the pages of history books. The hand that he had shaken was too much like the hand that had been red with Mexico's blood.

(He had washed his hands thoroughly after he had shaken hands with the admiral. He had called himself a superstitious fool, but he had rubbed his hands on the towel until they hurt.)

And Evan Schaefer. A quiet man, a man easy to underestimate. Sandoval had known men like him before, men who could not be pushed, men who stood by your side when the chips were down. Men like Schaefer were rare in any age. He liked Evan Schaefer and his wife, but he knew he would never tell them so. He had found some late wildflowers in the valley, and he would put them in Lee's cabin.

She would know who had given them to her, being the kind of woman she was. Sandoval had known many women, but never one like Lee. She made him sad for all the years that might have been.

He landed the copter by the ship.

He had not seen Schaefer for many months. He hoped Schaefer was doing all right. . . .

Almost a year had passed since he had first glimpsed the town of the people, which they called Home-of-the-World, and Evan Schaefer knew now what he had to do.

The old priest Loquav, with his clear-sighted eyes and silver fur, had taught him many things besides the language of the people. He had taught him a religion that on one level was an erotic cast of harvest-goddesses and rain-gods, and on another level was a moving symbol of man's ties to the land on which he lived, the air he breathed, and the sun that warmed him. He had taken him out into the streets of Home-of-the-World, and into the poor houses. There he had seen the suffering and privation he had not seen in the market square: the tired women, the empty-eyed men, the silent and hungry children. He had spoken to him of other times, when the people had been as the grass of the fields, and the granaries had been choked with food.

And old Loquav had done more than that. He had made Schaefer feel at home with the people. He had given him the warmth of friendship in a hard winter. He had looked at a being who was monstrous by his standards, and seen only the man who lived in that body. It was a trick than men of Earth often could not learn.

Loquav had said to him, "I know not if you are man or god or devil, but while we are together you are my brother."

Schaefer had seen Marin twice, and they had talked, but it was a touchy business.

One night, when the red sun had just dipped below the far horizon and the long shadows were painting the adobe roofs with flat black fingers, Schaefer stepped out into the streets alone. He walked toward the market square, where he heard the night-music striking up for dancing.

That was when he saw it.

There, in the shadows.

A man who was too big to be of the people, and a thick voice muttering in English. *"Come on, Baby, wrap those fine long arms around me. I've been away a long, long time. . . .*

A native girl, curious and afraid, not wishing to offend, standing with her back against an adobe house wall.

Schaefer felt a sickness in his stomach. He hurried on to the market square, where fires were burning brightly and drums were throbbing like heart-beats. He saw more of them, men from the ship, dancing with the girls.

And he saw men of the people, standing in the shadows, watching in silence.

Schaefer did not hesitate. He ran to his copter, climbed into the cabin, and took off into the twilight. There was a black fury raging inside him, and he pushed the copter as fast as it would go, toward the ship and Admiral Hurley.

V

Coming down past the great tower of the ship, he felt like a bug crawling down a flagpole. The copter hit with a puff of dust, and Schaefer was out and running almost before it was secured.

He went through the airlock, jerked his oxygen mask off gratefully, and walked straight to Hurley's quarters, his heavy boots leaving a trail of dust behind him on the polished floors. He had been back to the ship twice to see Lee but Hurley came first this trip.

There was an officer outside Hurley's door.

"Just a minute, sir," the man said. "I have strict instructions—"

"Get out of my way, please."

"Sir, the admiral said—"

"This is important. Just say in your report that I overpowered you." Schaefer brushed past the man, while the officer muttered under his breath about civilians in general and Schaefer in particular.

Schaefer knocked on the door, hard.

It opened after a moment.

Schaefer swallowed the remark he had ready. It was Mrs. Hurley who stood before him, a gray-haired, motherly type, with a gentle face made to order for beaming over blueberry pie.

"Yes? Carl is taking a nap right now. . . ."

"I'm very sorry to disturb you, but I must see him. Now."

"Well, I don't know. I do hope there hasn't been any trouble? You must be that anthropologist person Carl told me about."

"Yes, Mrs. Hurley. I'm that anthropologist person, fangs and all. Now, if you'll just—"

"I'll handle this, Martha." Admiral Hurley stepped before her, fully dressed but with signs of sleep still in his eyes. "I'll see you in my office, Schaefer. You know better than to come here."

"I'll be waiting," Schaefer said. He nodded politely to Mrs. Hurley. "A pleasure, ma'am."

He walked up to Hurley's office, seated himself, and waited.

The admiral let him stew for ten minutes and then came in and sat down behind his desk. His balding head gleamed in the light. His lean, sharp-featured face was expressionless, but his green eyes were cold as ice.

"Well, Mr. Schaefer?"

Schaefer forced himself to be calm. He fished out his pipe and tobacco that he had picked up in his copter and puffed on it until he could taste the fragrant smoke. The admiral had kept him waiting and he was determined to repay the compliment. He blew a lazy smoke-ring at the ceiling.

"Well, Mr. Schaefer? I'm not accustomed to—"

"Neither am I," Schaefer snapped.

The admiral shrugged. "No personalities, please. I assume you have something you want to say to me?"

Schaefer leaned forward, his pipe clamped in his teeth. "You know why I'm here, Hurley."

"I'm afraid I haven't the faintest idea."

"Your men are in the town."

Hurley waved his hand impatiently. "Oh, that. Yes, of course. They have my permission."

Schaefer stood up. "You've got to get them back here."

"I give the orders to my men, Mr. Schaefer. Please remember where you are."

"Dammit, man, this is important! You don't know those people over there. They are very proud. This could ruin everything. If they don't get out, there'll be trouble."

Hurley smiled. "*You* don't know my men, Mr. Schaefer. Men are men. They always know when there are women within ten light-years."

"You don't understand, Admiral. If they're that eager, stick 'em in the icebox until we get through here."

Hurley shook his head. "Can't do that. Regulations specify that a ship landed on alien soil must maintain its crew in constant readiness."

Schaefer felt a chill of despair. Talking to Hurley was like ramming your head against a block of cement. "The people won't stand for it, Hurley."

"I'll be the judge of that."

"Listen, Hurley—"

"No, *you* listen, Mr. Schaefer." The admiral paused, holding himself under control. "I am in command of this ship. I'll give the orders that pertain to the morale and welfare of my men. It is not my will that has kept us on this planet for almost a year. It is not my responsibility that your party took up space that might have been used for other men's wives. You evidently thought it necessary to bring *your* wife along, and I do not condemn you for it. We will leave this planet whenever you inform me that our mission has been accomplished. Until that time, I have a crew of men to handle. We are doing a lot for those savages, Mr. Schaefer, and it's costing a lot of money. They can spare a few native women. I know the type; they're all the same."

"You've never even been over to look at them. Is that all they are to you—savages?"

Hurley shrugged.

"Answer me!"

"You are the ones who make the definitions, Mr. Schaefer. The rest of us have work to do. No one is forcing the natives to do anything. If they are overflowing with virtue, they will conduct themselves accordingly."

"With a gang of sex-hungry crewmen? You know better than that, Hurley."

The admiral got to his feet. "Was there anything else you wished to see me about?"

Schaefer was suddenly conscious that his fists were clenched at his sides, clenched so tightly that his fingers ached. *Oh, to take just one swing at that damned supercilious jaw!*

He forced himself to calm down.

"There's going to be trouble. You've been warned, Hurley, and I'll hold you personally responsible for whatever happens."

"Thank you for your warning," the admiral said evenly. "I'll take it under advisement."

"Thanks a lot."

Schaefer turned and left

The thing had started now, and there would be no stopping it.

Hurry, hurry!

He found Lee in their cabin. She was pale and thinner than before, but she was OK. He knew she would always be OK, and that he never had to worry about her again. He stayed with her for two hours, and told her what had happened.

Then, he got back in his copter and flew off to find Sandy.

Hurry, hurry!

It was three days before he could return to Home-of-the-World.

Deep beneath the walled town, in the dark temple of the people, Marin the priest-king stood straight and still, his dark eyes burning like the lamps that ringed the chamber walls. His long arms were hidden beneath the folds of his robe and his canine teeth flashed in the light when he spoke.

"You told me long ago that you came as a friend to help my people, Schaefer. I took your words for truth, for no man lies to his friend. My people have taken you in, fed you through a hard winter when the sun was pale, taught you our tongue. Now men of your own kind descend on the people like a plague. They take our women in the shadows and mock our Home-of-the-World. This must not be, this cannot be. Speak, Schaefer, for you have many things to explain."

Schaefer felt the weight of a city on his back, doubly heavy because Home-of-the-World was his home now, just as the men of the ship were men who might have been his brothers. A man caught in the middle was seldom lucky, he thought, despite the old joke. "All my words to you have been true words, Marin. In your heart you know this. There are many men in my tribe and I cannot control them all. You must endure those of my kind who make a mockery of your people and your traditions. You must tolerate them. There is no other way."

"And why must I do these things?"

"If there is trouble, my friend, I cannot help you. You must believe me when I say that my people are very powerful. It is better to let them alone."

The priest-king shook his head. "They do not let us alone," he pointed out, "and you have not helped me yet, Schaefer."

Schaefer took a deep breath. It was now or never. Marin would not be put off much longer with promises, not with strange men walking the streets of Home-of-the-World.

"Will you come with me, Marin? Will you let me take you into the sky in my machine? Will you let me *show* you how we have helped you, if you no longer accept my word?"

The priest-king hesitated and seemed to withdraw into the shadows of the vault. "This would not be a good time to leave my people."

"Marin is not afraid?"

The priest-king drew himself up proudly.

"I will go with you," he said. "When do we leave?"

"Right now."

"Let it be so."

Side by side, the two men walked out of Marin's chamber, into the large cavern with its hundreds of lamps burning, its black altar waiting in the alcove, its little rings of dark woodpecker-scalps hanging on the walls. Then up through the long winding corridor, and out into the dazzling sunlight.

The copter was waiting for them under the open sky.

Spring had come again to the land of the people, a powder of green sprinkled across the plains, a scattering of tiny spots of red and blue and yellow that were flowers in the sun. It was not a spring as Marin had seen it in his youth, when he had run barefoot with the other boys through dew-wet grasses and swung with them on the strong forest branches that laced the roof of the world, but it was a better spring than he had seen these later years, and a spring he had feared he might never see again.

It marked a turning point. That was the important thing.

Marin stared down at the rolling plains, cool with the fresh delicate green of new grass. His quick dark eyes caught the sparkle of fresh water in the streams, not the yellow-brown floods of mud that roared to the river, but living water to give the world a drink.

The copter had not impressed him much; it was alien magic.

The miracle he saw below him did impress him. This was a magic worth knowing.

"The land is coming back," he said simply.

"Yes. Next year it will be better still."

"How have you done this thing, Schaefer?"

"That's what I'm going to try to show you. It will not be easy for you."

"My people will do anything. When the land dies, the people follow. I have looked long at our children, and wondered."

Schaefer landed in a valley where a young forest had been planted. Even with their artificial growth techniques, the trees were little more than shrubs. But they were growing.

He led Marin up a winding trail to where green shoots were searching for life in the ruins of a fire-blackened growth of dead conifers. New flowers covered the forest floor and there was a hum of insects in the air.

There was another sound, too, cutting through the silence like a million hammers.

Woodpeckers.

Schaefer ripped away a chunk of dead black bark. A horde of beetles scrabbled for cover in the riddled wood underneath. A brave woodpecker buzzed past his face, eager to get at the bugs before they vanished under the bark.

Schaefer found a stump and sat down. Marin stood watching the woodpecker a moment, then he sat down beside Schaefer.

"You talk," he said. "I will listen."

Schaefer groped for eloquence in a foreign tongue. He told Marin as best he could what had happened to the ghost of a forest they saw around them. It had been a combination of many things, but he simplified the story to get his point across. It only took a little thing to kill the land. A tiny thing, an insignificant thing.

Like a woodpecker.

The people hunted woodpeckers, because they valued their black scalps as a wealth symbol. Every house had some woodpecker scalps; without them, a man was a pauper. The temple had thousands of them hanging in circles on the walls. Under ordinary circumstances, this wouldn't have mattered. Ninety-nine times out of a hundred nothing would happen.

But it had happened this time.

Nature was a living fabric, a neatly balanced system in which every organism had a job to do. The woodpecker's job was to drill into the bark of trees to get the beetles that lived there. Not all of them, of course. Just enough to keep the beetle population down to where the living tree could handle it.

Take some woodpeckers away. Take them away in a bad year, when the remaining woodpeckers fail to rebuild the forest woodpecker families. A tree falls in a windstorm ,and then another. Their roots are broken, their sap runs weakly. The remaining woodpeckers cannot reach the beetles that attack the tree where it lies on the ground.

The beetles breed and thrive and multiply.

Other trees become riddled with the bugs, and they die and fall. They lie on the ground, and they dry out. Dead dry wood, waiting—

A storm. Dark clouds massed in a turbulent sky. A flash of lightning, a crash of thunder. Another stab of lightning, another—

The dry wood is ignited.

The forest is in flames. The winds blow, and carry the flames to other trees. An entire watershed is destroyed, and this happens in many places.

The snow falls in the winter, piling up in drifts. With the spring sun it melts, and there is nothing to hold it. It rushes down the mountains in torrents, across the plains in a flood, into the rivers that rage toward the sea in a yellow-brown torrent of land-destroying fury—

The land dies. The grasses and animals disappear. There is no life-giving water in the soil. The winds blow, and the dust swirls in ugly clouds through the deserted towns where the people once lived and laughed and hoped. . . .

There was a long silence, broken only by the hum of insects and the *rat-tat-tat* of the woodpeckers.

"It is hard to believe," Marin said finally. "All that from a few woodpeckers."

"There were other things. The woodpecker, as it happens, was critical here."

"But the woodpecker scalp is wealth to us." Marin spread his hands, his long arms outstretched. "You know how men are."

You know how men are.

I know, I know.

"I will show you greater wealth," Schaefer said slowly.

He led the way back through the dawning life to the copter. He reached into the cabin and pulled out a sack.

"Hold out your hands, Marin."

He poured a pile of glittering gold coins into the waiting hands.

"I will teach you to make these. And there are other things you must learn about the land you live on."

They got into the copter, and it lifted into the air. They flew back over the plains that were living again, pale green in the spring sun.

And all the way back the sunlight glinted on the shiny gold coins that the priest-king ran through his fingers, over and over again.

Another year rushed by in Home-of-the-World. For Schaefer, it was a year of hard work and worry. He pulled a lot of cultural strings, getting across the idea that his gold coins were pleasing to the gods, while the woodpecker scalps were not. He showed the people where to find the gold in the streams, and what to do with it when they had it. He had some of the UN men demonstrate what could be done with a plot of land if the people would adopt a few improved farming techniques. There was a great deal of disease in the town, but he knew better than to introduce modern medicines which would only result in a population explosion that would negate everything else that had been done.

He worried as hard as he worked. Perhaps he was a natural worrier; Lee had always told him that he was. But it was an explosive situation, and it was only a matter of time before the fuse caught fire. His only hope was to finish his work and get out before disaster struck.

Fortunately, there were no pregnancies among the girls of the town who were running around with the crewmen of the ship. The men had sense enough to take their pills, and that helped.

Unfortunately, it took time for grass to grow, time for forests to come back, time for the water to seep down into the reservoirs of the mountains.

Sandy and his men nursed the trees along, and readied the different animals for the grasslands and the forests.

And, miraculously, the thing that Schaefer feared did not come for many long months.

But it finally came.

It came with shattering abruptness.

Two men from the ship, drunk on native beer, attacked a respected daughter of a nobleman. The girl crawled home through the garbage in the streets, and she died horribly.

The young men of Home-of-the-World did not wait for Marin to tell them what to do. They had seen their women taken from them for too long and they had swallowed their pride until it stuck in their throats.

Their rage was a flame swinging along the walls of the town.

Hundreds of them shouted together and became a mob, an avalanche of vengeance. They caught four innocent crewmen in their streets and they killed them very slowly, pulling their bodies apart with their immensely strong arms.

Then they took the pieces and threw them into a dark shop where other men from Earth were drinking.

Riot thundered in the walled adobe town, and out into the fields beyond. Within two hours the streets were deserted, the square windows black. There was silence in Home-of-the-World, the silence of the death that had been and the death that was yet to be.

All but one of the living crewmen ran from the town and rode their copters back to the ship. But the people caught one of them, and kept him alive. A hundred men bound his arms and dragged him out into the fields. Torches were lighted and songs were chanted, and the whole mob set out across the plains toward the ship, waving their spears and bows and clubs.

Schaefer was hidden in a tiny room beneath the temple. He did not dare show his face in the streets, for his face was white and that was enough for the men of the people.

"We've got to stop them," he whispered. "We've got to stop them before they reach the ship. They'll be wiped out, every last one of them."

Old Loquav, his short-sighted eyes blinking in the dim light of the lamp, shook his silver-furred head sadly. "It is said among my people that death can race between two tribes faster than the wind."

"Could you stop them, if you could reach them in time?"

The old priest shrugged. "Marin has already left Home-of-the-World to advise his people. But words spoken in a storm are torn from the mouth and are not heard."

"He won't make it, Loquav. Is my copter safe?"

"The machine has not been harmed."

"Could we get to it?"

"There is a way."

The gloom pressed in upon them with the weight of centuries.

"Come on! We've got to do what we can."

Loquav shook his head. "I must do what must be done," he said, looking at Schaefer. "You, my friend, must rejoin your people. That is the way of the world."

There was no time for argument.

The old priest led the way, and the two men hurried along a dark twisting tunnel toward the stars.

The copter overtook the mob when it was a little over a mile from the ship. From the air, the people were a blaze of orange torches in the night, a nightmare of phantom shadows against the starlit silver of the plains.

"Put me down between my people and your people," Loquav said. "Be careful that you do not get trapped within range of the arrows, for an arrow asks not a man's motive."

Schaefer could not see the captive crewman, but he knew he was there. He toyed with the notion of trying to land the copter in the midst of the torches in an attempt to snatch the man to freedom, but he knew that the plan would not work.

He flew on, then skidded the copter to a halt on the level plains a few hundred yards from the marching men. He could hear the drums now, and the chants that filled the night with sound. There was grass under the copter where there had been dust two years ago, but that counted for nothing now.

Loquav touched his shoulder. "Goodbye, my friend," he said. "I will remember you with kindness in my heart."

The old priest climbed down from the cabin, turned his near-sighted eyes toward the torch-flames, and began to walk steadily to meet his people.

Schaefer skimmed the copter over the grass until he reached the ship. He left it with the other copters and the airlock opened to take him in.

"Glad you made it, Schaefer," an officer said. "We were worried about you."

Schaefer tore off his mask. "Where's Hurley?"

"Control room. They've got the negatives on the scope. Bill Bergman is still alive, but he looks bad."

"Bergman the one they caught?"

"That's right. He's a good kid, Dr. Schaefer."

"They're all good kids."

He ran through a ship tense with excitement and hurried into the control room. It was fully staffed and ready for action. Admiral Hurley stared at a viewscreen, his face taut with worry.

"Schaefer?"

"Yes."

"I want you to look at this."

Schaefer looked. The people were clear in the screen; he could see their thin faces, their long arms, their eyes burning in the torch-light. He saw Bill Bergman too—hardly more than a boy, with close-cropped hair and wide, terrified eyes. Four of the people were carrying Bergman, one for every arm and leg.

They were going to tear him apart.

He saw old Loquav, his back to the ship, waving his arms and talking to them. The people pushed him out of the way and came on.

The admiral's voice was surprisingly hushed when he spoke. It was the voice of an honest man who faced his mistake squarely. "I was wrong, Dr. Schaefer. That will not bring those boys back."

"No, it won't. It's too late now."

He stared at the people. A maddened mob of savages—yes, if you looked at it that way. But they were men as well, men who had taken all they could take, men who had been pushed too far. They were remembering their wives and daughters, and the men who had come among them in friendship.

"Our fire is accurate," Hurley said. "We can pick them off without touching Bergman."

Schaefer nodded, his stomach a sick knot inside him. A simple choice. A hundred men who would never have a chance for a boy who had meant no harm.

The torches came closer. The people stopped.

They held Bergman's body up, ready to pull it to pieces.

Hurley turned to Schaefer with a stricken face.

"You decide," he whispered.

The four men began to pull, slowly.

Schaefer closed his eyes. "Don't hit the priest," he said. "He was only trying to stop them."

The admiral straightened up.

"Fire!" he ordered.

VI

There on that shadowed night-land, beneath the radiance of the stars, the men of the people fell like wheat severed by the scythe. They fell one by one, the shock of amazement on their faces, when they still had faces. They fell and they writhed briefly in the cool green of the grass, and then they moved no more.

It was over in seconds.

Perhaps it was an accident, perhaps not. Schaefer never knew. But old Loquav fell with the rest, his close-sighted eyes at last giving up the struggle to see.

Only the boy named Bill Bergman remained on his feet, while the torch-flames flared and sputtered around him like the fires of hell. He covered his face with his hands and stumbled toward the ship.

"Go out and bring him in," Hurley ordered. There was no triumph in his voice.

"I'm going too," Schaefer said.

The admiral nodded. "Yes. Maybe we ought to see it up close. Maybe we owe them that, at least."

They left the ship and walked through the starlight across the grass they had planted. They walked up to the pile of bodies and there was nothing to say.

Schaefer found the old priest, and cradled Loquav's silver head in his arms. He could not even cry.

"Shall we bury them?" Hurley asked finally.

"No. No, I don't think so. We can't give them a burial that would have any meaning for them. These are not our dead. Their people will come for them."

"What can we do?"

"We can get the blazes out of here before there's any more killing. It's all over, Carl. I can never go back to the town again, even if Marin himself would be willing—he couldn't control the others after what's happened here tonight."

Hurley seemed to be searching for some words that didn't exist. He finally said, "Were you nearly finished?"

"It all depends. I think Sandy has his end pretty well taken care of. I thought I had Marin ready to do what was necessary—now I don't know."

"I wish there was something I could do."

You've done enough, pal, Schaefer thought, then choked off the feeling. Hurley at least knew when he had made a mistake, which was more than could be said for most men. "You can get this ship away right now, tonight, as fast as you can. That's all there is left to us."

Schaefer looked across the starlit plains toward the town the people called Home-of-the-World. He knew those rolling plains were far from empty. Out there in the long silence of the night, Marin was standing, watching him, wondering.

Don't let it all have been for nothing, old friend, Schaefer prayed. *Try to remember the good with the rest. Try not to think too badly of me when you grieve for your dead. Keep your land always, priest-king, and use it well.*

He touched Loquav's wet shoulder in a last goodbye. The flames of the torches hissed in the grass, burning themselves out. The other dead, the nameless ones, were stacked like cordwood in the shadows.

Schaefer remembered words from long ago. *"It is my prayer that there will always be friendship between your people and my people."*

Had there been other men, in other times, who had voiced that prayer in vain?

He turned and followed the living back toward the ship. The stars were bright above him, and they had never seemed so far away.

The men from Earth could not leave that night.

It was late the next afternoon before Sandy agreed to come in from his forest, where he had been adjusting the wildlife balance in the ecological system he had set up. When he got out of his copter he walked over to the terrible dark pile under the hot red sun and looked at it in tight-lipped silence.

He said nothing to Hurley when he entered the ship, and his only question to Schaefer was about Benito Moravia. After that he was silent and withdrawn, as though seeking to disassociate himself from the men around him.

The great ship lifted on the soundless power of her antigravs, a silver giant drifting up the ladder of the sky. She rose into flame-edged clouds, and beyond them through the peaceful blue of the atmosphere.

She entered the bright silence of space, and her atomics splashed white flame into the sea that washed the shores of forever.

She was going home.

Where the ship had been, there was a hushed quiet. It was a hot and windless day, and the grass hardly moved under the glare of the red sun. Miles away, toward the mountains, a herd of animals snorted nervously, and lifted their heads from the clean streams that chuckled down from the hills where new forests grew.

And the dead were very still.

The people came with the evening shadows. Brothers and wives and sweethearts and fathers and mothers, they picked through the bodies, searching for faces they had known. And then they carried their dead back through the merciful darkness to Home-of-the-World.

Marin the priest-king went directly to his temple, where torches flamed around the walls and he could not hear the mourning songs of his people. He knelt before the dark altar and closed his eyes.

He saw old Loquav, who had padded through these corridors when Marin was yet a boy. He saw all his people, who had trusted him, and now were gone.

He saw other things as well.

He saw sweet grass where there had been no grass. He saw streams with clear water, where you could count the pebbles on the bottom and drink until your eyes ached. He saw trees and flowers where there had been only naked fire-blackened ghosts.

He saw children of his people, no longer hungry and frightened, and he saw their children beyond them, fading into the gray mists of all the years that were to come.

Marin the priest-king prayed a very hard prayer. He prayed for the safety of the ship that had come from the skies, and now was going back to a land he would never see.

Then he opened his eyes and prayed a much easier prayer.

He prayed that the ship would never again come to the people who lived in Home-of-the-World.

The ship sailed a starbright sea, and the years whispered by like wind-blown sands where winds and sands could never be.

Schaefer lay frozen in his slot, with tubes in his nostrils and a mask covering his sightless eyes. He felt nothing now, and there are no dreams in death.

But before the nothingness had come, when the doctor had taken his body from the warm slab and the medics had carried him through the lock and into the glistening catacombs where he would spend the voyage to Earth in not-life, he had seen faces before his freezing eyes.

Lee's, framed by soft brown hair, warming him even as the blood slowed in his veins.

Sandy's, lost in self-accusation that reached far back into the past, back into a time when his own people had been visited by ships that had sailed strange seas.

Hurley's, lean and composed now beneath his balding head, hiding the failure that crawled through his chest.

Loquav.

Marin.

And, most of all, the haunted face and tortured eyes of Benito Moravia.

Moravia, waiting and wondering and fearing, as the long years crept by . . .

The ship touched down on Earth twelve years and two months from the day of its departure. It landed at night, in secrecy. No bands played, no one greeted them.

Its arrival was never publicly announced.

Moravia, of course, was informed that it had landed.

Schaefer and his wife hurried home, knowing that he would be waiting for them there.

Their house floated at five thousand feet, a cool green island in the gold of the sun. Time had passed it by, and it was unchanged, waiting for them.

This was like a thousand other homecomings they had know. They had gone out, perhaps to eat at Rocky Falls, as they had done so often now that they were alone. They were coming back, on an ordinary afternoon in a familiar world, with only a threat of rain blowing in from the west to hint at anything unusual.

Bur there was already a copter in the garage.

They landed and went inside. Schaefer held his wife's arm; Lee was very tired, although she was trying not to show it. Their home was soothing around them, its redwood walls warm and welcoming.

An old man rose from his chair as they entered. A cigarette trembled slightly in his blue-veined hand. The hair that had been black was a faded gray. The haunted brown eyes were tired, and the lines in the face had deepened.

For Benito Moravia, it had been twelve tough years.

"Lee," he said. "Evan."

Moved by an impulse she did not attempt to understand, Lee went to him and kissed him on the cheek. Schaefer stepped forward and gripped a hand that had little strength left in it.

"Hello, Ben," he said.

"I heard about everything," the old man said. "Got an abstract of Hurley's report. Is Sandy with you?"

Schaefer hesitated. "He didn't want to come," he said finally.

Moravia nodded. "I can understand that. I knew he would feel that way."

Lee broke the silence. "Can I get you a drink, Ben?"

"I could use one." He smiled faintly. "Ulcer or no ulcer. How does it feel to see a man get old while you stay young, Evan?"

Schaefer didn't answer that one.

They sat and sipped at their drinks, sensing the tension in the room. Schaefer could not face the old man before him and ask the questions that had to be asked. He was certain of the answers, and Ben had been hurt enough already.

The house swayed with a barely perceptible motion as a gust of wind hit it. It was darker outside now, and the sun was hidden behind a bank of black-edged clouds. It was going to rain, and rain hard. Schaefer could have lifted the house over the storm, but he made no move, letting it come.

They were on their second drink. An electric hush surrounded them, that breathless calm that welcomes the rain. Moravia looked at the floor and began to talk.

"You're wondering why I did it."

Schaefer waited, neither confirming nor denying the statement.

"I took a chance," Moravia said. "I took a long chance, maybe. A man has to do that sometimes. But I didn't know, I couldn't know . . ."

His voice trailed off.

They waited for him.

"More than a hundred natives. Four men from the crew. That's a lot of lives to have on your conscience." Moravia looked up at them, as though asking for their accusation.

Lee said, "Do you mean you *knew* what was going to happen? Is that what you're trying to say? Could you have—"

Her husband's hand silenced her with a touch.

The taut hush was unbearable, waiting.

"Go on, Ben," Schaefer said.

Moravia talked rapidly, wanting to get it out, wanting to get rid of it. "I knew when I first went to Dr. Schaefer that there would be trouble. I hoped it would be minor; I should have known better. But even the machines can't tell you *everything*. There *had* to be an incident, Lee. Can't you see that?"

He looked at her, his eyes pleading.

She looked away.

"A man in my position has to make decisions. That's what he's there for. They are seldom pleasant ones." He lit a cigarette, inhaled it deeply. "Here were a people facing ruin if I did not act. You saw the land, you know what would have happened to them. I could have closed my eyes, stuck to the letter of the law. I could have let them die, and no one would have questioned that course."

"I know that, Ben," Schaefer said.

The wind came up again, rustling through the room, heavy with the wet smell of rain. Thunder rolled gently in the west.

"The law said that the fourth planet of Aldebaran was forbidden to us." The old man bit the words out, hating them. "It's a good law, we all know that. That world is defenseless, and they have a right to be let alone. And yet I *had* to break that law, or hundreds of thousands of people would starve. You all saw that, but you only saw half the problem. I had to break that law—*and I had to break it in such a way that it would never be broken again.* I had to make absolutely certain that the only precedent I set was a bad one. There *had* to be trouble. Otherwise—"

"The story would have leaked out," Schaefer finished for him. "Men would point to what you had done the next time they wanted to go back to some helpless people. They could have used our trip as a justification for damned near anything. They could say that it had been tried once, and no one had suffered, so why can't we just get those minerals, trade with those natives, start just a *tiny* colony? It would have been the beginning of the end, for millions of human brings. I know why you did what you did, Ben."

Moravia went on as though he had not heard, speaking tonelessly as though reading an indictment. "I put Hurley in command of that ship because I knew he would make the mistakes he made. I picked the men of the crew, because I knew they would act as they acted. I sent *you* out there, knowing you might not come back. I wanted an incident, and I got one. We're safe on that score, for what it's worth. No government will ever speak out about this voyage, because they all share the responsibility. The UN will never talk. Hurley will keep his mouth shut or face a court martial. The law is safe, Evan. We spent a hundred lives and saved hundreds of thousands. I've tried to tell myself that's a good record. I've tried. . . ."

"If you had known how many would be killed—if you had known for certain that even one life would be lost—would you have gone ahead?"

The old man stood up. He was very thin and his head was bowed. "It's too much for any man to decide, Evan. I'm probably ruined—my career, everything—and I don't even know whether I did right or wrong. I don't know what the words mean any longer. I tried to kill myself when I heard what I had done, and I couldn't even do that."

Lee went to his side, touched his arm, not speaking, making no judgments.

Moravia turned and looked into Schaefer's eyes. "You were there, Evan. You saw it all. What should I have done, Evan? Tell me. *What should I have done?*"

Schaefer saw again the green grass of the plains, the trees of a new forest, a living land where there had been only death. And he saw old Loquav, and four crewmen ripped apart, and a dark pile of bodies under a hot red sun.

"No man can answer that, Ben," he said softly.

Almost blindly, Moravia stumbled out onto the porch, where the cool wind was fresh in his face. Schaefer joined him there, feeling the coming storm. They stood side by side, separated by a gulf no words could bridge.

A tongue of pure white lightning licked down from black clouds. The world held its breath and then the thunder crashed and boomed away with the wind. Lights came on like yellow fireflies in the darkness, and far below them the tree-tops danced in the shadows.

A gray wall of water swept over them, drenching them, but they hardly noticed.

They stood there on a house in the sky, each alone, looking down into the wildness of the wind, watching the driving sheets of rain that cleansed their Earth.

THE ONE THAT GOT AWAY

When Beaver Lodge burned to the ground, Charlie Buckner didn't pay particular attention. He was sorry that Al and Rita had lost their investment, of course, but to tell the truth he didn't figure he'd miss all that neon anyway.

When Bob Sanderford's brand new Mountain Super Service Station blew up and took Bob with it, that was a shade more serious.

When the Lazy T Dude Ranch caught fire and blistered a batch of dudes, Charlie began to worry a little. Elkhorn Valley couldn't spare any dudes, and neither could Charlie.

He was reading a letter when the news came, and the letter had him riled up anyhow. It was from Old Kermit Thompson over in Carson Creek, and it got Charlie so hot under the collar that his rimless spectacles fogged up.

The pertinent part of the letter read as follows:

Let me tell you something, Charlie boy, and you can pass it on to your hotshot Chamber of Commerce. The tourists over here in Carson Creek are catching so many trout that the game warden hasn't been to bed for a week. The streams are so full of fish that the water has to work up a sweat to get over them. They ain't no stock-pond babies, either. I thought you might enjoy the enclosed photos, which just represent an average catch over here.

The pictures were of trout, naturally. Lovely trout, in full color. Big, husky trout. *Piles* of trout.

When the phone rang, Charlie stuffed the letter and the pictures into the back pocket of his jeans and picked up the receiver.

"Gunnison Ranch," he growled. "Buckner speaking."

"Charlie? Earl here. We got another one. The Lazy T is on fire, and a couple of people got hurt before they got out. I swear I don't know what's going on around here."

315

"Anything I can do?"

"Nope, they got it under control now. But I'm beginning to think we've got a firebug on our hands. I thought you might want to check your cabins."

"Right. Thanks for calling, Earl. Let me know if anything else happens."

Charlie hung up, jammed on his battered straw hat, climbed into his new red jeep, and made the circuit of his tourist cabins.

Things seemed normal enough.

The people from Dallas in Cabin 5 couldn't get the coal stove going, so Charlie opened the draft for them, hauled out the ashes, and showed them how to strike a match. The salesman from Oklahoma in Cabin 3 wasn't catching any fish, and Charlie explained to him that it wasn't customary to use a sinker with dry flies. The nervous lady in Cabin 7 had heard a mouse running over the bed springs, and Charlie assured her that it was merely a bird on the roof, meanwhile making a mental note that he was feeding the cats too much. His two regulars in the end cabin insisted that he have a cup of coffee with them, which killed an hour.

Charlie had sharp eyes, but he saw no signs of any firebug.

Still, he could be next.

There had been six big fires in Elkhorn Valley in the past two years. In fact, come to think of it, just about every modern building in the town had burned down. Maybe he ought to be thankful he'd stuck to his rustic cabins with outhouses, because it sure looked as though something funny was going on.

Charlie decided that he had better think out the problem in earnest. There was only one way to do that, of course.

He told Mary where he was going, which didn't please her unduly because she was ironing sheets, and got his thinking equipment ready.

He put his rod, trout basket, net, and waders into the jeep and drove off to go fishing.

He drove up Beaver Creek Canyon past the old mine and parked the jeep on a dirt cutoff that was hardly more than a pair of tire tracks that veered off toward the stream. He got his gear ready, filled his antediluvian pipe with tobacco from a red can, and lit up with a wooden kitchen match.

Charlie puffed in satisfaction. The spring thaws on the slopes of the Rockies had filled Beaver Creek with clean cold water, and the willows that lined the stream were green and fresh. The sky was cloudy and the air was cool and crisp.

He was aware that the tourists hadn't been doing too well on Beaver Creek in the last few months, but that didn't bother him any. The way he figured it, it was a miracle they caught any fish at all. Anyhow, he knew the trout were in there; he had dumped them in himself when he served his annual time on the Fish and Game Commission.

He waded into the stream and got down to business, casting with an accurate and flexible wrist. He may have been putting on the pounds around the middle, he thought, but he could still work Beaver Creek with the best of them.

In two hours he caught two fish, both of which he threw back.

He thought of Kermit Thompson and his photographs and muttered a few phrases that should have boiled the water in the stream.

He tried every fly he had with him. The trout sneered at all of them.

Along about noon, when the dudes began swarming over the stream with their fancy tackle, Charlie did the sensible thing. He waded out of the stream, arranged himself comfortably behind the shelter of a pile of rocks, pulled his straw hat down over his eyes, and went to sleep.

When he woke up two hours later, the first thing he noticed was that it was raining. It was more of a drizzle, really; a fine gray mist that slanted down from the mountains and glistened on the willows and flowers.

Charlie yawned, stood up, and stretched. He looked out at the stream idly, stared, and suddenly sat down again. He crawled forward and peered between the rocks, hardly believing his eyes. Charlie was a lot smarter than he looked, and he had been around some in his time. Just the same, he had never seen anything like *this* before.

There were three fishermen that he recognized by the stream. They were all tourists from Elkhorn Valley, and he could see their cars parked up on the road. They were all dressed up in the latest fishing duds and they all had rods in their hands—but they weren't fishing.

They weren't even in the water, They were standing by the side of the stream, absolutely motionless. They didn't move a muscle, and their faces were as blank as so many slabs of salami.

They looked frozen—literally.

There was one other man on the stream, and *he* was fishing. Fishing? He was murdering the fish. He was working his way upstream, whistling a little tune, and at every cast a fat trout leaped at his fly as though it were the grandfather of all the juicy worms that had ever lived. He landed trout until his basket sagged on his shoulder, and they were beauties.

The three men on the bank stood like statues, never even looking at the fisherman.

Charlie stared until his eyes hurt, feeling rather like Rip Van Winkle. What was going on? The man in the stream looked ordinary enough, although his costume was rather like Churchill's zipper suit, but seemingly made out of plastic of some sort. Whoever he was, he was some fisherman.

Along about five in the evening, when the sun was thin behind the clouds and the air was growing cold, the man climbed out of the stream. He knelt down on the bank, took something metallic out of the pocket of his clothing, and punched what appeared to be a button.

At once, the other three gentlemen came to life. They blinked their eyes and began to walk as though unaware that anything had happened. They headed straight for their cars, shaking their heads.

Charlie overheard a snatch of conversation between two of them as they went by:

"Do any good today, Joe?"

"No luck at all. I never even saw a fish."

"Me neither. I'm going to try the lake tomorrow. I'm pooped."

The cars drove off.

The man in the curious suit hauled out a long knife and began to clean his fish, happily sawing off heads and tossing them into the stream.

That was when the *thing* appeared.

It looked like a gray metallic box about ten feet square. It came drifting lazily out of the sky without making a sound and landed by the bank of the stream. A door whispered open and yellow light spilled out. As far as Charlie could tell, the box was empty.

The man finished cleaning his fish, put his knife away, and stood up. He rubbed his cramped leg muscles, picked up his rod and trout basket, and started for the box.

Charlie had seen enough.

He got to his feet, spat accurately at a blue flower, and stepped out from behind the rocks.

"Hey, you!" he hollered. "Just a dad-blamed minute."

The oddly-dressed man stopped with one foot in the door of the metal box. He turned, his eyes wide with surprise. They were funny eyes, too.

Kind of violet, Charlie decided,

"Me friend," the man said rapidly. He looked just a trifle flustered.

"Like hell you are," Charlie retorted. "And what the devil kind of talk is that?"

The mail made an effort and collected himself. It took him a moment to digest the words, and he frowned. "I beg your pardon. Are you a minister?"

"No," Charlie said, "I ain't."

"I assumed from your use of sacred words—you must forgive me. You startled me, and I seem to be a bit confused."

Charlie, put his hands on his hips. "You got a license for those fish you caught?"

"Why, no. Of course not."

"You pay taxes?"

'No. I mean, I don't pay them *here*." The man groped for words. "Me friend."

"Don't start that again. I ain't no Indian. And you ain't no friend of mine. Who in blazes do you think you are, anyway?"

"My name is—ah—Onthal. I can explain—"

"You've got a powerful lot of explaining to do, Mr. Onthal. What did you do to those other fishermen?"

"The natives? Why, I merely immobilized them. Surely, Mr.—ah—er—"

"Buckner. Charlie Buckner."

"Surely, Mr. Buckner, you don't expect me to come all the way and fish with *others* on the stream. Get away from it all, that's the whole idea—"

"You own Beaver Creek?"

"Well no, not exactly—"

Charlie stuck his grizzled chin forward. "Mr. Onthal, we've been having a mess of fires over in Elkhorn Valley. You know anything about them fires?"

The man tried to back away and was stopped by the metal box. "Me friend," he said.

Charlie spat. "Sure, you're a real pal. Say, what kind of fly is that you were, using? It's dynamite."

Still off-balance. the man fumbled for it and held it up as though he had never seen it before. "This? Why, it's just a common green-tailed Buster."

Charlie peered at it, but the light was getting bad and it was hard to see. He considered asking Onthal to step away from the lighted door, but decided not to push his luck too far.

"A green-tailed Buster, eh? Common, you say?"

"Oh, extremely." The man swallowed, then pulled himself together. He seemed suddenly taller. "See here, Mr. Charlie. You're playing with fire."

"The shoe," Charlie informed him, "is on the other foot"

"Shoe? Foot?" The man hesitated, and for a moment Charlie was afraid that he was going to come out with the Indian-Paleface routine again. He got back on the track, however. "I mean, I could simply *obliterate* you."

"Why don't you?"

The man was taken aback. "It seems—well, crude."

"'There were people killed in those fires."

The man waved his hand. "Regrettable. But it was a mere side effect, we didn't intend—"

Charlie spat again. "Don't bother explaining. Instead, let me suggest a good reason for not harming me. I've got something you want."

"You? Have something *we* want?"

"Yeah, me. The colorful native."

"I find that hard to believe . . ."

"It's on the level, just the same." Charlie remembered that Onthal wasn't too hot on idioms. "It's the truth," he added.

"What is this—ah—item?"

Charlie settled his hat more firmly on his head. "Nothing doing, pal." He pointed vaguely up at the dark clouds. "You've got a ship up there, right?"

The man's mouth opened and closed but no sound came forth.

"I think you'd better haul me up there," Charlie said firmly, "and we'll talk a little turkey."

"Me—"

"I mean, I think we can make a deal. How about it?"

The man looked around for his voice and finally found it. "This is unprecedented."

"What have you got to lose? You can obliterate me up there if you've a mind to, can't you?"

"I suppose it could be done. Yes."

"Then let's get going. It's cold out here."

The man muttered something in an alien tongue and waved Charlie into the metal box.

Charlie stepped inside and took off his hat. The thing reminded him of an elevator.

Onthal joined him and the door shut.

There was a lifting sensation.

Charlie smiled.

As has been stated, Charlie was a great deal smarter than he looked . . .

The ship was just a spaceship, no more and no less. Of course, Charlie Buckner had never actually seen one before, but he read the papers and he knew what to expect. As a matter of fact, he didn't get to see this spaceship either; there were no windows in the box, and when the door opened again Charlie and Onthal were inside the ship.

"Quite a layout you got here," he said.

Onthal smiled. "Come with me. I will take you to the others."

Charlie followed him, keeping his eyes open. He was impressed, but hardly overwhelmed. The ship was on the plush side, just as he had anticipated.

When he saw the large room in which the other men were gathered, he relaxed. He was sure of himself now, on familiar ground. The room inside the spaceship had wooden panels with polished knotholes, a flashy bar—tended by a robot, but what the hell—and a big log fire blazing in a useless fireplace.

I know these birds, Charlie thought. *They're all the same, no matter where they come from.*

There was a sudden excited babble when Charlie made his entrance, all of it in an unfamiliar language.

Onthal held up his hand for silence. He cleared his throat, pleased with his own importance. "You know the rules, men," he said. "We speak only English when a native is present."

"What's he doing here?" a big balding man demanded, his face flushed with too many drinks. "What did you bring him here for?"

"He says that he—um—wishes to offer us a deal."

A slender blonde, whose function on a fishing trip was obviously other than piscatorial, giggled. "Isn't he quaint?"

To add to the local color, Charlie took out his pipe, filled it carefully, and lit it. Calmly, he flipped the match into the fireplace.

Another man, seemingly a person of some importance, stepped forward. "Your name, sir?"

"Charlie Buckner. And yours?"

"That does not concern you. We are not savages, Mr. Buckner. I will not pretend to offer you hospitality here. You will not be permitted to leave this ship alive."

"Glad to meet you, too." Charlie puffed on his pipe. "You're pretty jumpy, Clyde."

The man frowned. "You do not understand our position. We are not men of your world—"

"You can skip all that. I know all about you."

The man blinked. "You *do?*"

"Certainly. If you will be so good as to pour me a drink, I'll explain."

The man hesitated, then snapped his fingers. The robot rolled over with a tall glass on a tray. Charlie thanked him and sampled the drink. It was smooth. Definitely quality. Class.

Naturally.

"Well?" the man demanded.

Charlie sighed. "Back home, wherever that is, you people are successful businessmen. You work hard all the time, and the pressure builds up. When you take a vacation, you want to get away from it all. You like brief doses of unspoiled nature, and you like good fishing. Evidently, your own world is too citified for what you want, so you come to Elkhorn Valley. How am I doing?"

The man pursed his lips. "You're seriously suggesting that we'd bring a spaceship all the way from—well, all that way just to go fishing?"

"I'm not suggesting it. I know it. Look, amigo, I'm in the tourist business myself. I know how much money is spent every year just to go fishing somewhere. Why else would you come to our planet? You're way ahead of us in gadgets and machines, so we wouldn't have much to offer except scenery and fishing and hunting. I figured that right off. But why do you have to sneak around like you do? What are you afraid of?"

The man looked at the others who were gathered around and smiled. "You seem to be an intelligent man, Mr. Buckner. What do you think would happen to our fishing if the news got out that the Earth had been contacted from outer space?"

Charlie chewed that one over for a minute. It made sense. "You've got a point there. But I can't say much for the way you've conducted yourselves. You've got a lot to answer for."

"The Earth," the man said rather pompously, "is not yet ready for the galactic civilization. You would not be capable of accepting what we have even if it were offered to you—"

Charlie downed his drink, then gave the man explicit instructions as to how he could dispose of his galactic civilization. "I don't give a hang about all that junk. I'm talking about *me*. You don't pay taxes and you don't spend any money in Elkhorn Valley. You throw a fog around the other tourists so they don't get their share of fish. You burn buildings down—why, I don't know. Next thing, the other tourists—the paying customers—will stop coming. You call that fair?"

The man spread his hands with a we're-all-reasonable-men-here gesture. "Mr. Buckner, we have been visiting Elkhorn Valley for several of your years. It means a great deal to us. The problems of galactic administration and commerce—"

Charlie snorted.

"Well, never mind. You may find this hard to understand, Mr. Buckner, but we *love* Elkhorn Valley. We love it the way it is—primitive, unspoiled, rustic. You don't appreciate your own values. When you start putting up fancy clubs and internal combustion stations, you *ruin* Elkhorn Valley. We come a long way every year to find what we want, and we simply cannot permit this commercialization. That's what we're trying to get away from, don't you see?"

"So if we build something you don't like, you burn it down?"

"Naturally. Upon occasion, we like to wander through the village. It is a tonic to us. We don't *want* any changes here."

"I've felt the same way myself, Clyde. But I've got a living to make."

The man shrugged. "That is unfortunate."

"Isn't it, though?" Charlie helped himself to another drink. The robot, he decided, was the most friendly person on the ship. "But I think we can make a deal."

The man chuckled. "Really, Mr. Buckner. I don't mean to be insulting, but you have nothing that we want."

"That's where you're barking up the wrong tree." Charlie sensed that he had lapsed into idiom again and corrected himself. "I mean, you are mistaken. I have what you want more than anything else. But you won't get it without a promise that I will be returned safely to Elkhorn Valley."

"That's impossible. You know too much. I tell you, we absolutely *refuse* to get all tangled up with the local tribal governments. It would be the end of everything. We wouldn't get a moment's peace. Why, we might even have to go on television." The man shuddered.

"I can keep my mouth shut. Give me some tests or something if you don't believe it. I don't care a used salmon egg about men from another world, and I never worried any about Earth either. I care about my business and Charlie Buckner. Can't *you* understand that?"

"It sounds familiar," the man admitted.

"Okay. Deal or no deal?"

"Give him a chance," the blonde said, eying him speculatively.

"We'll see. What is this thing you have that you think we want, Mr. Buckner?"

Charlie smiled. He had them now.

He reached into the back pocket of his jeans and pulled out the letter from Old Kermit Thompson. He handed it over. Then he hauled out the photographs and handed *them* over.

The man's eyes widened. He read the juicy parts aloud:

> The tourists over here in Carson Creek are catching so many trout that the game warden hasn't been to bed for a week. The streams are so full of fish that the water has to work up a sweat to get over them. They ain't no stock-pond babies, either. . . .

He passed the photographs around.

There was a collective murmur of astonishment.

Charlie stoked up his pipe again and moved closer to the fire. "I know you people," he said. "A dude is just a dude, no matter where he comes from. You folks came down here in your fancy ship and found a spot you liked. Then you never looked no farther. You come back every year to the same place. You never bothered with the other side of the hill. You were too lazy to get off the beaten track. Well, just take a look at them fish. The *tourists* are catching 'em like that over in Carson Creek, and they don't have the equipment that you people have got. Now, you take one of them there green-tailed Busters up to Carson Creek . . ."

Charlie let his voice trail off. He had been dealing with tourists for a long, long time. He figured he knew how to handle them. If there was one thing they couldn't resist, it was news about better fishing somewhere else.

There was a mild pandemonium in the spaceship room.

There were *piles* of trout in those photographs—*big* trout.

Onthal pushed his way up to him, his violet eyes shining.

"Ah, Mr. Buckner?"

"Ummm?"

"How do we get to Carson Creek?"

Charlie hauled out the pencil and paper he always carried for just such occasions. He felt fine.

"Looky here. You just follow this road up Beaver Creek Canyon over the pass. Then, you go on due north about fifteen-sixteen miles. You'll come to a little lake shaped like a heart—you can see it plain from the air. Then you angle off to the left here . . ."

Charlie was feeling pretty good.

A man seldom obliterates anyone who tips him off to better fishing.

A month or so later, things had quieted down considerably in Elkhorn Valley.

There hadn't been any more local fires, and the Lazy T Dude Ranch had been repaired, The fishing was better than it had been in some years, and all of Charlie's cabins were full.

Charlie felt a faint twinge of regret when he read in the paper about Kermit Thompson's place over on Carson Creek burning to the ground, but that was the way the old ball bounced.

He waited until Mary was busy with her ironing, then loaded up his red jeep. He checked the tank. It was full—plenty for the run over the pass.

Charlie figured he'd just mosey on over to Carson Creek and sample the fishing.

Maybe he'd even run across Onthal again.

He filled his pipe and lit it with a sigh of satisfaction.

Onthal wasn't a bad guy when you got to know him.

Besides, he wanted to get a *good* look at that green-tailed Buster.

TRANSFUSION

The machine stopped.

There was no sound at all now, and the green light on the control panel blinked like a mocking eye. With the easy precision born of long routine, Ben Hazard did what had to be done. He did it automatically, without real interest, for there was no longer any hope.

He punched a figure into the recorder: 377.

He computed the year, using the Gottwald-Hazard Correlation, and added that to the record: 254,000 B.C.

He completed the form with the name of the site: Choukoutien.

Then, with a lack of anticipation that eloquently reminded him that this was the three hundred seventy-seventh check instead of the first, Ben Hazard took a long preliminary look through the viewer. He saw nothing that interested him.

Careful as always before leaving the Bucket, he punched in the usual datum: Viewer Scan Negative.

He unlocked the hatch at the top of the Bucket and climbed out of the metallic gray sphere. It was not raining, for a change, and the sun was warm and golden in a clean blue sky.

Ben Hazard stretched his tired muscles and rested his eyes on the fresh green of the, tangled plants that grew along the banks of the lazy stream to his right. The grass in the little meadow looked cool and inviting, and there were birds singing in the trees. He was impressed as always by how little this corner of the world had changed in fifty years. It was very much as it had been a thousand years ago, or two thousand, or three . . .

It was just a small corner of nowhere, lost in the mists of time, waiting for the gray sheets of ice to come again.

It was just a little stream, bubbling along and minding its own business, and a lonely limestone hill scarred with the dark staring eyes of rock shelters and cave entrances.

There was nothing different about it.

It took Man to change things in a hurry, and Man wasn't home.

That was the problem.

Ben took the six wide-angle photographs of the terrain that he always took. There were no animals within camera range this trip. He clambered through the thick brown brush at the base of the limestone hill and climbed up the rough rocks to the cave entrance. It was still open, and he knew its location by heart.

He well remembered the thrill he had felt the first time he had entered this cave. His heart had hammered in his chest and his throat had been so dry that he couldn't swallow. His mind had been ablaze with memories and hopes and fears, and it had been the most exciting moment of his life.

Now, only the fear remained—and it was a new kind of fear, the fear of what he *wouldn't* find.

His light blazed ahead of him as he picked his way along the winding passage of the cave. He disturbed a cloud of indignant bats, but there was no other sign of life. He reached the central cavern, dark and hushed and hidden under the earth, and flashed his light around carefully.

There was nothing new.

He recognized the familiar bones of wolf, bear, tiger, and camel. He photographed them again, and did manage to find the remains of an ostrich that he had not seen before. He took two pictures of that.

He spent half an hour poking around in the cavern, checking all of the meticulously recorded sites, and then made his way back to the sunlit entrance.

The despair welled up in him, greater than before, Bad news, even when it is expected, is hard to take when it is confirmed. And there was no longer any real doubt.

Man wasn't home.

Ben Hazard wasn't puzzled any longer. He was scared and worried. He couldn't pass the buck to anyone else this time. He had come back to see for himself, and he had seen.

Imagine a man who built a superb computer, a computer that could finally answer the toughest problems in his field. Suppose the ultimate in computers, and the ultimate in coded tapes; a machine—however hypothetical—that was never wrong. Just for kicks, suppose that the man feeds in an easy one: *What is two plus three?*

If the computer answers *six*, then the man is in trouble. Of course, the machine might be multiplying rather than adding—

But if the computer answers *zero* or *insufficient data*, what then?

Ben Hazard slowly walked back to the Bucket, climbed inside, and locked the hatch.

He filed his films under the proper code number.

He pushed in the familiar datum: Field Reconnaissance Negative.

He sat down before the control board and got ready.

He was completely alone in the small metallic sphere; he could see every inch of it. He *knew* that he was alone. And yet, as he had before, he had the odd impression that there was someone with him, someone looking over his shoulder . . .

Ben Hazard had never been one to vault into the saddle and gallop off in all directions. He was a trained scientist, schooled to patience, He did not understand the soundless voice that kept whispering in his mind: *Hurry, hurry, hurry—*

"Boy," he said aloud, "you've been in solitary too long."

He pulled himself together and reached for the controls. He was determined to run out the string—twenty-three checks to go now—but he already knew the answer.

Man wasn't home.

When Ben Hazard returned to his original year of departure, which was 1982, he stepped out of the Bucket at New Mexico Station—for the machine, of necessity, moved in space as well as time, As a matter of fact, the spatial movement of the Bucket was one of the things that made it tough to do an intensive periodic survey of any single spot on the Earth's surface; it was hard to hold the Bucket on target.

According to his own reckoning, and in terms of physiological time, he had spent some forty days in his check of Choukoutien in the Middle Pleistocene. Viewed from the other end at New Mexico Station, he had been gone only five days.

The first man he saw was the big M.P. corporal.

"I'll need your prints and papers, sir," the M.P. said.

"Dammit, Ames." Ben handed over the papers and stuck his thumbs in the scanner. "Don't you know me by now?"

"Orders, sir."

Ben managed a tired smile. After all, the military implications of time travel were staggering, and care was essential. If you could move back in time only a few years and see what the other side had done, then you could counter their plans in the present. Since the old tribal squabbles were still going full blast, Gottwald had had to pull a million strings in order to get his hands on some of the available Buckets.

"Sorry, Ames. You look pretty good to me after a month or so of old camel bones."

"Nice to have you back, Dr. Hazard," the M.P. said neutrally.

After he had been duly identified as Benjamin Wright Hazard, Professor of Anthropology at Harvard and Senior Scientist on the Joint Smithsonian-Harvard-Berkeley Temporal Research Project, he was allowed to proceed. Ben crossed the crowded floor of the room they called Grand Central Station and paused a moment to see how the chimps were getting along.

There were two of them, Charles Darwin and Cleopatra, in separate cages. The apes had been the first time travelers, and were still used occasionally in testing new Buckets. Cleopatra scratched herself and hooted what might have been a greeting, but Charles Darwin was busy with a problem. He was trying to fit two sticks together so he could knock down a banana that was hanging just out of reach. He was obviously irritated, but he was no quitter.

"I know just how you feel, Charles," Ben said.

Charles Darwin pursed his mobile lips and redoubled his efforts.

What they won't do for one lousy banana.

Ben looked around for Nate York, who was working with the chimps, and spotted him talking to a technician and keeping track of his experiment out of the corner of his eye. Ben waved and went on to the elevator.

He rode up to the fourth floor and walked into Ed Stone's office. Ed was seated at his desk and he looked very industrious as he studied the dry white skull in front of him. The skull, however, was just a paper weight; Ed had used it for years.

Ed stood up, grinned, and stuck out his hand. "Sure glad you're back, Ben. Any luck?"

Ben shook hands and straddled a chair. He pulled out his pipe, filled it from a battered red can, and lit it gratefully. It felt good to be back with Ed. A man doesn't find too many other men he can really talk to in his lifetime, and Ed was definitely Number One. Since they were old friends, they spoke a private language.

"He was out to lunch," Ben said.

"For twenty thousand years?"

"Sinanthropus has always been famous for his dietary eccentricities."

Ed nodded to show that he caught the rather specialized joke—Sinanthropus had been a cannibal—and then leaned forward, his elbows on the desk. "You satisfied now?"

"Absolutely."

"No margin for error?" Ed insisted.

"None. I didn't really doubt Thompson's report, but I wanted to make certain. Sinanthropus isn't there. Period."

"That tears it then. We're up the creek for sure."

"Without a paddle."

"Without even a canoe." Ben puffed on his pipe. "Blast it, Ed, where *are* they?"

"You tell me. Since you left, Gottwald and I have gotten exactly nowhere. The way it looks right now, man hasn't got any ancestors—and that's crazy."

It's more than crazy, Ben thought. It's frightening. When you stop to think about it, man is a lot more than just an individual. Through his children, he extends on into the future. Through his ancestors, he stretches back far into the past. It is immortality of a sort. And when you chop off one end—

"I'm scared," he said. "I don't mind admitting it. There's an answer somewhere, and we've got to find it."

"I know how you feel, Ben. If this thing means what it seems to mean, then all science is just so much hot air. There's no cause and effect, no evidence, no reason. Man isn't what he thinks he is at all. We're just frightened animals sitting in a cave gaping at the darkness outside. Don't think I don't feel it, too. But what are we going to *do?*"

Ben stood up and knocked out his pipe. "Right now, I'm going home and hit the sack; I'm dead. Then the three or us—you and I and Gottwald—are going to sit down and hash this thing out. Then we'll at least know where we are."

"Will we?"

"We'd better."

He walked to the elevator and rode down to the ground floor of New Mexico Station. He had to identify himself twice more before he finally emerged into the glare of the desert sunlight. The situation struck him as the height of irony: here they were worried about spies and fancy feuds, when all the time—

What?

He climbed into his car and started for home. The summer day was bright and hot, but he felt as though he were driving down an endless tunnel of darkness, an infinite black cave to nowhere.

The voice whispered in his brain: *Hurry, hurry—*

His home was a lonely one, lonely with a special kind of emptiness. All his homes seemed deserted now that Anne was gone, but he liked this one better than most.

It was built of adobe with heavy exposed roof beams, cool in the summer and warm in winter. The Mexican tile floor was artfully broken up by lovely Navaho rugs—the rare Two Gray Hills kind in subdued and intricate grays and blacks and whites. He had brought many of his books with him from Boston and their familiar jackets lined the walls.

Ben was used to loneliness, but memories died hard. The plane crash that had taken Anne from him had left an emptiness in his heart. Sometimes, late in the evening, he thought he heard her footsteps in the kitchen. Often, when the telephone rang, he waited for her to answer it.

Twenty years of marriage are hard to forget.

Ben took a hot shower, shaved, and cooked himself a steak from the freezer. Then he poured a healthy jolt of Scotch over two ice cubes and sat down in the big armchair, propping his feet on the padded bench. He was still tired, but he felt more like a human being.

His eyes wandered to his books. There was usually something relaxing about old books and long-read titles, something reassuring. It had always been that way for him, but not any longer.

The titles jeered at him: *Mankind So Far, Up from the Ape, History of the Primates, Fossil Men, The Story of Man, Human Origins, The Fossil Evidence for Human Evolution, History of the Vertebrates* . . .

Little man, what now?

"We seem to have made a slight mistake, as the chemist remarked when his lab blew up," Ben said aloud.

Yes, but where could they have gone wrong?

Take Sinanthropus, for example. The remains of forty different Sinanthropus individuals had been excavated from the site of Choukoutien in China by Black and Weidenreich, two excellent men. There was plenty of material and it had been thoroughly studied. Scientists knew when Sinanthropus had lived in the Middle Pleistocene, where he lived, and how he lived. They even had the hearths where he cooked his food, the tools he used, the animals he killed. They knew what he looked like. They knew how he was related to his cousin. Pithecanthropus Erectus, and to modern men. There was a cast of his skull in every anthropology museum in the world, a picture of him in every textbook.

There was nothing mysterious about Sam Sinanthropus. He was one of the regulars.

Ben and Gottwald had nailed the date to the wall at 250,000 B.C. After Thompson's incredible report, Ben himself had gone back in time to search for Sinanthropus. Just to make certain, he had checked through twenty thousand years.

Nobody home.

Sinanthropus wasn't there.

That was bad enough.

But *all* the early human and prehuman fossils were missing.

There *were* no men back in the Pleistocene.

No Australopithecus, no Pithecanthropus, no Neanderthal, no nothing.

It was impossible.

At first, Ben had figured that there must be an error somewhere in the dating of the fossils. After all, a geologist's casual "Middle Pleistocene" isn't much of a target, and radiocarbon dating was no good that far back. But the Gottwald-Hazard Correlation had removed that possibility.

The fossil men simply were not there.

They had disappeared. Or they had never been there. Or—

Ben got up and poured himself another drink. He needed it. .

When the Winfield-Homans equations had cracked the time barrier and Ben had been invited by old Franz Gottwald to take part in the Temporal Research Project, Ben had leaped at the opportunity. It was a scientist's dream come true.

He could actually go back and *see* the long-vanished ancestors of the human species. He could listen to them talk, watch their kids, see them make their tools, hear their songs. No more sweating with a few broken bones. No more puzzling over flint artifacts. No more digging in ancient firepits.

He had felt like a man about to sit down to a Gargantuan feast.

Unhappily, it had been the cook's night out. There was nothing to eat.

Every scientist knows in his heart that his best theories are only educated guesses. There is a special Hall of Fame reserved for thundering blunders: the flat Earth, the medical humors, the unicorn.

Yes, and don't forget Piltdown Man,

Every scientist expects to revise his theories in the light of new knowledge. That's what science means. But he doesn't expect to find out that it's *all* wrong, He doesn't expect his Manhattan Project to show conclusively that uranium doesn't actually exist.

Ben finished his drink. He leaned back and closed his eyes. There had to be an answer somewhere—or somewhen. *Had* to be. A world of total ignorance is a world of terror; anything can happen.

Where was Man?

And why?

He went to bed and dreamed of darkness and ancient fears. He dreamed that he lived in a strange and alien world, a world of fire and blackness and living shadows—

When he woke up the next morning, he wasn't at all sure that he had been dreaming.

Among them, an impartial observer would have agreed, the three men in the conference room at New Mexico Station knew just about all there was to know concerning early forms of man. At the moment, in Ben's opinion, they might as well have been the supreme experts on the Ptolemaic theory of epicycles.

They were three very different men.

Ben Hazard was tall and lean and craggy-featured, as though the winds of life had weathered him down to the tough, naked rock that would yield no further. His blue eyes had an ageless quality about them, the agelessness of deep seas and high mountains, but they retained an alert and restless curiosity that had changed little from the eyes of an Ohio farm boy who had long ago wondered at the magic of the rain and filled his father's old cigar boxes with strange stones that carried the imprints of plants and shells from the dawn of time.

Ed Stone looked like part of what he was: a Texan, burned by the sun, his narrow gray eyes quiet and steady. He was not a big man, and his soft speech and deliberate movements gave him a deceptive air of lassitude. Ed was an easy man to underestimate; he wasted no time on frills or pretense, but there was a razor-sharp brain in his skull. He was younger than Ben, not yet forty, but Ben trusted his judgment more than he did his own.

Franz Gottwald, old only in years, was more than a man now; he was an institution. They called him the dean of American anthropology, but not to his white-bearded face; Franz had small respect for deans. They stood when he walked into meetings, and Franz took it as his due—he had earned it, but it concerned him no more than the make of the car he drove. Ben and Ed had both studied under Franz, and they still deferred to him, but the relationship was a warm one. Franz had been born in Germany—he never spoke about his life before he had come to the United States at the age of thirty—and his voice was still flavored by a slight accent that generations of graduate students had tried to mimic without much success. He was the Grand Old Man.

"Well?" asked Dr. Gottwald when Ben had finished his report. "What is the next step, gentlemen?"

Ed Stone tapped on the polished table with a yellow pencil that showed distinct traces of gnawing. "We've got to accept the facts and go on from there. We know what the situation is, and we think that we haven't made any whopping mistakes. In a nutshell, man has vanished from his own past. What we need is an explanation, and the way to get it is to find some relatively sane hypothesis that we can *test,* not just kick around. Agreed?"

"Very scientific, Edward," Gottwald said, stroking his neat white beard.

"O.K.," Ben said. "Let's work from what we know. Those skeletons *were* in place in Africa, in China, in Europe, in Java—they had to be there because that's where they were originally dug up. The bones are real, I've held them in my hands, and they're still in place in the museums. No amount of twaddle about alternate time-tracks and congruent universes is going to change that. Furthermore, unless Franz and I are the prize dopes of all time, the dating of those fossils is accurate in terms of geology and the associated flora and fauna and whatnot. The Buckets work; there's no question about that. So why can't we find the men who left the skeletons, or even the bones themselves in their original sites?"

"That's a question with only one possible answer," Ed said.

"Check. Paradoxes aside—and there are no paradoxes if you have enough accurate information—the facts have to speak for themselves. *We don't find them because they are not there.* Next question: where the devil are they?"

Ed leaned forward, chewing on his pencil. "If we forget about their geological context, none of those fossils are more than a few hundred years old. I mean, that's when they were found. Even Neanderthal only goes back to around 1856 or thereabouts. Science itself is an amazingly recent phenomenon. So—"

"You mean Piltdown?" Gottwald suggested, smiling.

"Maybe."

Ben filled his pipe and lit it. "I've thought about that, too. I guess all of us have. If one fossil man was a fake, why not all of them? But it won't hold water, and you know it. For one thing, it would have required a world-wide conspiracy, which is nonsense. For another—sheer manpower aside— the knowledge that would have been required to fake all those fossils simply did not exist at the time they were discovered. Piltdown wouldn't have lasted five minutes with fluorine dating and decent X-rays, and no one can sell me on the idea that men like Weidenreich and Von Koenigswald and Dart were fakers. Anyhow, that idea would leave us with a problem tougher than the one we're trying to solve—where did man come from if he had no past, no ancestors? I vote we exorcise that particular ghost."

"Keep going," Gottwald said.

Ed took it up. "Facts, Ben. Leave the theories for later. If neither the bones nor the men were present back in the Pleistocene where they belong, but the bones were present to be discovered later, then they *have* to appear somewhere in between. Our problem right now is *when.*"

Ben took his pipe out of his mouth and gestured with it, excited now. "We can handle that one. Dammit, *all* of our data can't be haywire. Look: for most of his presumed existence, close to a million years, man was a rare animal—all the bones of all the fossil men ever discovered wouldn't fill up this room we're sitting in; all the crucial ones would fit in a broom closet. O.K.? But by Neolithic times, with agricultural villages, there were men everywhere, even here in the New World. That record is clear. So those fossils *had* to be in place by around eight thousand years ago. All we have to do—"

"Is to work back the other way," Ed finished, standing up. "By God, that's it! We can send teams back through history; checking at short intervals, until we *see* how it started. As long as the bones are where they should be, fine. When they disappear—and they have to disappear, because we know they're not there earlier—we'll reverse our field and check it hour by hour if necessary. Then we'll know what happened. After that, we can kick the theories around until we're green in the face."

"It'll work," Ben said, feeling like a man walking out of a heavy fog. "It won't be easy, but it can be done. Only—"

"Only what?" Gottwald asked.

"Only I wonder what we'll find. I'm a little afraid of what we're going to see."

"One thing sure," Ed said.

"Yes?"

"This old world of ours will never be the same. Too bad—I kind of liked it the way it was."

Gottwald nodded, stroking his beard.

For months, Ben Hazard virtually lived within the whitewashed walls of New Mexico Station. He felt oddly like a man fighting a rattlesnake with his fists at some busy intersection, while all about him people hurried by without a glance, intent on their own affairs.

What went on in New Mexico Station was, of course, classified information. In Ben's opinion, this meant that there had been a ludicrous reversion to the techniques of magic. Facts were stamped with the sacred symbol of *CLASSIFIED,* thereby presumably robbing them of their power. Nevertheless, the world outside didn't know what the score was, and probably didn't care, while inside the Station—

History flickered by, a wonderful and terrible film.

Man was its hero and its villain—but for how long?

The teams went back, careful to do nothing and to touch nothing. The teams left Grand Central and pushed back, probing, searching . . .

Back past the Roman legions and the temples of Athens, back beyond the pyramids of Egypt and the marvels of Ur, back through the sun-baked villages of the first farmers, back into the dark shadows of prehistory—

And the teams found nothing.

At every site they could reach without revealing their presence, the bones of the early men were right where they should have been, waiting patiently to be unearthed.

Back past 8,000 B.C.

Back past 10,000.

Back past 15,000—

And then, when the teams reached 25,000 B.C., it happened. Quite suddenly, in regions as far removed from one another as France and Java, the bones disappeared.

And not just the bones.

Man himself was gone.

The world, in some ways, was as it had been—or was to be. The gray waves still tossed on the mighty seas, the forests were cool and green under clean blue skies, the sparkling sheets of snow and ice still gleamed beneath a golden sun.

The Earth was the same, but it was a strangely empty world without men. A desolate and somehow fearful world, hushed by long silences and stroked coldly by the restless winds . . .

"That's it," Ben said. "Whatever it was, we know when it happened— somewhere between 23,000 and 25,000 at the end of the Upper Paleolithic. I'm going back there."

"*We're* going back there," Ed corrected him. "If I sit this one out I'll be ready for the giggle factory."

Ben smiled, not trying to hide his relief. "I think I could use some company this trip."

"It's a funny feeling, Ben."

"Yes." Ben Hazard glanced toward the waiting Buckets. "I've seen a lot of things in my life, but I never thought I'd see the Beginning."

The machine stopped and the green light winked.

Ed checked the viewer while Ben punched data into the recorder.

"Nothing yet," Ed said. "It's raining."

"Swell." Ben unlocked the hatch and the two men climbed out. The sky above them was cold and gray. An icy rain was pouring down from heavy, low-hanging clouds. There was no thunder. Apart from the steady hiss of the rain, France in the year 24,571 B.C. was as silent as a tomb. "Let's get this thing covered up."

They hauled out the plastic cover, camouflaged to blend with the landscape, and draped it over the metallic gray sphere. They had been checking for eighteen days without results, but they were taking no chances.

They crossed the narrow valley through sheets of rain, their boots sinking into the soaked ground with every step. They climbed up the rocks to the gaping black hole of the cave entrance and worked their way in under the rock ledge, out of the rain. They switched on their lights, got down on their hands and knees, and went over every inch of the dry area just back of the rock overhang.

Nothing.

The gray rain pelted the hillside and became a torrent of water that splashed out over the cave entrance in a hissing silver waterfall. It was a little warmer in the cave, but dark and singularly uninviting.

"Here we go again," Ed muttered. "I know this blasted cave better than my own backyard."

"I'd like to see that backyard of yours about now. We could smoke up some chickens in the barbecue pit and sample some of Betty's tequila sours."

"Right now I'd just settle for the tequila. If we can't figure this thing out any other way we might just as well start looking in the old bottle."

"Heigh-ho," Ben sighed, staring at the waiting cave. "Enter one dwarf and one gnome, while thousands cheer."

"I don't hear a thing."

Ed took the lead and they picked and crawled their way back through the narrow passages of the cave, their lights throwing grotesque black shadows that danced eerily on the spires and pillars of ancient, dripping stone. Ben sensed the weight of the great rocks above him and his chest felt constricted. It was hard to breathe, hard to keep going.

"Whatever I am in my next incarnation," he said, "I hope it isn't a mole."

"You won't even make the mammals," Ed assured him.

They came out into a long, twisted vault. It was deep in the cave, far from the hidden skies and insulated from the pounding of the rain. They flashed their lights over the walls, across the dry gray ceiling, into the ageless silence.

Nothing.

No cave paintings.

It was as though man had never been, and never was to be.

"I'm beginning to wonder whether *I'm* real," Ed said.

"Wait a minute." Ben turned back toward the cave entrance, his body rigid. "Did you hear something?"

Ed held his breath and listened. "Yeah. There it is again."

It was faint and remote as it came to them in the subterranean vault, but there was no mistaking it.

A sound of thunder, powerful beyond belief.

Steady, now.

Coming closer.

And there had been no thunder in that cold, hissing rain . . .

"Come on." Ben ran across the cavern and got down on his hands and knees to crawl back through the twisting passage that led to the world outside. "There's something out there."

"What is it?"

Ben didn't stop. He clawed at the rocks until his hands were bloody. "I think the lunch hour's over," he panted. "I think Man's coming home."

Like two frightened savages, they crouched in the cave entrance and looked out across the rain-swept valley. The solid stone vibrated under their feet and the cold gray sky was shattered by blasting roars.

One thing was certain: that was no natural thunder.

"We've got to get out of here," Ben yelled. "We've got to hide before—"

"Where? The Bucket?"

"That's the best bet. It's almost invisible in this rain, and we can see through the viewer."

"Right. Run for it!"

They scrambled down among the slick rocks and ran across the wet grass and mud of the valley floor. It was cold and the rain pelted their faces in icy gray sheets. The deafening roar grew even louder, falling down from the leaden sky.

Fumbling in their haste, they jerked up a corner of the plastic cover so that the viewer could operate. Then they squirmed and wriggled under the plastic, dropped through the hatch, and sealed the lock. They dripped all over the time sphere but there was no time to bother about it. Even inside the Bucket they could feel the ocean of sound around them.

Ben cut in the recorder. "Start the cameras."

"Done."

"Hang on—"

The shattering roar reached an ear-splitting crescendo. Suddenly, there was something to see.

Light.

Searing white flame stabbing down from the gray skies.

They saw it: Gargantuan, lovely, huge beyond reason.

Before their eyes, like a vast metal fish from an unknown and terrible sea, the spaceship landed in the rain-soaked valley of Paleolithic France.

The long silence came again.

Fists clenched, Ben Hazard watched the *Creation*.

The great ship towered in the rain, so enormous that it was hard to imagine that it had ever moved. It might have been there always, but it was totally alien, out of place in its setting of hills and earth and sodden grasses.

Circular ports opened in the vast ship like half a hundred awakening eyes. Bright warm yellow light splashed out through the rain. Men— strangely dressed in dark, close-fitting tunics—floated out of the ship and down to the ground on columns of the yellow light.

The men were human, no different physically from Ben or Ed.

Equipment of some sort drifted down the shafts of light: strange spider-legged machines, self-propelled crates that gleamed in the light, shielded stands that might have been for maps or charts, metallic robots that were twice the size of a man.

It was still raining, but the men ignored it. The yellow light deflected the rain—Ben could see water dripping down the yellow columns as though solid tubes had been punched through the air—and the rain was also diverted from the men and their equipment.

The men from the ship moved quickly, hardly pausing to glance around them. They fanned out and went to work with the precision of trained specialists who knew exactly what they were doing.

Incredible as it was, Ben thought that he knew what they were doing too.

The spider-legged machines stayed on the valley floor, pulsing. Most of the men, together with three of the robots and the bulk of the self-propelled crates, made their way up to the cave Ben and Ed had just left and vanished inside.

"Want to bet on what's in those crates?" Ben whispered.

"Haven't the faintest idea, but two-bits says you spell it b-o-n-e-s."

The great ship waited, the streams of yellow light still spilling out into the rain. Five men pored over the shielded stands, looking for all the world like engineers surveying a site. Others worked over the spider-legged machines, setting up tubes of the yellow light that ran from the machines to the rocky hills. Two of the robots, as far as Ben could see, were simply stacking rocks into piles.

After three hours, when it was already growing dark, the men came back out of the cave. The robots and the crates were reloaded through the ship's ports and the uniformed men themselves boarded the ship again.

Night fell. Ben stretched to ease his cramped muscles, but he didn't take his eyes from the viewer for a second.

The rain died down to a gentle patter and then stopped entirely. The overcast lifted and slender white clouds sailed through the wind-swept sky. The moon rose, fat and silver, its radiance dimming the burning stars.

The impossible ship, towering so complacently beneath the moon of Earth, was a skyscraper of light. It literally hummed with activity. Ben would have given a lot to know what was going on inside that ship, but there was no way to find out.

The pulsing spider-legged machines clicked and buzzed in the cold of the valley night. Rocks were conveyed along tubes of the yellow light to the machines, which were stamping something out by the hundreds of thousands. Something . . .

Artifacts?

The long, uncanny night ended. Ben and Ed watched in utter fascination, their fears almost forgotten, sleep never even considered.

Dawn streaked the eastern sky, touching the clouds with fingers of rose and gold. A light breeze rustled the wet, heavy grasses. Water still dripped from the rocks.

The uniformed men came back out of the ship, riding down on the columns of yellow light. The robots gathered up some immense logs and stacked them near the mouth of the cave. They treated the wood with some substance to dry it, then ignited a blazing fire.

Squads of men moved over the valley floor, erasing all traces of their presence. One of them got quite close to the Bucket and Ben felt a sudden numbing chill. What would happen if they were seen? He was no longer worried about himself. But what about all the men who were to live on the Earth? Or—

The squad moved away.

Just as the red sun lifted behind the hills, while the log fire still blazed by the cave, the ship landed the last of its strange cargo.

Human beings.

Ben felt the sweat grow clammy in the palms of his hands.

They floated down the shafts of yellow light, shepherded by the uniformed men. There were one hundred of them by actual count, fifty men and fifty women. There were no children. They were a tall, robust people, dressed in animal skins. They shivered in the cold and seemed dazed and uncomprehending. They had to be led by the hand, and several had to be carried by the robots.

The uniformed men took them across the wet valley, a safe distance away from the ship. They huddled together like sheep, clasping one another in sexless innocence. Their eyes turned from the fire to the ship, understanding neither. Like flowers, they lifted their heads to the warmth of the sun.

It was a scene beyond age; it had always been. There were the rows of uniformed men, standing rigidly at attention. And there were the clustered men in animal skins, waiting without hope, without regret.

An officer—Ben thought of him that way, though his uniform was no different from the others—stepped forward and made what seemed to be a speech. At any rate, he talked for a long time—nearly an hour. It was clear that the dazed people did not understand a word of what he was saying, and that, too, was older than time.

It's a ceremony, Ben thought. *It must be some kind of ritual. I hadn't expected that.*

When it was over, the officer stood for a long minute looking at the huddle of people. Ben tried to read his expression in the viewer, but it was impossible. It might have been regret. It might have been hope. It might have been only curiosity.

It might have been anything.

Then, at a signal, the uniformed men turned and abandoned the others. They walked back to their waiting ship and the columns of yellow light took them inside. The ports closed.

Ten minutes later, the ship came to life.

White flame flared beneath its jets and the earth trembled. The terrible roar came again. The people who had been left behind fell to the ground, covering their ears with their hands. The great ship lifted slowly into the blue sky, then faster and faster—

It was gone, and only the sound remained, the sound of thunder . . .

In time, that, too, was gone.

Ben watched his, own ancestors with an almost hypnotic fascination. They did not move.

Get up, get up—

The skin-clad people stood up shakily after what seemed to be hours. They stared blankly at one another. As though driven by some vague instinct that spoke through their shock, they turned and looked at the blazing fire that burned by the mouth of the cave.

Slowly, one by one, they pulled themselves over the rocks to the fire. They stood before it, seeking a warmth they could not understand.

The sun climbed higher into the sky, flooding the rain-clean world with golden light.

The people stood for a long time by the cave entrance, watching the fire burn down. They did nothing and said nothing.

Hurry, hurry. The voice spoke again in. Ben's brain. He shook his head. Was he thinking about those dazed people out there, or was someone thinking about *him?*

Gradually, some of them seemed to recover their senses. They began to move about purposefully—still slowly, still uncertainly, like men coming out from under an anaesthetic. One man picked up a fresh log and threw it on the fire. Another crouched down and fingered a chipped piece of flint he found on a rock. Two women stepped behind the fire and started into the dark cave.

Ben turned away from the viewer, his unshaven face haggard. "Meet Cro-Magnon," he said, waving his hand.

Ed lit a cigarette, his first in eighteen hours. His hand was shaking. "Meet everybody, you mean. Those jokers planted the other boys—Neanderthal and whatnot—back in the cave before they landed the living ones."

"We came out of that ship too, Ed."

"I know—but where did the *ship* come from? And why?"

Ben took a last long look at the people huddled around the fire. He didn't feel like talking. He was too tired to think. None of it made any sense.

What kind of people could *do* a thing like that?

And if they hadn't—

"Let's go home," Ed said quietly. They went out and removed the plastic cover, and then set the controls for New Mexico Station in a world that was no longer their own.

Old Franz Gottwald sat behind his desk. His white suit was freshly pressed and his hair was neatly combed. He stroked his beard in the old familiar gesture, and only the gleam in his eyes revealed the excitement within him.

"It has always been my belief, gentlemen, that there is no substitute for solid thinking based on verified facts. There is a time for action and there is a time for thought. I need hardly remind you that action without thought is pointless; it is the act of an animal, the contraction of an earthworm. We have the facts we need. You have been back for three days, but the thinking is yet to be done."

"We've been beating our brains out," Ben protested.

"That may be, Ben, but a man can beat his brains out with a club. It is not thinking."

"*You* try thinking," Ed said, grinding out a cigarette.

Gottwald smiled. "You are too old to have your thinking done for you, Edward. I have given you all I can give. It is your turn now."

Ben sat back in his chair and lit his pipe. He took his time doing it, trying to clear his mind. He had to forget those frightened people huddled around a fire in the mists of time, had to forget the emotions he had felt when the great ship had left them behind. Gottwald was right, as always.

The time had come for thought.

"O.K.," he said. "We all know the facts. Where do we go from here?"

"I would suggest to you, gentlemen, that we will get no answers until we begin to ask the right questions. That is elementary, if I may borrow from Mr. Holmes."

"You want questions?" Ed laughed shortly. "Here's one, and it's a dilly. There's a hole in all this big enough to drive the American Anthropological Association through in a fleet of trucks. What about the apes?"

Ben nodded. "You quoted Conan Doyle, Franz, so I'll borrow a line from another Englishman—Darwin's pal Huxley. 'Bone for bone, organ for organ, man's body is repeated in the body of the ape.' Hell, we all know that. There are differences, sure, but the apes are closer to men than they are to monkeys. If man didn't evolve on Earth—"

"You've answered your own question, Ben."

"Of course!" Ed fished out another cigarette. "If man didn't evolve on Earth, then neither did the apes, That ship—or some ship—brought them both. But that's impossible."

"Impossible?" Franz asked.

"Maybe not," Ben said slowly. "After all, there are only four living genera of apes—two in Africa and two in Asia. We could even leave out the gibbon; he's a pretty primitive customer. It *could* have been done."

"Not for all the primates," Ed insisted. "Not for all the monkeys and lemurs and tarsiers, not for all the fossil primate bones. It would have made Noah's ark look like a rowboat."

"I would venture the suggestion that your image is not very apt," Gottwald said. "That ship *was* big enough to make any of our ships look like rowboats."

"Never mind," Ben said, determined not to get sidetracked. "It doesn't matter. Let's assume that the apes were seeded, just as the men were. The other primates could have evolved here without outside interference, just as the other animals did. That isn't the real problem."

"I wonder," Ed said. "Could that ship have come out of *time* as well as space? After all, if we have time travel they must have it. They could do anything—"

"Bunk," Gottwald snorted. "Don't let yourself get carried away, Edward. Anything is *not* possible. A scientific law is a scientific law, no matter who is working with it, or where, or when. We know from the Winfield-Homans Equations that it is impossible to go back into time and alter it in any way, just as it is impossible to go into the future which does not yet exist. There are no paradoxes in time travel. Let's not make this thing harder than it is by charging off into all the blind alleys we can think of. Ben was on the right track. What is the real problem here?"

Ben sighed. He saw the problem all too clearly. "It boils down to this, I think. *Why* did they plant those fossils—and probably the apes too? I can think of fifty reasons why they might have seeded men like themselves on a barren planet—population pressure and so forth—but why go to all the trouble of planting a false evolutionary picture for them to dig up later?"

"Maybe it isn't false," Ed said slowly.

Franz Gottwald smiled. "Now you're *thinking*, Edward."

"Sorry, Ed. I don't follow you. You saw them plant those bones. If that isn't a prime example of salting a site, then what the devil is it?"

"Don't shoot, pal. I was trying to say that the fossils could have been planted and *still* tell a true story. Maybe I'm just an old codger set in his ways, but I can't believe that human evolution is a myth. And there's a clincher, Ben: why bother with the apes if there is no relationship?"

"I still don't see—"

"He means," Gottwald said patiently, "that the fossil sequence is a true one—*some place else.*"

Ed nodded. "Exactly. The evolutionary series is the genuine article, but man developed on their world rather than on ours. When they seeded men on Earth, they also provided them with a kind of history book—if they could read it."

Ben chewed on his pipe. It made sense, to the extent that anything made sense any more. "I'll buy that. But where does it leave us?"

"Still up that well-known creek. Every answer we get just leads back to the same old question. *Why* did they leave us a history book?"

"Answer that one," Gottwald said, "and you win the gold cigar."

Ben got to his feet. His head felt as though it were stuffed with dusty cotton.

"Where are you going?"

"I'm going fishing. As long as I'm up the creek I might as well do something useful. I'll see you later."

"I hope you catch something," Ed said.

"So do I," Ben Hazard said grimly.

The car hummed sleepily across the monotonous flatlands of New Mexico, passed through the gently rolling country that rested the eye, and climbed into the cool mountains where the pines grew tall and the grass was a thick dark green in the meadows.

Ben loved the mountains. As he grew older, they meant more and more to him. The happiest times of his life had been spent up next to the sky, where the air was crisp and the streams ran clear. He needed the mountains, and he always returned to them when the pressure was too much to bear.

He turned off the main road and jolted over a gravel trail; paved roads and good fishing were mutually exclusive, like cities and sanity. He noted with approval that the clouds were draping the mountain peaks, shadowing the land below. When the sun was too bright the fish could see a man coming.

He took a deep breath, savoring the tonic of the air.

Relax, that's the ticket.

He checked to see that no interloper had discovered his favorite stretch of water, then parked his car by the side of Mill Creek, a gliding stream of crystal-clean water that tumbled icily out of the mountains and snaked its lazy way through the long green valley. He grinned like a kid with his first cane pole.

Ben pulled on his waders, assembled his rod with practiced skill, and tied on his two pet flies—a Gray Hackle Yellow and a Royal Coachman. He hung his net over one shoulder and his trout basket over the other, lit his pipe, and waded out into the cold water of Mill Creek.

He felt wonderful. He hooked a nice brook trout within five minutes, taking him from a swirl of dark water shadowed by the bank of the stream. He felt the knots and the tensions flow out of him like melting snow, and that was the first step.

He *had* to relax. There was no other way.

Consider the plight of a baseball player in a bad slump. He gives it all he has, tries twice as hard as usual, but everything he does backfires. His hits don't fall in, he misses the easy grounders. He lies awake at night and worries.

"Relax, Mac," his manager tells him. "All you gotta do is *relax*. Take it easy."

Sure, but how?

It was the same with a tough scientific problem. Ben had long ago discovered that persistent and orderly logic could take him only so far. There came a time when no amount of forced thinking would get the job done.

The fresh insights and the new slants seldom came to him when he went after them, no matter how hard he tried. In fact, the more he sweated over a problem the more stubbornly recalcitrant his mind became. The big ideas, and the good ones, came to him in a flash of almost intuitive understanding—a flash that was conditioned by what he knew, of course, but a flash that did not come directly from the conscious mind.

The trick was to let the conscious mind get out of the way, let the message get through—

In Ben's case, go fishing.

It took him two hours, seven trout, and part of a banana to get the answer he sought.

He had taken a long, cool drink from the stream, cleaned his fish, and was sitting down on a rock to eat the lunch he had packed when the idea came.

He had peeled a banana and taken one bite of it when his mind was triggered by a single, innocuous word:

Banana.

Not just any old banana, of course. A specific one, used for a specific purpose.

Remember?

Charles Darwin and Cleopatra, two chimpanzees in their cages. Charles Darwin pushing his ape brain to the limit to fit two sticks together. Why?

To get a banana.

One lousy banana.

That was well enough, but there was more. Darwin might get his banana, and that was all he cared about. But who had placed the sticks in the cage, who had supplied the banana?

And why?

That was an easy one. It was so simple a child could have figured it out. Someone had given Charles Darwin two sticks and a banana for just one reason: to see whether or not he could solve the problem.

In a nutshell, a scientific experiment.

Now, consider another Charles Darwin, another problem.

Or consider Ben Hazard.

What is the toughest problem a man can tackle? Howells pointed it out many years ago. Of all the animals, man is the only one who wonders where he has come from and where he is going. All the other questions are petty compared to that one. It pushes the human brain to the limit . . .

Ben stood up, his lunch forgotten.

It was all so obvious.

Men had been seeded on the Earth, and a problem had been planted with them—a real problem, one capable of yielding to a true solution. A dazed huddle of human beings had been abandoned by a fire in the mouth of a cave, lost in the morning of a strange new world. Then they had been left strictly alone; there was no evidence that they had been helped in any way since that time.

Why?

To see what they could do.

To see how long it would take them to solve the problem.

In a nutshell, a scientific experiment.

Ben picked up his rod and started back toward the car.

There was one more thing, one more inevitable characteristic of a scientific experiment. No scientist merely sets up his experiment and then goes off and forgets about it, even if he is the absolute ultimate in absent-minded professors.

No.

He has to stick around to see how it all comes out. He has to observe, take notes.

It was monstrous.

The whole history of man on Earth . . .

Ben climbed into his car, started the engine.

There's more. Face up to it.

Suppose that you had set up a fantastic planetary experiment with human beings. Suppose that you—or one of your descendants, for human generations are slow—came back to check on your experiment. What would you do, what would you be?

A garage mechanic?

A shoe salesman?

A pool room shark?

Hardly. You'd have to be in a position to know what was going on. You'd have to work in a field where you could find out the score.

In a word, you'd be an anthropologist.

There's still more. Take it to the end of the line.

Now, suppose that man on Earth cracked the time barrier. Suppose a Temporal Research Project was set up. Wouldn't you be in on it, right at the top?

Sure.

You wouldn't miss it for anything.

Well, who fit the description? It couldn't be Ed; Ben had known him most of his life, known his folks and his wife and his kids, visited the Texas town that had been his home.

It wasn't Ben.

That left Franz Gottwald.

Franz, who had come from Germany and never talked about his past. Franz, with the strangely alien accent. Franz, who had no family. Franz, who had contributed nothing to the project but shrewd, prodding questions . . .

Franz.

The Grand Old Man.

Ben drove with his hands clenched on the wheel and his lips pressed into a thin, hard line. Night had fallen by the time he got out of the mountains, and he drove across an enchanted desert beneath the magic of the stars. The headlights of his car lanced into the night, stabbing, stabbing—

He passed the great New Mexico rocket base, from which men had hurled their missiles to the moon and beyond. There had been talk of a manned shot to Mars . . .

How far would the experimenters let them go?

Ben lit a cigarette, not wanting to fool with his pipe in the car. He was filled with a cold anger he had never known before.

He had solved the problem.

Very well.

It was time to collect his banana.

It was after midnight when Ben got home.

He stuck his fish in the freezer, took a shower, and sat down in his comfortable armchair to collect his thoughts. He promptly discovered yet another fundamental truth about human beings: when they get tired enough, they sleep.

He woke up with a start and looked at his watch. It was five o'clock in the morning.

Ben shaved and was surprised to find that he was hungry. He cooked himself some bacon and scrambled eggs, drank three cups of instant coffee, and felt ready for anything.

Even Franz.

He got into his car and drove through the still-sleeping town to Gottwald's house. It looked safe and familiar in the pale morning light. As a matter of fact, it looked a lot like his own house, since both had been supplied by the government.

That, he thought, was a laugh.

The government had given *Gottwald* a house to live in.

He got out of his car, walked up to the door, and rang the bell. Franz never got to the office before nine, and his car was still in the garage.

His ring was greeted by total silence.

He tried again, holding his finger on the bell. He rang it long enough to wake the dead.

No answer.

Ben tried the door. It was unlocked. He took a deep breath and stepped inside. The house was neat and clean. The familiar books were on the shelves in the living room. It was like stepping into his own home.

"Franz! It's me, Ben."

No answer.

Ben strode over to the bedroom, opened the door, and looked inside. The bed was tidily made, and Franz wasn't in it. Ben walked through the whole house, even peering inside the closets, before he was satisfied.

Franz wasn't home.

Fine. A scientist keeps records, doesn't he?

Ben proceeded to ransack the house. He looked in dresser drawers, on closet shelves, even in the refrigerator. He found nothing unusual. Then he tried the obvious.

He opened Gottwald's desk and looked inside.

The first thing he saw was a letter addressed to himself. There it was, a white envelope with his name typed on it: *Dr. Benjamin Wright Hazard.*

Not to be opened until Christmas?

Ben took the letter, ripped it open, and took out a single sheet of paper. He started to read it, then groped for a chair and sat down.

The letter was neatly typed. It said:

My Dear Ben: I have always believed that a scientist must be capable of making predictions. This is not always an easy matter when you are dealing with human beings, but I have known you for a long, long time.

Obviously, you are searching my home, or you would not be reading this note. Obviously, if you are searching my home, you know part of the truth.

If you would like to know the rest of the story, the procedure is simple. Look behind the picture of the sand-painting in my bedroom. You will find a button there. Press the button for exactly five seconds. Then walk out into my patio and stand directly in front of the barbecue pit.

Trust me, Ben. I am not a cannibal.

The letter was signed with Gottwald's scrawled signature.

Ben got up and walked into the bedroom. He looked behind the picture that was hanging over the dresser. There was a small red button.

Press the button for exactly five seconds.

And then—what?

Ben replaced the picture. The whole thing was a trifle too reminiscent of a feeble-minded practical joke. Press the button and get a shock. Press the button and get squirted with water. Press the button and blow up the house—

No. That was absurd.

Wasn't it?

He hesitated. He could call Ed, but then Ed would insist on coming over right away—and Ed had a wife and kids. He could call the police, but the story he had to tell would have sounded absolutely balmy. He had no proof. He might as well recite "Gunga Din."

He went back to Gottwald's desk, found some paper, and typed a letter. He outlined the theory he had formed and wrote down exactly what he was going to do. He put the letter into an envelope, addressed the envelope to Ed, stamped it, and went outside and dropped it in the mailbox on the corner.

He went back into the house.

This time he did not hesitate—not for a second.

He punched the button behind the picture for exactly five seconds. Nothing happened. He went out into the patio and stood directly in front of the barbecue pit.

The wall around the patio hid the outside world, but the blue sky overhead was the same as ever. He saw nothing, heard nothing.

"Snipe hunt," he said aloud.

Then, with breathtaking suddenness, something *did* happen.

There was an abrupt stillness in the air, a total cessation of sound. It was as though invisible glass walls had slipped silently into place and sealed off the world around him.

There was no perceptible transition. One moment the cone of yellow light was not there, and the next it was. It surrounded him: taut, living, seething with an energy that prickled his skin.

He knew that yellow light.

He had seen it once before, in the dawn of time . . .

Ben held his breath; he couldn't help it. He felt strangely weightless, buoyant, a cork in a nameless sea—

His feet left the ground.

"Good God," Ben said.

He was lifted into the yellow light, absorbed in it. He could see perfectly, and it didn't help his stomach any. He could see the town below him—there was Gottwald's patio, the barbecue pit, the adobe house. He began to regret the bacon and eggs he had eaten.

He forced himself to breathe again. The air was warm and tasteless. He rose into the sky, fighting down panic.

Think of it as an elevator. It's just a way of getting from one place to another. I can see out, but of course nothing is visible from the outside . . .

But then how did I see the yellow light before?

This must be different. They couldn't risk being seen—

Relax!

But he kept going higher, and faster.

The Earth was far away.

It was an uncanny feeling—not exactly unpleasant, but he didn't care for the view. It was like falling through the sky. It was impossible to avoid the idea that he was falling, that he was going to hit something . . .

The blue of the sky faded into black, and he saw the stars.

Where am I going, where are they taking me?

There!

Look up, look up—

There it was, at the end of the tunnel of yellow light.

It blotted out the stars.

It was huge even against the immense backdrop of space itself. It stunned his mind with its size, that sleeping metal beast, but he recognized it.

It was the same ship that had landed the first men on Earth.

Dark now, dark and vast and lonely—but the same ship.

The shaft of yellow light pulled him inside; there was no air lock. As suddenly as it had come, the light was gone.

Ben stumbled and almost fell. The gravity seemed normal, but the light had supported him for so long that it took his legs a moment to adjust themselves.

He stood in a cool green room. It was utterly silent.

Ben swallowed hard.

He crossed the room to a metal door. The door opened before he reached it. There was only blackness beyond, blackness and the total silence of the dead.

Ben Hazard tried to fight down the numbing conviction that the ship was empty.

There is an almost palpable air of desolation about long deserted things, about empty houses and derelict ships and crumbling ruins. There is a special kind of silence about a place that has once known life and knows it no longer. There is a type of death that hovers over things that have not been *used* for a long, long time.

That was the way the ship felt.

Ben could see only the small green room in which he stood and the corridor of darkness outside the door. It could have been only a tiny fraction of the great ship, only one room in a vast city in the sky. But he *knew* that the men who had once lived in the ship were gone. He knew it with a certainty that his mind could not question.

It was a ghost ship.

He knew it was.

That was why his heart almost stopped when he heard the footsteps moving toward him through the silence.

Heavy steps.

Metallic steps.

Ben backed away from the door. He tried to close it but it would not shut. He saw a white light coming at him through the dark tunnel. The light was higher than a man—

Metallic steps?

Ben got a grip on himself and waited. *You fool, you knew they had robots. You saw them. Robots don't die, do they?*

Do they kill?

He saw it now, saw its outline behind the light. Twice the size of a man, its metal body gleaming.

It had no face.

The robot filled the doorway and stopped. Ben could hear it now; a soft whirring noise that somehow reminded him of distant winds. He told himself that it was just a machine, just an animated hunk of metal, and his mind accepted the analysis. But it is one thing to know what a robot is, and it is quite another to find yourself in the same roam with one.

"Well?" Ben said. He had to say something.

The robot was evidently under no such compulsion. It said nothing and did nothing. If simply stood there.

"You speak English, of course?" Ben said, recalling the line from an idiotic story he had once read.

If the robot spoke anything, it wasn't English.

After a long, uncomfortable minute, the robot turned around and walked into the dark corridor, its light flashing ahead of it. It took four steps, stopped, and looked back over its shoulder.

There was just one thing to do, and one way to go.

Ben nodded and stepped through the doorway after the robot

He followed the giant metallic man along what seemed to be miles of featureless passageways. Ben heard no voices, saw no lights, met no living things.

He felt no fear now; he was beyond that. He knew that he was in a state of shock where nothing could get through to him, nothing could hurt him. He felt only a kind of sadness, the sadness a man knows when he walks through the tunnels of a pyramid or passes a graveyard on a lonely night.

The ship that men had built was vast, so silent, so empty . . .

A door opened ahead of them.

Light spilled out into the corridor. Ben followed the robot into a large, comfortable room. The room was old, old and worn, but it was alive. It was warm and vital and human because there were two people in it. Ben had never before been quite so glad to see anyone.

One of the persons was an elderly woman he had never seen before. The other was Franz Gottwald.

"Hello, Ben," he said, smiling. "I don't believe you've met my wife."

Ben didn't know whether he was coming into a nightmare or coming out of one, but his manners were automatic.

"I'm very pleased to meet you," he said, and meant it.

The room had a subtle strangeness about it that once more reminded Ben of a dream. It was not merely the expected strangeness of design of a new kind of room, a room lost in the lonely miles of a silent spaceship; it was an out-of-phase oddness that at first he could not identify.

Then he caught it. There were alien things in the room: furniture that was planned for human beings but produced by a totally different culture pattern, carvings that were grotesque to his eyes, rugs that glowed in curiously wrong figures. But there were also familiar, everyday items from the world he knew: a prosaic reading lamp, a coffee pot bubbling on a table, some potted plants, a framed painting by Covarrubias. The mixture was a trifle jarring, but it did have a reassuring air of homeliness.

How strange the mind is. At a time like this, it concentrates on a room.

"Sit down, sit down," Franz said. "Coffee?"

"Thank you." Ben tried a chair and found it comfortable.

The woman he persisted in thinking of as Mrs. Gottwald—though that was certainly not her actual name—poured out a cup and handed it to him. Her lined, delicate face seemed radiant with happiness, but there were tears in her eyes.

"I speak the language too a little," she said hesitantly. "We are so proud of you, so happy—"

Ben took a sip of the coffee to cover his embarrassment. He didn't know what he had expected, but certainly not *this*.

"Don't say anything more, Arnin," Franz said sharply. "We must be very careful."

"That robot of yours," Ben said. "Couldn't you send him out for oiling or something?"

Franz nodded. "I forgot how weird he must seem to you. Please forgive me. I would have greeted you myself, but I am growing old and it is a long walk." He spoke to the robot in a language Ben had never heard, and the robot left the room.

Ben relaxed a little. "Do you two live up here all alone?"

An inane question. But what can I do, what can I say?

Old Franz seated himself next to Ben. He still wore his white suit. He seemed tired, more tired than Ben had ever seen him, but there was a kind of hope in his eyes, a hope that was almost a prayer.

"Ben," he said slowly, "it is hard for me to talk to you—now. I can imagine how you must feel after what you have been through. But you must trust me a little longer. Just forget where you are, Ben—a spaceship is just a ship. Imagine that we are back at the Station, imagine that we are talking as we have talked so many times before. You must think clearly. This is important, my boy, more important than you can know. I want you to tell me what you have discovered—I want to know what led you here. Omit nothing, and choose your words with care. Be as specific and precise as you can. Will you do this one last thing for me? When you have finished, I think I will be able to answer all your questions."

Ben had to smile. *"Be as specific and precise as you can."* How many times had he heard Franz use that very phrase on examinations?

He reached for his pipe. For a moment he had a wild, irrational fear that he had forgotten it—that would have been the last straw, somehow—but it was there. He filled it and lit it gratefully.

"It's your party, Franz. I'll tell you what I know."

"Proceed, Ben—and be careful."

Mrs. Gottwald—Arnin?—sat very still, waiting.

The ship was terribly silent around them.

Ben took his time and told Franz what he knew and what he believed. He left nothing out and made no attempt to soften his words.

When he was finished, Gottwald's wife was crying openly.

Franz, amazingly, looked like a man who had suddenly been relieved of a sentence of death.

"Well?" Ben asked.

Gottwald stood up and stroked his white beard. "You must think I am some kind of a monster," he said, smiling.

Ben shrugged. "I don't know."

Mrs. Gottwald dried her eyes. "Tell him," she said. "You can tell him now."

Gottwald nodded. "I am proud of you, Ben, very proud."

"I was right?"

"You were right in the only thing that matters. The fossils *were* a test, and you have passed that test with flying colors. Of course, you had some help from Edward—"

"I'll give him part of the banana."

Gottwald's smile vanished. "Yes. Yes, I daresay you will. But I am vain enough to want to clear up one slight error in your reconstruction. I do not care for the role of monster, and mad scientists have always seemed rather dull to me."

"The truth is the truth."

"A redundancy, Ben. But never mind. I must tell you that what has happened on Earth was not a mere scientific experiment. I must also tell you that I am not only a scientist who has come back, as you put it, to see how the chimpanzees are doing. In fact, I didn't come back at all. We— my people—never left. I was born right here in this ship, in orbit around the Earth. It has always been here."

"For twenty-five thousand years?"

"For twenty-five thousand years."

"But what have you been doing?"

"We've been waiting for you, Ben. You almost did not get here in time. My wife and I are the only ones left."

"Waiting for *me?* But—"

Gottwald held up his hand. "No, not this way. I can show you better than I can tell you. If my people had lived—my other people, I should say, for I have lived on the Earth most of my life—there would have been an impressive ceremony. That can never be now. But I can show you the history lesson we prepared. Will you come with me? It is not far."

The old man turned and walked toward the door, his wife leaning on his arm.

"So long," she whispered. "We have waited so long."

Ben got up and followed them into the corridor.

In a large assembly room filled with empty seats, somewhere in the great deserted ship, Ben saw the history of Man.

It was, more than a film, although a screen was used. Ben lived the history, felt it, was a part of it.

It was not a story of what King Glotz did to King Goop; the proud names of conventional history fade into insignificance when the perspective is broad enough. It was a story of Man, of all men.

It was Gottwald's story—and Ben's.

Ben lived it.

Millions of years ago, on a world that circled a sun so far away that the astronomers of Earth had no name for it and not even a number, a new animal called Man appeared. His evolution had been a freakish thing, a million-to-one shot, and it was not likely to be repeated.

Man, the first animal to substitute cultural growth for physical change, was an immediate success. His tools and his weapons grew ever more efficient. On his home world, Man was a patient animal—but he was Man.

He was restless, curious. One world could not hold him. He built his first primitive spaceships and set out to explore the great dark sea around him. He established colonies and bases on a few of the worlds of his star system. He looked outward, out along the infinite corridors of the universe, and it was not in him to stop.

He tinkered and worked and experimented.

He found the faster-than-light drive.

He pushed on through the terrible emptiness of interstellar space. He touched strange worlds and stranger suns—

And he found that Man was not alone.

There were ships greater than his, and Beings—

Man discovered the Enemy.

It was not a case of misunderstanding, not a failure of diplomacy, not an accident born of fear or greed or stupidity. Man was a civilized animal. He was careful, reasonable, prepared to do whatever was ethically right.

He had no chance.

The Enemy—pounced. That was the only word for it. They were hunters, destroyers, killers. They were motivated by a savage hunger for destruction that Man had never known. They took many shapes, many forms.

Ben saw them.

He saw them rip ships apart, gut them with an utter ferocity that was beyond understanding. He saw them tear human beings to shreds, and eat them, and worse—

Ben screamed.

The Beings were more different from Man than the fish that swim in the sea, and yet . . .

Ben recognized them. He knew them.

They were there, all of them.

Literally, the Beings of nightmares.

The monsters that had troubled the dark sleeps of Earth, the things that crawled through myths, the Enemy who lived on the black side of the mind. The dragons, the serpents, the faces carved on masks, the Beings shaped in stones dug up in rotting jungles—

The Enemy.

We on Earth have not completely forgotten. We remember, despite the shocks that cleansed our minds. We remember, we remember. We have seen them in the darkness that lives always beyond the fires, we have heard them in the thunder that looms in the long, long night.

We remember.

It was not a war. A war, after all, is a specific kind of contest with rules of a sort. There were no rules. It was not a drive for conquest, not an attempt at exploitation. It was something new, something totally alien.

It was destruction.

It was extermination.

It was a fight between two different kinds of life, as senseless as a bolt of lightning that forked into the massive body of a screaming dinosaur.

Man wasn't ready.

He fell back, fighting where he could.

The Enemy followed.

Whether he liked it or not, Man was in a fight to the finish.

He fought for his life. He pushed himself to the utmost, tried everything he could think of, fought with everything he had. He exhausted his ingenuity. The Enemy countered his every move.

There was a limit.

Man could not go on.

Ben leaned forward, his fists clenched on his chair. He was a product of his culture. He read the books, saw the tri-di plays. He expected a happy ending.

There wasn't one.

Man lost.

He was utterly routed.

He had time for one last throw of the dice, one last desperate try for survival. He did his best.

He worked out the Plan.

It wasn't enough to run away, to find a remote planet and hide. It wasn't enough just to gain time.

Man faced the facts. He had met the Enemy and he had lost. He had tried everything he knew, and it hadn't been good enough. One day, no matter how far he ran, he would meet the Enemy again.

What could he do?

Man lives by his culture, his way of life. The potential for any culture is great, but it is not limitless. Culture has a way of putting blinders on its bearers; it leads them down certain paths and ignores others. Technological complexity is fine, but it is impotent without the one necessary ingredient:

Ideas.

Man needed new ideas, radically new concepts.

He needed a whole new way of thinking.

Transplanting the existing culture would not do the job. It would simply go on producing variants of the ideas that had already been tried.

Man didn't need transplanting.

He needed a transfusion, a transfusion of ideas.

He needed a brand new culture with fresh solutions to old problems.

There is only one way to get a really different culture pattern: grow it from scratch.

Sow the seeds and get out.

Man put the Plan into effect.

With the last of his resources, he outfitted four fugitive ships and sent them out into the wastes of the seas between the stars.

"We don't know what happened to the other three ships," Franz Gottwald said quietly when the projection was over. "No ship knew the destination of any other ship. They went in different directions, each searching for remote, hidden worlds that might become new homes for men. There is no way of knowing what became of the others; I think it highly unlikely that any of them survived."

"Then Earth is all there is?"

"That is what we believe, Ben—we have to go ahead on that assumption. You know most of the rest of the story. This ship slipped through the Enemy and found the Earth. We landed human beings who were so conditioned that they could remember little or nothing, for they had to begin all over again. We planted the fossils and the apes as a test, just as you supposed."

"But why? There was no need for such a stunt—"

Gottwald smiled. "It wasn't a stunt, my boy. It was the key to everything. You see, we had to warn the men of Earth about what they had to face. More than that, once their cultures had developed along their own lines, we had to share what we had with them. I need hardly remind you that this ship is technologically many thousands of years ahead of anything the Earth has produced. But we couldn't turn the ship over to them until we were *certain* they were ready. You don't give atomic bombs to babies. The men of Earth had to *prove* that they could handle the toughest problem we could dream up. You solved it, Ben."

"I didn't do it alone."

"No, of course not. I can tell you now that my people—my other people—never did invent time travel. That was a totally unexpected means of tackling the problem; we never could have done it. It is the most hopeful thing that has happened."

"But what became of the men and women who stayed here on the ship?"

Franz shook his head. "Twenty-five thousand years is a long, long time, Ben. We were a defeated people. We worked hard; we were not idle. For one thing, we prepared dictionaries for every major language on Earth so that all the data in our libraries will be available to you. But man does not live well inside a ship. Each generation we became fewer; children were very scarce."

"It's like the old enigma of the cities, isn't it?"

"Exactly. No city in human history has ever reproduced its population. Urban births are always lower than rural ones. All cities have always drawn their personnel from the surrounding countryside. The ship was sealed up; we had no rural areas. It was only a matter of time before we were all gone. My wife and I were the last ones, Ben—and we had no children."

"We were so afraid," Mrs. Gottwald said. "So afraid that you would not come before it was too late . . ."

"What would you have done?"

Franz shrugged wearily. "That is one decision I was spared. I did cheat a little, my boy. I was careful to give you no help, but I did plant some projectors near you that kept you stirred up. They broadcast frequencies that . . . ah . . . stimulate the mind, keep it in a state of urgency. Perhaps you noticed them?"

Ben nodded. He remembered the voice that spoke in his skull:

Hurry, hurry—

"Franz, what will happen now?"

Gottwald stroked his beard, his eyes very tired. "I can't tell you that. I don't know the answer. I have studied the men of Earth for most of my life, and I still don't know. You are a tough people, Ben, tougher than we ever were. You have fought many battles, and your history is a proud one. But I cannot read the future. I have done my best, and the rest is up to you."

"It's a terrible responsibility."

"Yes, for you and for others like you it will be a crushing burden. But it will be a long fight; we will not live to see more than the beginning of it. It will take centuries for the men of Earth to learn all that is in this ship. It's an odd thing, Ben—I have never seen the Enemy face to face. You will probably never see them. But what we do now will determine whether mankind lives or dies."

"It's too much for one man."

"Yes." Gottwald smiled, remembering. "It is."

"I don't know where to begin."

"We will wait for Edward—he will be here tomorrow, unless I don't know him at all—and then the three of us will sit down together for one last time. We will think it out. I am very tired, Ben; my wife and I have lived past our time. It is hard to be old, and to have no children. I always thought of you and Edward as my sons; I hope you do not find this too maudlin."

Ben searched for words and couldn't find any.

Franz put his arm around his wife. "Sometimes, when the job was too big for me, when I felt myself giving up, I would walk up into the old control room of this ship. My wife and I have stood there many times. Would you like to see it?"

"I need it, Franz."

"Yes. So do I. Come along."

They walked for what seemed to be miles through the dark passages of the empty ship, then rode a series of elevators up to the control room.

Franz switched on the lights.

"The ship is not dead, you know," he said. "It is only the people who are gone. The computers still maintain the ship's orbit, and the defensive screens still make it invulnerable to detection—you wouldn't have seen it if you had not been coming up the light tube, and there is no way the ship can be tracked from Earth. What do you think of the control room?"

Ben stared at it. It was a large chamber, acres in extent, but it was strangely empty. There were panels of switches and a few small machines, but the control room was mostly empty space.

"It's not what I expected," he said, hiding his disappointment.

Franz smiled. "When machinery is efficient you don't need a lot of it. There is no need for flashing lights and sparks of electricity. What you see here gets the job done."

Ben felt a sudden depression. He had badly needed a lift, and he didn't see it here. "If you'll forgive me for saying so, Franz, it isn't very inspiring. I suppose it is different for you—"

Gottwald answered him by throwing a switch.

Two immense screens flared into life, covering the whole front of the control room.

Ben caught his breath.

One of the screens showed the globe of the Earth far below, blue and green and necklaced with silver clouds.

The other showed the stars.

The stars were alive, so close he could almost touch them with his hand. They burned like radiant beacons in the cold sea of space. They whispered to him, called to him—

Ben knew then that the men of Earth had remembered something more than monsters and nightmares, something more than the fears and terrors that crept through the great dark night.

Not all the dreams had been nightmares.

Through all the years and all the sorrows, Man had never forgotten.

I remember. I remember.

I have seen you through all the centuries of nights. I have looked up to see you, I have lifted my head to pray, I have known wonder—

I remember.

Ben looked again at the sleeping Earth.

He sensed that Old Franz and his wife had drawn back into the shadows.

He stood up straight, squaring his shoulders.

Then Ben Hazard turned once more and looked out into the blazing heritage of the stars.

I remember, I remember—

It has been long, but you, too, have not forgotten.

Wait for us.

We'll be back.

GUARDIAN SPIRIT

The small gray metallic sphere drifted down through the night sky of Pollux V, twenty-nine light-years from Earth. The eery pinkish glow of the two moons glinted softly on the floating sphere against its backdrop of silver stars. Already, invisibly far out in space, the ion drive of the mother ship from Earth's CAS fleet had flared into life again, carrying the great ship back into the lonely darkness between the words.

The sphere was alone.

It dropped gently through the atmosphere on its antigravs toward the dark surface of the planet below. It made no sound, drifting through the strange moonlight as insubstantially as a ghost from some forgotten world. It hovered above the branches of a stand of trees for a moment, shifted course slightly, and settled in a field of grass and shrubs. It barely disturbed the grass at first and then, as the antigravs shut off, it crushed into the ground with its true weight.

A circular port slid open and two men stepped out. The light from inside the sphere beamed through the port and mixed with the rose of the moonlight. The two men were clearly visible and made no effort to conceal themselves.

Even physically, the two men were a contrast, and their first actions on the unknown world merely underlined the differences between them. Arthur Canady, tall and lean and dour, leaned back against the side of the sphere and lit his pipe with hardly a glance at the new world around him. Frank Landis scurried around like a newly-released puppy, his stocky body scuttling back and forth between dimly-glimpsed rocks and shrubs and night-blooming flowers, his sandy hair like a feverish halo over his open, eager face.

"Look at this, Art," he said, retrieving a delicate white flower that looked like an orchid. "How about that? Isn't it something?"

Arthur Canady puffed on his pipe solemnly. "I knew a man once who ate flowers," he said.

"Why'd he do that?" Frank asked, falling into the trap as usual.

363

"To get to the other side," Arthur Canady explained patiently.

Frank Landis looked at him, blankly. "Sometimes I just don't get you, Art."

"I'm not always contagious, I guess."

"I mean, what the *hell*. Here we are, the first civilized men ever to set foot on a new world—it's an historic moment—and you're not even interested."

"I wouldn't say that," Canady said, uncoiling himself from the side of the sphere. "It's just that botany is a little out of my line. For instance, unless you're too set on making a little speech about the Mission from Earth and the Great Terran Father, I suspect that there's something important going on over there right now that we ought to see." He pointed toward the west.

Frank looked and saw nothing. "What's over there?"

"Among other things, if our survey map is accurate, there's a good-sized stream. On the banks of that stream, the natives have a camp—a big one. And they're having a ceremony of some sort."

"What makes you think so?"

"See that glow over there, through those trees? Unless you happen to believe in a horde of giant lightning bugs that means a series of large fires. And if you'll turn up your hearing aid a bit you can hear what sounds like a chant of some kind. Tired hunters aren't very apt to be just practicing their harmony around the old campfire, so I assume there is some type of ceremony going on. And I think we ought to be there."

"Now?" Frank asked.

"Why not?"

Frank stared at his companion. He had never worked with Canady before and knew him only by his reputation, Dammit, no matter how good an anthropologist he might be, the man wasn't *comfortable*.

"You're not afraid of a few hundred natives, are you?" Canady asked, smiling.

"Of course not! I'm sure you know what you're doing. It's just that—well, we just got here—seems like rushing it a bit . . ."

Canady tapped his pipe out against his boot, carefully smothering the hot ashes with dirt. He had rather suspected that Frank, for all his too-frequent sermons about his love for primitive peoples, preferred to deal with natives from a position of massive strength. Well, he had a point there and this was no time to start a silly argument. "Don't worry, Frank. We'll wait until tomorrow and run through the customary contact routines. I'm just going to sneak over there and have a look through the glasses. You can stay here if you like."

He got his glasses out of the sphere, locating them under Frank's demonstration steam engine, and stuck a pistol in his belt. Then, without another word, he struck off to the west toward the sound of the chanting. He would really have preferred to go alone, to savor this new world without the bubble-bath of Frank's somewhat shrill enthusiasms, but he hadn't gone fifty yards before Frank panted up behind him and fell into step.

"This is really something," Frank exclaimed. "I feel like Robinson Crusoe!"

Canady toyed with a vision of a suitable desert island but held his tongue. His long legs covered the ground with an easy, effortless stride. He felt rather than saw the lovely moons in the star-sprinkled sky, felt the alien wind in his lungs, felt the strange and wonderful sounds and smells and impressions that tugged oddly at his heart.

He entered the darkness beneath the trees, silent as a shadow, and slipped toward the orange glow of the firelight. The chanting was closer now; it had a weird and haunting atonality to it, a subtle rhythm that was hard to catch—

Canady quickened his steps, all thoughts of Frank forgotten. There was a sadness in him, and a nameless hunger.

Twenty-nine light-years from the planet Earth it had begun again.

Hidden in a clump of thorny bushes on a low hill. overlooking the stream-cut valley, Arthur Canady held the glasses to his eyes and stared down upon a scene of wild magnificence, a scene that filled him with wonder and the sense of a life beyond his knowledge, a life glimpsed far away, a life he could never enter.

It was something that the survey charts and the planted microphones had not prepared him for. He was a man who was seldom surprised but he was surprised now. It was the difference between a faded photograph and the reality, the difference between a set of statistics and the miracle of human beings. All the expected culture elements were there, but the *intensity* of the thing was astonishing. And there was something more . . .

The stream coursed through the moonlit valley, pink and silver beneath the moons. Tremendous fires blazed along the river banks, hissing and crackling with the rich juices of fresh sap, shooting spectacular showers of sparks high into the air. The orange glow of the flames bathed the rows of tipi-like skin tents in lambent, living light.

There must have been close to a thousand men and women camped by the river, which was an amazing number of people for a hunting culture. Every last person was taking part in the ceremony: dancing, preparing food, singing. They were a tall, robust people; they moved proudly with their heads held high. They were dressed in a wild and barbaric splendor: fur robes and feathers and intricately painted designs on their graceful bodies.

The chanting was continuous. It was a joyful, happy kind of music, serving as a chorus behind the whirling forms of the dancers. Most primitive music, Canady had always felt, was just that: primitive and incredibly monotonous. But this was something else: a lively, complex wave of counterpoint and rhythm that set a man's blood racing in his veins. And the dancing was no mere shuffling of feet in a circle; it was abandoned and yet controlled, graceful as a ballet but with a rough sexuality to it that was strangely innocent, strangely pure.

The happiness and the joy were tangible things; you could feel them in the air. It was a time of rejoicing, a time of release, a time of thanksgiving. And yet there was a dark undercurrent to it, a shadow that moved in and out among the firelit dancers like a whisper of remorse. . . .

In the precise center of the camp one fire blazed higher than all the others. A constant stream of men fed fresh wood to it, tossing mighty logs into the flames. It was a hot, roaring fire, a pivot around which all else revolved. It drew the eye like a magnet.

The two men from Earth lay silent, watching. Both of them knew that they had a once-in-a-lifetime opportunity and they took full advantage of it. Tomorrow their work would begin, the work that would spell the end of the life they were watching, but for now it was only something to see, something to remember when the old days were gone.

The dancing and the chanting continued. It went on for hours, rising in intensity all the time. The dances grew wilder, the chanting rose to a climax that was almost unendurable. The fires blazed and the moons arced across the night sky, shaming the distant light of the stars.

When it happened, it happened with a startling abruptness.

The chanting stopped, as though cut off with a switch. The dancers stopped in mid-step. The natives moved into a silent circle around the central fire. A hush fell over the night, a hush of expectancy. . . .

One man stepped out from the others, framed in the leaping flames. He was naked, free of ornament of any kind. He raised his right hand and then his left. He bowed to the four directions. He looked up, out into the night and the moons and the stars. His face was radiant with a supreme peace.

Calmly, without hesitation, he walked into the roaring fire.

He climbed up the searing logs, his hair already aflame. He lay down on his back on a bed of fire. He did not move. He did not cry out. His body disappeared in a mass of flame, even the bones lost in the red-hot coals that fed the fire.

The fire blazed higher, crackling and hissing.

It was done.

The natives turned silently and filed back to their tents by twos and threes. No one looked back at the funeral pyre. Within minutes there was not a human being to be seen anywhere. The stream wound through the valley, gliding smoothly in the fading light. The fires blazed for a remarkably short time, then died away into glowing coals. The great fire that had eaten a life was the last to go, flaring and sparking as though reluctant to give up its moment of splendor, but it finally faded and collapsed into a pile of smoking embers.

The night stole in again, covering the tents with darkness.

The two men from Earth eased themselves out of the concealing bushes and walked back under the stars to their waiting sphere. Even Frank had nothing to say

Canady felt the strange world around him, felt it as a palpable presence, and was filled with an excitement that had no name. He felt that he stood on the edge of marvels, of wonders that dwelt in an abyss of dreams.

One thing he knew: this was no ordinary hunting culture, no matter what the survey charts showed.

He slept badly, impatient for the morning sun.

II

The sun was a red glory in the sky and by its harsh light the world of Pollux V lost much of its ethereal quality and resolved itself into a matter-of-fact land of rolling plains, distant mountains, and stands of tall trees that followed the river valleys. After a breakfast of concentrated coffee and powdered eggs, Canady found it difficult to recapture his mood of the night before. What he *had* seen had been unprecedented, but perhaps he had attached too much importance to it.

Still, it was odd. The man who had walked into the flames had seemed to do so of his own free will; he had not been forced. He had not been a sacrifice in the usual sense of the word, and in any event human sacrifices were normally a luxury restricted to higher types of culture with larger populations. The man had *wanted* to go into those flames. Why? And why had his death been the occasion for such rejoicing on the part of the rest of the people? There had certainly been more than one band present; people must have come in from miles around to share in the festivities. . . .

Canady shook his head. It was folly to speculate on such things until you knew enough about the culture to make sense of them. He put the incident from his mind and settled into routine.

And routine it was. The first contact between Earth and a primitive culture was always a dramatic event but the procedure was cut and dried.

The scientists of Earth's Cultural Aid Service had worked out a plan for every known type of culture and all the field men had to do was to follow the proper plan in simple ABC fashion. All the plans, based on centuries of experience on Earth and on the nearer planetary systems, were designed to do two basic things: show the people that the newcomers were friendly, and show them that they were too powerful to be attacked. It was a neat example of the age-old technique of putting a big smile on your face and carrying a sharp knife in your toga.

While Frank set up his equipment in the sphere, Canady took a high-powered rifle and set out across the plains toward a small herd of grazing animals. The animals (called yedoma in the local native dialect) were large beasts that looked like the American moose, save that the horns on the males were short and stubby affairs like those of domestic cattle. The economic life of the natives—as best the CAS could gather from photographic and microphonic survey—was based on the herds of yedoma that roamed the plains; yedoma meat, fresh or dried, was the food staple, yedoma skins were used for tents and clothing, yedoma sinew was used for thread. It was a neat parallel to the reliance of the ancient Plains Indians upon the buffalo, and it offered an exceptionally easy situation for cultural manipulation.

Canady kept the wind in his face and it was a simple matter to get close enough to the herd for a shot. The animals had had no experience with a weapon that killed at long range and were aware of no danger. Canady dropped a yedoma calf with one shot and could easily have killed half the herd if there had been any point in it. He dragged the calf back to the sphere and lifted it inside.

They were ready.

Frank Landis took the controls and lifted the sphere into the morning sky with the effortless ease of a man to whom all things mechanical were second nature. There was little sensation of movement within the sphere as it floated over the plain toward the native camp.

Canady sat quietly, smoking his pipe. It was crowded inside the sphere, crowded with portable steam engines and sacks of seeds and repeating firearms and that greatest of all invasion threats, crates of sewing machines. He thought of the wild and free scene the night before, the tents and the fires and the dancing, and he thought of it as a way of life already gone, destroyed by the bland deadliness of sacks of seeds and crates of sewing machines. The old regret saddened him, and he was unable to comfort himself by the neat-sounding official phrases that cloaked the operation of the Cultural Aid Service.

In theory, they were helping the natives. The fact that the natives had asked for no help was not mentioned. The speeches at the United Nations were fairly dripping with high-sounding phrases about underdeveloped areas, primitive misery, and the moral obligation of the strong to help the weak. There was much oratory about starving children and the glorious benefits of civilization.

Behind the scenes, oddly enough, much of the talk was along the same lines. All men wear cultural blinkers which condition them to curiously inevitable chains of reasoning. Given certain premises, certain conclusions follow as certainly as fish swallow worms. The goals and aspirations of a man's own culture just naturally seem *right* for all other cultures as well, and surely you are doing the other fellow a service by passing on the joys that you yourself have known. . . .

And then, of course, there *was* the fact that primitive areas make poor markets for an industrial civilization. The development of the ion drive had made trade commercially sound, and Earth's factories were not geared to mass-produce arrow points. If you want to sell a man a tri-di set, it helps to have electricity first. If you want to sell a man a tractor, it is nice if agriculture has already been invented. If you're thinking in terms of consumers, a large and prosperous population is better than a small and poverty-stricken one.

The human mind is infinitely capable of rationalization; it can justify anything from crusades to slavery on the basis of Good, Pure, and Noble Motives.

Canady had never considered himself a romantic man. He was a product of his culture and he had to live in it. He had found a job that interested him, a job that offered good pay and prestige, and he did his job honestly. But he had never been able to convince himself that he was a knight in shining armor by reciting a string of platitudes. He was too wise a man to believe that he could change the universe by a one-man fight against injustice, so he simply did what men have always done—he did the best he could to ease some of the pain along the way.

Right now, as the sphere floated over the tree-tops, he was not unduly proud of himself. Even the argument that he was gaining valuable data for his science failed to reassure him, and it was a mark of his honesty that he did not even consider the argument that if he didn't do the job somebody else would.

Frank looked up from the controls, his blue eyes disturbed. He was not an insensitive man and many of the same thoughts had been bothering him. Frank, however, could always sell himself on the rightness of what he was doing. It was not dishonesty on his part; his brain just worked that way.

"Seems kind of a shame," he said. "I guess they like their life pretty well the way it is."

"Maybe not," Canady said, helping him out. "After all, Frank, that's an argument that might have kept us all in the caves."

"That's right." Frank's eyes brightened. "Hell, if you don't believe in *progress,* what can you believe in?"

Canady could think of several answers to that one but he just shrugged as though the problem were insoluble. The blind faith in progress—which normally, if you tried to pin it down to anything approaching preciseness, meant increased technological complexity—was so deeply ingrained in Earth's cultures that it had become an automatic response. Even children believed in progress. How could you not believe in progress?

"I look at it this way," Frank said slowly. "We're taking something away from them, sure. We're asking them to change their way of life on a purely voluntary basis—we're not *forcing* them to do anything. In return, we're offering them things they've never had before: comfort and good health and security. What's wrong with that?"

"Your insight is very comforting," Canady said without smiling. "Got the bomb ready?"

Frank looked at him sharply, disturbed by the juxtaposition of the two sentences. Canady, however, smoked his pipe without expression. "It's ready."

Canady studied the terrain below in the viewers. They were over a cleared area near the native camp. He checked the safety detectors. There were no people in the target area, but it was close enough so that they could get an eyeful.

"Let go the convincer," he said.

Frank tripped the switch and the bomb fell. It went off with a satisfying bang and set off a cloud of smoke out of all proportion to any damage it might have done. It was not atomic, of course. There was no need to use a block-buster when a firecracker would serve.

"Set her down," he said.

Frank jockeyed the sphere into position above the rows of skin tents and landed it in the precise center of the camp. They waited until the natives had had time to form a cautious circle around them and then they opened the port.

The two men from Earth stepped out, smiles on their faces and their right hands raised in gestures of peace.

Canady's troubled green eyes took in the whole works with one swift, experienced glance. Anthropologists who have spent long years in the field tend to be more impressed with the similarities between cultures than with their obvious differences. It is only the untrained eye that seizes upon the somewhat superficial oddities and cannot see beyond the seemingly bizarre to the deeply-rooted universals that underlie all human social systems. A nomadic hunting culture *has* to have certain characteristics for the excellent reason that it will work in no other way. This, as Canady was well aware, is just as true twenty-nine light years from Earth as it was in aboriginal Asia, Africa, or North America. A scientific law is binding no matter where you find it.

He saw a great deal in that one quick check. He saw not only the scene before him but saw it projected against a backdrop of facts and figures, saw it nearly divided up into familiar categories. Even if he had not already known a great deal about the natives from the planted microphones that had enabled him to learn the language, he could have predicted rather closely what these people would be like. Now as always in the moment of initial contact, he was on the alert for anything off-key, anything that didn't fit. It was the unexpected that could make for trouble.

At first, he saw nothing unusual.

The natives stood in a loose circle, waiting. There were fewer of them now than there had been the night before; obviously the other bands had dispersed after the ceremony. Canady estimated the crowd at about sixty-five men and women. They were a tall, healthy-looking group with that robustness of bone and muscle that comes from an outdoor life and a predominantly meat diet. The men were dressed in skin leggings and had ornate bone combs stuck into their long dark hair. The women wore a simple skin tunic, tied at the waist with beaded thongs.

Canady spotted his first oddity: none of the natives was carrying a weapon of any kind. He filed the fact away.

Canady lowered his hand. "We visit The People in peace," he said loudly in the native language. "We come among The People as friends. We come from the sky to bring honor to the Old Ones and many gifts to The People."

Precisely on cue, Frank dragged the yedoma calf out of the sphere and placed it on the ground before the natives. There was a low murmur from the people. A man stepped forward, his dark bronzed skin glistening in the sun. He was dressed exactly like the rest except that his head-comb was blue rather than white. He raised his right hand. "You are welcome among The People," he said quietly. "We thank you for your gift. Our food is your food, and our camp your camp."

It was all according to formula but Canady felt again the stirrings of uneasiness. The natives were too calm, too self-assured. Surely the bomb had had *some* effect. . . .

"We bring not only friendship to The People," he said. "We bring many useful gifts to make your days easier. We bring a hunting stick that kills with a sound like thunder."

Frank stepped out again with a repeating rifle in his hand. He lifted the weapon to his shoulder, took aim on a small tree, and fired six shots in rapid succession. The trunk of the tree splintered neatly and a fragment of bark fell to the ground. The staccato sound of the shots died away and there was silence.

The natives watched impassively, giving him their courteous attention. They were neither frightened nor impressed.

Canady finished his speech rather lamely. "It is our hope that this day
will mark the beginning of a long friendship between The People and our
own people. It is our hope that the Old Ones will look with favor upon
our visit, and that we may each learn many things."

The native with the blue comb nodded. He waited to make sure that
Canady had finished speaking, and then stepped forward and took his
arm. He smiled, showing fine, even teeth. "Come," he said. "You must be
tired and hungry after your journey through the sky. Let us eat of the
yedoma and talk to one another as men."

Canady hesitated, more and more unsure of himself. The *tone* of the
thing was completely wrong. It was not that the natives were unfriendly,
but there was certainly none of the usual gods-from-the-sky business. It
was almost as though The People had visitors from space every day in the
week. He looked at Frank out of the corner of his eye. Frank was smiling,
still playing the Great White Father role.

"Bring the rifle," he said in English.

The native turned and led the way toward his splendidly painted tent.
Canady and Frank walked along behind him. The native men and women
watched them with no great interest and then went about their business.

"Well, I'll be damned," Canady said.

"This is really something," Frank whispered.

"It's something right enough," Canady agreed. "But what the devil *is* it?"

He followed the native into the tent, and he sensed once more that
he stood on the edge of marvels, of wonders that dwelt in an abyss of
dreams. . . .

The days that followed were easily the strangest of Canady's life. Psychologically, it is never a simple matter for a man to be uprooted from all
that is familiar to him and set down in a way of life that is not his own.
Previously, though, in his work in the Alpha Centauri system, Canady
had at least been supported by the knowledge that his task was going well,
that the situation was fully under control. And Dave, who had shared
those years with him, had been much more of a friend than Frank Landis
could ever be.

Canady had never felt so utterly alone. Even in his troubled adolescence in New Chicago he had had understanding parents who gave him
an anchor in a bustling world. Later, there had been a series of women—
though he had never married—and the quiet contentment of summers
in the unspoiled national forests of Colorado. His interest in his work
had sustained him when all else failed, and now even his confidence in
his knowledge was shaken.

It was made all the more difficult by the fact that there was nothing wrong with The People that he could put his finger on. There were no signposts erected in the village that advertised BIG MYSTERY HERE. The People were friendly enough in their fashion and they were more than willing to cooperate. They did all the things that they were supposed to do. The men rode out of the camp on their camel-like mharus in hunting parties, searching for the grazing herds of yedoma which they brought down with their bows and arrows. The women cooked and worked long hours in preparing skins and gathering wild plants from the river valleys. Often, at night while the two moons sailed among the stars, stories were told around the campfires, stories of the Old Ones and the Long Walk and the heroic deeds of the warriors of The People.

It was all very normal on the surface. But the nuances were all wrong, completely beyond Canady's understanding. The grace notes of the culture were subtly alien in a way he could not fathom. Frank was merely puzzled and a little hurt by the reception given to his bag of tricks, but Canady was deeply disturbed.

He tried to drive a wedge of understanding into the culture by falling back on the most reliable of all techniques. He began by employing the genealogical method, a safe introductory gambit for centuries. He sat down with Plavgar, the blue-combed native who seemed to have the high status of a headman. He asked him all the innocuous, surefire questions. What was the name of his wife? What had been the names of her parents? What had been the names of his parents? What were the names of their children, if any? This sort of thing was practically guaranteed to set any native off on a long chain of reminiscences about his family for generations back, and in the process the anthropologist could gain a valuable key to the various kinship connections that were so important in a primitive society. Plavgar, however, simply did not respond. He gave his wife's name, and explained that she had been obtained by raiding a neighboring band. He gave the name of his father and mother—and then proceeded to name almost everyone in the band, calling them all father and mother, and offering to introduce them to Canady. The idea of brothers and sisters appeared to puzzle him. As for generations past, he was a complete blank. Since peoples without a means of writing always made a point of remembering relatives to a really amazing degree, this was manifestly impossible.

He did get a typical culture hero story, about a man who had led an almost legendary mharu raid against the Telliomata, swiping their entire mharu herd from right under their eyes. But then Playgar blandly offered to introduce Canady to the culture hero, who could be seen at that moment calmly gnawing on a steak in front of his tipi.

Frank set up his steam engine and showed The People the work it could do. They watched the demonstration politely, as one might watch a child putting together a model airplane, and then ignored it. Frank got out his battery-powered sewing machines and played his trump card. He took the women aside and showed them how they could cut their work-day in half. The women tried it out, smiling and eager to please, and then went back to their bone needles.

Even the rifles, so demonstrably superior to the native bows and arrows, failed to have the desired effect. The natives admired Frank's shooting and that was all. This was a serious business, because the rifle was a lever that the men from Earth had relied heavily upon. Once you substituted rifles for bows in a hunting culture you had a ready-made market. Not only would the natives become so dependent on the rifles that they would in time forget how to make bows, but the introduction of the rifle would set off a chain reaction that would completely upset the balance of power between the native groups. A band with rifles was unbeatable. Then, the mere threat of taking the rifles away or withholding ammunition was all the threat you needed. . . .

Try as he might, Canady could get no information about shamans. At first, he put this down to an understandable tabu against referring to the supernatural. But the natives did not shy away from his questions: they simply assured him that they didn't *have* any curers or healers or medicine men. He got a lot of patient talk about the Old Ones, and that was that. He shook his head. He had never heard of a primitive culture without shamans—it was as unthinkable as a copter without an atmosphere. What did they do when they got sick?

It was not until he had been on the planet for two full months that the truth hit him in the face, the truth that should have been obvious from the first. It was so simple, so utterly out in the open, that its significance had completely escaped him. And it was so fantastic that the very idea was automatically rejected by the mind.

It all began when Lerrie, the wife of Rownar, announced that she was pregnant.

III

A fever pitch of excitement ran through the camp of The People and Canady found himself caught up in it despite himself. He had lived long enough to know that true happiness was the rarest of all gifts, and the natives around him were almost delirious with joy. Even the certain knowledge that he was on the verge of a tremendous scientific discovery paled to insignificance. There was a smile on every face and work was impossible. A sense of miraculous well-being permeated the very air. It was a holiday mood and Canady surrendered to it.

The People had stayed long in one place and it was time to move on. The warm summer months were fading into the chill of autumn and the yedoma herds were migrating to the south across the grassy, rolling plains. The People would have had to follow them in any case, but it was definitely the news about Lerrie that triggered their departure.

The great tents were struck and the hides were lashed to pack mharus. The tent poles were tied to the flanks of the beasts so that their tips dragged along the ground. The tips were securely lashed together, travois-fashion, to form a V-shaped platform upon which The People placed their few belongings. The men and women mounted their mharus and they were ready. Leaving home was as simple as that.

The People moved out at dawn on a cold, gray day. A light rain was falling and the yedoma robes were welcome against their shoulders. Canady, moved by an impulse he hardly understood, rode with the natives. His camel-like mharu was a spirited mount and he felt oddly at peace on the scrap of hide that served as a saddle. His tall, lean body had grown hard in his months with The People and the wind-swept rain in his face was fresh and cool, the breath of life itself.

Dammit, he thought, *I feel like a man again.*

Frank followed along behind the tribe, piloting the sphere. He held it just above the level of the grass and its soundless presence was curiously unreal. The People ignored it and whenever Canady glanced back and saw it hovering over the plain behind him he felt a wild urge to laugh. The thing was somehow comical, for all the engineering skill that had gone into it. When compared with the magnificent vitality of the world around it the sphere became a kind of cipher, colorless and blatantly trivial. It seemed to sail along in a void, trying without success to attract attention to itself. It was a loud-shirted tourist in a forest of cool pines and it didn't matter, it was overwhelmed. . . .

A day and a night and a day The People rode. They did not seem to hurry and they dozed in their saddles and chewed on dried meat and berries as they traveled but there was a definite direction to their wandering, They crossed the windy plains and struck a trail that wound up into the foothills of a range of purple, snow-capped mountains. They rode into a sheltered canyon where a small stream trickled out of a glacial spring, a canyon where the trees were tall and dark and green. They moved through the evening shadows, pitching their tents and building great yellow fires that warmed the chill air.

Canady was sore and red-eyed from lack of sleep. The trick of dozing in the saddle looked easy enough when the natives did it, but he had discovered that the jerky gait of the mharu was anything but soothing. He decided that perhaps the rugged outdoor life was not an unalloyed joy after all and stumbled into the sphere with relief. The warm, dry bunk pulled him like a magnet and he fell into it without bothering to take off his damp, dirt-streaked clothes.

Frank, neat and clean and freshly-shaven, wrinkled his nose. "You smell like a fertilizer factory, my friend," he said. "Remember, I live here too."

"Make yourself at home," Canady said. He yawned, too tired to argue. "Call me early, will you? I have a feeling that something's going to pop, and I don't want to miss it."

Frank said something else, then looked more closely at his companion and gave up. Canady was already snoring lustily. Frank smiled and managed to haul off the sleeping man's boots, which he held at arms-length and deposited outside on the ground. He gently placed a blanket over Canady's body and sat down to write up his field notes for the day.

He shook his head. Canady was a funny guy.

Outside in the night, a single voice was raised in a plaintive chant. It was a woman's voice, soft and lovely in the silence. Frank listened to it for a long time and then he too went to bed.

The woman chanted on, her voice liquid and true, and it was hard to tell whether it was a song she sang, or a prayer. . . .

The next day dawned clear and cold with a thin wind whining down from the mountain snows. The sheltered valley, dark with tall fir trees, was slow to warm and the tipis of The People stood like frozen sentinels on the canyon floor.

Arthur Canady stood surveying the scene, his long legs wide apart, his work-roughened hands on his hips. There was a respectable black beard on his face and he had let his hair grow long. He shivered a little in the cold and tried to determine his next move. There was no doubt that they had failed utterly in their mission to date; the natives had shown no interest at all in the fancy gadgets they had brought from Earth. This didn't bother Canady—in fact it gave him a secret satisfaction—but what did bother him was the fact that after months with The People he was still a stranger. He felt a keen sense of not belonging, of being an outsider. He had made no friends and this had never happened to him before. The People were not hostile and they treated him with every courtesy, but they did not *accept* him.

That hurt.

He walked along the line of tipis, smelling the rich odors of yedoma steaks broiling over the cook-fires. He saw Lerrie, the wife of Rownar, washing her face in the cold waters of the mountain stream. She looked up at him and smiled. She looked radiantly beautiful as though filled with an inner joy that stamped itself upon her every feature. Her eyes sparkled in the morning sunlight. She shook the water from her face and began to comb out her long black hair.

"Good morning," he said.

"It is a lovely morning, Ar-thur." It was odd to hear his name on her lips and the sound of his name took on a strange music.

"The Old Ones have been kind," he said, following the formula. "I rejoice for you."

She smiled again. "I am to be a mother," she said, as though this were the most wonderful thing in the world. "I, Lerrie, am to have a child!"

"That is good." Canady hesitated, searching for the right words. "It is your first?" he asked.

She stared at him and then laughed aloud. "My first! Surely you are joking with me? Of course it is my first. How could it be otherwise?"

"Forgive me; many of your customs are still strange to me. Lerrie, in my world it is sometimes dangerous to ask a woman how old she is. Do you mind if I ask you? How old are you, Lerrie?"

She frowned as though puzzled. "How . . . *old?*"

"How many seasons have you lived?"

She shook her head. "I do not know," she said simply. "We do not count such things. I am alive. That is all."

"Many seasons?" Canady persisted.

"Yes, Ar-thur. Many seasons."

"Do you remember when you were a child, Lerrie?"

She pursed her lips. "It was long ago. I remember little." Her face brightened. "I do remember the Coming of Age, when I became one of The People. I will never forget that. I was so frightened. I had heard stories of the Long Walk, even then." She paused. "My child will be a good child, Ar-thur. He will have a good heart."

"I'm sure he will, Lerrie." He looked at the woman before him. She was hardly more than a girl. By Earthly standards she could not have been more than twenty-five years old. And yet she could not remember her childhood?

She had lived—how long?

Many seasons.

"I rejoice for you," he said again, and walked on to find Plavgar, the headman of The People. He found him sitting cross-legged in his tipi while his wife busied herself mending clothing. Canady was invited inside and seated himself on Plavgar's right, which he knew was proper etiquette for a guest. He said nothing until Plavgar's comely wife had served him a wooden bowlful of stew, which he dutifully sampled.

"Please smoke if you wish," Plavgar said. "I have noticed that it makes you more comfortable."

Canady pulled out his pipe, filled it, and lit it with a burning stick from the fire. The inside of the tipi was surprisingly roomy and spotlessly clean. The ground was covered with yedoma skins and the air smelled sweet and fresh. Canady took his time, puffing on his pipe. Plavgar sat quietly, watching him. He was a man of great dignity but except for the blue comb in his hair there was nothing about him to show his office of leader. He was still a young man in the prime of life, and yet his bearing was that of a man who had lived long and thought of many things.

"May I ask you some questions?" Canady said slowly.

Plavgar smiled. "That is your custom."

Canady flushed faintly. "I am sincere in wanting to know about The People. There are many things that I do not understand. As I stay with you longer, I find that I know less and less."

"That is the beginning of wisdom, my son." It was first time that Plavgar had ever called him son and it pleased Canady. Of course, he himself was thirty-five, older than Plavgar looked, but the term seemed fitting.

"Do I have your permission to ask you anything I wish?"

Plavgar nodded, a faint twinkle in his eyes. "We have no secrets. I will help you all I can."

Canady leaned forward. "What happens to the children of The People?" he asked.

Playgar frowned. "What happens to them? Why, they grow up into adult members of the tribe."

"They *always* grow up into adult members of the tribe?"

"Almost always. When a child is born he must learn many things. He must live among The People and learn their ways. If he has a good heart, he is sent out alone to Thunder Rock, high in the mountains. There he fasts for four days and there the Old Ones send a guardian spirit to him. He sees the guardian spirit and they become one. Then he goes through the Coming of Age, and he is one of The People forever."

"And if he does *not* have a good heart?"

"That does not often happen, my son. If he does not have a good heart, if he does not believe in the ways of The People, then the Old Ones are sad and will not accept him. His guardian spirit does not come to Thunder Rock and he is alone. If he has no guardian spirit, it would be unthinkable for him to take part in the Coming of Age."

"What happens to him?"

"He takes the Long Walk."

"You mean—he is expelled from the tribe?"

"He was never one of The People. He takes the Long Walk alone. He is alone forever or until his heart is good. A man cannot be a man until his heart is good."

Canady kept his face expressionless. His profession had taught him patience, if nothing else. It was always like this: the answers freely given that explained nothing. The guardian spirit complex was a familiar one, of course; it was the idea of a personal vision that came after fasting, a contact with the supernatural that gave a man a kind of personal phantom ally that accompanied him through life. If you were told throughout your childhood that you would see a spirit on zzzzzzzzzthunder Rock, and if you went without eating for four days alone in the mountains, you would see a spirit right enough. Particularly if you could not gain admission into adult status in the tribe if you did *not* see a spirit. Still—

"I have heard much of the Old Ones. Can you tell me about them?"

"The Old Ones lived in the world before men came," Plavgar said, as though instructing a small child. "They were mighty beings and they live still in the high places. We cannot see them in our day-to-day life, but they are always there. They show themselves to us on Thunder Rock if we have a good heart. The Old Ones watch over our people and protect us from harm. The lives of the Old Ones and those of The People are one. We live together in harmony, and each is a part of the other."

That tells me exactly nothing, Canady thought.

He tried to bring the conversation down to a more concrete level. "Why is it that I have seen no children among The People?" he asked.

Plavgar smiled. "They have all grown up. The children are The People now."

Swell.

"And Lerrie?"

"The Old Ones have been kind. We rejoice for her, and we are thankful to Mewenta." Plavgar eyed him shrewdly. "You will stay with us long, my son?"

"Perhaps." The mother ship was due to pick them up twenty-two terrestrial months from now.

"Then you shall see for yourself what happens to the children of The People." Plavgar's face glowed. It seemed to be impossible for any native to refer to the coming child without a kind of inner ecstasy. "The Old Ones have been kind!"

"I rejoice with you," Canady said politely. There was a question nagging at him, something about what Plavgar had said. He tried to put his finger on it and failed. There were so many strange things—

He stood up. "I thank you for your time, Plavgar."

"I hope I have helped you," the headman said.

I hope so too, Canady thought, feeling far from certain.

He took his leave and went back to the sphere to dictate the text of his conversations with Plavgar and Lerrie.

All that afternoon, while Frank was busy trying to interest someone in his sewing machines, Canady puzzled over the data he had obtained. He felt that he had at least made some progress: he could pinpoint the areas in the culture that were causing the trouble. He could ask the right questions, and he knew that the answers were only a matter of time.

He smoked his pipe thoughtfully and as he worked he sensed a growing excitement within him. Approached solely as a puzzle, The People were more intriguing than any culture he had ever encountered. And if his hunch was right—

Looked at on a superficial level there was nothing at all extraordinary about The People. They formed a small hunting society based on the yedoma, they lived in tipis, they told stories about the Old Ones and believed in personal guardian spirits. There was nothing obviously wrong. But—

Item: None of the Earth's techniques for manipulating the culture had had the slightest effect. The culture was stable beyond belief. They not only had no interest in technology as such—they actively opposed any technological change. They wanted to keep their way of life the way it was. This was frequently the case in areas like social organization and religion, but Canady had never heard of a group that would not take to firearms and sewing machines like ducks to water. It was as though The People *knew* that the introduction of new technological elements would inevitably change their total way of life.

Item: Lerrie looked like a young girl. Yet she could not remember her childhood. She had no idea how old she was. And the notion of having more than one child had struck her as being ridiculous.

Item: There were no old individuals among The People. Canady had not seen a single person who looked over thirty. Even the leaders like Plavgar were young men.

Item: There were no children among The People. At first, Canady could hardly credit this, but there could be no doubt of it now. There were no babies, no adolescent boys and girls. Lerrie's pregnancy was a great event. Her child would be the only one in the tribe. . . .

Item: There were no shamans. There were no techniques for dealing with sickness.

What did it all add up to?

Suddenly, Canady remembered the phrase of Plavgar's that had troubled him when he first heard it. What had Plavgar said?

"We rejoice for her, and we are thankful to Mewenta."

Mewenta? But the husband of Lerrie was named Rownar. Who was Mewenta, and what did he have to do with the coming birth of Lerrie's child?

Canady snapped his fingers. Of course! He knew who Mewenta had to be, and that meant—

He got to his feet, the blood racing in his veins. He hurried outside into the twilight shadows. He knew the question now. It was time to get an answer.

Canady soon found that it was easier to determine upon a course of action than to carry it out. He had worked over his data longer than he had thought and twilight was already deepening into night when he tried to find Plavgar for another conference.

He found him quickly enough but Plavgar was busy.

The hunters had all come in, loaded down with yedoma meat, and smooth firm-fleshed fish had been taken from the mountain streams. The women had prepared the evening meal and built up the fires against the night. The People had gathered in knots around the fires and Canady saw at once that there was some kind of ceremony going on.

It was not the sort of thing that a man could interrupt gracefully. Canady stayed in the shadows and watched.

It was a curious ritual, a mixture of wild abandon and solemn, highly stylized movements that were as old as time and performed with an immemorial artistry. There was a definite rhythm to the ritual, but it was a rhythm of motion rather than of music; no instruments were used and the only sound came from cadenced human voices.

The women sat in groups of four around the fires. In the center of the camp, dressed in a long blue tunic, Lerrie stood on a low platform of logs. Her skin gleamed like gold in the firelight and her long black hair glistened around her shoulders. She turned slowly on the platform, facing each group of women in turn. There was a happiness in her eyes that was good to see.

The men danced in a great circle around Lerrie, their deep voices chanting a song that was old when the very mountains were young. Every few minutes one man would detach himself from the circle and visit each of the woman-fires. At each fire he would raise his bare arms and address the women in a ritual speech. He would tell of the events of his life, taking care to mention the incidents he had shared with each woman, and then give an account of his personal exploits: coups he had counted on raiding parties, his moment of contact with his guardian spirit, stories of Long Walks and Old Ones. When he had completed the circle of the fires, he would choose one woman for his ceremonial mate and take her into the trees beside the mountain stream. After a time, the two of them would come back to the fires, the woman would seat herself in her group of four, and the man would resume his place in the circle. As far as Canady could determine, the only rule was that a man could not choose his own wife.

Canady watched in silence, feeling far more than a scientific interest in the proceedings. He felt desperately alone, desperately out of things, like a penniless child with his face pressed tight against the cold window of a toy shop. He stood in the shadows of the firelight, half in darkness and half in light, and he chewed on the stem of his pipe with a longing and bitterness that racked his soul. The stars were frozen above him, the night was chill, and he had been long without a woman. . . .

The tireless chant continued and The People filled the darkness with their rejoicing. Only Lerrie was alone, and no man touched her. She stood smiling on the log platform, radiantly lovely with the new life that was stirring within her. Canady felt a strange kinship with her, the kinship of the outsiders, but he resented her too. She was the center of everything, and he simply did not count.

He shook his head. This was a hell of a time for self-pity.

He waited until dawn streaked the sky with gray, waited until he could sense the great red sun hovering beneath the mountain horizon. When the ceremony was over and The People were laughing and talking together in normal voices, he sought out Plavgar.

Plavgar smiled and touched his shoulder with something like pity. "Welcome, my son. I thank you for your courtesy in waiting. It has been a long night for you."

Canady nodded. "The longest of my life, I think. May I ask you one more question, Plavgar?"

"We have no secrets, my son."

"You told me earlier that you rejoiced for Lerrie, and that you were thankful to Mewenta. Who is Mewenta?"

Canady tensed. He knew the answer to the question but he had to ask, had to be *sure*. He listened to Plavgar's words with a thrill of confirmation.

"Mewenta was a great man of The People. On the night before you came to visit us, Ar-thur, he did a wonderful thing for The People. He walked into the fire and his spirit now lives here in the mountains. Because of his deed, the Old Ones smiled. That is why Lerrie now will have a child."

Canady remembered that night. They had hidden in a clump of bushes, looking down on a scene, of wild magnificence. A thousand natives had gathered around a roaring fire and the tipis had shone in the moonlight. A naked man bowed to the four directions, gave a last farewell look out into the night and the moons and the stars. His face had been supremely peaceful, the face of a man who had reached the end of a long, long journey.

He walked into the roaring flames. . . .

Mewenta.

Canady turned and walked back to the sphere. He should have been tired but nothing was further from his mind than sleep. He felt an electric excitement in his muscles, an almost supernatural clearness in his mind.

He shook Frank's shoulder.

"Frank, wake up."

Frank sat up in bed, rubbing his eyes. "What's the matter? What time is it?"

"Frank, I've got it. I know about The People now."

Frank Landis groped for a cigarette, eyeing his companion sleepily. "Know what about The People? What is there to know?"

Canady laughed. "God, and we tried to impress them with sewing machines!"

Frank waited, puffing on his cigarette. "Well?"

"Frank, don't you see? We've walked right smack into the middle of the biggest discovery ever made by man. Frank, The People *don't die.*"

"What?"

"They don't die, at least not naturally. They're immortal, Frank. They live forever."

Frank stared at him, the cigarette forgotten in his hand.

"Immortal," Canady said again.

He walked over to the port and looked out at the red splendor of the morning sun.

IV

Two hours later, while the camp slept around them and the warmth of the day inched up toward the mountain snows, the men from Earth were still at it. The sphere was blue with stale tobacco smoke and the coffee dregs had turned gummy in the cups.

"I did *not* say you were crazy, Arthur," Frank said."That's not fair."

Canady watched him and had to smile. Despite the words that tumbled from his lips, Frank obviously thought he was trapped with a lunatic—or at best with a man on the thin edge of sanity. And Canady was finding it very difficult to *talk* to Frank. Frank's eager, friendly personality and his guileless blue eyes just didn't belong in the same room with talk about immortality. It was like trying to explain to a three-year-old child that the Earth wasn't *really* flat but only looked that way.

"It's true, Frank. Our opinions won't change it any."

"But look." Frank nodded his head up and down solemnly, determined to explode the fallacies in the argument. "It just doesn't stand to reason. You say these natives live practically forever. OK. That means that they are maybe thousands of years old. Think what a man could learn if he lived to be a thousand years old! Dammit, he wouldn't be living like a savage. He would have developed a superior, advanced kind of culture. Isn't that true?"

Canady stoked up his pipe. He was feeling light-headed from the long hours without sleep. But if he could just make Frank see—

"I agree. He wouldn't be living like a savage. And he would live in a very advanced type of culture."

Frank threw up his hands. "Well?"

"Well what?" Canady leaned forward. "Think a minute. Are The People *really* living like savages, and what the devil does that mean anyhow? Do you mean they are savages because they hunt animals for food? Or because they live in tents instead of skyscrapers? Or because they use bows and arrows instead of rifles or atom bombs?"

"But their technology *is* simple. You can't deny that."

"I don't have to deny it. Just the same, simple isn't savage. After all, what's a technology for? How do you judge it? I would think you have to rate it by seeing what it does in terms of its own cultural context. The only real index of technological advancement is one of relative efficiency. What do you want a rifle for if you don't need one? What do you need a doctor for if you never get sick?"

"It isn't an efficient technology. You can't tell me a bow is more efficient than a rifle for a hunter. It *isn't*."

"It is in a special situation, and this is one of them. Look, it's obvious that for some reason these societies must be kept small. Not only that, but they must be peaceful. If they've hit a perfect balance in ecological terms with a bow and arrow, a rifle would just foul everything up. The one cardinal fact about an immortal society is that it must survive. If it doesn't, it's not immortal. And therefore anything that *in the long run* does not contribute to survival cannot be tolerated. Hell, you can't argue with the thing. It *works*."

"All right, all right." Frank poured himself another cup of coffee, "But all that is theory, speculation. It doesn't prove that those natives live forever."

"True enough. But try this on for size: there is not a single child in this village. There is not a single elderly person. The People can hardly remember when they were young, it was so long ago. And until Mewenta chose to destroy himself, Lerrie could not have a child. When Mewenta died it was such a singular event that natives for miles around came into camp just to witness it. When Lerrie announced that she was pregnant, the whole tribe went into a delirium of joy. It can only mean one thing: this is a rigidly controlled population. No child can be born until the death of an adult makes room for a new member of the society. It would *have* to work that way. If nobody dies and children keep on being born The People would breed themselves into extinction."

"I'll go along with that up to a point. I think you have demonstrated that we have a rigidly controlled population here. I admit that I've never heard of anything like it. But that still doesn't prove all this immortality stuff."

Canady sighed. He was talking to a stone wall. "Look, Frank. *Why* didn't The People accept those sewing machines and rifles? *Why* weren't they impressed with that bomb we dropped, or with this sphere for that matter? *Why* have we failed to make the slightest impression on them?"

"You said it yourself. If you destroy a perfect ecological adjustment . . ." Frank stopped.

"Exactly. *But how do they know that?* Who told them about ecological adjustments? How could they possibly know what effect a rifle will have on their culture? You started out by saying they were a bunch of savages. Now you're saying they know all about the effects of acculturation and cultural dynamics. You can't have it both ways."

Frank lapsed into silence.

"It's more than just ecology, Frank. I'm convinced that this immortality angle is *part* of their culture—a product of it. It isn't a mutant gland or a shot of wonder drug in the gizzard. It comes about *because* they live the way they do. They know that. So of course they're not going to jeopardize it by changing their culture. What's a rifle or a spaceship against the prospects of living forever? Think of it, Frank! No lying awake nights wondering if that ache in your belly is cancer. No sitting in a hospital room wondering if your wife will live until morning. No certain knowledge that you will see your father and mother buried in a hole in the ground. No waiting for your muscles to turn flabby and the saliva to drool from the corners of your mouth when you eat. No watching a friend get skinnier day by day, no watching the light go out of his eyes. My God, would you trade that for a sewing machine?"

Frank shook his head. "I always read that if you lived forever you would be unhappy and bored stiff. How about that?"

Canady laughed. "Man, that is the rationalization of the ages. You can't live forever, therefore you don't want to. You can't have a steak, therefore you aren't hungry. Are The People unhappy? I'd say they're a million times happier than most men and women on Earth. And would you *really* fight against it if you knew you could live forever? I wouldn't! My life hasn't been any screaming ecstasy but I'll hang onto it as long as I can. And if I could live forever, if I could really do the things I love—"

How do you speak of these things to another? How do you tell of blue skies and sunlight and the laughter of love? How do you tell of the joys of just being alive, of knowing that the world of winds and trees and mountain streams is yours to cherish forever? How do you tell of a love that endures for all the years, all the springs?

"Mewenta killed himself," Frank said bluntly.

"Sure. Not all people are happy, and these natives *are* people. And perhaps a man might even sacrifice eternal life to bring joy to his fellow man, the joy of children. I have heard that when a man of The People feels restless or discontented, he sets out on a Long Walk alone. He gets close to the land to cleanse his heart. It usually works. If not, there's always the fire."

"You spoke of peace. How about all this raiding that goes on?"

"You mean counting coups?" Canady shrugged. "Sure, they go off and rustle the mharu herds. They have real knock-down fights too. But who said a culture like this has to be dull? It *couldn't* be dull. They don't kill each other in the fights. Have you noticed the combs the men wear in their hair? That's what they take instead of scalps. It serves the same purpose. You don't kill a guy in a football game either, but you can get plenty steamed up about it. *Everything* in the culture is set up to avoid boredom. They alternate roles, for one thing. Every five years or so everyone switches positions. Plavgar is the headman now, but that is only one of the many parts he has played in his life. And all the ceremonies, the periods when the sex tabus are lifted—they all serve the same purpose. Dammit, The People like to have *fun.* "

Frank lit another cigarette. "If it's true, Arthur—we've got to find out how it's done. We've *got* to."

Canady smiled. "Have The People ever lied to us?"

"No, I guess not."

"How do they say it's done?"

"I don't follow you."

Canady go up, stretched, and yawned. "I think you better brush up on your guardian spirits, Frank. I think you better start thinking about the Old Ones."

Frank stared. "But that's all superstition—"

"Is it? *How do you know?* Have you ever fasted on Thunder Rock?"

Canady turned before Frank could answer him. He peeled off his clothes and fell into his bunk. He closed his tired eyes.

And he thought—

The world of winds and trees and mountain streams yours to cherish forever . . .

V

The days flowed into weeks and the weeks became months. The People drifted south along the sheltered slopes of the blue mountain range and the cold winter snows settled on the grasslands in a blanket of white. Only the brown and black tips of the grasses showed above the rolling sea of snow and the yedoma herds turned their backs to the wind and pawed at the frozen soil with cold and bleeding hooves.

Arthur Canady lived as though in a dream. He was not himself and he felt the very foundations of the world he had known crumbling away beneath him. Subtly, without any clear time of transition, he found himself caught between two different ways of life. He lived in a cultural twilight, an outsider, belonging neither to the world of his past nor to the world that had suddenly opened up before him.

I'm a marginal man, he thought. *Me, Arthur Canady, a scientist. I don't fit anywhere. Maybe I've never fit in, not really. Maybe I've been searching all my life, never finding, never knowing what it was I sought. . . .*

He spent part of his time in the sphere with Frank, surrounded by the familiar gadgets he had always known, both attracted and repelled by the personality of his companion. The man was such a mixture of receptiveness and bull-headedness. Like most naive men, Frank prided himself on being utterly practical. He was tolerant and respectful of new ideas, but he could never change beyond a certain point. His personality was a finished thing; it had nowhere else to go. Canady envied him in a way, but he was unable to communicate with him except on a very superficial level.

He spent part of his time with The People, riding with them on the winter-thin mharus, facing the wind-driven snows with Plavgar and Lerrie and Rownar. He learned to bring down the mooselike yedoma bulls with an arrow behind the left shoulder, learned to cut the blood-warm hides from the bodies with a stone knife, learned to drink the hot blood against the cold of the winter plains. He sat in the smoke-hazed tipis at night, sweating with the others around the tiny fires of yedoma chips, listening to the stories of The People.

Still, he did not belong.

The People smiled at him and seemed glad to see him, but there was a barrier he could not cross. The men were friendly without being his friends, the women cordial but invincibly remote. Canady let his hair and beard grow long and began to dress in the skin clothing of the natives. There were many times when he set out across the plains alone, eyes narrowed against the cold, and there were many nights that he looked up at the frozen stars and wondered which one was the sun he had known on Earth. . . .

And the dark, terrible irony of the thing that was happening gnawed at his mind day and night. He would sit and smoke his pipe staring at Frank. Didn't he *know?*

Canady had always been a lonely man, lonely not only for companionship but for a richness and a fullness he had never found in life. His loneliness was made doubly unbearable by the vitality of the life around him. The People offered him nothing, denied him nothing. They made no overtures. They were simply there.

And life everlasting . . .

Canady abandoned all pretense of scientific investigation. He went to see Plavgar. He seated himself in the tipi on Plavgar's right, ate of the ritual food, and groped for words.

"The Old Ones were here before The People came," he said, thinking like a native. But his mind refused to stay on that level. He thought: *Everything they have told me has been the literal truth. There are Old Ones. What are they? In the vastness of the universe, life must take many forms. Do they co-exist with men, manifesting themselves only in visions? Could they have existed on Earth, serving as the basis for primitive legends? Who knows what we destroyed when we sailed into strange harbors with our ships and our diseases? We never saw our natives until we had corrupted them.* "They must be powerful beings. Did they not try to defend their world?"

"Conquest is a delusion of the young, my son," Plavgar said slowly. "There is room for all. The lives of the Old Ones and the lives of The People touch in only a few places. We are equal but different. To them, as to us, harmony is the highest law of the universe. We all must live so that we *blend* with one another, Men and Old Ones and plants and birds and animals and sky and water—all must work together to make a world fair and good. The Old Ones have given life to us. In return, we give them happiness. They can *feel* the warmth of our lives. They need our presence, just as we need theirs. We live together, and we are both the better for it."

Canady leaned forward. "You too once came to this world in ships?"

Plavgar smiled. "It was long ago. Yes, once we were civilized and advanced, just like yourself."

The irony of the headman's words was not lost on Canady. He brushed it aside. "Plavgar, what is the secret? What is the price a man must pay for eternal life?"

Plavgar looked at him steadily. "We do not live forever, my son. A very long time, yes, but not forever."

"But there must be a secret! What is it?"

"There is only one rule. *You must learn to have a good heart.*"

Canady swallowed hard. "A good heart?"

"That is all. I have told you the truth. I have concealed nothing from you. We have no secrets. There is no magic pill, no gadget that will bring you what you seek. You must *believe,* that is all. You must have a good heart."

"But—" Canady's mind was dizzy with what Plavgar was saying. A good heart? He had learned many things in many schools, but no one had taught him this. How did a man go about getting a good heart?

"A man's heart is within himself," Plavgar said simply. "You must look around you, at the mountains and the skies, at the plants and the animals. You must look within yourself. You must feel that you are a part of all life, and respect it. You must find peace. Then you must go to Thunder Rock and fast for four days. And if you believe, if your heart is good, you will see the Old Ones. The guardian spirit will come to you. Then, my son, you will be one of The People—for always."

The yedoma-chip fire flickered brightly in the tipi. The shadows closed in around Canady, shadows and something else . . .

"Thank you, Plavgar," he said.

He got up and left the tipi, walking out into the cold night air. Hs boots crunched the snow under his feet.

All he had to do was to believe. All he had to do was to reject all he had ever known. All he had to do was to get a good heart.

Simple!

And there were other problems, other loyalties.

He walked back alone to the sphere.

When he told Frank what he was going to do, Frank hit the ceiling.

"You can't do it, Art." Frank's face was very pale. He backed away from his bearded, wild-looking companion as though Canady was a carrier of some frightful disease. "It's against the law."

"Whose law? We're a long way from Earth, my friend. I'm not a soldier. I'm a scientist."

"You're a fool! Dammit, can't you see what you're doing? You've got a wild bee in your brain and all that talk about being a scientist is so much hogwash. You're going native! You, Arthur Canady, hotshot scientist!"

"All right. I'm going native."

"Look, Art. It's more than that. It's—it's disloyal, that's what it is. You can't just turn your back on your own people for a bunch of wild hunters."

"I can try."

Frank's anger got the better of his caution. "You act like you're so damned superior to everyone, you and your sarcasm! And look at you! What the hell is a good heart? You'll park yourself up on the mountain and starve to death waiting for some native gods to come and hand you immortality, It's crazy, Art! I won't let you do it"

Canady smiled. He stood there, tall and lean and toughened by his life on the plains. His green eyes were cold. "You can't stop me, Frank. Don't try."

"Forget about me. How about your own people, your friends? Don't you owe them something? You're always spouting off about ethics, but what are you doing? You're a traitor!"

Canady sighed. "You still don't see it, do you?"

"See what? There's nothing to see."

"Yes, there *is* something to see. You spoke of ethics. Have you ever heard a phrase about doing to others as you would have them do unto you? I suggest you think about it a little."

"What are you talking about?"

"Look, Frank. We came here from Earth with a lot of high-sounding notions about helping the natives, didn't we? What was it that we offered them, essentially? We offered them what we thought was progress for a price. We would give them technological advancements if they would simply agree to change their culture, their way of life. All they had to do was learn to live the way we do and we would give them something of what we had. Of course, we didn't put the offer to them honestly. We tried to trick them into it—all from the very highest motives, naturally. Was that ethical?"

Frank shrugged. "You tell me."

"I am telling you. If it was ethical, then you can't damn the natives for giving us a dose of our own morals. If it wasn't ethical, then it's pointless for us to prattle about right and wrong. Don't you see, Frank? They've turned the tables on us. They're offering us exactly what we offered to them. The joker is that the *they* seem to have the superior culture, if that adjective means anything. They'll give us what they have: eternal life. And the price we have to pay is the same price we were going to charge them: all we have to do is change our culture and live the way *they* do. It's beautiful and neat and maybe a little frightening. But at least they were honest about it: no tricks, no high pressure salesmanship. The choice is there. What we do with it is up to us."

"It's fantastic! You can't believe—"

"I've *got* to believe. That's the whole point. And don't make the mistake of underestimating these natives, They are far from helpless. They have the best of all defenses: a good offense. They protect themselves by *giving*. We could destroy their culture, sure. But if we do we throw away our only chance for immortality! We *need* their culture. Oh, they're safe enough."

"Art, even if you believe all that stuff you still have a duty to your own people. You signed on to do a job. You can't just walk out on it."

"I'm not going to walk out on it. That's why I came back here. I'm going to write up precisely what I have discovered, leaving out nothing. There will be no secrets. I am going to tell our own people exactly what I have found. Hell, I'm giving them the secret of practically eternal life! What man ever did more for his people? If they don't believe me, that's their business. I'm giving them the chance. And I'm giving them the key that may one day unlock this culture, if they will only use it. You see, we made our big mistake in trying to impress The People with technological gadgets. They just don't *care* about technology. Perhaps if we had tried something else—Shakespeare, poetry, art, music—they might have listened to us. I don't know."

Frank shook his head. "You need a doctor."

Canady smiled. "Not any more, pal. And I'll tell you something else. I hope everyone *does* think I'm cracked. I hope they dismiss my report and toss it in the trash file. My conscience is clear. I've found what I want. All I want now is to be let alone."

"You're really going?"

Canady walked over and sat down at his desk. "I'm going to write this report. It will take a couple of days. After that, I'm going out alone."

"To get a good heart?"

"To get a good heart."

Canady assembled his notes and went to work.

Frank Landis stared at him and ran his hand through his sandy hair. Almost desperately, he picked up two battery-powered sewing machines and went out into the snow to peddle his wares.

VI

The lakes and ponds were still frozen solid and the mountain streams were still glazed with ice. The barren black brush of the plains was still skeletal and gaunt against the drifts of silver snow and the winter winds still whined down the canyons and froze the sweat on your face into little drops and rivulets of ice.

Yet the worst was over when Arthur Canady left the sphere and the camp of The People and set out alone into the wilderness. The snow-choked blizzards and the rivers of knife-edged winds had passed. The winter was resting, holding its own, waiting for the spring thaws and the return of green to the land. The gray winter skies had turned to cloudless blue and the great red sun was warm again on his back.

You must feel that you are part of all life. . . .

It was a strange Odyssey and Canady felt that strangeness keenly. It was a quest for the intangible, a search for the unknown. Canady was a trained man and he felt competent to search for many things: success in a field he knew, material prosperity, the solution to a scientific problem. He was enough of a product of his culture to feel at home looking for gold or uranium or a prize set of horns to hang over an old-fashioned fireplace.

But a good heart?

That wasn't so easy, Where did you look? How did you go about it? His scientific training got in his way. What was a good heart? It was a phrase he would have denounced as meaningless in a seminar discussion. It was mysticism. It was something for philosophers and theologians and politicians to kick around. It was fuzzy, slippery. . . .

You must look within yourself.

He rode out across the white-coated plains, drifting with the yedoma herds that offered him meat and warm furs. He watched the tiny tracks that criss-crossed over the crust of the snow. He watched the great birds that soared high in the sky on motionless, splendid wings. At night he pitched his small tent in whatever shelter he could find. He sat before his tiny fire and watched the twin moons float down the cold arc of the stars.

He rode into the far mountains, climbed the ageless rocks and stood with his head in the sky looking down upon the vastness of the land below him. He listened to the wind, rode through the whispers of the trees.

You must believe, that is all.

Perhaps he had help; he did not know. The Old Ones lived still in the high places, and perhaps they looked upon him with compassion. Canady felt a great peace growing within him, a peace he had never known in the cities of Earth. It was a hard life but he too became hard. He took a secret pleasure in the toughness of his body, in the sharpness of his eyes. He awakened with the sun, grateful for the life in his body, eager to see what the day would bring. Smiles came easily to his face and he was relaxed, free from worry.

Why had his people thrown all their energies into bigger buildings, more powerful ships, more intricate engines? Why did his people spend all of their lives grubbing at jobs they detested, their greatest joys coming from a slickly gutless mediocrity on the tri-di set? What had they mistaken for progress, what had they sacrificed to that strange god? How had it come about that pleasure had become something to snatch on the run, between business appointments, between the soggy oblivion of sleeping pills?

Progress.

Could it be that true progress might be found on a simple pathway through the trees and not on a super freeway at all? Could it be that eternal life had always come from a kind of faith, from being close to the land and the world of living things?

If you believe, if your heart is good, you will see the Old Ones. The guardian spirit will come to you. Then, my son, you will be one of The People—for always.

Canady rode alone across the rolling plains and up twisting mountain trails. Winter lost its grip on the land and the streams leaped from their banks, fed by the melting snows. Patches of green came again to the lowland valleys and the first wildflowers poked up their heads toward the sun.

When he thought he was ready, Canady turned and rode high into the mountains. The warm spring wind brushed at his face and he filled his lungs with it in a kind of ecstasy. He was at peace, with himself and with the world around him. If nothing else, he had found that much.

He rode toward Thunder Rock to begin his fast.

Thunder Rock thrust its dark, wind-scarred bulk up into the sky high above the timber line where the last stunted trees clung to their precarious holds on the face of the mountain. There was a small cave in the side of Thunder Rock, a cave that opened upon a level sheet of stone that extended to the sheer face of a black glass-smooth cliff. Standing on that shelf of stone, a man could look down on the rivers of clouds that wound around the lower peaks.

Canady had tethered his mharu far down in a mountain valley where there was plenty of grass and water. He could see the valley from Thunder Rock, and once in a while he caught a glimpse of his mount, little more than a black dot on a stamp of green far below.

He allowed himself a few swallows of icy water from a nearby snowbank and that was all. He ate nothing. In the daylight hours he stood on the shelf of rock and looked down on the world, and at night he shivered in his cave. He had his fur robes but there was no material with which to make a fire.

The air was thin and seared his lungs. His joints were sore and stiff. The days without food left him weak and giddy, and he looked down at the black dot of the mharu and wondered whether he would ever be able to climb down the mountain again. He was surprised to find that his mind lost none of its sharpness. In fact, it worked with an almost preternatural clarity, as though all problems were easy and all questions could be answered. He felt as though he were running a fever and he was reminded of the sensation of heightened awareness that sometimes comes with fever dreams. And then he remembered that when the fever was gone a man would wake up and everything that had seemed so clear would vanish like bubbles on the wind. . . .

The days and nights blurred together. He lay quietly in his cave and he had never felt less alone. It gave him an eery sensation to think that each man and woman of The People had once slept where he was sleeping, walked where he was walking, thought where he was thinking. There was no visible sign that they had ever been here but he could see memories of them in every stone, in every stain of dampness, in every tongue of sunlight that licked at the cold surfaces of the rocks. He sensed a continuity of life that he had never appreciated before, a linking together of living things in an endless procession over the plains and into the wild mountain ranges.

On the fourth night, the rains came.

A sea of swollen clouds washed over the stars. For long minutes the moonlight gleamed on the edges of the clouds, setting them aflame with pink and silver light, and then the darkness was complete. There was an electric hush as the world held its breath.

Then the lightning came, jagged white forks of frozen fire that flashed down from black cloud masses and hurled themselves with livid fury at the stolid bulk of the mountains. The thunder crashed on the heels of the lightning, splitting through the skies with a tearing, ripping explosiveness that tore the very air apart.

Canady huddled in his cave, blinking at the savagery of the storm. The walls of the cave were white with the continuous flashing of the lightning, his ears roared with the brute power of the thunder.

Thunder Rock!

The rain came down in solid sheets, hissing on the ledge of stone, pouring in torrents down the cracks and crevices of the mountains. The stone shelf outside the cave became a puddle, a lake, and the water washed into the cave itself, soaking his feet.

Canady stood up, his head almost touching the roof of the cave, He did not fear the storm. He ignored the water at his feet. He stared out into the raging night.

The guardian spirit will come to you.

His skin crawled. A prickling sensation ran up and down his spine. He narrowed his eyes, tried to see, The white flashes of the lightning were everywhere. The thunder beat at his ears.

He *felt* them. He felt them all around him. He closed his eyes. There! He could almost see them—

The Old Ones.

Mighty, powerful, old when the mountains were young. And yet friendly, respectful, equals—

Canady clenched his fists.

He whispered the hardest prayer of all: "Let me believe! Oh, let me believe!"

There was a long moment when nothing seemed to happen. Then, abruptly, the lightning and the thunder died away. The storm rolled off into the distance, muttering and grumbling to itself. There was silence except for the soft patter of the rain outside the cave.

Canady opened his eyes. There was a sinking sensation in his chest. Had he failed? Was it all for nothing?

Then he saw it.

A great bird flew out of the darkness and perched on the rain-wet shelf of rock. He looked like a hawk, an eagle. He was a mighty bird, raven-black, bold eyes glittering in his head, great wings folded at his sides. There was nothing supernatural about him. Canady could see the drops of water on his feathers, hear the faint whistle when he breathed.

And yet—

The guardian spirit will come to you.

The eagle walked toward the cave.

Canady stepped forward to meet it.

Suddenly, the cave was alive. He saw them now, all around him, glowing like creatures of light and energy. They touched him and they were warm. They seemed to have faces and they were smiling, smiling. . . .

Canady felt tears in his eyes, tears neither of happiness nor of sorrow, tears that came from an emotion too strong to be borne, too mighty to be named. He stood up straight as a man stands among his friends.

And the night was dark no longer and the stars looked down on him from a bright and peaceful sky.

VII

The small gray metallic sphere lifted from the camp of The People but now it carried one man instead of two. It gleamed dully in the light from the great red sun. It hovered high above the surface of Pollux V, looking down on a world flushed with green. It paced the planet as the world rotated on its axis.

It seemed a puny thing as it awaited the arrival of the mother ship from the CAS fleet of Earth, dwarfed by the vault of the heavens and the vast expanse of the land below it. One day it might return, but there were easier worlds for contact. And hidden in its tapes and papers and records it carried a secret no man would believe, a key that could have unlocked one of the hidden secrets of the universe.

Frank Landis sat on his bunk, surrounded by his sewing machines and rifles and model steam engines. He fingered them each in turn, his blue eyes blank and staring, thinking about the crazy man he had left behind. . . .

And the man who had been Arthur Canady came down from Thunder Rock and rode out of the mountains onto the wind-swept plains. The land was green with the promise of spring, the promise of world renewal, the promise of budding trees and fresh grasses and air so clean you could taste it.

His every sense was heightened, he was alive as he had never been alive before. His heart was a song within him. He knew that the wife of the great Mewenta would be stolen by the Telliomata to make room for him, and he knew that this was a good thing, a happy thing.

The ship was not going home. *He* was going home.

And when he rode into the village of The People there was a smile on every face, and there was a new tipi in the camp circle.

And Plavgar came to meet him and raised his arms in welcome.

And the Old Ones who walked at his side forever whispered to him as he rode, whispered down the winds and across the fields, whispered down from the free skies where the eagle flew, whispered to him alone—

"Welcome, brother, welcome."

THE GIFT

The swollen white sun drifted slowly down toward the horizon, more than eleven light-years from earth. Long black shadows striped the land. The shadows seemed alive, shifting with the strong winds that blew through the undulating grasses and stunted trees of the fifth planet of the Procyon system.

On that vast windswept plain that stretched away to encircling mountains of naked rock, creatures moved. There were squat and heavy-footed grass-eaters, walking slowly in dense defensive clusters. There were sleek, catlike carnivores, drinkers of the wind, prowling in pairs waiting for the night.

And there were manlike things that could not have been mistaken for men. Hairy they were, with long and powerful arms. They crouched around tiny fires in crude pithouses: round holes dug into the ground and roofed with branches and mud. They worked on their hunting spears and nursed their babies and told lengthy and intricate stories. Sometimes, they laughed. They were waiting for the winds to die.

There was a structure on that plain, a shining alien thing that did not belong. It had been there for half a century, but it was an intrusion. It stood apart and alone, a giant gleaming hemisphere of unyielding glassite.

Around that arching dome, the land was sterile. Nothing grew there and no animals ever came.

Sealed inside the great dome, faintly visible through the thick glassite, there was a small city.

People lived there: isolated, abandoned, forgotten.

There were soft shadows in the city now, indistinct patches of fugitive shade thrown by the lowering sunlight that filtered weakly through the treated glassite dome. Soon, the shadows would be gone and the illumination would be even again.

There was no wind, of course.

The winds never blew in the city.

Lee Melner ran through the pale Colony streets, his heart pounding. The evening shadows had dissolved under the steady thrust of the overhead lights. There was no cover. He simply had to run through the empty lanes, run as fast as he could, and trust to luck.

He might not be seen.

If he were seen, he might not be recognized.

And if they did report him—

Well, he would face that when the time came. He *had* to go.

He turned in to the last street, an avenue broader than the others. He could hear chanting ahead of him in the Square. He slowed his pace, catching his breath. He eased along the smooth wall that lined the inner-city street, hugging it. His throat was dry. He trembled with excitement.

Lee Melner had spent all of his seventeen years in the Colony. The dome-covered city was his world. It was a controlled world: gray, precise, safe, and stable. There were no surprises. There was no action. Even the seasons never changed. It was always the same temperature. There was no darkness. There were no storms.

(Sometimes, when the lighting was right, he could see great sheets of water washing over the dome. Twice in his lifetime, there had been tremendous crashes of thunder so loud that he could actually hear them. Once, he had thought he heard the far whining of the wind. That, he knew, was probably his imagination.)

There was nothing to *do*.

Most of the time, except with Ellen, Lee was bored stiff.

That was why he had to be in the Square tonight. It was not that he was particularly impressed by Edson Hewitt's revelations. It was the color and motion and sound that drew him. It was the smells, the jostlings, the tang of the forbidden.

It was something *different*.

He pressed into the back of the crowd, losing himself. Nobody looked at him. Edson Hewitt was going full blast, and he held every eye.

He stood there on a platform, his tall, thin body shrouded in the black cape he always wore. Four flaming torches burned at the corners of the platform; Lee could smell the acrid chemical smoke. A woman in a shimmering white gown stood behind him. Her hands were clasped as though in prayer. Her head, framed by a cloud of long unfashionable blond hair that seemed to glow in the torchlight, was tilted back. She was staring intently up at the high underside of the dome.

Pretty corny, Lee thought. Just the same, it was effective.

"Citizens!" Edson Hewitt boomed in his deep, stentorian voice. "It is not too late for men of good will. You must have faith!"

"Faith," chanted the crowd, right on cue.

"The ship will come!" Edson Hewitt lifted his skeletal arms in supplication. "The ship will come again, but it is not enough just to wait and hope. We have had enough of waiting! We must take action!"

"Action," echoed the crowd.

"There is no limit to the power of the human mind. There is no barrier that can stand against its force. No, my friends, the light-years are as nothing! We must *project* the purity of our thought. We will be heard! There will be an answer!"

"Answer."

"The ship will come again. It may be out there now, out in the great darkness, listening. We must put aside all evil things. We must cleanse ourselves. We must be worthy. We must project, project, project! And we must do it together!"

"Together!"

There was more, much more, in the same vein. The man's presence was hypnotic; the people in the Square were like puppets, desperate to believe. The woman in the white gown never moved, staring up and out with blank and lovely eyes. The torches hissed at the platform corners; they were like the jets of a ship, pushing out orange columns of flame . . .

Lee wanted to let himself go, wanted to be caught up in it all, to be *part* of it. Something in him yearned to surrender, to float, to be absorbed. But he could not believe. There was a wall in him that would not break. Behind that wall, he knew that he needed something he had not yet found. He did not know what that something was, but he knew that Edson Hewitt wasn't it.

"Join hands, citizens! Touch! The time has come!"

"Come!"

Lee was startled as hands sought his. He found himself clasped by an old man on his right; the hand was frail and dry like a wad of long-dead skin. A woman—no longer young, but not yet old—caught his left hand. Her palm was moist and strong. Her fingers contracted convulsively. There seemed to be an irregularity in her hand, a patch of different texture, a small object—

Lee kept looking straight ahead. His own palms began to sweat. He had lost his anonymity; he might be remembered. Of course, the meeting was not really illegal; free speech was still protected in the Colony. It would have been impossible to hold a large clandestine meeting anywhere in the Colony, especially not in the Square. There were no secrets in this world. Still, an activity can be forbidden whether it is illegal or not. Young people were supposed to stay in their homes during the night hours. His father had expressly warned him about attending this gathering. Old John Melner had strong opinions about Edson Hewitt . . .

"Now! Project! The ship will come! Make it aware!"

"Aware!"

The torches flared higher. There was a scent like perfume, a sweetness that animated the still air. Moans came from the crowd.

A man quite close to Lee began to babble. The sounds that came from his mouth resembled words, but the language was unknown to Lee. In the dancing torchlight, Lee saw flecks of white foam on his lips. A woman fainted. She sank to her knees and was kept from falling by those who held her hands. Somewhere, there was a cry of anguish, then sobbing.

The torches brightened into a final blinding flash. With an abruptness that was shocking, they went out. There was only the steady pale light of the city. Edson Hewitt and the blond woman in the white gown were gone.

The ceremony was over.

Lee disengaged his right hand; the old man simply stood where he was, whimpering softly. The woman on his left had vanished.

Lee became conscious of something sticking to the palm of his left hand.

An irregularity, a small object—

He closed his fist around it.

He turned and ran.

Old John Melner glanced at his watch. He lifted his thin hand and stroked his thatch of fine white hair. He noticed that his hand was trembling slightly. He felt the weight of his years.

"Give him another thirty minutes to be on the safe side," he said. His voice was steady, but it took an effort. "Then I'll go home."

"Are you sure it worked?" Dana Bigelow paced nervously back and forth across the sparsely furnished antiseptic room. His back was bent; Dana was in constant low-level pain.

John Melner shrugged and settled himself in his chair. Dana's fretfulness always made him try to relax; it was like an antidote. "I know my son. Lee knew about the meeting. I was carefully not at home. My wife was conspicuously asleep. So Lee went to hear Edson Hewitt pour out his garbage. He couldn't possibly stay away—don't you remember when you were seventeen years old?"

"No," said Dana Bigelow.

"*I* do. I would have gone just to look at the blonde. Lee is no different; he's a good boy. Okay. I know Paula, too. She found him, just as she was supposed to do. She found him if she had to crawl through that crowd. So Lee has got the note, and he got it under suitably dramatic circumstances. He'll take it from there, or I have terribly misjudged my son."

Dana Bigelow continued to pace. "Are you sure we're doing the right thing? We're taking an awful chance. The computers can't figure all the variables. I'm worried about Lee, even if it works. And I just don't know about us—"

John Melner scowled. He looked formidable despite his age; the man had a will that had grown stronger with the years. "*We* don't have a vast amount to lose, you and I. In any case, the threat to us—and to the Colony—is minimal. As for Lee, *of course* we can't be sure we're doing the right thing. That's the trouble with us, anyway—we always have to be so *sure.* The only certainty, my friend, is death—and that's about what we've got here. The time has come to take a chance or two. We can't take it; we're too old, too set in our ways, too secure. We value our security too highly, miserable as it is. That's a penalty of age. Lee is different: he's young, dammit, and full of juice and crazy romantic dreams. Lee suffers from the disease of youth—he thinks he's immortal, that agony can never touch him, that the world can be changed. Okay; that's what we need. You say you are worried about Lee. So am I—worried if he stays, worried if he goes. Lee is my son, remember? My only son, and a son that came late in life. That's my answer to you, Dana. If he knew the whole story, do you doubt which choice *he* would make?"

Dana Bigelow stopped pacing. His eyes flashed from beneath his bushy brows. "I know what he would do. That's not the point. By definition, the young lack experience. They have no basis on which to judge. It's up to us to protect them."

"Protect them from what? From life? What do all our experiences amount to? Have they been all that salutary? Dana, we're a bunch of zombies living in a glass cage. What kind of record is that?"

"The Colony has survived. We're alive."

"Are we? It's a matter of definition. Anyway, we're two old men locked in a senile argument. The thing is done. The decision has been made. What we have to do now is get out of the way and let it happen."

"You're very confident."

"No, not that. Call it by another name."

Old John Melner sat quietly then, looking at nothing, waiting to go home.

Lee Melner ran back through the pale streets of the city. His face was flushed with excitement. He felt like a fugitive, although he could not believe that he had done anything really wrong. He did not look at the object clutched in his hand.

His home was a unit in a housing complex not far from the edge of the Colony; the great dome was closer to him now, starting its downward curve to meet the ground and form the seal of the city wall. The apartment was substantial, occupying three levels of the eight-story building, but from the street it was indistinguishable from the other units. There was, of course, no yard. The only grass and the only trees in the Colony grew in a tiny park not far from the Square. Sometimes—three times since Lee had been alive—flowers grew there.

He slipped the object into his pocket and pressed the combination of the door. The door hissed open. Lee moved inside, trying to control his harsh breathing. The house was silent; the lights were on as always in the lower level. He glanced at the familiar room. It was large and had a kind of warmth that came from long acquaintance. At the same time, there was almost nothing in it that was unusual or unique. There were no paintings, no books, no curious oddments of furniture. Everything had been made in the Colony, mass-produced by singularly unimaginative machines.

Everything but one item.

In the center of the room, on a stand protected by a plastic cover, there was an empty glass jar that had once held instant coffee. It had a faded red label on it with yellow lettering. It still had a lid.

It had come from earth.

It was more than an antique. It was something from a now unreachable world that seemed sometimes to be a dream.

It was priceless.

Lee activated the field lift that carried him silently to the third level. He did not pause at the second floor; he assumed that his mother was still asleep. If she had awakened, or if his father had returned and found him gone—

Well, he would soon know.

He stepped out into his room. He had no brothers or sisters; hardly anyone did. The third level was his alone.

Everything was exactly as he had left it. The bed was rumpled with pillows under the warmer to look—hopefully—like a sleeping body. His desk was neat and clean, the computer terminals off. The photograph of Ellen was on the stand by the bed, as always. The globe of earth glowed softly in the corner: deep blue and gentle green and rich brown. It was nothing like the world he knew.

Lee shrugged off his clothes and put on his sleeping tunic. He rearranged the pillows and switched off the overhead lights. He dug into the pocket of his discarded clothing and felt the small wadded object.

He carried it into the bed with him.

Carefully, trying to control the shaking of his hands, he unfolded the packet and smoothed it out. As he had suspected—indeed, known with a certainty that left no room for doubt—it was a message.

He examined it in the faint illumination of the bed light.

The note read:

Lee, you have been chosen. Your selection has involved years of study and analysis. We have chosen you because we know that you can be trusted and because your personality profile shows that you can succeed.

Much depends on you. Much has been kept from you. There has been no word from earth for thirty-five terrestrial years. Earth may no longer exist. The ships will never come.

You have your life before you. If you wish to live as others have lived, huddled in fear in this Colony prison and waiting for extinction, disregard this message.

If you want more than that—if you have the courage to follow your heart— you have only to act.

Lee, there is another world out there, beyond the Colony dome. It is waiting for us. The air is good, the white sun shines, the strong winds blow. There are people out there. Not people like us, but they are humanoid. They have not forgotten how to laugh and how to dream. We have much to offer them. They have more to offer us. One man can make the contact, if he is the right man.

There is a way out, contrary to what you have been taught. In addition to the main lock, there is a small emergency exit. It is simple to operate, from both the inside and the outside. The directions are engraved in a panel just to the left of the exit.

There is always danger in the unknown. You must be aware of this when you make your choice. If you choose not to go, you will live in comfort and security. You must decide whether that is all you want.

We will not contact you again if you stay in the Colony. If you do go Outside, and if you do not fail, you will be contacted by someone you know.

You will be the first. Remember that. Our trust in you is great.

Go to the house of Gilbert McAllister on the edge of the Colony not far from your home. The house is empty now. The door combination has been altered so that it is the same as your own. The lift in the main chamber on what appears to be the bottom floor will go DOWN *if you press the control marked* EMERGENCY *It will take you to the exit.*

The rest is up to you, Lee.

Good luck from all of us.

The message was unsigned.

Lee got up, concealed the refolded packet in his desk, and returned to bed.

He switched off the bed light.

Lee Melner never closed his eyes that night, but he dreamed many dreams.

Although it seemed an eternity, it actually took him two months to make up his mind.

He went many times to the house of Gilbert McAllister. Twice, he checked the combination on the door. It worked, and he found that he was not surprised. He did not go in.

He lived in a state of constant turmoil. Outwardly, he was calm enough; he sleepwalked through the set routines of his gray life. Inwardly, he was seething. He could not think and yet his mind was racing. He ached to tell someone, share what he knew. He came very close to taking Ellen into his confidence. Something made him hold back; he was afraid to involve her.

Not yet, not yet.

Long before he was aware that he had made a final decision, Lee caught himself making plans. This time would be safe; that time would not. What to wear, what to take. How to carry food and water. Whether or not to leave a message in case he did not return . . .

A night came. He could not sleep. That day there had been rain Outside; he had seen the sheets of water washing across the dome. That night, as he lay in his bed, he heard the distant roar of thunder. It was the third time in his life that he had heard it. He shivered and his heart pounded. He knew that he had to go.

A week later, he went.

Very early in the morning, while the Colony slept, Lee returned to the house of Gilbert McAllister. He pressed the combination and the familiar door whispered open.

He stepped inside, and the door closed behind him. The house was nothing special—a unit like all the others. It was neat and clean and had an empty smell about it.

He moved through the pale interior illumination and located the lift. There was a small switch on the bottom of the control panel. It was clearly marked: EMERGENCY. DO NOT TOUCH.

He threw the switch.

The lift went down. It went farther than he had expected, and then stopped.

He was in a large, barren chamber. The walls and floor and ceiling were all a muted brown. There was nothing in the room. There was no sound except for a gentle hissing from the air vents. The room was a little cold.

A sealed airlock portal was set flush into the wall that was closest to the edge of the dome. It was not large—just big enough to admit two men at once—but it was the same general type as the huge main lock that Lee had seen many times.

There was a panel just to the left of the lock. When Lee stepped in front of it, a red warning light appeared. Words flashed on the panel: DANGER. THIS IS AN EMERGENCY EXIT. DO NOT OPEN WITHOUT AUTHORIZATION

The directions were engraved on the panel.

The instructions were not complicated.

Lee took a deep breath and activated the lock.

John Melner sat with his head in his hands. He was desperately afraid. He could not lie to himself. The ultimate responsibility was his.

"Lee never had a chance," he said. His voice was tired and barely audible. "The message was too calculated. He was an iron filing drawn to a magnet, a starving man moving toward food. We made the decision for him."

Dana Bigelow paced as always, his face a frozen mask. "We have switched roles, John. It is futile to blame yourself for what had to be done. The thing may work, you know. I have every confidence in Lee. His prognosis is strong."

"Yes, but we *manipulated* him."

"We had to. The Colony is staring down a dead-end tunnel. We are stagnant, static, afraid to act. *We* know what the problem is and what caused it. We were abandoned here; God knows why. We were dumped and left. We found ourselves on an alien world and none of the fancy plans were ever implemented. We knew how to survive: stay put, don't make waves, don't take chances. We had it drilled into us. It was all we knew. We were too infernally wise and experienced to break out of the shell. We needed something we did not have. We needed a man of action . . ."

"We needed a hero," John Melner said quietly. "A quaint, old-fashioned primordial hero. A bringer of fire, a slayer of dragons, an opener of the way. A man who ignored the odds, took the long chance, welcomed a challenge. A dreamer, a doer, a man of impulse. In short, a *young* man whose mind was not too cluttered up with the knowledge of what he couldn't or shouldn't do. We had the young man. We worked on him a little, but basically he was what he was. We provided the *opportunity.* It is the situation that creates the hero—or breaks him. We set it up. We baited the trap."

"There was no alternative. Most of us exist in a kind of paralysis of routine. We worship order because it has kept us alive. The rest of us—

Edson Hewitt and his cape-flapping friends—have retreated into sheer ceremonialism and mystical flapdoodle. Harmless, maybe, but it won't get us anywhere. We had to *try*. If we didn't, we wouldn't last more than a generation or two. We'll just curl up in a ball and whimper ourselves to death."

"But he's my son, Dana. Logic won't help me now—and it won't help him. The world out there is tougher than Lee can possibly know. And those—savages—*are* dangerous. There were—troubles—when we first came here. You remember young Tom Bailey. *He* was going to make friends with them. They tore him apart and ate him."

"That was a long time ago, John."

"Yes, a long time ago . . ."

They could remember, both of them. Fifty years, half a century, a lifetime. They had come from a crowded earth, more than eleven light-years to the fifth planet of the Procyon system. There had been great plans then, plans to start a new life, plans to work with the inhabitants of Procyon V, plans for visits back to earth.

Plans . . .

For seven years the ships had come on schedule, driving through the gray reaches of space prime. The Colony had been successful. For a while, it was a good place to be: alive, creative, sure.

And then the ships had stopped.

There was no warning; there could be no warning. The ships from earth simply did not come.

Messages, yes. But they were old transmissions, long outdated. It took better than ten years for radio waves to span the gulf between earth and Procyon V. It took more than twenty years to send a message and receive a reply.

There was no clue to what had happened in any of the messages. There had been no word at all for the last thirty-five years. That meant, of course, that the transmissions from earth had ceased even before the last ships had come . . .

The colonists were cut off, isolated, forgotten. It was a shock beyond belief, and it hurt. The scars went deep.

It was anybody's guess what had happened. A political revolution, possibly, a revolt against the exploration of space. A religious upheaval and a creed that space travel was evil. A plague, a war, a lapse into barbarism.

It made no difference.

They were alone, more alone than men had ever been. For all they knew, they *were* the human race. There might be survivors in other colonies on other worlds. There might be people left on earth.

And there might not.

They had to preserve what was left. They had to be careful. They could not afford the luxury of experiments.

They survived. They imitated life. That was all.

They knew a fear that was beyond calculation.

And now, finally, they were stirring. They had found the strength to break the pattern, to make a gesture, to try, to seek . . .

"He's out there now," Dana Bigelow said. "If only we could help him—"

Old John Melner shook his head. "We've done what we can do. You know the analysis. He has to be alone. He has to be romantically—idealistically—motivated. He has to believe that it is in his hands. The decisions must be his to make. We can't help. We can only get in his way."

"What *can* we do?"

John Melner managed a bitter old man's smile. "We can wait," he said.

Lee Melner stepped Outside.

Something hit him, spun him around. He fell to his hands and knees, gasping.

Wind. He knew what it was; he had studied about it. He was not prepared for the reality. He had known only still air.

This was different. Raw, wild, strong! It smacked him like a thousand fists. It howled at his clothes. It ripped at his flesh.

Lee's mind reeled; he was assaulted by sensations. He could not sort them out. Smells of green and growing things, smells of wetness, smells of immense quantities of free and moving air. Light: intense flaming white light that seared his eyes. Colors: vivid greens and blacks and browns and blues. Sounds: the wind that moaned, the trees that creaked, the grasses that cracked and slithered . . .

He struggled to his feet, rocking, bracing himself.

He narrowed his eyes to slits, trying to absorb what he saw.

Behind him, the vast arch of the dome. He could not see it all, of course. It looked peculiar to him, somehow reversed. It gleamed in the light. He could not see through it; it was a gigantic bubble of reflective glare.

Ahead of him was a band of sterile ground, gray and grimy, that circled the bottom of the dome wall. It was narrow, less than seventy yards in most places, but it seemed formidable to Lee. There were few open spaces in the world he knew.

Beyond that was a tremendous green plain, alive in the rivers of wind, huge beyond comprehension. Bare and jagged mountains of dark, shining rock, far away, so distant that he had no concepts to judge them by.

And a sky, the first sky he had ever seen, a sky without a roof, a sky that went on forever, a sky that dwarfed him, a sky that held a swollen white sun that burned—

Lee drank it in. He was beyond fear, beyond excitement. He was alive, out of the tomb! He could do anything, go anywhere.

He yelled a wild animal yell.

The wind ripped it from his mouth, hurled it away.

He ran, stumbling and falling, across the sterile band. The gritty gray stuff stuck to his shoes, worked into his feet. It smeared itself on his jacket, his knees, his hands.

He reached the green grasses and collapsed. He rolled in the damp, tough stems, feeling the moist soil beneath him. He sniffed the juices of life. The wind moaned at him, but he was under it now and it was lessening. He laughed like a madman, laughed with a strange glee that was sweeter than anything he had ever known.

He surged to his feet, challenging the wind. He moved through the grasses at a pace somewhere between a fast walk and a trot. He felt strong, confident, and eager. He had no fixed destination; he simply moved away from the Colony. He could not get lost. The dome was so big that it hardly diminished in size no matter how far he went. Within a day's range it would still be visible.

He paused. The first note of caution intruded on his mood. He did not want the night to catch him Outside. He had never experienced that kind of darkness, in the open, with an invisible world pressing in on him . . .

Still, there was plenty of time.

He moved on. The sun burned his face and hands, but it was not yet painful. The wind was cool and the grasses danced, and the thick, stunted trees whispered a song to him . . .

Abruptly, he came to a small clearing. There was a tiny spring of crystal-clear water that bubbled up from a rock formation. There was a path that led away from the spring, and tracks in the soft soil, many tracks.

And there was someone—or something—in the clearing.

Lee stopped short. He dropped to his belly and held his breath. Somehow, he had not expected this. He knew about the savages that lived Outside, of course. He had planned to contact them, one day when he knew more. But not now, not so soon, not the very first time . . .

Why not? Why not today?

He lay very still and studied the figure in the clearing.

It was a female, he decided, and very old. She was sprawled on her side, her eyes closed. Her breathing was so shallow that she almost seemed dead. Her arms were thin and very long. Her knees were flexed under a stained yellow tunic of animal skin. There was hair on her wrinkled face.

She was not human. She was neither good to look at nor ugly. She was just there, a half-alien thing in the dirt.

Half alien, yes. And half something else. An old woman, alone, more dead than alive.

Sick?

Lee stood up. There was nothing to fear here. He came from a world where illness was something rare, and curable when it happened. He was not afraid of it. The old woman certainly could not harm him. They were alone in the clearing.

He took a cloth and moistened it in the spring. The water was cold. He knelt beside the woman and gently bathed her wrinkled face. He made soothing noises.

She smelled. There was an old deep scar on her forehead.

She opened her eyes. They were astonishingly clear and a bright, hard green.

She hissed, horribly. She raked at him with her claws.

Lee moved back, not too fast. He saw a cluster of purple berries on a nearby bush. He had no idea whether or not they were edible, but that was unimportant. He needed to make a gesture that she would understand.

He picked a handful of the fat berries. He bit into one, tasting it. It was sweet and juicy. He placed the berries near the woman's head and stepped back again.

He waited, not rushing her. The wind had died and the clean air was almost still. He could see thin eddies of blue smoke curling up in the distance. The trampled path led in that direction.

The old woman shook her hairy head and groaned. She reached out and grabbed the berries. She crammed them into her mouth, all of them. She chewed with stained and worn-down teeth. She swallowed.

She tried to get up and failed. She looked at Lee with those strange metallic green eyes. She seemed puzzled and confused now. Her eyes came in and out of focus.

She tried again to rise. She could not make it. She fell back on her side.

She said something harsh and guttural. It might have been a curse or a prayer or nothing at all.

She stopped speaking. She lay perfectly still, barely breathing.

Lee made his decision. He did not know what the old woman was doing here. He was not a fool, and he had studied something about primitive peoples; the Colony school was a good one and Lee—although he was unaware of it—had received special attention. The old woman might be sick; she could have been separated from the others to protect the village. She was very old; she could have been abandoned or crawled out herself to die. She might have come to the spring and simply been unable to return. She might be lost, although that was unlikely.

There was no way to tell. What was certain was that he had *already* made contact. That had not been his plan, but plans were made to be changed.

Lee picked up the woman and cradled her in his arms. She stiffened but had no strength to fight. There was not much meat on her bones. She smelled of sweat and soil and age.

Carrying the woman in his arms, Lee started down the path toward the tendrils of blue smoke.

A cluster of pithouses covered with roofs of branches and plastered mud. Hives, like miniature domes. Blending into the landscape: natural, weathered, timeless. Smells of burning wood and fire-dripping meat.

A great white sun, blazing at the zenith.

Sounds: cries, screams, whistles.

People: squat hairy men with hugely muscled arms dangling below their knees, half-naked women, bright-eyed children peering from doorways.

Weapons: long spears with stone points, clubs, flaked-stone knives with leather handles.

Lee put the old woman down and stepped slowly back. He made no sudden moves. He kept his hands in plain sight.

He was defenseless, of course. He had no knowledge of killing.

He waited, looking into hard unreadable alien eyes.

The thought came to him that he was very close to death. He felt it, deep down, but his mind rejected it. He stood quietly, resisting the impulse to run.

The old woman groaned and stretched out a bony hand toward her people.

A man grunted something, put down his spear, and walked to her. He stared straight at Lee but did not speak. He picked the woman up—casually, as though she were a stick of firewood—and carried her back. He put her down by the hide-covered hole that served as a doorway to one of the smoking pithouses. Hands reached out and pulled her inside.

Lee waited. He could do nothing else.

Time passed, slowly. The great white sun moved in the sky.

After an age, a man moved. He was old but not feeble. He stepped into a pithouse, a knife in his gnarled hand. He emerged in a moment with a charred dripping hunk of meat impaled on the knife.

The man walked up to Lee and stopped. Lee could smell the grease in his hair. The man extended the knife.

Carefully, Lee put out his hand. He grasped the chunk of meat. It was hot and slippery. He pulled it from the flaked-stone blade of the knife.

He bit into it. The meat was tough, and the flavor was strong. He chewed it as best he could and managed something resembling a smile.

The old man smiled back. He sheathed his knife. He reached out and touched Lee, gently.

The other men put down their spears and clubs. The women began to chatter. Children emerged from doorways.

The vast river of wind stirred, gathering its power. Long black shadows crept across the land. The heat of the sun was fading.

Lee did not care. He grinned broadly now.

Something, perhaps, was over.

Something else was ready to begin.

Many times, Lee Melner went through the hidden exit and rejoined the Outside People.

He studied them, hunted with them, ate with them, laughed with them. He came to know them, little by little.

They were both less and more than he had imagined. Less, because they were not romantic creatures of an idyllic world of dreams. They were tough, brutal, and hard.

The old woman he had saved had indeed crawled away to die; she had too many years and had become a burden. She went out again and this time she did not return.

There was death, too, among the very young. Infants rarely survived very long. Death came to them in many guises: sudden, sure, unsentimentalized. Lee had never seen young people die before.

But the people were more than that . . .

It was curious. In the midst of death—and uncertainty and sickness and desperate hardship—there was life. There was promise. There was a quickening of the blood, laughter that eased pain, new dreams, new beginnings.

And there was the sun and the great wind and the enormous sky and the stars and the rain . . .

The contrast with the Colony was stark and clear. Inside the dome, there was order, security, peace—and decay. Under the dome, there was no real tomorrow. There was only a slow ending.

Lee learned who had sent him from the Colony and why. He knew that he had a decision to make. The decision was not easier with his father involved.

It was not easy, period.

He could not just run away. *He* was the alien on this world, even though he had been born here. He was drastically different from the Outside People. And he was a man, with a man's sexuality. He needed a woman of his own kind. He needed Ellen.

He could not bring the Outside People into the Colony. They could never adapt to it, and it would be wrong to try. There was no point at all in inflicting a dead end on them.

He could not bring the Colony to the Outside People. It was utterly impossible. The citizens of the Colony lived on a pyramid of technology; they could not move. And they were set in their ways, frozen, more fearful than any savage child huddled in the darkness and the howling wind . . .

Lee knew something of history; he had been carefully taught. He knew the dangers of contacts between an advanced civilization and bands of primitive hunters. It was rough on the hunters, always. Rough, and usually fatal.

On earth, the hunters had been obliterated. Technological civilization had triumphed.

And now, perhaps, there was no life on earth.

It was not an easy decision that Lee Melner had to make.

But he made it.

John Melner looked at his son. "Well," he said, his voice carefully neutral. "You have something to tell me."

Lee searched for the words that would not come. Old John seemed so frail, his lined face sunken beneath his fine white hair, his thin hands trembling slightly even when supported by the top of the table . . .

The small room was very still.

"It was my decision to send you out, Lee. There were no strings attached. You have had nearly a year to make up your mind. We have put no pressure on you. You asked for this audience. Come on, lad. Spit it out."

Lee stood there, his skin roughened by the sun and the wind. He felt strange, an outsider in the house of his own father. He could not find words that did not carry pain.

Old John snorted. "Dammit, boy, I was born on *earth*. I crossed the gulf between the stars. I had the rug pulled out from under me on an alien planet. You can't hurt me, Lee, except with silence."

"Okay," Lee said slowly. "I think there is just one thing to do. I don't like it, but there it is."

Old John smiled. "Where?"

Lee did not return the smile. He had to force himself to speak. "There is no future here, in the Colony. The ships will never come back. We cannot bring the Outside People into the dome; it would kill everything that they are. The Colony itself cannot change; it is too precariously balanced, and the adults are locked into a life way they are afraid to alter. It has sustained them too long."

"It is a good analysis, if a trifle grim. And so?"

Lee took a deep breath. "And so," he said, "the young people must go Outside. They must go and try to make a new life, and they must go soon."

"Before they become too wise?"

Lee shrugged. "Before they reach the same conclusions that your generation reached. Before they begin to—repeat."

Old John stared at his son. "*All* of the young people?"

"All who wish to go. That will be most of them. It makes no difference, really. There will not be enough left behind to sustain the population."

"You've thought of that, have you?"

"Yes."

"You are pronouncing a sentence of death."

"Yes. If there were some other way—"

"But there isn't. Either some die, sealed in this mechanical prison, or all die. Is that it?"

"That's about the size of it."

Lee hung his head. He could not face his father's eyes. He kept remembering the emaciated old woman, out there by the spring in the sun and the wind. She, too, had faced death alone. She, too, had been abandoned by those who were young and strong . . .

"When will you go?"

"Soon. When we are ready."

"And will you—say goodbye?"

"Yes, of course. And we will come back to see you."

"Occasionally. That would be—helpful."

A long silence fell between them.

John Melner broke it. "We will be comfortable; that is something. Extinction, after all, is just an inability to change. You are right; *we* cannot change. But we can let you go, if we are big enough. We can give you the gift of hope. And perhaps, one day, you will remember . . ."

"We'll remember," Lee whispered.

Old John stood up, his face composed. "I'm getting maudlin in my senility," he said. "I'm proud of what you have done, Lee—and of what you will do. Now go and leave me alone for a while. We both have much to do."

Lee left the room and the door hissed shut behind him.

John Melner sat down and closed his eyes. He felt very tired.

He did not try to fool himself; he had never done that. His son's decision was probably the right one, the only one. He would support it. But the young could be cruel, cruel . . .

He shook his head. Lee had not reckoned with the possibility that he might fail. It was all very well to march off into the sunrise filled with brave hopes and dreams. But there would be many sunrises and many sunsets. Dreams had a way of fading with age. He was not optimistic.

Still, they had a chance.

That was the only gift he had left to give.

And the alternative—

"The alternative," he said quietly, "is to be like me."

He opened his eyes. He felt the half-forgotten tears, the tears for what was lost and for what might have been.

Old John Melner looked at the closed door.

"Lee, Lee," he whispered. "God, if I could only go with you!"

Slowly, the old man turned back to the papers on his desk and began to do what had to be done.

TO WHOM IT MAY CONCERN

Call it a hunt.

If that is too simple, call it a quest.

They were coming.

They had searched through an ocean of darkness, a night sea that floated worlds upon worlds, stars beyond number, universes that began and ended and flowed into yet other universes.

They were after something. Otherwise, they would not have been there.

They needed something. Not technology, certainly. They had plenty of that. They understood technology and respected it, but that was not enough. Endurance was the problem. Call it continuity.

They would know it when they found it. They would know what to do with it. They had a wisdom that went deeper than intelligence. They had other senses.

They were not beyond self-interest. They were driven by their own needs. Otherwise, they would not have been there.

But there was room for others. They knew they were not alone. They knew that it was all linked together.

The seeking was urgent. The journey had been long.

They were ready. They would not quit. They could not afford to miss.

They were coming.

Call it a hunt.

Jerry Hartshorn felt rotten. He wiped the sweat out of his eyes with a sand-streaked hand. He said, "So this is how it ends."

Nobody heard him, of course. He was talking to himself again, which was not a particularly good sign.

He tugged his stained hat down more tightly over his damp hair and squinted into the African sun. It was the same old sun that rolled around the sky everywhere else. Nothing special. It wasn't the sun that was getting to Jerry Hartshorn. It was a bug, despite all the pills and all the shots. He was sick. Not sick enough to go down. Just sick enough to be miserable.

He also did not like what he was seeing.

He swung up his camera, noting that the brown strap across his shoulder was fraying to the danger point. He checked the settings—always the same at this time of the day, but Jerry was a careful man—and snapped a couple of shots. He hated the photography angle; taking pictures made him feel like a tourist. It was a part of his job, but the plain truth was that he was always disappointed with his slides and prints. They were clear enough, barring a disaster here and there, but the magic eluded him. The pictures were flat and literal. The significance and the emotion never got through the camera lens; they stayed behind, locked up in his head and his gut.

In any case, how did you photograph the end of a world? It didn't end with a bang and it didn't end with a whimper. It just stopped.

"Chins up," he said. "Duty and all that. Posterity and tenure."

This is what he photographed:

There was a battered thick-trunked baobab tree that cut the glaring sunlight enough to provide a puddle of shade. There was the flat rust-red earth of southern Kenya, mottled by bedraggled flat-topped acacia, the cactus-caricature of euphorbia, and very ordinary dusty brush.

There was a lot of open country—plains, really—and an enormous bowl of blue sky. It was as though clouds hadn't been invented yet.

And there were the people.

They did not seem to be doing anything dramatic. Small, brown, and leather-tough, they had gathered in the dubious shade of the baobab. It was the last day, and they were spending it as they had spent so many others. Waiting.

Most of them were there, clustered near the camp. Jerry did not have to count them. Fifteen people: old men, women that ran the gamut from ancient Klu to the young smooth-skinned Twee, a few children who were blissfully unaware both of what they were and what they were about to become.

Three men were not present. They had left before dawn, smearing poison on the foreshafts of their arrows and joking loudly. They were not likely to find anything, but their spirits were always good at the start of a hunt. Even the last one. George Ndambuki, Jerry's African colleague, was with them.

Taking pictures, Jerry thought ruefully. *Good ones.*

He shut the protective case over his camera and adjusted the shoulder strap. He had photographed what there was to see.

Nothing much. Even the clothing would have discouraged the true devotee of the supposed romance of primitive life. For the most part, the people were dressed in what might politely be called contemporary fashion. Torn shorts and carefully washed undershirts for the men, long cotton dresses and bandana-turbans for the women. Only the youngest children had style. They wore nothing at all.

The People. That is what they called themselves, in common with God only knew how many human societies that had lived and died on this planet. In what was pompously referred to as the scientific literature, they were the Kwaruma. It was not the right name. In their own language, the word for People was Xhagit. The first sound was a click phoneme. However, they had been dubbed the Kwaruma by their Bantu-speaking neighbors, and they were stuck with it.

Tomorrow, the trucks would come. The Kwaruma were going to be "resettled" on farming plots in a development scheme. The television crews would be on hand, because this was no small matter.

As far as anyone knew, the Kwaruma were the last hunters and gatherers left on earth.

A jet smashed through the African sky. The symbolism was so pat that Jerry Hartshorn tried to ignore the racket. He had lived with these people for nearly a year. He did not need a jet aircraft to remind him of what was happening.

He still felt rocky. No matter; a couple of aspirins would get him through the remaining hours. Ah, wonder drugs! The true blessing of civilization. . . .

He checked his field notebook and moved in closer to do what had to be done.

The last camp of the Kwaruma was like most of the camps that Jerry had seen. It had a slapdash quality to it and it had *temporary* written all over it. Compared to the camp, the scarred baobab tree looked eternal.

The structures weren't houses. They were simple lean-tos made of crooked poles and brush. There was almost nothing in them: a few iron pots the Kwaruma had scrounged, some digging sticks, traditional ostrich eggs used as water containers, small cracked hide bundles of treasured heirlooms, a few trade knives and two old wood-pointed spears.

The People lived outside. In any case, when you have to move frequently and do it on foot you get down to essentials. The People did not even have dogs to help them.

Old Klu already had a small fire going. It was partly a sign of confidence and a show of respect for the departed hunters. But Jerry knew that there was another reason. Warm as it was in the African sun, Klu was thinking about the coming night. She suffered from the cold, and it took more than memories to sustain her.

Jerry was working—taking notes—but he found the time to exchange small-talk with everyone. He speculated with the elder men about the possible success of the hunt. He joked with Twee, confining himself to acceptable brother-sister themes. He admired the roots the women had gathered. It made him feel somewhat better. The Kwaruma were a friendly people and they had more or less accepted him. He was proud of that. Who knew? Maybe they even liked him.

If he could help them, later—

Well, he would not forget. But this was not the time. There were so few hours left. . . .

He walked over to Jane's tent, which was pitched a short distance from the camp. He could hear the clicking of the portable typewriter inside.

Not for the first time, he reflected on the percentages. Eighteen Kwaruma and three anthropologists. It was a peculiar world.

The tent was open, of course. There was no breeze, and it was like an oven in there.

"It's Tarzan," he said. "Jane busy?"

Jane Schubauer went right on with her typing. "Come on in," she said.

Jerry picked his way through the clutter and perched on a camp chair that had one slat missing. He removed his hat and used it to fan himself.

Jane finished a paragraph—she always typed up her notes with indecent speed—and turned to face him. Her eyes widened slightly. "You look like a walking corpse," she said.

He shrugged. "Beastly tropical heat. The throb of native drums. You know."

"You can't die now. You're cooking the feast tonight."

"I will not falter. Two aspirins would help the ape-man."

Jane rooted around and produced the aspirin bottle. She handed it to him with a canteen of water. The water was warm and tasted ominous but he got the pills down.

"Just wanted to check," he said. "You go over the life-history with Klu, I measure the amounts of plant foods and meat after the hunters get in, and George writes up the last hunt. Then we eat and kick it around to see if we've forgotten anything. That cover it?"

She nodded. "Sounds okay to me. We've just run out of time, that's all. Jerry, you do look awful."

"I'll make it."

They eyed each other. There were other words to be said between them, but they might never be spoken. They were either beyond that or had never gotten there.

No computer would ever have put them in the same pile, Jerry thought. Jane—she loathed the name—was a tall raw-boned woman who could look attractive when she bothered. She was brilliant and she was difficult. When she laughed, Jerry chalked it up as a triumph.

Jerry was short, wiry, and thin. He had a brownish beard that itched, He had a bad habit of cracking jokes at the wrong times. Even those who knew him well had trouble telling when he was serious—which was all too often—and when he was kidding. He believed in what he was doing.

They were competitors, of course, Back at the University, they were on the Harvard system. Hire six, terminate five, keep one. They were also friends: they liked and respected each other. Once, they had even been lovers. It had been a mutual disaster.

"See you later," Jerry said.

Jane went back to the typewriter. The clicking resumed. "Be careful, Tarzan," she said.

The hunters returned in the late afternoon. Jerry could hear them coming, and knew that the hunt had been good. When the hunters had been successful, they made a lot of noise. When they failed, they came silently back to the camp and nobody ever asked them what had happened.

Jerry went to meet them.

They came out of the earth, shadows among shadows. Kwi, still walking lightly after a long day in the bush. Tuwa, who could be spotted at a distance because of his limp. Gsawa, taller than the others, walking a little apart, lost in his private world as usual.

George Ndambuki brought up the rear. Incredibly, he still had a tie on. He was visibly tired, but he had his camera out and ready. He was going to photograph the end of the hunt or perish in the attempt.

The women began to ululate. It was a haunting sound. It seemed as ancient as humanity itself.

Jerry stayed out of the way until George had his final pictures. Then he moved in to examine the kill.

Kwi, who was the nearest thing to a leader that the Kwaruma had, gave him a big smile. Kwi had an upper incisor tooth missing; he liked to tell the story of how he had lost it. He also had a safety pin in his ear. He was a delightful man, solid as a rock but with a consistent good humor that was contagious. Kwi had pulled Jerry through some difficult times, just as he had done for the rest of his people.

"See," Kwi beamed. "Did I not tell you? It was Gsawa's arrow that went home."

The hunters had divided their kill for easier transport and they had not bothered to bring in the head and horns. Still, Jerry could identify the animal at a glance. Rather surprisingly, it was a Tommy. They were not common in this part of Kenya.

"*Gazella thomsonii thomsonii,*" Jerry said. He was not showing off; this was a little running joke he had with Kwi.

"*Swala tomi,*" Kwi agreed. He spoke Swahili when he was having fun with the anthropologist, which was frequently.

Jerry figured it up in his head; he would weigh the meat later. A Tommy was one of the smaller African antelopes. This one was a male. It might go sixty pounds, and that meant something like thirty pounds of edible meat. Close to two pounds of meat for every adult. Meat was always shared.

"We will provide," Kwi said. He slapped his bow. "No more Spam."

Jerry nodded gratefully. "No more Spam," he agreed.

George Ndambuki could not stay out of the conversation. "I timed the poison," he reported. "One hour less thirteen seconds."

"Great," Jerry said. "I know it wasn't easy." He found it awkward to talk to George; he felt much closer to Kwi. George Ndambuki was so impressed with his own Ph.D. that he sometimes forgot to be human. it was understandable—George had sacrificed a great deal for the degree that had come fairly easily for Jerry and Jane—but his everlasting dignity got on Jerry's nerves.

"I will cook," Jerry said to Kwi. "That was the agreement."

Kwi laughed. "The women will cook," he predicted. "You get the beer."

Jerry fell back on a Kwaruma saying. "Friends do not argue."

Kwi laughed again and Tuwa and Gsawa joined in. It paralyzed them to hear Jerry's Kwaruma accent.

"You have much to learn," Kwi said. It was a statement without malice. "I must teach you while I can."

It was a scene not quite as old as time.

The fires were orange and cheerful. There were good smells and the shadows danced. The camp was an island of brightness. The air had cooled and the stars were near.

Jerry Hartshorn chewed on the tough but tasty meat. His head was throbbing but he was strangely content.

He was a part of something.

How many times over how many millions of years had this small ritual been enacted? Fire and food, hunters who had returned and women who had waited, collected, and prepared. Children who watched and listened and dreamed.

It was ancient, it stretched back unbroken to a world older than humanity. Australopithecines and those who had preceded them must have known nights like this.

It was only ten thousand years ago that the human animal had begun the flirtation with agriculture and domesticated animals. Two cheers for the Neolithic! It was only five thousand years since the first cities had stained the earth.

Always, the hunting and gathering peoples had continued. Their numbers had dwindled and they had retreated into remote areas that the manswarm did not covet. But they had survived.

Until now.

The Kwaruma were distant relatives of the San of Botswana and the Kalahari Desert. Once, these people had been dominant throughout Eastern Africa. They were called the Bushmen by those who never bothered to learn their proper name.

The San were finished. They had not been exterminated physically; there were still plenty of them around. But in terms of their traditional culture they were extinct. The San were gold-miners, hired herders, servants, squatters in city slums. They had adapted.

Only this tiny remnant group of Kwaruma were left. Anywhere. They were anachronisms.

Kwi had been right, or nearly right. The antelope meat had been broiled by the Kwaruma women; they had allowed Jerry to weigh it, but they were adamant about the cooking. Jerry had done his best. He had promised the people a feast and he delivered after a fashion. He heated up canned corn. He passed around tins of pineapple. He opened cans of pork and beans; the Kwaruma preferred it cold. He made coffee and dumped in cups of sugar.

And he supplied the beer.

He felt at home with the Kwaruma but he did not delude himself. He was an intruder, along with Jane and George. He had come from a distant land on his own kind of hunt. When he had his quarry—information, knowledge—he would go away again. And then—

Ah yes, that was the question.

Well, save it for tomorrow. Save it for all the tomorrows.

The three of them managed to squeeze into Jane's tent together. It wasn't much of a conference. George Ndambuki was out on his feet; he had walked far with the hunters. Jane Schubauer was having trouble with the wick on her lamp and she still had notes to type. Jerry Hartshorn was discovering that the mixture of beer, meat, and fever verged on the lethal.

The camp was anything but festive. They could hear subdued voices and an occasional rattling of pots and cans around the dwindling fires. That was all. The Kwaruma had no drums—just wooden whistles and bows that they tapped with sticks—and they were not in a mood for dancing. Basically, like all the world that was beyond the reach of electricity, the Kwaruma were a daylight people. The night was for sleeping,

"Well." Jerry spoke because somebody had to do it. "Last chance and all that. Have we forgotten anything?"

"Probably" Jane said. She did not sound unduly worried. She wanted to get back to her notes.

"I think we have done extremely well," George offered. "We have all that there is to get." George's opinion of the Kwaruma was not high. Having made something of a transition himself—his own parents had lived in a thatched hut and sacrificed goats to the ancestors in Ukambani— he viewed primitive lifeways with a slightly jaundiced eye.

"So we have it all." Jerry could not allow himself the luxury of laughter and he didn't feel up to it anyway. "Okay. Meeting is adjourned. See you in the morning."

He ducked out of the tent. The night was chilly and he had to wait a long minute to let his eyes adjust to the darkness. The little fires were not much help now. He shivered and tried to decide what to do.

He went to his own tent and fished out a warm jacket. He retrieved his last bottle of Scotch from under a pile of dirty clothing. He had not exactly been hiding it, but he had been saving it. Scotch was still relatively inexpensive in Kenya—unlike the rare imported bourbons—but it nevertheless put a dent in the budget.

He supplied himself with a tin cup and went outside to sit on a stump.

Jerry had no more questions to ask. This was not because he knew everything there was to know about the Kwaruma. That was George's fantasy. It was because he had gone as far as his educated ignorance would take him.

He looked up at the stars. They were very close and there were lots of them.

He waited.

Jerry was feeling better. The Scotch had something to do with that, of course. But much more than whisky was involved. Jerry was young. Even with the bug in him, he could handle the Scotch.

He felt like this sometimes. Open, receptive, expectant. Once in a while, you had to relax and get out of your own way. You had to let things happen.

He did not know how long he had been sitting there. He didn't care. The stars had moved. The camp was silent.

Jerry waited.

It happened.

A shadowy form materialized out of the night. A familiar voice spoke. "Doctor Jerry?"

It was Kwi. The question was a formality. Kwi knew perfectly well who he was; the hunter had eyes like a cat. But a man did not approach another person at night without an invitation.

"Old friend," Jerry replied in Kwaruma. Kwi had just used up most of his English. "I am glad that you have come. Please join me."

Jerry shifted his position on the stump to make room. He should have known better. Kwi dropped down into a squatting position, his heels beneath his body and his elbows on his upper legs. He could sit like that for hours. He had something in his right hand. He did not put it on the ground.

Jerry smiled. He *was* glad that Kwi had come, and that had nothing whatever to do with his work. He enjoyed his company. He could barely see the safety pin in Kwi's ear glinting in the starlight.

Jerry extended the tin cup. "Drink?"

Kwi laughed softly. He liked to show his missing tooth. He took the cup in his left hand, sipped politely and without comment, and returned the cup to Jerry. Kwi did not care for Scotch. They had found that out long ago.

The ensuing silence was long but not uncomfortable. Jerry did not push at it. Kwi would say what he had to say when he was ready.

Jerry studied the man without seeming to look directly at him. He did not need more light than there was. He knew every wrinkle in that prematurely lined face. He knew every scar on that leather-skinned body. He had photographed his friend hundreds of times; Kwi would be famous one day. He had interviewed him, hunted with him, joked with him.

Oh, he knew all about Kwi. He could tell the story of his life. He knew how Kwi had become the headman of the Kwaruma. (The Kwaruma had no chiefs. Nobody had selected Kwi as headman; "he just got to be that way.") He knew how Kwi had lost the incisor tooth. (Let Kwi tell *that* story.) He knew how Kwi could double as a shaman. ("I can leave my body, Dr. Jerry. It is a gift. When the Others tell me what to do—when the power is right—I can heal.")

And he knew nothing about Kwi. They shared the bond of a common humanity and something in their personalities meshed. But Kwi had lived a life that Jerry could not share. Kwi knew much—and felt much—that he could not communicate to a well-intentioned alien. It worked both ways. Jerry had been unable to explain what a Department of Anthropology was. Somehow, that did not seem very important.

Jerry poured himself a bit more Scotch. He waited. He was very good at that.

Finally, Kwi broke the silence.

"You say that we are the last," he said.

"Yes. It is true."

"That is a hard thing to believe."

"You do not lie to me. I do not lie to you."

Kwi sighed. It was as close as he had come to expressing regret over what was passing. He was not a man given to self-pity. "No," he said. "You do not lie."

The silence came again. Jerry said nothing, prepared to wait it out.

This time, the silence was short.

"There is something I want you to have, " Kwi said. "My People have always had it. It will be lost where we are going."

"I will protect it. You honor me with your gift." The words were Kwaruma. They sounded inadequate. The thoughts that churned in Jerry's head were not Kwaruma. They didn't fit the occasion either.

Kwi rocked forward slightly on his toes. He was more serious than Jerry had ever seen him. "I have listened to the stories you have told me," Kwi said. "I have heard other stories. Understand me. My people have always had it. I do not mean just the Kwaruma. *All* my people."

Very slowly, Jerry put the tin cup down. His hand was shaking. He thought he understood what Kwi was saying. That was the problem.

He picked his words with care. "All of your people? Do you mean all of the hunters and gatherers? Everywhere?"

Kwi smiled his gap-toothed smile and relaxed. Communication had been easier than he had figured. "You have it right. That is what I was told. I have not seen it with my own eyes. Only for some."

Jerry stared at the object in Kwi's right hand. It appeared to be a hide wrapping of some kind. "What is it?" he asked inanely.

"It is yours now," Kwi said. He gave it to Jerry as though ridding himself of a burden.

Jerry took the thing and held it gingerly. It was a skin container; he could tell by the texture. It was small, only a little larger than his hand. There was something hard inside it.

Jerry went into his tent and got a flashlight. He came back and placed the object on the stump.

He unfolded the creased hide and there it was.

He didn't know what he had expected, if anything. But not this.

It was old, chalk-white, and ridged. It had been much used; it had finger smudges on it.

It was the shell of a turtle.

Well, what do you do? Laugh? Cry? Tell shaggy dog stories?

Jerry felt drained. A pragmatic man, he had somehow believed that he was on the edge of revelation. He should have known better. This was the real world.

A turtle!

The damned thing was not even ancient—certainly not an object handed down from the beginnings of mankind. The shell was dry and brittle, not fossilized. It was at most a century or two old.

Was Kwi joking?

Perhaps sensing his disappointment, Kwi said: "It was given to me by my father. He received it from his father."

No, he was not joking.

Jerry studied the shell. He knew next to nothing about turtles. *Testudo something.* What was the difference between a turtle and a tortoise? Let's see, the upper plates formed the carapace, and the bottom plates were the plastron. . . .

So what?

"It is not clear in my mind," he said. That was putting it mildly. "Your people have always had *this* turtle shell?"

Kwi grunted. He gave Jerry a look reserved for backward children and dim-witted anthropologists. "The shell of the *churi* is not strong when it dries. There is nothing inside. It will break if you drop it. If you put something on top of it, the shell will shatter. This one has lasted a long time. It is lucky. There were many others before this one. That is what I was told."

"So it has been replaced? Many times?"

Kwi did not bother to answer.

"And it is not *this* turtle shell that all of your people—all of the hunters and gatherers—had?"

Kwi stood up. He was getting tired. It may have been that he too was disappointed. Doctor Jerry could be a little slow in the head.

"My meaning was that they all had a *churi.* That is what I was told. I have seen some, long ago. Not this same shell. But like it. They all work the same."

Jerry took a deep breath. They were back in the real world. It was just barely possible—

"Work the same?"

"The *churi* is medicine," Kwi said slowly. "It is power. It connects things."

Jerry did not know how to respond to that. The real world was getting fuzzy again.

"Protect it," Kwi said. "You will see."

The last of the Kwaruma headmen had said all that he cared to say. He had done what he had to do. That was the story of his life.

He turned and vanished into the night.

A great weariness descended over Jerry Hartshorn. The stars seemed heavy. He stumbled into his tent, taking his gear with him.

A half-empty bottle, a tin cup, a flashlight.

And an old turtle shell wrapped in hide.

Sleep would not come.

Tired as he was, Jerry's mind was racing.

It may have been the extraordinary day he had been through. It could have been the illness. It might have been the Scotch.

Who knew? Maybe it was the turtle shell.

He felt it there, right under his cot.

He had made a classic mistake, and he knew it.

He had trapped himself in the real world without asking the key question. *Whose real world?*

His? A world choking with billions of people, a world beset with problems that had no solutions, a world of science that had no room left for miracles?

The world that Kwi had known? Hunters and gatherers had populated the earth, but not harshly. There had been no population explosion. There had been no wars. There had been no destruction of the land. There had been no alienation from other living things. They had killed, yes, but they had not exterminated. They had endured for millions of years. For all Jerry knew, that was a record that had no counterpart in the entire universe. Certainly, as far as mankind was concerned, it had no equal on the planet earth. It was a world that had its own rules: sharing, accommodation, fulfillment. It was a world in which miracles could happen.

The world of the turtles? Well, why not? The turtles were older than humanity, older even than the primates. They were as old as the earliest dinosaurs. Frozen in their shells, they had waddled and paddled down through the eons. They had changed very little; they had developed a mechanism for retracting their heads instead of tucking their necks along the sides of the shells. That was about all. They knew something about endurance. Indeed, they were close to immortality. . . .

Oh yes, the real world.

Did Jerry Hartshorn have a part to play in it?

(*Hartshorn.* Even his name was a link with the past. Was that an accident?)

He could sense the turtle shell under him. *Churi.* What had Kwi said? *"It is power. It connects things."*

Question: Could they have missed something like this? Something crucial? All the anthropologists who had worked with hunting and gathering peoples for more than a century?

Answer: Absolutely. It was precisely the kind of thing that would have been overlooked. Something seemingly without significance. Something that their training never mentioned.

Who asked questions about turtles?

Who listened if the subject came up?

Jerry twisted in his sleeping bag. The cot was singularly uncomfortable.

"Friend," he said aloud, "you've been out here too long. You're headed for the old laughing academy."

The words hung there in the cold night air. They were alien.

He had the sensation that something was trying to get through to him. Something pecking away at the traditional barriers of his mind. . . .

"You're sick, old buddy," he said.

Maybe.

Get out of the way. Let it happen.

He tried. Feeling almost guilty, he even put his hand down and touched the hide container beneath his cot.

Nothing happened. Or had it already happened? Or—

"The hell with it," Jerry said.

He closed his eyes and attempted to sleep.

Dawn was streaking the African sky with color. Inside the little tent, Jerry Hartshorn was neither asleep nor awake. His hand still rested on the skin-wrapped turtle shell.

He had not prayed since he was a child. He was not sure that he was praying now.

His mind seemed clear—unnaturally so—but he had trouble with the proper form of address.

God? No: too culture-bound.

Great Spirit? Never: too corny

To Whom It May Concern? Not bad. It covered a lot of territory, supernatural and otherwise.

He sent his message, silently. He did not want to be overheard babbling in his tent. Tenure and all that.

I don't know who you are or if you are. I'm new at this game. I have this damned turtle shell and I don't know what it means. If you understand it, if it can help you or it can help us, please find me. The turtle shell and I will be together. We'll be waiting.

There was no answering message. He hadn't expected one.

Just the same, he felt better.

He opened his eyes and examined the pale light.

"Might as well get up," he muttered.

He had a lot to do today.

It was mid-morning before the television crews arrived and Jerry did his best to ignore them. He was in no shape to give interviews. Jane made a perfunctory appearance before the cameras, but George Ndambuki was in his element. He was magnificently glib and he managed to work in all of the proper catch phrases: A Human Tragedy, The Promise of Tomorrow, The Heritage of Mankind, The New Africa, and The Responsibility of Science to Society.

Splendid.

The relocation trucks finally rolled up in the heavy heat of afternoon. Nothing ever happened on time in Kenya. As symbols of The Promise of Tomorrow the trucks did not inspire unlimited confidence. They were coated with dust and they wheezed and clanked like tanks that had been on the wrong side of a tough battle.

The television people insisted on a brief ceremony—a Farewell to Eden kind of thing—and that was the end of the Kwaruma.

The last of the hunters and gatherers were politely herded into the trucks. The adults were very subdued and old Klu was crying. The children were wide-eyed and lively. For them, this was an adventure.

Jerry had said all his farewells and he could not say them again. He walked out into the searing sunlight and stood there with his hat in his hand.

When the trucks pulled away, Jerry waved his hat.

He never saw Kwi again.

The baobab tree that had marked the last camp of the Kwaruma was far behind them now. There was tarmac under the wheels of the Land

Rover. After bouncing around in rough country for so long, they seemed to be gliding.

Nairobi was one hundred miles ahead of them: a straight shot. It was still light enough to see but neither Jane nor Jerry gave the scenery so much as a glance. They knew it by heart.

George Ndambuki's vehicle was behind them. It would turn off at Machakos.

"Are you tired?" Jerry asked. "I could drive."

"The hell you say." Jane gripped the wheel until her knuckles whitened. "When we get to the big city, Tarzan is going to the hospital."

"You've been a mess through this whole rotten brick," Jerry said. His voice was so weak that it frightened him a little. His moist hand reached out and touched the hide container that rested between them.

"What is that thing? Why didn't you pack it away with the other gear?"

"It was a gift from Kwi. It's a turtle shell."

"You're kidding."

"Not this time. Neither was Kwi."

Jane Schubauer didn't know what to say to that. Wisely, she said nothing.

"Jane?"

"I'm here."

"In case I pass out, I have a favor to ask of you."

She was really worried now. "You don't have to ask, Jerry. Just tell me what you want."

"The *churi*. The turtle shell. I think it's important to us. Keep it for me, will you? It mustn't be lost."

"Done. Save the explanations for later. Try to get some sleep."

It was growing dark. The first faint stars dusted the African sky. Jane switched on the headlights.

Jerry closed his eyes. He trusted Jane. He felt good about that.

When you get close to the edge, you do not worry. You just hang on. Your mind works.

There was a kind of contact.

Jerry knew that he would not die. Not yet. They wouldn't let him.

He was a link. (Missing? No, just a shade fragile.) There was continuity. Something flowed between him and all the countless generations of mankind, those that were gone and those that were yet to be. Something flowed out, touching, connecting. . . .

His own kind of search was ending.

Perhaps he knew what was coming, perhaps not.

He did know that he had found something and that he too would be found.

He was certain enough to smile.

Nairobi was not the end of the trail.

They had searched through an ocean of darkness, a night sea that floated worlds upon worlds, stars beyond number, universes that began and ended and flowed into yet other universes.

They were after something. Otherwise, they would not have been there.

They would know it when they found it. They would know what to do with it.

The seeking was urgent. The journey had been long.

They were ready. They would not quit. They could not afford to miss.

They were coming.

Call it a hunt.

A Stick for Harry Eddington

The giant photographs set into the panels of the office walls were striking anachronisms: an Eskimo crouching on blue ice, a harpoon ready in his right hand, staring intently at a bone splinter stuck into the thin partition of a seal's breathing hole; an African man, his teeth filed down to sharp points and the lobes of his ears distended, leaning on a staff in the butter-yellow sunlight and gazing at a herd of skinny, hump-backed cattle; a Polynesian, his golden body drenched with spray, guiding an outrigger canoe through white surf that foamed like liquid cotton under a twilight sky. . . .

Harry Eddington jerked his attention away from the pictures. "Say that again," he demanded.

The man behind the polished desk, whose name was Richard Mavor, smiled and interlaced his well-manicured fingers. "About the financial arrangements?"

"About the price, yes," Harry said.

"The Exchange does not dicker. Our contract is a standard one, as I told you. For clients whose net worth is over one million dollars—and we don't accept any other kind of clients, Mr. Eddington—the client is allowed to retain one-third of his wealth. This is to enable him to provide for his wife, his children, his charities, and whatnot. The rest is signed over to the Exchange. In return, the Exchange guarantees to place the client in the form, location, and situation that has been mutually agreed upon. There can be no refunds, of course, because what we are offering you is by necessity a one-way ticket. We can put you where you wish to go, but you will then be a pauper by our standards; we can't bring you back again at our own expense. That's simple enough, isn't it?"

Harry Eddington ignored the advice of his doctor and lit a cigarette. "Very simple. I give you about seven million bucks. You give me a life of poverty. Is that it?"

437

"Give or take a few hundred thousand dollars," Richard Mavor said agreeably. "We will insist on a thorough audit, of course."

"Isn't that a little steep?"

Mavor chuckled. "You can't take it with you, Mr. Eddington. Either way. If you live out your life in your present circumstances, what is left after taxes will do you no good in your coffin. If you choose to accept our services, we have to insist on a clean break. This is for your own welfare, believe me. If the transfer is incomplete and tentative, you would be nothing but a rather peculiar tourist. Besides, it's illegal to set aside a kind of emergency fund in case you change your mind."

"You can't take it with you, either, but *you* want it."

Mavor managed to achieve a hurt expression. "I only work here, as I'm sure you understand. *I* don't get the money."

"You get a commission, don't you?"

"Well, yes."

"I wasn't born yesterday," Harry said.

"In that case," said Richard Mavor, who had no intention whatever of letting this particular fish get off the hook, "you will certainly appreciate that our positions are different. You are—or were—a businessman, Mr. Eddington. You don't expect to get something for nothing. The service we provide is highly specialized; it costs money. You came to us. We did not come to you."

"You sent me a letter," Harry said stubbornly.

"Come now. We do not advertise at random, but when we have reason to believe that a man is a potential client we offer him an opportunity. The fact that you came here is proof that you are interested."

"Okay, I'm interested. I don't expect to get something for nothing. On the other hand, I don't intend to get nothing for something. A whole hell of a lot of something. I worked hard to get where I am today."

Mavor smiled and moved in for the kill. "And where are you today, Mr. Eddington? That is the heart of the matter, it seems to me. You are fifty-one years old and you cannot work because of the retirement laws. You have no real interests apart from the business from which you are barred. Your children are married and you seldom see them. Your wife is younger than you are, and she has—ah—lost interest in you. A divorce would cost you a fortune, and your chances for happiness would be no better than they are now. You have made a great deal of money, I grant you that. If your money could buy you what you want—call it happiness, dignity, contentment, whatever you please—then you would be a fool to sign it over to us. If, however, your money is useless to you in your present circumstances, why try to hang onto it? You recall the story of the Spanish at Tenochtitlan, of course?"

"Can't say that I do," Harry said, thinking that the man across the desk knew entirely too much about him.

"Well, in brief, when Cortes was sacking the Aztec city, some of his men got themselves so loaded down with treasure that they were at a distinct disadvantage when the going got rough. In fact, when they had to swim for it across the canals, they sank like stones. You follow me?"

"I get the picture."

"I'm sure you do, Mr. Eddington. Now, let's put our cards on the table. There is really just one thing for you to decide. How much is your happiness worth to you? The choice is yours—your money gives you that choice. We don't expect you to decide today. We *would* like for you to take some of our literature home with you—here, these four spools will do for a starter. Check them out and make up your own mind.If you feel that our offer is a good one for you, come back with your lawyer. I'll be glad to answer any of your questions at any time, of course."

Harry hesitated. "Just one question for now. This is a true exchange, right? If I go, someone will—ummm—take my place?"

Richard Mavor smiled his ready smile. "Nature abhors a vacuum, Mr. Eddington."

"Meaning?"

"Well, Mrs. Eddington will not be left alone, I can assure you of that."

Harry grinned. "That has possibilities, doesn't it?"

Richard Mavor looked at him sharply. "Our experience has been that it works out very satisfactorily for all parties concerned."

Harry stood up and pocketed the spools. "I'll be in touch."

Richard Mavor extended his smooth hand. "We'll be expecting you, Mr. Eddington."

Harry Eddington woke up early the next morning, as always. All his life he had gotten up at dawn and had been in his office before eight. Now that there was no need for him to get up, he could not cultivate the habit of sleeping late.

He faced the day with a total lack of enthusiasm. He glanced at the door of Emily's bedroom. It was closed and probably locked. He didn't try it. He killed an hour in the bathroom, dressed with elaborate and pointless care, and went downstairs.

The great house seemed empty, and for an excellent reason: it *was* empty. He rattled around in it like a marble in a mahogany barrel.

He sat down alone at the dining table and jabbed the breakfast buttons. In eighty seconds—no more, no less—the serving cart rolled in from the kitchen with two poached eggs, four pieces of bacon, toast, and coffee. It all tasted like sawdust except for the coffee. The coffee tasted like dishwater.

Harry got up and wandered through the deserted house. He had the whole day ahead of him and absolutely nothing to do. He had eaten breakfast. The next big item on the agenda would be lunch. Then would come the interminable wait until dinner. After that, God alone knew.

He went into the TV room and stared at the blank gray screen that covered one wall. He decided that he wasn't desperate enough yet for daytime television. He sat down and picked up the morning paper. It was a printed one; Harry was something of a traditionalist. He was not eager to read it, but a man had to do something.

He checked the financial pages with a practiced eye and found that he had made about five thousand dollars while he slept. He glanced at the comics. Orphan Annie was the only one that had survived from his youth, and he was mildly reassured to find that she had developed neither eyeballs nor progressive political attitudes. He tried to get through the sports section to see how the Cards were doing. Not bad, but they still weren't about to catch the General Dynamics Giants. The G.D. Giants, as they were known in the trade, had just enticed too many good ball players with fancy stock deals.

There was nothing much in the news. The Mars Colony, staffed entirely by men and women under twenty, announced that it would be self-sustaining next year. Harry had heard that one before. The President, who was a mature old gentleman of twenty-five, had made a speech vowing to end conflict of interest contracts in the development of the Antarctic. The appearance of the Field Mice, a quartet of nine-year-old folk singers, had caused a near riot in New York. Critics had praised the group's "purity of line" and "intuitive understanding" of such hallowed ballads as *Pistol Packin' Mama* and *Three Little Fishes*. Harry hadn't much cared for the songs the first time around. Scientists at the National Institute stated that human gills for undersea living could now be obtained at reasonable cost, and held out the distinct hope that there could now be "increased social interaction" between interested citizens and sperm whales. Harry wasn't interested.

He read the ads with a feeling somewhere between disgust and despair. Harry had nothing against advertising—quite the contrary—but the *tone* of the ads annoyed him. All of the models in the photographs were either bright-eyed children or impossibly virile men and women in their teens. Old people simply didn't exist. The prize ad showed two women in seductive nightgowns stretched out side by side on a bed with silken sheets. WHICH GIRL IS THE GREAT GRANDMOTHER? asked the caption. ONLY THE FAMILY DOCTOR KNOWS FOR SURE! Bully for him, Harry thought. He read on. It seemed that regular injections of beeswax, Lunar dust, and apricot juice would keep a woman perpetually young and "active," apparently right up to the time when she conked out from old age in the midst of an orgy.

"Damnation," he said, and lit a cigarette.

It had been different in the old days, Harry knew that. His father had not been any senior citizen at fifty-one. He hadn't been this much out of things as an invalid of eighty.

Still, if you were thinking about the good old days, you had to go back to Grandfather Eddington. Harry's kids called him Harry when they bothered to speak to him at all. Harry had called his father Dad or Pop. Harry's father had called *his* father just that: Father. And he had usually added that obsolete word, *sir*.

Harry remembered Grandfather Eddington, remembered him vividly. He remembered him from those long-ago Sunday dinners in the big white house when he was a child, and he remembered him from the stories his father had told him. Grandfather Eddington had been an awesome figure of a man. He had ruled his household like a king.

Harry could see him now, striding down the sidewalk on a Sunday afternoon, going to the park to feed the birds. He always dressed in white; he looked like a military snowman with his shock of white hair and his bushy white eyebrows. He carried a walking stick, a carved staff of ornate polished wood, and he twirled it as he walked. Family legend had it that Grandfather had cracked a skull or two with that stick when people had not gotten out of his way fast enough to suit him.

When Harry had been very small, dressed in his hated Sunday suit of blue coat and knickers, he had been allowed to tag along behind Grandfather on those walks to the park. He had admired that walking stick more than anything else on earth. One day, he had promised himself, he would have a stick like that. He would be *somebody*.

It hadn't quite worked out that way.

Harry had no walking stick, and people would have considered him balmy if he had bought one. Nobody walked anywhere these days. His authority in the family approximated absolute zero. As for being a wise old man whose advice was sought by all, that was a very large laugh. Nobody gave a hoot in hell what he thought about anything. The Field Mice? He still thought that Benny Goodman had been pretty hot stuff. The Mars Colony? He didn't know an asteroid from a hole in the ground, and didn't care. Baseball? He remembered Musial and Williams and Ol' Diz—what could he possibly say about a Yankee first baseman who was fifteen years old? Sure, he knew that players came along much faster with all the organized pre-school training they got now, but after all. . . .

Face it. He was *out* of it, and that was that.

He leaned back in his reclining chair. The massage started. He lapsed into daydream. He was doing that a lot lately—not quite asleep, not quite awake. . . .

Harry was walking briskly down the sidewalk, his white suit shining in the sun. His stick felt good and solid in his right hand, and he twirled it expertly as he strode along. "Good afternoon, sir," a man said, touching his cap. Harry nodded indifferently; he had a decision to make. Now, about the new park that had been proposed. They could clear that shoddy area between Main and Fulmore, run a little rustic bridge over Clear Creek. put in some nice fat goldfish—

"Harry!"

He looked up with a start. Not a goldfish, alas. Emily had arisen.

"Harry, you're spilling ashes all over the rug."

"Oh. Sorry, dear."

"I'm going out," Emily announced.

He looked at her. She wasn't hard to look at by any means. Her clear skin was unlined, her blonde hair soft but expertly waved, her figure young and appealing under her clinging green dress.

"Going to see the swami?" Harry asked.

"He's not a swami, and you know it. He's a certified Interpreter of Mysticism, and he's a *very* fine man."

Emily had been going in for assorted cults of late, which really wasn't like her at all. The cults all seemed to advocate abstinence from what they persisted in referring to as pleasures of the flesh, or so Emily said. That certainly wasn't like Emily either, and Harry had his doubts.

"Give the swami my regards," he said.

"I'll do that." Her voice was cool and unconcerned. "And try not to drink too much this afternoon, Harry. We're going out tonight."

"Out?"

"To the club. We're playing Bingo."

Oh *boy*, thought Harry.

Emily swished out, her hips swinging engagingly.

Damn it, Harry thought, she does that on purpose. He had been forced to try other women from time to time—a couple of years of abstinence could be a very long time indeed, and Harry wasn't all that old—but they hadn't worked out very well. Basically, Harry was a decidedly conservative man.

He went in and ate lunch by himself, as usual.

He returned to his chair, dialed himself a bourbon and water, and took out the spools that Richard Mavor had given him.

Harry Eddington had just about made up his mind.

Still, he wasn't a man who liked to rush into things.

He didn't entirely trust Mr. Richard Mavor.

He intended to be very sure that he knew what he was doing before he put his John Henry on any contract.

The spools, as he had feared, were rather heavy going.

"You'd think," he said aloud, "that with all the money they make they could afford some decent writers."

He stuck with them. The projections, he found, were oddly convincing despite their murky language. Harry could spot a phony pitch a mile away, and the spools struck him as being on the level. The problem was in trying to decipher what it was that they were saying.

The first one was wittily entitled, *The Sociocultural Concomitants of Status and Role Transformation.*

Translated into a rough approximation of English, it said that every social system was marked off into a series of positions—statuses—and that for every status there was a role, the latter being the part that a person was supposed to play when be occupied a particular status. So far, so good. It seemed that status was determined in a variety of ways, depending on the culture of the group in question, but that much the same ingredients were used elsewhere in calculating status: age, sex, birth, property, personality characteristics, and so on. However, the *value* assigned to the various factors changed from society to society. Some systems gave high status to the old, some to the young; in some cultures it was great to be a man, in others it was better to be a woman. Harry began to get a headache. In addition, certain *kinds* of persons were more highly valued in one system than in another. A warrior was a big man among the Plains Indians, but if you were a Hopi you were supposed to be peaceful. There were rather too many examples along the same lines; Harry got the general idea without undue difficulty. It seemed that the role that went along with the status also varied at different times and places. The basic point was simple enough: the problem of individual happiness and contentment was largely a matter of being the right sort of person in the right place at the right time. In effect, Harry figured, the business of the Exchange was to match a given person with the culture that happened to value what that particular person had to offer.

He followed it all the way through. Then he dialed another drink and tackled the second spool.

It too, had a racy title: *A Thematic Analysis of the American Culture Pattern.*

"Oh, brother," Harry said.

The idea this time hit close enough to home to be moderately interesting. The spool stated that the American culture in 1995 was classified as a dynamic, driven system: it was the precise opposite of a stable, passive culture type. The system retained a number of fundamental ideas that had characterized it for many years: an emphasis on very rapid technological and social change, a focus on youth, an isolation of the individual as a kind of social atom. "That's me," Harry said. The ideal in the old American culture, the spool projected, was the man of action, the go-getter, the practical man who got things done. Nowadays, the legacy of this notion still survived. The elderly—legally defined as those past fifty years of age— were in a tough spot because they were thought of as obsolete. They didn't have much to offer in the way of traditional wisdom because the culture had literally passed them by: the culture changed so fast that the culture in which they were expert no longer existed. If they had money, they could function as consumers. "Don't I know it," Harry said. Beyond that, they could only try to "think young" and masquerade as pot-bellied teen-agers. The passing of the frontier had put more economic power in the hands of women. The role of the male was becoming ambiguous. . . .

Harry felt worse than ambiguous. His headache was assuming classic proportions. He scanned the last two spools with something less than complete dedication.

One was called *The Legal and Ethical Aspects of Ego Exchange,* and it was primarily a summary of a series of court decisions. The key point seemed to be that personality transfers were legal as long as both of the parties concerned had given their consent to the transaction. On the ethical side, the U.N., after a long procedural wrangle, had given its blessing in the form of its *Manifesto Regarding the Rights of Individuals to Cultural Self-Determination,* which sounded reasonably lofty,

The final spool was *The Dynamic Mechanics of Personality Transfer,* which boasted a preface by the retired head of the American Medical Association. (A lengthy footnote said proudly that the good doctor was now a shaman on Tierra del Fuego.) The projection was a maze of circuit diagrams and obscure mathematical symbols, and it was all Greek to Harry.

Well, no matter.

Harry was ready for Mr. Mavor.

"We want to be completely satisfied," said Richard Mavor the next day.

"That makes two of us."

"I believe you said that you had some specific questions?"

"A few, yes. Let's suppose that I agree to make the switch. Does the Exchange guarantee my future happiness?"

Mavor pursed his lips. "That's a large order."

"It's your business, isn't it?"

Mavor leaned forward across the polished desk and chose his words with great care. "We can guarantee two things, certainly. First, we will put you—

the essential you, so to speak—in a body that will—ah—harmonize with the new surroundings you choose. Second, we will place you in a functioning culture that will maximize the attributes you happen to possess."

Harry considered. "Okay, I'll buy that. Why can't you put me in a young body?"

Mavor looked shocked. "It doesn't work that way. We are not in the immortality business, Mr. Eddington. The transfer is only possible—mechanically and legally—between two persons of the same physiological age. We have a leeway of a week or two at best. If you had studied *The Dynamic Mechanics of Personality Transfer.* . . ."

"I'll take your word for it. Look, if this is such a good deal for me, how come the other guy is so willing to take my place?"

Mavor waved at the pictures on the walls. "People are funny, Mr. Eddington. One man's meat, you know."

"It can't be that simple."

"It is and it isn't. Look at it this way. What we have in the modern world is a situation in which most of the people—numerically speaking, if that isn't overly redundant—live in what amounts to the same basic culture, the urban, industrialized, technologically sophisticated culture that you and I grew up in. The rest of the people—small in total numbers, but rich in diversity—live in the remnants of primitive societies or in peasant enclaves. In your case, there is no point to shifting from one area to another within the same basic culture pattern. You have to go elsewhere, into the primitive world. Now, to most primitive peoples, romantic gush to the contrary, the chance to have a shot at this glittering outside world of ours is overwhelmingly attractive. Such a man, perhaps regrettably, doesn't think much in terms of subtle satisfactions and delicate personality adjustments. He hasn't got much of anything, by our standards, and he wants a car, a copter, a big house with a fancy bathroom, a TV, money, power. In short, he wants what you have got. You have to live as a poor, powerless man before you can appreciate the other side of the coin. And you have to live as a rich, lonely man to understand the rewards of other ways of living. Neither man can tell the other one anything, but we have found that both are eager and willing to make the exchange."

"It doesn't cost the other guy anything?"

"He hasn't any wealth, in our terms. It has to be paid for at this end."

Harry nodded slowly. He thought he would know a snow job when he heard one, and Mavor seemed to be giving him straight answers. "I thought these—uh—savages were dying out. What if there's no place to go? Suppose the culture fizzles out while I'm still alive?"

Richard Mavor, who wouldn't see forty again, was an experienced man. He had a lot at stake, and he had the answers to tougher questions than the ones that Harry Eddington was asking. "It's a funny thing, actually.

You'd be surprised how many primitive cultures there are left, to say nothing of peasant societies. We always tend to think that the whole world is like ourselves; that's been true all through history. But God knows how many cultures there were on this planet that never even heard of the Roman Empire, say. Even now, there are quite a few cultures kicking around that are radically different from our own—in Africa, in India, in South America, in New Guinea and other places. Our job is to know where those cultures are and what they are like. We employ as many anthropologists as the ten leading universities in this country combined, and we spend a great deal of money to ensure that those cultures will survive for a reasonable length of time. But let's be frank about this, Mr. Eddington. If you're looking for a romantic, untouched island full of beautiful, happy people who are totally uncontaminated by any taint of contact with the outside world, you can forget it. It doesn't exist. All we have to offer are real people and real places. We have no convenient time machine at our disposal. We can't put you in Utopia. But you certainly wouldn't be happy in never-never land anyway, believe me. There have to be a few problems or there is no zest to living—and that's the whole idea, isn't it?"

Harry felt a growing sense of excitement. There might be a catch in it somewhere, but he couldn't see it. It was a little like heaven; nobody ever came back to give you a first-hand report. But what did he have to lose?

"Where could I go?" he asked. "What would it be like?"

Richard Mavor smiled with considerable relief. He knew exactly where Harry was going. He even had the agreement ready with the man Harry was scheduled to replace. The man's name was Wambua. Mavor was pleased for a number of reasons, not the least of which was that he felt a certain kinship with Harry. Of course, it wouldn't do to move *too* fast. He had to be careful.

"We'll have to run some tests, match you up with what we have available. We want you to be completely satisfied, as I told you. Until the contracts are signed, however—"

Harry stood up. "My lawyer is outside," he said firmly. "Let's get on with it."

Two weeks later, on Harry's last night as Harry Eddington, he took Emily to a movie. It was a very modern movie: it was filmed in jerky movements like a silent film, it was equipped with smell and sensations, and it had neither beginning nor ending. Harry didn't care; his mind was on tomorrow.

When they got home, both of them seemed preoccupied. Emily smiled at him, which was unusual. "Goodnight, Harry," she said, and went into her own room and locked the door.

"Goodbye, Emily," said Harry.

He was smiling too.

The African sun gave little warmth in April. It was the middle of the long rains in Kenya, and the hills of Ngelani were damp and chilly. Wambua wa Mathenge, who had once been a man named Harry Eddington, pulled his tattered gray blanket around his naked shoulders and shivered.

"I will have more beer," he said, extending his tin cup.

Ndambuki poured from the calabash without comment. Wambua's cup was clean, as usual, but then Wambua had been a little peculiar lately.

Wambua took a sip of beer and spat it on the ground for the *aimu,* the ancestors. The *aimu* were welcome to it, in Wambua's opinion; the beer, made from quickly fermented sugar cane juice, was a far cry from Budweiser.

He looked around. The fields, each one marked off by a hedge of sisal, stretched forlornly over the treeless hillsides. Even now the women were working with the crops, as was fitting. A group of boys walked along the valley trail, pushing a herd of skinny hump-backed cattle. Wambua smiled, showing his filed and pointed teeth. He liked to look at cows. Cows were wealth, and cows could pay the bride-price for his sons when Wambua was good and ready for them to marry.

A jet screamed through the sky, flashing over the huts of sun-dried brick and thatch, headed for Nairobi. Wambua's smile vanished. Those damned American tourists . . .

"Wambua!" It was Kioko who spoke, Kioko of the splendid beard. "You are dreaming, *mutumia.* Have you forgotten that we have a case to decide when the council meets tomorrow?"

Wambua felt a small glow of pleasure. Kioko had called him *mutumia,* elder. He *was* an elder, of course, as were most men of his age among the Kamba. All of the men seated around the little fire and sharing beer from the calabash were elders, as was only proper. "I am giving the matter much thought. More beer, Ndambuki?"

Ndambuki, who was the junior elder present, poured again.

Wambua was thinking; that was true enough. But it was hard to concentrate. He was sure that a witch was after his cows. Two of them had gone lame in the past week alone. It was high time he went to the *mundu mue* and had the doctor cast his bead. Of course, he was not unmindful of his duty. His opinion had been sought in an important legal case. If the elders did not maintain law and order, who would?

He sipped his beer thoughtfully. "I will tell you this, Kioko," he said. "When you need nine men, Wathome is number ten."

The elders gathered around the calabash chuckled. That was a good proverb, very apt indeed.

"A frog cannot stop a cow from drinking," Wambua continued. "Moreover, a neighbor makes a smelling sheath."

Ndambuki slapped his thigh. Wambua might be acting a little strange, but he was no dumb Masai when it came to legal cases.

Wambua delivered his opinion on the case at some length. He was enjoying himself hugely. Let the women work the fields and haul the firewood on their backs, this was a job for a *man*. This took real skill.

"Never fight a war with your finger," he concluded solemnly.

The discussion went on all afternoon. The beer dwindled in the calabash until nothing was left but a sticky residue for the flies. The fire died down to an orange pile of hissing coals.

Wambua glanced up in time to see Muema, the first son of his first wife, walking down the trail toward him. Muema stopped at a respectful distance from the knot of elders. "Father," he said, "your food has been prepared, if you desire to eat it."

Wambua grunted. It was the duty of a son to assist his father when his father had been long at the beer calabash, but Wambua felt perfectly capable of navigating. Still, it would be pleasant to walk with his son. He stood up and checked his charms. The ball of lion hair and the small antelope horn were in their proper places, along with his cigarette lighter and package of filter-tips. Wambua had not yet adapted to snuff.

"Do you wish me to take your arm?" asked Muema.

"I can walk," Wambua assured him. The boy was being very careful with his manners. He had better be, Wambua thought. Otherwise, Wambua would not give him any cows, and that would be a disaster. No cows, no bride.

Wambua picked up his elder's staff. It was made of hard brown wood, smoothly polished from years of use. It was seven feet long and had a little fork at the top end. Only an elder could carry such a stick.

His son fell in behind him and Wambua started up the steep trail that led to his cluster of huts. He blinked his eyes against the gray drizzle. The huts would be warm and pleasantly smoky. He had not yet decided which wife he would favor tonight. A man should try to be fair. It was really Syomiti's turn. There was too much witchcraft around to take needless chances. On the other hand, Mbinya was young and appealing. . . .

He gripped his stick firmly and hummed a little tune.

Wambua did not regret the choice he had made, not for a moment.

He would not have changed places with anyone else in the world.

Emily Eddington stared out of the window of the TV room and frowned with annoyance. The damned cows were still there in her backyard, standing placidly in the moonlight. She could smell them right through the air conditioner.

What was worse, she could smell Harry too. Harry wasn't much of a one for taking baths.

Harry wasn't much of a one for anything, if it came to that. He spent his time staring at the TV or zooming through the city air in his copter. Emily had been expecting a bit of a thrill from being married to a man who was, after all, something of a savage. She had been disappointed, to say the least. Harry treated his cows with more consideration than he showed her.

Emily turned away from the window. She had on her most seductive negligee and her sexiest gown under it.

"I'm going to bed, Harry," she said softly.

Harry Eddington, who had once been a man named Wambua wa Mathenge, continued to gaze with rapt fascination at a western program on TV. There were *lots* of cows in the show. He did not bother to look up at Emily.

"I will inform you when you are wanted," Harry said.

Emily went up the stairs, boiling mad.

Tomorrow, she was going to have a good long talk with dear old Richard.

"I can't stand it, do you hear?" Emily said.

"It won't be for long, dear," Richard Mavor said patiently. "You really shouldn't come here to the office. It's too dangerous."

Emily began to cry. "You don't love me any more," she said, crossing her admirable legs.

Mavor kissed her gently. "You know better than that, Emily. I don't like this waiting either. But we have to be careful. If the Exchange finds out about that kickback—"

"You said you could work everything out."

"I am working everything out. Be reasonable, darling. When you first came to me about Harry—the first Harry, that is—I told you that I could arrange it so that you would get part of that seven million back. You got it, didn't you? You are still a very wealthy woman, Emily."

"I don't care. I did it for you, Richard, you know that. And now here I am stuck with that—that cowboy—"

Mavor felt a warm glow. She *did* care for him, at least a little. He knew Emily's faults; he had no illusions about her. But he had fallen hard for Emily Eddington. He had wanted her from the first moment he had seen her, and he still wanted her. Their clandestine meetings were not enough, not nearly enough. . . .

Mavor put on his most convincing manner, which could be quite convincing indeed when he set his mind to it. And he set his mind to it without reservation: his whole future depended on it. "We can't stretch the law too far, darling. We have to wait until Harry—the second Harry, that is—

gets tired of his new toys and starts thinkin. It will take a few years, that's all. Then, when you've made him thoroughly miserable, we can plant that ad about the cattle ranch where he'll be sure to see it. I've explained all this before, sugar; we both agreed to the plan, and we have to stick with it. Harry Number Two is not Harry Number One, not quite. He won't put up with a difficult wife, and he won't be tempted by any primitive society—he's been there. Harry Number Two will take the divorce route, which will be just fine. He'll have his cattle ranch, you'll *still* have plenty of money, and we can get married."

Emily dried her eyes. "Oh, I know—you're right, dear—but I hate this waiting. . . ."

"So do I. But it's the only way. Our time will come."

"Kiss me again, Richard. Really kiss me."

Mavor did so. It was quite a kiss.

"I'll go now," she said, her spirits much restored. "Same time and place as usual?"

"I'll be there."

"Don't forget about me, Richard."

"Not a chance," he assured her.

He showed her out, his heart pounding.

Richard Mavor sat behind his polished desk and smiled with pardonable pride. He figured that by any reasonable standard he had done pretty well for a mere wage-earner faced with retirement.

"Everybody wins," he said aloud.

Harry Number One, he was sure, was a happier man today. He knew all about Harry Number One; they were a lot alike in many ways, even down to such details as having fallen for the same woman. Harry Number Two was having a good time, and would enjoy himself even more with his cattle ranch. And Emily—

Well, Emily Eddington was as probably as happy as she could ever be. She was a restless woman, she would always move from one man to another, but she was basically satisfied in a culture that completely suited her.

Richard Mavor wanted his woman to be happy. He was going to marry her as soon as it could be arranged, and he was going to do his best to make the marriage a good one. But he did not delude himself. Emily had not been content with Harry Number One, she was not content with Harry Number Two, and she would not be content with Richard Mavor when she got him.

Well, that was the way it was. A man had to be practical.

At the very least, he would have Emily to himself for a few years. He would have a taste of luxury while it lasted.

And when she tired of him, or he of her—

He smiled. There was a remedy available. He was an expert in that particular field.

He looked up at his favorite picture. The African man in the butter-yellow sunlight was still leaning on his staff, gazing out at the herd of thin, hump-backed cattle.

"Save a stick for me, Harry," Richard Mavor said quietly.

OLD FOUR-EYES

It was not fear that she felt. Fear was natural to her. Fear was a part of the innate caution of her species.

This was terror.

Her liquid brown eyes stared without hope from her gray-streaked mask of fur. Her long flattened ears quivered against her shoulders. Her old-ivory claws dug convulsively into the dry grass that lined her nest. She could not retract them.

She had never known loneliness but she knew it now. He was not coming back to her. He could not come back.

She had never been trapped. There had always been a way out. So casually, it seemed, so uncaringly, there was nowhere to go.

The sounds of death were all around her. Death? Worse than death. Extinction. She knew the concept.

There was a hunger in her to climb the sky. If she could fly, she could escape. She often watched the birds. It seemed to her that the higher they flew the more freedom they had. If she could soar above the sun and beyond the stars, she might live forever.

But she could not fly. Not alone. The best she could do was to climb a tree. That wasn't good enough.

The noises surrounded her, tearing at her guts. The steady unyielding clank of machinery. The whine of car tires on the hot hard road slashes. The betrayal of barking dogs. And the worst sound, the one that lanced her heart: the screeching high-pitched *beep-beep-beep* of the metal construction dragons running in reverse.

She understood what was happening. It was not mysterious to her.

The strongest instincts she had urged her to wait, to blend, to make no moves. That was the way.

But she could smell the Enemy in the windless oily air, and the Enemy was swarming. The Enemy controlled the technology and it was too much to fight. She could not hide. There was no space.

453

The Enemy. Was he not always and eternally the same? A killer, a chopper, a mindless destroyer? Once, long before the complex machines, he had eaten anything that moved. Lizards, snakes, bugs, turtles. Her own kind he had stone-boiled alive. She could call up the images from the meshing of memories. Now, she was not even meat. Boys who neither knew nor cared what she was fired pellets at her for sport. Steel blades tried to scoop her up for garbage. Metallic treads crushed her nests so completely that sometimes she could not locate them.

She was not in the way, not really. She was too small for that.

She was simply ignored. She did not count. The Enemy had no name for what she was. In his world, to be nameless was to be nothing.

She shivered. She tried to wrap herself in her curled tail. There had been a time when that had given her security. It did not work on this day, in this place.

The terror was too great.

Part of it was the loss of her mate. They had been bonded for many seasons. But there was more.

She had a child within her. *One* child. She had been a mother before, but never the mother of a single child. That was unnatural. It was as though the end of her species was known. Nothing could be spared, nothing wasted.

Her universe was not the same.

Ancient wisdom whispered to her to be still, to merge with the earth and the grass and the wood of the trees.

She could no longer listen.

Slowly, slowly, she extended her white-tipped brown tail. Painful as it was, impossible as it was, she had to act.

The old ways would not work.

She had to make her move, or die.

Even his friends often referred to him as Old Four-Eyes. It was a tag that had been hung on him as far back as high school.

Paul Shudde's thickish wire-framed glasses were fogging up from the humidity, but that was no big deal. There was nothing to look at anyway.

The hearing room was the same one the City Council used, and it fitted the standard pattern: comfortable padded swivel chairs behind the long table for the board members, hard wooden benches for the unfortunate petitioners.

Paul Shudde was waiting his turn. The Planning and Zoning Board, known not too affectionately as PAZBO, had to follow the posted agenda. But there was no way to tell how long each item would take. The hearings sometimes went on well past midnight. They were not well attended. If you didn't have to be there, you weren't.

At the moment, Big Buddy was holding forth. It was not the first time. "I love the environment," Big Buddy purred. "Nobody in Lakeview Oaks has done more to protect nature than I have."

Paul Shudde knew what was coming. He wished he could shut it out. Big Buddy was about to regale PAZBO again with the enthralling tale of how he had blown the whistle on the commercial doughnut enterprise sneaking into the rich shaded streets of Lakeview Oaks. Not a quaint and upscale little doughnut shop, mind you, but a chain called Soppin' Sinkers. Good Lord, next thing you know the hamburger franchises would creep around the corner and there might be Belt Busters and Mustard Whoppers in Paradise.

The doughnut story bored the socks off everyone but Big Buddy, but Earl Collins—Big Buddy's real name—was decidedly cozy with the dedicated volunteers of PAZBO. He cultivated them tirelessly. He practically lived in the hearing room, his spotless alligator boots never scuffing the carpet, his belt buckle flashing as big as a hubcap, his creased cowboy hat that had never known sweat or felt the sun being doffed respectfully now to this board member, now to that. Big Buddy's aftershave lotion was sweet enough to draw flies, which it did. PAZBO would listen as long as Big Buddy wanted to talk, and then they would grant him his variance.

That was the way it was.

It was after ten when Paul Shudde got his shot. He expected to lose, of course. He was up against Money. In his experience, which was considerable, Paul Shudde versus Money was a case with a predetermined outcome.

Lakeview Oaks didn't quite know what to make of Paul Shudde. A syndicated columnist for small-town newspapers wasn't a real writer. He didn't produce fat books about Texas that were bound in cowhide and placed proudly on coffee tables. Just the same, he had a handful of loyal readers. That meant at least some publicity, and PAZBO thrived on thundering silence.

"Mr. Chairman," Paul said. He reached into his scruffy pants, pulled out a handkerchief that had seen better days, and wiped off his glasses. "I will be brief, although my worship of the environment is possibly equal to that of the previous petitioner."

The PAZBO chairman frowned. He didn't appreciate sarcasm, whether in Paul Shudde's column or in person. This was serious business to him, and the chairman had nothing if not dignity. He wasn't a real porker, but he was amply fleshed enough to show that he had not missed many meals in his lifetime. He had one of those ruddy complexions that could have been attributed to earnest outdoor activity, high blood pressure, or good whiskey. He had blue eyes as dead as marbles.

"Mr. Shudde," he said, spreading his arms as though in benediction, "I fervently hope that you have something new to say to us tonight."

"I do, Mr. Chairman." Paul managed to get it out with a straight face: "I am pleased to report that the hotplate has been removed from the loft over the carport."

Mrs. Langley, the only female on PAZBO, actually smiled. She was very nearly human.

The chairman tapped his pencil on the long table. "That leaves us with the somewhat related problems of square footage and exterior trim," he intoned. He said it precisely as he might have said, "You give us no other option, Shudde. We will have to blow up the planet."

Paul did the best he could. He identified deeply with every bewildered peasant who had ever confronted a mindless bureaucracy. "I have a plan to put up rock facing over the tarpaper section," he said. "I can enclose the breezeway between the house and the carport. That will pick up close to another two hundred square feet."

That caused a stir. The PAZBO representatives were forced to confer in whispers. It wasn't that Paul's response to their edict was satisfactory, of course, but Paul was *moving toward compliance.* That had legal implications.

The chairman finally asked, "How long do you think these alterations will take?"

"Exactly six months," Paul Shudde said. He had no intention whatever of doing the work, but he was buying time. If he asked for a continuance of no more than six months and appeared to be working on a solution, the board had to grant his request.

The chairman's ruddy complexion flushed to beet red. He was between a rock and a hard place.

It was no secret in Lakeview Oaks that this whole idiotic mess was a result of political agitation against the grandfather clause. That was the one that allowed older residents of the area considerable latitude in conforming to new building codes. It was the principle that permitted Paul Shudde's antiquated overgrown cabin to exist in the posh bedroom community of Lakeview Oaks.

The stink about the hotplate was that it raised the awful specter of someone actually taking in *boarders* in Lakeview Oaks. The nonsense about exterior trim and square footage was to ensure that only the right people— that is, wealthy ones—lived in the area.

Paul Shudde had *tarpaper* on his house.

If, miraculously, he snookered PAZBO this time, there were other ways to get rid of Paul Shudde.

Nothing dramatic like concrete overshoes and a body in the lake. Just a slight zoning change here, a bit of a property reappraisal there.

Tax him out.

That was the civilized way.

Paul Shudde did not belong in Lakeview Oaks. It was no place for mavericks.

"Six months," the chairman said and banged his gavel.

Paul Shudde pushed his way out into the warm Texas night. He felt neither triumph nor sadness at his latest skirmish with PAZBO.

He felt lost.

He was losing his home, and he had nowhere to go.

She had not chosen the old house by the lake at random.

There were several things that attracted her to it. First, there was no dog. Paul Shudde (she knew his name) had a cat that was so relaxed it spent most of its time dozing on the ground with all four paws folded into the air. It responded to all challenges with near total indifference. Squirrels ate out of its food dish with impunity. Second, there was the house itself. It was different from all the others. It had a worn, comfortable smell to it. Third, the house did not have a true yard. There was fairly thick brush around it and a tangle of sharp-needled cedars. There was cover, if it came to that. Finally, there was the lake. Even with all the power boats that raced madly from nowhere to nowhere, she liked the water. She could not swim as well as the raccoon, for whom she was often mistaken, and she did not eat as many fish. But she knew her way around in the lake.

She could swim across to the other side, of course. The lake was only a wide river controlled by the great concrete dams the Enemy had built. The problem was that both sides of the lake were the same. One side was as crowded and stinking and blotched with manthing structures as the other.

Her heart pounded wildly as she belly-crawled down the side of the driveway to the edge of the carport. Her damp cold nose filled with the sharp scent of the Enemy. The warning signs of the manthings almost smothered her. It was hard for her to breathe.

Every ancient urge within her screamed to her that she was wrong. She was built for concealment, designed to look like many other creatures. She could freeze more completely than any possum.

She was not weak. She could fight when the odds were reasonable. She had done so more than once. But that was not her way.

To call attention to herself deliberately, to crouch in a carport, where headlights would be certain to pick her out—well, that was crazy. That was suicide.

Wasn't it?

Her brown lustrous eyes opened wide. Even by star-glow, she could see her own muzzle and tactile hairs.

She hated the brain and the sensing that had forced her to this place. It would be far easier to do what her kind had always done. It would be easier to pretend that the old ways were still working. Yes, it would be easier to die and be done with it.

It was living that was hard.

She knew that the true suicide was to refuse to change when the time had come. She was not like a deer, who could adapt reasonably well to crowding. A deer could coexist with the Enemy right up to the time when he got his antlers blown off in hunting season. She could not do that. She was not put together that way. She needed room to live her life. She needed her own space to create what she was.

It was all gone.

She had been so shattered by the horror and noise and confusion around her that she was pregnant with a single child. *One.*

She could not hide from herself.

She needed help. There weren't many places she could look. She did not know what would happen.

She tensed. Her soft glowing eyes opened still wider.

See?

The headlights were turning into the driveway.

In moments, she would have her answer.

The Ford pickup with the camper shell on the back was quite ordinary except for the discreet lettering on the door on the driver's side. It read:

PAUL SHUDDE
FAMOUS OUTDOOR WRITER

Nobody ever got the joke, of course. That was the point.

Paul knew a man in Kerrville who had managed to sell a grand total of two stories about hunting polar bears. He had promptly put his name and the legend FAMOUS OUTDOOR WRITER on both his Jeep and his stationery. Paul had figured that the man was insane, but then the freebies had started coming. Whenever the mighty hunter wrote to a manufacturer and used his letterhead, he was deluged with rods, guns, and tents.

So Paul had tried his own version, with a notable lack of results.

His mind still on the PAZBO meeting that would eventually take his home away from him, Paul rolled into his driveway and stopped just short of the carport.

He spotted the animal right away. It was caught in the pickup headlight beams. It did not pull back. It did not cower. It simply crouched there like a child's play-bear made out of gray-brown fur. Its eyes were unblinking. They looked as big as saucers.

Paul noticed that his prudent cat had vanished.

Paul set the transmission on park and switched off the engine. He kept the headlights on but he did hit the dimmer switch.

He climbed out of the cab, carefully.

At first, Paul was not much interested in what the animal looked like. It was its behavior that concerned him.

The animal should have tried to run away. At least, it should have retreated into some of the carport junk. It might even have attacked if it was startled and trapped.

The creature did nothing at all.

It did not act like a normal animal.

Rabies?

Paul took a closer look at it, positioning himself so that he did not cover the creature with his shadow. It did not look sick. Eyes were bright, tongue was not coated or dripping, fur was clean and healthy.

What the animal looked like was—well, weird.

Paul gave one of those insincere smiles that people try out on small children and unfamiliar animals. "What in the world are you?" he asked.

The thought occurred to him that the question might not be rhetorical at all.

Paul Shudde was not a trained zoologist but he was a native of Texas. He had a writer's curious eye and he had spent enough time outside the cities to know a chuck-will's-widow from a common whippoorwill. He had also read a few books in his time.

This beast was a new one on him.

It was about the size of a coon—a female, not a male—and it had a grayish bandit's mask that was very coonlike. (He had no idea whether this particular specimen was a male or a female, and he was in no hurry to pick it up to find out.) The ears would have horrified a raccoon; they were long, soft, floppy things that belonged on a rabbit of some sort. The tail was not ringed; it was a white-tipped squirrel tail and it arched over the animal's back as he had seen squirrels do with their tails so many times. While it crouched, Paul could not tell much about its legs or feet. The most striking thing about the wide brown eyes was that they were clearly intelligent.

This was no dummy he was looking at.

He realized that if he had not framed the animal in his headlights and looked closely at it he would have mistaken it for something else. It resembled many other things. Nobody would ever look at it twice, unless—

Unless the animal *wanted* to be examined.

Was that possible?

Paul Shudde took a deep breath, moved slowly back to the pickup, and cut the lights.

"Come on in if that's what you want," he said softly. He was quite sure the beast could understand every word. "Or you're welcome to bunk in the carport."

Taking his own sweet time about it, Paul walked along the breezeway, opened the door to his house, and switched on an inside lamp. Yellow light splashed out into the darkness.

Paul could hear the gentle splashing of a small ripple against the lakeshore.

He crossed his fingers.

If that thing was what it appeared to be, his troubles were over.

He sank into his favorite chair and held his breath.

Slowly, hesitantly, reluctantly, the animal moved inside. It was very frightened.

Paul Shudde exhaled and smiled a big genuine smile.

Unless he was very much mistaken, salvation had just followed him through the door.

Run!

She had no experience with the interior of a manthing's house. She was confused. The conflict between what she wanted to do and what she had to do was tearing her apart.

Run! Get out! Fade into nothingness! That was what millions of years of her heritage shouted to her. She was no longer an insect-eater who stayed in the trees. The great stinking lizards were gone, all of them. But the feelings were the same.

To expose herself in artificial light was a horror to her. It was more than that. She was using the other side of her innate talent. She was actually forcing the Enemy to focus on her.

He had to understand what she was. Had to!

She did not know whether she had made a fatal mistake or not. The four-eyed Paul Shudde was not like the others, she was sure of that. But what *was* he like?

He was smart. In some ways, he was even smarter than she was. Allowing for what he was, he was not really vicious or bloodthirsty. He probably would come down on her side, more or less.

But was he a shade too cunning? Had he searched for angles so long that he couldn't see something straight and simple?

She was not at all certain that she trusted Paul Shudde. Not with her life. Not with the life of her unborn child.

But there was no one else.

Nothing.

She crouched on the floor in the house of the Enemy. She let the light hit her smack in the eyes.

She desperately hoped that if she didn't look interesting she at least looked cute.

Endangered species. The two words burned themselves into Paul Shudde's brain.

It took him a few days to see all the ramifications, but Paul Shudde was not slow on the uptake. He was not a man who required a crowbar blow to the head before he grasped things. Old Four-Eyes was a pretty fair country poker player, and the pale blue eyes behind the thick glasses were sharp.

A minnow could stop a giant dam from being built, if it was the right minnow.

How about a species that was not only endangered but previously unknown? How about a brand-new kind of threatened animal that had chosen to live in Paul Shudde's house?

He laughed out loud. He thought about PAZBO and he smelled something profoundly unusual: victory.

He waved at his visitor, who was hunkered down in the kitchen. The animal was watching him with those strange brown eyes. He had figured out her sex by now—she was a mammal, after all—and it seemed to him that she was a bit fatter than she had been. She had eaten everything that he had given her except for spinach, broccoli, and beets. She did not care for vegetables.

She was death on bugs. Paul Shudde's house was extraordinarily free of flies, mosquitoes, ants, spiders, and ticks. He was properly grateful.

He had not named her. That seemed wrong to him. She was not a pet. He did not own her.

"Friend," he said, "you are about to become famous."

She stared at him. He knew that she understood most of what he said to her. He did not know how she did that, but she did. He could also usually sense her reactions to what he said. She did not communicate through language, but she was not ignorant of how it worked. And she could influence his perceptions a little. He could get happiness or sorrow, pleasure or pain, agreement or dissent.

At the moment, he was getting annoyance.

The cat, who had modified its habits to the extent that it slept on its belly with its eyes slitted open, eased to its feet and flowed away on silent paws.

"Something wrong?" Paul asked her. "You understand that you're free to leave just as you came? You understand that I'd never put you in a zoo or anything? You're not worried about a lab, are you? Some kind of experiment? Hey, I'm on your side."

He thought, but was somehow ashamed to say: *This is me, Old Four-Eyes. I'm not a monster. If you thought I was, what are you doing here?*

She did not get any of that. She could not read his mind.

She just looked at him with hurt eyes. She looked through him. The claws on her somewhat humanoid hands dug into the linoleum.

Paul had noticed those claws before. Put nails on those fingers instead, and you were maybe looking at a primate. Did that matter?

Whatever she was, she would get the job done.

"Are we friends or aren't we?" Paul asked.

She stared at him doubtfully.

Paul Shudde moved to his desk, which was in one cleared corner of the cabin's cluttered main room. He sat down at the worn straight-backed chair where he had always done his best thinking. He took the cover off his typewriter. He did not intend to write anything yet, but it was a part of the ritual. He stuck his pipe in his mouth but did not light it. She hated tobacco smoke.

He reflected that it was not unusual for him to have trouble with females in this house. Ladies had moved in with him from time to time, but it had never lasted. As several of them had informed him with some asperity, Paul Shudde was a man destined to live alone.

"No secrets, okay?" Paul said. "I'll tell you exactly how all of this looks to me."

She waited.

Paul held nothing back.

For one thing, he told her, it was very funny. He started to say as funny as hell, but he decided that using such phrases might lead them into murky water indeed.

Imagine! While the eager Americans spent lifetimes searching for the mythical Bigfoot in Asia, and good old Nessie in the Loch Ness of Scotland, and dinosaurs in the swamps of central Africa, they couldn't even recognize what was in their own backyard.

A completely unknown species.

Oh, her kind must have been seen countless times. She could not be completely alone; there had to be enough of them to form a breeding population. But seeing is one thing. Identifying is another.

Almost always, when she did not succeed in blending into invisibility, she would have been taken for something else. Something common, something familiar. Nothing out of the ordinary. A raccoon, a rabbit, a squirrel, a fox, a dog, a rat . . .

And if someone did grasp that she was different, who would pay any attention? There never was a hunter without yarns to spin, and most of them were about unusual animals. The stories were received as tall tales; hunters were notorious liars, just like fishermen.

There never was a child whose imagination did not kick into high gear once in a while. Who took children seriously? That was part of what it meant to be a child: you did not have to stick to the literal truth.

Sure, there were birdwatchers and butterfly collectors and wildflower counters, but even near a large university how many people kept tabs on rabbits and squirrels—when they weren't rabbits or squirrels?

Her bones must have turned up now and again. Her kind was not young, Paul was certain of that. But small mammal bones were a dime a dozen. If there were no artifacts with them, or something distinctly un-usual, even paleontologists would not look at them twice. They would be filed under that old standby, Miscellaneous. Paul would have wagered a tidy sum that her skeleton was as nondescript as the rest of her appeared to be. It was obvious to him that her brain was remarkable for its struc-ture, not its size. Paul had once been involved in an ill-fated affair with a book club. He remembered it well: one handsome volume free, then two a month at one hundred dollars each for a thousand years . . .

He had received a two-volume set on mammals of the world. He had thumbed through it casually. Now, he studied it at some length.

It was his opinion that even the experts would have disagreed about what she was. A mammal, yes. But then what? Where did she belong?

Insectivora? She ate bugs like candy.

Carnivora? She was not averse to meat, either.

Lagomorpha? Who could miss those rabbit ears?

Rodentia? She had a lot in common with a squirrel.

She was much more special than she looked, and that was a part of the puzzle. Her uniqueness was not apparent at a glance. Even after days in her company, Paul could not spell it all out.

She couldn't transmit polychrome pictures into a man's mind with a twitch of her whiskers. She could not use her long ears to communicate in sign language. She wasn't an alien from the stars, complete with a magic satchel containing cancer cures and recipes for world peace.

She was home folks.

"We need each other," Paul finished. "I can give you a home where you won't have to worry. You can give me *my* home. I know something about publicity. Friend, there's even a book in this! When they find out what you are, and where you are, they won't be able to touch this house with an order from the Supreme Court!"

She did not look impressed.

"Come on!" Paul said. He was getting a little impatient. "I tell you, it's even better that you look kind of ordinary. No offense. If we do this right, people will fall in love with you. They'll send you money. You'll become a symbol of all the lost things, all the helpless creatures shoved aside by progress. You and I, we'll be Big!"

She closed her luminous brown eyes. It was as though she could not stand to look at him any longer.

Paul Shudde took off his glasses and wiped them on the same handkerchief he had used in the PAZBO hearing room. He was disgusted. Maybe he was giving her credit for being more than she was.

Maybe he wanted so badly for all of it to be true that he was just kidding himself.

There had been more than a little disappointment in Paul Shudde's life.

"Maybe," he said out loud, "you're just another damned animal."

The words hung in the still air.

Another.

Damned.

Animal.

Why did the words seem to mock him?

Was he blind?

She padded across the breezeway, her claws clicking a little against the concrete. He made no attempt to hold her in his house.

There were times when Old Four-Eyes seemed stupid. Not cruel. Not evil. Not tainted like so many of them.

Just stupid.

Her kind had to know the Enemy. It was essential to their survival. As they all did, she had put in a great deal of time and effort in observing and studying human beings. You cannot hide effectively if you do not know who the hunter is.

She knew manthings rather well, both in general and in particular. She knew Paul Shudde, up to a point.

That was what made communication between them possible, such as it was.

With her own kind, blending between them was close enough so that they could predict what each one was thinking, or would think in a particular situation. It was not so much direct contact between several minds as it was different minds working in exactly the same way. There was no need for words, and she was incapable of vocal speech. She was not put together that way. The blending was not perfect, but she was aware that no communication system was ever perfect.

When she interacted with a human being like Old Four-Eyes, she had to use another technique. She could utilize her blending talents slightly to nudge impressions here and there, but basically she had to *show* Paul Shudde what she wanted him to see. Their minds were not similar enough for deeper meshing. But most of the words he used were no mystery to her, whether she could speak them or not. Knowing languages was a part of knowing the Enemy. Her kind had done a lot of listening. Words had been around for a long, long time. The languages of the manthings were not as different from one another as they fondly believed; there was an underlying structure that was built into the species.

In any case, she did not have to understand all human languages. Just most of the words of Paul Shudde.

Knowing what she did, it was difficult for her to see why Old Four-Eyes was being so obtuse.

Did he not understand that publicity would kill her as surely as a bullet? It would take a tougher manthing than Paul Shudde to keep out the reporters, the photographers, the scientists. She knew what tourists were, too. If she survived, which she wouldn't, she would be a freak. Her child might as well be stillborn.

There was more. She was not quite the last of her kind. There were others, and some of them were fairly near. The only protection they had, fragile as it was, was that the Enemy did not know they existed.

It would be the end. They would be hunted down, one by one, until there was nothing left. Hunted down not just by the casual killers, the rare-trophy shooters, but by all the nature lovers, all the idle curiosity seekers, all the questers after knowledge . . .

She herself would have no chance at all.

Ah, would they try to mate her in a cage if they brought one of the others in alive? Would they wire her up and take notes? Would they do *research?*

Would they slice her up, oh so painlessly, in a sterile white anatomy lab? Or would they perhaps catch enough to establish a hopeless colony with electric fencing? They could introduce all kinds of wonderful diseases. They would have only the purest of motives—for themselves.

She could end her life as part of an experiment.

Her velvet ears quivered uncontrollably. She curled up in a fluffy shaking ball against the warm earth outside the garage. She tried to wrap herself in her white-pointed tail, to disappear.

She knew that she was nearly invisible. A human being could almost have stepped on her without seeing her. That talent was still strong. They had it even in death. Their lifeless bodies were usually ignored along with the rest of the trash.

It wasn't good enough. Not any longer.

If they came after her kind, knowing that they were there, they would find them. They would know exactly what they looked like. They would know something about their habits.

The best way to hide, and the only way to do it over a very long period of time, was to have no one looking for you. Even infants knew that.

She smelled Paul Shudde's pickup truck in the garage. It did not bother her as much as before. She was getting to where she could endure the scent of dirty grease and oil.

But the truck was a machine, and it was mind-linked to Old Four-Eyes. The truck sharpened her awareness of memories she would have preferred to suppress. Her kind was not lacking in humor, but they seldom thought in terms of jokes. One running amusement that they had, a theme that recurred in their legends, was the idea of the Enemy so preoccupied with his machines that he was devoid of common sense. The standard story was the one about a manthing confronted by an elementary task such as catching a fish. Instead of doing it directly, he would invent a massively complex technology to do the job. He would develop fiberglass and graphite industries to make his rods, reels that were marvels of engineering, lines that were strong enough to snare elephants, lures that were baffling in their ingenuity. Or he would invent fleets of boats, nets that could stop whales, canning factories to preserve the fish, highway networks to distribute the fish. . . .

Her kind had not been successful with technology. They had experimented with it once, long ago, and they had failed. Ever since that time, they had been contemptuous of machines. They had their own ways. Size up the pattern, see the interconnections, make the right move at the right time. Simplify, simplify—

She had believed that it took one kind of mind to live with technology, and another kind to live without it. Her kind had spurned it.

She hated it. It was alien to her. But it was terribly strong. It was defeating her and everything like her. She was coming to a clear understanding of that.

It was not the pickup truck itself that frightened her, not its smell or its feel or its unyielding shape. It was the mind-link between the machine and Paul Shudde. They were connected.

Had she made a disastrous mistake with him? Was he too much like the rest of them? She did not think that he had been. He had been different. She would never have gone to him otherwise.

But now—

She trembled and tried to calm herself. This ceaseless panic was not good for the life within her.

And Old Four-Eyes?

She had developed a certain affection for him, despite his blindness. He probably meant well.

The question was not what would become of Paul Shudde.

No.

Rather, the question was what Paul Shudde might become.

Paul Shudde actually had the paper in the typewriter to write the story. He did not plan on a blockbuster. His idea was to plant just enough teasers in his column to attract the attention of a few sharp-eyed readers. There were quicker ways to do the job, but he had nearly six months. That was time to allow the story to build.

He came that close.

When the chips were down, he could not do it. Sanity splashed over Old Four-Eyes like a bucket of icewater. It was the curse of his life.

"Crap," he said. He never would amount to anything, and he knew it.

He yanked the carbon-sandwiched sheets out of the antediluvian machine. He was horrified, as though the paper itself had become contaminated. He put in fresh paper.

He had, he figured, come perilously close to thinking exactly like the good citizens of PAZBO. That was the way their minds worked. Get what you want at any price, convince yourself that nobody will be hurt by your actions, sleep the dreamless sleep of the innocent. . . .

"Partner," he said to his guest, deliberately lapsing into the toothless-old-sidekick talk that television believed to be characteristic of all Texans, "we came powerful close that time to burning down the barn."

She looked up at him from her favorite curl-up place next to the refrigerator. She seemed puzzled but some of the bleak anxiety drained out of her soft brown eyes.

Paul Shudde typed a blue streak. He could work fast when he had to, and he did have a living to make.

He understood that whatever she was, she could not actually read his mind. He didn't know whether she could read typed words or not, and he preferred not to think about it. In any case, it seemed wiser to tell her out loud what he was writing.

"You remember how the folks at PAZBO got their bowels in an uproar about my hotplate in the room over the carport," he said. She got some of that. She liked it better when he spoke simply and directly. "That was because the hotplate turned the room into the equivalent of an apartment with kitchen facilities, you understand?"

She looked doubtful.

"Well," Paul went on, "this column I'm writing takes off from there. It doesn't mention you at all. It's all about how I took that old hotplate and used it to heat up some tar. Boiled that tar right in the loft over the carport! Used it to repair my tarpaper house on the elegant shores of Lakeview Oaks." He laughed. It was a real knee-slapper of a laugh, not a civilized snicker. "That ought to make me really popular around here. PAZBO may have to go into emergency session!"

She could not smile. She did not have the anatomy for it. She was not sure why the story struck Old Four-Eyes as so funny, but it obviously tickled him. She curled her lip a little to show her appreciation. That was as close as she could come to a visible laugh.

As he wrote, Paul's mind was racing. When he was finished, he tried out his thoughts on her.

"There is a way," he said finally. "I think there is a way. You're going to have to trust me again. Do you think you can do that?"

She gave him her doubtful look.

"I did the right thing before it was too late, didn't I? Do I have to be elevated to sainthood?"

She let that one alone.

"What do you have to lose, my friend? Nothing, right?"

She got up and paced around, her claws clicking on the linoleum. She looked profoundly uncertain.

Paul Shudde told her what they had to do.

Getting into the pickup truck was as hard for her as anything she had ever had to do. It was a completely alien act. Even after a solid month of practice runs, she could not tolerate being back in the camper shell. The fake nest made out of boxes and blankets was comfortable enough most of the time, but the closed-in feeling and the stench of the exhaust got to her. Twice, she threw up. She was ashamed of herself, but she could not control it.

Her panic returned whenever she tried to ride in the camper. The little side and rear windows were too high for her to see out of, and that was part of it. The jouncing isolation was the worst. She could not signal to him in the cab. Even when she could reach him, there were things she could not communicate.

He did not know that she was pregnant. He did not know that her time was near. He did not know that she was convinced that her child would not survive a birth in the back of the truck.

She had to ride up front, flop ears and all.

That was not easy either. It was not that anyone bothered them. It was the sheer horror of being trapped in a moving metal machine on a highway choked with cars and trucks.

Death surrounded her. The sounds and stinks she had avoided all her life twisted at her guts. She was right in the *middle* of them.

Old Four-Eyes kept up a running commentary. He was attempting to calm her down.

"Cedar Park," he said. "Practically part of Austin now, like Lakeview Oaks."

She had her eyes narrowed to slits. She was hurting and the pain was getting worse.

"Leander," Old Four-Eyes said. He knew that something was very wrong. He was not sure what it was.

"Seward Junction," he said. She was breathing a little easier despite her spasms. The traffic's greasy whine was diminishing. She could almost smell green plants and living air.

Hold on, she told herself. *Hold on!*

She had never been this far from her birthplace.

When the truck rattled across the first of two bridges that spanned the San Gabriel River, she opened her red-flecked brown eyes enough to look. The cab window was low enough so that she could see. She could have reached out her handpaw and touched the lettering: FAMOUS INDOOR WRITER

They were out of the cities, through the towns.

She saw long grass and shade trees and rolling hills.

She sniffed the gentle tang of wildflowers.

Hold on!

She did not know whether she could make it or not. Somehow, the pain was worse with only a single child.

They came to a locked gate. It took Paul Shudde forever to open it. She considered jumping out of the cab, but they were still too close to the narrow paved road. It was too far to cover.

She nearly cried out in agony. She bit her tongue with her sharp, strong teeth. She tasted blood.

Dirt road now. Just a track. Rough, bouncing across a field of flowers. She could smell flowing river water. She could see stands of cedar, clumps of oaks, fans of feathery mesquite.

She caught the green smell of pecan trees. Close!

They came to a gray-white cutstone wall as high as the truck. It went on for miles. It was old, constructed without mortar. It had been built to keep something out or keep something in. She didn't know which. She hurt too badly to care.

There was a cut in the stone wall. It was just big enough to let the truck through. It was marked by slabstone towers on each side. The towers were a couple of feet higher than the rest of the wall.

The truck started a downgrade toward the river. She could smell the fishy scent of slow-moving stream water beneath a fierce, clean sun. She could hear a faint stirring in the trees that lined the river.

Hold on!

She could not hold on. The pain was too much.

She reached for the door handle. She was able to get her clawed fingers around the handle. She did not have the strength to operate the mechanism.

She uttered a hissing scream. It was loud and it was insistent.

Old Four-Eyes looked startled. He hit the brakes, reached across the seat, and shoved the pickup door open.

She fell out of the truck, hit the ground running, and was gone.

Paul Shudde knew that he might never see her again. Pulling a disappearing act was her major talent. She had plenty of room now.

Suddenly, it was unreasonably important to him for her to stick around. If she vanished, there would be a hole in his life.

He eased the pickup to the clearing on the bank of the San Gabriel. He drank a fair amount of Scotch as he checked out his land and got a small fire going. He did not get drunk. On the other hand, he was not cold sober either.

He was not overly impressed with what he had done. He probably could not have saved his house anyway. Exploiting her would have delayed things, that was all.

It was no gigantic sacrifice.

He had gotten these eighty acres on the San Gabriel in one of those can't-miss Texas land deals that had been prevalent a few years ago. Surprisingly, this particular deal had actually worked out. He owned the property and it had not cost him an arm and a leg.

He called it his ranch. Anything in Texas that was bigger than an acre was called a ranch. It was in fact undeveloped land a good many miles from anywhere.

There would be no construction on his ranch in his lifetime. It was not a guarantee of forever, but it was a start.

The ranch had water and fish and brush and trees and nuts and berries. It had birds nesting in the cottonwood trees. It had free animals that left criss-crossing tracks in the earth—

Everything she needed.

As for himself, he found a measure of peace here. He needed living water and growing trees and untouched animals too. They kept him at least partially sane.

Economically, he could survive. It wouldn't be big-time, but he could make it. His lakefront lot in Lakeview Oaks was worth something even in a depressed economy. He could sell it and move into one of the empty condos that were all over Austin. They were so desperate to fill those condos that they would accept almost any offer, even one from Paul

Shudde. A change of pace would be helpful for his column. It would all work out.

He could drive out here to the San Gabriel now and then. It only took a couple of hours. The ranch was his retreat from a world where he was not entirely comfortable. *He* wanted it left wild.

He wasn't doing it all for her. He told himself that he wasn't a complete idiot.

Just the same, she had exploded from his truck as though she could not stand his presence a moment longer. He hadn't wanted or expected cringing gratitude. What the hell. But she might have made some slight gesture of farewell.

Something.

Way down inside, it hurt him.

He slept in the camper shell on the back of his pickup. He had a mattress in there and he had cleaned out the mess she had involuntarily made in her fake nest. He left the tailgate door up. It was warm enough so that the light breeze was welcome. He enjoyed listening to the liquid glide of the. river. There wasn't much water in the San Gabriel this time of the year, but that would change with the rains that marked the end of summer.

Without his glasses, he could not see the stars.

He was tired and the whiskey worked on him some. Still, he slept restlessly. He was pleased when he woke up in the morning without a hangover.

He could not face the day without coffee, but once that task was done there was no real reason to stick around. There was no point in looking for her.

He started up the truck and headed out. There was morning moisture on the grass. The tires left distinct tracks. The trail would remain until the sun burned it away.

He kept his gaze fixed straight in front of him. He did not want to seem to be searching.

He was going through the cut in the stone wall when he saw her. She was on top of the slabstone tower on his left. The driver's side.

He stopped, hard.

She was a little higher than he was. He had to look up at her. His glasses were playing tricks on him.

She wasn't alone.

"My God," Paul Shudde said. His tone was somewhere between blasphemy and reverence. "Look at that!"

Old Four-Eyes looked up. Four old eyes looked down. She had given birth. There was a child on the tower with her. It had a small bandit's mask and still-wet velvet ears that drooped on its shoulders and ancient wondering brown eyes. . . .

How had it gotten up there? It was less than a day old. She must have carried it—

She was trying to explain things to him. Doing it the only way she could.

Paul Shudde did not spoil it. Sometimes, he did things right. He did not get out of the truck. He did not try to pet her. He did not frighten the child.

"Hey," he said. "I'll be back."

She did not move. Her gaze was steady. Her white-tipped tail may have twitched, but just barely. She wasn't going to make a spectacle of herself.

Paul Shudde eased the truck past the stone wall. He took it slow and steady on the dirt road that wound toward the locked gate. The last thing he wanted was to alarm them.

"Old Four-Eyes," he said aloud. He knew that she was out of hearing range, but he was getting into the habit of articulating his thoughts for her. "Another Old Four-Eyes!"

He laughed. It made no sense, but there it was.

It was the first time in years that there had been this much happiness in him that did not come out of a bottle.

She sensed the presence of an unattached male somewhere in the area. She was not sure exactly where he was, but she could tell that he was lonely.

He had been by himself for a very long time. Their kind did not cluster. They needed space to live. But it was not good to be totally alone.

He would find her. No matter how secure her hiding place, he would find her. There could be no secrets between them.

She nuzzled her cubchild. She was as relaxed as she had ever been. She knew instinctively that when they bonded it would be like the ancient times.

There would be more than one child. There would be a litter. That was as it should be.

The sunlight warmed her fur. She looked up and watched a soaring red-tailed hawk riding the thermals across the vault of the sky.

She thought about the childless man whose name was Paul Shudde. He was and was not the Enemy. They had shared pieces of their lives. There was a kind of link between them.

The manthings were not all the same. She had been right about that.

She owed him something. Whatever her life was worth. And she sensed that there was more than that.

There was a partnership here. It was not fully formed and it was something new and untested after all the countless years. It was only a beginning.

The two of them could not change a world much by themselves. But they could make a start. One controlled the immense power of technology. The other saw patterns and had the ingrained cautious wisdom to avoid the catastrophic mistake. Together—

She had no idea where the partnership might take them. She was certain that with a little luck it would go far, far beyond the banks of the San Gabriel River.

There was hope.

Call it that.

She did not know what difference, if any, the existence of one species more or less might make. Her mind did not compute in those terms. She had a sense that when one was saved it was somehow better for all of them.

There was a deep joy in her from being alive. She snuggled down into her nest. She licked her lonechild lazily. It did not lessen her love to understand that in another year or two there would be a litter.

The unbonded male was getting closer. She could feel him.

She thought again of Paul Shudde.

She was happy for him.

Old Four-Eyes was going to have lots of company.

THE NEW ENGLAND
SCIENCE FICTION ASSOCIATION (NESFA)
AND NESFA PRESS

Recent books from NESFA Press:

- *Far From This Earth* by Chad Oliver (vol. 2) $24
- *A New Dawn: The Complete Don A. Stuart Stories* $26
- *Cybele, with Bluebonnets* by Charles L. Harness $22
- *Entities* by Eric Frank Russell $29
- *Major Ingredients* by Eric Frank Russell $29
- *Dimensions of Sheckley* by Robert Sheckley $29
- *From These Ashes* by Fredric Brown $29
- *Martians and Madness* by Fredric Brown $29
- *First Contacts: The Essential Murray Leinster* $27
- *His Share of Glory* by C. M. Kornbluth $27
- *The Best SF: 1964* $25

The Complete SF of William Tenn
- *Immodest Proposals* (Vol. 1) $29
- *Here Comes Civilization* (Vol. 2) $29

The Essential Hal Clement:
- *Trio for Slide Rule & Typewriter* (Vol. 1) $25
- *Music of Many Spheres* (Vol. 2) $25
- *Variations on a Theme by Sir Isaac Newton* (Vol. 3) $25

Details and many more books available online at: www.nesfa.org/press

Books may be ordered by writing to:
NESFA Press
PO Box 809
Framingham, MA 01701

We accept checks, Visa, or MasterCard. Please add $3 postage and handling per order.

The New England Science Fiction Association:

NESFA is an all-volunteer, non-profit organization of science fiction and fantasy fans. Besides publishing, our activities include running Boskone (New England's oldest SF convention) in February each year, producing a semi-monthly newsletter, holding discussion groups relating to the field, and hosting a variety of social events. If you are interested in learning more about us, we'd like to hear from you. Write to our address above!

Acknowledgments

Books don't happen without a lot of volunteer effort: Attention must be paid!

Proof reading was provided by a stalwart band of NESFAns: Dave Anderson, Bonnie Atwood, Lis Carey, Pam Fremon, Deb Geisler, David Grubbs, Lisa Hertel, Tony Lewis, Mark Olson, Kelly Persons, Sharon Sbarsky.

But this book wouldn't have made it to the proof readers without the efforts of Tony Lewis (research and advice) or Rick Katze (scanning). George Flynn (Proofmeister) cleaned up the mistakes in remarkably little time, and Mark Olson kept the computers (and the editor) up and running.

And special thanks to George Zebrowski for persuading me to do it, and smoothing the way.

—Priscilla Olson
June 2003